The SEXTON BLAKE Casebook

Galley Press

A COLLECTION OF ADVENTURES FEATURING THE OTHER WORLD FAMOUS DETECTIVE
COMPILED BY MIKE HIGGS

For
CYNTHIA

Compiled and designed by Mike Higgs

Published in this edition in 1987 by
Patrick Hawkey & Co. Ltd., Suite 411, 76 Shoe Lane, London EC4.
for GALLEY PRESS
an imprint of W.H. Smith & Son Ltd., Registered number 237811,
England, trading as W.H. Smith Distributors, St. John's House,
East Street, Leicester LE1 6NE.

ISBN 0 861 36616 6

Printed in England.

CONTENTS

First Published in the Sexton Blake Library in 1923

THE MYSTERY OF GLYN CASTLE

CHAPTER 1.
Owen Glyn Comes to Glyn Castle.

"HOLD on for your life, Vic—there's some rocks just ahead!" Crash!

The speaker's voice was completely drowned amid the roaring of the waves, and the hissing, blinding spray. A moment later the ominous rending of splintering timbers sounded, and the little sailing boat, after one drunken lurch, slithered from the rocks upon which she had been driven.

The frail craft fell back helplessly into the seething smother of angry waters which boiled and churned furiously at the base of the treacherous headland, and almost disappeared beneath a tremendous wave.

She emerged after a second, and bravely tried to ride the mighty breakers which were rolling shorewards with relentless, pitiless force. But it was evident that the little vessel was doomed—she could never hope to live in such a sea after her buffeting and pounding on the cruel rocks.

A fitful moon was shining dully above the black and threatening cloud-bank which scurried across the heavens, and the pale glimmer only served to make the raging storm more hideous and terrible. The time was late evening, but it might have been midnight to judge by the deserted appearance of the foreshore.

The little headland against which the sailing-boat had struck was situated on the bleak and desolate coast of Gower — some little distance west of Langland Bay, not far from the great port of Swansea. This part of the rock-bound shore was completely destitute of habitations, by all appearances, and as far as the eye could reach nothing could be seen but tremendous crags and cliffs.

The tiny craft, her sails long since ripped to shreds, was tossed hither and thither in the giant waves, and her two drenched occupants clung desperately to whatever they could manage to grasp. Their plight was extremely serious, for the boat was rapidly becoming waterlogged, and all efforts to control her were useless and futile.

Owen Glyn, one of the luckless adventurers in the plunging cockleshell, was a London journalist, and his companion was a kindred spirit named Victor Spalding. Glyn was a sturdy young Welshman—a fine fellow in every way, and of a rather serious turn of mind. His friend, although similarly decent, was exactly the opposite in temperament, and somewhat inclined to be a humorist. He was one of those exuberant fellows who seemed to make light of everything, under way and all conditions. Being of the happy-go-lucky sort, light-hearted and care-free, he was famous in Fleet Street for his facetiousness.

Even under the present conditions Victor Spalding found it impossible to be serious, although he knew well enough exactly how perilous their position actually was. His good looking face broke into a grin as he glanced at his friend.

"Looks as if we're in for a considerable wettin' before we reach land again, old man," he yelled, in order to make his voice heard above the lashing waves. "It strikes me we're booked for a dip in the briny pretty soon! This old tub is crackin' up."

"She'll be a total wreck inside the next two minutes," agreed Glyn, with a grim nod. "Unless we can manage to keep her off the rocks, we shall be dashed to smithereens. Look out, man!"

Glyn's voice carried a note of warning, for he could see that their craft was being driven periously near the menacing rocks once more. Like a cork the boat was lifted on the crest of a tremendous wave, and in another second she would be sent crashing to her doom.

Fortunately for the two amateur mariners, the little boat was turned completely upside down as she was swept upwards by the surging waters. And before the craft was finally dashed to pieces upon the rocks, its occupants were precipitated into the sea, gasping and floundering helplessly like a couple of straws in a cataract.

In a moment they were completely submerged in the boiling foam, and they knew that they would have to battle with all their strength to keep clear of the deadly rocks and crags which foamed the headland. Fortunately they were both expert swimmers, but even so it would be touch and go with them. In a storm such as this it was well nigh impossible to keep their heads above water, to say nothing of controlling their direction of progress.

It seemed quite a long time before either of the young men bobbed to the surface once more. But they appeared after a few moments, spluttering and panting for breath. As they did so they saw their little boat flung with terrific violence against the rocks, where it was battered to pieces like a hollow eggshell.

Spalding grinned again.

"Of two evils, choose the lesser!" he panted, striking out strongly against the racing ride. "I'm not kiddin' myself that we're in clover, old man, but we're a dashed lot better off in the water than we should have been in that bally boat. All we've got to do is to keep our heads above water, and let the ragin' ocean do the rest. We shall be chucked ashore before long, whether we like it or not."

Glyn was tossing about in the angry surf close to his friend, and he nodded as he heard the words.

"You're quite right, Vic," he agreed. "But you must remember that the greatest danger lies in being hurled against the rocks. We must do our utmost to clear this headland, and try and steer a course to the beach. It's our only chance. Got ready to meet this chap!"

Glyn broke off as a huge mountain of water came towards them, its crest bubbling and seething with white foam. Quick as a flash, the pair turned and dived clean into the monster wave, and succeeded in getting through it without coming to any harm.

After it has passed, Glyn struck out grimly in an effort to round the treacherous headland of rocks, followed very closely by his friend. Once they could get clear of this, they would have a much better chance of reaching the mainland, although, even then, they would be extremely lucky if they succeeded in reaching the beach without injury. For the whole foreshore was studded with sharp, jutting masses of rock, which stood out menacingly in the boiling surf. For miles along this rugged coast these rocks reared themselves out of the sands, and many an unwary seafarer had met his death upon their relentless and murderous spikes.

Owen Glyn and Victor Spalding now commenced a deadly battle against the forces of nature, and struggled desperately to make their way inshore. They managed to keep fairly close together, but they were forced to continually dive into the great rollers head-on in order to keep themselves from being carried upwards, and dashed upon the rocks, as their little craft had been.

But by adopting these tactics, and swimming with all their strength, they gradually made headway out of the danger zone formed by the rocky headland, and succeeded in getting into the more open water beyond. Even here they were by no means out of danger, for the great waves came surging over them in a continuous succession, tossing them this way and that like little bits of cork in a mill-race.

Glyn, who was by far the more experienced of the two, knew quite well that they were in the most deadly peril, for any moment they might be dashed to death against an unseen rock. But, although he uttered no word of complaint, he reflected bitterly that their predicament had been brought about by the headstrong caprice of his companion.

The pair had started out from Mumbles for a sail in the evening—entirely against the advice of Glyn. The project had been Spalding's idea from the first, and he, no doubt, had been lured on by the brightness of the evening weather. He had scoffed at the very idea of a storm being near, as Glyn had hinted, and in the end the couple had set out.

For a while they had enjoyed their cruise immensely and had smoked and chatted together lightheartedly. But then, with unusual suddenness, a squall had come up, and had quickly turned into a raging storm, accompanied by thunder and lightning, and torrents of rain.

The two young men had turned and raced for port with all speed. But the storm had overtaken them, and had smashed the rudder of their little craft, and had carried away her flimsy sails, leaving them utterly helpless. They had been forced to run before the storm, unable to steer their vessel, and to face whatever lay in their path.

Luckily, they had been carried straight towards the coast, instead of out to sea, where they would have stood no chance whatever of living through the tempest. As it was, things were quite bad enough, for the luckless pair knew quite well that the rugged coast was crammed with dangerous rocks and crags. But they were helpless, and could do nothing but put up with whatever lay in store for them.

So far they had been extremely fortunate. Their boat was splintered to matchwood, it is true—but they themselves were still in the land of the living, and uninjured. But they were fighting for their very lives against the sea and the rocks, and if they finally succeeded in getting ashore they would have ample cause to congratulate themselves.

And it now began to look as if they would, indeed, manage to reach land. Glyn was still leading the way, with Spalding struggling gamely in his wake. The pair were gasping and panting with their efforts, and they were obliged to gulp in hurried breaths as opportunity offered. Three-fourths of the time they were under the surface of the angry waters, but they were slowly but surely getting nearer to safety.

They would not be able to endure the strain much longer, for their struggle had sapped their strength. And they knew that the worst was yet to come. Every moment brought them nearer to the treacherous rocks, and unless they could manager to prevent themselves being flung violently against them, their fate would be sealed. Their only hope lay in steering a course between the masses of rocks, and this would be no easy task, with such a sea running.

But the shipwrecked pair floundered gamely on, and more by luck than anything else succeeded in choosing a spot where the rocks were fewer. Glyn was the first to be cast ashore, and he was flung upon the beach by a mighty wave which carried him almost high and dry. He lay panting and spent upon the dripping sands, and he was conscious of a dull, numbing pain in one of his legs.

The next minute Victor Spalding, hurled shorewards by the next great roller, came toppling helter-skelter upon the beach. He was flung completely over a jutting point of rock, where he rolled over and sat up with his usual nonchalant unconcern. He glanced over to where his friend was lying and grinned.

"Bet you couldn't do that, old scout!" he remarked.

This was quite characteristic of Spalding, nothing seemed to make him serious. He always took dangers lightly, with a joke of some kind on his lips. In the present instance he was quite aware that both himself and his friend had had an almost miraculous escape from death—but the very manner of his landing had caused him to see the humorous side of their adventure.

Both the young men were feeling somewhat weak and used up, but their hearts were filled with a great thankfulness. They had managed in spite of all, to reach safety, and they were content.

Glyn looked up as Spalding made his remark, and his face was white and drawn with pain. In the pale, fitful moonlight, this was evident enough to his friend, who crossed over to him at once, his expression now one of acute concern.

"Hallo! What's up, Owen, old man?" he asked quickly. "You're looking a bit groggy."

Glyn smiled painfully.

"I—I'm all right, Vic," he said. "I think we're a couple of the luckiest chaps on earth to get out of this mess as we have done! Why, I never expected to get ashore at all, so I can't grumble at the little graze on the shin which is giving me beans just now! One of those blessed rocks caught me as I whizzed past it on the wave, I think, and it's pretty painful."

Spalding nodded, and bent down at once. In a moment he had pulled up Glyn's trouser leg, and was looking at the injured limb. There was no wonder that Glyn had winced with pain, for his shin was pretty badly hacked, and he was bleeding rather profusely.

"Bally nasty sort of wound, old chap, but we'll soon have it bound up," commented Spalding, taking out his handkerchief as he spoke. "If you can manage to walk, it's up to us to scout round and find some sort of place to spend the night. Hanged if I relish campin' out in the rain just now! I don't mind bein' shipwrecked, but I draw the line at sleepin' in the open when there's about half-a-ton of wetness comin' down every five minutes or so!"

Glyn smiled, and watched his friend deftly bind the handkerchief round his injured shin.

"I agree with you, Vic'" he said. "But we shall have to take our chance of finding accommodation. Don't forget that we're on a bleak and desolate part of the coast, and I shall be surprised if we come across any habitation hereabouts. We may be miles and miles away from the nearest house!"

Spalding snorted disgustedly.

"That's right—be cheerful!" he said. "Hang it all, give us a chance to look round before you dash our hopes to the ground! But I've got a notion you're wrong, old thing! I fancy I saw a glimmer of light at the top of the cliffs here while I was bein' buffeted about in the briny—an' I'm going up to investigate! Do you think you can manager the climb—or shall I hoist you on my manly back?"

"Oh, I can manage to walk all right—don't worry," said Glyn, getting to his feet as he spoke. "I only hope you're right about that, light, Vic. I can do with a rest and a feed, I can tell you!"

Spalding licked his lips.

"Don't talk about it, old boy!" he said, placing his hands upon his stomach. "I feel absolutely empty, somehow—although I'll admit that it's queer, considerin' that I've swallowed about half the ocean! Hallo! There seems to be a sort of pathway up the bally mountain here! Come on—I'll bet this is the way to the grub and a bed!"

He grabbed hold of Glyn, and assisted him along a beach towards the path he had discerned in the pale moonlight. It was a rough, rugged kind of stairway leading up the cliff side, and had obviously been cut by human hands. This gave the two adventurers renewed hope that there was some sort of habitation quite near to the spot, and they lost no time in making the ascent.

Glyn found that he could walk with the help of his friend, although each step caused him to suffer intense agony. The wound upon his shin was more serious than he had thought at first, but it was no use giving way to despair. Spalding, in spite of his offer, could not possibly have carried Glyn up the steep cliff, although he would have been quite game enough to make the attempt. And so Glyn bravely set his lips, and allowed himself to be half-hauled up the rough and slippery stairway.

The rain was pouring down in torrents, and an occasional flash of lightning showed them their surroundings with remarkable clearness. Below them, the incoming tide roared and crashed against the rocky beach, and Spalding and Glyn felt a renewed thankfulness in their hearts at their deliverance. After all, they had had a remarkable escape from death, and they were extremely lucky to have escaped with only the injury to Glyn's leg.

The fitful, pale moonlight was quite sufficient to show the steps in the pathway, and inspite of their sodden condition, the two castaways managed to negotiate them without mishap. After five minutes climbing, they reached the summit, and they were surprised to see a huge building situated practically at the edge of the cliff itself.

It was an extremely picturesque old place, with turrets and towers galore—evidently an ancient castle which had withstood the storms and winds for hundreds of years on that bleak, exposed spot. It was a welcome sight just now to the two soaked and exhausted young men, and Spalding pointed eagerly.

"There you are, old bean—what did I tell you?" he exclaimed. "There's the light I saw right enough—the friendly old beacon which spells rest, shelter and grub! Our luck's in after all, and we'll soon be comfortably housed within this musty old fortress! I'm just beginning to enjoy myself, Owen, old chap—and I'm hanged if I anticipated any adventure of this kind when we started out from London!"

This was undoubtedly true.

The two young journalists had travelled to Swansea in connection with a murder case which was attracting great public attention at the moment, and they had had no thoughts beyond that. Spalding's idea of going for a sail was solely responsible for the adventures which they were now experiencing—and which were to lead to many strange events.

The light which had been visible from the sea came from one of the castle windows overlooking the cliffs, and as Glyn and Spalding approached the great building they could see that the entrance was upon the opposite side of the old house. Very soon they had reached the great, iron-studded door, and Spalding seized the massive knocker and hammered loudly.

Rain and wind whistled round them as they waited for a response, and as nothing happened within the first minute, the knocker was again put into action by the irresponsible and impatient Spalding. He thudded virorously and repeatedly upon the door, and at last the two visitors heard the sound of movements within.

"Woke 'em up at last!" said Spalding, with a grin.

A moment later the tremendous door was pulled open, and a little, wizened, bent old man stood facing them, looking rather scared and startled. He gazed at the newcomers stupidly for a few seconds, and then spoke in a husky, trembling voice.

"What—what do you want?" he muttered querulously, looking from one to the other apprehensively.

Spalding stepped forward.

"Well, if you'll be kind enough to oblige us, we'd like some food and shelter for the night," he said. "We've been shipwrecked on the rocks just below here, and we feel pretty well used up! In addition, my friend has injured his leg, and he wants attention rather badly. Anything doin'?"

The old man seemed slightly at a loss how to act, and he half shook his head.

"I'm—I'm sure I don't know what to do, gentlemen!" he mumbled. "You see, it's this way——."

"Are you the owner of the place?" interrupted Spalding.

"No, no, sir—my name's Llewellyn, and I'm the caretaker," answered the old fellow. "This is Glyn Castle, and I'm quite alone in the old house. But if you have suffered shipwreck, as you say, I can do nothing less than admit you."

Owen smiled to himself as he heard the old man's words. Glyn Castle—his own name! The thought passed through his mind that they couldn't have come to a better place.

The caretaker opened the door wide as he spoke, and the two sodden and bedraggled adventurers entered the ancient castle with somewhat mixed feelings.

As they did so, the heavy door closed behind them with a dull, sinister slam, while the gale whistled shrilly and fiercely outside.

CHAPTER 2.
The Face in the Picture.

"COME this way, gentlemen," said the old caretaker, after closing the door, and casting a scared glance into the gloomy recesses of the great entrance hall. "I suppose you will want to take your wet clothing off as soon as possible, and warm yourselves by the fire!"

Owen Glyn nodded.

"That will certainly be our wisest plan," he agreed. "We're sorry to put you to so much trouble, and we'll help you light the fire——."

"There is quite a large fire burning in this room, sir," broke in the old fellow, striding across the hall, and flinging open the door of a great apartment as he spoke. "If you will make yourself at home here, I will hurry away and bring some blankets."

"Good man!" said Spalding, with a nod of approval. "Thanks very much! Ah! What a sight to cheer a couple of half-drowned men, eh? That's what I call a fire! One of the old sort—hot enough to roast a bally bullock!"

He, and Owen had followed the caretaker into the large room by this time, and their chilled hearts were greeted by the sight of a tremendous fire which burned on the open grate, radiating a cheerful glow of light and heat. The soaked pair hurried over to it, and were soon warming themselves near the crackling flames.

Llewellyn left the room, promising to return with blankets and a bandage for Owen's leg. And while the old chap was absent the two friends commenced to undress, spreading their sodden clothing in front of the fire to dry. The caretaker reappeared before they had stripped, and he brought them a couple of thick, warm blankets apiece, and placed the bandage upon the table.

"There you are, gentlemen—I hope you will be able to manage," he said, still with that peculiar scared look on his face. "I am quite unable to offer you a bed, and you will have to make shift in this one room for the night. But I will prepare you some food and bring it to you as soon as possible."

The two friends thanked him and went on with their undressing. The warmth of the fire had already made them feel much better, and when they had finally divested themselves of their wet clothing and had wrapped themselves in the blankets, they were almost themselves again—except for Owen's wound.

Victor now devoted his attention to this, and soon had it neatly and firmly bandaged up. The gash was really a serious one, and gave Glyn considerable pain. But he bore it bravely, and assured his friend that it was very much easier for the attention he had given it.

Llewellyn now returned once more, this time carrying a large tray, on which reposed a huge plate of sandwiches, some cups and saucers, and a large jug filled to the brim with steaming hot coffee. He set this burden down upon the table near the shaded lamp, and turned to the two blanket-swathed visitors.

"I don't think there is anything more I can do for you, gentlemen," he said in his trembling voice. "I hope you will like the food I have brought. It is plain, I know, but it is wholesome, and the coffee is hot. If you require any more, just ring the bell."

Victor eyed the tray hungrily, and the caretaker moved towards the door.

"Gosh! I shouldn't think we can manage more than you've provided here, Llewellyn!" he exclaimed. "We're tremendously obliged to you, and we'll drink your health in the coffee without the slightest delay! I've got an idea that we're going to enjoy this meal better than any we've had for many a long day. Bein' shipwrecked may have its drawbacks—but I can thoroughly recommend it for givin' a fellow a first-class, number one appetite!"

Owen smiled at his friend's irrepressible good humour, and the hungry pair fell to with a will. After their recent experiences they were badly in need of something strengthening, and the steaming coffee was the best stimulant they could take. Its grateful warmth seemed to make new men of them, and after drinking a cup each, they discussed the sandwiches. They were plain, as Llewellyn had remarked, but the luscious ham, liberally wedged between the slices of bread and butter, were tremendously enjoyable to the nearly exhausted young men.

Within ten minutes they had literally cleared the board, and were feeling like giants refreshed. They had been so busy attending to the wants of the inner man they had scarcely had an opportunity of studying their surroundings or of discussing the strangeness of the caretaker's manner. Llewellyn had vanished from the room immediately after bringing in the tray, and he had done so with a furtiveness which was somewhat uncanny.

Victor rose to his feet with a satisfied sigh, and looked round the large room. It was of such a size that he could only dimly see into the far corners of it, for the shaded paraffin lamp gave but an indifferent light. But what little light there was showed the room to be furnished in a very old-fashioned style, with solidly made furniture of a bygone age.

"We seem to have struck a ducededly queer sort of show," he remarked, gazing round him with interest. "I'll admit that we ought to be jolly grateful to Llewellyn for takin' us in and feedin' us up—but why did the old chap seem so startled when he opened the door?"

Owen shook his head.

"Goodness knows!" he replied. "There's evidently something strange about this place, old man—and about Llewellyn, too. He seems to be frightened out of his wits at our being in the house at all. That's why we're confined to this one room, I expect."

Spalding wheeled round in mock horror.

"Here, hold on, old sportsman—I'm dashed if I like the sound of that word 'confined'!" he protested. "Hang it all, this isn't a blessed prison, even if it looks like one. But wait a minute! I seem to have a hazy recollection of a curious sound as that old caretaker left the room, but I was too busy packing my interior to take much notice at the time!"

As he was speaking Victor crossed the room to the door and turned the handle. In a moment he knew that his suspicion was correct, and he turned back to Owen with a peculiar expression on his good-natured, open face.

"I thought so!" he observed, with a faint grin. "You were right, old top—we're confined right enough! The bally door's locked!"

Owen Glyn rose from his chair in consternation and surprise, and looked at his friend rather excitedly. The realisation that they were prisoners was somewhat astonishing, and for a moment he said nothing.

"You must be mistaken, Vic!" he said at last. "What possible reason can that old caretaker have for locking us in here? It's—it's preposterous!"

Spalding nodded.

"I think the same as you, Owen," he said. "But there you are! The door is locked right enough, and the window looks as if it wants a bit of opening! This adventure seems to be turnin' out in a rummy way when you come to think of it! Why did the old bird lock the door—that's what I want to know!"

He strolled over to the window and examined it. The casement was situated high up in the wall and seemed to be composed of coloured glass. Thick curtains divided the window recess from the room, which explained why they had seen no glimmer of light from the outside.

Owen's leg was paining him considerably, but he hobbled over to Victor's side, and the pair examined the curious room together. Glyn seemed to be strangely silent and preoccupied, and Spalding wondered at the reason for it. But he said nothing as they walked round the room, looking at everything with great interest.

There was nothing very much to see, and in any case the light was so weak that very little could be discerned with any clearness. They discovered that the great room contained a large amount of very antique, beautiful furniture, consisting of bureaux, bookcases, tables, and articles of that kind. And after a merely cursory glance round they returned to their chairs before the fire and fell to talking over the situation.

"Our ancient friend Llewellyn has evidently got the wind up rather badly over something or other!" said Spalding, making use of his usual free and easy slang expressions. "But why should he be so scared, I'm dashed if I can understand! I daresay that you and I looked a pretty pair of scarecrows when we first appeared at the hall door—but, hang it all, we surely weren't hideous enough to make the old buffer act in this queer way! It's bally mysterious, and I'm filled with curiosity to discover what's up!"

"So am I," he agreed. "But there's something else which is very mysterious— to me, at any rate. Do you know, Vic, that this old place seems to be strangely familiar to me? I can't for the life of me understand why, but I've just got that feeling. Curious, isn't it?"

Spalding looked up at his friend and grinned.

"Perhaps it's not quite so curious as you seem to think, old man," he said. "You've told me more than once that there's some sort of a mystery connected with your past life, and for all you know this old castle may be your ancestral home! Your name's the same, anyhow—and that may be a clue! Of course, we know that Glyns are about two a penny in this part of the country, but you never know your luck! There are stranger things happen in real life than any of the stunts they shove in stories!"

"Don't be such an ass, old man!" he said. "There's certainly something missing with regard to my past history, but it's ridicuous to suppose that this old place has anything to do with it. Even coincidence hasn't quite such long arms as to literally cast me up on the shore at the very foundations of my boyhood's home—absolutely unknown to me!"

Spalding shook his head doubtfully, and the two friends began talking over the strange blank in Owen Glyn's life. It was quite true that some mystery surrounded his parentage, and this was always a point of acute worry on the young man's part.

During the war Owen had served as a lieutenant in the Army, but beyond that fact he knew absolutely nothing about himself. He had been found in Germany, a prisoner of war, and he merely knew that his name was Owen Glyn. It was quite evident that he had suffered severely from shellshock, and he had been brought to England and cared for in a Home for more than eighteen months.

Eventually he had recovered his full health and strength; but even now he knew nothing about his parentage or home. He had advertised pretty extensively, but all to no purpose. He had never succeeded in discovering anything whatever about himself, greatly to his regret.

He had always carried a photograph of an elderly man, signed "your loving Father"; but, of course, this told him nothing, and he could not even say how he came to possess it. But he had never ceased in his efforts to find out something regarding his past life. War Office records had been ransacked, in vain, and at last he had almost given up hope of ever learning the truth concerning himself.

Owen was of a literary turn of mind, and he had soon commenced to make a good living with his pen. He now shared a flat with Victor Spalding in a quiet turning off Fleet Street, and was perfectly contented and happy. But for the blank page regarding his early life, Owen Glyn would have been absolutely in his element. He loved his work, and he loved the comradeship of his one staunch friend; but it was only natural for him to wistfully long for his parents, and to know whether he possessed brothers or sisters.

Up to the present moment he had never experienced the strange feelings which possessed him now—that of being in vaguely familiar surroundings. He told himself again and again that it was all fancy, but he could not shake the queer sensation from him.

He told Victor that he was a senseless idiot for even suggesting that this old place was anything to do with his early life; but at the same time he had a peculiar feeling that his friend's words had some truth in them. And yet such a thing was impossible, ridiculous, fantastic! After all the efforts he had made to find some trace of his old home it was simply out of the question to suppose that he had stumbled upon it by the merest chance, by the simple process of being cast ashore from a wrecked sailing boat!

Owen regarded the very idea as preposterous; but Victor persisted in declaring that it was at least a feasible hypothesis.

"It's all very well for you to scoff and cackle, old chap, but how the dickens do you account for this queer sense of familiarity about this room which has got hold of you?" he asked. "That wants a bit of answering, to my mind. And you seem to overlook the fact that this old pile possesses your very name. What about that, eh? Hang it all, coincidence can go a long way, but it can't go so far as this! You're a Welshman, your name's Glyn, and you feel at home in Glyn Castle, which is on the Welsh coast. What more do you want! You're on the trail of your past, old thing, and it's up to us to follow it to the end! What about it?"

Owen tried to laugh again, but his face became twisted with pain as his wound throbbed. Spalding noticed it, and jumped to his feet with alacrity.

"That leg of yours wants another good dressing," he declared. "I'll get that fossilised caretaker to bring some water and some fresh bandages. We can't afford to neglect a thing like that, or else we'll have you laid on your back for weeks to come!"

He walked over to the door and grasped the handle. The door was still locked, and Victor was just about to hammer upon it to draw Llewellyn's attention, when he happened to glance at the wall to the left of the doorway. A big oil painting hung there, almost hidden in the shadows, and neither of the young men had observed it before

For some reason which Spalding couldn't explain, he walked over to the table and grasped the lamp. Then he carried it towards the picture, and held it as high as he could, so that the rays of light fell upon the grimy canvas. The picture was now illuminated with a fair amount of clearness, and as Victor Spalding gazed at the painting he drew his in breath with a sharp little hiss of excitement.

"Great Scott!" he shouted eagerly. "Come and have a look at this, old man! I've made a discovery which I think will start you jumpin' for joy—in spite of your wonky leg!"

Owen rose to his feet painfully, and glanced at his friend in surprise.

"What on earth are you getting so excited about, Vic?" he asked. "Anyone would think that you've discovered a valuable masterpiece—a Romney or a Rembrandt——"

"So I have. A masterpiece of more interest to you than any of the works of the two jokers you've just mentioned!" interrupted Spalding. "Come and have a squint for yourself!"

Wonderingly, Owen hobbled across the room to his friend's side. There had been something in

Spalding's tone which hinted more than his words implied, and Glyn was at a loss.

"Now, then, what's this marvellous find of yours?" he began. "You're——"

"Look here!" interrupted Spalding tensely. "What do you make of this, Owen?"

He pointed towards the old oil-painting as he spoke, and Glyn looked at the canvas in some curiosity. He stared at it for a moment or two fixedly, and then gave utterance to a great gasp of surprise.

"Good—good heavens!" he muttered, scarcely able to believe his eyes. "It's—it's——. But it can't be, Vic! It's impossible! And yet the likeness is too striking to be mere imagination. Oh, I don't know what to think!"

Forgetting his wounded leg in the excitement of the moment, Owen Glyn ran across the room to the spot where the clothing was spread out to dry, and feverishly searched in one of the pockets. In a moment he had withdrawn a pocket-book from the sodden coat, and was re-crossing the room. As he went he took something out of a little pouch at the back of the book, and held it up beside the oil painting as he came to a halt.

It was the photograph of his father, and as the two friends compared the pictured features they were both struck by the great similarity between the painting and the photograph.

Owen was trembling with excitement, and he turned to Spalding with an eager light on his flushed face.

"The—the tremendous likeness, Vic. Do you see it?" he exclaimed breathlessly. "What can it mean? Is—is it possible that Glyn Castle is really connected in some strange way with my past life?"

Victor nodded, and looked at Owen queerly.

"There's no doubt about it, to my way of thinkin'," he replied. "This old painting is almost exactly like the photograph of your guv'nor, and you can bet your life that——. Hallo! That bally door's opened at last!"

As Spalding was speaking, he became aware that the locked door had suddenly been opened, and that the caretaker was looking at them.

There was a strange, sinister light in the old fellow's eyes.

CHAPTER 3.
Sexton Blake Accepts a Commission.

VICTOR SPALDING walked briskly along Oxford Street, Swansea, and abruptly swung himself into the foyer of the Hotel Majestic. There was a look of acute worry on his usually smiling features, and he was in a state of considerable untidiness.

Evidently the young journalist was feeling very far from himself

The hour was a very early one for him to be abroad, and scarcely anybody was stirring, even in such a busy thoroughfare as this. A couple of milkmen were visible as they went on their morning rounds, and a sleepy-looking porter was shaking mats a few doors away from the hotel.

But Spalding scarcely noticed his surroundings at all in his present pre-occupied frame of mind, and his wrinkled brow spoke eloquently of the anxiety which filled him.

He passed through the foyer and made his way to the lounge. He glanced round in an absent kind of manner, but almost instantly his eyes focussed themselves upon the figures of two people whom he obviously recognised at once. One of them was tall and rather spare, with clear-cut, strong features, and his companion was an alert-looking youth, with bright eyes and a shrewd expression.

Spalding hurried over to them at once, his face showing the pleasure and relief which surged through him.

"Mr. Blake and Tinker!" he exclaimed, his eyes sparkling and his hand outstretched. "By gad! I've never been so pleased to see you in all my life! This is the most amazing piece of luck I've ever experienced—absolutely!"

The warmth of Spalding's greeting seemed to take the famous Baker Street criminologist a trifle by surprise, and he looked at the young journalist in some curiosity. But he shook hands cordially enough, in spite of the fact that he seemed a little at a loss to exactly place the identity of the new-comer.

Sexton Blake and Tinker had come to Swansea in connection with the same crime which was responsible for Spalding's presence in the great Welsh port, and they had already concluded their inquiries. They were, as a matter of fact, upon the point of leaving for London by an early train, and had been just setting out for the station when Spalding had appeared.

The detective eyed the journalist with a little frown of puzzlement on his brow.

"I must admit that your face seems quite familiar to me," he observed pleasantly, "but at the same time I cannot quite——"

"Oh, that's all right, Mr. Blake!" interrupted Victor. "My name's Spalding, and I had the pleasure of makin' your acquaintance when you were investigatin' that affair of Lady Wynchester's stolen pearls, at Berkeley Square. I'm up against somethin' in this neighbourhood which knocks spots off anything I've ever struck in the way of a mystery, and I'm hopin' that you'll undertake to help me—seein' that I've been fortunate enough to meet you in this unexpected manner! Anything doin'?"

Sexton Blake smiled, and shook his head.

"I remember you perfectly now, Mr. Spalding, but I'm afraid I shall be unable to do as you ask," he said. "Tinker and myself are just starting for London——"

"Oh, hang it all, can't you just hear what I've got to say before you turn me down?" interrupted Spalding, his face the picture of dismay. "I assure you, Mr. Blake, this affair is just in your line! But, quite apart from that, my pal has disappeared, and I want you to help find him! The whole thing is appallin', and I'm nearly worried to death!"

The famous detective looked at his watch.

"Well, I can give you just ten minutes," he said, "After that Tinker and I must hurry off to the station."

"Oh, thanks tremendously, Mr. Blake."

The young journalist had not met Tinker before, and after a brief introduction to the lad, the trio made their way to the smoking-room, where they were soon comfortably seated.

Spalding plunged at once into his story, and related as briefly as possible the events of the preceding night. He told his hearers exactly how he and Owen Glyn had been cast ashore on the rocks, and the subsequent visit to the ancient castle on the cliffs.

He also explained the strangeness of the caretaker's manner at Glyn Castle, and touched lightly upon the mystery which surrounded the past life of his friend. Spalding omitted no essential details, and told Blake and Tinker how he had discovered the oil painting which bore such a striking resemblance to the photograph of Glyn's father.

"Just as Owen and I was discussin' this picture," he went on, "we became aware that the door had been unlocked, and that the ancient caretaker was gazin' at us with his peculiar, sinister-lookin' eyes. There's somethin' dashed queer about that old fellow Llewellyn, Mr. Blake!"

"Evidently!" murmured the detective, who had been listening with great interest. "Did he give any explanation as to why the door had been locked?"

"No, he may have been going to do so, but somethin' happened just then which prevented him from goin' into any details," said Spalding. "Poor old Owen was so excited about the picture of his father that he forgot the wound on his shin, and he went blundering into a stool, and stumbled over it. There would have been nothin' serious in that, only he happened to catch his injured shin on the bally thing, and started the wound bleedin' most alarmingly. He simply laid on the floor groanin' in agony, with the blood runnin' down his leg in the most shockin' manner. I could see that the thing was serious, and quite beyond my powers of attention, and I told Llewellyn that a doctor's presence was absolutely essential.'

"Quite so," agreed Blake.

"Well, I bound up Owen's leg again, and started gettin' dressed in my sodden clothes, meanwhile makin' inquiries from the caretaker as to where a doctor could be found." continued Spalding. "The old fellow told me that a doctor lived in a village two miles away from the castle, and I set out post-haste to bring him along. There's no need to weary you with my adventures in discoverin' the village, and the medical man's house, but I found 'em at last, and succeeded in inducin' the doctor to come back with me. It wanted a bit of doin', Mr. Blake, for even a doctor doesn't like to be hauled out of warm bed and carted off in the pourin' rain for a two-mile walk!"

Spalding paused, and grinned.

"But he was a thorough sportsman, and he came without a murmur," he resumed. "I took him back to Glyn Castle, and we hammered at the door for admittance. Old Llewellyn opened it after a few minutes of waiting, and I could see at a glance that his expression had changed completely."

"In what way?" asked Blake.

"Well, he looked tremendously surprised when he saw me," replied Spalding. "He gazed almost stupidly from me to the doctor, and I asked him what the dickens was the matter. But instead of replying, he asked a question.

"'Why—why have you come back here?" he asked in quavering tones.

"Of course, I stared at him rather blankly, thinking he had gone off his chump, or something like that.

"'I've brought the doctor to attend to my friend's injured leg,' I replied.

"'But your friend isn't here!' said Llewellyn, looking at us in surprise. 'He seemed to be angry with you for troubling about fetching the doctor, and he got dressed immediately after you had left, and followed you!'

"This was a bit of a shock to me, Mr. Blake, and I scarcely knew what to do. I couldn't believe the caretaker's words, and I began to question him rather closely. But he simply stuck to his story, and insisted that Owen had dressed and gone out after me. What could I do in face of that? Llewellyn swore that Owen wasn't in the castle, and there was nothing for the doctor and myself to do but clear off!"

Sexton Blake nodded.

"Your position was decidedly awkward," he admitted.

"Awkward isn't the word for it," said Spalding. "I felt startled and angry, and I was tremendously worried about poor old Owen. I didn't believe for a moment that he had left the castle of his own accord, but to satisfy a sort of forlorn hope, the doctor and I searched about the cliffs for a long time. I thought it just possible that the poor old chap had fallen and hurt himself afresh, but we found no sign whatever of my pal."

He paused, and the expression of acute worry returned to his face. Blake and Tinker had been listening with great interest to the journalist's story, and it was clear that they were impressed.

"It's jolly queer where Mr. Glyn could have got to," said Tinker thoughtfully. "Why did he go out after you at all, when he knew you'd be returning shortly with the doctor?"

"That's just the point which puzzles me," said Spalding. "I had a long talk with the doctor as we were searchin' the cliffs, and told him just how we had come to visit the old home. He gave me the information that Glyn Castle had been standin' empty for years and years, and until I told him he didn't even know that a caretaker was on the premises. When you come to think of it, Mr. Blake, the whole series of circumstances are bally strange, particularly when you take into consideration that Owen recognised the old painting, and Llewellyn's peculiar manner all along. What do you think of it?"

The detective stroked his chin thoughtfully.

"It is rather difficult to say at this stage," he replied. "Your story has all the elements of a profound mystery, and I will admit that I am greatly interested. Do you think Mr. Glyn's injury was sufficiently serious to prevent him leaving the castle without assistance?"

"Yes, that's just what I do think, Mr. Blake!" answered Spalding promptly. "Moreoever, I've got a pretty good idea that Owen has met with some sort of foul play—there's no other explanation of the matter, to my mind. When I walked into Swansea this morning I had intended to go to the police, but I haven't much faith in their methods, especially in a case of this kind, where there's no actual, concrete proofs to offer 'em. But as soon as I set eyes on you and Tinker—Well, there you are! Will you look into the mystery and find my pal, Mr. Blake? For heaven's sake don't say no, for you're the very man for a job of this sort!"

Sexton Blake smiled, and looked from Spalding to Tinker, and back again.

"Well, I don't deny that I am greatly interested in the strange business you have placed before me," he said, "and I am inclined to agree with you that your friend has met with foul play. It is scarcely conceivable that Mr. Glyn would dress himself and hurry out after you as the caretaker stated, especially as such a proceeding would be pointless. He would have done far better to remain where he was until you returned with the doctor. And this, in my opinion, was what he intended to do."

Spalding looked up quickly.

"You mean that Owen was either forced to leave the castle, or that he is being detained there against his will?" he asked.

"Exactly!" agreed Sexton Blake. "And, since you and the doctor made a thorough search of the countryside in the immediate vicinity of the castle, there is little doubt in my mind that your friend is being kept within the castle—probably a prisoner!"

"But what on earth for?" asked Spalding in perplexity.

The detective shook his head.

"If we could answer that question, I don't think there would be much more mystery to solve," he replied. "Tell me, Spalding, did this caretaker strike you as being unusual in any way, apart from his queerness of manner?"

"It's difficult to say, Mr. Blake—he's such a wizened, bent little man," answered the journalist. "He's evidently tremendously old, and now you come to mention it, he did seem to be scared and frightened when we first went to the castle. And, in addition, he locked us in that room, as I told you, which seems to be a strange sort of thing to do."

"Very strange," agreed Blake. "You said that he unlocked the door just as you and Glyn were discussing the picture of his father, did you not?"

"Yes."

"Do you think Llewellyn overheard what you were saying?"

"Oh, yes, he must have done so!"

"Humph! I thought so," murmured the detective thoughtfully. "Well, my dear fellow, I am more than half inclined to delay my journey to London and to have a look into this business. Undoubtedly there is some sinister mystery connected with that old castle, and I am rather curious. What do you say, young'un?"

He turned to Tinker as he uttered the last words of his sentence, and his assistant promptly nodded with great vigour.

"It's a great idea, guv'nor!" he said. "I vote we stay behind and get busy in the Glyn Castle mystery! We can just do with a few days on the rugged coast of Gower—after slogging away in London as we've been doing lately. Besides, you can't refuse to help Mr. Spalding to find his chum—it wouldn't be playing the game?"

Blake smiled and glanced at the eager Spalding.

"Tinker's words appear to have clinched the matter, and we will accompany you to Glyn Castle at once," he said.

The young journalist jumped to his feet and grasped Blake's hand warmly.

"Gosh, Mr. Blake, you're a brick!" he exclaimed delightedly. "I feel too overwhelmed with gratitude to thank you properly now, but I've got an idea that some dashed strange events are goin' to occur. I'm chiefly concerned about the fate of poor old Owen, for I'm absolutely certain that he didn't leave Glyn Castle of his own free will. Goodness only knows what's happened to him, but if anybody's harmed him they'll have to answer to me for it!"

Spalding's face took on a grim expression as he uttered the words, and Blake and Tinker could do nothing but admire him for his staunch loyalty to his friend. There was no pretence about Victor—he meant what he said, and he would certainly make things hot for those responsible for Owen's predicament.

The trio discussed the arrangements for the immediate future, and a little later they set off for the old castle upon the cliffs. Blake and Tinker, now that they had consented to make an investigation into the strange mystery which surrounded the old building, were quite as eager to reach the spot as Spalding himself.

But Victor, of course, was actuated by a double motive. He was anxious to solve the queer mystery, but he was more anxious regarding the whereabouts of his friend.

What could have happened to him?

CHAPTER 4.
The Rusted Grating.

SEXTON BLAKE paused upon the wind-swept cliff and looked into the near distance with interest.

"Quite an imposing structure, Spalding, and undoubtedly of tremendous age," he remarked, pointing to Glyn Castle as he spoke. "The general outline of the building suggests that it was erected in the latter part of the Middle Ages, and I daresay its grim old walls have concealed many a stirring little drama from the eyes of the world."

Victor nodded.

"Yes, Mr. Blake, a mediaeval castle of this sort seems an ideal settin' for blood-curdlin' dramas!" he replied. "But, all the same, I hope poor old Owen isn't goin' through anything of that kind! In the daylight the castle looks picturesque and beautiful, but last night, in the darkness and rain, its sinister appearance was enough to give a fellow the shivers!"

"Hanged if I can see anything particularly attractive about the old show—daylight or not!" put in Tinker, eyeing the old pile critically. "Looks more like a prison than a residence, and it seems to have a sort of forbidding appearance about it. Ugh! Fancy living in a place like that!"

The trio had just come in sight of the ancient castle as they walked along the cliffs from the direction of Langland Bay. There was no proper roadway hereabouts, but merely an indistinct pathway through the grass. It was possible to approach the castle from the road leading to the village near by, but Blake and his companions had preferred the more pleasant method of traversing the cliff path.

The stormy weather of the previous night was still in evidence, although the rain had ceased to fall. A strong wind was blowing, inland from the sea, and angry, scudding clouds overhead seemed to give a hint of more rain in the near future.

Glyn Castle, viewed in the strong light of day, was certainly a fine old building. Its massive and imposing architecture, its lofty turrets and towers, gave it an appearance of grandeur and majesty which had been entirely lacking during the hours of darkness, when Spalding and Glyn had first approached it.

But, in spite of its beautiful and artistic form, there seemed to be a hint of grim and sinister mystery about the ancient place, even in the full light of the morning. Its great towering walls and ornamental masonry were all in a remarkable state of preservation, but the building as a whole certainly seemed to be forbidding and uninviting, as Tinker had said.

After pausing for a few moments the three interested spectators continued on the way. They were quite near to the spot where Spalding and Glyn had come to grief upon the treacherous rocks below, and the young man pointed out the roughly hewn stairway which led from the beach to the cliff top. This evidently had been made for the convenience of the inhabitants of the castle, and was probably as old as the building itself.

The whole country-side, apart from the castle itself, was bleak and barren, and consisted chiefly of coarse, grass-covered stretches of ground, with an occasional tree or mass of rock to break the monotony. No other human habitation was within sight, and Glyn Castle was about as isolated a dwelling as one could find in the British Isles.

"Cheerful lookin' sort of shanty, isn't it?" remarked Spalding as the trio drew nearer to the great iron-studded doorway. "Reminds me of the stories I used to read when I was a kid, Mr. Blake! I never dreamed that I should one day be mixed up in a real adventure with an ancient castle as the scene of operations, but I've got a strong sort of feelin' in my bones that somethin' queer is going' to happen here!"

Tinker grinned.

"It strikes me that something queer has already happened here!" he said. "Mr. Glyn's imprisonment, for example. It seems obvious that he's being detained—that yarn about his going away last night is too thin to hold water. Even if he had been turned out, he would have waited for you."

"Of course he would," agreed Spalding, with a worried frown.

"Well, we'll interview the caretaker for a commencement," said Sexton Blake, halting in front of the door and grasping the knocker.

He gave it a few business-like thwacks, which echoed within the great hall eerily, and then waited for the door to be answered. In a very few seconds footsteps sounded, and then the massive door was opened a few inches, and the scared face of the old caretaker appeared. Llewellyn evidently intended to take no chances, for he was careful to keep a heavy chain in position, which effectually prevented the door opening more than a distance of three or four inches.

Through this narrow aperture his apprehensive old features could be seen gazing out upon the three visitors. Blake and Tinker were strangers to him, of course, but it was clear that he recognised Spalding instantly, for he fixed his eyes upon the young journalist with none too friendly an expression.

"Why—why have you come here?" he quavered. "I cannot tell you anything more——"

"We have come to see Mr. Owen Glyn," interrupted Sexton Blake briskly, stepping closer to the door, and looking at the caretaker intently. "Kindly open the door, and let us in!"

The old man shook his head.

"Mr. Glyn left the castle last night—as I told this gentleman," he said, indicating Spalding. "I have no idea where he went to but he is certainly not here. Why do you persist in thinking he is?"

"Because we are quite convinced that Mr. Glyn was in no fit condition to leave unassisted!" said Blake. "He was physically unable to do so, and in any case there was no object in his leaving when he knew that Mr. Spalding had gone to procure the services of a doctor. It is useless for you to stick to your story, Llewellyn—we don't believe it!"

"Not a word of it!" put in Spalding warmly. "Look here, man, you'd better let us in, or else you'll find yourself in trouble! Where is my friend?"

"Mr. Glyn left the castle shortly after you did, sir!" persisted Llewellyn, his voice faltering and trembling. "I—I told you last night that he was annoyed at your going, and he insisted upon going after you! That is all I can tell you!"

"Why was Mr. Glyn annoyed?" demanded Blake. "He knew that Mr. Spalding had gone for a doctor, did he not?"

"Yes, I suppose so." faltered the caretaker. "But he—he said his injury was not sufficiently serious to need medical attention."

Spalding grunted angrily.

"Look here, Llewellyn—you're lying!" he exclaimed. "When I left, Mr. Glyn was groaning in agony, and quite unable to walk—as you know well enough! What's the idea of springing' this cock-an-bull story on us, eh? Why are you keepin' Mr. Glyn in the castle? Come on—you'd better tell the truth before I lose my temper! I know he wouldn't leave until I returned—so it follows that he's still here! Now then—are you goin' to tell us the truth and open the door?''

The caretaker shook his head, but it was noticable that the frightened look in his eyes became more pronounced.

''I—I have told you the truth,'' he said tremulously. ''Mr. Glyn is not here, and I cannot open the door to you. I have wasted far too much time already in this useless talk, and I must go about my duties!''

Slam!

The massive door closed with a bang, and Victor Spalding clenched his fists angrily as he glanced at Sexton Blake.

''Well, of all the confounded nerve!'' he exclaimed heatedly. ''What do you think of it, Mr. Blake? That miserable old reprobate actually banged the door in our faces! By gosh! I'll—I'll——''

Sexton Blake looked grim.

''There is no object in losing your temper, Spalding,'' he said smoothly, cutting the young journalist's angry speech short. ''It is quite obvious that the caretaker was lying in order to induce us to go away. I am perfectly convinced that he knows all there is to know about Glyn—and I am also fairly certain that Glyn is within the castle!''

''So am I!'' declared Spalding. ''That's what makes me so infernally wild! The position is simply frightful: we're as helpless as kittens, so far as I can see! It's impossible for us to get into this blessed fortress in order to rescue poor old Owen; an' yet we must, Mr. Blake! It's absolutely up to us to get him out, or perish in the attempt! What do you suggest?''

Spalding looked at the detective anxiously as he spoke, and it was quite evident that he was vastly concerned regarding the fate of his friend. Blake's expression was one of concentrated thought, and after a few moments he turned to the journalist keenly.

''The position is somewhat curious, as you remarked, Spalding,'' he said. ''But it may not be altogether hopeless, in spite of the impregnable appearance of the castle. Our best policy will be to take a walk completely round the building, and see if we cannot find some method of entering. Llewellyn, evidently has no intention of admitting us, so we must discover a means of entering without his assistance.''

Victor shook his head doubtfully.

''Might as well try an' break into Dartmoor prison as get into this blessed place!'' he muttered. ''Still, that seems to be about the only thing to do, so we'll have a shot at it! That is to say, you will, Mr. Blake! I'm no bally good at the burgling stuff, but I'll bet that if any man can break into this old castle, you can!''

Sexton Blake made no reply, but merely smiled as he commenced the circuit of the building. This was quite an easy matter, for the castle was planted directly upon the cliff, with no surrounding grounds or gardens whatever. The walls rose sheer from the grass-grown earth, and they were free to walk close beside the old house without hindrance.

But as they went there seemed to be little prospect of gaining an entry into the grim interior, for all the windows were set high up, and were, in addition, securely barred and shuttered. The whole place was like a fortress, and after examining three sides of the building they were forced to the conclusion that no hope whatever existed of gaining admittance, unless some means could be found of attaining their object upon the fourth side—that which overlooked the sea.

Spalding was becoming somewhat dejected; a state of mind entirely foreign to his usually sunny nature. He was extremely worried and anxious regarding his friend, and he blamed himself—quite unjustly—for being the cause of what had taken place.

''I was a bally idiot for leaving poor old Owen in a place like this!'' he said. ''But I had no idea that he'd be trapped as soon as my back was turned. What's to be done, Mr. Blake? We simply must get the dear old chap out, even if we have to blow a hole through the wall! And that, by the look of things, is about the only way we shall be able to get inside!''

''Don't be in too much of a hurry, my dear fellow,'' and Blake quietly. ''There is still the seaward side of the castle to investigate, and until we have thoroughly examined that we must not give up hope.''

Tinker snorted.

''Not much hope of doing anything on that side, guv'nor,'' he remarked. ''Why, the castle wall rises sheer from the cliff edge!''

''I fancy you are mistaken, Tinker,'' replied the detective, making his way to the seaward side of the building. ''Ah! You see? There is quite enough room on this ledge for us to walk from one side of the castle to the other. Be extremely careful, though; the earth may be loose and treacherous.''

Blake pointed to a narrow ledge which ran between the end wall of the house and the edge of the cliff itself. It was barely more than three feet wide at its broadest part, and in places this was narrowed down to something under two feet where miniature landslides had occurred from time to time. From this ledge there was a sheer drop of a hundred feet to the rocky beach below, while the lofty wall of the castle rose into the air from the opposite edge of the narrow shelf.

To negotiate this perilous path steady nerves were required, but without a moment's hesitation Sexton Blake commenced walking unconcernedly along it, followed closely by Tinker and Spalding. And once they had fairly started, they could see that, after all, there was not a great amount of danger owing to the fact that tough, strongly-rooted ivy grew profusely along practically the whole width of wall. This, in the event of any of the trio slipping owing to a false step, would afford an excellent hand-hold.

Blake, as he led the way along, kept a keen look out for any signs of a means of gaining an entry. But the windows on this side were precisely similar to the others—high up, barred and shuttered. To attempt to make an entry by either one of them would be futile—a mere waste of time.

The detective observed, as he edged his way along the ledge, that the castle wall did not continue in an unbroken line to the further extremity, but that a kind of recess was situated in the centre. He further noticed that, from this recess, a massive tower reared itself heavenwards, like a grim sentinel on guard. No doubt this had been used, in days long gone by, as a watch tower, for a grimy window, almost hidden among the ivy, was situated rather more than half way up.

Blake saw all this as he made his way towards the base of the towering column of masonry, and he smiled grimly to himself. He had an idea that this spot might afford them a means of attaining their object, for his keen eyes had already noted the possibilities which the window in the tower offered.

A few moments later the detective reached the recess, Tinker and Spalding joining him immediately afterwards. They found themselves in a little weed-grown backwater, as it were, completely isolated from all human observation—with the exception of the shipping at sea, which they could well afford to ignore entirely.

Sexton Blake glanced round with great interest, and then turned to his two companions, at the same time producing a pair of powerful binoculars from his coat pocket.

"Splendid!" he murmured. "We have reached a point from which we cannot be observed from the castle windows, with the single exception of that situated in the tower. And that, I fancy, is going to prove more of a help than a hindrance."

Blake focussed his glasses upon the window as he spoke, and Spalding and Tinker looked at one another.

"By Jove! Mr. Blake's right!" exclaimed the journalist. "That bally window in the tower is the only one visible from here! All the same, I don't see how it's goin' to help much. It's barred, like the others, to say nothin' of bein' about twenty-five feet over our heads!"

Tinker nodded.

"Yes, and those iron bars look pretty solid, too," he remarked, eyeing the casement dubiously. "It would need either a Samson or an acetylene welding set to get into the castle through there——"

"No, Tinker, you are mistaken," interrupted Sexton Blake smoothly, lowering his binoculars and turning to his assistant. "These glasses show quite clearly that some of the bars are almost rusted through, and it ought not to be a very difficult matter to wrench a few of them out."

"Oh, good!" commented Tinker. "That simplifies matters considerably, guv'nor. This is the only window we can hope to get in by, and if those iron bars are weakened by rust, it ought to be comparatively easy."

Spalding looked at Blake eagerly.

"Don't you think it would be as well if I fetched the police, Mr. Blake?" he suggested. "They could force an entry by this window, and demand the instant release of poor old Owen."

"That would not be of the slightest use, Spalding," interrupted the detective, shaking his head. "The police, in the first place, would probably refuse to take any action, and even if they did they would find nothing. It is quite evident that the old caretaker is no fool, and he would not be caught napping so easily. No; our only hope is to take the law into our hands, and force our way into the castle."

"But do you thing it's possible?" asked Victor.

"Yes," said Blake. "The wall of the tower is partially ivy-green, and the stone-work, in addition, is exceedingly rough, with many crevices and niches which will afford excellent hand-hold, as you can see."

Tinker cocked his eye at the tower wall, and nodded.

"I can shin up to what window in about a couple of ticks, guv'nor!" he observed. It'll be a pretty easy climb, with the ivy stalks and the cracks in the stone-work to grab hold of. Shall I have a shot at it?"

"Yes; but be as careful as possible, my boy," said the detective. "The ivy may not be as strong as it seems."

Tinker, thus bidden, lost no time in commencing his climb. Naturally, it would not be quite so simple as he made out, but he had often negotiated more difficult and perilous ascents than this. Blake and Spalding remained at the base of the wall, holding themselves in readiness to lend assistance in case Tinker had a mishap.

But the lad seemed to be as sure-footed as a cat as he mounted upwards, making use of every thick branch of the ivy to assist him. Now and again, when the ivy looked uncertain, Tinker inserted his fingers in one of the many fissures in the stonework, and managed to draw himself nearer to the window with every second that passed.

In some places the ivy was quite useless, being much too think and weak to bear the weight of even a child, and in these circumstances Tinker was obliged to trust entirely to his grip upon the face of the wall itself. He clung on with hands and feet, and gradually mounted higher and higher. He noticed, with great satisfaction, that a thick branch of the ivy—one of the main stems of the plant—ran a few feet beneath the window itself, and he knew that when he reached this his position would be comparatively secure. The ivy, in fact, would give him a good foothold while he operated upon the window bars, for it curved gracefully under the window-sill as it stretched upwards from the ground at an acute angle.

Tinker safely got over the difficult portion of his climb, and breathed a sigh of relief as his fingers at length grasped the firmly-rooted ivy branch. Once he had done so, he pulled himself up with the greatest ease, and rested his feet upon the giant creeper, at the same time securing a good grip of the window-ledge itself. He found that he was now able to reach the iron bars without trouble, and he waved his hand to Blake and Spalding as a signal that all was well.

"Good for you. Tinker!" called the journalist delightedly. "Hang on tightly, an' see if you can shift a few of those bally iron bars!"

Tinker lost no time in devoting his attention to them, and a brief examination showed that the detective had been right in his surmise. Several of the bars were almost completely rusted away by the action of the weather, and grasping the first bar he bent it upwards quite easily, after first severing it by a hefty tug. The bar was so rotten near the base that it parted at once.

The removal of this one bar did not widen the space between the others sufficiently to admit of Tinker's passage through the window, so the lad at once devoted his attention to another. This was not quite so easy to dislodge, but after a few powerful wrenches it began to give way in a similar fashion to its neighbour. A final hefty pull succeeded in parting the decayed iron, and, incidentally nearly precipitated Tinker to the ground. The sudden jar he received as the bar parted almost made him lose his balance, but he just managed to retain his hold of the bar and pull himself to safety once more.

He merely gave a grunt of relief, and then proceeded to force the bar upwards, out of the way, as he had done with the other. Then he took a firm hold of the remaining bars, and commenced to haul himself through the window, which was open and unshuttered. Within a few seconds he was through, and his first consideration, after a preliminary glance round, was to turn and widen the space between the bars by the removal of a third. This was necessary, if Blake and Spalding were to enter, and Tinker found the task much easier now that he was in a secure position.

In fact, he managed to force another two of the rusty bars upwards, thus making the space amply wide enough to admit a full-sized man without difficulty. And, that done, Tinker waved to his companions once more, and then disappeared within the tower.

There was plenty of light here, for another window was built into the wall directly opposite the one by which Tinker had entered. He found himself in a tiny, square room, absolutely bare of furniture, and smothered in thick dust and hanging cobwebs. Evidently the place was nothing but a look-out tower, and had long since ceased to be used for any purpose whatever.

Tinker looked round curiously, and saw that a circular stone staircase led downwards, and he wondered what his best plan would be. He listened intently, but could hear nothing, and he decided to descend and investigate further before reporting to his master.

Instantly he commenced to put his thoughts into action, and silently made his way down the dusty stone stairs. As he went it became darker and darker, for there appeared to be no windows whatever upon the staircase. After going down about thirty stairs, however, he saw that daylight was filtering in somewhere lower down, and a little later he came upon another grimy window, situated at the base of the staircase, in a sort of lobby.

At the end of the lobby—which was not more than six feet long—a massive oaken door was situated, and Tinker's heart sank. He would never be able to force a tremendous door of this sort, and he began to think that all his efforts had been in vain. For, unless he could get beyond that doorway, he would be no better off than before he entered the castle at all. It was a galling thought, and Tinker set his teeth grimly as he approached the door, and listened.

Not a sound of any sort reached his ears and the silence of the dismal place was almost tomb-like. But Tinker was not a lad who was much troubled with nerves, and he began to examine the door which barred his further progress. It was a solid structure of oak and iron, with a cumbersome lock, and a circular, twisted iron handle. Tinker grasped this in a forlorn hope that the door would yield, and turned it gently.

The clumsy catch rose with a clumsy click, which echoed through the little lobby like a pistol shot. Tinker's heart almost stood still for a moment, least the sound had been heard within the castle. But nothing happened, and he gently pushed upon the great door.

To his intense surprise and joy it began to open, and he realised that it was not locked after all. This discovery made him feel greatly elated, and he pushed the door open a little wider—just sufficient for him to peep through. Then he smiled to himself, for there was nothing to be seen but a long stone passage, into which the daylight filtered only dimly. The passage was quite deserted, and at the far end it apparently took an abrupt turn to the left.

Tinker gazed along the sombre corridor for a few moments, considering the best method of procedure. He reflected that in all probability he was below the ground level, and that this passage was but one of a series which honeycombed the basement of the castle. He might easily lose his way if he started on a tour of investigation alone, to say nothing of other dangers which might beset him. So he decided to go back to the tower window, and obtain his master's assistance before proceeding further.

Accordingly, he silently closed the oaken door, and ran back up the circular staircase. When he arrived at the window he leaned out, and beckoned to the detective, who was still standing below with Spalding. Tinker signalled for Blake to make the ascent of the wall, at the same time cautioning him not to shout. Tinker deemed it wisest to make as little noise as they could, for it was impossible to tell where Llewellyn was situated, and whether he was within hearing distance.

Sexton Blake understood at once, and waved back to Tinker. Then he turned to Spalding, and spoke in a low voice.

"Tinker evidently has discovered a way into the castle," he said. "You had better remain here on guard while I join him."

"Right-ho, Mr. Blake—if you say no, that's good enough" agreed Spalding. "I won't deny that I'd like to come along, but you're the leader of this burglin' outfit, so I'll proceed to carry out orders! I suppose you're goin' on the principle that too many cooks'll spoil the broth, eh? In other words, too many of us overrunnin' the castle might give the show away!"

Sexton Blake smiled and nodded.

"Exactly," he said. "But it's just possible that you way be of much greater use here, Spalding. In a matter of this kind, one never knows what is going to crop up."

He grasped the ivy as he spoke, and was soon climing up towards the window. Blake was much heavier than Tinker, of course, but he was an expect athlete, and he found no difficulty in making the ascent. He had observed exactly where Tinker had planted his feet on the way up, and this simplified matters for the detective. He used the same crevices and fissures, and accomplished the climb in less time than Tinker had done. Within three minutes of the start he was clambering in through the window, assisted by Tinker.

The lad lost no time in telling his master of his discoveries as they went down the circular staircase.

"I expect that passage leads right into the castle, guv'nor," he went on, "and if we have any luck at all, we ought to be able to locate Mr. Glyn without much trouble. According to Mr. Spalding, there's nobody here except that ancient caretaker, and once we're inside the place it ought to be easy enough to settle with him."

Blake nodded thoughtfully.

"Llewellyn is the only individual here so far as is known," he said. "But there may be others, Tinker. It is quite evident that a mystery surrounds this old place, and we must go carefully until we are a little more certain of our ground."

The pair had by this time reached the bottom of the circular staircase, and approached the oaken door. Tinker opened it as he had done previously, and he and Blake stepped into the passage with the silence of mice. Without hesitation, but walking on tiptoe, they traversed the dimly-lit passage until the end was reached, and cautiously looked round the corner. Here the corridor continued at right-angles, and seemed to be an exact replica of the other—only shorter.

The utter silence of the place was uncanny and almost weird, but Blake and Tinker continued on their way, turning several times at right-angles. The passages seemed to be endless, and Tinker had evidently been right in his first thought—that the castle was undermined by an extensive series of similar corridors. They were all dismal and badly lit, being neither pitch dark nor light, but in a sort of semi-twilight. What little daylight did penetrate into the place came from a number of perforated gratings let high up into the walls.

Blake and Tinker conversed very little as they explored the queer tunnels, and what few words were spoken were whispered in scarcely audible voices. After turning sharply for about the fourth time, the detective's keen ears caught a slight sound, and he instantly touched Tinker's arm as a signal for him to halt. The lad did so, and the pair stood listening intently.

The sounds were more distinct now, and Blake looked at Tinker tensely.

"Footsteps!" he murmured. "They are coming this way, too, by the sound of them!"

Tinker set his teeth grimly.

"Then we shall be spotted, guv'nor!" he breathed. "There's no escape from this passge unless we double back—and there's no time for that. What are you going to do?"

For answer Sexton Blake stole silently forward. He and Tinker were only a few feet away from another bend in the corridor, and they crept towards it and cautiously peeped round.

Blake pursed his lips in a grim smile as he beheld the bent figure of the old caretaker coming towards the spot. Llewellyn was carrying a tray, upon which was a supply of food and drink—and it was this circumstance which made the famous detective smile in that peculiar manner.

For it proved beyond question that a prisoner was close handy. The caretaker, evidently, was even now on his way to feed the captive—whom Sexton Blake had no doubt was Mr. Owen Glyn himself.

Events were moving slowly—but there seemed something tangible to go upon at last!

CHAPTER 5.
Down in the Dungeons.

SEXTON BLAKE'S keen brain summed up the situation quickly.

He knew that what Tinker had said was right—there was no time to retreat along the passage, and it was equally impossible for them to move forward without being seen by the oncoming caretaker. The corridor itself was absolutely bare of recesses, or other means of concealment, and there was only one possible thing to do.

Bold action was essential, and Blake decided to confront Llewellyn without a moment's delay.

Abruptly, and without any preliminary warning, the detective stepped out directly in the caretaker's path, closely followed by Tinker. The pair halted in the centre of the passage, and waited with some curiosity to see what effect their sudden appearance would have upon the decrepit and mysterious Llewellyn.

The result was somewhat startling.

A couple of ghosts could scarcely have made the caretaker jump more effectively. Blake and Tinker had stepped out so silently and quickly that Llewellyn was scared out of his wits for a few seconds, and after uttering a gasp of surprise and dismay, he allowed the tray of food to drop from his nerveless fingers.

The crash of the breaking crockery failed to bring Llewellyn back to earth, and he seemed almost paralysed with apprehension. There was no doubt that his surprise was genuine, and it was clear that he regarded the appearance of the two strangers within the castle with chagrin and concern. But he was too much startled to utter a single word for a brief space, and simply stared stupidly at the forms of Blake and Tinker, as if unable to believe the evidence of his own eyes.

After a few moments, however, the new-comers observed that the expression in the old man's eyes were changing from surprise and dismay to furious anger, and when he had recovered himself a trifle, he looked from one to the other with fierce glint in his curious, sinister eyes.

"What—what is the meaning of this?" he demanded hotly, his voice tremulous and quivering. "How did you force yourself into the castle? You—you have no right here whatever, and your audacity is amazing! What do you want?"

Sexton Blake stepped forward, and looked at the old caretaker sternly.

"You know very well what we want, Llewellyn!" he exclaimed. "Since you refused to admit us in the ordinary manner, we had no other course but to let ourselves in——"

"You are breaking the law!" interrupted the old man. "You have made yourselves liable to prosecution for burglary?"

The detective smiled.

"Possibly!" he admitted. "You are quite at liberty to inform the police—if you think fit! But before you do so I intend to find Mr. Owen Glyn—whom I am quite convinced is within this building—imprisoned against his will! Do you deny it?"

Llewellyn nodded quickly.

"Yes, I do!" he replied. "You—you must be mad to say such a thing! I told you before that Mr. Glyn left the castle last night, soon after his friend, and that——"

"Precisely!" cut in Sexton Blake smoothly. "That's what you told us, Llewellyn! But it doesn't follow that your statement was true, or that we believe what you said! As a matter of fact, I am quite convinced that you are lying! Mr. Glyn is here, and I demand to see him at once!"

The caretaker looked at Blake somewhat fearfully, but stuck to his point.

"He—he is not here!" he said feebly. "Why should you persist——"

"Then for whom was this food intended?" demanded the detective quickly, pointing to the mass of broken china and the ruined meal upon the floor. "Do you still insist that Mr. Glyn is not here?"

Llewellyn shrugged his shoulders with a helpless gesture, and remained silent. It was evident that he had been lying all along, and that he could not hope to keep up his attitude of deception. Blake noted the old man's discomfiture, and he smiled again.

"It is useless for you to keep up this farce a moment longer," he said curtly. "I have been exceedingly patient with you so far, Llewellyn. It is not my way to threaten—but unless you act promptly, and lead us immediately to the spot where Mr. Glyn is imprisoned, I shall send my assistant to fetch the police at once."

There was no mistaking the tone of Blake's voice, and the caretaker realised that he was cornered. He cast a surly and vindictive glance in the detective's direction, and gave vent to an angry grunt.

"Suppose I admit that Mr. Glyn is here—what business is it of yours?" he growled, altering his tactics, and eyeing the detective with a cunning look.

"That is entirely beside the point!" snapped Sexton Blake. "I demand to see Mr. Glyn at once—that is sufficient for you! Now then, are you going to show us the way to Mr. Glyn's apartment?"

The old man nodded eagerly.

"I am in your hands, gentlemen, by the look of things!" he muttered. "There is nothing for me to do but admit that you are right, and show you the way to the prisoner's cell! Come this way!"

Llewellyn's demeanour was now totally different, and Sexton Blake immediately suspected that the old man intended to lead himself and Tinker into a trap. But the detective gave no sign of his suspicions as he commenced following the caretaker along the dim passage. Nevertheless, he was alert, and well on his guard against any such move on Llewellyn's part.

Blake watched the old man closely as he led the way along, and kept within a few inches of his side, so as to obviate any possibly of his slipping away down some unforeseen tunnel or passage. In an ancient building of this kind, there was no telling what Llewellyn might be up to. He, obviously, was familiar with every nook and cranny of the old castle, whereas Blake and Tinker was completely in the dark regarding the lie of the land, as it were.

But the old fellow led the way along the passage in quite a straightforward manner, turning several times abruptly, until the top of a flight of stone stairs was reached. Llewellyn commenced the descent without a pause, and Blake made a sign to Tinker to be careful as they followed him down into the black depths which confronted him.

The staircase seemed to lead down into the very bowels of the earth, and an earthy, dank smell assailed their nostrils as they descended deeper. The air was sweet and wholesome, however, and the caretaker continued unconcernedly on his way, as if quite familiar with his surroundings.

After going down two flights, with abrupt turns at the bottom of each, Blake thought it advisable to have a little light upon the scene. The darkness here was intense and absolute, and the detective produced his electric torch, and switched it on. A second later Tinker followed his example, and the dual beams of light showed them the way with startling clearness after the intense gloom.

Llewellyn halted abruptly as the darkness was dispelled, and turned round, apparently disconcerted and upset. Obviously, he had not bargained for anything of this sort, and he was at a loss.

"Those torches are quite unnecessary!" he muttered, blinking in the bright glare. "I can find my way easily enough in the gloom——"

"That is very probably true," cut in Blake sharply. "But we prefer to see where you are leading us to, my friend!"

Llewellyn said no more, but the apprehensive look in his eyes became more pronounced. It was clear enough to him that these two strangers were highly suspicious of his motives in taking them into lower regions of the castle, but he turned once more, and continued on his way.

The bright torch lights showed Blake and Tinker that they were nearing the bottom of the staircase now, and they glanced round with interest. The stairs themselves, and the walls and floors, were all composed of solid stonework, massively built, and evidently of great age. But, apart from the earthy smelling atmosphere, the place appeared to be quite dry and well preserved.

At the foot of the staircase the caretaker emerged upon the floor of a long passage—a dark, tunnel-like corridor, with a series of iron-studded doors running along either side. The very appearance of these sinister-looking portals was depressing, and the gloom and chilly air merely served to enhance this unwelcome sensation.

Tinker shuddered.

"Ugh! What a ghastly place!" he exclaimed looking round with a shiver of disgust. "It's worse than the cells of old Newgate!"

Sexton Blake paused, and nodded.

"Much worse!" he agreed. "There is no doubt that we are in the dungeons of Glyn Castle, my lad. In the old days they were not over particular regarding light and ventilation, and I daresay some of these loathsome cubicles have housed many a brave martyr. Which of the cells is the present apartment of Mr. Owen Glyn, Llewellyn?" he added, turning upon the old caretaker quickly.

But the man, in spite of his age and stooping aspect, was not to the caught napping, and he shook his head.

"You won't find any trace of Mr. Glyn down here!" he declared emphatically. "I told you he wasn't in the castle, and you'll find that I'm right! You are welcome to search the dungeons to your heart's content."

As he spoke, Llewellyn threw open the heavy door of the first dungeon, and waved his hand towards the interior.

"Go in and assure yourselves that I am speaking the truth, gentlemen!" he exclaimed.

Sexton Blake smiled.

"Certainly!" he agreed. "We will follow you in, Llewellyn."

The caretaker cast a keen look at the detective, and it was quite apparent to him that Blake had no intention of allowing himself to be trapped unawares. The criminologist was, in very truth, highly suspicious of the old fellow, and determined to give him no opportunity of playing tricks.

Without hesitation, Llewellyn entered the dark, evil-looking chamber, and Blake and Tinker went in after him. A glance was sufficient to assure them that the dungeon was empty of all human presence; it was completely bare, with the exception of a couple of rusty, ominous chains, fitted with leg-bands, which had at one time been used to manacle some poor creature who had been condemned to eke out a terrible existence in the ghastly prison.

Blake and Tinker left the cell and re-entered the passage once more, the caretaker following at once. Llewellyn immediately opened the door of the next dungeon, and went in. Just inside the door he turned, and faced round with a knowing leer upon his wrinkled features.

"Empty—like the first!" he exclaimed. "You will find that all the dungeons are the same, and you are merely wasting your time in searching down here for Mr. Glyn!"

Sexton Blake pursed his lips.

"I don't believe you, Llewellyn," he said. "And I can assure you that I shall not be satisfied until I have made a very thorough investigation. Come along, open the door of the third cell."

The caretaker smiled to himself, and did as he was ordered. Blake and Tinker had not entered the second dungeon, for a brief scruntiny of the interior, clearly defined in the light from their torches, had assured them that it was as empty as the first.

Llewellyn closed the door and walked to the third cell, which he opened by drawing back the heavy bolt. He was just about to enter, with a grumble upon his lips regarding the futility of the whole proceedings, when Sexton Blake gave him a gentle push from the rear, which sent him stumbling into the dungeon before he realised what had occurred.

Blake slammed the door and shot the bolt with a thud, totally regardless of the caretaker's furious shouts of protest. There was no doubt that Llewellyn had received the surprise of his life, and he was giving vent to his feelings in no uncertain words.

But the detective merely smiled, while Tinker grinned broadly.

"Well, I must say the old chap asked for what he's got, guv'nor," he remarked. "I believe he was only waiting for a suitable opportunity to shove us into one of these blessed dungeons. He'd have done it, too, if you hadn't been so wide as to see through his little game."

"Undoubtedly, young'un. He brought us down here for the sole purpose of trapping us, as you say," agreed Blake. "But we cannot have our movements hampered and hindered by him indefinitely. He will come to no harm where he is, and, meanwhile, you and I can make our search for Glyn without interruption."

Tinker nodded.

"You think he's down here then, sir?" he asked.

"In my opinion there is no question about it," declared the detective. "These dungeons are extensive, and probably cover the whole basement of the castle. They are practically soundproof, too, and however loudly Glyn shouted he would not be heard, I am convinced that we shall find him, but whether we shall discover the reason for his imprisonment is quite another matter."

Sexton Blake was quickly throwing the beams of light from his torch into the dungeons as he spoke, one after the other. But drew a blank at each one—there was no sign of any living soul in any of them.

Tinker, after standing at Blake's side for a few moments, crossed the passage, and commenced searching in the dungeons upon the opposite side. These were exactly similar in every way, and they were all empty.

As the pair made their examination of the long line of cells, they could faintly hear the furious voice of Llewellyn demanding to be released. But they took no notice of him, and by the time they had reached the further end of the corridor they were no nearer to the object of their search. Owen Glyn was certainly not here, and Tinker looked at Blake dubiously.

"No luck so far, guv'nor!" he exclaimed. "But I daresay there are a good few more of these beastly places to look into yet. The whole foundations of the castle seems to be composed of 'em. What horrible cells to place human beings in! As bad as the black hole of Calcutta, I should think. Ugh! It strikes me that the good old days were the bad old days in some respects, if this is a fair sample of the prisons they used to use."

Tinker was certainly right, the dungeons were terrible places in every respect. Not a trace of daylight penetrated to them, and the only ventilation appeared to be afforded by the passages—which circulated a current of fairly sweet air by means of gratings connected with the open. The cells themselves were merely solid stone boxes fitted with doors, completely bare of furniture, and containing only the hideous iron manacles and chains attached to the walls. These spoke eloquently enough of the tortures which at one time were inflicted upon evildoers, and Tinker felt thankful that he was not living in an age when such things were allowed to take place.

After examining every cell in the passage, the two searchers found that the dungeons extended at right angles, another long corridor containing almost as many as they had already looked into. It took them a further ten minutes to flash their torches into all of them, but by the time they had reached the end they had still found no trace of the missing man.

There seemed to be no end to the series of dungeons, for a third passage was discovered at the end of the second, and this, also, was composed of the gruesome stone prisons. Blake and Tinker began to lose hope a little as they commenced upon them, and for the most part they searched in silence—one on either side. The atmosphere of the place was depressing in the extreme, and this, added to their non-success, seemed to take away their desire for conversation.

Blake judged, as he neared the end of the passage, that the dungeons were formed in a rectangle, or, to be exact, in three sides of the rectangle. The fourth side was merely a passage, with a stone staircase leading upwards at each end. It was by one of these staircases they had descended, and it thus became clear to Blake that they were nearing the spot where they had first commenced—only at the opposite end of the black passage. The detective shrewdly began to suspect that their quarry would be unearthed in one of the cells as yet unsearched; for the caretaker, in order to throw them off the track, would naturally lead them to the series of cells which were entirely unoccupied. No doubt he had planned to imprison Blake and Tinker in one of these, and he would have succeeded if the pair had not been strictly upon their guard.

Somewhat encouraged by his deduction, Sexton Blake continued looking into the dungeons with renewed hope of success, and his astute conclusion was proved to be correct within the next few moments. Tinker also had been hurrying to finish his side of the passage, and as he reached the end cell he gave vent to a delighted shout of triumph.

"Here he is, guv'nor, I've found him!" he exclaimed, flinging open the dungeon door as he spoke. "Mr. Glyn is here, chained up to the wall!"

Blake was at Tinker's side in a second, and together they entered the cell. The lad's words were quite true, as the detective saw at a glance. Owen Glyn—for it was he right enough—was sitting upon the floor of his prison, securely manacled by the ankles, and chained to a great ring in the wall, exactly as the prisoners of a bygone age had been incarcerated. Blake murmured angrily as he saw the helpless position of the unfortunate man, but before he could speak Glyn himself jumped to his feet with a clanking of chains and a joyous-shout.

"Thank Heaven!" he exclaimed fervently. "I don't know who you are, but I'm absolutely overjoyed to see you! Dare I hope that you have come to release me, or are you in league with the scoundrel Llewellyn? But I can see you're not."

Blake smiled.

"Quite right, Mr. Glyn, we have come to get you out of this unfortunate predicament," he said, looking at the young man keenly. "Your friend Spalding is responsible for our presence here, and——"

"Good old Vic! I knew he'd move heaven and earth to get me out of this mess," interrupted Glyn. "I've had a most fearful time, I can assure you, and somebody's got to go through the mill for shoving me down here like a caged animal! By George! A few more hours of this, and I should have gone raving mad, I believe."

The detective nodded.

"I can quite believe it," he agreed. "No doubt you have had a most trying experience, and it will be interesting to discover why you have been imprisoned here."

"That's the very thing which has been puzzling me, Mr.———" Glyn paused, and looked at Blake intently, and with a puckered brow. "I feel certain that I have seen your somewhere before, and yet—— Why, Great Scott! Of course, you're Mr Sexton Blake, aren't you? What an idiot I am not to have recognised you before?"

Owen Glyn's pleasure was genuine and unaffected, and he grasped Blake's hand heartily. After he had wrung it warmly, and had been briefly introduced to Tinker, he again turned to the detective with surprise in his eyes.

"I am tremendously delighted to meet you, Mr Blake, especially under such conditions as these!" he exclaimed. "But I can't understand how Vic enlisted your assistance so quickly. It's—it's amazing!"

Blake chuckled, and explained how Spalding had met himself and Tinker at the Hotel Majestic, and how he had induced them to visit Glyn Castle. As the detective related the incidents he deftly picked the locks of the ankle-irons, and managed to free the prisoner without the aid of keys. By the time he had finished Glyn had been informed of all that had taken place, and the young man was overwhelmed with gratitude at the efforts which had been made on his behalf.

"The whole business is a perfect mystery, Mr. Blake," he declared. "I haven't the slightest idea why I was locked up in this ghastly place, and I can only conclude that Llewellyn, the caretaker, must have gone mad."

Sexton Blake shook his head.

"I'm afraid I can't agree with you in that supposition," he said thoughtfully. "In spite of his obvious age, there is no sign of insanity about Llewellyn, so far as I can see. No, Mr. Glyn, there is some deep mystery at the back of the curious incidents which have taken place here, and the finding of the solution should prove to be a most absorbing little problem. To be quite frank, I am greatly interested."

Owen Glyn looked at Blake eagerly.

"Does that mean that you are going to make an investigation—professionally?" he asked.

"Certainly—if you wish it," returned the detective.

"If I wish it!" repeated Glyn. "Why, Mr. Blake, I'd rather you looked into the matter than anybody! There's evidently something confoundedly fishy about the whole business, and if you can clear it up—

well, I'd feel a lot more comfortable.''

No doubt Owen Glyn was thinking of the mysterious blank in his past life as he was speaking, and of the strange likeness of the old oil painting upstairs to the photograph of his father which he always carried.

A peculiar little thrill went through him as the thought crossed his mind that now, perhaps—with the celebrated Baker Street criminologist at work on the case—the mystery of his parentage would be cleared up. That was his dearest wish, and if only it could be accomplished, he would be the happiest fellow in the country.

But dare he even hope for such a satisfactory outcome of Sexton Blake's inquiries?

He scarcely knew what to think.

CHAPTER 6.
Who is Mr. Godfrey Jarrow?

''TINKER, I think you may as well run upstairs and inform Mr. Spalding of our discoveries,'' said Blake, turning to his assistant. ''Better go out by the front door, and being him back with you.''

Tinker nodded, and hurried off up the stone stairway on his mission. The rambling old castle was so vast in size, and in the number of passages and turnings, that it was quite an easy matter to become lost if one was not very careful.

But Tinker had a rather acute instinct for the sense of direction, and after making one or two false excursions, he found himself in the dimly-lit passage from which the oaken door gave access to the circular staircase which led to the tower by which he had first entered.

Arrived here, he made his way towards the spot from where Llewellyn had appeared carrying the tray of food, and soon afterwards Tinker emerged into the great hall of the castle. The front door was heavily bolted and barred, but Tinker had these unfastened within a few seconds, and passed out into the sweet-smelling open air. After the depressing atmosphere of the dungeons this was a welcome contrast, and he lad hurried off round the building to the spot at the rear where Victor Spalding was still mounting guard at the foot of the tower.

The journalist faced round sharply as Tinker appeared round the angle of the stone wall of the recess, and his face broke into a grin as he recognised the newcomer.

''Oh, it's you, is it?'' he exclaimed. '''Bout time you showed up, I think! What the deuce have you and Mr. Blake been doin' all this time? I was beginnin' to think you'd fallen victims to the same fate which had overtaken poor old Owen, and I was just goin' to shin up the ivy on a tour of investigation! Anythin' doin' in the discovery line, by the way?''

''Yes, rather!'' said Tinker. ''We've found Mr. Glyn—chained up in one of the beastly dungeons! He's quite all right, and the guv'nor told me to fetch you in!''

''Oh, ripping!'' exclaimed Spalding in a relieved voice. ''It's great news to hear that Owen is safe an' sound! I suppose that antiquated caretaker merchant was responsible for the whole business, wasn't he? By jingo, I'd like to give the madman a taste of his own medicine——''

''Don't worry—he's having it now!'' cut in Tinker, with a delighted grin. ''The guv'nor got fed up with Llewellyn's lies and procrastination, and shoved him into one of the dungeons. He's safe enough for a while!''

''Great!'' chuckled Spalding, as he followed Tinker back along the ledge to the side of the castle. ''Mr. Blake is a man of action, and knows exactly the right kind of goods to hand out. I'm dashed glad I met him this mornin' in Swansea—to say nothin' of you, old top! You're the very pair to handle a mystery in a mouldy old show of this sort, and I'll bet things are going to hum before we're very much older!''

Tinker nodded, and explained how he and Blake had discovered the unfortunate Glyn as they hurried round to the front entrance to the building. Spalding, of course, was just as mystified as the others regarding Llewellyn's motive for acting as he had done, and he was equally anxious to learn the solution of the outrage.

By the time the pair arrived in the upper passage on their way to join Blake and Glyn in the dungeons, they found that the detective and the late prisoner had already emerged, and were even now making their way towards the main part of the castle. Spalding hurried forward as he caught sight of his friend, and grasped his hand in a warm and hearty grip.

"I hear you've been havin' a taste of the dungeon stuff, old scout!" he exclaimed in his usual facetious manner. "Incarceration in the black hole, and all that kind of ghastly rot! But thank Heaven you're not hurt, old man! I've been in a most frightful state of anxiety since you disappeared—nearly demented with worry, to tell the truth! Any idea why that confounded old caretaker performed the locking-up stunt?"

Glyn shook his head.

"Not the slightest," he replied. "I received the surprise of my life when Llewellyn suddenly turned upon me! But we'd better go down to the room where the incident happened, and I'll tell you all about it!"

All four of them now descended the stairs, and walked towards the room Glyn had mentioned—that huge apartment into which the caretaker had showed himself and Spalding the previous night. Glyn had briefly told Sexton Blake about the oil painting, and about the strange blank in his memory regarding his past.

The detective was very interested, but so far had made very little comment. He intended to thoroughly search the old castle before he allowed himself to form any opinion regarding the matters in hand, but before he commenced upon this task he would hear Glyn's account of what occurred after Spalding's departure from the castle the night before.

The great reception room was soon reached, and after a preliminary glance round, and a quick scrutiny of the oil painting, Blake turned to Glyn.

"How did it happen that such a feeble old man as Llewellyn managed to overpower you?" he asked.

"That's the very thing which has been puzzling me!" climed in Spalding. "Owen is a pretty hefty sort of fellow, and can usually take care of himself as well as the best of us. Llewellyn must have had help—or else have used a bally dose of dope!"

Glyn smiled and shook his head.

"He neither had help, nor used a drug," he said. "He simply collared me by a trick. You know, Vic, that I hurt my injured shin pretty badly by falling over that stool, and you—like a good pal—bound it up before you went for the doctor?"

"Yes, rather—you looked so groggy that I felt absolutely bound to fetch the doc," said Spalding, with a nod. "What happened after I'd gone?"

"Well, Llewellyn seemed to be tremendously upset and concerned over me," said Glyn. "He fussed about, fetching all kinds of things I didn't want, until at last he unearthed some embrocation, with which he offered to rub my leg. I was in pretty acute pain at the time, so I accepted his invitation, and allowed him to get busy with the stuff. He propped my leg upon a stool while I sat in a chair, and set to work in quite a professional style."

"Queer!" commented Spalding. "If he intended to shove you in a cell, why did he doctor you up first?"

"He was probably doing so to gain time in which to mature his plans," said Sexton Blake shrewdly.

Glyn nodded.

"Just what I thought, Mr. Blake," he agreed. "Llewellyn was silent while he worked—scarcely spoke a word. Evidently he was forming the scheme which he afterwards carried out. Of course, I was entirely unsuspicious, and after he had rubbed my leg for a while, and then left me, I thought he was merely preparing a bandage or washing his hands. But the artful old scoundrel was engaged in something much deeper! To be exact, he was getting a noose of rope ready, and he threw this over my head and shoulders and drew it tight before I could even guess what was happening!"

"Great Scott!" exclaimed Victor. "The bally old fraud!"

"Of course, I struggled," went on Glyn. "But Llewellyn had taken care to get the rope low down, and so made me pretty nearly helpless. My arms were fastened to my sides, and I couldn't free them, however much I tried. And while I was struggling the caretaker yanked me to my feet, confound him! My injured leg let me down at once, and I collapsed upon the floor from sheer agony."

Glyn pulled a wry face at the thought of it, and it was evident that he had suffered severely from his lacerated shin.

"What did the murderous old blighter do next?" asked Spalding.

"Bound me more securely," said Owen. "He trussed me up like a plucked fowl, and then literally dragged me down into that foul dungeon. Goodness only knows how the old chap managed to do it, but he did. The journey was a pretty painful one for me, I can tell you; for I was simply hauled and bumped down the stone stairs like a sack of rubbish! Once the dungeon was reached, Llewellyn fixed those ankle-irons in position, and then removed the ropes. He gave me no explanation as to why he imprisoned me, but simply locked the door and cleared out. I've been lying down there ever since, wondering at the cause of it all, and you can tell how pleased I was when I saw Tinker unlock the door and call out to Mr. Blake. There you are, that's the whole yarn. Why the deuce the caretaker—who is a perfect stranger to me—should attack me and chain me up like that is a complete mystery. I've been trying to work out a probable explanation until my head ached, and I'm going to leave it to Mr. Blake to have a shot at."

The detective smiled.

"Your story is very interesting, Mr. Glyn," he said. "Without a doubt, there is something big behind Llewellyn's conduct, and we must do our best to discover it. As a commencement, I do not think we can do better than explore the castle. By the way, let me glance at the photograph of your father, will you?"

Glyn produced it at once and handed it to the detective. Blake took it, and examined it as he walked over to the oil painting, at which he gazed intently for some moments. But he said nothing as he handed the photograph back to Glyn, rather to the young man's surprise.

Sexton Blake next took a keen glance round the large room, noting everything it contained in his comprehensive manner, but did not go to the length of examining the interior of drawers, or anything of that kind. He simply observed the various articles of furniture, and the obvious fact that they had been in disuse for a great length of time. Blake also saw that the contents of this one room alone were of considerable value, each piece of furniture being a veritable gem of antiquity.

The next twenty minutes were spent in a tour of investigation through the various rooms in the rambling old castle. Neither of the explorers were familiar with the interior of the old place, and so Sexton Blake led the way, leaving the other three to follow at their leisure, as they chatted together Glyn's injured leg was still giving him pain, but it was very much better for his enforced rest in the dungeon. No doubt the caretaker's application of embrocation helped to take away the acute pain, for Glyn found that he could now use the limb with comparatively little inconvenience.

The trip through the great building was of absorbing interest, and in every room the little party found something to excite their curiosity and excitement. Glyn Castle, with the exception of Llewellyn, was completely empty of any human presence apart from themselves; but it was filled with antique and extremely valuable furniture of all descriptions. The old building was a treasure house of beautiful articles, some of them a trifle musty, perhaps, but splendidly preserved on the whole. The interior of the castle itself, too, was magnificent, and, taken altogether, it was a unique and lordly dwelling.

Sexton Blake, however, came across nothing whatever which would throw the most obscure light upon the strange events which had taken place, and it looked as though the mystery was to remain as deep as ever, in spite of the exhaustive search he had made.

The party, after going over every room in the castle with the exception of the domestic regions, now entered this domain of the servants, and these quarters showed the same signs of disuse as the rest of the place. There was one little room, however, which was quite different, and this evidently was the particular little den of the old caretakers. Everything here was fresh and clean, and there was no doubt that Llewellyn believed in making himself as comfortable as possible.

Blake's attitude became very much more keen as he entered the doorway, and for a few moments he stood gazing into the room intently, taking in every detail. The caretaker obviously used this apartment for his every need, for a small camp bedstead stood against one wall, while nearby there was a table upon which rested an oil cooking-stove, crockery, and pots and pans of various kinds.

Opposite to this, against the other wall of the room, there was a second table. This was used for the storage of books and papers, and for writing purposes, to judge by appearances. Pens and ink were there, writing blocks, envelopes, a spectacle case resting upon a few newspapers, and finally a bunch of telegraph forms.

Blake's eyes narrowed a trifle as he caught sight of this miniature "office," and he crossed over to the table quickly. Here, if anywhere, he would be likely to find at least something which would serve as a slight clue to the caretaker's actions, and the detective's hopes were soon proved to be well-founded.

Tinker and the two journalists followed closely upon Blake's heels, and they crowded round him as he made a search of the loose papers which littered the table.

"This is where the startlin' discoveries are goin' to be made!" exclaimed Spalding, gazing at the table with interest. "After searchin' all through this mouldy old castle and findin' absolutely nix, we arrive at the spot where the bally clues are absolutely piled up in heaps! There you are, Mr. Blake's clicked already!"

The others laughed and looked at the detective eagerly. He had certainly grasped one of the papers in a fashion which indicated that he had found something of importance, and his alert manner only served to confirm what Spalding had facetiously pointed out.

"Humph! I fancy you are not very far from the truth when you say that we have discovered our first clue," said the detective smoothly. "It may be very slight, but it is certainly something!"

"What is it, guv'nor?" asked Tinker.

"It's is a copy of a telegram which Llewellyn evidently despatched this morning," replied Sexton Blake. "That, at any rate, indicates that he is not acting alone, and it ought to give us something to work upon."

"What does it say, Mr. Blake?" asked Glyn eagerly.

"And who's the joker it's addressed to?" chimed in Spalding. "That's the most important thing, in my opinion."

The detective smiled.

"Undoubtedly," he agreed. "But if you will listen, I will read the wire to you. It is addressed to Mr. Godfrey Jarrow, Jermyn Street, London, W., and it merely says, 'Please come to the castle by first available train.—LLEWELLYN.' The message, you see, is very brief and to the point, and it seems to indicate that we may expect further developments before the lapse of many hours."

Spalding puckered his brows.

"Wonder who the dickens Mr. Godfrey Jarrow happens to be, anyhow?" he said musingly. "Ever heard of the chap, Owen?"

Glyn shook his head.

"Not to my knowledge," he replied. "The name is quite unfamiliar to me, but I should say that he's the man who employs the caretaker—in all probability the owner of the castle. That seems to be the most feasible explanation of the matter. What do you think, Mr. Blake?"

The detective looked thoughtful.

"Somewhat difficult to say," he answered evasively. "In any case, the chief point of interest seems to be Llewellyn's anxiety to bring this Mr. Jarrow down here in such a hurry."

Thud! Thud!

Sexton Blake was interrupted at this point by the sudden banging of the knocker upon the front door, and the members of the little party looked at one another questioningly. Spalding, of course, was the first to break the silence, and—as usual—he could not refrain from trying to be funny.

"Talk of the devil!" he exclaimed. "I expect this is the Jarrow merchant himself, comin' to make a personal investigation——"

"Don't talk rot!" said Glyn. "How the thunder could anybody get from London in such a short time as this! Why, it couldn't be done by aeroplane!"

"Quite right, Glyn, but I should not be surprised if the visitor proves to be a messenger boy with a wire from the mysterious Mr. Jarrow," said Blake, striding towards the door as he spoke. "However, I will soon ascertain whether I am right or not!"

The detective was right, for he found a telegraph boy waiting at the hall door, with a telegram for Llewellyn. Blake took it, tipped the boy, and closed the door. Then, feeling perfectly justified in so doing under the circumstances, he tore open the envelope and withdrew the flimsy form.

Before he had time to unfold it, Tinker, Glyn and Spalding were by his side, all eager to read the contents of the wire. It was exceedingly brief, and ran: "Arrive during evening.—JARROW." Just those four words, but Sexton Blake's face assumed a grim expression as he read them.

"We certainly shall have to look a good deal further into this matter," he said crisply. "It is just beginning to get interesting! I fancy there is a rather deeply-laid plot at the back of the incidents which have already occurred, and it would be a pity if we failed to seize upon such a unique opportunity to probe it to the bottom."

The detective spoke thoughtfully, and it was clear that he had already formed some sort of scheme for the furtherance of his plans even in this short time. The others looked at him with puzzled expressions as he walked back to Llewellyn's little den, and it was evident that none of the trio could quite understand Sexton Blake's meaning.

They watched him in silence for a few moments as he made another search of the caretaker's table—which brought forth no further results, however—and then Spalding turned to the criminologist with an exaggerated frown upon his brow."

"Subtle, deucedly subtle, in fact!" he exclaimed. "I've been rackin' my brains to discover just what you meant by that last remark of yours, Mr. Blake! That is to say, I've been tryin' to find where the unique opportunity for probin' the mystery comes in! Dashed if I can see one!"

Blake smiled.

"You'll understand in a few moments, my dear fellow," he said. "It seems to me that our best policy will be to act the part of hidden watchers—for a time, at any rate—until we are a little more certain of our ground. And in order to carry out a plan of that sort, it is essential that Llewellyn should remain entirely unsuspicious of what we have discovered, including your prison cell, Glyn!"

The young man stared at the detective in some amazement, and it was evident that Spalding and Tinker were equally surprised.

"But, that's impossible, Mr. Blake!" protested Glyn. "How can we make the caretaker believe that I'm still in the dungeon, when I'm not?"

"Quite simply," said Blake. "All you have to do is to go back there!"

"What!" exclaimed Glyn, gazing at Blake with a blank expression. "Go back to that ghastly hole! No fear! Why, you must be joking——"

"On the contrary, I am deadly serious!" interrupted the detective quickly. "You must remember that Llewellyn, so far, is totally in the dark as to what we have been doing since we locked him in the dungeon, and it is my intention that he should remain unenlightened. If you will consent to go back to your prison, Glyn, it will be quite an easy matter to hoodwink the old man—until such time as we are ready to take action."

Spalding grinned.

"There you are, old man, easy!" he exclaimed. "Ripping chance for you to distinguish yourself, and all that sort of rot! Hanged if I can see what Mr. Blake is drivin' at, but that's nothin' to do with the question! All you've got to do is to go back into the dark hole, and sit tight!"

Owen Glyn took very little notice of Spalding's remarks. But it was beginning to dawn upon him that Sexton Blake really meant what he said. It seemed an extraordinary thing, and the young man was totally at a loss to see through the detective's plan.

"I can see you're serious, Mr. Blake," he said. "But what on earth is the idea? What good will it do if I go back into the cell? There seems to be no point in such a thing!"

"I think you will admit there is, when you've heard what I've got to say," replied Blake smoothly. "We now kow that Llewellyn is in communication with this mysterious Mr. Jarrow. We also know that Jarrow is arriving here to-night. That, in point of fact, is all the information we have been able to gather, and in order to discover the exact connection between these two men we shall have to act warily. Therefore it is essential to put Llewellyn entirely off the track, and allay his suspicion."

"Of course," said Tinker. "But how are you going to do it, guv'nor?"

"By replacing Mr. Glyn in his original prison, and releasing Llewellyn!" said the detective. "It will be easy enough for us to make the old man understand that our search for Mr. Glyn has been in vain, and we will apologise for locking him up, and take our departure from the castle!"

Tinker slapped his thigh enthusiastically.

"By jingo—that seems simply a terrific wheeze!" he exclaimed. "Llewellyn will think we're blithering idiots, and he'll feel absolutely secure when he finds that Mr. Glyn is still in the dungeon—just as he left him!"

"Exactly!" agreed Sexton Blake. "The caretaker will put us down as a pair of incompetent noodles, and after our departure he will act in precisely the same manner as he would have done if we hadn't entered the castle at all. He will, in fact, put us out of his calculations entirely. But you and I and Mr. Spalding will be very much on the alert—outside the castle—waiting and watching for whatever developments occur."

Sexton Blake's plan was a sound one in every respect, and quite easy to put into operation. Llewellyn, of course, was totally ignorant of the fact that Glyn had been found and released, and if he discovered the young man still imprisoned when he visited the dungeon after the departure of Blake and Tinker, he would naturally assure that Glyn had been there all the time. Spalding, who had been on guard outside, had not been seen by the caretaker at all, so would not enter into the old man's calculations.

The scheme was pronounced first rate by all three of Blake's companions, although Owen Glyn certainly did not relish the part assigned to him. But the whole thing depended upon his consent to be re-imprisoned, and he agreed with obvious reluctance. This was not to be wondered at, for he had already spent several hours of extreme discomfort in the terrible dungeon, and to voluntarily go through the trying ordeal again was asking a good deal of him. But he could see that it was the only way.

It was quite evident that Glyn had not been imprisoned by Llewellyn without a reason, and the young man was just as keen to discover that reason as Blake and Tinker and Spalding. Perhaps of the four, he was the most anxious of them all—for he was beginning to think that the ultimate explanation of the mystery would concern him very intimately.

And so Glyn agreed to fall in with Sexton Blake's plan.

He consoled himself with the thought that his second sojourn in the dungeon would only be of short duration, and that his friends would be very near to him the whole time—crouching in the gloom of the old castle walls to see what events the evening would bring forth.

CHAPTER 7.
The Man From London.

GLYN CASTLE, dimly outlined against the sombre background of storm-swept sky, appeared eerie and sinister in the evening gloom.

Darkness had descended upon the majestic old pile which reared itself heavenwards from the lonely cliff-face, and with it had come the rain and the wind—heralding a storm similar to that of the previous night.

Down below, on the treacherous rocks and crags, the great rollers came dashing inshore with tremendous force, hissing and roaring, and sending vast sheets of vapour-like spray high into the air. The sounds of the angry waters, beating monotonously against the mountain of rock which formed the cliff-face, could be heard above the howling of the wind and the patter of rain upon the sodden ground, which added to the dismal and black outlook.

In spite of the stormy weather and the desolation, however, a man presently came striding towards the old building, enveloped in a dripping mackintosh. He was evidently a big, burly individual, heavily built and vigorous; so much was obvious from his generous outline and his swinging, quick tread. He was looking ahead of him as he progressed, and he made straight for the massive front door of the lonely castle.

No doubt the solitary visitor imagined himself to be the only person abroad in that wind-swept, exposed spot; but if such was the case he was mistaken. For his every movement was intently watched by two pairs of sharp eyes, which gazed out from behind a low pile of rocks situated in the nearby dripping grassland.

Tinker and Victor Spalding were the owners of the eyes, and they had been concealed in their present position for the last hour—ever since the first signs of approaching darkness had made themselves apparent. Their vigil had by no means been a pleasant one, for with the coming of the rain and the wind they had been soaked and chilled to the bone. But it was impossible for them to desert their post, and they had accepted the inevitable with the best grace possible.

"Hallo! Somethin' doin' at last!" whispered Spalding, nodding towards the big man. "This merchant must be the mysterious Jarrow—and I must say he looks a formidable sort of blighter! Old Dempsey would have somethin' of a job to knock him flat!"

Tinker nodded and grinned.

"Yes—he's certainly a decent-sized chap!" he returned. "But mere weight isn't everything, you know. I daresay he's flabby enough when it comes to the pinch!"

"Let's hope so, anyhow," said Spalding. "We may have to come to grips with him before the night's out. I shouldn't be surprised if there's a bally lot of dirty work in the offing! Wonder how your guv'nor's farin'?"

"No need to worry about him," said Tinker. "He'll be able to look after himself easily enough—dirty work or not! All the same, I wish we were with him!"

Sexton Blake had gone off alone to carry out a little scheme he had in mind, and Tinker and Spalding were forced to keep watch alone. But they had very little doubt that the detective was very much on the alert somewhere within the castle and they were quite easy in their minds concerning his safety.

The burly pedestrian had now reached the front door of the building, and he applied the heavy knocker in no uncertain manner—wishing, do doubt, to get in out of the rain as quickly as possible. Tinker and Spalding saw the bent old figure of Llewellyn as he opened the door, and a moment later the man in the mackintosh had passed inside, and the door was reclosed.

"Phew! What a night, Llewellyn!" exclaimed the visitor as he entered the dim hall. "Rain, wind and darkness—to say nothing of stony pathways!"

"Yes, sir—the weather is terrible," agreed the caretaker, helping the stranger off with his dripping mackintosh. "But, all the same, I am very glad you have come so quickly. Several strange happenings have taken place, and I thought it advisable to wire you as I did.

Mr. Godfrey Jarrow—for the visitor was obviously he—nodded, and followed the caretaker into the little living room. He was a very large man of about forty-five years of age, somewhat distinguished-looking, and decidedly gentlemanly. Evidently he was a man who believed in getting down to business without loss of time, for he seated himself in a chair near the shaded reading lamp, and looked at Llewellyn inquiringly.

"Now then—what's the trouble?" he asked. "Why have I been brought down here in such a hurried manner? You say that strange happenings have taken place, and I'm quite anxious to learn what they are."

The caretaker seated himself some little distance from the newcomer, and stroked his stubby grey beard a trifle nervously. Then, speaking in his habitual trembling manner, he entered into a long account of all that had taken place in the old castle. He told Mr. Jarrow about the arrival of the two shipwrecked young men the previous night, and how they had begged for shelter.

He explained all the incidents as they had occurred; how Glyn had stumbled over the stool and reopened this wound, and how his friend Spalding had set off for the doctor. Llewellyn then related how he had imprisoned the young man by roping him up, and dragging him down into the dungeon.

Mr. Jarrow listened to the caretaker's story with great intentness, and it was clear that he was vastly interested—and not a little puzzled. He stared at Llewellyn somewhat blankly, and there seemed to be traces of acute annoyance in his glance.

"But—I don't understand!" he exclaimed. "What on earth is the meaning of all this, eh? Why did you take it upon yourself to lock this young man up in the dungeon?"

Llewellyn smiled.

"I think that point will be quite clear to you, sir, when I tell you that the young man's name is Glyn—Owen Glyn!" he said quietly.

Mr. Godfrey Jarrow jumped to his feet quickly.

"What!" he exclaimed. "Do you mean to tell me that one of the two shipwrecked men was Glyn himself—Owen Glyn! I—I can't believe it, Llewellyn! It's altogether too fantastic to suppose that he would be cast ashore here—of all places!"

The caretaker shook his head.

"However queer it is, sir, I am quite convinced that the man I have imprisoned is Mr. Glyn—the owner of the castle!" he declared. "I was just as much amazed as you are when I first discovered the truth; but there is no doubt that I am right, as I think you will agree when I relate what occurred to arouse my suspicions."

And Llewellyn proceeded to tell the agitated Mr. Jarrow about the oil-painting, and its striking likeness to the photograph which Owen carried in his pocket-book. He also related the manner in which Spalding, accompanied by two strangers, had revisited the castle during the morning, and had demanded admittance.

"You didn't allow them to enter, of course?" asked Jarrow sharply.

"No, sir; but they were very persistent, and I had to finally bang the door in their faces," said the caretaker. "It was impossible to make them believe that Mr. Glyn had departed the night before, and I was greatly worried as to the best course to take."

Jarrow nodded with approval.

"You did quite right, Llewellyn—quite right," he exclaimed. "And now——"

"But I haven't told you everything yet, sir," interrupted the caretaker. "A little while after I had refused to admit the strangers I prepared some food for Mr. Glyn, and then started off for the dungeons. But in the upper passage I was suddenly confronted by the same two strangers who had called earlier, and I was absolutely flabbergasted!"

"Good heavens!" muttered Jarrow. "How did they get in?"

"I don't know, sir; but they gave me to understand that they did not intend to take their departure until they had found Mr. Glyn," replied Llewellyn. "Of course, I told them he wasn't here, but they wouldn't believe me. At last, while they were searching the dungeons, they pushed me into one of the cells, and locked the door! I was helpless, and almost an hour passed before I saw them again. But then they returned and let me out, saying that they could not find Mr. Glyn, and apologising for making a prisoner of me!"

"That was extremely fortunate, and we must congratulate ourselves," said Mr. Jarrow grimly. "You have done exceedingly well, Llewellyn, and I am greatly pleased at the neat manner in which you captured Mr. Glyn. It is most essential that he should be held safely. But what happened to the strangers—did they leave quietly?"

"Oh, yes, sir—they went away at once," said the old fellow. "Possibly they thought they might get into trouble if they remained, for they had broken into the castle unlawfully. What do you intend to do with the prisoner now, sir?"

Jarrow paced up and down the small room once or twice before replying, deep in thought. The caretaker's story had obviously upset his equanimity, and he seemed somewhat at a loss.

"It is most extraordinary," he muttered. "The fact that Glyn should come here in such a strange fashion is amazing! But one thing is certain, Llewellyn," he added, in a louder voice. "He cannot remain here! We must get him away out of the country at the earliest possible moment. I don't see exactly how it's going to be done—but I shall soon think of a way, and make plans accordingly. Meanwhile, of course, Glyn must be kept securely imprisoned in the dungeon."

Llewellyn nodded.

"Yes, sir, he'll be safe enough there,' he said. "But I am very glad that you have come; the responsibility of keeping him a prisoner without your knowledge was very trying to me."

Mr. Godfrey Jarrow agreed and proceeded to ask the caretaker a string of questions connected with the strangers who had entered the castle without permission. But Llewellyn affirmed that he knew nothing about them whatever, not even their names. Spalding, of course, he spoke of as Mr. Glyn's bosom friend and companion in the shipwrecking incident. But with regard to the others—Blake and Tinker—he was entirely ignorant.

Jarrow and the caretaker discussed the matter for some little time, and finally decided that the strangers were merely chance acquaintances of Spalding's, whose aid he had enlisted in his search for his friend. Now that they had gone, there was nothing further to worry about.

"Are you going down to see Mr. Glyn, sir?" asked Llewellyn.

Jarrow shook his head.

"No, I don't think I had better do so," he replied. "Such a proceeding would be most unwise, and no good would come of such an interview, so far as I can see. By the way, how is Mr. Glyn taking his enforced imprisonment——"

Mr. Godfrey Jarrow paused abruptly and a startled look appeared in his eyes as he glanced over the caretaker's shoulder. For there, framed in the doorway, was an exact replica of the old caretaker himself! Every detail was the same—the figure, the stoop, the grey-bearded features — everything with the exception of the clothing, which was slightly different. For a few seconds Jarrow continued to stare at the apparition with his mouth agape, and then he uttered a gasp of surprise.

"What—who—— Am I dreaming?" he stammered hoarsely.

Llewellyn, attracted by Jarrow's strange manner, faced round sharply, and then drew in his breath with a quick little hiss. At the same time he smiled to himself and rose to his feet, his attitude and demeanour changed entirely. He was no longer the bent and shrivelled old man he appeared, but stood up tall and erect. In a flash he had removed the short grey beard which adorned his chin, and almost in the same movement a false wig was drawn from his head. Then he stepped backwards a few paces, and as he did so a revolver miraculously appeared in his right hand, held in a steady and unwavering grip.

"I think, Mr. Jarrow, that the time has arrived when a formal introduction of myself is necessary!" he said in a cold, firm voice. "My name is Sexton Blake, and the best advice I can give both you and Llewellyn at the moment is to put your hands up without delay!"

The detective, as he spoke, watched the two men narrowly. There was no doubt that he had sprung a very complete surprise upon them, and he did not anticipate any trouble. The old caretaker promptly raised his hands above his head and advanced into the room trembling with fright. But Mr. Godfrey Jarrow was made of sterner stuff, and instead of complying with Blake's order, he uttered a bellow of fury and bewilderment.

"What does all this theatrical tomfoolery mean?" he roared angrily.

Blake smiled.

"I fancy that what you are pleased to term theatrical tomfoolery is in reality something far more useful!" he said pleasantly. "What I have learned by impersonating your caretaker, Mr. Jarrow, convinces me that you are playing a rather deep game—at the expense of Mr. Owen Glyn! I suspected all along that something decidedly fishy was in the wind, and so I prepared this little scheme in order to make certain of my ground. I found it quite a simple matter to re-enter the castle after releasing Llewellyn from the dungeon, and to imprison him afresh in one of the turrets which abound here!"

Jarrow breathed hard.

"You—you——" he began in a voice choking with fury.

"Quite so," said the detective blandly. "I must admit that my efforts at disguise succeeded far beyond my expectations, but by the aid of the wig and beard you were completely deceived, no doubt owing to the fact that you have not seen Llewellyn for some months, and also to the lack of adequate illumination! However, you have told me something of the true state of affairs, and but for the unfortunate appearance of Llewellyn, I daresay we should have progressed even better! The caretaker's escape has upset my plans considerably, but—since he has regained his freedom—we must make the best of it!"

Sexton Blake, although he spoke in this manner, was in reality feeling greatly chagrined at the partial failure of his plans. He had been quite as surprised as Jarrow when Llewellyn had appeared at the doorway, for the detective fondly imagined that the caretaker was safely locked in a remote turret.

Sexton Blake had conceived this new scheme some little time after he and Tinker and Spalding had left the castle, and in order to carry it out successfully it was necessary that Llewellyn should be disposed of for the time being. So Blake had again climbed the tower by means of the ivy, and had taken the old caretaker unawares, and had imprisoned him securely. But, by some means or other, he had managed to make his escape, thus completely spoiling the further plans which the detective had in mind.

It was very annoying, but now that the secret was out, Blake could do nothing but act boldly, and face both Jarrow and Llewellyn squarely. He was not exactly sure how the little episode was going to end, but he determined to learn all he could while he held the upper hand.

Mr. Godfrey Jarrow glared at Blake vindictively.

"What business is it of yours what I do in my own house?" he growled furiously. "What right have you here at all?"

"Never mind that at the moment," answered Sexton Blake. "I strongly advise you to tell the truth in a straightforward manner, Mr. Jarrow, before you get yourself into further trouble. "Tell me—why are you so anxious to get Mr. Owen Glyn out of the country?"

Jarrow scowled.

"I do not see why I should submit to your impertinent questioning!" he said warmly. "You have forced your way into the castle unasked, and you have apparently taken it upon yourself to pry into my private affairs! I refuse to put up with it, sir, and I refuse to answer any of your confoundedly personal questions!"

Sexton Blake set his lips firmly.

"It is quite obvious to me that you are deliberately trying to defraud Mr. Glyn!" he said quietly. "I would suggest, Mr. Jarrow, that you immediately abandon any such idea, and give up any schemes you have in mind to carry out your object. I can assure you that it will be far better to restore to Mr. Glyn the property which is rightfully his! Do you understand me?"

Jarrow glanced at the detective fiercely. But he seemed to realise that he was cornered—that he was playing a losing game.

"Perfectly!" he muttered sullenly.

"Do you agree to discontinue your campaign against Mr. Glyn and his inheritance? asked Blake.

"What else can I do?" growled Jarrow. "You have got the upper hand of me and I am forced into a corner! Confound you—you have ruined everything!"

Sexton Blake smiled and strolled a few steps nearer to the centre of the room. As he did so he noticed that Llewellyn was reaching upwards to where a little stone projection protruded from the wall. The detective instantly became suspicious, and his voice snapped out sharply:

"Hold still, Llewellyn—and keep your hands above your head!" he commanded. "Remember that I have warned——"

Blake suddenly realised that he had been a fraction of a second too late. For even as he uttered the words he felt the solid stone flooring beneath him give way.

Before he could even throw out his hands in an effort to save himself, he knew that he was shooting downwards into the utter blackness of the lower regions—utterly helpless to stop his headlong descent!

CHAPTER 8.
The Enemy's Strategy.

SEXTON BLAKE'S fall was arrested a moment later by the hard, unyielding stonework of the lower floor.

His hurtling body crashed down with tremendous force, and it seemed impossible that he could have escaped without serious injury. He realised in a dazed kind of way that he was suffering considerable pain and that he was in pitchy darkness, with the exception of one small square of dim illumination which was apparent high above his head.

Even as he glanced up towards the spot the lighted aperture gradually grew smaller, and the detective knew that the movable stone slab in the floor of Llewellyn's room was sliding back into position—operated no doubt by some secret mechanism. Finally it closed with scarcely an audible click, and Blake's prison became even more intensely dark.

The detective, after lying upon the floor for a few minutes, in order to regain the breath which had been practically knocked from his body, slowly began to rise to his feet. He found, somewhat to his surprise, that he was able to stand, and a brief overhauling of his limbs was sufficient to tell him that no bones were broken. He was stiff and sore, however, and bruised practically all over. But, upon the whole, he considered that he had escaped lightly, for he had fallen from a great height.

The very distance of the drop told Blake that he had landed in one of the dungeons of the castle, and the knowledge made him furious. All his plans had apparently miscarried in the most unfortunate fashion, just at the moment when he had expected to accomplish so much!

His only comfort was in the thought that Tinker and Spalding were outside, keeping a close watch upon the building. He could rely upon them to get busy within a reasonable time, and this aspect of the matter caused Blake to cheer up a trifle.

Although the detective was feeling extremely annoyed at the simple manner in which he had been caught, he could not, with justice, censure himself for what had occurred. He had not blundered in any way, and it had not been possible for him to suspect the existence of a trap in the stone flooring of the caretaker's room. It had seemed absolutely solid in every way, and the moveable slab was so ingeniously constructed that it was quite out of the question to detect its presence.

The catatrophe had occurred solely on account of Llewellyn's unforeseen appearance, for the cunning old rascal was responsible for the opening of the hidden trapdoor. But Blake realised, with a somewhat bitter tightening of the lips, that worrying would do no good.

Painfully he felt in his pocket for his electric torch. Every movement of his arms and legs caused him to wince slightly, for his fall had shaken him up pretty considerably. But he managed to grasp the torch after an effect, and pressed the switch hopefully.

But no light appeared, as he had half feared. The fall had broken the filament of the tiny bulb, and the instrument was put out of action for the time-being. So the luckless detective was forced to fall back upon the less effective, but extremely useful, box of matches. He struck one of the matches at once, and the little blaze which resulted showed him his suspicion was correct.

He was imprisoned in one of the gruesome dungeons, without a doubt, and this knowledge did not add to Blake's peace of mind. For he knew that these cells were so strongly constructed that escape was completely out of the question. Just to make assurance doubly sure, however, he quickly examined the place by the aid of the matches, but soon found that there was no hope of getting out. The door was barred upon the outside, and the walls were composed of solid slabs of stone. Nothing short of dynamite would loosen one of them, and the trapdoor by which he had entered was all of a couple of dozen feet behind his reach.

With feelings too deep for words, Sexton Blake seated himself upon the hard stone floor. There was absolutely nothing he could do to help himself, and it only remained for him to wait, with as much patience as possible, for Tinker to get into action. The position was galling in the extreme; but it was no use railing against the inevitable. He was a prisoner, and he must remain in captivity until he was released.

Meanwhile, Mr. Godfrey Jarrow—in the room over Blake's head—looked at Llewellyn with great approval as he flopped himself into a chair breathing hard. The excitement of the last few minutes had made Jarrow go somewhat pale, but he was rapidly recovering his composure.

"That was a smart move of yours, Llewellyn!" he exclaimed admiringly. "I must congratulate you heartily upon your amazing astute action! You have managed to turn the tables completely, and that interfering detective is absolutely out of harm's way! He can't escape, I suppose?"

Llewellyn, looking pleased and somewhat excited, smiled and shook his head.

"No, sir, Mr. Blake is undoubtedly a very clever man, but I don't think, he is capable of escaping from the dungeons," he said. "It is lucky for us that he is ignorant of the pecularities of the castle, for if he had been familiar with them, he would assuredly have succeeded in attaining his object, and releasing Mr. Glyn!"

"Yes, he would—confound him!" he agreed. "But how did you manage to escape from the turret Blake mentioned?"

The old caretaker smiled again. He was one of the most aged of the Glyn family retainers, and he had lived in the castle all his life. There was not a secret about the old place of which he was not aware, and in these circumstances it was not surprising that he had regained his liberty.

"Mr. Blake locked me in the turret of the west wing," he said. "Naturally, the place seemed to be absolutely secure to him, sir, and it was pure chance that made him choose that particular turret for my prison. I don't suppose he would have been so easy in mind had he known about the secret stairway which leads from it to the upper passage; but it was by that means that I made my escape. However, it was impossible for the detective to know that I could leave the turret whenever I pleased, and I felt quite unconcerned sir. But I received something of a shock when I commenced the descent."

Jarrow looked up quickly.

"Shock!" he repeated. "You don't mean that Blake's assistants are inside the castle——"

"Oh, no, sir, nothing of that sort," interrupted Llewellyn. "I was referring to the condition of the secret stairway. Shortly after I left the turret I found my progress barred by a mass of fallen masonry, which must have come dislodged years and years ago. I began to think that Mr. Blake had made me a prisoner in reality, but I set to work upon the wreckage, and after some hours of hard work, I succeeded in forcing my way through. That is the reason I did not make my appearance earlier, sir."

Jarrow nodded.

"Perhaps it was just as well that you didn't, Llewellyn," he said. "Everything has turned out very well indeed as things are, and you came upon the scene at the precise moment to upset Blake's little game. It was a lucky thing for us that we happened to be in this room, where the trapdoor is situated."

"Very lucky indeed, sir," agreed the caretaker. "I could not force Mr Blake to walk upon the trap, but I was waiting in readiness to act as soon as he did so. At the same time, I was a little dubious as to whether the central stone would answer to the touch of the knob, for the device which actuates the trap was made in the sixteenth century. But, fortunately, it is still in working order."

Llewellyn, owning to his long association with the members of the Glyn family spoke in almost a refined manner. He was an exceedingly well-trained servant, and he appeared to regard Mr. Jarrow with as much respect as his former employers. Much of the sinister appearance which had so drawn the attention of Owen and his friend had now left the caretaker's face, and in all probability he had assumed the expression for reasons of his own.

Mr Godfrey Jarrow, now that the excitement of the moment was over, was rapidly recovering his composure. He certainly had not bargained for anything of this nature when he had left London, but now that events had turned out as they had, he was bound to deal with them.

"Look here, Llewellyn, we can't leave matters as they are," he declared, looking at the old fellow thoughtfully. "Now that we have gone so far in this affair, we're absolutely forced into going further. Not only must we get Glyn out of the country, but Sexton Blake as well. That is essential, and the sooner we can manage it the better. No harm will come to them, of course; but we must arrange to keep them away for at least three months."

Llewellyn listened gravely to what Jarrow said, and then shook his head.

"I am afraid the matter is not quite so simple as that, sir," he said. "You see, Mr. Blake is not the only one concerned. There are others, one of them the detective's assistant, and the other, Mr. Glyn's own particular chum."

"But I don't see what——" began Jarrow.

"I think it highly probable that these two young men are even now waiting outside the castle," interrupted Llewellyn. "Very likely they are keeping watch, and if that is the case, it will be very difficult to do as you suggest. You see, sir, they know that Mr. Blake and Mr. Glyn are inside the castle, and it is not to be supposed that they will go away without further investigation. The very fact that Mr. Blake does not rejoin them will cause them to be more suspicious than ever."

Jarrow gave vent to a low curse under his breath.

"Confound it! This will ruin everything!" he muttered savagely. "But you're right, Llewellyn—absolutely right! "Something will have to be done at once about those chaps outside. We can't allow their presence to upset all our arrangements, that's certain. By James!"

He broke off abruptly, and slapped his thigh. A cunning expression appeared in his eyes as he looked at the old caretaker, and it was evident that Jarrow had thought of some new dodge for the furtherance of his plans.

"An idea, Llewellyn, a really splendid idea, as I think you'll agree!" he exclaimed, rubbing his hands together with a satisfied air. "If those two fellows are really outside, as you say, I think it will be a simple matter to fool them."

The caretaker looked at Jarrow quickly.

"Fool them, sir?" he repeated.

"Exactly! Nothing will be easier, Llewellyn," went on Jarrow. "All you have to do is to go outside, find them, and bring them in here."

The old man stared blankly, and looked very mystified.

"But I don't understand——" he began.

"You would understand easily enough if you considered the position for a moment," interrupted Jarrow briskly. "Blake came in here disguised as yourself, Llewellyn, and it's only natural to suppose that his friends outside are aware of his plans. Assuming that to be the case, it follows that they will mistake you for Blake as soon as they see you, for it is impossible for them to know that Blake is imprisoned."

The caretaker nodded his head quickly as he realised Jarrow's meaning, and his face expressed some amusement.

"Of course, sir, of course!" he exclaimed. "It is a remarkably smart idea of yours. I am to go outside and find Tinker and his companion, and tell them to come in? In your opinion they will accept me as the disguised Mr. Blake, and will follow without hesitation."

Jarrow nodded.

"That's it—precisely," he agreed. "They'll take you for Blake without question, and they'll enter the castle like a couple of lambs! They can't possibly have the slightest suspicion of you, and the very fact of your inviting them to enter will make it appear that Blake has gained the upper hand. But they'll soon find out their mistake."

Jarrow grinned to himself as he spoke, and Llewellyn nodded his head approvingly. The dodge was certainly a cute one, and there was every prospect of it succeeding.

Tinker and Spalding, of course, were fully aware that Blake had entered the castle in thue personality of the caretaker, and they would naturally assume—when they saw Llewellyn—that they were confronting the disguised detective. Jarrow's scheme, undoubtedly, was a master stroke of finesse, and he hastened to put it into operation.

Llewellyn accordingly—after receiving a few parting words of instruction from Jarrow—equipped himself with a storm-lantern, and made his way out of the gloomy old building into the darkness of the night. He had no notion in which direction to look for his victims, but he shrewdly concluded that a few softly-spoken hails would have the effect of making Tinker and Spalding disclose their whereabouts.

The old caretaker was no fool, and he called Tinker's name in quite a fair imitation of Sexton Blake's own tone of voice. He was now familiar with the detective's manner of speaking, and he did his best to simulate it without betraying his real identity. He concluded that any little flaws would pass unnoticed by Spalding and Tinker, under the circumstances.

There was no response to his first hail, and Llewellyn peered into the darkness, holding the storm-lantern at arm's length as he did so. He walked along beside the castle wall for a short distance, and then halted again.

"Tinker!" he called softly. "Tinker!"

He looked round anxiously as he spoke, and almost immediately he was gratified to observe two dim forms detach themselves from among the rocks which were dimly visible upon the grassy patch nearby, and hasten towards him.

Tinker and Spalding, as a matter of fact, were thoroughly tired of their uncomfortable vigil in the mind and rain, and were only too glad that there was something doing at last. They hurried towards Llewellyn without hesitation, and joined him within a few moments.

"Thank goodness you've made a bally move at last, Mr. Blake! exclaimed Spalding. "Tinker and I have been havin' a most deuced time out here, I can tell you! What's happenin'?"

Llewellyn had now lowered the storm-lantern, so that its dim rays should not illuminate his features too clearly as he confronted Tinker and Spalding. He had no fear that his real personality would be suspected, but it was as well to be cautious.

"A good deal has been happening, my dear fellow," he said in a whisper to Spalding. "But I cannot explain now. Everything is all right, and you and Tinker had better come inside at once."

Tinker breathed a sigh of relief.

"Oh, good!" he exclaimed. "We've had enough of skulking out here in this beastly weather. How did you manager to get the better of Jarrow and that ancient caretaker, guv'nor?"

Llewellyn's eyes gleamed with satisfaction as he heard Tinker's words. It was quite evident to him that he was accepted as Sexton Blake without question, and he turned and led the way back towards the castle door without answering Tinker's query.

Spalding and Tinker followed him at once. Neither of them had the the slightest doubt regarding the old man, although they wondered why the detective continued to adhere so closely to the character of Llewellyn. Cute as Tinker undoubtedly was, he could scarcely be blamed for remaining unsuspicious of the cunning plan which was being carried through. The darkness and the rain all helped to make Jarrow's scheme a success, and the trio hurried to the castle without loss of time.

Llewellyn had left the door ajar, and he was the first to enter—pushing the door wide open, and halting just inside the hall. Tinker and Spalding followed close upon his heels, and immediately they were inside the caretaker closed the great door with a sinister clang.

Tinker looked round sharply.

"I say, guv'nor, rather unwise to bang the door like that," he exclaimed, in a tone of surprise. "What about Jarrow and——why, Great Scott! The—the rotter's here!"

Tinker caught sight of Mr. Godfrey Jarrow as he uttered the words. He was standing in such a position that the open front door had concealed his presence from the newcomers. But now that the door was closed, he stood plainly revealed in the light of the storm-lantern. Jarrow was smiling with triumph, and in his had he grasped a wicked-looking Browning.

"Exactly. I am here, right enough, as you remark, Tinker!" he exclaimed blandly. "It may interest you to know that your master is already a prisoner in my hands, and that you and your companion are about to join him in captivity."

CHAPTER 9.

Mr. Godfrey Jarrow Takes Action.

TINKER stared at Jarrow blankly for a few seconds, and then transferred his gaze to the features of Llewellyn, who was smiling in a self-satisfied fashion at the success of his ruse.

"By Jingo! They've tricked us, Vic!" roared Tinker angrily. "This old scoundrel is Llewellyn, the caretaker, and not the guv'nor at all!"

Spalding nodded.

"That appears to be quite evident, old son," he agreed. "But I must remark that we've been caught being in a deucedly neat manner. There seems to be nothin' else for it but to get busy on that little scrap I hinted at a little while ago. What about it?"

Victor Spalding, in spite of his somewhat affected manner, was quite ready to put up a fight when the necessity arose, and he considered that the time had come for drastic action.

He and Tinker were rather staggered at the turn of events, and they were a little at a loss to understand exactly what had happened. It was quite evident to them that some disaster had occurred, and that Sexton Blake had in some way been disposed of by Jarrow and Llewellyn. The pair were mystified and chagrined at the neat manner in which they had been tricked, and they faced their enemies angrily.

"What have you done with the guv'nor, you blackguard?" shouted Tinker, turning on Jarrow like a flash, and striding forward with clenched fists. "If any harm's come to him, I'll—I'll——"

"You'll do precisely nothing!" interrupted Jarrow, dropping his air of bland amusement and pressing his Browning into Tinker's chest. "Understand that I'm top-dog just now, and I'm not standing any nonsense from you! This pistol is fully loaded, and if you and your friend show the least sign of causing trouble, I shan't hesitate to use it!"

Tinker breathed hard, and Spalding stepped forward as if to send his clenched fist crashing into Jarrow's face. But as he did so, Llewellyn also produced a revolver, and indicated that Spalding had better submit to the inevitable. It was thus made quite clear to the two helpless prisoners that resistance would be futile, and they were forced to accept the situation with the best grace possible.

Any attempt to make a fight of it would be worse than useless under the circumstances, and Tinker and Spalding could do nothing but glare at their captors impotently. It would be the height of folly to risk being shot, and their best policy would be to submit quietly and await an opportunity to turn the tables.

Jarrow observed their attitude of resignment and smiled approvingly.

"That's better," he said, with a nod. "I am glad you are sensible enough to realise when you are beaten. No harm will come to you if you'll do exactly as you're ordered; but I'm afraid you'll have to be imprisoned in a similar fashion to Mr. Blake for the time being."

"What for?" demanded Tinker angrily. "What's the idea of all this mystery, anyhow? Where's Mr. Glyn?"

"He is also a prisoner," said Jarrow. "But I have no time to argue with you, my lad. Your presence here is inconvenient to me, and since you have chosen to meddle in my affairs, I must take whatever course I think fit to get rid of your interference!"

Tinker and Spalding looked at one another helplessly. Jarrow's words told them absolutely nothing, and even now they were no wiser regarding the mystery which surrounded the old castle. There was nothing for them to do but take whatever came and trust to luck.

Victor Spalding shrugged his shoulders expressively.

"Dashed lively endin' to our pleasant little vigil in the bally rain!" he remarked. "Poor old Owen is down in the depths, an' now Mr. Blake has been shoved into the clink! It's our turn to pay a visit to the nether regions now, by the look of things, old scout!"

Tinker nodded gloomily and cast a glance at Jarrow. He was watching the two young men warily, and he took care to keep his pistol ready for instant action. Evidently he had no intention of allowing them the slightest opportunity of making a bid for liberty.

"Come on, Llewellyn, bind their hands behind them with that cord!" he rapped out briskly. "Once these fellows are safely imprisoned we can get about our business!"

The caretaker nodded as he pocketed his revolver, and proceeded to do as Jarrow ordered. A length of strong cord was lying upon the floor, and with this Llewellyn bound the hand of Tinker and Spalding securely behind their backs, rendering them completely helpless.

They were then ordered to march forward into the caretaker's little room, where they were halted beside the movable stone slab in the floor. Jarrow directed Llewellyn to touch the knob which operated the slab, and when the apeture was uncovered he flashed a light downwards, and told Tinker and Spalding to take a look.

"You will observe that Mr. Blake is comfortably housed in this little apartment," he remarked blandly. "It is just as well that you should see one another, to make the position clear!"

Tinker gazed down the shaft and dimly saw the form of his master in the dungeon below. Blake, attracted by the opening of the slab, and by the light, looked up quickly, and it was evident that he recognised his assistant.

"That you, Tinker!" he asked anxiously.

"Yes, guv'nor; but I can't help you!" answered Tinker. "Jarrow and Llewellyn deceived Mr. Spalding and I by a trick, and we're in their power!"

Blake gave vent to a low exclamation of annoyance, and it was clear that he was disappointed in his hopes. This was totally unexpected, and he realised at once that the position was rapidly growing worse. But he gave no indication of what was passing in his mind, and assumed a hopeful air.

"Never mind, Tinker, cheer up!" he called. "Jarrow will not have everything his own way for long. It is certainly unfortunate that you and Spalding have been trapped, but don't worry."

Jarrow muttered an oath under his breath.

"We'll see that that!" he growled. "I've got the four of you now, Blake, and I mean to take steps to keep you where I want you! You came here interfering in my affairs unasked, and you've only got yourselves to blame for what's happened. Close the trap, Llewellyn, and get these two fellows safely locked up in the dungeon!"

Mr. Godfrey Jarrow spoke impatiently, evidently somewhat puzzled by Sexton Blake's optimistic tones. He knew that the detective was securely imprisoned, with no chance whatever of making his escape, and he couldn't understand the lightheartedness of his captive.

The famous detective was also aware of his unfortunate predicament, but he was not the man to give way to despair. He had been in many a tighter corner than this, and had always managed to wriggle out of it by some means or other. Blake habitually looked upon the brightest aspect of any given situation, and he found that his optimism usually brought its own reward.

Llewellyn again produced his revolver after he had closed the stone trap-door, and he and Jarrow between them marshalled Tinker and Spalding towards the gloomy lower passage in which the chilly stone dungeons were situated. With their hands securely bound behind them, the prisoners were forced to march ahead with no possibility of eluding their armed captors, and they descended the great stone staircase to the cells with feelings too deep for words.

Everything seemed to be going wrong in connection with this strange case, and Jarrow and Llewellyn appeared to be doing precisely as they liked. All Blake's plans had miscarried, through no fault of his own, and now Tinker and Spalding were put out of the running, thus making the situation ten times worse. For, instead of being free to render aid to Blake and Glyn, they were themselves deprived of their liberty.

The position was galling in the extreme, and all four of the prisoners felt a little dejected, particularly as they were none the wiser regarding the mystery which surrounded the old castle and its strange occupants. They had discovered absolutely nothing, and they were even ignorant of Mr. Godfrey Jarrow's exact status, or what his purpose was.

The dungeon passage was soon reached, and Jarrow's voice, now harsh and with no trace of its former blandness, rapped out an order to the caretaker.

"Lock them in separate cells, Llewellyn!" he exclaimed. "There's no fear of them making their escape, so you may as well unbind their wrists!"

The old man smiled to himself as he proceeded to carry out the instructions, for none knew better than he how true Jarrow's words were. The dungeons of Glyn Castle had never been known, in all their history, to allow the escape of a prisoner, and they were equally as strong and secure now as they were when first built.

Jarrow stood nearby, with his Browning at the "ready," while Llewellyn removed the cords from each prisoner in turn and locked them securely in separate cells. Once they were inside, Jarrow and his henchman took their departure without further ado, leaving Tinker and Spalding to their own devices and in total darkness.

All four captives were now within close proximity of one another, but as totally isolated as if separated by miles, so far as conversation was concerned. The walls of the dungeon were of tremendous thickness, and no amount of shouting would penetrate them.

Owen Glyn had been in captivity the longest, and he was anxiously waiting to be released by Blake and his companions. He had submitted voluntarily to this second spell of imprisonment, and he expected every minute to regain his liberty. He was, of course, totally ignorant of the misfortunes which had overtaken his friends, and perhaps this was just as well. Had he been aware of what had actually occurred, he would probably have felt like giving way to despair; but, as things were, he was cheerfully anticipating a speedy release.

Blake and Tinker and Spalding, however, knew differently, and their spirits had consequently fallen to a somewhat low ebb. Each of them was utterly helpless in his own particular cell, and they were deprived of the slight consolation of talking to one another. There was nothing for them to do but sit upon the hard stone floor and review the situation, and this they did without deriving the slightest satisfaction.

Sexton Blake, particularly, felt angry with himself for allowing this catastrophe to occur, although he was not in any way to blame. Jarrow had gained the upper hand by the unforeseen escape of the old caretaker from the turret, and this was a circumstance against which the detective could not possibly provide. But it had changed the whole aspect of the situation, and fresh plans would have to be made.

Exactly how to set about doing this was the immediate problem to solve, and Blake knew well enough that the task would be difficult. In fact, he realised that action of any sort was out of the question while he and his companions were locked within their prison walls, and there was nothing to do but await events.

The four discomfited prisoners were busily engaged with their separate thoughts for some little time before anything occurred to interrupt them. But after half-an-hour had passed Llewellyn again made his appearance in the passage outside, and proceeded to dump blankets and food into each of the occupied cells, taking great care, as he did so, to open the doors only just sufficiently for his purpose. The old man, also, kept a firm grasp of his revolver as a means of preventing any attempt at escape.

Llewellyn carried out his task quickly, and without wasting words. In fact, he scarcely uttered a syllable during the whole time he was occupied in attending to the prisoners, and when he had done he took his departure once more, in the same grim silence.

The fact that blankets and food had been supplied to the four helpless captives told them plainly enough that their immediate release was by no means contemplated, and this knowledge did not serve to cheer them up at all. Under the circumstances, however, they were thankful for small mercies, and they wrapped themselves in the blankets and proceeded to partake of the sandwiches which Llewellyn had provided.

The caretaker rejoined Mr. Godfrey Jarrow in the little room above, and glanced at the big man questioningly. Llewellyn was a little dubious as to how events would turn out eventually, and he was clearly pertubed regarding the four charges which had been placed in his care below.

"How long will it be necessary to keep the prisoners here, sir?" he asked, taking a seat opposite Jarrow. "We shall need a considerable quantity of food if they are to be here for any length of time——"

"They won't be kept here a moment longer than necessary, Llewellyn," interrupted Jarrow. "We must consider ourselves very lucky that things have turned out as satisfactorily as they have, but something must be done immediately, of course. Now that we have captured all four of them I feel much easier in mind, for I don't suppose their plans were known to any others. There is every need for drastic and rapid action, but it is unnecessary to worry ourselves unduly over the situation.''

Llewellyn nodded.

''What do you propose to do, sir?'' he asked.

''I am going to Swansea at once to carry out a little plan I have in mind,'' replied Jarrow. ''It is absolutely essential that those four interfering busybodies must be got completely away—and kept away—for at least four months! Otherwise my plans will all fall to the ground. And, as I have no intention of allowing that to occur, I am going to see about the removal of the prisoners without delay!''

The caretaker looked a little startled.

''But—but how is it possible for you to arrange a matter of that kind, sir?'' he asked. ''I don't see——''

''There's no need for you to see, either!'' broke in Jarrow. ''All you've got to do, Llewellyn, is to guard the prisoners closely until I take them off your hands! I shall hold you absolutely responsible for them, remember! We can't afford to have any hitch occur now, and I shall look to you to see that everything is all right while I am away!''

The old man shifted uncomfortably in his chair, evidently not relishing the task allotted to him. But he made no comment as he listened to Jarrow's final instructions before he took his departure from the castle. But then, when Llewellyn was finally left alone, he paid a visit to the dungeons to assure himself that the prisoners were secure, and afterwards settled himself down in any easy chair—with his revolver ready—to await the return of Mr. Godfrey Jarrow.

★ ★ ★

Some two hours after his talk with the old caretaker, Jarrow was comfortably seated in the back room of a dingy quayside inn near Swansea Docks. He was facing a couple of rough-looking, weather-beaten individuals, who obviously followed a seafaring profession, and who were pulling vigorously at their pipes as they confronted Jarrow.

These two men were respectively Captain Shanks and his son, Joe, a burly young fellow of about twenty. They were the owners of a little seagoing cutter named the Ocean Sprite, a sturdy vessel capable of making voyages of considerable length. Jarrow had been aboard her on one or two occasions, and he was therefore fairly well acquainted with her owners.

Consequently he had sought out the father and son as the very men he required to undertake the task he had in mind, and for the past fifteen minutes he had been explaining exactly what he required them to do. Both the men had listened with the greatest interest, and they now regarded Jarrow with somewhat dubious glances.

''Remember, captain,'' said Jarrow in conclusion, ''I'm going to foot the bill for all the expenses for the trip, and pay you and your son a clear five hundred pounds for your services. You must admit that my offer is a generous one, and will pay you much better than carrying your usual cargoes.''

''Maybe!'' said Shanks cautiously. ''But I want to git all the details o' this business thoroughly clear before I commit myself to anything, Mr. Jarrow! I understand that we git two hundred pounds down, an' another three hundred at the end of the trip? Is that it?''

Jarrow nodded.

''Yes; in addition to the money for expenses, you'll get three hundred at the close of the voyage, provided everything goes well,'' he said. ''But if you allow the prisoners to escape, you'll get nothing beyond the original two hundred! Now then, what do you say?''

Captain Shanks scratched his head.

''Don't 'urry me, Mr. Jarrow, don't 'urry me!'' he exclaimed. ''Your proposition has took me off my feet a little, an' I want to consider it calm an' peaceful afore I agree! Let's go over the main points again—just to freshen my memory!''

His son leaned over with an impatient expression on his face.

''Everything's clear enough, dad!'' he said. ''Mr. Jarrow explained everything quite distinctly. All we've got to do is to fetch four prisoners from Glyn Castle, and take them for a cruise in unfrequented waters for four months. We've got to carry enough food, and a fresh water machine, and we ain't got to touch land, or approach any other vessel during the trip.''

''Exactly!'' agreed Jarrow. ''That's enough, surely!''

''Simple enough, to be sure,'' said the captain. ''But I don't reckon to git myself into no trouble with the police, mind you! You said we'd got to treat the prisoners well and that no 'harm ain't to come to 'em! Well, I like that all right, an' I've a darned good mind to close with your offer, Mr. Jarrow! No questions ain't got to be arsked, I s'pose?''

Jarrow smiled.

"Well, the less you know about the affair the better for you," he said. "I can give you my word that there's nothing in it to get you into trouble with the police. These four prisoners stand in the way of a little business I've got on hand, and I want them put out of harm's way, for the time-being. You are to treat them as well as you possibly can, but keep them afloat for four months. That's all there is in it. Do you agree?"

Captain Shanks looked thoughtfully at Jarrow, and from him to his son Joe. The skipper was evidently in two minds about accepting the commission, and was considering the matter well before committing himself. Finally, he leaned over to Joe, and carried on a whispered conversation for a few minutes before again turning to the anxious Jarrow.

"Well, guv'nor, me an' Joe reckon we'll undertake the cruise, bein' as 'ow there ain't going to be no dirty work connected with it!" he said. "I ain't goin' to say as I like the job, mind, but we needs the money. So if you'll jest 'and over that two 'undred pounds right away, we'll call it a deal!"

Mr. Godfrey Jarrow smiled with satisfaction and at once produced his pocket-book, and took from it a sheaf of banknotes, which he passed over to the captain.

Within half an hour the three men had arranged all the final details of the scheme which so vitally affected the helpless prisoners in Glyn Castle, and when Jarrow finally took his departure, he was feeling elated and satisfied.

For his plans, in spite of Sexton Blake's activities, were working extremely well!

CHAPTER 10.
Shanghaied!

SEXTON BLAKE paced his dungeon cell impotently.

He was feeling furious and enraged at the way things had turned out, and he was chafing enormously at his inability to make any headway in connection with the mystery which he had undertaken to solve.

He had been confined in the dungeon only a comparatively few hours, but to him it seemed as if he had been there for days and days. The position was made all the more uncomfortable by the knowledge that escape was entirely out of the question. It was absolutely useless for him to even make the attempt—for he knew before that any such attempt would be doomed to failure. he was therefore deprived of even this slight consolation, and had perforce to remain in the cell, totally inactive.

There was nothing he could do to ease the position of himself and his companions, and the great detective fumed and fretted like a caged lion. The cell was pitchy dark by night and by day, and not even the faintest glimmer of light penetrated so far beneath the old castle floors. The uncanny silence, too, was well-nigh unbearable to a man of Blake's active mind, and it was no wonder that the detective patrolled his cell in a fever of angry resentment.

"Oh, this is intolerable—unbearable!" he muttered to himself, for the hundredth time." Blake had been imprisoned by his enemies many times before, but never in such a hopelessly impregnable place as this. There was not even a sporting chance of freeing himself, and he scarcely contain his impatience.

Moreover, he was curious and greatly puzzled as to the cause of it all. Why had he and his friends been cast into the dungeons in this fashion? What was Jarrow's object in acting in this manner? What, indeed, was Jarrow doing at the castle at all?

All these questions, and many others, passed through Blake's mind as he paced his cell, and he promised himself that they would be answered at the very first opportunity.

Tinker and Spalding and Glyn, all separately imprisoned quite near to Sexton Blake, were undergoing very similar sensations in their respective cells. They were all mystified and angry at the unexpected turn of events, and were wondering when their uncomfortable imprisonment was to cease. Their isolation was the hardest part of their burden—for each was unaware how his companions were faring. The whole position, in fact, was becoming intolerable, as Blake had said—but they were totally helpless to move a finger in their own aid.

And while the luckless captives were bewailing their fate in the cruel dungeons, old Llewellyn, the caretaker, was comfortably seated in his little room above, calmly scanning the pages of a newspaper. He was evidently looking for some particular item of news, for he made no attempt to read more than the bare headlines. Presently, however, he found what he sought, and he commenced chuckling over a certain paragraph which gave details of the mysterious disappearance of four individuals from London.

Several similar reports had appeared in the papers regarding the sudden vanishing of Sexton Blake, Tinker, Spalding, and Glyn. All four of them, it was stated, were known to have visited Swansea, but since their arrival in the great Welsh seaport all traces of them had been lost. They had disappeared, utterly, and all sorts of suggestions and surmises were contained in the various reports which appeared in different newspapers.

Llewellyn had read them all, and seemed to be in no way perturbed at the news contained in this latest paragraph, to the effect that the police were making very minute investigations as to the whereabouts of the four missing people. The caretaker knew well enough that they would never be likely to reach Glyn Castle in their search, and he was quite easy in mind regarding his prisoners.

When he had finished reading the newspaper, he busied himself in preparing some food for the captives, and carried it down to the dungeon passage. There was no necessity for Llewellyn to unlock the cell doors to hand the food to the prisoners, for a small grating was fitted into the centre of each. These gratings were strongly made and hinged—which made it a simple matter for the food to be passed into the interior of the cells. Llewellyn merely unfastened the hinged gratings, and handed each prisoner his portion, afterwards locking the grills securely in position once more. Since the caretaker had opened the doors to throw in the blankets, they had remained locked and barred, and the prisoners had had no opportunity of "rushing" Llewellyn during his visits to them.

The food which the caretaker supplied was wholesome and tasty, but none too plentiful. He doled out just sufficient to meet the demands of nature, and supplied each prisoner with enough to keep the pangs of hunger away. As a beverage they were sometimes allowed coffee, and sometimes tea—but they had either one or the other with practically every meal. Upon the whole, they were by no means badly treated in this respect, and they usually ate and drank very heartily of whatever was given them.

This occasion was very similar to the previous ones, and the four prisoners were soon busily engaged in demolishing their rations. They were, of course, quite unable to see what they were eating, owing to the intense darkness, but their meals usually tasted quite good, and they made short work of them—in spite of the various drawbacks under which they were compelled to eat. Blake, as a rule, felt quite satisfied with his portion—but Tinker and Glyn and Spalding, being young and healthy and vigorous, could quite easily have tucked away at least double the quantity, if they had had the opportunity.

A couple of hours after consuming the food Sexton Blake began to feel strangely sleepy, and his suspicions were at once aroused. Nothing like this happened before during his imprisonment, and he instantly suspected that some sort of drug had been introduced into his tea or sandwiches. He had tasted nothing unusual, it is true—but he was well aware that certain narcotics could be administered without their presence being detected.

At all events, he felt quite certain that his drowsiness could only be accounted for in this way, and he wondered for what purpose the drug had been given. He had no doubt that the other three prisoners had been treated in a similar fashion to himself, and his keen brain endeavoured to cope with the probable reason.

The detective, in spite of his iron will and strong character, found himself unable to shake off the slowly creeping stupor which was gradually overpowering him. He fought against it with all his might, but he knew that his efforts would end in failure. The drug had taken too great a hold on his system to admit of being successfully combated by force of will, and he felt himself sinking by slow degrees, into a state of unconsciousness.

It he had had only the slightest inkling of what the food contained he would have refrained from eating it. For he realised that something important was evidently afoot, and he would have given anything to retain his full faculties. It would probably mean an opportunity of turning the tables upon his enemies, and Blake strove hard to keep himself from succumbing to the insidious drug which was surely robbing him of his senses.

But, as he feared, his efforts were useless. Almost before he knew it he had dropped off into a deep slumber—a dreamless, sound sleep, from which he would not be likely to awaken for some considerable time. And as Blake had surmised, Tinker, Spalding, and Glyn were all in a similar condition—stretched at full length on their blankets, oblivious to their surroundings.

The explanation of this state of affairs soon became apparent. For, within the next hour, Jarrow and Llewellyn made their appearance in the dungeon passage, accompanied by Captain Shanks and his son Joe. They had come to carry out their contract with Jarrow, and no time was lost in setting about the transfer of the four prisoners to the waiting cutter.

The skipper had received full and precise instructions how to proceed, and he and his son commenced operations by grasping one of the captives—it was Owen Glyn—and carrying his unconscious form out of the dungeon into the passage. Llewellyn, equipped once more with his storm-lantern, showed his light upon the scene, and proceeded to illuminate the way out of the castle.

The old caretaker, carrying his lamp, directed Shanks and Joe up the great stone staircase into the upper passage, and so on until the entrance hall was reached. The skipper and his son seemed to make very little trouble of carrying their burden, for they were both strong, brawny men.

Llewellyn opened the front door for them to pass out, but he made no attempt to accompany them with the lamp, as this would have been somewhat risky. The night was pitchy dark outside, but the owners of the Ocean Sprite were used to the gloom, and they carried their unconscious prisoner towards the cliff path without the slightest hesitation.

Negotiating the steep and broken stairway to the beach below as a little more difficult for Shanks and his son, but they accomplished the task without accident, and hurried across the rock-strewn stretch of sand to the spot where the cutter was moored. The hour was very late at night, and the whole coast was deserted—so the conspirators had no fear of their actions being observed.

Owen Glyn was soon hoisted aboard the Ocean Sprite, and dumped into a fairly comfortable bunk situated in the forepart of the vessel. He was snoring loudly and peacefully sublimely indifferent to what was happening around him. Joe Shanks grinned as they left the sleeping man.

"No fear of him waking up for a few hours, dad," he remarked easily. "If the other three are no more troublesome than this one, we shall have a pretty easy time gettin' them aboard."

The skipper grunted.

"Easy or not, I shall feel a durned sight more comfortable when we git 'em to sea," he said. "This is a queer sort o' job, an I don't relish being pulled up by no coastguards. So we'd best hurry."

Joe nodded, and the pair returned to the castle with all speed. The task before them was no light one, for it is by no means an easy matter to carry the inanimate form of a man for such a distance. But they had accomplished the first journey without mishap, and they set about bringing the other three prisoners down to the cutter as speedily as possible.

One by one they were taken from their cells and transferred to the vessel, in the same way as Glyn had been. Llewellyn met the two seamen each time they returned, and escorted them to the dungeon passage with his lamp. Jarrow merely acted the part of onlooker, occasionally giving Shanks a word of instruction or advice as it occurred to him.

Sexton Blake was the last of the prisoners to be removed from the castle, and after he had been safely stowed into the little for'ard cabin with his companions, the Ocean Sprite put to sea without the loss of a moment. Jarrow and Llewellyn were heartily glad to see the last of their unwelcome captives, and locked themselves within the castle with more contented minds than they had had since Owen Glyn and Victor Spalding had first made their appearance at the door of the old building after their shipwrecking incident.

Mr. Godfrey Jarrow considered that he had disposed of the prisoners in a masterly manner, and that he was now free to pursue his mysterious plans without hindrance. In any case, he was quite certain that he had nothing further to fear from Sexton Blake—for at least four months. And by that time he would be quite willing for the detective to make what investigation he wished.

Jarrow was quite convinced that, whatever his motives were, they were quite unknown to Blake and his companions. And in this he was undoubtedly right. For Blake, in spite of his efforts, had been baffled at every turn, and he was even now quite ignorant of the mystery which surrounded Glyn Castle and its two strange inhabitants.

Captain Shanks, after the smart little vessel had cast her moorings and was ploughing through the water at a good pace, busied himself on deck while his son took the wheel. The Ocean Sprite was a swift-sailing, sloop-rigged craft of graceful appearance, but just now there was something about her which seemed strangely out of place. There was a wooden erection which had been specially built for this particular trip, and the skipper grinned to himself approvingly as he surveyed it.

Meanwhile, the four prisoners from Glyn Castle were still sleeping as peacefully as ever, proving that Llewellyn had done his work with more efficiency than discretion. The effects of the drug were still very apparent and none of the victims showed the least sign of awakening. It was not until another three hours had passed that the first of the prisoners began to recover, and this in itself was a somewhat slow process.

Sexton Blake showed the first signs of returning consciousness, and his sensations were peculiar and hard to define. His head ached and buzzed abominably, and for some little time he lay trying to collect his scattered wits. The drug had numbed his senses, and he could not remember much for some minutes after awakening.

But gradually his faculties returned to him, and as they did so he became aware that he was no longer lying upon a solid stone floor. It was pitch dark, the same as the dungeon had been, but everything else was different. The air was not so chilly and stuffy, and strange gurgling and swishing noises came softly to his ears. Lastly, Blake felt the rolling motion of the boat, and in a flash of understanding he realised that he was at sea.

The detective was still feeling bemused and fuddled by the action of the drug, but he lost no time in scrambling to his feet as soon as this knowledge of the change of prisons fully dawned upon him. It was not difficult for him to reconstruct what had taken place while he lay drugged and helpless, and he determined to discover exactly what class of vessel he was aboard of.

Accordingly he rose to his feet somewhat shakily, and found to his satisfaction that he was not bound. He also discovered, by his sense of touch, that he had been lying in a lower bunk of the cabin, and was consequently able to step out upon the floor without any trouble. His head seemed to be swimming as he gained an upright position, but after a few moments this unpleasant sensation began to pass away.

The detective was rapidly recovering his customary alertness of manner, and he struck a match and looked round the little apartment. The spluttering flame showed him a clean and neat little cabin, fitted with four bunks, a table with a scrubbed top, and various lockers and chests. But Blake had no interest in anything but the bunks, and he investigated these at once.

As he had thought, three of them were occupied by Tinker, Spalding, and Glyn—all of them were still in the deep sleep induced by the drug. Blake made no attempt to awaken them, but he was keenly delighted that they were here with him, safe and sound.

The match burnt out in a few seconds, and the detective crossed the cabin to the door. He had expected it to be locked, but somewhat to his surprise, he found it unsecured in any way except for the usual latch. This seemed to point to the fact that he and his three companions were no longer prisoners—but Blake was soon to learn differently.

He opened the door at once, and passed out upon the open, wind-swept deck. The keenness of the air which blew into his face did more than anything else to dispel the remaining effects of the narcotic, and Blake felt better after the first few moments under the stars than he had done since falling into the stupor.

He looked round him with great interest, and the first faint streaks of dawn showed him, with fair distinctness, that the vessel upon which he was standing was well out in the open sea—completely out of sight of land. This was positive proof that a good long time had elapsed since the coast had been left behind.

Blake next turned his attention to the craft itself, and he saw at a glance that the cutter was a good, seaworthy vessel of substantial build. The cabin from which he had just emerged was situated in the extreme bows of the little ship, and within six feet of the door, stretching right across the deck, was a heavy wooden barrier—completely blocking the passage to the after part of the boat.

The detective's eyes narrowed as he observed the obstruction, and its significant presence was not lost upon him. Obviously the barrier had been erected as a means of preventing himself and his companions from having the free run of the vessel, and he saw at once that the strongly-made fencing would effectively confine the prisoners to this allotted portion of the deck.

The barrier was built after the style of trellis work, but strong enough to withstand the heaviest storm, if appearances went for anything. There was no apparent gateway, or other opening, in the formidable-looking barrier, and there was no doubt in Blake's mind that its purpose was intended solely to keep himself, and the other prisoners from leaving this position of the cutter.

Sexton Blake smiled grimly to himself as he took in all these details, and he marvelled at the completeness of the arrangements which had been made to render himself and his companions helpless. Mr. Godfrey Jarrow, of course, was responsible for them, and the famous detective promised himself a satisfactory settlement with that gentleman at the earliest opportunity.

Meanwhile, he suddenly became aware that a figure was moving towards him along the deck—upon the further side of the trellis barricade. It belonged to Captain Shanks, and he nodded cheerfully to Sexton Blake as he came to a halt upon the heaving deck.

"Mornin', sir!" he greeted pleasantly, at the same time drawing an enormous revolver from his pocket. "I see you're 'avin' a look at the alterations wot we've made for your benefit. I'm sorry you'll 'ave to be content with such a small bit o' dec, but orders is orders, as the sayin' is."

Sexton Blake smiled.

"No doubt we have to thank our friend Jarrow for this little trip?" he suggested. "But as we are apparently booked for a prolonged journey on your vessel, I should like to know who you are, and where you are taking us."

The skipper nodded.

"Well, I don't think they'll be any 'arm in obligin' you with an answer to all you want to know, sir," he replied. "My name is Cap'n Shanks, an' this cutter is owned by me an' my son Joe. We've been 'ired—as you reckoned—by Mr. Jarrow, an' we've got orders to take you an' your friends for a long cruise. We're bound for the South Atlantic, an' if you an' the other gents will only behave sensible, there ain't no reason why we shouldn't all enjoy ourselves. You won't come to no 'arm whatever—provided you don't try no tricks:"

The detective pointed to the revolver.

"That, I presume, is intended to add a little weight to your arguments—in case my friends, or myself, attempt any of the tricks you mention?" he asked drily.

"Exactly, sir—you've hit it fust go!" answered the skipper blandly. "I think I ought to explain the position at the beginnin'—so's there can't be no misunderstandin' later on. You an' your friends 'ave got to keep to your own side of this 'ere barrier—that's about all there is to it! Me or my son will always be on deck, fully armed, an' if any of you gents make an attempt to git past this blamed fence, we shall be compelled to act drastic. But there won't be no need for nothin' of that sort, sir—if you'll only act sensible. You'll 'ave plenty of good food, which we shall pass through this 'ere slit in the fence, an' you won't 'ave no cause to worry over nothin'."

Captain Shanks spoke in a tone of voice which indicated that he wished everything to be on amicable terms between himself and his prisoners, and Sexton Blake looked at him sharply. The detective could see that the skipper was by no means of a scoundrelly nature, as might have been expected, and he took some trifling consolation from that fact. But Blake was certainly surprised at this move on Jarrow's part, and he did not know quite what to make of it.

He regarded the captain fixedly.

"How long is this cruise intended to last?" he asked.

"Well, my orders is to keep afloat for four months, sir—without touchin' land, or approachin' any other craft," answered the skipper deliberately. "So it's up to you to git kinder resigned right away. You an' your friends won't 'ave no 'ardships to suffer, an' you'll be takin' a good long 'oliday without no expenses to pay."

Sexton Blake's lips set in a firm, grim line as he heard the captain's words, but he gave no indication of the astonishment which filled him. He was also greatly angered at the helpless position in which he had been placed by the cunning Jarrow.

Action on the part of the prisoners was rendered impossible—for with a constant watch being kept by armed men nothing could be done to improve the situation. Apparently, the four of them had been pitched out of the frying-pan into the fire—for they were certainly no better off aboard the cutter than they had been in the dungeons of Glyn Castle—so far as taking action against Mr. Godfrey Jarrow was concerned.

The famous Baker Street detective had never found himself quite so thoroughly thwarted at every turn than at the present moment, and a great rage welled up within him. Matters had been quite bad enough at the castle, but to be drugged and shanghaied in this outrageous fashion was almost beyond endurance. But he realised the utter futility of railing against the inevitable, and he turned abruptly on his heel and entered the little cabin once more.

The daylight was now much stronger, and it revealed the fact that the other three victims of Llewellyn's drug were all showing signs of recovery. Glyn was stretching himself drowsily as Blake entered, and Spalding was sitting up and looking round him with a dazed and vacant expression. Tinker was still lying in his bunk, but his eyes were open wide, and the astonishment in them spoke eloquently of the fact that he had regained his wits to a sufficient extent to know that he was no longer in the dungeons of Glyn Castle.

"What's happened, guv'nor?" he muttered recognising Blake at once. "I—I feel absolutely rotten! My head's buzzing like a blessed saw-mill, and I can't see straight."

Victor Spalding turned his head and nodded.

"That's dashed queer!" he remarked "You've described my feelin's exactly old son. Hanged if I know what to make of this! The bally room seems to be heavin'—just as if the castle is topplin' over! If I hadn't been confined in the dark and dismal dungeon for hours an' hours, I should be inclined to put this ghastly sensation down to a considerably strengthy gargle."

Sexton Blake chuckled, and turned to the little washstand which was screwed to one of the walls of the cabin. Here he found a bottle of water and a glass, and he proceeded to give each of the three dazed youngsters a drink of the clear, reviving liquid.

Its effect upon them was immediate and beneficial, and within the next five minutes they had recovered sufficiently to listen with amazement and interest to Blake's account of his interview with Captain Shanks. The detective recounted everything which had passed, and his three hearers were staggered at the turn events had taken.

"This is simply ghastly, Mr. Blake!" exclaimed Glyn. "Do you mean to say we're going to be cut off from civilisation for four solid months?"

"According to the skipper—yes!" answered Blake. "This man Jarrow is responsible for our predicament, and I am quite at a loss to understand his motives in acting as he has done. However, it is no use worrying ourselves unduly, we must await our opportunity of reversing the position."

Spalding grunted.

"But, according to what you've just told us, that seems to be pretty hopeless," he observed. "This adventure appears to be a fair knock-out for unexpected surprises, Mr. Blake, and I'm dashed if I can see where it's goin' to end! First we're messed about by that old fossil of a caretaker, an' then incarcerated in the noisome dungeons of the castle. Now, to cap the lot, we're ballywell shanghaied like a set of drunken longshoremen. Goodness only knows what it all means, but we seem to be up against it this time with a vengeance!"

Owen Glyn nodded gloomily.

"Just when I had hoped for so much, too!" he muttered brokenly.

Sexton Blake tapped him on the shoulder reassuringly.

"It is early yet to give way to despair, my dear fellow," he said. "I don't think there is any cause for undue anxiety—at any rate, at present. I will admit that the position is extremely galling, but something may turn up to alter the whole aspect of affairs at any moment."

This was quite true, and the detective's cheerful attitude soon reflected itself on his companions—at least, to a certain degree. They discussed the whole situation in detail, but it was impossible for them to arrive at any satisfactory explanation of Jarrow's strange actions, or to make plans for the immediate future.

A little later they went on deck in a body, and surveyed the formidable barricade. Upon the other side of it Captain Shanks was busy with some coils of rope, but he turned and faced them as they appeared. His revolver was stuck in his belt ready for instant action, and it seemed that the skipper was determined to give his prisoners no opportunity of passing the barrier.

"Joe is gettin' some breakfast ready for you gentlemen now," he exclaimed pleasantly. "He'll pass it through to you in a few minutes, an' I 'ope you'll enjoy it. We're goin' to make things as comfortable as we can for you while you're aboard our craft, an' all we asks you to do is to keep over in your own quarters. If you do that, things will go on smooth an' amicable."

Spalding grinned.

"Well, it's cheerin' to learn that we're goin' to have some grub, at any rate," he remarked. "This bally trellis-work arrangement reminds me rather forcibly of the Zoo, you know. Caged animals, and all that sort of rot. Fancy bein' stuck here for four months! Ye gods and little bloaters!"

Spalding's facetious remarks really voiced the sensations of his three companions. They were all feeling somewhat like caged animals as they regarded the strongly-made barrier which confronted them, and they realised the utter helplessness of the position. The barricade itself could be easily surmounted were it not for the fact that Shanks or his son were continually on the watch with firearms ready for action. Any attempt to climb the fence would be doomed to failure at the outset under such conditions, and the four prisoners set their teeth grimly. There was nothing for them to do but accept the situation as philosophically as possible, and hope for the best.

The cutter was now ploughing through the choppy sea with exhilarating swiftness, and under different circumstances the little party who stood in the forepeak would have enjoyed themselves immensely. As things were, however, they felt very little pleasure in the enforced voyage, and for the most part they stood surveying their surroundings in silence.

Not a sail of any sort was in sight, and their vessel was quite alone upon the vast waste of waters, her sails bellying out in the stiff breeze which blew strongly from the north-east. Sexton Blake cast a comprehensive glance at the scurrying clouds above, and turned to his companions.

"I fancy we're in for a spell of rough weather," he commented. "There is every sign of a storm blowing up within a few hours, and Shanks and his son will have all their work cut out to manage this craft, small as it is. Possibly we may find an opportunity of obtaining control of the boat, but we must be very cautious, and take no action until we are quite certain of success."

The detective's words seemed to cheer the others. They promised a sporting chance of reversing positions, and the little party discussed the possibilities of escape while they partook of breakfast in the little cabin. Joe, as his father had promised, prepared a really substantial meal for them, and they enjoyed it immensely. After their recent experiences in the dungeons of the castle, they were feeling invigorated and freshened by the keen sea breezes, and their appetites responded accordingly.

Blake's forecast of the weather conditions looked like proving correct, for as the morning wore on the sea became appreciably rougher, and the wind blew almost a gale. By the time dinner was over, and the afternoon was well advanced, the storm threatened to swoop down upon them at any moment, and the four prisoners observed that Captain Shanks was looking anxious and worried.

He and Joe had shortened sail several times during the last few hours—a sure indication that they anticipated a spell of bad weather. The sea was rising rapidly now, and the wind was howling through the rigging with a shrieking intensity which foretold of worse to follow. But the Ocean Sprite, in spite of her rolling and plunging, seemed to be easily manageable by the skipper and his mate, for Joe acted in that capacity. They were both experienced seamen, and handled the vessel with ease and assurance.

Blake and his three companions spent most of the afternoon on their little stretch of deck, interestedly watching the skilled manipulation of the various ropes and tackle. The boat was now speeding through the waves at a tremendous speed, running before the wind with scarcely a dozen yards of sail set. Now and again she shipped formidable seas, and the spray continually roared up from her sharp bows, and soaked the occupants of the forepeak. But they preferred to weather the storm in the open, rather than be confined to the tiny cabin.

Tinker cocked his eye skywards, and surveyed the heavens dubiously.

"This is only the beginning of what we're in for!" he remarked, with a nod. "There's a hurricane coming up in a few minutes, guv'nor—and it's going to be a regular blighter, if I know anything!"

Blake nodded.

"I'm afraid you're right, Tinker," he agreed. "There is every sign of a very severe storm, and I think it will break shortly after sunset. In all probability we shall have to lend a hand with the running of the boat, but we will do nothing whatever for the present. Just wait and see how events turn out."

Spalding and Glyn were looking serious, as well as Blake and Tinker. They were quite experienced enough in the ways of the sea to know when the elements threatened danger, and they fully realised the gravity of the situation. The skipper and Joe were doing their best, and so far they had matters well in hand. Joe was at the wheel, and his father was busy with the gaff-lines and other gear which required attention. The skipper had already securely lashed everything possible, and was now going over his work a second time to make everything doubly sure before the storm broke upon them.

The dusk was gathering quickly now, and the wind howled more fiercely than ever. Then, with scarcely any warming, the rain began to descend in a blinding sheet, hissing down upon the decks with a fury which was almost incredible. At the same time, the seas became rougher than ever, and the little Ocean Sprite tossed and plunged like a wild thing. At one second she was high up upon the crest of a giant wave, and the next she was floundering in the trough, with her timbers creaking and groaning under the terrific strain.

Mountainous seas crashed upon her decks in a continuous succession, and the little Ocean Sprite lurched and shivered drunkenly under each terrific impact. Blake and his companions, huddled together in the bows, were compelled to cling tightly to the rails to prevent themselves being flung overboard. The ship was floundering in the throes of a particularly nasty squall, and seemed to be in imminent danger of turning turtle. But the wind and the seas, between them, brought her back on a comparatively even keel, and sent her scurrying forward into the spume and spray like a frightened bird.

Disaster, however, was not to pass them by entirely.

Sexton Blake, as he clung to the rail, suddenly became aware of a tearing, rending sound from overhead, and he glanced up quickly. There was still sufficient light for him to discern the quivering mast, and even as he looked he saw a portion of the rigging in the act of falling to the deck. A warning cry arose in his throat, but before he could give utterance to it the mass of cordage hurtled downwards with tremendous force.

Joe Shanks, apparently, saw the incident at the same second as the detective. But, unfortunately for him, he was standing directly beneath the loosened rigging. He saw his danger in a flash, and made a sudden sideways dive in order to clear the descending missile. But he was just the fraction of a second too late, and he was sent crashing to the deck with a heavy thud.

He lay just where he had fallen, ominously still. There was no doubt that he was gravely injured, and his father came running towards him, careless of anything else. He bent over Joe anxiously, and the first glance told him that the lad was unconcious—perhaps dying.

Captain Shanks was almost stunned by this disaster. Even with Joe's aid the task of managing the boat was no light one, especially during stormy weather, but with his son rendered helpless, the skipper knew that he was lost. And Joe must be attended to at once—he could not be left upon the sea-swept deck, exposed to the fury of the elements. The captain looked round him almost wildly, scarcely knowing which way to turn.

Sexton Blake, watching from the other side of the barricade, saw Shanks' predicament at once, and—with characteristic generosity—determined to go to the rescue. He could do no less under the circumstances.

"If you want any help, captain," he called, raising his voice above the roar of the wind, "I am perfectly willing to do anything I can!"

The skipper looked round quickly.

"Thank you sir, thank you!" he said gratefully, forgetting everything else in the anxiety he felt for his son. "Joe is pretty badly injured, by the look o' things, an' if you can do him any good I shall be more obliged than I can say!"

The detective nodded, and prepared to climb the barrier, now without the slightest fear of hindrance. As he did so he could not help feeling that Fate seemed about to turn the tables, and that the fortunes of himself and his three friends were altering for the better.

CHAPTER 11.
Unforeseen Disaster!

CAPTAIN SHANKS was obliged to take the wheel, and to leave his injured son in charge of the detective.

He could not be in better hands than those of Sexton Blake, although the skipper was unaware of this at the moment. Shanks was only too glad to have Joe attended to at all, under the circumstances, and he cast a grateful look in Blake's direction as he saw the famous detective gently lift the stricken man into his arms and make his way below.

Within five minutes Joe was made snug and comfortable in the skipper's cabin, and Sexton Blake quickly examined his injuries. As skilfully as any doctor, and with a face equally as grave, Blake attended to the unconscious man. He was bleeding profusely from a jagged wound upon the head, and after staunching the flow of blood and temporarily bandaging the injury, the detective left the cabin once more and ascended to the deck.

Shanks was still at the wheel, looking worried and grieved; but he was not alone now. As Blake had surmised, Tinker and Spalding and Glyn were now doing everything in their power to assist the skipper in the running of the vessel, and they were proving themselves to be extremely useful hands in this emergency. Without their timely aid, the Ocean Sprite would in all probability have foundered; but, as things were, they had managed between them to save the gallant little cutter from destruction.

Under the skipper's directions, they had done everything necessary to ensure the safety of the ship, and even now they were running into smoother water. By the look of things, they had weathered the worst part of the storm, and by dawn there was every prospect of their making calm waters once more.

Blake looked round approvingly as he emerged on deck and quietly walked to the skipper's side. Shanks turned an eager face as he approached, and it was evident to the detective that a great bond of affection existed between father and son.

"Well, sir, how is he?" he asked anxiously scanning Blake's features in an endeavour to learn the worst. "Don't—don't tell me that my poor boy is—is——"

"No, captain; Joe is unconscious, but he is not dead," interrupted Blake quietly. "He has received a very severe blow upon the head, and I'm afraid the matter is serious."

Captain Shanks swallowed hard.

"Not—not in danger of dyin', sir?" he gasped chokingly. "Oh, don't say that I'm to lose my son!"

Sexton Blake placed a hand on the old man's shoulder.

"I'm sorry, captain," he said softly, but it is only right that you should know the worst at once. Joe is in danger of death, as you feared. He has received a fracture of the skull, and there is a small piece of bone pressing upon a vital nerve centre. Such a condition of things is extremely serious, and it is unfortunate that we are so far out to sea."

The skipper passed a hand across his forehead and looked at Blake with moist eyes.

"Do you mean that nothin' can be done to help my boy, sir?" he breathed. "Do you mean that we've got to stand by an' watch him die, without bein' able to do nothin' for him? Heaven grant that such is not the case! I'd willin'ly give my own life it it would save Joe, an' I can't bear the thoughts of him goin' like this! What can we do to help him, sir; what can we do?"

The detective looked at Shanks squarely.

"There is only one thing which will save the life of your son, captain," he said.

"An' what's that, sir; what's that?" asked Shanks tremblingly.

"An operation," answered Sexton Blake. "An operation performed within the next hour is the only hope, but I think that would almost certainly be the means of preventing Joe's death."

The skipper ran his fingers through his hair with a hopeless gesture as he comprehended the purport of Blake's words. The realisation of the utter impossibility of obtaining medical aid in time to be of any use almost drove him frantic, and he clutched at the detective's coat-sleeve in an agony of fear and consternation.

"An hour?" he repeated dazedly. "My son will die if we don't git an operation performed within an hour? By heavens, it's—it's impossible, sir! We're more'n six hours from the nearest land, an' the wind an' tide's against us. The seas are so heavy that he couldn't be taken off by another vessel, even if we sighted one, an' we can do nothin' but run afore the wind. An' Joe, my boy, has got to die within—— Are you sure sir, that there's no other way to save him? Can't we——"

He broke off, too miserable and grief-stricken to say more. The words seemed to choke in his throat, and he turned a tear-stained face to the detective which spoke more eloquently of his feelings than any mere words could have done.

Sexton Blake felt genuinely sorry for the old skipper, and he rapidly came to a decision.

"There is only one other suggestion I have to make, Shanks," he said, looking at the skipper with his keen eyes. "The operation on your son is the only hope of pulling him through, and I am perfectly willing to perform it, if you are agreeable. I cannot, of course, promise success, but I will do my best to save Joe's life."

The detective spoke in a quiet voice, but it seemed to carry the hope of success. Captain Shanks clutched at the unexpected offer as a drowning man clutches at a straw, and he turned to Blake with a new-found look of joy in his glance.

"Thank Heaven for your kindness, sir!" he said chokingly. "I—I know I don't deserve to be treated like this, but if you'll only save the life of my boy, I'll—I'll do anythin' in my power to repay you! Agree, sir? O' course I'll agree, an' only too thank ful o' the chance! Go—go an' perform the operation on Joe, sir, an' may good luck go with you!"

The skipper's voice was filled with relief and hope, and he gently pushed Sexton Blake towards the companion-way in his eagerness for him to commence on his delicate task. Shanks did not even think of questioning Blake's ability to perform the operation; he took this much for granted, and, in any case, it was better for the captain to know that at least some efforts were being made on behalf of the injured man, rather than to leave him to die without everything possible done.

And so, Blake, having gained the captain's consent, descended once more to the little cabin alone, and prepared to begin on the fight for Joe's life. The famous detective was very greatly skilled in surgery and medicine, but he realised that everything was against him in this instance. He had no drugs or instruments of any sort which were suited to the matter in hand, and he would have to manage as best he could with what few articles he carried upon his person.

Chief among these was a strong but delicately made pocket-knife which contained other implements in addition to the usual two blades. It was fitted with scissors, tweezers, and a couple of sharply-pointed instruments which Blake had often found useful in minor operations previously. He had never been compelled to use the crude tools for such an important occasion as this, when a life hung in the balance; but they were certainly better than nothing.

The detective set about his task with a businesslike alertness which indicated that he was a perfect master of the situation, in spite of the many drawbacks with which he had to contend. He removed his coat and rolled up his shirt-sleeves as a commencement, and then procured a bowl of water and some bandages. The bandages he had discovered in a locker during his first visit to the cabin, but there was nothing else in the surgical line which would assist him.

Joe Shanks was breathing evenly, but was still totally unconscious as Blake began his task. It was necessary to remove the matted hair from around the wound before doing anything else, and while the detective was thus engaged he became aware that the skipper had softly entered the cabin. Blake made no comment, for he had no objection to the father of his patient being present. After all, it was only natural that Shanks should be tremendously anxious regarding his son, and he felt compelled to leave the ship in the hands of the late prisoners and to watch by Joe's side.

He took up his position by Blake's elbow, but made no attempt to enter into conversation, realising with shrewd common-sense that it was far better for the detective to be left to concentrate upon his work unhampered. But if he did not speak with his lips, his eyes glowed with an expression of gratitude which told plainly enough what he left.

Sexton Blake went about his intricate task with a dexterity which surprised the old seaman, who gazed fascinatedly at the skilful fingers of the great detective as they performed their mission of restoring life and health to the injured man. Blake had not yet begun the actual operation so far, but was still engaged in preparing the way for it. Perfect cleanliness was vital before he could hope to raise the fragment of bone which was pressing upon the nerve centre, and in order to make a success of the work he had set himself to accomplish, Blake took great pains to cleanse the wound of all foreign bodies.

At last he was ready to make the great experience, and he braced himself for the ordeal. The detective's nerves were as firm as steel at all times, but he realised that he would be testing their strength severely during the next few minutes. For not only had he to perform the operation with inadequate implements, but he had also to contend against the continual rolling and pitching of the vessel as she was buffeted about by the tremendous seas. One false move on Blake's part would seal Joe's doom for ever, instead of saving his life, and he set his lips in a firm, grim line as be prepared himself for the supreme moment.

Captain shanks watched him breathlessly, scarcely daring to move a finger, lest he should disturb the man who was fighting for the life of his only son. He marvelled at the apparent calmness and impartiality which characterised Blake's every move, but the skipper could never fully realise the enormous strain under which the detective was labouring in reality.

Quietly and methodically, and seeming to act without effort, Blake fought for the ebbing life of the captain's son. Joe was lying upon a pad of folded blankets, which Blake had spread upon the firmly-clamped table, and the only illumination which served to show him what he was doing came from a shaded oil-lamp which rocked and swayed overhead.

And under these primitive conditions, the great detective patiently probed and manipulated his instruments with a decisiveness which was nothing short of miraculous. The only sign which showed what he was undergoing in the way of nerve-strain was the perspiration which slowly formed upon his brow. He did nothing without first weighing its consequences in his mind, and every tiny movement was made with a deliberation which proved that Sexton Blake, had he so desired, could have become one of the world's most famous surgeons.

In absolute silence—except for the howling of the wind and the swish of the water against the ship's side—the detective carried on his work, watched by the anxious eves of Captain Shanks. For almost fifteen minutes Blake bent closely over his patient's inanimate form, battling for his life with all the skill at his command, and at the end of that time he raised himself with a little smile of satisfaction upon his features, and commenced wiping the instruments he had used.

The skipper noticed the change in Blake's attitude but he dared not risk asking for information, in case the reply he received was the one he dreaded to hear. But he soon found that it was unnecessary to question the detective, for Blake turned to him almost at once.

"I fancy your son will recover now, captain, and be little the worse for his mishap," he said, quietly. "The operation was a somewhat troublesome one to perform, but I think we may regard it as successful."

Captain Shanks groped for Blake's hand through his tear-dimmed vision, and wrung it warmly and fervently. He was quite unable to utter a word for a few moments, but when at last he found his voice he spoke huskily and brokenly.

"Mr. Blake, I shall never be able to repay you properly for what you've done for me an' my boy to-night!" he muttered quaveringly. "It—it seems too good to be true, sir! To think that you have done this for me—after the shameful way I've treated you an' your friends! I—I didn't know such kindness could be found in this world, an' I feel properly ashamed to look you in the face!" But it's larnt me a lesson—by gosh, it has. I'll take my oath that I'll never undertake another shady job o' this sort, an' to prove that I mean what I say—jest watch me, sir!"

The skipper dragged his heavy revolver from his pocket as he spoke, and walked towards the ship's side. Then, raising it above his head, he flung it with all his force through the open porthole, emitting a grunt of disgust at the same moment.

"From this moment onwards. Mr. Blake, I'm your friend till the day I die, an' I'm ready to take any orders you like to give!" he exclaimed, with evident sincerity. "I'll take you back to the nearest land as soon as you give the word, an' the man who paid me to keep you afloat can go to blazes, for all I care! I've finished with 'im an' all his blamed kind, an' from now on I'm goin' to play a straight game!"

Sexton Blake smiled as he shook the skipper's brawny fist. He had half expected something of the sort, and he was highly delighted at the wholehearted manner in which the captain had admitted his wrong-doing. Blake was a remarkably shrewd judge of character, and he knew from the first moment of seeing Shanks that he was not a bad fellow at heart.

"I am extremely glad to hear you speak in this way, captain," he said. "and I shall be very interested to learn the details of Jarrow's contract with you. Have you any idea what his motive is in getting you to keep us aboard this boat for so long a time?"

Shanks shook his head.

"No, sir—I don't know nothin' about that," he replied. "Jarrow ain't the sort o' man to tell no secrets to the likes o' me!" But I'll tell you everything I can as soon as you like, an'——"

Shanks paused as a knock sounded on the door, and the next moment Spalding and Glyn entered the cabin. They were both grinning in spite of the uncomfortable wetness of their clothing, and they approached Blake and Shanks at once.

"Deucedly glad to see that you an' the skipper are gettin' more friendly!" exclaimed Spalding. "Owen and I heard you talkin' after the long spell of silence, an' we concluded that the critical stage of the proceedings was over. So we've just popped in to offer congrats!"

"You're right, sir—dead right!" said the skipper, heartily. "Mr. Blake has pulled my boy right out o' the grave, as you might say, an' if any gentleman deserved to be congrat'lated, it's him. Why, I can't hardly believe that he's done such a wonderful thing—although I see 'im do it with my own eyes!"

Spalding and Glyn were elated when Blake explained the change in their fortunes, and while Tinker remained at the wheel—where they had left him—Shanks explained exactly what had passed between himself and Jarrow. The skipper did not spare himself in the slightest degree, but related everything in detail—finally producing the two hundred pounds which had been paid to him as the first instalment of what he was to receive for his services.

"He can have his dirty money back now!" he concluded, looking at the wad of notes disgustedly. "After what's 'appened, I wouldn't think o' touching a blamed penny of it—not me! I'm sorry that I ever took it in the fust place, an' that I ever 'ad anythin' to do with Mr. Jarrow! 'E might 'ave been the cause o' my losin' my boy, if it 'adn't been for you, sir!"

Blake nodded thoughtfully, and proceeded to put a few questions to the skipper regarding Jarrow's underlying motives. But he soon found that Shanks knew absolutely nothing of what lay at the back of Jarrow's move, and could not enlighten him in way way whatever. The captain could recall nothing of any hint which Blake thought it possible Jarrow had let fall, and after a few minutes the detective was compelled to give up his quest for information.

Shanks, obviously, knew nothing beyond the fact that Jarrow required the four prisoners kept out of his way for the period he had stated, and it was therefore of little use to question him further. The old skipper was quite sincere in his self-condemnation, and could be relied upon to prove himself a staunch comrade to the late prisoners, from now onwards.

It was a remarkable fact that even now, after all that had taken place since Glyn Castle was first entered by Spalding and his chum, nothing was known of the queer mystery which surrounded the old building. It seemed incredible, but it was true. Blake and his friends were practically none the wiser, in spite of their adventures on the rugged Welsh coast, regarding Glyn Castle. All they knew was that Mr. Godfrey Jarrow and Llewellyn were opposed to them, and Sexton Blake vowed that he would solve the puzzle at the earliest opportunity.

The skipper looked up as a heavy sea thudded against the ship's side, effectually reminding him that the storm had not yet blown itself out.

"Bless my life! I must get back to my duties, gentlemen!" he exclaimed. "I have been so interested in Mr. Blake's operation on my boy that I clean forgot the Ocean Sprite, an' everythin' else! I'll soon 'ave our position worked out, an then I'll be able to tell you 'zactly how far we are from the nearest land."

"Good!" said Spalding. "Bally good, in fact! Land is the stuff I want to see more than anything else just now. I've had quite enough of the jolly old sea to last me for years an' years, and I don't want to see the inside of a boat again for——. Gadzooks! I believe something has got in our beastly way, and we've hit it with a considerable bash!"

Crash! Crash!

Even as he finished speaking, Spalding was sent sprawling upon the floor of the cabin, while an appalling series of grinding, splintering sounds came to his ears. Shanks and Glyn had also been flung to the floor, but Sexton Blake had just managed to grasp the table, and to save himself from being pitched over. Incidentally, he instinctively saved the unconscious Joe from sliding off the table, and so meeting instant death.

The Ocean Sprite, after heaving and tossing for a few seconds amid the din of rending timbers, became strangely still, and the startled occupants of the skipper's cabin scrambled to their feet and looked at one another with serious faces. There could be only one explanation of this occurrence, and with one accord they dashed for the companionway, and literally tumbled on deck.

The night was inky black, and a thick sea-mist enveloped everything at a distance of a dozen yards or so. Giant seas were dashing into the air on either side of the little cutter, and Blake set his lips grimly as he saw them. They could only mean one thing—and Tinker's anxious voice confirmed the detective's worst fears even as he gave free rein to his thoughts.

"Guv'nor, we're on the rocks!" exclaimed. Tinker, his voice full of blank amazement and consternation. "We ran into this bank of fog only a couple of minutes ago, and I couldn't see a blessed thing! Oh, what rotten luck! Are—are we badly damaged, do you think?"

"Yes, Tinker, I fancy we are very seriously damaged!" answered Blake, in a low voice. "You are in no way to blame, however, and there is no need for you to condemn yourself. This fog-bank, evidently, is hanging over some rocks, and we seem to have become firmly wedged upon them——"

"You're right, Mr. Blake!" cut in the skipper, with a sad note in his voice. "The Ocean Sprite is done for this time, without a doubt! She's blamed near high an' dry on the rocks, an' I shouldn't wonder but what there's a hole in her bottom big enough to drive a carriage an' pair through! Well, it serves me right for usin' the craft for Jarrow's dirty work—bust my buttons if it don't!"

In spite of the seriousness of the situation, the others were forced to smile at Shanks' philosophic manner of regarding the catastrophe. There could be no doubt that they were in a most precarious position, and this aspect of the disaster was not lost upon the free-and-easy Spalding.

"That's all very well, cap'n," he protested. "But what I want to know is—how are we goin' to make the shore again? Bein' stranded on the bally rocks is a deuced awkward sort of accident, you know, just when things were lookin' so rosy, too! Dashed if our luck isn't dead out all the way along!"

Victor certainly seemed to have hit the nail upon the head by that remark, for misfortune was dogging the little party relentlessly and persistently, by all appearances.

Dawn would be breaking very shortly now, but at the moment the early morning was dark and chilly. The rain had ceased to fall, but the seas were still running high, and the wind had dropped almost to a dead calm—which accounted for the thick mist. The storm had blown itself out, and the rough seas were merely the aftermath of the hurricane which had raged during the night.

This, at any rate, was something in their favour, for there was now no danger of the vessel being washed off the rocks. A brief investigation showed that the Ocean Sprite had become firmly wedged between two towering fangs of rock, and she seemed to be in no danger of sliding off. Captain Shanks announced that the tide was rapidly running out, and he was proved correct within a very short time.

By the time the first faint streaks of dawn showed themselves in the Eastern sky the rocks upon which the cutter was impaled were only just awash, and a little later she was absolutely high and dry. And in the growing light of the new day the little party scrambled overside with the intention of ascertaining the extent of the damage to their vessel.

A prolonged examination of the cutter's bottom was quite unnecessary, for the first glance told them the worst. Practically half the Ocean Sprite's keel had been ripped away, and the damage was so extensive that the hope of refloating her was utterly out of the question. Captain Shanks was almost broken-hearted when he saw the havoc which had been wrought on his beloved little craft, but no amount of wailing would help to mend matters.

And a worse discovery was yet to follow.

The ship's party, after they had investigated the damage to the cutter, went for a tour of inspection over the rocks with the intention of ascertaining their whereabouts. And it did not take them long to find out that they were on an island—a tiny rock of a place, barren of trees, and desolate in the extreme. It was composed chiefly of towering, jagged formations of rock, and a more bleak and uninviting refuge could scarcely be imagined. At high tide the greater part of the island was pretty well submerged by all appearances, for sand and seaweed were strewn everywhere among the lower crags and boulders.

"Well, of all the dismal, wretched, an' barren islands in the world, this is the bally limit!" exclaimed Spalding, looking round with an air of disgust and disappointment. "Bein' shipwrecked on an island filled with coconuts an' bananas an' things wouldn't have been so bad, but this——! Ugh! It makes a fellow shudder to gaze at the landscape! Where the deuce are we, anyhow?"

Captain Shanks was looking serious as he turned to answer the question.

"If I ain't mistaken in my reckonin'," he said gravely, "we're somewhere not very far off the coast of Portugal. But we might jest as well be in the middle of the Pacific for all the help we're likely to git! We're stranded on about the worst o' rocks in the Atlantic—an' it looks as though we're booked for a considerable stay!"

The others looked at the skipper with anxious glances, but it quickly dawned upon them that Shanks was right.

They were marooned—marooned on a barren island of rocks!

CHAPTER 12.
The Voyage on the Raft!

OWEN GLYN looked at Sexton Blake with a wistful expression in his eyes.

"Surely there must be some means of making our escape from this wretched place," he said. "I know we've no cause to grumble, really—for we're jolly lucky to have come off as well as we have done. But I'm fearfully anxious to get back and see what's happening at the castle. I—I can't help feeling that the mystery of my parentage is going to be cleared up there, Mr. Blake, and this set-back is galling and exasperating."

Blake took a pull at his pipe, and nodded thoughtfully.

"I am quite as anxious to get back to civilisation as you are, my dear fellow," he replied. "As a matter of fact, I have been seriously thinking of building some sort of raft, and attempting to reach land by that means. It is impossible for us to remain here indefinitely, and something will have to be done."

The famous detective was lying upon a pile of blankets and cushions as he spoke, and appeared to be extremely comfortable. The wisps of smoke from his pipe curled upwards towards the lofty arches of a tremendous cave in which he was reclining, and for a shipwrecked man he was undoubtedly doing himself remarkably well.

Two days had passed since the Ocean Sprite had wrecked herself upon the rocks, and during the interval the six castaways had managed to make themselves a comfortable home upon the barren island. Or, to be more exact, five of them had done so—for Joe Shanks, of course, was quite incapable of taking any active part in the proceedings.

A brief search of the island had revealed that fact that a large cave existed high up in the centre of the great formation of rocks, and the party had at once decided to make their home there. The cave was lofty, and quite out of the reach of the tide, and it was situated in such a position that it would afford them ample protection from the keen winds which blew across the Atlantic.

Within a couple of hours of discovering the cave they had made plans to transport all the available stores from the cutter, and they had set about this task without a moment's delay. Their craft had not been absolutely wrecked when she had first struck the fangs of rock, but there was no telling when another storm might come along and break her up completely. It was, therefore imperative to land all the food and other material from the Ocean Sprite as quickly as possible, and the five marooned adventurers had set to work with a will.

Before darkness had fallen they had accomplished the greater part of the business. Every scrap of food had been carried ashore first, and this had been followed by blankets and clothing, cushions, crockery, and cooking utensils, and even a couple of tables and some chairs and stools. The galley stove had been taken to pieces with some difficulty, carted into the cave and re-erected. Everything possible which could be taken from the cutter had been landed, and the result was a remarkably comfortable island home.

Joe Shanks, under Blake's direction, had been very carefully taken ashore, for his condition was as yet extremely critical. There was no doubt about his recovery provided he was allowed to rest, but any sudden jar or shock might easily prove fatal.

And so the skipper's son had been carried from the cutter's cabin—still reclining upon the table on which the operation had been performed. He had been securely lashed to the woodwork by strips of sheeting to avoid any possibility of his slipping off, and the legs of the table had then been removed—thus forming the table top into a stretcher. The patient had been safely carried into the cave, and seemed to have suffered no ill-effects whatever—greatly to the captain's joy.

The six castaways had spent the night's in peaceful and well-earned slumber, and the following day they had again visited the wreck, and had brought ashore a few more articles which might prove useful. Upon the whole, they regarded themselves as being extremely fortunate, but they were all chafing somewhat under the enforced imprisonment—the duration of which they could not even make a guess at.

No ship had been sighted since their arrival on the island, and Captain Shanks had stated that, according to his reckoning, the nearest land was some ten or twelve miles away at a rough estimate. The skipper also caused a little gloom to settle upon his companions when he mentioned the fact that the island was situated in treacherous waters which were studiously avoided, and that in consequence they were not likely to be sighted by any passing vessel.

But, in spite of these drawbacks, the little party were exceedingly lucky to have come off so well. They had every necessity—and a good many luxuries into the bargain—for a long stay upon the rocky island if necessary, and so they had nothing to grumble about.

The Ocean Sprite, while the rough seas had subsided considerably, was still getting a pretty severe buffeting at each high tide, and was fast becoming a total wreck. She was still firmly wedged between the treacherous fangs of rock, and seemed to be in no danger of slipping off. But the seas had left their impression upon her injured hull, and were relentlessly rending her to pieces.

Practically all the timbers which had been torn from the once proud little vessel had drifted ashore, and had been hauled high above the reach of the waves, in readiness for use as fuel, or for any other purpose which might be necessary. A good deal of the wood was sound, and serviceable, and Sexton Blake determined to make good use of a quantity of it as a means of escape. There was plenty of strong rope available, and he saw no reason why a raft should not be constructed, as he had just suggested.

Owen Glyn seized the idea with alacrity, and his eyes gleamed with pleasurable anticipation.

"A raft!" he repeated. "Why, of course—that's a splendid suggestion of yours, Mr. Blake! There's plenty of timber here, and we could build one large enough to carry the whole six of us easily——"

Sexton Blake shook his head.

"No, no, Glyn—that would never do," he interrupted. "It would be extremely foodhardy for more than two of us to venture into the open sea under such conditions. A raft such as we could construct would be a frail contrivance at the best, and there is no necessity to risk more lives than is absolutely necessary."

"Mr. Blake's right, Owen—absolutely right," cut in Spalding. "A trip on the briny ridin' a bally raft may be great fun for healthy fellows like us—but just imagine what it would be like for poor old Joe here! The exposure an' the tossin' would finish him off long before land was reached. No, old son, a couple of us must make the journey, and send help back for the others."

"Exactly," agreed Blake. "That is my idea precisely, Spalding. And, since the suggestion came from myself, I think Tinker and I will make the attempt to reach the coast as soon as we can prepare the raft. I am particularly anxious to settle accounts with Mr. Godfrey Jarrow, and Tinker and I will make all haste to Glyn Castle—if we are lucky enough to make land without mishap."

The others looked at the detective with disappointed glances. Clearly, both Spalding and Glyn had hoped to be chosen to accompany Blake—but they realised that it was more fitting that Tinker should go. He was Blake's assistant, and would no doubt be more useful to him than either of them.

Captain Shanks approved of the plan, too, and volunteered to do everything in his power to make the building of the raft a success. He would have liked to make the journey himself, but it was out of the question for him to leave his injured son. Joe was making good headway, but it would be some little time before he was his old self again.

And so the little party of five fell to discussing the details of the plans for the immediate future. The evening meal was just over, and night was almost upon them, so nothing further could be done until the next morning. Fortunately, there had been plenty of blankets aboard the Ocean Sprite, and in consequence each member of the little camp had two or three in which to roll themselves up for the night.

Very soon they were all sleeping soundly. They had all been working like navvies during the whole of the day, with the exception of Joe, and as a result they slumbered deeply. The keen sea breezes also helped to induce heavy sleep, but at the same time they were extremely refreshing and beneficial. So much so, in fact, that by dawn the castaways were astir once more, feeling invigorated and ready for anything.

Tinker and Spalding volunteered to prepare breakfast, while Blake and Glyn went off with the skipper to choose the most suitable lengths of timber for the construction of the raft. It was their intention to use as much as possible of the wood which had been cast ashore, and to supplement this by taking whatever further supplies they required from the cutter. The vessel would never be fit for use again, so it did not matter about disfiguring her a little more.

For two whole days Sexton Blake and his companions worked upon the building of the raft, and succeeded in turning out quite a serviceable looking craft. The keel was made out of heavy pieces of securely lashed timber, and upon this was built up a solid platform of planks and spars.

There were several layers of these, all bound tightly together, so as to give the raft a good floating body. Upon the topmost of all—which was really the "deck" of the raft—flooring boards had been placed, which made the little vessel much more comfortable than the usual roughly-built raft.

Moreover, sides had been added to the flooring, so as to prevent as far as possible the shipping of heavy seas, and also to make the craft more water-tight. By the time she was ready for launching, she was practically a complete little boat, with seats for the passengers, a locker for the storage of food and water, and a mast and sail. A couple of roughly-made oars were included, and altogether the raft looked quite capable of doing what was required of her.

Blake and Tinker surveyed the clumsy stack of timber and cordage with critical eyes, and the latter nodded his head with great approval.

"She'll do, guv'nor," he observed. "I wouldn't mind trusting myself on this raft for a three-hundred-mile trip, let alone ten or twelve. She'll carry us to land without any trouble at all."

Blake smiled.

"It will never do to be too certain in a case of this sort," he answered. "The raft certainly looks capable of anything now, but a little rough weather will probably alter her appearance considerably. However, I certainly think we shall stand a fair chance of making the coastline, and we'll make a start at dawn to-morrow."

Everything was prepared before darkness fell. A large keg of water was placed in the locker, and sufficient food for several days' rations was stowed on board. Nothing was overlooked, and by the time the little party turned in they were all feeling satisfied that the journay would prove to be a successful one for Blake and Tinker.

They were astir before the break of dawn the next morning, and Blake made a brief examination of Joe Shanks before he left the island. There was no telling when the detective would be able to send help to the four marooned castaways, but he promised that help would certainly come if he and Tinker succeeded in making a safe journey.

Blake was pleased with the progress of his patient. Joe was mending in a remarkably rapid manner, showing that he was the possessor of a fine, healthy constitution. He was not allowed to talk much as yet, and he had been told very little of the adventures which had befallen the Ocean Sprite's party. Joe was in no need of further medical aid, and his complete return to health was simply a matter of time. This in itself was a remarkable tribute to the detective's prowess as a surgeon, and Captain Shank's gratitude was something extraordinary.

After a hasty breakfast the raft was launched, and Blake and Tinker, after shaking hands all round, took their places on the deck. They found that the raft floated evenly, and seemed to be in every way thoroughly seaworthy.

When Blake said the word, Shanks and Glyn and Spalding gave the raft a mighty push off, which sent her swaying and rocking on the tide. But in a few moments she settled down to the swell, and as the wind caught in her flapping sail, she sped out almost gracefully into the open sea.

"Good-bye and good luck!" sang out Spalding, waving his hand in farewell. "Buck up an' send the bally old rescue party along!"

Glyn and the skipper added their parting words of good cheer to those of Spalding, and Blake and Tinker answered and waved in return. They kept on waving at intervals until the island was a mere speck in the distance, and the figures of the three castaways looked no bigger than insects. The adventurers had fairly started on their perilous cruise now, and they would have to trust to Providence to see them safely through.

For some hours they allowed themselves to drift with the wind and tide, for they had no exact idea in which direction the mainland lay. In any case, the oars would be of very little use as a means of propelling or steering such a heavy and clumsy craft, and their best policy was to simply drift. So long as they were travelling in something like the right direction—which Blake reckoned should be northwards—they were pretty certain to strike land sooner or later. And, provided they did so within reasonable time, they would be quite content.

The weather was now fine and sunny, which made the first part of their trip almost enjoyable. By noon they had seen no sign of any other craft, and they were absolutely alone on the vast expanse of waters—apparently cut off from civilisation for all time. The comparative frailness of their floating refuge made the pair feel strangely insignificant as they rode upon the heaving breast of the ocean now so placid and calm. It was difficult to realise that this same gently rippling stretch of water, aided by the wind, could lash itself into such an appalling power of destruction as that which had sent the gallant little Ocean Sprite high and dry upon the rocks—a shattered wreck.

Blake and Tinker enjoyed a hearty lunch as they bobbed and floundered along in their queer vessel, and discussed the possibilities of making the land by the time darkness had fallen. As far as present appearances went, there was not much possibility of any such good luck befalling them. But they continued to hope, and to scan the horizon in all directions.

The fact that they had been so many hours at sea without sighting any other vessel indicated plainly enough that they were either making very slow progress, or else that the rocky island on which they had been marooned was further out of the track of ships than Captain Shanks had supposed, Blake and Tinker, at any rate, had certainly expected to see some little indication that civilisation had not been left entirely behind them, even if they did not sight land.

But for another couple of hours they drifted along in the same sluggish manner, still without seeing so much as a fishing smack. Matters were now beginning to look a trifle serious, and Blake was grave. It was impossible for them to sail along indefinitely in this ridiculous little vessel, that much was obvious.

The detective was gazing idly overside when he suddenly became aware that the raft was gradually changing its direction of travel. Her sails were still set, but instead of drifting in the same direction as the slight wind, she was moving at right angles to it. There could be only one explanation of this, and Blake turned to Tinker.

"We're being carried out of our course by some sort of current, young'un," he said, pointing into the water. "I think we'd better unship the oars, and see what can be done in the way of steering. I am quite convinced that the nearest land does not lie in the direction in which the current is taking us, and our best policy will be to——"

"But I can't understand it, guv'nor!" interrupted Tinker, "I always thought that sea-currents were caused by rivers emptying into the sea? If that's the case, we ought to be somewhere nearer land than we supposed! Hadn't we better let the current take us along?"

Blake smiled.

"I think not, Tinker—if we can help it!" he replied. "You see, the current may be caused by a river entering the ocean fifty miles or so away. Or it is caused, possibly, by something entirely different. There is no telling with these mysterious currents, for the Atlantic is full of them."

Tinker nodded, and unshipped the oars, as his master had directed. They took one apiece, and commenced pulling strongly in an endeavour to turn the raft out of the current. But their efforts seemed to make very little impression on the clumsy craft, for it continued to glide smoothly along with the eddying swirl.

The pair rowed until the perspiration streamed down their cheeks, but they made no progress whatever. It was evident that they would have to give up the attempt, and allow themselves to be carried along helplessly. The raft, being a practically square structure, was difficult to steer, and absolutely refused to answer the pull of the oars.

"Phew! This is rotten!" gasped Tinker. "It's hopeless, guv'nor! We might as well try to shove the Olympic along with a couple of oars as this old tub! She won't budge an inch!"

"So it seems," replied Blake, resting upon his oar, and wiping his face. "The current is too strong for us, Tinker. We must drift along with it, that's all. Perhaps it will prove a blessing in disguise—but I'm doubtful! However, we're in the hands of the gods, and we can only hope for the best."

They shipped their oars once more, and sat in the raft regaining their breath. The current was not carrying them along at any amazing speed, but it was certainly taking them more swiftly than the wind had done. Blake and Tinker were by no means perturbed, but they were naturally somewhat anxious regarding their ultimate destination. But there was nothing for them to do but await events.

The evening was well advanced before any change in the outlook occurred—and by that time they had been drifting along with the current for several hours. The dusk was just beginning to gather when Tinker's keen eyes detected a smudge of smoke upon the horizon, and he let out a frantic yell of delight. Excitedly he pointed out his discovery to Blake, and the pair wondered anxiously whether they would be seen.

The detective calculated that the raft would not be very far distant from the steamer by the time she passed their bows, as it were, and he reckoned that it would be possible to attract attention—provided the light did not fall too soon. He and Tinker spent a rather excited three-quarters of an hour while they waited for the supreme moment to arrive, and during this interval one or other of them continually waved their sail about in an effort to attract the attention of the steamer's crew.

At last the large vessel drew within hailing distance, and both Blake and Tinker commenced shouting at the top of their voices. But even as they did so they observed that the steamer was slowing down, and that a small boat had been lowered, and was being rowed in their direction. The tramp steamer's officers had evidently seen their signal of distress long before they had heard their hail, and Blake and Tinker both offered up a little prayer of thankfulness. They were saved!

An hour later both Sexton Blake and Tinker were seated in the skipper's cabin on the tramp steamer, and the former gave the captain a brief account of their plight. Blake did not deem it necessary to explain everything in detail, but he told just enough to satisfy the skipper that everything was in order.

The rescued castaways found, to their delight, that the vessel was bound for Tilbury, and Blake, when he at last found an opportunity of a private talk with Tinker, informed the lad that he was exceedingly pleased that things had turned out as they had.

"As events have happened in this way, Tinker, we have now a splendid opportunity of making a few enquiries before sending out help to our friends on the island," he said. "They are perfectly safe, and have plenty of food—sufficient for four months, if necessary. Moreover, Joe Shanks cannot be moved for another fortnight, and during that time you and I can find plenty to employ our time, I have no doubt!"

Blake spoke in a significant tone of voice, and Tinker looked at him sharply.

"What do you mean, guv'nor?" he said. "Are you going to leave those chaps on the island while you deal with Jarrow?"

The detective nodded.

"Exactly, Tinker!" he agreed. "I mean to find out exactly what is happening at Glyn Castle without a moment's delay. There is something extremely peculiar in the incidents which have occurred there, and I shall not be content until I have discovered their meaning."

"Good!" commented Tinker. "That means that we shall get our own back on Mr. Jarrow! By jingo, the scoundrel will receive the surprise of his life when he sees us walk in as large as life! I suppose we shall start for Wales as soon as we touch port?"

"By the first available train!" answered Sexton Blake.

CHAPTER 13.
The Rescue of the Crusoes.

VICTOR SPALDING looked out across the deserted horizon with a somewhat dejected expression upon his usually sunny features.

"Not a sail!" he muttered. "Not even a bally smudge of smoke to gladden the old optics! Dashed queer why Mr. Blake and Tinker have deserted us like this! I can't bring myself to believe that they came to grief on that toppin' little raft! The idea's too ghastly, old scout!"

Owen Glyn nodded.

"It may be ghastly, Vic, but it seems to be true," he replied. "There's no other possible explanation of their long silence that I can see. Why, man alive, do you mean to say they'd leave us here like this if they had reached land?"

Spalding looked thoughtful.

"Well, you'd scarcely think so," he admitted. "But these detective Johnnies are queer fellows when they get busy on the solvin' of a bally mystery, you know! At any rate, I'm not going' to believe that Blake and Tinker are payin' a visit to Davy Jones yet awhile! Hang it all, Owen, the very idea of that makes a cold shiver run up an' down my beastly spine!"

Glyn turned his face seawards and glared into the distance, obviously unable to agree with his friend's point of view. The two young men had indulged in similar conversations on many occasions recently, and there was certainlyu some excuse for them.

Queerly enough, they were both looking tremendously bronzed and healthy, and their clothing seemed to have undergone many changes for the worse since the departure of Sexton Blake and Tinker.

Other changes were apparent on the island, too. A little, roughly-built house stood near the entrance to the great cave—obviously constructed out of the timbers of the ill-fated Ocean Sprite. The wreck of that gallant little craft was no longer visible upon the jagged fangs of rock, for the very good reason that the majority of its woodwork had been utilised upon the island by the castaways.

Outside the shack, sitting in deck chairs, the figures of Captain Shanks and his son Joe could be plainly seen from the spot where Glyn and Spalding were standing. Joe appeared to have lost all traces of his illness, and was just his former vigorous self again. Even as Spalding turned to glance inland, Joe rose from his chair and strode across to where a little wooden hut had been constructed. From the base of the hut a large armoured hose ran down the rocks to the sea below—evidently a supply pipe to the apparatus which was installed within the hut.

This was nothing less than a fresh-water machine which had once been in use in the cutter. There was no spring water whatever upon the rocky island, and the castaways had been compelled to make use of this apparatus in order to obtain the vital liquid. It was a lucky thing for them that the machine had been among the equipment aboard the Ocean Sprite, for otherwise their predicament would have been hopeless.

Joe turned the circular handle of the pump which drew the water from the sea and delivered it, fresh and pure, into the pail which he had placed under the valve. Then he picked up the pail and made his way to the little wooden house, in which the cooking arrangements were carried on.

Spalding had observed Joe's movements, and he knew that the skipper's son was setting about preparing a lunch for the four inhabitants of the island. Since his recovery he had acted as chief cook and bottle-washer of the party, and he was becoming quite an expert.

The four marooned men, in spite of the comparative luxury of their quarters, were becoming sick and tired of their monotonous existence upon the island, and this was not to be wondered at. For weeks had elapsed since Sexton Blake and Tinker had sailed away in their raft in order to bring assistance, and during the whole of that time the castaways had received no message from them.

This disappointment had made them—with the exception of Spalding—fear that the worst had happened to Blake and Tinker. They believed that their voyage upon the raft had ended in disaster, and that the detective and his assistant had perished before land could be reached. Victor Spalding, however, did not share this view for some reason, and nothing would convince him that they had seen the last of their two brave friends. He admitted that he had no grounds upon which to found his belief—but he just stuck to his opinion.

Certainly Glyn and Shanks and Joe could not be blamed for believing as they did. For it seemed incredible that Blake—if he had really escaped death—should leave them alone on the island for such a long period.

Once or twice they had thought that help would arrive—only to meet with disappointment. Ten days after Blake and Tinker had left, they had caught sight of a small motor-boat just after dawn, and they believed that it had been cruising near the island. But, in spite of frantic efforts, they had failed to attract the attention of the occupants.

They had also found some mysterious footprints in the sand, which proved conclusively that somebody had landed on the island. They had seen no trace of the visitors themselves, and they had been greatly puzzled and chagrined. It was a very queer circumstance, and one which the castaways were totally unable to account for.

And since that time the same thing had occurred on two or three occasions, greatly mystifying the marooned unfortunates. They were totally at a loss to account for these uncanny visitations, which appeared to be absolutely pointless. Nothing was ever taken away from the island, and nothing, so far as they could discover, was left behind except a few blurred footprints in the sand.

Apart from these somewhat extraordinary happenings, the life of the four Crusoes was humdrum and monotonous in the extreme. But they were, nevertheless, growing quite accustomed to it by this time, and were healthy and bronzed and full of vitality and vigour. They were well supplied with food and drink, and plenty of fuel was available from the wreck of the cutter. Moreover, they had practically everything necessary for their individual comfort in the way of razors and soap, for they had been able to rescue everything which the Ocean Sprite had on board.

The only fly in the ointment, as Spalding put it, was the uncertainty of what had happened to Blake and Tinker. There is an old saying to the effect that no news is good news, but in this particular instance it didn't seem to fit. The lack of tidings indicated that disaster of the worst possible kind had overtaken the detective and his assistant, for if they had reached land they would assuredly have sent help to their marooned friends. That, at all events, is how the castaways had regarded the matter.

Spalding and Glyn had visited the rock upon which they now stood many hundreds of times during their stay upon the island, and had always looked in vain for the hoped-for sail. This occasion proved to be the same as the others, and the pair turned dejectedly back towards the centre of the place they had been compelled to call home for so many weeks.

"Oh, I'm fed-up!" said Glyn. "Absolutely and thoroughly fed-up!"

His friend chuckled.

"Well, I'm in high hopes that I shall be in the same agreeable condition in a few minutes!" he remarked. "I observed that the excellent Joe disappeared into the cook-house a little while back, an' I'll bet he's preparin' a thunderin' good feed, as usual! It's simply amazin' the way that chap knocks up the grub!

Glyn couldn't help grinning at Spalding's facetiousness. He was always the same, no matter under what conditions he happened to find himself, and nothing ever seemed to ruffle his habitual good temper. This was just as well, especially in the present circumstances, for a man of Spalding's character could usually be relied upon to dispel any gloominess which happened to be in the air. Indeed, his good-humour and cheery spirit had done much to make life on the island bearable for his three companions.

During lunch Captain Shanks brought up the one important topic of conversation—as he usually did. This, of course, was upon the subject of rescue—how long it was likely to be delayed, or whether it would come at all. The skipper made some reference to this important question at practically every meal, and he never seemed to tire of talking about it.

He was just as mystified as the others regarding Sexton Blake's silence and inaction, and the only explanation of it which occurred to him was that the detective had perished. Yet Shanks could not understand this, for the weather had been exceedingly good upon the day Blake and Tinker had left the island, and he would have staked his life that the pair would reach land in safety.

And yet they had heard nothing.

This very obvious fact usually had the effect of bringing the mealtime discussions to a close, for the simple reason that a dead wall confronted the. But each day brought renewed hope to the four castaways, and it was only natural that they should voice their thoughts.

The weather to-day was particularly fine and sunny, and when lunch was over Glyn and Spalding set about doing their share of the "housework," as they termed it. All four of them worked splendidly together, and the task of washing up was mostly performed by Joe, while Glyn and Spalding dried the plates and dishes after him.

Spalding grasped a pile of clean "crocks" with the intention of stowing them away in readiness for the next meal, when he happened to glance seawards. As he did so he gave a sudden start, which had the effect of scattering about half the plates up the floor.

Glyn and the skipper and Joe looked round quickly, but before they could inquire the cause of the sudden clatter, they were surprised to see Spalding deliberately fling the rest of the plates he held haphazard into a corner and wave his arms wildly.

"A sail—a sail!" he yelled. "By the Lord Harry, a bally boat is comin' in sight at last! Hooray!"

His companions followed the direction of his glance with excited looks, and they saw at once that his words were true. A large motor-launch was making for the island at a smart pace, and she presented a magnificent spectacle to the eager castaways as they watched her ploughing through the waves towards them. This was the first vessel they had seen for weeks and weeks, and they became almost frantic with excitement as they beheld her.

Owen Glyn drew in his breath with a sharp little hiss of doubt.

"I—I wonder if she's really coming here with the intention of taking us back to civilisation?" he breathed.

"Of course she is, you idiot!" said Spalding. "Look at the way she's steerin'—absolutely in a bee-line for us! I'll bet Mr. Blake and Tinker are aboard of her—you can tell that by the direct manner in which she's headin' this way! If strangers were visitin' the island, they wouldn't be buzzin' landwards at this rate; they'd come crawlin' up to see what sort of a show they were up against!"

Captain Shanks nodded quickly.

"I believe you're right, sir," he exclaimed tensely. "No motor-launch would be in these waters without a good reason—— But my buttons! Did you see that?"

"See what?" asked Glyn.

"Why, there's somebody wavin' to us from the launch's deck!" yelled the skipper. "That proves that Mr. Blake is on board! Oh, thank Heaven, he an' the boy got ashore safely!"

The captain was undoubtedly right, as the others saw immediately. There was certainly somebody on the launch who was waving a white handkerchief, and in all probability it was Tinker's greeting to them. As if with one accord, the four castaways commenced running madly down to the water's edge waving frantically as they went.

The motor-launch was now much nearer, and they could see that she was much larger than they had at first thought. In fact, she looked more like a fair-sized yacht than a launch—a yacht capable of great speed, to judge by her graceful lines and racy build.

She dashed up to within five hundred yards of the treacherous rock shore, and then dropped anchor. Within a couple of minutes a small boat was lowered overside containing two figures, who commenced rowing towards the island with swift and powerful strokes.

The four marooned men were now so excited that they could scarcely contain themselves. As the little boat drew near to the beach they waded in and pulled her high and dry, at the same time confirming their hopes as to the identity of the visitors.

"Mr. Blake an' Tinker!" shouted Spalding delightedly. "I knew all along you'd come back sooner or later!"

"I—I can scarcely believe it!" said Glyn brokenly. "After we'd given you up for lost, too! Oh, this is too good to be true!

Captain Shanks and Joe greeted the newcomers with respectful pleasure and expressed their gratitude at the safe return of the wanderers. So far Blake and Tinker had had no opportunity of getting in a single word, but the detective, when he had at last finished shaking hands with everybody, did manage to make himself heard.

"My friends, I am delighted to find you all looking so well," he exclaimed. "It is exceedingly gratifying to me to know that you have suffered no ill effects from your long stay here, and I declare that Joe is even better than he was before his accident!"

"Yes, rather—Joe's all right!" said Spalding. "We're tremendously pleased to see you an' Tinker, Mr. Blake, but we can't understand why you left us here such a bally long time! You don't know what we've been conjecturin' about you——"

"I don't wonder at that, my dear fellow," interrupted the detective. "But Tinker and I could not possibly come sooner. We reached civilisation quite safely on the raft, but there are some very good reasons why we could not return here before this. We have come to take you back with us now, however, and I can promise you a good time after your lonely existence on this rock."

Glyn looked at Blake with a curious expression in his eyes.

"Have you been prevented from returning here by that fellow Jarrow?" he asked. "Have you been inquiring into the mystery of the castle——"

"Yes, Glyn—I have!" interrupted Blake, with a nod. "But I do not intend to enter into any long explanation regarding that matter just now. You can take it from me that everything will be well before long, and I propose to take you straight to the castle at once, although I think it will be as well to spend a few days in the open sea to begin with. Tinker and I have been working fairly hard of late, and a little cruise in the yacht will do us both good. I am sure you will not mind a little delay of that sort, in spite of your impatience to return!"

Glyn smiled.

"Mind, Mr. Blake?" he echoed. "Great Scott, I don't care if we spend a month in the yacht so long as we get off this beastly rock! I'll admit that we've had all the necessities of life here, but the monotony and the loneliness have been frightful! The pleasure of seeing you and Tinker again, and the knowledge that we're going back to the castle at all is good enough for me! What do you say, Vic?"

Spalding grinned.

"I echo your sentiments exactly, old scout!" he remarked. "The mouldy old castle can rip for all I care! Any old time will do to continue out bally investigations there—so long as we're back in a civilised community I don't mind if it snows! I've got an idea, accordin' to Mr. Blake's observations, that he has done all the investigatin' necessary, an' he's goin' to spring a stunnin' surprise on us! I may be wrong, but—there you are!"

Sexton Blake smiled quietly to himself when he heard Spalding's words, but he made no comment. He seemed to be strangely uncommunicative considering his long and unaccountable absence, but he appeared to be in no hurry to enlighten the castaways as to his doings. And they, on their part, were too excited and relieved at their rescue to pay much attention to this aspect of the matter.

They were heartily glad that the time had come for them to leave their rocky island home at last, and arrangements were quickly made for all four of them to go aboard the yacht. This was a simple matter, for they intended to leave everything just as it was upon the island. Captain Shanks, if he so desired, could come along and collect anything he needed at some future date.

Within half an hour the whole party were comfortably installed on the magnificent motor yacht, and were speeding away from the lonely little isle which had been their home for so many long weeks. Glyn and Spalding were supplied with new suits of clothing which Blake had thoughtfully brought for them, and the pair looked forward eagerly to enjoying themselves.

They were a little mystified at Sexton Blake's peculiar reticence regarding his adventures during the last three months, but they did not dream of pressing him for details. They knew well enough that the detective would confide in them when he thought fit, and meanwhile they gave themselves up to having a glorious time aboard the yacht.

She was truly the last word in luxurious motor launches, and carried a crew of seven or eight. She was equipped with a spacious dining saloon and a large billiard-room, and lighted throughout by electricity. Everything possible was provided for the comfort of her passengers, and Glyn and Spalding were not at all sorry that Blake had suggested the cruise before returning to port.

They all spent a most enjoyable five days aboard the swiftly-moving craft, speeding through the waters in glorious weather. For the most part the yacht kept clear of the usual shipping lines, and no land had been sighted since the start. But Glyn and Spalding were quite content, caring very little where they were taken. Sexton Blake was conducting the cruise, and that was good enough for them. They knew that they would finish by being taken to the castle, and they were quite content.

At dinner on the sixth day Blake made the long looked-for announcement.

"I intend to steer straight for the rugged cliffs at the base of Glyn Castle to-night," he said quietly. "You have been exceedingly patient, Glyn, but there is no reason why we should delay our return any longer."

"Oh, good!" said Owen, looking at the detective with a puzzled face. "I had no idea we were anywhere near the Welsh coast, Mr. Blake. Have you made any arrangements as to what you're going to do when we get there? What about that scoundrel Jarrow? And Llewellyn—the old humbug?"

Blake smiled.

"I think we can afford to ignore them on this occasion, my dear fellow," he replied. "However, we will see how events turn out."

He said no more, and some time later he and Tinker, accompanied by Spalding and Glyn, left the saloon and went on deck. The night was pitchy dark, with no moon, and with dense cloud banks obscuring the stars. The yacht was even now nearing the frowning cliff upon which Glyn Castle was perched, and the travellers strained their eyes shorewards to discern their whereabouts. It was difficult to see anything at all, but Glyn judged that they were no more than a mile from the treacherous, rocky coast.

"I say, Mr. Blake, you surely don't intend to make a landing to-night?" he exclaimed. "It's not far off midnight now, you know, and I should think it will be better to wait till the morning."

The detective shook his head.

"No, Glyn, we will go ashore at once," he declared. "I fancy there is a little surprise waiting for you in the castle, and I have a mind that you should pay a visit there as soon as possible!"

Glyn was greatly puzzled, but he made no further comment. Blake's words, as a matter of fact, had aroused his curiosity, and he was now quite eager to go. And, within the next ten minutes, the yacht was anchored, and a small boat lowered overside. Blake, Tinker, Spalding and Glyn took their places within it, and pushed off for the shore.

Only a few hundred yards had to be traversed, and the nose of the boat grounded upon the beach in a few seconds, and the little party scrambled out, and made their way towards the cliff path in the darkness. They had no difficulty in finding it, and they mounted the summit of the cliff in single-file.

At the top the dull, grim walls of the old castle could be dimly seen, standing gaunt and lonely in majestic solitude, its ancient turrets and towers rearing themselves heavenwards with proud aloofness. Owen Glyn looked at the great building with quickly beating heart, and as he did so he started slightly. A change had come over the castle since he had last seen it by night, and he knew at once what it was.

Practically all the windows were now brilliantly illuminated, whereas previously they had always been

CHAPTER 14.
An Amazing Discovery.

VICTOR SPALDING grinned to himself as they halted at the massive hall door. It was clear that he had observed the difference in the aspect of the castle, as well as his chum, and he turned to Glyn as Sexton Blake gave a hearty peal at the bell.

"Somewhat more cheery lookin' exterior—what?" he remarked. "Brilliant lights everywhere in honour of the prodigal's return, an' all that sort of rot! If only the fatted calf is roastin' on the spit, I shall be perfectly contented. By gad!"

He broke off in surprise as the hall door was flung open by a liveried flunkey, who stepped aside to allow the visitors to pass into the wide hall. As they did so they were too astounded to utter anything for a few moments, for an amazing change had taken place. The wide hall was now superbly furnished, and soft electric lights gleamed everywhere.

The whole place seemed to be transformed entirely. The same picturesque old walls were unaltered, but countless improvements had been made to everything. But, although the furniture was new and magnificent, there was nothing modern in the appearance of the whole—with the exception of the electric lighting. And this had been carried out in such a way that it resembled the old-fashioned candles and lamps.

Sexton Blake and Tinker were smiling delightedly and the detective took it upon himself to conduct Glyn and Spalding from room to room. The pair were almost speechless with surprise, for the same amazing changes had taken place everywhere. Every apartment they entered had some fresh revelation for them, although the castle still preserved, practically intact, its former appearance of tremendous age. But the whole place was improved in an astounding degree, and Glyn and Spalding wandered about with the keen enjoyment of a couple of schoolboys.

At last they returned to the big hall once more, and Owen Glyn turned to Sexton Blake for enlightenment.

"What does it all mean, Mr. Blake?" he asked. "Who is responsible for all the amazing changes which have taken place here since we saw it last? It's absolutely wonderful, and the castle is scarcely recognisable as the same old building."

The detective chuckled.

"You will soon know everything, my dear fellows," he said. "But now that you have had a look round, and have seen what has been done, I want you to take a walk into Langland Bay at once—if you think you can manage it after all the excitements of the evening!"

Glyn looked surprised.

"Certainly, Mr. Blake, I don't mind," he said. "But what's the idea——"

"I have a letter here, addressed to the Langland Bay Hotel," interrupted the detective. "If you wouldn't mind delivering it, I should be greatly obliged."

"But, look at the time!" said Glyn, more puzzled than ever. "It's past two o'clock in the morning, Mr. Blake!"

"Never mind that, my dear fellow," answered Blake. "The time makes very little difference, for when you reach the hotel you will find that the letter is expected!"

"That's good enough, Owen, old man," cut in Spalding. "Come along, I'll go with you! It's a dead cert that Mr. Blake wouldn't want the bally letter delivered at this unearthly hour unless it was important, so let's get a move on! What about it?"

Glyn nodded abstractedly, and the pair left the castle once more, and started off on their mission. They were quite unable to understand the attitude of Sexton Blake, but they both obtained the impression that there was something significant in the letter.

The night was intensely dark, and for a few moments the two young fellows had some difficulty in keeping to the path. But after a short time their eyes became more accustomed to the gloom, and they progressed more quickly.

After they had walked along in silence for a minute or two, Glyn turned to his chum.

"Look here, Vic, there's something thundering queer about everything, in my opinion!" he said. "It's all different, somehow——"

"Rather!" said Vic emphatically. "The whole bally castle is changed in a stupendous manner——"

"Yes, I know," interrupted Glyn. "But other things are different as well, and I'm blessed if I can make it out! The cliff path didn't seem quite the same, I remember, and I'm jolly certain this road is altered!"

Spalding looked round him.

"Altered!" he repeated. "How the deuce can the road be altered, old son? An' yet, now you come to mention it, it does seem a bit different! Dashed queer thing, you know, to find alterations outside as well as in! By gad! I—I thought there was a wood, or somthin', just away to the right there!"

Glyn nodded.

"So there is," he agreed. "There's a road through that wood leading to a village with a name about ten yards long——. Why, the wood doesn't seem to be here, Vic! Surely we haven't come the wrong way? Hanged if I can make out exactly the lie of the land!"

He paused, and looked round him in astonishment. He could have sworn that he and Spalding had taken the usual cliff path which led to Langland Bay, and yet he didn't seem to recognise his surroundings. Moreover, the wood which Spalding had mentioned was no longer visible. It was really a peculiar experience, and he didn't know what to make of it.

"I say, Owen—there's something deucedly fishy about all this!" said Spalding, gazing ahead intently. "First we miss the bally woods, an' now I see there's a lot of gleamin' lights in the sky over there! They were never there before, so far as I know, an' I've been wonderin' what they mean! See 'em?"

He pointed in front of him as he spoke to a spot where a glimmer of reflected lights gleamed in the heavens. Glyn looked in the same direction, and scratched his head in perplexity.

"By jingo—so there are!" he exclaimed. "Hanged if I can made head nor tail of this affair I've never been so fogged up in my life! I know we're going in the right direction; and yet we seem to be on unfamiliar ground all the time! Nothing is exactly as it ought to be to-night, and I've got half an idea that we're asleep and dreaming!"

"No fear, old scout; dreams don't alter the bally landscape in this fashion!" replied Spalding. "We're up against somethin' deucedly queer, an' I propose that we ask some joker what's happened when we get into Langland Bay——. Hallo! There's a stranded motor car just ahead, by the look of it!"

The two friends had been walking onwards as they conversed, and they now observed that a motor car was standing stationary in the roadway a little distance in front. They saw that the driver was repairing a tyre as they drew nearer to the spot, and he took very little notice of them as they halted within a few yards of him.

This seemed queer to the newcomers, and Spalding determined to interrogate the stranger with an idea of ascertaining their exact whereabouts. In ordinary circumstances such a thing would have seemed ridiculous, but both Spalding and Glyn had an unaccountable feeling that they were lost.

"Sorry to trouble you, old man—but can you direct us to the Langland Bay Hotel?" asked Spalding leaning forward and bending over the kneeling motorist. "We seem to have lost our bearin's a trifle!"

The driver of the car looked up, and shook his head.

"The Langland Bay Hotel!" he repeated. "Say guess I've never heard o' such a place!"

It was quite evident that the man was an American, for he had an accent one could almost cut with a knife. Glyn and Spalding looked at one another disappointedly.

"Oh, well, if you're a stranger in these parts, I don't suppose you would know it," said Spalding.

The man laughed.

"Stranger nothin'!" he exclaimed. "I reckon I've lived around here ever since I was born, an' there ain't no hotel within a hundred miles which I couldn't direct you to without thinkin' twice! Guess you've got hinder mussed up with the name o' the place you're searchin' for, son!"

Spalding and Glyn were absolutely astounded to hear the man speak in this manner, and they again looked at one another queerly.

"If you've lived here all your life, you must know the Langland Bay Hotel!" said Glyn. "It's not much more than a mile from here——"

"Cut it out, pard!" interrupted the motorist. "I reckon you must be lookin' for the Centerville City Hotel, sure! You'll find it right in the middle o' Centerville City, two miles further on! That's the nearest hotel you'll strike around this locality!"

The two friends stared at the speaker blankly, seriously wondering if they had encountered a madman.

"Centerville City!" repeated Spalding. "What on earth are you talkin' about, old chap! You must be thinkin' of your own home town across the bally water, or somethin'! We want Langland Bay——"

The motor driver rose to his feet, and looked at the pair strangely. He was evidently puzzled, but he grinned broadly.

"Say, you guys talk as if you think you're located in England!" he said. "I guess it's time you're put wise——"

"Nothing of the sort," cut in Glyn. "We're in Wales!"

"Look here, sonny, I don't allow no blamed Britisher to pull my leg—it ain't healthy!" growled the man, staring harder than ever. "This place is Center County, in the State of Maine, U.S.A.! I dunno what sort o' bees you've got buzzin' under your cap, but you can take it from me that the only hotel hereabouts is in Centerville City!"

The driver seemed to be quite sincere, and he did not strike them as being at all like a lunatic. But Spalding and Glyn could not believe the evidence of their ears, and they looked at the man blankly.

"You—you must be mad!" muttered Glyn. "We're on the Gower Coast, in Wales—eight miles from the port of Swansea! We can't possibly be anywhere else, and it's ridiculous for you to say we're in America!"

The motor driver spat into the darkness impatiently.

"Gee! You guys sure want a tarnation amount of convincin'!" he exclaimed. "I tell you you're in the State of Maine, an' if you don't believe me, jest get aboard my auto! I'll soon show you that you're barkin' up the wrong blamed tree—sure!

He busied himself with the tyre without more ado, and Spalding and Glyn gazed at one another in a perfect chaos of mind. They had never experienced anything so extraordinary as this in their lives before, and they didn't know whether to accept the motorist's offer or not.

"Well, if this doesn't beat the bally band!" murmured Spalding. "I certainly feel inclined to accept this gentleman's offer to take us for a trip in his 'auto'—just to see what's goin' to happen next! By gad! Are we travellin' on our heads or our heels, old scout?"

Glyn shook his head helplessly, but followed his chum into the car. The driver finished whatever he was doing to the tyre within a couple of minutes, and he drove off in the direction of the spot where the lights were gleaming in the sky.

The occupants of the car sat as if dazed. Every minute they were forced, against their better judgement, to accept the driver's statement that they were, in very truth, really upon American soil. Astounding as this undoubtedly was, there was ample evidence that it was a fact.

The road upon which they were speeding was different, as they could now see, from the Langland Bay road. It was broadening out into quite a respectable thoroughfare, whereas it ought to have remained narrow and tortuous. And, almost before they knew it, they had entered a small town—which could not be mistaken for anything but a purely American "city,"

Its main street was wide and long, and the buildings upon either side were chiefly those known as "frame" houses—mostly built of wood. A few brick structures were scattered here and there, but the whole place was typically American in style. The street was brilliantly lighted by means of electric standards; and it was the glare from these which Spalding and Glyn had seen reflected in the sky.

The car halted abruptly at a level crossing, in the roadway, and the next moment a train roared by—a train which could not, by the wildest stretch of imagination, be mistaken for a British one. It's great towering locomotive was fitted with an enormous cow-catcher, and a bell upon the boiler clanged out its warning to users of the road as the engine flashed on its way, pulled a long train of brightly lighted Pullman cars behind it. No doubt the express was the Something-or-other Limited, bound for New York.

Victor Spalding and Owen Glyn rubbed their eyes, and gazed at one another in a manner which was really comical. They had every cause for their amazement, but there was no doubt that they were at last convinced of the truth of the motor driver's statement.

"By gad—it's true, Owen!" gasped Spalding. "We're absolutely in the United States, old man—not a doubt of it! This is one of Mr. Blake's little tricks—an' he's had us on toast with a vengeance!"

Glyn gulped.

"But—it's impossible, Vic!" he protested. "Remember the castle! Great Scott! Haven't we just come out of it? How can we be in America when Glyn Castle is just along the road!"

"Dashed if I know, old top—but we are!" returned Spalding. "There must be two bally castles—exactly alike, or somethin' of that kind! Anyhow, that express was American enough—an' so is this town!"

Glyn nodded dazedly.

"Yes, that's so," he admitted. "But I'm hanged if I can understand it, Vic. Talk about surprises! Fancy finding ourselves in America when we thought we were in Wales! We had no suspicion whatever—— Hallo! Here's Mr. Blake himself!"

At that moment another car had whizzed up and halted alongside the one in which the two friends were seated. It contained Sexton Blake, Tinker, and a smiling stranger.

"Well, my dear fellow," said the detective, "I hope you delivered the letter safely at the Langland Bay Hotel——"

"A bit too deuced thick to play a joke like this on us, Mr. Blake!" put in Spalding. "You're a bally fraud, absolutely!"

Blake chuckled.

"I think it wil be as well if we all go back to Glyn Castle," he suggested. "A few explanations, I fancy, will not be at all unwelcome!"

CHAPTER 15.
The Mystery Solved—Conclusion.

OWEN GLYN and his friend looked tremendously relieved when they heard Sexton Blake's words.

His promise of enlightenment bucked them up wonderfully, and made them feel quite cheerful. The mystifying experiences they had recently undergone had almost taxed their patience to the limit, and they had seriously begun to wonder whether they were mad or sane.

Blake's hint that satisfactory explanations were shortly to be forthcoming put the pair at their ease once more, but at the same time it whetted their curiosity in no uncertain manner. Truly, the amazing series of recent happenings would require a vast amount of clearing up, and Spalding and Glyn were quite anxious to get back to the castle.

Glyn Castle, Blake had called it, but surely he must be wrong! And yet it seemed to be the same in every way to Spalding and his chum, and they were puzzled beyond measure. They couldn't for the life of them understand how this particular circumstances was to be explained, but they realised that idle conjecture was useless.

Blake's car had by this time turned round, and was speeding back along the road, closely followed by the vehicle in which the two friends were seated.

They had given no instructions to the driver whatever, and they shrewdly suspected that he had received them earlier—probably from Sexton Blake. It was all part of a pre-arranged plan—that much was obvious now—and Spalding and Glyn marvelled at the thoroughness and subtlety of the famous detective's surprise.

They had been completely hoodwinked into believing that they were being taken to the Welsh coast in the motor yacht, whereas in reality they had been brought to America. This, of course, accounted for the "cruise," which had really been substituted for a speedy Atlantic crossing. Sexton Blake had stage-managed everything admirably, and had succeeded in keeping up the little deception to the very last.

The two cars quickly reached their destination, and Spalding and Glyn looked at the old building with a new interest. Either their eyes were deceiving them, or else some sort of miracle must have happened, but they could not doubt that it was Glyn Castle itself which stood before them. The old towers and turrets, the gables and chimneys, everything was identical, with the exception of the brilliant lights which shone from the mullioned windows. The ancient, weather-stained walls stood out in the same grim manner, frowning as darkly as they had always done.

Sexton Blake and Tinker alighted from their car, and followed the beaming stranger who accompanied them to the door of the castle, beckoning to Spalding and Glyn as they did so. A couple of minutes later the whole party of them were assembled in the great lounge hall, and the famous detective—who was still wearing an expression of smiling amusement—turned to the two mystified young men

"I trust you will forgive us of the harmless little deception which has been played upon you, my dear fellows," he said, with a merry twinkle in his keen eyes, "but the opportunity was much too good a one to miss. However, before we enter into any further details, I want to introduce you to Mr. Oscar T. Williamson, the famous millionaire. He is quite anxious to make your acquaintance, I assure you."

Glyn and Spalding were presented at once to the affable looking stranger whom they had first seen in the car, and when these formalities were over the millionaire seated himself, and beamed upon them. He seemed to be an extremely jovial individual, and his visitors liked him instantly.

"Mr. Blake is quite right when he says that I'm pleased to meet you two boys," he began. "As a matter of fact, I'm real delighted to know you both, but I'll admit at once that it's you, Mr. Glyn, in whom I'm particularly interested. You see, I've got a fixed notion in my head that you and I are kinsmen——"

"Kinsmen!" repeated Glyn in astonishment. "Well, I'm jiggered! But I—I don't see exactly how we can be related, Mr. Williamson——"

"That's not at all surprising," interrupted the millionaire smoothly. "but when I tell you that my great grandfather was one of the Glyns, of Glyn Castle, no doubt the position will be a littler clearer to you. I happened to be born here in the States because my parents were located here, but you can bet that I've always had a pretty considerable interest in my ancestral home 'way back in the Old Country. To be quite frank, the yearning to see it for myself took a great hold on me, and during the early part of last summer I crossed the Atlantic for a holiday in England. And about the first thing I did when I landed was to buy a ticket for Swansea."

Mr. Williamson paused, and looked round. Everybody was listening to him with the greatest interest, and Owen Glyn seemed absolutely absorbed in his newly-found kinsman's story. He felt that the narrative was being related chiefly for his benefit, and he was right.

"I guess I didn't lose much time in hitting the trail for Glyn Castle, sonny," went on the millionaire, "and I found the old place to be about ten times as magnificent as I had anticipated. I had imagined it as a ramshackle, tumbled-down ruin, and I was agreeably surprised when I saw that the castle was in a splendid state of preservation. Well, to cut a long story short, I took such a fancy to the old building that I determined to have it—lock, stock and barrel, complete as it stood! I was in a position to buy it, whatever the price might be, and I got busy at once——"

"Do you mean that you wanted the castle as a residence?" asked Glyn.

"Exactly!" nodded Mr. Williamson. "But it was no use to me for that purpose where it stood in Wales, and I reckoned to have it transported, and rebuilt right here on my Maine estate!"

"What—what an extraorindary idea!" he ejaculated.

"Amazing'!" put in Spalding.

"Extraordinary or not, I reckoned the scheme was quite possible, and I began making inquiries," went on Mr. Williamson blandly. "I found, eventually, that a Mr. Godfrey Jarrow, of London, was the owner of the castle—at least, he told me that he owned the place, and he agreed to sell out his interest for the sum of twenty thousand pounds. We fixed the deal, and everything was signed, and all arrangements made to get the transporting arrangements in hand. But just about this time you and your friend here slid into the landscape, and slightly disorganised the whole bag of tricks, by all accounts!"

The millionaire smiled, and Sexton Blake took up the story from this point.

"Mr. Williamson is quite right, Glyn," he said. "By an extraordinary series of coincidences, the incidents which took place at the castle—the happenings which caused you and Spalding and myself and Tinker such mystification—occurred just after Jarrow had put the deal through with Mr. Williamson. Naturally, Jarrow was anxious and furious when you appeared upon the scene so unexpectedly, for if you succeeded in making out your right to the property he would lose the twenty thousand pounds purchase money!"

Light at last began to dawn upon Owen Glyn, and he nodded.

"I see just what you mean, Mr. Blake"' he said, "But Jarrow was absolutely on the wrong track really. I had no intention of putting in a claim for Glyn Castle, for the simple reason that I was not aware that I had any right to it! I will admit that I was in high hopes of establishing my identity when Vic discovered that oil painting of my father, but beyond that I was not interested."

"I quite understand that, my dear fellow," agreed Blake. "But Jarrow was not to know your intentions. As a matter of fact, I have proved beyond question that you are the rightful owner of the castle, and it is obvious that Jarrow was quite aware of this also. He was your late father's trustee, and he took every advantage of your unfortunate loss of memory to benefit himself financially.''

''The confounded old swindler!'' chimed in Spalding. ''That accounts for his terrific anxiety to get us all out of his way so quickly!''

''Precisely!'' agreed Sexton Blake. ''Jarrow as soon as he realised the position, did everything possible to get you, Glyn—and Spalding, Tinker and myself as well—out of harm's way. It was essential to his interests that we should be disposed of for a sufficient length of time for the castle to be taken down, and shipped to America. After he had received his money, of course, he would promptly vanish, and he wouldn't care a jot then what we did. And so the cunning scoundrel arranged with Captain Shanks and his son to take us aboard the Ocean Sprite for a four months' cruise.''

Sexton Blake paused, and looked at Glyn. It was clear enough that the famous detective's news had pleased the young man considerably, and his face was flushed and excited. At last his burning desire was satisfied, and he knew for a fact that he was really Owen Glyn, heir to Glyn Castle. This had been quite an unexpected and un-looked-for development in his fortunes, and it would be futile to ignore the fact that he was overjoyed. But before he could pour out his gratitude for what Blake had done for him, the detective resumed.

''As you know,'' he went on, ''disaster overtook the little Ocean Sprite of the coast of Portugal, and the whole party became marooned on the rocky island. But Tinker and myself succeeded in reaching England by means of the raft, and we hurried without the loss of a moment to Wales. When we arrived at Glyn Castle we discovered that the work of taking the building to pieces was already in progress, and we were greatly surprised.''

Glyn nodded.

''I should think you were!'' he exclaimed. ''Why, I've never heard of such an astounding idea in my life as the complete removal of a huge place like Glyn Castle! The task must have been a colossal one to accomplish! But what about Jarrow, Mr. Blake? What did you do to him?''

''Nothing—so far!'' replied the detective, with a grim note in his voice. ''Tinker and I kept our presence entirely secret, and even to this moment Jarrow is under the impression that we are all cruising in the Atlantic! You see, he is quite ignorant of the fate which had overtaken the Ocean Sprite, and I saw no reason to enlighten him! But I sought out Mr. Williamson with all possible speed, and explained the whole position to him. Naturally enough, he was extremely angered when he learned of Jarrow's duplicity, and suggested that we should at once inform the police with a view to his immediate arrest. Afterwards the plan was to bring you and the others back from the island at once, and to go through all the formalities for the purchase of the castle a second time. I agreed to this arrangement readily enough, of course; but Mr. Williamson thought it better to make a slight alteration!''

Sexton Blake paused and glanced at the millionaire, who was still smiling in his former bland manner.

''That is quite correct,'' he agreed easily. ''I am one of those individuals who believe in the old saying that second thoughts are best, you know, and I suggested to Mr. Blake that we should leave all existing arrangements as they were, and carry the thing through—but at record speed! You see, sonny, I thought it possible that you might refuse to sell, and I couldn't afford to risk a disappointment of that sort!''

Glyn shook his head.

''You needn't have feared anything of that nature, Mr. Williamson,'' he said, with a smile. ''I should have agreed readily enough——''

''Perhaps so,'' broke in the millionaire, ''but there was an element of doubt about the matter, and I was determined to have the castle in any case. And I guessed that it would be safer, from my point of view, to move it first, and offer to buy it afterwards! But doing that I reckoned that I should be pretty certain to keep it, for I can hardly imagine that you'd be enthusiastic about the place as to have it shipped back to Wales!''

''I should think not!'' said Glyn, with a laugh.

''Well, Mr. Blake jibbed a bit at first,'' went on Williamson, ''and I could only get his consent to the plan by undertaking to pay you whatever price you cared to ask for the castle—no matter what it was. I agreed to this at once, naturally, and we soon got busy. A literal army of workmen were turned loose upon the old building, and the task of transplanting it across the water was got under way as quickly as possible. Huge gangs of men were kept working at the double day and night in order to get the job finished before your store of supplies ran out on the island, and they succeeded. They succeeded far beyond my expectations, and they carried out the work in an amazingly complete manner, as you can see for yourself."

The millionaire waved his hand as he spoke, indicating the walls around him. The others glanced at them and marvelled. Even after Mr. Williamson's explanation it was difficult to realise that the building in which they were seated was actually the identical castle which had stood upon the coast of Wales for hundreds and hundreds of years.

But it was true.

Every brick and stone which had been used in the making of Glyn Castle centuries ago had been transported across the Atlantic in the most careful manner by experts, and the castle was now rebuilt in its original form. All the valuable carved panelling has been scrupulously packed, and was now back in position, looking as exquisite as it had ever done.

Only the brain of an American millionaire could have given birth to a notion of this description, and only his unlimited supplies of money could have accomplished such a colossal task. The transplanting of Glyn Castle must have cost Mr. Williamson a tremendous sum altogether, but he considered the result to be well worth it.

For some few minutes there was silence in the great hall. Owen Glyn and Victor Spalding having been only just acquainted with the true state of affairs, needed a little time to recover their composure, which was not to be wondered at under the circumstances. Surprise after surprise had been showered upon them, and they were a little swept off their feet.

One little point seemed to be worrying Spalding, and he looked at Mr. Williamson and Sexton Blake in turn.

"You may think it funny," he said, with a grin, "but I've been wonderin' what's become of that blitherin' old fossil known as Llewellyn! He richly deserves to be boiled in oil or somethin' pleasant of that sort for the fearful way he behaved when the bally castle was on the other side of the ocean!"

"I'm not sure that I don't agree with you, Spalding," he said. "But Mr. Williamson merely 'fired' the old caretaker as a punishment for his sins. Not doubt Llewellyn would have been brought over here if he had been of a different character, but Mr. Williamson very sensibly refused to have any dealings with a traitor."

The millionaire nodded.

"Absolutely," he agreed. "That fellow Llewellyn may have been an old retainer of the Glyn family, but his conduct in helping Jarrow to swindle our friend here of his inheritance disgusted me so much that I kicked him out neck and crop."

Glyn nodded.

"Well, he got much less than he deserved," he said. "And now there's something that I want to know—from you, Mr. Blake! Why did you bring Vic and myself here in such a mysterious manner? Why weren't we told that we were in America instead of Wales! You can't imagine what a couple of idiots we felt when we were questioning the driver of that motor-car! We thought he was a madman, and no doubt he thought the same of us!"

The detective chuckled.

"I fancy Mr. Williamson can answer your question far better than I!" he observed.

The millionaire laughed.

"Yes, I'm the culprit!" he exclaimed. "I'm afraid I can do but little but beg an apology, but it was a whim of mine to bring you and your friend here at night just to see if you'd be deceived!"

"Well, I'm jiggered!" exclaimed Glyn.

"At any rate, you succeeded all right, Mr. Williamson," said Spalding. "To be quite exact, you diddled us very neatly! We hadn't the faintest notion that we were anywhere but on the coast of Wales, an' when we discovered that we were on Yankee soil—well, there you are! Surprise wasn't the word to use at all!"

"Yes, I'm quite satisfied," nodded the millionaire blandly. "I chose this particular portion of the coast because it resembles the Welsh cliffs so closely. It is not exactly the same, of course, but there is so little difference that you were unable to detect it in the darkness. I am absolutely proud of the castle, now that it's safely rebuilt and installed with electric lighting, and I'm only waiting for you to mention a figure which will satisfy you, Mr. Glyn, to complete the business!"

Owen looked a little bewhildered and uncomfortable. Everything had been sprung upon him with such suddenness that he wasn't prepared to discuss money matters just now, and he turned red.

"Well, I scarcely know how to answer you, Mr. Williamson," he exclaimed. "I think it is fairly certain that I should have sold the castle in any case when I found that I owned it, and I also think that I should have been quite eager to accept the twenty thousand pounds you mentioned. Therefore we may as well——''

''By gad, you're a rotten sort of business man, Owen!'' cut in Spalding. ''Here's a gentleman absolutely rollin' in wealth an' eager to carve off a chunk of it for you in return for the bally castle, an' you don't attempt to drive a bargain! Why, man, you ought to stand out for double the sum you just talked about, if only for compensation as the way you've been imprisoned, shipwrecked, marooned, an' what not!''

Glyn looked more uncomfortable than before.

''Shut up, you old Shylock!'' he hissed. ''What do you mean by suggesting anything like that? You ought to be— Why, you bounder, you're only pulling my leg!''

Mr. Williamson smiled more broadly than before and commenced writing out a cheque. He handed it to Glyn a few seconds later, and the young man nearly fell back off his chair when he read the amount.

''Great Scott! What's this for?'' he gasped. ''Fifty thousand pounds! It's—it's too much, Mr. Williamson, and I couldn't think of——''

''Put it in your pocket and say no more about it!'' broke in the millionaire. ''I agree with your friend's views, whether he was pulling your leg or not! I regard the castle as cheap at forty thousand, and the extra ten is just a little appreciation of your good-natured way of taking everything. I guess over three months of isolation on the island was worth ten thousand, to say nothing of all the rest!''

Glyn shook hands with Williamson as if in a dream. He was almost too affected to speak, for he had never expected anything like this. In one stroke he had regained his identity and obtained a fortune, and he was dumb with amazement and joy.

''Speaking of the island,'' said Blake, ''I omitted to tell you that you were not quite so much out of touch with civilisation as you supposed. I sent a small party of men there on several occasions, just to watch over you and see that everything was all right. They had instructions not to speak to any of you—in case you questioned them. They reported to me that things were going well, and I was relieved of any anxiety on that score.''

''By gad! That accounts for the mysterious footprints we found in the sands!'' said Spalding.

''Exactly!'' said Blake, with a smile. ''We couldn't possibly leave you marooned for all that time without assuring ourselves of your well being, so I adopted this plan. It was the only way, and it proved quite successful.''

★ ★ ★

Nothing now remained but to deal with Mr. Godfrey Jarrow, the rascally trustee of the Glyn estate. He was still in ignorance of the true state of affairs, and he was due to arrive at the castle at nine o'clock, much to the surprise of Spalding and Glyn. Williamson had arranged for Jarrow to call in person on this particular morning for the purpose of receiving the balance of his money. So far he had merely been paid a deposit, and he was not likely to overlook the appointment.

The night had long since passed, and the time was almost seven o'clock when the little party finished their conversation in the great lounge hall. Mr. Williamson suggested that they should all partake of an early breakfast while awaiting the arrival of Jarrow, and so, after a refreshing wash and brush up apiece, they enjoyed a hearty meal together.

They were just finishing when Jarrow was announced. He came in, looking as brawny and cocksure as he had done in Wales, and he was smiling broadly as he entered. But as soon as he caught sight of Sexton Blake and Owen Glyn, his features underwent a remarkable change. He staggered drunkenly in his amazement, but before he could utter a word, Mr. Oscar T. Williamson told him exactly what he thought of him in no uncertain manner. The millionaire adopted a grim attitude and spoke in harsh tones; but he spoke to such good purpose that Mr. Godfrey Jarrow—metaphorically speaking—completely shrivelled up.

He was beaten—just at the very moment when he had expected to triumph. His eyes glinted angrily when he realised his position, and it seemed as if he was about to become violent. But at that moment Mr. Williamson touched a bell, and an American police officer, accompanied by a Scotland Yard detective, entered the room, and promptly arrested Jarrow on charges of conspiracy and fraud.

The humiliated trustee cast venomous and vindictive glances at the assembled party as he was being led out, but he was sensible enough to make no attempt to break away from his captors.

Spalding breathed a sigh of relief as the door closed.

"Well, that's that!" he observed. "Old Jarrow has got his all right this time, without a bally doubt!"

Tinker grinned.

"And he deserves it, too," he said. "Jarrow must be a pretty low down sort of bounder to try and rob a chap of his inheritance! What's more, he'd have succeeded if you and Mr. Glyn hadn't been shipwrecked at the foot of the castle cliffs that night!"

"Absolutely!" agreed Spalding. "An' it strikes me that he'd have won the day in spite of that if you an' Mr. Blake hadn't got busy an' rounded him up! But it's all over now, thank goodness, an' dear old Owen has come out on top! Good luck to him!"

At this point Mr. Oscar T. Williamson rose to his feet, his bland smile very much in evidence.

"My friends," he said. "it is entirely owing to my somewhat bizarre notion of transporting Glyn Castle to America that you are gathered here this morning, and I guess I shall be tremendously disappointed if I can't persuade you all to spend at least a week with me as my guests. I can promise you a rattling good time, and I reckon a brief holiday of that sort will be a fitting termination to all your recent adventures. Now then, what do you say?"

With one accord the millionaire's guests said "Yes"; and the week which followed amply repaid them for their decision. For Williamson was as good as his word, and gave the members of the party an almost-royal time.

Glyn Castle—that ancient structure which had withstood so many storms on the rugged coast of Wales—was now a brilliant palace of light and activity; and was not at all likely to degenerate into its former condition of loneliness and gloom. But in spite of the new condition of things, the old building still retained something of its sombre stateliness, and this added very materially to its charms.

Mr. Oscar T. Williamson, at any rate, was more than delighted with his new possession, and that, after all, was the main thing to be considered.

THE END.

First Published in the Sexton Blake Library in 1925

THE CASE OF THE SOCIETY BLACKMAILER

THE PROLOGUE.
CHAPTER 1.

THE sun was sinking to the west, and the cool of the evening had set in. The day's toil was over at the estancia of San Pablo, belonging to the Senor Hernando Lopez, and the gauchos, as cowboys are called in Uruguay, had finished their supper, and were sprawled lazily on the grass outside of their quarters, smoking and chatting, while a couple of them strummed on guitars.

Not far from them was the house of their employer, built of stone, and surrounded by a wide veranda, and shaded by a clump of williows and acacias which grew by a stream of water.

In all directions stretched the grassy uplands, where thousands of sheep and cattle were grazing; and beyond the ranges was the bare, wind-swept pampa, rolling away to distant mountains, and to wooded valleys.

They were much of the same type, these gauchos, of mixed Spanish and Indian blood, with reddish-bronze skin, and straight, black hair, and beady eyes.

They wore sombreros and cotton pantaloons, and the upper part of their bodies were draped in ponchos, squares of woollen cloth with slits cut in the middle to admit the head.

Their spurs were of silver, and at each man's waist hung a lasso or a bola the latter a rope with a round ball at the end of it.

They were not all Uruguayans, however. Amongst them were two Arizona cowboys, and a Mexican vaquero. And there was also an English youth, Oliver Douglas by name, a handsome young fellow of twenty-five, tall and broad-shouldered, clean-shaven, with a florid complexion and fair hair, and dark blue eyes.

A visitor had arrived at the estancia that day, an English sportsman who had come up-country from Montevideo to shoot deer and ostrich, and he was spending the night with Hernando Lopez.

The gauchos had seen him, and they were talking of him with laughter and jest, and Oliver Douglas was listening to the conversation with vague unrest, when one of the household servants approached the group.

"I have a message for you, Douglas," he said in Spanish. "The senor would have you come to him at once."

"He wants to see me?" asked the English youth, with a slight start.

"Yes, that is what he told me," the servant replied.

"What for, Morale?"

"That I do not know. But you had better be quick, for the senor is not in a good temper."

The servant departed, and Oliver Douglas rose from the ground, shrugging his shoulders. The news of the arrival of the visitor—he had not laid eyes on the Englishman himself, or learned his name—had caused him a little uneasiness.

It was very silly of him, he had felt. There wasn't a chance in a million of that which he feared happening.

But his suspicions had been roused now, and there was a worried look on his face, and a sinking at his heart as he crossed over to the house.

He mounted to the veranda, and passed straight from it into the large living-room, which was furnished comfortably and luxuriously as befitted a wealthy stockraiser.

Two persons were seated here at a table littered with dishes. They had dined, and now they were drinking red wine and smoking black cigars.

One was Hernando Lopez, big and burly, swarthy of skin, with a bushy black beard and moustache; and the other was the English guest—a slim, fair gentleman of perhaps thirty, with aristocratic features, and a blonde moustache that drooped over his lip.

One quick glance at him, and Oliver Douglas knew what to expect. But he did not show any emotion.

"You sent for me, senor?" he said quietly to his employer.

Hernando Lopez nodded, and looked inquiringly at his guest, who lifted a monocle that was suspended from his neck by a silk cord, and screwed it into his eye.

For a moment he closely scruitinised the youth.

"Yes, Senor Lopez, I was right," he declared in a slow, drawling voice. "I thought I recognised the fellow when I had a glimpse of him this afternoon, and now I am quite sure."

"He is the same rascal you told me of, then? said Hernando Lopez."

"He is the same," Hugh Anstruther replied. "Not a doubt of it. We were members of the same club in London before he was kicked out. His real name is Denis Sherbroke, and he is the son of Julian Sherbroke, the millionaire. He led such a reckless and dissolute life that his father cut off his allowance, and turned him adrift. Shortly afterwards the fellow got into very serious trouble. He and the other two rogues tried to obtain a large sum of money by fraud from Sir Harry Royce, a friend of mine. While under the influence of drink Royce was induced to sign his name to a paper which he believed to be an IOU for a small gambling debt, and he subsequently discovered he had backed a bill for three thousand pounds. At the same time the discounted bill had not fallen due. Sherbroke's accomplices escaped abroad, and he was arrested.

"But the affair was hushed up. With great difficulty, through the influence which Mr. Julian Sherbroke exerted in high quarters, he had his son released. There was a strict condition imposed by the police, however. It was understood that the boy was to leave the country at once, and that if he ever ventured back he would be rearrested and charged."

Hugh Anstruther paused.

"That was three years ago," he continued, a sneering smile on his lips, "and now I find young Sherbroke here, at your estacia, in an assumed name."

Hernando Lopez's face was as dark as a thundercloud.

"What have you got to say for yourself?" he demanded of the youth. "Do you admit you are Denis Sherbroke, or do you deny it?"

"I don't deny anything," Oliver calmly, replied. "All you have been told is true."

"So you deceived me, eh? You brazenly lied to me! You led me to believe you were an honest young fellow who had fallen on bad times through no fault of your own!"

"Can you blame me, senor? I had to have employment, and you wouldn't have given it to me if I had told you the truth. Haven't I been worthy of your trust? You gave me a chance, and I was grateful. I have led a straight and honest life since I have been with you, and if you will keep me on——"

"Keep you on? Is it likely I would, knowing what you are? I'll have no rogue and swindler working for me! It wouldn't be safe! I dare say you have been waiting and watching for an opportunity of——"

Hernando Lopez chocked with rage.

"You're discharged!" He cried, striking the table with his fist. "I've finished with you! I paid you your wages this morning, and you won't get another peso from me! And now begone, you impudent, lying rascal! I'll give you a quarter of an hour, and if you haven't cleared off by then I'll have you thrashed with whips! You'll get no employment elsewhere in Uruguay! I'll see to that! This is an honest country! Take my advice, and cross the border into Brazil or the Argentine, where you'll find plenty of rogues as bad as yourself!"

Appeal would have been useless, and Oliver Douglas knew it. He stepped to the door, hesitated, and looked at the man who had betrayed him.

"You have done a cruel and heartless thing, Anstruther," he said, in a sullen tone. "If I go clean to the devil it will be your fault. Remember that!"

"Clear out, you crooked dog of a swindler!" roared Hernando Lopez. "Don't stand there! Begone!"

The youth left the house, and more in sorrow than in anger. He could not justly blame his employer. He went to the men's quarters, and came out a few moments later with his blanket strapped to his back, and his automatic-pistol in his belt.

The gauchos had meanwhile heard of his discharge, and they mocked him and jeered at him, calling him vile names as he passed by them.

Oliver did not reply to their taunts. He walked rapidly on, scarcely hearing the abuse that rang to his ears, and did not stop until he was beyond the limits of the San Pablo estancia.

Then he sat down on a stone to consider his plans. He was far up-country, two hundred miles to the north of Montevideo, in a remote province of Uruguay.

He had a month's wages in his pocket, and the meagre savings of three years as well; and to the south-west of him, within a couple of days' journey was a railway-station.

"I'm not going over to Brazil or the Argentine," he doggedly reflected. "It will be Montevideo for me. I'll have a good time there while my money lasts. When it is gone I'll try to get work at the docks, and if there should be nothing doing, I'll have to beg or starve."

He set off again as the sun was touching the horizon, and while he held to his course, bitter thoughts of the past crowded into his mind.

What a heavy price he was paying for his sin—for the crime which had made him an outcast from his native land! Yet he had no right to complain, even if he had been spoilt by an indulgent parent.

No, his punishment was deserved. All Hugh Anstruther had said of him was true. He was a criminal.

Heedless of remonstraces and warnings, he had led a life of unbridled extravagance and dissipation until he had exhausted his fathers patience and been turned adrift from home.

His allowance cut off, craving for money to gratify his desires, he had fallen in with evil companions, and been easily persuaded to join in their plot to swindle the wealthy young baronet, Sir Harry Royce, out of a large sum of money.

The trick prematurely discovered, his accomplices had fled the country, leaving him to bear the brunt. He had been arrested—had suffered the indignity of having his finger-prints taken at Scotland Yard—had been set free through his fathers influence, and had been banished to South America on conditions which forbade him ever to return to England.

He had nearly starved in Montevideo before he met Herman Lopez there and induced the stock-raiser to give him employment at the estancia of San Pablo.

Three years ago that was; and since then he had been working hard, almost cheerfully, and clinging to a very slender ray of hope—the hope that he might some day redeem his character and go home, win his fathers forgiveness, and marry the girl be loved.

Muriel had loved him, too, with a steadfast and loyal love, yet her influence had not saved him.

She had often pleaded with him, and the last time he had seen her, on the eve of his departure, she had pleaded with him again, told him she still had faith in him, and made him promise to turn over a new leaf for her sake.

For three years he had kept his promise, and had clung to the slim hope. But now——

"There's no use in hoping any longer!" Oliver said to himself aloud, an angry glitter in his eyes. "Curse that fellow Anstruther! He has ruined the one chance I had of making good! I don't suppose I'll ever get another, I may as well go straight to the devil, and be done with it! That's all that's left to me!

He had been tramping for more than an hour, and now, in the dusk of the evening, he had reached the crest of a wooded hill. He would not go any farther to-night, he decided.

He climbed down into a deep glade, where tall pine-trees grew, and a stream trickled from beneath a mossy rock, and pink, and purple, and golden flowers spangled the grass.

And as he was gazing about him, looking for a suitable place to make his bed, he was startled by a stealthy, rustling noise behind him.

Swinging quickly round, he saw the shadowy figure of a man, and at the same instant he was struck on the head with a blunt weapon.

He staggered and fell, half-stunned by the blow. He was not unconscious. He was dimly aware of rough hands fumbling at him, tearing at his clothes, but he was utterly helpless.

At length, by a sudden and strenuous effort, he scrambled to his feet, and grappled with his assailant.

"Let go, curse you!" a voice snarled in Spanish. "Do you want me to kill you? Let go, I say!"

A violent jerk broke Oliver's hold, and another blow from the weapon sent him reeling to the ground again. He was completely stunned this time.

For a little while his mind was a blank, and when he came to his senses, with an aching head, he was alone, and all was quiet. He could not hear a sound.

He got up, weak and dizzy, and leaned against a tree. He was still somewhat dazed, and as he was wondering why he had been attacked, and by whom, a sickening fear flashed upon him.

He thrust his hands into his pockets, and withdrew them empty. He had been robbed. The envelope containing his month's wages, and a wallet in which he had hoarded his savings, had been stolen.

His pistol was gone also. He had been left with only his blanket, and his pipe and tobacco-pouch. It was a heavy, disastrous loss—between sixty and seventy pounds, reckoning pesos in English money.

Oliver had no doubt the thief was one of the gauchos, who had warily followed him from the estancia.

"It must have been Garcia, the Mexican greaser?" he cried in a fury. "The rest are decent enough fellows! Yes, I am sure it was Garcia. He has hated me since I knocked him down for kicking a young calf. And he knew I had been saving! He saw me put a wad of peso-notes into my wallet one day!"

There was nothing to be done. If the Mexican was the thief he would waste no time in hiding his plunder. Moreover, Oliver had not recognised his assailant, and could not swear to his identity.

It would be useless for him to go back. He must make the best of his loss. Remembering he had had some loose silver, he searched his pockets again, and found half a dozen small coins which had been overlooked by the thief. They were of trifling value, but they would be a help to him—a great help.

He had to reconsider his plans now. He could not travel by rail, and he was afraid to follow the line to Montevideo lest he should be arrested as a vagabond, and clapped into prison.

"I had better strike due south, over the lonely country," he said. "There is a sort of bridle path to guide me. It will be a tremendously long journey on foot, but I shan't starve. There are a few villages on the way, I believe, and what little silver I have will buy enough food to keep me alive until I reach the city."

And what then? Would he be able to find work? He was too ill to worry about that now.

Having slaked his thirst at the stream, he stretched himself on the grass, spread his blanket on top of him, and presently dropped off to sleep.

CHAPTER 2.

A WEEK later, after night had fallen, Oliver Douglas came over the brow of a hill, and saw below him, bathed in the glow of the moon, a village of small adobo houses.

They were scattered about, and in the midst of them was a fairly large building, white-walled, and with a square tower. It was a church, commonly called a mission chapel in Uruguay.

Day by day Oliver had been on tramp, and he had covered more than half the distance to Montevideo, in good weather and bad.

He was footsore, tired and hungry, and disreputable of appearance, for his clothing had been torn by thorny bushes, and soiled with mud; his boots were in a wretched state, hard rains had battered and bleached his sombrero, and there was a growth of stubbly beard on his cheeks.

He wanted a meal badly, but the prospect of getting one was not encouraging.

As not a glimmer of light showed anywhere, he was sure the people of the village were all in bed and asleep, and he dared not waken any of them.

He had tried that before, and had been put to flight with a vicious dog snapping at his heels.

"I'll have to stay hungry until morning," he said to himself. "I must find a place of shelter, though. I can't walk any farther to-night."

He wearily descended the hill, went by a number of the dark and silent dwellings, and stopped at the mission chapel.

The door was not fastened. He entered quietly, with a feeling of reverence, and passed between rows of rude benches, guided by the moonlight which streamed in at the windows, to the rear of the sacred building. There was an altar here, and beyond it, at the base of the tower, was a small door.

Oliver meant to sleep on one of the benches, but as he was about to unstrap his blanket from his back he heard footsteps; and at once, on a prudent impulse, he glided behind a massive, upright beam which supported the roof.

At the same moment the front door was pushed open, and two dusky figures appeared. They came straight forward, and paused within a few paces of Oliver, who could see them clearly.

They were two well-dressed men, and to the youth's surprise they looked like Englishmen. One was tall and lean, with shrewd features, and a black moustache, and the other, a plump little man of less than average height, was clean-shaven, and had a jovial, good-humoured countenance.

"Well, Hewitt, here we are at last," said the latter in English, in a squaky voice. "Up in the wilds of Uruguay. It's the longest trip the chief has ever sent us on—eh?"

"And the most risky," the other replied, in a surly tone. "I wish I was back in London, Carey. This is a devil of a country!"

"Mustn't grumble, my boy!" chuckled the little man. "Mustn't grumble! It's worth the risk. Think of the pay we get!"

"And think what the chief gets," muttered the tall man. "He takes the larger share."

"Oh, no, he doesn't. You don't believe that, and neither do I. As I've often told you, Hewitt, there is some big pot behind the chief—some person in a high position in Society who drags family skeletons from their closets, and rattles their bones, and chooses the pigeons to be plucked, and pulls the strings, and pockets most of the spoils."

"You are right about that, no doubt."

"I am sure I am. The chief couldn't nose out the dark secrets of Mayfair and Belgravia, though he is a bit of a swell himself. As for the game we are working on now, I would like to know how much Mr. Julian Sherbroke will have to fork over."

"It won't be less than a hundred thousand pounds, I'll bet. Perhaps more, Carey."

"A hundred thousand! My giddy aunt! And we'll be lucky if we get five hundred each, over and above our expenses! Still, that's not to be sneezed at, Hewitt. We can't complain."

Mr. Julian Sherbroke! Oliver was breathing hard, and his brain was reeling. It was all he could do to keep quiet. Had his ears deceived him? No, it was impossible.

These two Englishmen, thousands of miles from home, had mentioned his fathers name in connection with the business which had brought them to this lonely Uruguayan village. Julian Sherbroke would have to pay one hundred thousand pounds, one of them had said. And they had talked of their chief, of Mayfair and Belgravia, of somebody in Society, of family skeletons.

"Good heavens! what can it mean?" the bewildered youth reflected. "What on earth can it mean? My father has never been in South America in all his life. Not as far as I know. Yet there can't be two Mr. Julian Sherbrokes in London."

The first shock over, he pulled himself together, and remembered that he was in an awkward, if not dangerous, position.

His curiosity had been roused to the keenest pitch. He wanted to learn more—he must—but he would have to be very careful, else he would be discovered; and in that event he would have to beat a rapid retreat, or put up a fight.

There had been no further conversation between the men. The little man was filling a pipe, and when he had lit it the two of them stepped to the small door at the base of the tower.

Then tall man tried the knob, and, finding the door locked, he promptly and deftly wrenched it open with an implement like a jemmy.

"On with the glim, Carey!" he bade.

A shaft of golden flame stabbed the darkness. It was a flashlight in the hand of the little man, and as it played to and fro it revealed to Oliver, from his hiding-place by the beam, a tiny room with damp-stained walls, a slanting shelf at the rear of it, and chained to the shelf a musty volume bound in leather.

He had no doubt what the volume was. It must be the chapel register—the chronicle of births and deaths, and marriages.

The tall man moved to the shelf, and while his companion held the light steady for him, he opened the book, and turned the pages over one by one, slowly scanning each.

"Ah, here we are!" he murmured at length.

"Have you found one of them?" the little man asked eagerly.

"I've found the two, Carey. They are both on the same page."

"How can that be, Hewitt?

"Because there is only an interval of a year between the two entries. One is at the top, and the other is near the bottom."

"Well, hurry up. This is a spooky sort of a place, and it is getting on my nerves. That shadow on the wall looks like a skeleton."

Oliver's bewilderment had increased. He knew with what object the intruders had entered the church.

Taking a knife from his pocket, the tall man Hewitt carefully cut the page from the volume, folded it, slipped in into his breast-pocket, and shut the book. Then he came out of the room with his companion, and closed the door.

"The next thing is to search the padre's house, Carey," he said.

"I don't like the idea," the little man replied uneasily. "Isn't the leaf from the register enough?"

"It's not enough for the chief. You know what his orders were. He believes the padre has some letters and papers in his possession, and we've got to get them. I don't like the idea myself, though, Carey. The village people are half-breeds, descendents of the savage and bloodthirsty Charrua Indians, and they would hack us to bits if we were to be caught."

"Oh, heavens!" groaned the little man, rolling his eyes. "Cheerful, isn't it? What a Job's comforter you are, Hewitt, to be sure! But if we've got to go through with it——"

"What's that?" the other interrrupted.

A loose board had just cleaked under Oliver's foot. The flashlight played around him, showing his protruding elbows; and at once, knowing he had been discovered, he stepped from behind the beam, and raised his arms.

"It's all right," he said. "You needn't be afraid of me."

The tall man pointed an automatic-pistol at the youth's chest, and the little man Carey kept the light on him.

For a few seconds they stared at him in silence, scrutinising him from head to foot; and in that brief interval Oliver thought quickly, and decided what part he would play.

For his own safety, for his very life—and for another reason as well—he must contrive to deceive these men. Moreover, he must not let them know or suspect he was an Englishman.

"I guess you needn't be afraid of me," he repeated. "You might as well put that gun down."

"Who are you?" demanded the tall man. "I'm a tramp," Oliver replied, with a silly grin. "That's all. Just an ornery tramp."

"English or American?"

"I'm an American. Been starving out here three years."

"Where did you come from? What are you doing here?"

"I've come from up-country, and I crept in here to sleep, and to hide. I've been chased."

"Chased?" said the tall man. "Who's been after you?"

"A band of Redskins on horseback," Oliver answered. "Hundreds of them. They had tomahawks, and bows and arrows.

They wanted my scalp, but I scared them away. I whistled like an army bugle, and you should have seen them run! It was funny!"

The youth laughed—a cackling, idiotic laugh. His captors glanced at each other and nodded.

"He's a looney?" said the little man, in a low tone.

"A bit cracked, Carey," the other assented.

Oliver laughed again.

"That's what they all say," he muttered. "And they're all liars. I'm no more cracked than they are, I reckon, if I do see ghosts and things. Give me some grub, will you?" he continued. "Or give me some money."

"We'll give you nothing," said the tall man. "You'll have to shift for yourself."

"Then tell me where I am? What's the name of the place?"

"You are at the village of San Jacinto. Where are you going from here?"

"I don't know. Anywhere. I'm only a tramp."

"Have you been watching us? Did you see what we did?"

"I saw you go into that little room, and read a book. But its no business of mine."

"No, it jolly well isn't! if I thought——"

The tall man broke off. He drew his companion aside, and for several minutes they carried on a whispered conversation that was inaudible to the youth.

Then the little man turned to him.

"Do you want a job, Mr. Vagabond?" be asked.

Oliver shook his head.

"No, I dont," he sullenly answered. "Work ain't in my line. It never was."

"There won't be any work about it."

"You're trying to fool me, ain't you?"

"No, I'm not. I'll talk straight to you. Gavin Carey is my name, and my pal is Mack Hewitt. The old padre of this village, Father Jose Amaral, has some papers which don't belong to him, and we have instructions to get them. We are going to his house now to search, and we want you to come with us."

"What for? What am I to do?"

"Watch and listen. That's all. If you'll do that we''ll take you down to Montevideo with us, and give you enough money to put you on your feet. We have a couple of horses tethered yonder, out on the pampa, and you can ride behind me. How does it strike you—eh?"

Oliver was elated. It was with difficulty he kept a stolid, stupid countenance. The true motive of the proposition was quite obvious to him.

Though he had deceived these men, led them to believe he was a looney, they weren't taking any chances. They did not dare kill him, for one thing; and on the other hand, they were afraid to leave him at San Jacinto because of what he had seen and heard. That was why they had suggested he should help them, and go with them to Montevideo.

All this swiftly occurred to the youth, and as quickly he formed a desperate resolve. For the sake of his father, whom he judged to be threatened with blackmail, he must get from the men the leaf torn from the church register, and what papers they might steal from Father Amaral.

And he would have an opportunity of doing so if he accepted their proposal.

"Well, how does it strike you?" the little man repeated, after a short pause. "Are you standing in with us?"

"Sure thing," Oliver replied, in an indifferent tone.
"And you'll go with us to Montevideo?"
"Sure thing. I don't care where I go."
"Come along, then. We're in a hurry to finish the business.

CHAPTER 3.

HAVING left the mission chapel, and gone with stealthy tread along the village street for a couple of hundred yards, Oliver and the two men stopped by an adobe dwelling which was larger than the rest; and was like the others, in darkness.

The door was not secured, for Father Amaral had no need to be afraid of thieves. Mack Hewitt pushed it softly open, and his companions followed him into a room that was dimly lit by the glow of the moon.

Gavin Carey played his fashlight, and the little group saw that they were in the living-room of the house.

It was furnished with Spartan simplicity. No carpet or rug was spread on the stone floor, and the walls were bare, except for two or three religions pictures.

There was an armchair, a stool, a rude table on which were several books, a pipe, and a tobacco-jar. And in a corner, resting on a bench, was a small, rusty chest of iron.

Gavin Carey pointed to it.

"The papers will be there, I'll bet," he chuckled.

"Shut up, you fool!" bade Mack Hewitt in a whisper. "Do you want to waken the padre?"

All was quiet. Not a sound could be heard. Oliver and the little man stood by the table, the latter holding the flashlight, and Mack Hewitt glided warily over to the iron chest.

It was unlocked. He raised the lid, and when he had rested it against the wall he rummaged amongst the contents of the chest, on which the flare of light shone.

"A lot of trash!" he murmured. "Old clothes, a photograph of a Spanish girl, a rosary, a bronze statue of the Virgin, and——"

He paused.

"Ah! What's this?" he added as he held up a packet of letters, losely tied together with a cord.

He took one of the faded envelopes out, and glanced at the letter it contained, then replaced it, and thrust the packet into his breast-pocket, with the leaf from the church register.

"Are they what the chief told you to look for?" asked Gavin Carey, in a low tone.

Mack Hewitt nodded.

"Yes, I've got them," he replied. "The letter I looked at is signed by Mr. Julian Sherbroke, and the others are in the same handwriting."

"Good business! That's all, isn't it?"

"That's all, Carey. We've finished here."

"Let's get a move on, then. I shan't feel easy until we are in the saddle, Mack."

"Wait a bit! we mustn't leave any traces."

Mack Hewitt rearraged the disordered contents of the chest and lowered the lid.

As he straightened up, a noise was heard, and the next instant a door at the rear of the room was opened, and there appeared the figure of a venerable old man, with white hair and clean-shaven, wrinkl-ed features, carrying a lighted candle.

It was Father Jose Amaral, robed in black, and with a cow! on his head.

"The padre!" gasped Gavin Carey.

Father Amaral lifted one hand in sten rebuke. "Wicked and sacreligious men!" he exclaimed, ut-terly unafraid. "Is this a place for you to come to with evil intent? The abode of a priet of God? Would you rob me, who have devoted my life to——"

"Hold your tongue, padre!" Mack Hewitt bade fiercely as he pulled his automatic from his belt. "We don't want to do you any harm, but if you say another word——

"Don't shoot him, Mack!" Gavin Carey broke in. "I won't have it!"

Oliver's fists were clenched, and he was in a boiling rage. He would knock the two men down if ıe could, he resolved, and capture them, with the help of the priest.

But before he could make a move Father Amaral, overcome by the shock, tottered against the wall, ınd let the candle slip from his limp grasp.

He gave a husky shout, and now, realising that he would be unable to clear himself should he be caught, Oliver hastened from the dwelling with his companions.

"A nice mess we're in!" muttered the little man.

"Shut up, and save your breath!" said Mack Hewitt. "We must run for our lives!"

Father Amaral was still shouting, louder and louder. An alarm had risen, and it was spreading. Excited voices were heard from all directions, and as the fugitives raced along the village street two of the inhabitants rushed from a house in front of them—two big, swarthy men, wearing ponchos.

Carey felled one with his fist, and Hewitt rapped the other on the skull with his automatic.

"Come this way, Carey!" he bade as he swerved to the right. "And keep an eye on the looney! Don't let him give us the slip!"

The three darted amongst the scattered dwellings, running as fast as they could, and they were soon clear of the village and out on the open, grassy pampa.

They were not so frightened now. They believed they could escape. Looking back, they saw behind them in the moonlight, in hot pursuit, at least a score of shouting, yelling people.

But beyond them and to the west, at a lesser distance, they could see the two tethered horses.

"Ha! The steeds await us!" panted Gavin Carey, who was jovial sort of a villain. 'Once in the saddle and——"

As he spoke an old-fashioned gun roared like a blunderbuss. A slug whistled by Oliver's ear, and at once, to the consternation of the fugitives, the horses jerked up their picket-stakes, and went galloping off in terror.

"Oh, heavens, that's done it!" deplored the little man. "We've lost them, Hewitt! They'll gallop for miles before they stop!"

"Curse the luck!" Mack Hewitt cried. "What the blazes are we to do now? We can't put up a fight against that mob of greasy natives! They are too many for us, even with our pistols!"

"We have just one chance," said Oliver, pointing to the south. "There are woods yonder. We must try to reach them."

"Yes, it's the only chance!" Hewitt assented. "Here goes!"

Altering their course, they ran fleetly, with a hue and cry ringing in their ears. They had drawn their pursuers after them, but by hard efforts they gained a little, and they were a couple of hundred yards in the lead when they plunged into the belt of timber.

It was not very wide. They got through it in half a mile, and broke from the cover on to open and rugged ground.

And now, to their relief, they could scarcely hear the clamour. It was growing fainter, they were sure.

"Our luck's in!" Gavin Carey cheerfully declared. "The natives are going back to the village to find out what the alarm was about."

"Yes, it sounds as if they were," replied Mack Hewitt. 'And when they learn that we broke into the padre's house, they will be after as again."

"Do you think so, Mack?"

"It's pretty much of a certainty. We had better push on until we are a long way from San Jacinto."

Oliver agreed with his companions. They stopped for a few moments to recover breath, and then continued their fight.

For an hour they trudged across a rolling plain, which brought them to a stretch of scrub, and when they had traversed that they climbed a steep hill, clothed with grass, and came at the top of it to a sandy hollow that was rimmed around with boulders, and shaded by a clump of pinetrees.

"We'll stop here for a time," said Mack Hewitt. "I'm dead tired, and I'm going to snatch forty winks of sleep. You and the looney can keep watch, Carey, though I don't believe we have anything more to fear from the village people.

"It may be days," he added, "before Father Amaral discovers that the letters have been stolen from his chest, and that a page is missing from the chapel register. And it will be so much the better for us!"

Gavin Carey nodded.

"I'll wake you in an hour," he said, "and get a few winks myself. I'm as tired as you are, Mack."

CHAPTER 4.

MACK HEWITT stretched himself at the bottom of the hollow, with the sand for a pillow, and fell asleep at once. And Oliver and the little man lay down on the brow of the hill, with their backs against the trunk of a big pine-tree.

Gavin Carey was in a cheery mood, and it was difficult for the youth to believe he was such a scoundrel as he undoubtedly was.

He cracked jokes, and talked of one thing and another. He seemed to have taken a liking to Oliver.

"It will be no use trying to find our horses," he said. "We''ll have to walk to the nearest railway station, and travel by train to Montevideo. And we'll leave you there, with a few shillings in your pocket, for we've got to get back to England. Take my advice, my boy, and find work. You don't want to be a tramp all your life, do you?"

He did most of the talking. Oliver played the part of a looney, saying little or nothing, and now and again mumbling incoherently.

But he was thinking—and thinking hard. He knew what he meant to do, after Mack Hewitt had been roused, and Carey had gone to sleep.

He would snatch Hewitt's pistol from his belt, and cover him with it; threaten to shoot him if he uttered a word, and make him promptly hand over the packet of letters—the letters the man had said had been written by Mr. Julian Sherbroke—and the page from the register.

Then he would take to rapid flight, go back to the village of San Jacinto, and give the letters and the leaf to Father Amaral.

"The padre will surely believe my story," he reflected, "and he will be able to explain the mystery about my father, I dare say. I can't imagine what it is. It is the strangest thing I have ever known."

Oliver's opportunity was to come sooner than he had expected, as it happened. Presently, as he was speaking of something, Gavin Carey's voice trailed into a whisper.

His chin sank on his breast, and he began to snore. He was sound asleep.

And now, with a different plan in mind, Oliver crept cautiously into the sandy hollow, and knelt by the prostrate figure of Mack Hewitt.

He could see the letters and the page sticking from the breast-pocket of the man's coat, which was partly open; but as he was reaching them, when his fingers were almost touching them, Hewitt suddenly awoke.

With a startled exclamation he sprang to his feet and struck at the youth, who dodged the blow and scrambled from the hollow. His attempt had failed, and his life was in peril now.

Stop him, Carey!" Mack Hewitt shouted. "Stop him!"

Gavin Carey jumped up at once, but by then Oliver had darted past him, and leapt over the crest of the hill. He went tearing down at reckless speed at the risk of his neck; and as he ran the two men yelled at him, and Hewitt opened fire with his automatic.

Two shots missed, and with the third report Oliver felt a burning pain. The bullet had grazed one side of his head. He floundered on for several yards, staggered blindly, pitched on to a mossy shelf or rock, and lay there limp and motionless.

He was only slightly stunned, though he was unable to rise. He had his senses, and could hear the voices of the two men who were standing above him.

"You've killed the poor fellow!" cried Gavin Carey.

"It serves him right!" Mack Hewitt declared, with an oath. "He's no looney. He's as shrewd as they make them. He's been playing a game with us from the first, else he wouldn't have tried to steal the letters and the leaf. But perhaps he isn't dead. He may be only shamming."

"He isn't, Mack! I'm sure you killed him!"

"I'd better go down and see to make certain."

"No, no, don't! We had better clear out of this as quickly as we can! Come along!"

"Very well, Carey. If any of the village people are searching for us they would have heard the shots I fired."

The talk ceased, and retreating foot steps were heard. Mack Hewitt and Gavin Carey were gone, crossing the top of the hill, and both strongly believed that the young tramp who had tricked them was dead.

The steps faded to silence, and with a thankful heart Oliver sat up. He put his hand to the spot the blood was trickling from, and found the bullet had merely broken the skin.'

"I'll be getting on now," he thought.

He felt better now, and was able to rise. But his limbs were shaky, and at the first step a fit of giddiness seized him, and he swayed on the edge of the rocky shelf and topled headlong over.

He could not check himself. Down the hill he went, now rolling and now sliding, clutching at tufts of grass, and at the bottom of the slope he landed lightly in a soft copse of bushes.

He was not hurt. He lay there for a little while, gasping for breath; and when at length he scrambled out from the thicket and got to his feet, he heard rustling, crackling sounds in the scrub beyond him, and saw a number of dusky figures rapidly approaching.

They were already close to him, and before he could take to his heels he was surrounded by a score of the village people.

He was in fear of these swarthy, fiercevisaged natives who were descended from Uruguay. They meant to kill him, he was sure; but they did him no harm, though they handled him roughly, and reviled him in the Spanish tongue.

"You come with us," said one of them, a big man whose poncho was richly embroidered. "You will be punished for trying to rob the holy padre whom we love."

In the wilds of Uruguay the punishment for thieves was summary death, as Oliver knew, and he realised that he was in a desperate plight.

As he had failed to recover the stolen letters he could not prove his innocence. Father Amaral would disbelieve his story, and presume him to be as guilty as were the men he had been with.

He offered no resistance, and said nothing. He would wait, he reflected, and appeal to the padre, who might be inclined to mercy.

In the grasp of the big man, and with the rest of the party trailing behind, Oliver was marched back through the scrub and the woods, and across the pampa to the middle of the village of San Jacinto.

All of the people flocked from their dwellings, and there was a hostile demonstration against the prisoner. A yelling mob pressed about him on all sides. He was cursed and threatened, menaced with knives, and he had no chance of speaking to the padre.

Father Amaral was visible in the background waving his arms and calling loudly, but his voice was drowned by the shrill and angry clamour, and the crush was so great he could not get near the youth, hard though he tried.

Oliver shouted to him, appealed to him, until the big man whom the others called Chica, dealt him a blow and bade him hold his tongue.

"You are a dog of a thief," he cried striking him again, "and you must die! Such is our law! At sunrise to-morrow you will be shot!"

It was a staggering sentence. To be shot at sunrise without the formality of a trial! Would the padre allow that? Could he, would he, prevent it?

No, it wasn't likely. The man Chica, it seemed, was the ruler of San Jacinto. In vain Oliver protested, assested his innocence, demanded to see Father Amaral.

His wrists and ankles were bound with thongs of rawhide, and he was picked up and carried to a sort of a shed and thrust into it. Chica pulled the door shut, remarking that the English dog was securely tied and needed no guard.

The clamour ceased, and the crowd gradually dispersed. Soon all was quiet. The people had returned to their beds.

"There's no hope," Oliver told himself. "The padre can't save me. I'll be shot in the morning.

He thought of home, of his father, of Muriel. Bitter anguish swept over him, and was succeeded by hot wrath. What right had these half-civilised brutes to shoot him? He would escape! He must!

He struggled madly at intervals, making frenzied and futile attempts to loosen the thongs which bound him, until he was completely exhausted.

And he was about to drop off to sleep in sickening despair when the door opened and a black-robbed figure appeared. It was Father Amaral.

"Hush!" he bade in a whisper. "Not a word! Do not speak now! I have come to set you free. You are only a boy, and too young to die in your sins. Moreover, I think you have been led astray by evil companions older than yourself."

The padre was kneeling on the floor. He had no knife, but with his slim, white fingers he tugged and twisted at the youth's fetters, untying the knots.

"It will be better so," he murmured. "Though my people are devoted to me, they will not allow me to interfere with their laws, and they would be very angry if they were to know I had released you. I would have them think it was by your own efforts."

It was done at last. The thongs were all untied. Oliver rose on his cramped limbs, and Father Amaral pressed a parcel in his hand.

"Food for you," he said. "And here also is a little money—as much as I can spare. Get as far on your journey as you can before you stop to rest. And for my sake try to lead a better life in future."

"May Heaven bless you, holy father!" Oliver replied, his voice tremulous with emotion. "I will never forget what you have done for me. I will remember you with deepest gratitude as long as I live. But——"

"The night is drawing to an end," the padre interrupted. "Time is precious to you, and you must not waste it in talk."

"But I must speak! I beg you to listen! You wrong me! I am not as evil as you believe! Not willingly was I with those wicked men!"

"It may be so. I trust it is."

"It is the truth, I swear! I had crept into the church to sleep when the men entered. I saw them go into the small room under the tower, and saw one of them cut a leaf out of the register. Afterwards they discovered me, and had I not pretended that——"

"A leaf cut from the register!" repeated Father Amaral, in a tone of bewilderment. "Can it be possible?"

"You will find it missing," Oliver continued. "That the men took, and more than that. They have stolen a packet of letters from the iron chest in your house."

"What? The letters written by the English senor? This is indeed a most strange thing! I can hardly believe they have been stolen! I will look when I get home!"

"You will not find them in the chest. They are gone, And now, before we part, tell me what it all means. It is a matter which concerns me. What could be the motive for stealing the letters, and the page from the register?"

"Truly, my son, I know not any more than you do."

"You must know, holy father. The men are English, as I am also, and they mentioned a name which——"

"Say no more," bade the padre. "Your life is in peril, and you must be on your way. At any moment we may be discovered. As for the strange things you have told me of, I will consider them. Did I know what they meant I should tell you. Go now, my son! And my blessing go with you, whether you be good or evil!'

Father Amaral spoke the truth. Oliver could not doubt his word. Not from him, it appeared, could he learn the explanation of the mystery.

He was very anxious to question him further, but he dared not delay. He clasped the noble-hearted padre's hand, fervently thanked him again, and slipped from the shed, the gift of silver in his pocket, and the parcel of food under his arm.

When he had walked a few yards, he glanced over his shoulder and saw Father Amaral gliding in the opposite direction.

"I hope I'll be able to repay that good man some day," he said to himself.

There was nobody about, and the moon had gone down. Treading noiselessly, and skulking in the shadow of the dwellings Oliver stole through the slumbering village and when he was clear of it, and out on the open pampa, he put his mind seriously to the position he was in.

In the space of a few hours his whole outlook on life had changed. He had a definite object in view. He must—no, he was going to—checkmate Mack Hewitt and Gavin Carey, and wrest from them the spoils which were to be used as an implement of blackmail.

But how? And when and where? He must think it out carefully. And he did.

There was a railway some miles to the west, and the men would doubtless hasten to the nearest station and go by train to Montevideo, from which port it was their intention to sail for England.

"Those crooked scoundrels believe I am dead," Oliver reflected, "and it will be best to let them think so for a while. I haven't the money to travel as a passenger, but I'll bet I can get down to the city on a goods train, hidden in a truck. It would be no use trying to get the better of the men in Uruguay, though, by legal means or otherwise. So there is only one thing for it. I'll have to sail on the same boat with them as a stowaway. I'll contrive that somehow. I've got to."

It was all planned in Oliver's shrewd head, the daring and reckless scheme. He had a dogged nature. Should there be difficulties, he would conquer them.

Cost him what it might, at the risk of arrest and imprisonment, he was going to return to England with Hewitt and Carey, keep track of them after they landed, learn what the secret was, foil the villains and their chief, and save his father from being blackmailed.

And perhaps he would win back all he had lost by his folly, and marry the girl he loved.

Thus thinking, cheer and hope in his heart again, he trudged across the lonely pampa, weary and footsore, yet resolved to put many miles between himself and San Jacinto by sunrise.

He would be safe then, if his escape had not meanwhile been discovered. And there was little or no likelihood of that, he was confident.

His life had been saved by Father Amaral, and it occurred to him, as he went on, that the loss of his employment at the San Pablo estancia, and the theft of his money, had been blessings in disguise.

But for those misfortunes he would be new at Montevideo, with no knowledge of the sinister secret, and with no prospects for the future.

CHAPTER 5.

WHEN a goods train from the far north pulled up in the railway-yard on the outskirts of Montevideo at early dawn one morning, a tarpaulin which covered a truck filled with grain sacks was cautiously lifted, and from beneath it crawled Oliver Douglas.

Having descended from the truck and stretched his stiff and aching limbs, he threw a glance around him, peering into the murky gloom in all directions.

He had his chance. Sure that he would not be observed by any of the train-hands, he darted across half a dozen lines of metals, climbed a grassy embankment, scaled a fence, and bore to the left by a deserted road.

"Well, here I am at last, thank goodness!" he said to himself. "If only those rascals haven't sailed yet! It isn't likely they have."

Oliver was covered with dust and grime, and his stomach craved for food. For three days he had been travelling south, hidden in the truck, and for twenty-four hours he had not eaten a bite.

He still had the few silver coins the kindly padre had given him, however, so he wouldn't starve. But he had no chance of getting food now, at this early hour.

He tightened his belt to stifle the pangs of hunger, and struck into a brisk pace along the road, which presently brought him to the suburbs of the big Spanish capital of Uruguay.

He had a weary tramp before him. He went by miles of small and modest dwellings inhabited by the working classes, by miles of broad avenues lined with stately residences in which immensely rich people lived in Parisian luxury and refinement, and so, finally, to the business quarter of the city, where were restaurants, theatres and cafés, splendid shops, and buildings worthy of any European capital.

At a small place in a side street Oliver brushed the dust from his shabbly clothes, washed his face and hands, and ate a hearty meal.

Then he set off again, refreshed and strengthened, and tramped, move weary miles; until, about the middle of the afternoon, he came to the vast docks of Montevideo, which stretched along the River Plate as far as the eye could reach, and were crowded with shipping from every part of the world.

With an object in mind, Oliver followed the docks for some, distance, scanning the various vessels, watching them being loaded and unloaded; and at length, with a slight start, he paused behind a tier of casks and looked over the top of them.

"My word, if it isn't the Trinidad!" he muttered. "The boat I came out to Uruguay on! I wonder if Neil Rankin is still the Purser?"

Yes, there she was, the large ocean liner Trinidad, belonging to the Bannerman Line of Liverpool. For a little while Oliver stood there, gazing wistfully at the vessel; and then he gave another quick start, and ducked his head.

A taxi had just stopped beyond him, and two well-dressed men were getting out of it. They were Mack Hewitt and Gavin Carey, and each carried a kitbag.

The chauffeur having been paid, the men walked straight to the Bannerman Line boat, showed their papers to an officer at the foot of the gangway, and mounted to the deck.

Oliver stared after them.

"They must have booked their passages," he reflected. "They could have got to Montevideo a couple of days, ago by a passenger train. They are going home on the Trinidad, and so am I. I've simply got to. That's all there is about it. But how the deuce can I?"

It was a hard problem, and Oliver sat down on an upturned cask to consider it. Though it would be no difficult matter for him to slip on board the vessel and find a hiding-place, he would amost certainly be discovered during the voyages, and that would spoil his plans.

What was he to do? He gazed into vacancy, his chin resting on his hands; and as he was cudgelling his brains, trying to solve the problem, footsteps approached, and a man stopped in front of him—a lean, rakish little man in a blue uniform and a peaked cap, with a small, scrubby moustache, and a pointed tuft of beard.

"By jingo, it's Dougles, isn't it?" he said with a dry chuckle.

"It isn't anybody else," Oliver replied. "How are you, Rankin?"

"As fit as a fiddle. How's yourself?"

"Is is any use asking that?"

"No, it isn't. So you haven't made good, laddie, eh?"

Oliver shook his head gloomily, and the two were silent for a few seconds. They had been intimate friends on the voyage from England on the Trinidad three years ago.

Neil Rankin, the Scotch purser of the boat, had taken a liking to the youth. He had known him only in the name of Douglas, and had been led to belive that he was going to Uruguay to make a fresh start in life after a quarrel with his father because of his wild and extravagant habits.

"What have you been doing all the time?" he resumed, taking close stock of the shabby young fellow. "Not loafing?"

"No, I've been at an estancia up-country, punching cattle with a lot of greasy gauchos," said Oliver. "I didn't mind the work. I made good right enough. But I got sick of it and cleared out. I hit the trail for the nearest railway-station, and I hadn't gone far when I was attacked and robbed by some scoundrel. He stole my month's wages and all my savings."

"Hard luck that was, laddie."

"It was rough, Rankin. I hadn't any money, so there was nothing for it but to steal a ride in a truck on a goods train. That's how I got down to Montevideo. It was only this morning I——"

Oliver broke off abruptly. Somethin had occurred to him—a hopeful, cheering inspiration. He hesitated for a moment, thinking quickly.

"When do you sail, Rankin?" he inquired.

"At ten o'clock to-night, with the tide," said the purser.

"Well, I want you to do me a favour—a great favour," Oliver continued. "I'll talk straight to you. I've been a fool, and I'm sorry for it. It was my fault I quarrelled with my governor. I'm going home to tell him what an ass I was, and ask him to forgive me. But I'm dead broke except for some small silver. I can't stay in Montevideo without money, and I can't cable to have some sent to me. So will you—will you hide me on board the Trinidad?"

Neil Rankin shrugged his shoulders.

"You're not asking much, are you?" he said, in a sarcastic tone. "A fine lot of trouble you'd get me in!"

"There wouldn't be any risk," Oliver pleaded. "You could see to that. Don't refuse, there's a good fellow! I can't stay out here another day. You wouldn't leave me in Montevideo to starve, would you? It's a cruel city. I've got to get home as quickly as I can, and the Trinidad is my only chance."

"I'm sorry, laddie, but it can't be done. You know how strict the law is. If you were discovered you would be shipped back to Uruguay, not having any papers, and I would be in a devil of a mess."

"It has often been done before. Listen, Rankin! My name isn't Douglas. I'll tell you who my father is. You may have heard of him. He is Mr. Julian Sherbroke."

The purser whistled through his teeth.

"Mr. Julian Sherbroke!" he repeated, looking at the youth incredulously. "The millionaire! And you say you're his son!"

"So I am," Oliver declared, "It's the truth, Rankin. I swear it is, on my honour."

Neil Rankin was wavering now. He was a good-tempered generous fellow, and he was sorry for the unfortunate youth.

"I'll do it!" he said gruffy.

"You will?" Oliver exclaimed eagerly. "It's awfully decent of you. I don't know how to thank you. How are you going to arrange it?"

"I'll have to hide you somewhere in the hold," the purser answered. "I'll see that you get enough to eat and drink during the voyage, and when we're in the Mersey I'll contrive to smuggle you ashore."

"And will you lend me enough money to travel third-class from Liverpool to London? I'll pay it back. I promise."

"Yes, I don't mind."

"But how am I to get on board here Rankin, without being seen or questioned?"

"I'm not sure. You may have to slip into the water, and climb a rope to the ship's bow. We'll talk of that later. You meet me at this spot, laddie, at exactly nine o'clock. I'll have found a hiding-place for you by then. And now I must be off. So long!"

Neil Rankin nodded and was gone, bending his steps towards the boat. And Oliver, who was hungry again, crossed the docks to look for a cheap restaurant.

He thanked his lucky stars he had fallen in with his old friend the purser. In something like three weeks he would be in England.

★ ★ ★ ★ ★ ★

Between ten and eleven o'clock that night Mack Hewitt and Gavin Carey, attired in evening-dress, sat in the saloon of the big vessel, eating and drinking and talking of their adventurous trip up-country.

And far beneath them in the hold, in a cramped nook amongst the passengers' luggage, Oliver Douglas was reclining cosily, with a blanket for a pillow, listening to the faint sound of rippling water.

The voyage had begun. The liner Trinidad was gliding down the River Plate, homeward bound.

The End of the Prologue.

THE STORY.

CHAPTER 1.

THERE was a look of deep concern on Secton Blake's face when he stepped from a taxi at eleven o'clock one morning in front of a pretentious dwelling in Chesham Place, Belgravia.

His arrival was expected. The butler, an elderly man with a sad countenance, let the famous detective into the house, spoke a few words to him, took him upstairs, and showed him into a bed-room on the first floor.

Inspector Widgeon, of Scotland Yard, was standing by the window.

"Good-morning, Blake," he said, in a low tone. "Mrs. Milvern told me on the 'phone she was going to ring you up as she wished us both to be here."

"And she told me," Blake replied, "that she had telephoned to the Yard, and you were coming on. Rather an unusual proceeding under the circumstances, don't you think?"

"Yes, I did think so," the inspector assented. "I had no explanation from her. She merely informed me of what had happened."

"As she did me, Widgeon. Have you seen the lady yet?"

"Not yet. I am waiting for her."

"A doctor has been sent for, I suppose?" Blake continued.

"He has been and gone," said Inspector Widgeon. "He could not do anything. He is returning later, I believe."

They stood in silence, gazing at a loungechair that was close to the fireplace. Huddled limply in the chair, fully dressed, was the body of a clean-shaven man who was about forty years of age. One of his hands rested by his side, and in the other, which hung from the arm of the chair, and automatic pistol was tightly clenched.

There was a bullet hole in the front of his jacket, over the left breast, and the edges of it were scorched and stained with blood.

The body was that of Mr. Eric Milvern, a younger son of Lord Branksome.

"He was an intimate friendof yours, I think," said the inspector.

"Fairly intimate," Blake answered. "I liked him very much."

"Have you any idea why he should have shot himself?"

"None in the least, Widgeon. He was in prosperous circumstances—he inherited a considerable sum of money from an aunt—and he was happily married. No, I can't imagine why——"

"She is coming!" the inspector interrupted.

The rustle of skirts was heard. The door was opened, and Mrs. Milvern entered the room and quietly shut the door behind her.

She was a fair woman of thirty, tall and graceful, and a recognised society beauty. Her white, tear-stained cheeks told how terribly she had suffered from the shock. Apparently she hadrecoveredfrom it.

She was calm now, strangely, amazingly calm; but there was a curious glitter in her dark blue eyes—a look which was more than grief. She came slowly forward, her gaze averted from the motionless object in the lounge-chair.

"I will tell you at once why I sent for you, Mr. Blake," she said, in a dull tone. "You were my husband's friend, and I want you and Inspector Widgeon to avenge his murder."

"Murder?" Blake repeated, in surprise. "Surely not!"

"Not legal murder," said Mrs. Milvern, very softly and coldly. "No, it can't be called that. But none the less Eric was cruelly, wickedly murdered, and I wil never rest until justice has been done."

"What do you mean? Am I to understand that some trouble, some worry, preyed on his mind and drove him to——"

"Yes, Mr. Blake, he was hounded to death—hounded and harried and persecuted, until in despair he took his own life. I know now that was the reason. I did not know before. I did not guess. Until a month ago my husband was his normal self, always happy and cheeful, and in bright spirits. Then I noticed a change in him—a sudden change. He was depressed. He never laughed or smiled. He took no pleasure in anything. He lost his appetite, and moped about the house. I thought he was ill, but he assured me he was not.

"Day by day, week by week, he grew more depressed. I knew he must be greatly worried over something, but I could not persuade him to tell me what it was. He would not even admit he was worried. He said I was talking nonsense."

"I was at the theatre last night with some friends," she resumed, in the same dull, firm tone, "and when I came back my husband had left word that he had gone to bed. This morning he did not come down to breakfast at nine o'clock, our usual hour. I waited half on hour, and then, feeling alarmed, I went up to Eric's room. And here I found him dead, just as he is now, shot through the heart. No one heard the report of the pistol in the night. The shot must have been fired while heavy traffic was passing the house.

"I was distracted with grief. I swooned, and was unconscious for a little while. The servants hurried in, and a doctor was sent for. When I recovered I saw an envelope on the table addressed to me. It was a letter written by my husband. Here is is, Mr. Blake. It will clearly explain to you the reason for——"

Pausing again, Mrs. Milvern took the letter from her bosom, and gave it to the detective. It was a very short one, and it ran as follows:

> "My Darling Angela,—I am nearly mad. I have deceived you. I wanted to tell you the truth, but I could not. I have been worried and persecuted until I can endure it no longer. My life is an intolerable burden to me. It is blackmail—that old affair which I believed to be dead and buried for ever.
>
> "I can't pay the money demanded of me, and for your sake I can't face exposure. There is only one thing to be done, and I am doing it. Forgive me, darling, I beg of you, and try to forget me. Good-bye.
>
> "From your broken-hearted husband.
>
> "ERIC."

Blake's face was very stern and harsh when he had read the pitiful letter. It had stirred him deeply. He handed it to the inspector, and spoke to Mrs. Milvern.

"I am reluctant to put any personal questions to you—questions which will hurt," he said, "but it is important that I should. What is the old affair your husband refers to? I think you know."

"Yes, I know," Mrs. Milvern replied. "And I am quite willing to tell you. It happened long ago, years before I was married. My husband was wild in those days and fond of pleasure. He was in Paris, and he went to a night gambling club, and there was a fight there. Several persons were badly hurt, and the police came in. Eric had nothing to do with it. He was perfectly innocent. But he was arrested, and for a little while he was in prison, in false name which he gave to the police. He confessed to me when we became engaged, and I laughed at him, and told him it didn't make any difference to me."

"How many years ago was it?" asked Blake.

"At least fifteen years. It may have been more."

"Well, somebody must have recently learned of the matter, and started blackmailing your husband. As a rising young politician the publication of the fact that he had been in prison would be fatal to his prospects. Have you no suspicious? Can you imagine who the person might be?"

"No, Mr. Blake, I can't. I haven't any idea. I never told anybody of what happened in Paris, and I am sure Eric never did. He was too much ashamed."

"Can't you give me any help at all?" said Blake. "I would like to know how the negotiations were conducted. Has your husband any visitors who were strangers to you?"

"No, only intimate friends of ours," Mrs. Milvern answered. 'Eric has frequently been out, though."

"Perhaps there are letters in his desk which would throw some light on the mystery."

"There are none, Mr. Blake. I searched his desk thoroughly before the inspector came."

"Did you search his pockets also?"

"I had the butler do that. He found no letters or papers. If Eric had any he must have burnt them. I wish I could help you. If only I could! I have lost the best husband any woman ever had. There was never an angry word between us. Oh, how I shall miss him! How can I live without him? I say again he was murdered—cruelly murdered by somebody who ought to be hanged! You know that as well as I do, Mr. Blake. You were one of his best friends, and——"

Mrs. Milvern's voice rose to a higher pitch.

"You must avenge Eric's death!" she cried, her eyes flashing with passion. "You can, and you must! If you don't, I will! Oh, my poor husband!"

She made a move towards the loungechair, but Blake quickly intercepted her, and seized her by the arm.

She struggled with him, and tore herself from his grasp; and then, bursting into a flood of tears, she turned to the door and went out of the room, sobbing bitterly.

Inspector Widgeon shook his head.

"Poor lady!" he remarked. "I don't wonder she is so distressed, and in such a vengeful mood. It is a very ugly business."

"Very ugly indeed," said Blake, whose brows were knit. "And not the first one of the kind. I have just been thinking of several things, and I will recall them to you very briefly. It is less than two years since Sir Bruce Maitland secretly and hurriedly sold his residence in Portman Square, and what other property he had, and utterly disappeared. Why? Nobody knew. He has not been heard of to this day."

"I remember the affair," the inspector observed.

"Some months afterwards,' Blake went on, "the Marquis of Barleven, a wealthy young man in rugged health, engaged to a princess, went over the Brussels, and was there found dead in his bed at an obscure hotel—dead of poison administered by his own hand. Why? No one knew. There was no explanation."

"None at all," Inspector Widgeon assented. "It was a mysterious case."

"And last spring," Blake resumed, "the Hon. Gertrude Haysboro, a beautiful girl of twenty, daughter of Lord Danesmere, and the fiancée of a duke's son, was found drowned in a pond on her father's estate in Norfolk, on the morning after a big dance at the house. The pond was very shallow. The girl's footprints were traced straight to the edge of it, and into the water. It was so obviously a case of suicide that the coroner would not entertain any other theory."

"I remember that also," said the inspector. "Miss Haysboro had not quarrelled with her fiancée, and she was in perfect health. None of her family or friends could suggest any motive for her rush act. it was another mystery."

Blake nodded.

"Three unsolved mysteries," he said. "Sir Bruce Maitland, the Marquis of Barleven, and Gertrude Haysboro were all prominent in London society, and moved in the same exclusive circle; as, indeed, did Eric Milvern. And of those three people not one left any letter, any written statement, to throw light on their different motives.

"As for poor Milvern's letter, it shows why he shot himself. And it strengthens a suspicion I have had in mind for some time—that the three other persons we have been speaking of were victims of blackmail, and of the same blackmailer."

"I quite agree," replied Inspector Widgeon. "And now I will tell you something which will interest you. Months ago, shortly after the suicide of Lord Danesmere's daughter, our chief at Scotland Yard was informed by one of the cleverest of our C.I.D. men that there was strong reason to believe a secret blackmailer was at work in Society."

"At about the same time," he said, "I made an entry in my notebook which was precisely to the same effect. And I am sure we were both right—the Scotland Yard man and myself. Yes, for the last couple of years some ruthless and crafty scoundrel, some person of high position in the most exclusive circles of Society, a person with an amazing and cunning ability for gleaning dark secrets of the past, has been rattling the dry bones of family skeletons in Mayfair and Belgravia, and blackmailing members of his own class."

"I haven't any doubt of it," said the inspector. "The letter we have just read is plain proof. The blackmailer may be a woman, though."

"That is possible, even likely. Yet a woman would hardly have worked the game on her own."

"You haven't made any investigations, I suppose?"

"No, Widgeon, I have not. I have been too busy. But I shall take the matter up now that my friend Milvern, like the Marquis of Barleven and Gertrude Haysboro, has been driven to suicide. We know of four persons who have baffled the blackmailer, three at the cost of their lives, and one by disappearing; but we do not know how many have yielded to the demands, and paid for silence. Eric Milvern refused to pay—the price was probably too heavy for his means—and I am determined to bring to justice the human fiend who hounded him to his death."

"You will have the stiffest kind of a task, Blake."

"I know that. Of all criminals the blackmailer is the most secure—and the most merciless, remorseless, and diabolical. He is well safeguarded, hedged about by a ring of steel which almost invariably defies the law. But I will get my man sooner or later. It is only a question of time. It will be slow work, as I have not the slightest clue to help me. What a pity poor Milvern did not——"

Blake broke off, a glitter in his eyes.

"Come, Widgeon, let us go," he added. "There is nothing more to be learned from Mrs. Milvern."

With a glance at the huddled figure in the lounge-chair, they left the room and went downstairs; and a low, anguished cry—the cry of a woman whose heart was breaking with grief—came to their ears as they passed out from the house of tragedy into the bright, autumn sunshine.

"I believe the world is getting worse instead of better," Blake gloomily remarked, as he hailed a taxi.

Inspector Widgeon shrugged his shoulders.

"You are in a pessimistic mood to-day," he said.

CHAPTER 2.

A CHURCH clock in the neighbourhood was striking the hour of six in the morning when a burly, broadshouldered man, with a face like a boiled lobster, and a ragged moustache that was chewed at the ends, pounded noisily up the stair of a cheap lodging-house at the top of the West India Docks Road, and flung open the door of a big, dingy room that was as cheerless as a barn.

At first sight one might have taken the room for a large mortuary, for ranged along the walls were numerous low, wooden boxes shaped like coffin-cases, and in each box was a motionless, recumbent figure covered with a blanket.

The man put his hand to his mouth.

"Now, then, it's time to be shifting!" he bellowed like the bull of Bashan. "Wake up! Hustle yourself! Get a move on! D'you bear me, you lazy dogs! What d'you expect for a tanner a night? Come now, hurry along!"

The slumbering figures came to life. They stirred, awoke, and sat up—a motley crew of ragged, dirty vagrants of all ages, from boys to venerable greybeards.

They coughed and yawned; stretched their limbs and rubbed their drowsy eyes. Some grumbled loudly, and some protested in whining tones.

"Hustle yourselves!" the burly man yelled at them. "Clear out of this! D'you hear?"

In fear of Black Mike, as he was called, the lodgers got up stiffly to their feet, and adjusted their tattered garments. By twos and threes they shuffled to the door and slunk sullenly from the room, until only one was left behind.

A youth in soiled and shabby clothes and a grimy shirt, with unshaven cheeks and unkempt hair, was still sitting in his box. He was gazing into vacancy, his thoughts confused, his mind wandering.

The burly man approached him, an oath on his lips.

"Where do you think you are?" he cried in a mocking voice. "At the Hotel Ritz? What are you waiting for, my lord? For the valet with your shaving-water, eh? Or your morning cup of tea? Or a half-pint of champagne and a biscuit?"

He clenched his fist.

"Why the blazes don't you get up?" he bawled. "Do you want me to chuck you out of the window?"

Oliver Douglas collected his scattered thoughts, and suddenly remembered where he was. He scowled resentfully at the man, but did not answer him.

Throwing off his filthy blanket, he snatched his greasy cap and rose. And then, dodging a kick from Black Mike, he slipped by him, ran down the stairs and passed out of the dwelling into a grey, chill gloom of the early morning.

"The insolent ruffian!" he muttered. "It's the last he'll see of me! I'll have to find another place to sleep, and I dare say it will be the Embankment, unless I go without food."

It was hardly daylight as yet, and the air was cold and biting. Oliver felt it the more because he was so recently from the warm climate of Uruguay.

When he had inhaled deep breaths through his nose and slapped his chest with his arms, he went by the group of shivering, homeless vagabonds ejected from the lodging-house, who were loitering on the pavement, and turned from the West India Docks Road into the Commercial Road East.

Presently he stopped at acoffee-stall, and while he sipped a cup of steaming coffee, and munched a stale bun, he considered things.

He had a lot to consider, too. All had gone well with him since he had sailed from Montevideo on the liner Trinidad.

On the arrival of the boat at Liverpool, early the previous morning, he had been smuggled ashore by Neil Rankin; and the purser had lent him enough money for a third-class ticket to London.

Having waited and watched on the Princess Landing Stage, Oliver had seen Mack Hewitt and Gavin Carey come down the gangway—had warily shadowed them to Lime Street Station—and had travelled up to Euston with them.

There he had been very apprehensive, fearing he would lose all trace of the men; for they had got into a taxi, and he could not afford one.

He had ventured close to them, however, and by good luck he had distinctly heard the address they had given to the chauffeur—the name of a street and the number of a house.

And Oliver, knowing as he did that the street was in a fashionable part of the West End, in expensive Belgravia, knew also that the house must be a private residence.

Did Hewitt and Carey live there? No, that was not to be credited.

It was almost certainly the residence of the mysterious chief, the person who had sent the men to the Uruguayan village of San Jacinto; and the packet of letters stolen from Father Amaral, and the leaf cut from the chapel register, would remain in that person's possession.

Thus Oliver had logically reasoned. His primary object had been accomplished, and he did not take the trouble to go to the address he had learned.

For economy's sake, and because he had a nervous dread of the West End police, he had tramped from Euston to the East End—he had gone slumming there when a boy—and had drifted to Black Mike's lodginghouse, attracted by a sign which offered beds for sixpence.

And now, after an uncomfortable night, he was up against a stubborn proposition.

He was a disreputable-looking figure, and the price of the coffee and the bun left him with exactly a shilling.

To keep the house in the West End under survellance, watch the movements of the chief, ultimately get the packet of letters and the register page, and give them to his father—such were Oliver's nebulous plans.

But if he was to carry them out he must have money—and plenty of it—to buy respectable clothes, and to live in decent comfort while he was engaged on his task.

How was he to get it, though? He had pondered over the question during the voyage, and had foreseen that there was only one way. He thought of that way now, and hesitated.

There was no alternative. He must appeal for assistance to the Society girl, the daughter of wealthy parents, who had vainly tried to be his guardian angel. He was not too proud to do so, under the circumstances, as it would not be an appeal for charity.

"I will write to Muriel, and have her meet me somewhere," he reflected. "I can trust her, and if I tell her part of my story she will believe me.

Oliver was sure she would. He had always been truthful with her, and she had been like a sister to him, though she had loved him as well.

He meant to write at once, at the nearest post-office, but when he had finished his frugal breakfast he changed his mind..

He would wait until evening, and, meanwhile, he would go to West End, where he might possibly meet the girl.

Moreover, he was keenly desirous of seeing the parts of London which had been so familiar to him in the past.

His dread of the police had faded to a mere shadow of uneasiness. Shabby and unshaven as he was, he felt there would be little or no danger of his being recognised by anybody as the son of Julian Sherbroke.

He went on foot. He could not afford to ride, with only a shilling in his pocket.

At a slow pace, his hands thrust into his pockets he slouched along the Commercial Road, reminded of the country by the loads of hay, and carts filled with vegetables, which passed him.

At Aldgate he entered the City at the hour when thousands of people—the advance army of the day's toilers—were hastening to their employment; porters and office-boys, strutting junior clerks, and pretty girl-typists, who mostly wore biscuit-coloured stockings and brown and yellow plaid-coats.

It seemed to Oliver that the crowds were greater than they had been before. Everything interested him.

He gazed in wonder at the new buildings, at the larger and improved types of motorbuses, at the orange-painted cabs which flamed conspicuously amidst the traffic.

He thought of the vast wealth stored around him, in the safes and strong-rooms of banks and business houses, as he tramped through Cornhill and Cheapside.

At the end of Newgate Street he glanced at the Old Bailey—he had very nearly been tried there—and on the Viaduct he paused to look at Blackfriars Bridge in the distance.

Beyond Holborn Circus, where were mammoth shops, he loitered at the plate-glass windows.

He traversed New Oxford Street and passed Oxford Circus; and as he held on to the west his heart ached now and again, and he smiled bitterly.

He was a ragged vagrant, outside the pale of society, with the shadow of a crime hanging over his head. He was close to his home, but if he were to go there he would be turned away.

At length coming to the Marble Arch, he went into Hyde Park. He walked along the main avenue, to the south, until he got a glimpse of his father's palatial residence in Park Lane; and then with a lump in his throat, he bore to the right and struck across the grass.

He was tired now, and presently he sat down on a bench at a secluded spot. It was the hour of noon, and the air was warmer, though the sun was veiled by a soft, pearl-grey mist.

There was nobody in the vicinity. Over on the Serpentine, wild-fowl squawked and cluttered, and from Rotten Row throbbed the sound of smooth gliding vehicles.

A trumpet pealed at Knightbridge Barracks. Motor-horns blared raucously in Piccadilly.

When Oliver had been sitting there for a little while, thinking of the huge city that stretched for miles and miles on all sides of him, he grew drowsy, and fell asleep.

Roused by approaching steps, he opened his eyes, and gave a quick start. A man was standing in front of him—a man with shrewd, clean-shaven features.

"What are you doing here?" he asked, in a suspicious tone.

Oliver stared, and was tongue-tied for a moment. His heart was thumping, and he could feel his cheeks flush.

He had often seen this man before, in the West End. He knew him to be Charles Fenner, a C.I.D. detective, attached to Vine Street,

"What are you doing here?" the man repeated.

"Nothing," Oliver numbled. "Only having a rest. I'm one of the unemployed."

"I daresay. One of the kind that wouldn't take employment if it was offered. Hyde Place isn't the place to look for work. You had better be moving on."

"All right."

Oliver rose, and shuffed off. Through apparently, he had not been recognised—he had feared he would be—he was still apprehensive. He was afraid his identity was suspected.

He walked slowly for some distance, and when he had got to the eastern end of the Serpetine, he yielded to the impulse to glance back, and perceived that the detective was following him.

And now seized with sudden terror, he lost his head, and did a foolish thing. He took to his heels, and with the man in chase of him—he looked back again—he scrambled through the shrubbery, darted amongst the trees, and emerged on to the footpath that skirted the Row.

A few yards to his left was a blue car, and a pretty, fashionably-dressed girl was in the act of stepping into it.

Oliver had a glimpse of her face, and the next instant, as the car moved, he raced after it, and caught it up.

Leaping to the footboard, he jerked the door open—slammed it shut as he sprang in—and dropped on to a seat opposite to the startled girl.

"Don't be frightened. Muriel!" he panted. "It is I—Denis Sherbroke! Don't you know me?"

Muriel Treverton uttered a low exclamation, and, leaning forward, she gazed closely at the shabby youth.

"Yes, I know you," she said quietly. "I do now. I didn't at first. You have changed."

"And I look like a tramp, Muriel. I'm not fit to be here with you. I'm sorry, but I had to——"

"Why did you jump in, Denis?"

"I was in danger. I was chased by a Vine Street detective—a man who knew me in the old days. I wonder if——"

Pausing, Oliver stood up, and peered through the oval glass at the rear of the car.

"I'm safe," he declared. "I can't see anything of the fellow. He ran after me because. I was so stupid as to run away from him. I was afraid he might recognise me. I am sure he didn't, though."

The car was gliding through the gates at Hyde Park Corner. Muriel Treverton reached for the speaking tube, and gave instructions to the chauffeur, who drove west towards Knightsbridge.

There was short interval of silence. The girl's face was very grave and troubled.

"We are going for a long ride," she said, "so we will have a chance to talk."

"It-it is awfully kind of you," faltered Oliver, who felt his position keenly. "What do you think of me?"

"I think you have made a great mistake," Murriel replied. "You ought to have stayed out in South America. You have broken your promise. Why have you been so foolish as to come back to England, where you are in danger of arrest?"

"I had to come. There was a reason."

"Not a good one, Denis, I am afraid."

"Yes, it was a good one, When you have heard what it is I am sure you won't blame me for——"

Oliver stopped for a moment. "There's one promise I've not broken," he continued. "The one I made to you the night before I sailed, when you said you still had faith in me, and begged me to turn over a new leaf for your sake. And I did, Muriel. I kept my word. I've been honest and sober. I haven't done the least thing one could be ashamed of.

"Soon after I went out to Uruguay, I got work at an estancia a couple of hundred miles up-country, herding and branding cattle with a lot of uncouth gauchos. For three years I've been working hard, and saving money. I made good, and tried to comfort myself with the hope of being allowed to return to England some day—the hope that I could redeem my character, and earn my father's forgiveness, and justify your faith in me.

"And I should still be on the estancia, playing the straight game, if it hand't been for an Englishman who had known me in London turning up there on a visit. I won't tell you his name, though he did a low, caddish thing. I wouldn't have thought he was capable of it. He denounced me to my boss, Hernando Lopez and I was discharged on the spot, and sent adrift. I hit the trail down-country, and I hadn't gone far when I was attached and robbed by one of the gauchos, who had followed me in the dark.

"He stole my money and my pistol, and I had to do the journey on foot instead of travelling by rail to Montevideo, as I had meant to. It was all for the best, as it turned out. For a week I tramped over the pampas, and one night, when I reached the little village of San Jacinto——"

Oliver paused, and hesitated. It has been his intention to confide only partly in Muriel Traverton, but he changed his mind now, and concluded he would give her his full confidence.

Having told her of his adventure in the mission chapel at San Jacinto, and the amazing conversation he had overheard, and the theft of the packet of letters at Father Amaral's house, he related in detail everything which had happened since; from his flight from the village with his companions, to his arrival at Euston from Liverpool, and the address to which the men Hewitt and Carey had been driven.

In the course of the narrative he had made clear what his plans were, and when he had finished, he looked appealingly at the girl.

"Do you believe my story?" he asked.

"Of course I do,' Muriel replied. "I believe every word of it. You were always truthful with me."

"And do you think now I did right in coming home?"

"I certainly do, Denis. You had your chance, and you took it. Yes, the proper thing was for you to come back, and try to save your father from being blackmailed, in spite of the risk of being arrested. It was splendid of you! How brave and courageous you were! What narrow escapes from death! If that noble priest hadn't set you free you would have been——"

The girl's voice choked with emotion, and, clasping Oliver's hand, she drew him over to her side. And for just a moment she threw her arms around him, and pressed her lips to his stubbly cheek.

"Poor boy!" she whispered, as she released him.

"That was sweet of you!" Oliver said, in a husky whisper. "You are the one and only friend I have in the world! I was afraid you had forgotten me!"

"You knew I wouldn't," Muriel answered. "I will always be the same to you. Didn't you mean to write to me?"

"Yes, I was going to, this evening. And I found you instead."

"Well, Denis, we have a lot to talk about. What a bewildering mystery you discovered out in Uruguay! What can those stolen letters, and the leaf cut from the register, have to do with your father?"

"I have no idea. I can't imagine any more than you can. To my knowledge, father was never in Uruguay. I feel sure of one thing, though, Muriel. There is no shameful secret in his past life."

"I don't believe there is. There can't be. Whatever the mystery may be, it isn't disgraceful. But it is a serious matter, if those wicked men expect to make him pay one hundred thousand pounds. What a pity you can't put the police on the track of the men But if you told them, I suppose you would be arrested. You must carry out your plans, Denis. And you must succeed. If you get the letters and the leaf, that will prevent the men from blackmailing your father, and he will gladly forgive you, and will see that you don't get into trouble with the police for coming back from Uruguay."

"Yes, that's the way I look at it. That is why I returned, Muriel. It will be a difficult task, and a dangerous one, perhaps, but it will be worth the risk. If I succeed it will mean everthing to me, I think—all I have lost through my mad follies."

"Yes, Denis, all you have lost. I am thinking of that, too."

There were tiny wrinkles on Murie! Treverton's brow, beneath the drooping ringlets of chestnut brown hair.

Her light brown eyes were bent in pity—and more than pity—on the shabby figure of the youth to whom she had been faithful and loyal for years, refusing to believe, even in the darkest hour, that he was beyond redemption.

"I am going to talk to you bluntly," she went on. "You are obsolutely destitute, and I must help you, else you won't be able to do anything at all. Don't let foolish pride stand in your way."

Oliver winced. The words hurt. Yet the offer had spared him the humiliation of asking for assistance.

"I am not too proud to accept help from you," he meekly replied.

"It wouldn't make a bit of difference if you were," said the girl. "You are badly in need of money, and you must have some at once."

"You may lend me some, Muriel. I will repay every penny of it some day."

"It will be a loan, of course."

Opening her vanity-bag, Muriel took out a gold chain-purse, and look from the purse a bunch of crumpled banknotes.

"There are thirty pounds here," she said, slipping the notes into Oliver's hand. "That will be enough for the present. Get shaved, and have your hair cut, and buy a complete outfit of clothes. Find decent lodgings somewhere—I should try Bloomsbury—and come to my house at nine o'clock to-night, for supper."

Oliver's eyes were dim.

"You are an angel of mercy, dear!" he murmured. "Heaven bless you! But I daren't come to your house, much as I should like to. It would not be safe."

"It will be perfectly safe," said Muriel. "Father and mother have gone to the South of France for a month. There are only Aunt Mary and I at home, and my aunt is an invalid, and doesn't leave her room. As for the servants, they are all fairly new, including the chauffeur. Not one of them was with us when you used to call in the old days, so you won't have anything to fear. We will have another long talk, Denis, about your plans. I will give you a bearer cheque for a couple of hundred pounds, to get on with, and perhaps I shall be able to do more than that for you."

"You can't help me to baffle the blackmailers, Muriel."

"I know I can't. I was thinking of something else. I won't tell you now what it was."

During the conversation a number of miles had been covered. The car had crossed part of Putney Heath, and was running along the Portsmouth road.

The chauffeur turned it round at the bidding of his young mistress, and while he drove back to town, the girl, wishing to divert Oliver's mind from sad thoughts, induced him to talk of his life on the estancia in Uruguay, and listened to him with interest.

They were in the Brompton Road, near Sloane Street, when they were held up in a block of traffic. And now Oliver rose.

"I will leave you here,' he said. "And you must see that your chauffeur does not talk of to-night's affair."

"Do not worry about that," Muriel replied. "He is a good man and will act discreetly. Good-bye!

Nine o'clock tonight, remember. I will expect you."

Oliver nodded. He opened the door and stepped out. Closing the door behind him, he dodged between a lorry and a cab and gained the pavement.

He walked over to the north side of Knightsbridge, and a few moments later he was rising towards Piccadilly on the top of a red General, his heart full of gratitude to the girl who had helped him in his sore need.

He was cheeful and confident. Muriel Treverton still loved him. He could not doubt that. For her sake and for his own, difficult and dangerous though his task might be, he would win through.

CHAPTER 3.

SEXTON BLAKE filled in the pink slip of paper, tore it from his chequebook, and put it in his pocket. He was leaving town shortly, and he needed some money.

He picked up a letter he had received that morning, and when he had read it again he thrust it into a pigeon-hole, lowered the lid of his desk, and rose.

"Where are you off to?" asked Tinker.

"I am going to my bank to cash a cheque," Blake replied. "I am short of cash."

"And when do we go to Plymouth, guv'nor?"

"Not until this evening. We will travel by the night express. You might ring up Paddington and book a couple of sleeping-berths. Inspector Henshaw wants my help and I can't well refuse, as he has done me one or two good turns. And, what's more, I am interested in the case. I doubt if the murder was committed by the escaped convict from Dartmoor, though the evidence against him is very strong."

Blake went to the door as he spoke.

"I probably won't be back for luncheon," he added. "I have some business to attend to in the City."

Tinker turned to the scrap-book in which he had been pasting newspaper clippings, and Blake left the house and hailed a taxi, and drove to the London and Northern Capitals Bank in Cheapside.

As he entered the long, marble-paved lobby he noticed that a door straight beyond him was open to the width of an inch or so, and that somebody was peering from it; and the next instant the door was opened a little wide, and Mr. Randolph, the manager, made a quick and furtive sign to Blake, who judged at once that something was amiss.

He strolled forward carelessly, not glancing to right or left, and as soon as he had passed into the private office Mr. Randolph softly shut the door.

"I'm glad I got a glimpse of you," he said, pointing to another door which was open, and led to the inner premises of the bank. "I want you to see somebody. A gentleman who is at the third window from my office. Take a good look at him Hurry!"

The doorway was at right angles to the front fo the building. Blake stepped to it, and, craning his neck to one side, he saw the person who had been mentioned.

Standing at the third window, talking to a clerk who was inside the grill, was a tall, well-dressed man of middle-age, with a florid complexion, a heavy, fair moustache, and a bushy beard that drooped to his chest.

There was a short conversation between the two. Then the gentlemen nodded, shrugged his shoulders, and left the bank.

Blake turned to the manager.

"Well?" he said, in a puzzled tone.

"Wait a moment," bade Mr. Randolph. And with that he spoke to the clerk, who was approaching him. "What did the gentleman have to say about it, Wilkins?" he inquired.

"He was a bit irritable at first, sir," the clerk answered. "and then he said it didn't matter, and he would come back before three o'clock."

"He didn't appear to be uneasy?"

"No, sir., he was quite cool."

"Very well. That's all, Wilkins. I shall be engaged for a little while. See that I am not disturbed."

The clerk withdrew, closing the door behind him. Blake took a chair, and Mr. Randolph sat down a this desk.

"Did you ever see that gentleman before?" he asked.

"No; to the best of my knowledge I never have,' Blake replied. "He was an entire stranger to me. Why did you want me to look at him?"

"I had a reason," said Mr. Randolph. "A stupid one, perhaps. At all events, I'll have your opinion. I would like to know what you think. You are acquainted with Mr. Julian Sherbroke, who is a customer of the bank. I had a visit from him several days ago. He instructed me to sell some securities of the value of seventy thousand pounds, and put the money to his credit, which I did.

"And to-day this gentleman comes in and presents Mr. Sherbroke's cheque, drawn to bearer, for fifty thousand pounds. The clerk brought it to me. The signature was genuine. I could not dispute that. Yet I hesitated. To gain time, I had Wilkins tell the gentleman there was not sufficient cash available at the moment, and asked him to return later. I was inclined to ring up Mr. Sherbroke. Immediately afterwards you came in, and it occurred to me to——"

The manager paused and laughed.

"Everything is in order, of course," he continued. "You heard what Wilkins told me. The gentleman was perfectly cool. No doubt he will come back. As for the securities, why shouldn't Mr. Julian Sherbroke have instructed me to sell them? Even millionaires can't always lay their hands on large sums of money when they want them."

"Not always," Blake assented. "But it is rather an unusual thing, I imagine, for a millionaire to fill in a cheque, payable to bearer, for so large an amount as fifty thousand pounds."

"Yes, it is," said Mr. Randolph. "Very unusual. That is what I had in mind at the first. You have roused my suspicious again, Blake. What do you think of the matter?"

"It is a trifle queer, I will admit."

"Then you must advise me what to do. Shall I pay the cheque if it is presented again?"

"You can't refuse to pay, Randolph, if you are satisfied the signature is genuine. On the other hand, Mr. Sherbroke has rather a hot temper, and if you were to question him about the matter he might——"

Blake broke off, and for a few moments he was silent, puffing at a cigar the manager had given him. The fact that Julian Sherbroke was an immensely wealthy man, and prominent in society, taken in connection with the sale of the securities, and the fifty-thousand-pound cheque—these things had started a vague train of thought in the shrewd detective's mind.

He was thinking of Sir Bruce Maitland, of the Marquis of Barleven, of Gertrude Haysboro, and of Eric Milvern.

Could it be possible that Julian Sherbroke was being blackmailed? If so, what was the reason? He certainly would not have consented to pay a large sum of money—any money at all, indeed—under a threat to expose the shameful and criminal part of his son had played in the affair of Sir Harry Royce.

He would have stubbornly refused, for though young Denis Sherbroke's disgrace had been kept out of the newspapers, it had been common talk in Society at the time, and amongst some of the general public as well.

"What do you advise me to do?" Mr. Randolph repeated.

"Leave it to me," said Blake, rousing from his reveries. "I'll see Mr. Sherbroke. I will slip round to his offices, and mention the matter to him."

"I will be more than thankful. Suppose I ring him up after you go, and tell him you are coming to see him."

"Very well. You can do so if you like."

"And you will come back to tell me what he said, Blake?"

"Yes, I will come back. There will be ample time before the gentleman returns with the cheque."

"You believe he will?"

"I haven't a doubt of it, Randolph. I am certain he will return."

Blake rose, and produced his own cheque. And when the manager had brought him the money he left the bank and walked round to the large building in Throgmorton Street, in which were the office of Mr. Julian Sherbroke, the millionaire financier.

He was known there. It was not his first visit. The clerk to whom he gave his card took him to a waiting-room and left him there; and almost at once he came back, looking very startled.

"I am afraid Mr. Sherbroke is ill, sir!" he exclaimed. "Will you please come?"

Blake jumped up and hastily followed the clerk, who led him along a passage and threw open the door of the private office.

Within, huddled in a limp attitude in an armchair behind his desk, was an elderly gentleman of stoutish build, clean-shaven except for short, sandy whiskers.

He appeared to be in a state of collapse. His head was thrown back. His face was very white, and he was breathing hard.

One hand clutched the receiver of the telephone on the desk, and with the other he was tugging at his collar.

Blake surmised at once what had happened, and as quickly he realised, was convinced, that his vague suspicious had been correct.

"It is nothing serious,' he said quietly to the clerk. "Mr. Sherbroke will soon be all right. I know what has upset him; he has been worrying over a certain matter, and I have called to have a talk with him about it. You can go now. Don't annouce anybody else while I am here."

CHAPTER 4.

THE clerk did not hesitate. Knowing who the detective was, and believing what he had been told, he promptly withdrew, shutting the door behind him.

Blake stepped forward, and stood by the desk. Mr. Julian Sherbroke was recovering now. The colour ebbed back to this cheeks, and he straightened up in his chair.

He pulled himself together, but he could not conceal the shadow of apprehension in his eyes. He frowned at Blake, though he had been on friendly terms with him for years.

"I would like to know what excuse you have for meddling in my private affairs, sir?" he said curtly.

"I supose you refer to my visit to your bank," Blake replied. "You have been talking to the manager on the telephone."

"Yes, sir, I have been!" snapped Julian Sherbroke.

"And what did he tell you?"

He didn't want to tell me anything, except that you were coming round to see me. But I got more than that out of him. A most inquisitive and impertinent fellow, is Randolph! He is not fit for the position he holds! And I let him know it! He had no right to utter a word to you about the fifty-thousand-pound cheque I drew yesterday! Not a word! he should have paid it on the spot, without questioning!"

"I don't agree with you. Under the circumstances, Sherbroke, I think the manager was justified. You must not blame him for trying to guard your interests. In the first place, I have more than once been retained by the bank, and I enjoy their confidence. Furthermore, it was an unusual thing for a cheque for so large an amount to be presented, and drawn to bearer at that."

"Haven't I the right to draw what cheques I please, as long as the money is there to meet them?"

"Of course you have. In this instance, though, there was ground for some slight suspicion."

"Suspicion be hanged! I am amazed that——"

The millionaire broke off, flushed with anger, and hammered the desk with his fist.

"You have had your trouble for nothing, Mr. Sexton Blake!" he declared. "I have instructed Randolph to pay the cheque when the holder of it returns, and that is the end of the matter!"

"You have told him that on the telephone?" Blake said heatedly.

"Yes, I have!"

"You can cancel your instructions. Take my advice, Sherbroke. Ring up the bank and tell Randolph you have changed your mind, and wish to stop payment of the cheque."

"Stop payment? I will do nothing of the sort, sir! How dare you dictate to me? You must be stark mad, Blake, to come here and tell me how to conduct my own business! The matter is at an end, as I said before!"

"No, Sherbroke, it is not at an end. It is only at the beginning."

The two men measured glances, gazing at each other steadily. They were at cross-purposes. Julian Sherbroke's face showed both uneasiness and defiance.

Blake knew just what was in his mind, and he wanted badly to draw him out. But how was he to do so? It was a stubborn character he had to deal with.

What should be his next move? It would be useless to handle the millionaire with gloves on. No, he would have to bully and browbeat him.

"When I came in," he said, after a brief pause, "you were almost in a state of collapse. You looked as if you had a fit of apoplexy."

"Absurd!" muttered Jilian Sherbroke, "Ridiculous! I had been talking excitedly to Randolph, and I was suddenly overcome by the heat of the room."

"That was not the reason," Blake went on. "You were upset by what the bank manager told you—that I had learned of the fifty-thousand-pound cheque, and was coming round to question you about it. To put it bluntly, you were afraid of me."

"What utter nonsense! Why should I be afraid of you?"

"I will tell you why, Sherbroke. Because you are too much in fear of the scoundrel to expose him."

"Blackmailed? Me? It's a lie! Confound your impudence, Blake! I'll tolerate no more of it! Clear out of this! Begone, or I'll—I'll——"

Julian Sherbroke's voice chocked. He sprang to his feet, his cheeks purple; and as he was spluttering with rage and shaking hsi fist at the detective, he swayed like a reed-turned pale—sank down in the chair—and tugged at his collar again.

There was a carafe of water on the desk. Blake poured some into a glass and gave it to the agitated man, who drank it, and presently sat up, his features twitching.

He was not angry now. There were only fear and appeal in his eyes.

It's no use trying to keep anything from you," he said in a husky tone. "I'm sorry I spoke to you as I did, Blake. You were quite right. I am in the clutches of a cursed blackmailer. You can't help me. I won't let you. But I will tell you the whole story."

"Before you do that," Blake replied, "ring Radolph up, and instruct him not to pay the cheque."

"No—no, I won't!" Julian Sherbroke cried.

"I say you will! You must!"

"And I say I won't Not if you clapped a pistol to my head! I dare not stop that cheque, Blake!"

"Then I will——"

"No, you shan't! Keep away from the telephone! I'll smash it if you come near!"

"You fool! Will you let that scoundrel rob you of fifty thousand pounds?"

"I can't help it! if you try to stop the payment of the cheque I will tell you nothing! And you will find out nothing!"

Blake shrugged his shoulders. He had to give in. He knew it would be a waste of breath to press his demand any farther.

"You will be sorry for this, Sherbroke," he said as he sat down. "Very sorry. And now let me have your story." he added.

"It will be in confidence," replied the millionaire. "Is that understood?"

Blake nodded. Julian Sherbroke drank another glass of water, and then, speaking in a low tone, he began his narrative.

Many years ago, when he had barely laid the foundation of his fortune, and was unknown in Society, a City company with which he was connected had sent him out to Uruguay to purchase large tracts of cattle lands.

"I was little more than a youth at the time," he continued. "I was fond of adventure, and In enjoyed the rough life out there. Though I travelled on horseback to distant places, I made my headquarters at the village of San Jacinton, where I lodged with the Spanish padre, Father Amaral.

"He had living with him an orphan niece, Mercedes Amaral, who was the loveliest girl I had ever seen. I fell madly in love with her. I proposed, and was accepted; and when I asked the padre's consent to our marriage, he told me the history of his niece, saying he felt it was his duty to do so.

"It appeared that Mercede's surname was Valdez, not Amaral. Her mother, the sister of Father Amaral, had run away and married a notorious ruffian and bandit, Pedro Valdez, who was a low-caste half-breed. Several years afterwards Valdez was caught and hanged, and his wife returned with a child to her brother's house, where she died a month later.

"Such was the story, and it was a very ugly one. But it did not turn me against Mercedes. I loved her just as much. We were married at San Jacinto by her uncle, in the mission chapel, and for the better part of a year we led a perfectly happy life. Then I went far up-country to the borders of Brazil.

"I was absent for some weeks, and when I returned to the village—I had meanwhile written a number of letters to my wife—a terrible shock awaited me.

"Mercedes was dead and buried. She had died of a fever, leaving a baby girl who was only two or three weeks old. Father Amaral wanted to keep the child, but I loved it for my wife's sake, and refused to give it up entirely. The girl was christened Carmen, and I left her with her grandfather and came home. I did not tell anybody of my marriage. I kept the secret, though I had no particular reason for doing so."

Julian Sherbroke paused for a moment.

"To shorten the story," he went on, "my little daughter lived with Father Amaral for some few years, and then he sent her to England, at my request, and I took her to a convent-school in France to be educated. At about that time I married again, but I did not tell my wife of my previous marriage.

She did not know, nor did any of my friends, that I had ever been in Uruguay.

"My son Denis was born, and a few years afterwards my love for Carmen having increased, I took a step I had been contemplating for a long while. I brought her to my home in London, letting it be understood that she was my ward, the daughter of a very old friend of mine who had recently died in France. She was then eighteen years of age, and she had grown to be a beautiful and accomplished girl. She could speak English as fluently as French, and——"

"Your ward?" Blake interrupted, with a slight start. "You mean Miss Evelyn Kerr?"

"Yes, that was the name I gave her," assented Julian Sherbroke.

"And she married Lord Morpeth?"

"She did, Blake. Seven years ago."

"Did she know you were her father?"

"No, I let her believe that she was really my ward. As for her early childhood, the three of four years she spent with Father Amaral at San Jacinto, she had forgotten all about that short period of her life."

Blake nodded gravely.

"Go on," he bade. "The blackmailing affair is next. How did that come about?"

Julian Sherbroke hesitated, his face sombre. "Somebody learned of my first marriage," he replied.

"So I supposed. How could the information have leaked out after so many years?"

"I have not the remotest idea, Blake. It is a mystery to me. At all events, less than a week ago, I had a visit from a man who dealt me a staggering blow. He had in his possession, he declared—and I could not doubt him—the letters I had written to my wife while I was up-country in Uruguay, the chapel record of my marriage to Mercedes Valdez, and the record of my child's birth. And he also said he knew, and could prove, that my wife was the daughter of a half-breed bandit who had been hanged for robbery and murder. The fellow demanded a hundred thousand pounds, threatening that unless I gave him the money, and swore to hold my tongue, he would go to Lord Morpeth and tell him the whole story. And I had to come to an agreement with him."

"You had to, Sherbroke?"

"Yes, there was nothing else for it. Yesterday I gave the man a cheque for fifty thousand pounds, and when I have given him another cheque for the same amount, a month from now, I am to receive the letters and the leaf which was cut from the church register at San Jacinto."

"Who is this man?" asked Blake. "You know his name."

"I know what he calls himself," Julian Sherbroke admitted. "But I won't tell you."

"I dare say you have been to see him. Where does he live?"

"I won't tell you that, either, Blake. I have told you too much as it is. I have broken my promise."

"Your promise?' exclaimed Blake, his eyes flashing with scorn. "A promise to a filthy blackmailer! You are a fool! The biggest fool I have ever known! You must stop the cheque, defy the scoundrel, and help me to have him arrested!"

"No, I can't!" cried Julian Sherbroke. "I daren't! I won't! It's no use trying to persuade me!"

"You must, for your own sake."

"It is impossible I tell you! I am too much afraid, Blake! You don't realise the position! It is not a question of my own sake at all! I would willingly pay twice as much money rather than——"

Julian Sherbroke broke off, a look of keen distress in his eyes. He leaned forward, his hands clutching the edge of his desk.

"You don't understand!" he said hoarsely. "I will tell you what I am afraid of! Carmen is everything to me! I love and adore her! She is just like her dead mother, except that she shows no trace of Spanish blood! She is happily married! She is devoted to her husband, and he is devoted to her! But Lord Morpeth is a member of the Government, and he is a proud man! He believes in caste! It is his religion! He boasts of his Norman blood, of his titled ancestors, of their valorous deeds through the past centuries, of their favour with kings and courts!

"What would he think—what would he do—if he were to learn how he had been deceived—if he were to find out that his wife's grandfather was a half-breed Uruguayan bandit who had been hanged for murder?

"He would be furious! He would forgive neither me nor Carmen, ignorant thought she is of the deception! He would have nothing more to do with her! He would cast her off, find a means of divorcing her, and break her heart! Yet you want me to let her suffer shame and disgrace for my sin!

"You would have me run the risk, for a few paltry thousands of pounds, of Lord Morpeth learning the truth! I won't do it! By heavens, I won't I shall protect my daughter if it costs me my whole fortune! You understand now! Don't say any more! I won't listen to you!"

Blake shook his head impatiently. He did not think the millionaire's fears were exaggerated. He knew himself that Lord Morpeth was a man of intense, unbending pride—as proud as Lucifer.

But that consideration did not weigh with him. He was determined not to let the matter rest as it was, for he was almost certain he had got on the track of the secret blackmailer of Society, the atrocious scoundrel who had hounded Eric Milvern to suicide, and other persons as well.

"You are unreasonable, Sherbroke," he said in an irritable tone.

"No, I'm not," replied Julian Sherbroke, who was calmer now. "I am thinking of Carmen. I won't give you any further information. Not that I could. I know little enough."

"If you stop that cheque," said Blake, "the man will put the screws on, and I can have him tripped up, and his claws cut."

"I told you I wouldn't do it, and I won't. If I stopped payment of the cheque the fellow would go straight to Lord Morpeth."

"He would not. Don't you believe it, Sherbroke. He would have another shot at you.'"

"Let us drop the argument. You can't change my mind. I would like you to help me, though, if you will."

"You are talking in riddles," Blake complained. "How can I help you if you refuse to help me! You need help pretty badly. You don't know what it means to yield to the rapacious demand of a blackmailer, as you have done. In all probability, when the month has expired, the man will get another fifty thousand pounds from you, and trick you out of the letters and the marriage and birth records. And he will keep on blackmailing you."

"The same thing has just occurred to me," said Julian Sherbroke. "That is why I asked for your help. You go ahead with the matter, quite on your own. I won't give you any assistance. If I did I might show my hand, and in revenge the scoundrel would go to Lord Morpeth. But I think you are clever enough to lay him by the heels, and force him to give you the letters and the other proof."

"You think so, do you? I've got to find the man first, remember."

"You had a good look at him at the bank, I believe."

"Yes, Sherbroke, I did."

"Well, you have seen him, and I don't mind telling you he lives in the West End. So you have two clues, so to speak, to start with."

Blake considered. He was exasperated by the obstacles which had been put in his way, and by the millionaire's stubborn folly. He had some valuable information, however, and he felt that he stood a chance of success.

Moreover, if his efforts should fail, he would have an oportunity at the end of a month, when the time came for payment of the second cheque.

Yet he could not be sure of that. He made another futile attempt to persuade Mr. Sherbroke to open his lips, and then, on a sudden impulse, he jumped up and stepped over to the telephone.

"What are you going to do?" exclaimed Julian Sherbroke, thrusting out his arm.

"I want to talk to Randolph,' Blake replied.

"You shan't countermand my instructions!"

"Don't be alarmed. I merely wish to put a question to the manager."

"Very well."

The arm was withdrawn. Blake picked up the receiver, and was promptly connected with the Northern Capitals Bank in Cheapside. He recognised the voice that answere his call.

"Blake is speaking," he said. "Has that fifty-thousand-pound cheque been presented again?"

"Yes—presented and cashed," the manager replied. "I paid it by Mr. Shebroke's instructions."

"How long ago?"

"Not more than ten minutes. It is all right, Blake, isn't it?"

"Quite all right, Randolph. Good-bye."

Blake dropped the receiver on its hook. He was keenly disappointed, and he did not hesitate to say so.

"The cheque was paid ten minutes ago, Sherbroke," he declared. "Otherwise I should have waited outside the bank, and shadowed the man."

"I thought that was your idea in telephoning," Julian Sherbroke replied.

"And you are glad it didn't come off, eh?"

"I am not sorry, Blake. The fellow might have discovered you were following him, and he would have suspected I had set a police-trap for him. And there is no telling what he would have done in revenge. I have reason to be afraid of him."

"You are a coward. Sherbroke! I am disgusted with you! You want my assistance, yet you put stumbling-blocks in my path! How do you expect me to accomplish anything? I will throw the case up, and leave you to make the best of your precarious positions, unless you will——"

Blake paused abruptly.

"You've got to give me further information!" he said sharply and sternly. "Who is the blackmailer? Tell me for your daughter's sake! Be quick! What is his name?"

Julian Sherbroke was frightened into compliance.

"The man calls himself Charles Desboro," he faltered.

"Where does he live? What is his address?"

"He lives at No. 189A, Ponter Street. Now you have got so much out of me, what steps do you propose to take? If the man is led to suspect I put you on the track he will go to Lord Morpeth."

"You needn't worry about that."

"I can't help worrying, Blake. Do be careful, I beg of you."

Blake sat down, and lit his pipe. Somewhere or other, he was pretty sure, he had heard the name of Charles Desboro memtioned. When or where it was the could not remember.

Who was this Charles Desboro? Was he the real blackmailer, or was he a go-between? he was most likely the latter, and, if so, it was to be presumed that the letters and the marriage and birth records were not at his residence in Ponter Street.

Be that as it may, it would be extremely difficult if not impossible, to get at the man. Blackmailers were strongly entrenched, safe from arrest and punishment, unless they should be exposed by their victims.

And Julian Sherbroke was determined not to expose Charles Desboro. He was very foolish, but there was some excuse for him. He was willing to be bled extortionately rather than risk his daughter's happiness.

Thus Blake reflected for a little while, and at length he rose, shrugging his shoulders. He would have to work on his own. He knew he could not induce Mr. Sherbroke to take action against the blackmailer.

"Leave the matter to me," he said as he picked up his hat from the desk. "I will do what I can."

"It is very good of you," Julian Sherbroke answered.

"And meanwhile, if you have any communication from or with the man Desboro you must let me know."

"I will, Blake, you can depend on that."

Blake stepped to the door, and paused. His thoughts had drifted to the affair of three years ago, in which he had played some part.

"By the way," he asked, "have you heard anything of your son since he went out to South America?"

Julian Sherbroke's face darkened.

"Nothing whatever," he replied, "and I don't wish to hear. I have finished with him."

"He wasn't vicious. He was weak, and easily led. I hope he has made good. Perhaps he found employment in Montevideo, and has stuck to it."

"More likely he is begging in the gutters. I don't care which. It is a matter of indifference to me. Oddly enough, I imagined I saw him standing outside a window of my house one night this week."

"It was only a delusion, Blake. The boy would not have dared to come back to England."

Blake nodded.

"I must hurry off." he said. "I am going down to the West County to-night on professional business. I will see you again when I return. Good-afternoon, Sherbroke. Try to keep cheerful."

CHAPTER 5.

BLAKE and Tinker were not long absent from London. On the fourth day after their arrival at Plymouth they succeeded in tracing and arresting the murder of an old farmer at Yelverton Junction—the crime had not been committed by the escaped convict from Dartmoor, as the detective had shrewdly surmised—and that night they travelling back to town.

Blake found no letter from Julian Sherbroke awaiting him, and at noon the next day he went down to Scotland Yard to see Inspector Widgeon.

The inspector was alone, sitting at this desk in the room overlooking the Embankment and the river, with a disorderly litter of papers in front of him.

He took a cigar from his mouth, and turned to Blake with an odd sort of grin, which was almost invariablya sign that he had something up his sleeve.

"Hallo!" he said. "Sit down! What have you been doing since I saw you last at Chesham Place? Searching for the society blakmailer?"

Blake shook his head.

"I am about ready to tackle that job," he replied. "You haven't put any of your men on to it. I suppose?"

"No, they have been to busy," said Inspector Widgeon. "They haven't had any time to look for blackmailers, with this crime wave sweeping London. I wish you luck. Let me know how you get on, will you?"

"Not until I have made some progress. Then I may come to you for assistance."

"I doubt if you will. Set a thief to catch a thief! Unless one of the blackmailer's victims should squeal, you won't stand an earthly chance of——"

The inspector broke off, and grinned again.

"I am going to give you an interesting piece of news," he continued. "As I have often told you before, you missed your vocation. You are too tender-hearted, Blake and too easily deceived by human nature, to be a good detective. You ought to have founded a home for penitent crooks, with all the luxuries of Broadmoor, and an abundance of cigars and champagne and truffles. Oh, you and your Dartmoor shepherds!"

"Oh, why do you think that?' murmured Blake, wondering what was coming.

"You remember the affair of young Denis Sherbroke three years ago," Widgeon answered. "It was as much due to you as to his father's influence that he was discharged from custody, and allowed to go abroad, on the strict understanding that he would never return. It was his first offence. He was weak and easily led. There was good in him. It would be a great pity to send him to prison. That's what you said about him, didn't you?"

"Yes, I did," Blake assented. "And I believed it."

"Well, you were wrong, and I was right. The boy was rotten to the core!"

"What have you heard of him, Widgeon?"

"What have I heard? Mr. Julian Sherbroke's scapegrace son is back in London, and he has broken into a house in the West End, with intent to commit a burglary."

"I am amazed to hear it, and very sorry," said Blake. "Can it be true?"

"Of course it is true!" declared the inspector. "I know what I am talking about, The fellow broke in a house in Ponter Street."

"In Ponter Street? Whose house?"

"The residence of a Mr. Charles Desboro."

Blake gave a quick start, but Inspector Widgeon did not notice it. He chuckled and rubbed his hands. He was enjoying his triumph.

"I will give you the facts," he went on. "It is a modern house of red brick, semidetached, with a small patch of garden at the front, and a narrow passage running along one side to a large garden at the rear of the premises.

"Between ten and eleven o'clock last night a constable who was on duty in Ponter Street—Gibbon by name—heard shouts, and saw a man slip out of the front gate of Mr. Desboro's residence and take to his heels. He chased him for a short distance, lost him in the darkeness, and returned to the house, which was in a state of excitement.

"Mr. Desboro let the constable in, and told him what had happened. The burglar had got access to the house through the kitchen, crept upstair to a study on the first floor, and forced open a roll-top desk. A servant discovered him. She called for help, and by the time Mr. Desboro had rushed up the fellow had dropped from a window into the passage at the side of the dwelling and made his escape. Gibbon examined the desk, and found clear impressions of finger-prints on it. He warned Mr. Desboro not to let them be disturbed, and subsequently he reported the affair to his superintendent, who telephone to Scotland Yard. One of our men went to Ponter Street, and photographed the finger-prints. And after the plates were developed here this morning——"

The inspector paused and chuckled again.

"The finger-prints corresponded exactly," he added, "with those which were taken of Denis Sherbroke three years ago. There can't be the slightest doubt that he was the burglar. You see the mistake you made, now, don't you?"

Blake shrugged his shoulders and smiled. He was not irritated, not even chagrined. He was so interested in what he had learned that he didn't care a rap for the inspector's jibe. Furthermore, he

was inclined to believe that the joke was not on himself.
"He who laughs last laughs best," he quietly remarked.

"You have a hide as thick as a rhinoceros!" Inspector Widgeon retorted.
Blake's eyes twinkled.
"I suppose I'll have to admit I was wrong about young Sherbroke," he said. "By the way, have you had from Gibbon's superintendent the full report made to him by the constable?"
Widgeon nodded.
"The full report," he replied.
"Had Mr. Desboro's desk been ransacked?" Blake asked.
"Yes, the contents were in confusion."
"Was anything stolen?"
"Nothing at all, Blake."
"Was there any money in the desk?"
"Thirty pounds in Treasury notes, in a small drawer. The young rascal must have been frightened away before he had a chance to find the money."
"I dare say," murmured Blake. "Does Mr. Desboro know that the finger-prints have been identified?"
"Yes, he does," the inspector answered. "He rang up a couple of hours ago to inquire."
"You told him whose finger-prints they were?"
"I did,, Blake. And I also told him not to mention the fact to anybody, and he promised he wouldn't."
Blake knit his brows.
"It is rather a pity," he said, half to himself.
"A pity?" repeated Widgeon. "What do you mean?"
"Nothing in particular. I was just thinking. What are you going to do about the matter? I should not inform Mr. Julian Sherbroke if I were you."
"No, I shan't. I'll spare him the blow at least for the present. As for the boy he will catch it hot for breaking his promise. It may be difficult to find him. But it won't be long until he is tripped up, and then I'll put him through the mill on the old charge. His position is that of an arrested and accused person who has escaped and fled the country and returned. The charge still hangs over him. It has not been withdrawn. He can be taken straight before a magistrate and remanded."
Blake had scarcely been listening to the inspector.
"It will be much more difficult to find young Denis," he said, "if he should learn that his finger-prints have been identified at the Yard. You will be wise to keep the Ponter Street affair out of the newspapers."
"I am going to keep it out," Inspector Widgeon replied. "I have already seen to that. I am sorry I told you, come to think of it."
"Why are you sorry?"
"Because you will probably search for the boy yourself, and if you find him you will repeat the good Samaritan act, and smuggle him of abroad again."
Blake laughed.
"Once bitten, twice shy!" he said.
Once!" sneered the inspector. "More times than I can count on my fingers and thumbs!"
This was a gross exaggeration, though it was true that, astute as Secton Blake was in his judgement of character, he had on several occasions been deceived.
But he was sure he had not been deceived in young Denis Sherbroke, and he would have liked to tell Widgeon so. That would have been indiscrect, however.
He resisted the temptation, and, leaving the inspector to his work, he drove home and told Tinker what he had learned.
"There's an easy problem for you,' he continued, when he had finished the story. "Did Denis Sherbroke return to lead a life of crime or not? Was it merely a curious concidence that he should have broken into the house of the man who is blackmailing his father or was it not? Was robbery his motive, or had he another motive?"
For only a moment Tinker was perplexed.
"It was more than a coincidence!" he exclaimed. "That is too far-fetched! My word, guv'nor, he must have broken in to search for the letters and the other evidence. It is almost incredible, though."
Blake shook his head.

"No, it isn't incredible," he declared. "There is a simple explanation. Denis Sherbroke was in Uruguay, and Charles Desboro sent someone out there to get the letters Julian Sherbroke wrote to his wife and the leaf from the register in the chapel of San Jacinto. And by some accidental means, either at the village up country or down at Montevideo, Denis encountered the man, got wind of his game, sailed for England on the same vessel with him, shadowed him after he landed, and traced him to Desboro's house, in Ponter Street."

"That's the explanation," Tinker assented. "It was plucky of the fellow, wasn't it? I'll bet I know what his idea was. To do his father a good turn, and have him forgive him, and get him out of the scrape that forced him to leave the country three years ago.'

"Yes, no doubt. Creditable motives. The boy has risked his freedom, a term of imprisonment, to foil the blackmailer."

"Well, guv'nor, here's wishing him the best of luck!"

"I wish him the same, Tinker. And with all my heart. And I hope he will elude the police."

Blake sat down as he spoke, his brows wrinkled.

"Things are rather complicated, aren't they?" he said. "Charles Desboro will be alarmed, and on his guard, since ke knows it was Julian Sherbroke's son who got into his house, and must suspect what his object was. I wonder if the young fellow will make a second attempt? I shouldn't be surprised if he did. There is going to be work for you to do, Tinker. You knew Denis. You might try to find him, and if you succeed you will bring him to me. And we must set a watch on Mr. Desboro. That is the main thing. I don't believe he is the actual blackmailer, and if I am right he hasn't got the documents. They will be in the possession of——"

Blake paused.

"Here comes Mrs. Bardell with the luncheon," he added, as he heard the stair creaking to a ponderous tread. "We will finish our conversation later."

CHAPTER 6.

BITTERLY disappointed by the failure of his attempt in Ponter Street, Denis Sherbroke stayed in the seclusion of his lodgings for several days, mooding over his troubles and wondering what he should do next. He was not discouraged. Failure had not weakened his resolve to achieve the object on which so much depended.

He meant to make a second attempt shortly, for he had been frightened away before he had throughly searched Mr. Desboro's desk, and he believed that the letters and the document were there.

Meanwhile he had spent a very dull time, and at eight o'clock one evening, tempted to take a little pleasure in the West End, and trusting that the false moustache he wore would protect him from recognition, he left the house in Bloomsbury and strolled down to Piccadilly Circus.

Concluding to go to Odler's Brasserie in the Quandrant—it was an old haunt of his—he went in by the rear entrance in Glasshouse Street, and paused on the threshold to take a furtive survey.

He threw a sweeping glance beyond him, and, seeing no one whom he knew, he seated himself at a small, unoccupied table close to the door.

He was facing the Quadrant entrance, and presently, after he had ordered a glass of beer and a sandwich, he looked over his shoulder to see who were behind him.

For a moment his attention was drawn to a couple of Frenchmen who were having a heated argument, and when he looked the other way his heart gave a quick throb.

In the brief interval somebody had taken the vacant seat oposite to him—a well-dressed gentleman, clean-shaven, with ruddy, good-humoured features. It was Mr. Charles Fenner, of Vine Street.

"Hallo, Sherbroke!" he said cheerfully, smiling at the youth.

Denis felt his cheeks burning. It would be useless for him to deny his identity; he knew that.

His first impulse was to take to flight, but he checked it,thinkinghe might have a better opportunity later.

By an effort he pulled his wits together and tried to appear at ease.

"How are you, Mr. Fenner?" he replied, as calmly as he could.

"Quite well, my boy, said the C.I.D. man. "And you look the same."

"Yes, I'm all right," said Denis. "Can I offer you a drink?"

"No, thanks. I just stopped to have a little chat. I hope I'm not intruding."

"Not at all. I'm glad to see you, Mr. Fenner."

"Very good of you. By the way, I believe I saw you in Hyde Park the other day."

"Yes, you did," Denis assented. "I am sorry I couldn't wait to talk to you. I was in a hurry."

"I noticed you were," Charles Fenner replied. "So you have come back to England, eh?"

"Yes, I got homesick out in Uruguay. There is no place like the old country."

"I'd have stayed out there, my boy, had I been you. It was a healthier climate for you."

"I had my reasons for not staying there any longer; and they were good reasons."

"What about your promise, and the penalty for breaking it?"

"That's up to you, I suppose."

Charles Fenner nodded.

"You were a fool to come back, knowing you were liable to be arrested on the old charge," he said dryly, dropping his bantering tone. "And you were a bigger fool to break into that house in Ponter Street the other night."

Denis stared open-mouthed.

"What—what house?" he gasped.

"The resident of a Mr. Charles Desboro," said Charles Fenner. "They have you nailed at Scotland Yard for that job."

"I don't believe it! How could they have——"

"By the finger-prints you left on the desk, Sherbroke. Amateur cracksmen are usually careless in that way."

Denis was hard hit. His position has been bad enough before, and now it was much worse. There were two charges against him, and he would probably be sent to penal survitude.

Should he tell the detective the whole story, and throw himself on his mercy? No, even should his statements be believed, the police would be powerless. They would have no legal right to enter Charles Desboro's house, with or without a search-warrant. They could take no steps whatever against him.

It rested with him, Denis, to recover the documents, and baffle the blackmailer; and if he were to do so he must escape.

He thought of all this very quickly, and pretended to be more frightened than he was. With a shaking hand he lifted his beermug to his lips, and spilt some of the contents as he put it down.

'You've got me, Mr. Fenner," he said in a husky voice. "What are you going to do with me?"

"I'm going to take you round to Vine Street, my boy," the detective replied.

"Right you are, sir. I'll——"

Like a flash Denis was on his feet, and as quickly, in two strides, he was at the door.

Out he went, and when he had darted across Glasshouse Street, dodging at the peril of his life between two cars, he sped past the Monico, whipped round the corner of Shaftesbury Avenue, and ran as fast as he could, pushing roughly and swiftly through the crowd on the pavement.

He did not pause to look over his shoulder. Whether or not he had eluded the detective he did not know. He thought he heard shouts, but he was not sure, as the traffic was making a deafening noise.

He hesitated at Denman Street, and ran on as he observed a taxi crawling slowly beyond him, opposite to the Trocadero.

He overtook it—sprang to the footboard—jerked the door open—and called to the chauffeur:

"The Scala, Fitzroy Square! Hurry, please! I have an appointment!"

The cab shot off as Denis tumbled in and shut the door. Was he safe? He waited until he had gone by Rupert Street, and then, peering from the plate of glass behind him, he had a glimpse of Charles Fenner getting into an orange taxi at the corner of Denman Street.

His heart sank. The detective had been in pursuit of him, and was on his track.

"I'll be run down in the end, I dare say," he muttered. "But I'll give the fellow a chase for it. He may lose me."

The two cabs raced up Shaftesbury Avenue and round by the Palace; and they were about the same distance apart—a couple of hundred yards—as they drew near to the top of the Charing Cross Road.

And now an idea suddenly accured to Denis. He might easily escape, he reflected, if he had a little time. Even a minute would be enough.

He lowered the window and spoke to the chauffeur.

"I've got to go home for something I forgot," he said. "Take me to No. 58, Doughty Street, Bloomsbury."

The taxi swerved to the right, into the flaming lamps of New Oxford Street; thence to Hart Street, and from that to the Theobald's Road.

Denis looked back again, and his spirits rose.

"I believe I can do it," he said to himself. "I am pretty sure I shall."

The orange-coloured taxi had been held up by the traffic at Southhampton Row. It was clear now, and was keeping to the pursuit; but it had lost some ground, and was farther behind than it had been before.

The chase was nearing its end now. Soon the leading taxi turned to the left, throbbed along John Street, and stopped in front of No. 58, Doughty Street.

Denis leapt out, gave the chaufeur five shillings, hastened across the pavement, and pulled his latchkey from his pocket as he stepped into the wide portico of the oldfashioned dwelling.

The orange cab had not yet appeared at the corner of Theobald's Road as he opened the door.

He pushed it shut, and shot the bolt, rapidly mounted the stairs, and entered his comfortable bedroom, which was at the back of the first floor.

"That's done it," he thought. "I'm all right now, and I can take some things with me, though I haven't much time to spare."

He took a small kitbag from the wardrobe, and hurriedly filled it with clothes and boots and toilet articles.

Then he went to the window, and raised the sash, and as he swung over the ledge, his bag in one hand, he heard shouts in Doughty Street, and loud hammering on the front-door of the house.

He let go and dropped, and landed lightly in a thick clump of shrubbery beneat him.

He was in a large garden which stretched at the rear of the dwelling, and when he had raced to the bottom of it—he could still hear the detective hammering on the front-door–he unlocked a gate in a high wall, and slipped through into Doughty Mews.

He glanced right and left, saw nobody, and glided from the mews to a deserted street, along which he walked at a rapid pace.

He turned corner after corner, and paused at a dark spot. All was quite behind him. He was safe, at least for the present.

"That was a near thing," he reflected. "What a fool I was to go to the brasserie to-night! The police will be inquiring for me at Lodging-houses all over London tomorrow. Well, there is only one thing to be done, and I'll have to do it. I hope it won't come to that, though. I had rather have stayed in doughty Street."

He prudently held to the north, thinking of what he had learned from the Vine Street detective, until he came to Euston Road. Then he hailed a taxi.

"The Marble Arch, please," he said to the chaueffeur.

CHAPTER 7.

MR. CHARLES DESBORO, a handsome, middle-aged gentleman with a blonde moustache and steel-blue eyes, had risen later than his usual habit; and by the time he had tubbed and dressed, and finished his breakfast, it was nearly eleven o'clock.

Having glanced at the newspaper, he rose from the table, and went upstairs to his study on the first floor, taking with him unopened the one letter he had received by the morning delivery.

A fire was burning in the luxuriously-furnished room, and between the two windows was the roll-top desk Denis Sherbroke had broken into.

He would not have found what he was after, however, even if he had not been interrupted in his search.

There was nothing in that desk—or in the house—which Mr. Desboro would have been afraid to let the police see, or anybody else.

He unlocked it, and raised the lid, and carefully chose a cigar from a box of Rothschilds; and when he had set it alight he tore open the sealed envelope, and took from it a printed card of invitation to an exhibit at a Bond Street art gallery of a collection of paintings of the Black Forest in Germany, by an English artist.

Mr. Desboro did not care a rap for the Black Forest, but he was none the less very much interested in the card. He held the reverse side of it to the heat of the fire, and gradually there appeared in pale purple, word by word, a number of lines of fine writing. And this writing, which had been done with invisible ink, ran as follows:

"It was a difficult task, but I have succeeded. I went to Oxford to make inquiries, and after a long search I found at a shop a good photograph of Julian Sherbroke's son, taken in a group when he was in the cricket team of his college. He is the same boy who was hiding in the mission chapel at San Jacinto that night. There isn't any doubt about it at all. As for other matters, your instructions have been carried out, Carey has made such arrangements as you wished, and all is in readiness. We are waiting for further orders

"HEWITT."

The letter pleased Charles Desboro, and it did not please him. He smiled rather sourly, then frowned. He had been clinging to the very dim hope that his suspicions might be wrong.

He tossed the letter into the fire, and he was thoughtfully pacing the floor when the telephone bell rang.

He picked up the receiver.

"Hallo!" he cried.

"Is that you, Charles!" replied in French a clear, mellow voice—obviously afemininevoice.

"Yes, he is speaking," Charles Desboro answered in the same tongue. "How are you this morning?"

"Don't ask conventional questions. It is stupid. Have you any news for me about Julian? It is several days since I talked to you last. You remember what you told me you were going to do."

"I have done it, Highness. Julian is safe proposition. I have had him under strict surveillance. He has been leading he: normal life. He has not been to Baker Street—you imagined he might go there—nor has been to Scotland Yard. He will give no trouble, be assured."

"I am glad to hear it. He is a man of violent temper, and I feared he might yield to it, and make up his mind to fight. So he has been taking it quietly, has he?"

"Yes, it would seem so," said Charles Desboro. "And now I will have a report from you, if you please. You know what about, If there is one man in the world of whom I and again, by cleverness inconceivable, he has got on my track, and has beaten me. It is impossible, certainly, that he can get at me, much less at you.

"Yet it sticks in my mind that the events of the last couple of years, and in particular the recent suicide of his friend Milvern—I was strongly opposed to that affair, you will recall—may have aroused Blake's suspicious, and that he is working secretly.

"You promised to find out what his movement were, if you could. I left that to you because of your opportunities, and because it would have been no safe task for any of my staff of assistants. They would rather, one and all, swim across the Styx than keep watch in Baker Street."

A little short laugh floated over the wires.

"You can disabuse yourself of the least apprehension, my friend Charles," the woman replid. "I know that Monsieur Blake is not engaged on any secret work. On the contrary, he has been leading a life of idleness and pleasure, as is his habit when he has nothing else to do."

"You are sure of that, Highness?"

"Absolutely. Of late Monsieur Blake has been much in the public eye, as by chance I have seen and learned. Last Tuesday night I nodded to the distinguished gentleman at Lord Carchester's reception. On Wednesday night he dined at the Ritz—I was two tables removed from him—with Sir Algernon Chetwynd, our High Commissioner in Borneo. The day before yesterday, I have been informed, he was one of a party who had luncheon at the Maison Jules at the invitation of Cavedish Doyle, the Secret Service man, who has for the past month been reveling in hairbreadth escapes in Moscow. And last night, as it happened, I saw him at Her Majesty's Theatre, in the Duches of Shetland's box. Voila! Are you satisfied?"

"My mind is relieved," said Charles Desboro. "When Sexton Blake works he does not play, as I am well aware."

"Be cheerful, then," the woman answered. "I would like to have a personal chat with you. But I must shun Ponter Street as I would a pestilence. You will have to wait until I give another party. Perhaps I won't invite you, though. At the last one I had, which you attended as the Count de Roncelles, you neglected me shamefully."

"I will atone for it next time. And now to business again, Highness. I have just had a report from Hewitt. It is in regard to the matter I spoke of at the beginning of the week.'"

"Yes, I remember. And what does Hewitt say?"

"He has discovered positive confirmation of my suspicious—a photograph of Julian's son. It was the boy Denis who played the spy on Hewitt and Carey in the mission chapel at the Uruguayan village of San Jacinto."

"I am not surprised," said the woman. "I was certain of it from the first. I wonder if Julian knows his son is back in London?"

"I am sure he does not," Charles Desboro replied. "And it would make no difference if he did. He would be little or none the wiser for what his son could tell him. It would not induce him to fight.'

"You don't think it is a serious matter, then?"

"Of course not, Highness. The boy won't dare go near his home in Park Lane. He knows he is in danger of arrest, and he will lie low."

"He may try to break into your house again."

"I am hoping he will. I shall be prepared for him."

"What do you mean? Don't be too rash. Are you thinking of——"

"Never mind about that, Highness. My judgment is better than yours."

"Well, if you have nothing more to tell me I will ring off. That dodering old bore, the Earl of Griffenhurst, is waiting downstairs. My maid has just brought me his card. I believe he is going to propose to me again. What a pity he hasn't a family skeleton, too! He is worth a million, you know. Good-bye! But wait a moment! A word of advice! Do you think you could find a desert island thousands and thousands of miles from anywhere?"

"Why do you ask such a silly question, Highness?"

"Because one of these days, my dear Charles, you will have Sexton Blake so hot on your track that you will have to utterly disappear—if you should be lucky enought to get the chance. Good-bye!"

There was a rippling peal of laughter—and silence. Charles Desboro swore as he dropped the receiver on its hook, and for an instant a golden glint flashed in his steel blue eyes. He did not relish the lady's jest.

"One of these days it will come to a final issue," he reflected. "That is true. But I will get Sexton Blake before he can get me."

The golden glint was still in his eyes, and had the detective of Baker Street seen it he would at once have known the man's real personality. For under another name—his right one—Charles Desboro was the most daring and notorious of crooks, one of the cleverest of criminals and rogues.

"No, I am not afraid of Sexton Blake!" he muttered.

He lied to himself. He was afraid, and his face was clouded as he sat down at his desk. He had told her Highness he was afraid.

He quickly recovered his confident spirits, however. He wrote a letter, and when he had sealed and stamped it, and addressed it to somebody in the East End—it was written with invisible ink—he pressed an electric-bell. His valet shortly appeared—a lean wiry man, dark and clean-shaven.

"Yes, sir?" he said.

"You remember the matter I spoke to you about the other day?" Charles Desboro replied.

"I remember, sir," the man assented.

"Well, Croxted, I propose to carry out my plans. I have written to Hewitt. He will get the letter this evening, and will come promptly bringing with him the things which will be necessary. And night after night hereafter, beginning with tonight, you and Hewitt will set a watch, and will be ready for immediate action."

"Very good, sir."

"I don't believe the trap will fail, though it may be some days before anything happens. As for Carey, whose assistance will be needed, he already knows just what he is to do, and he has made the necessary arrangements. Each night he will be at a garage in this neighbourhood, and a telephone message will fetch him quickly with a cab."

Charles Desboro paused.

"That's all for the present," he added. "here is the letter, Croxted. Take it at once to the nearest post-office, and put a sixpenny special-delivery stamp on it."

The valet departed with the letter. Charles Desboro finished his cigar, lit a fresh one, and went downstairs to the library.

He took a volume of travels from a bookcase, and as he settled comfortably in a lounge-chair by the fire, a raucous shout rang to his ears:

"Extry! Speshul'dishun! All the latest racing tips! Extry!"

A ragged and grimy lad, with a bundle of newspapers under his arm, was passing by the house. He loitered for a moment, and went slowly on, crying his wares:

"Speshul'dishun! Latest racing tips!"

He did not go very far. He presently turned into a side-street, and entered a dairy-shop, where he took a seat at a marble-topped table, and called for a glass of mild and a bun.

"It's a hard life, isn't it?" he facetiously remarked to the waitress who brought his order.

"If you're referring to me——" began the girl.

"I mean myself, miss," said the lad, with a sigh.

"You look as if you led pretty hard life. I dare say I'll have to scrub the chair you're sitting on, to get the dirt off. You might have found a coffee-stall open if you'd gone down Victoria way.

"I'm quite comfy where I am, thank you. And please don't be impertinent. If you was what they call world-wise you'd know fine feathers don't make fine birds. Suppose I was to tell you I was a detective in disguise. What would you think?"

"I'd think you were balmy. And I believe you are. What kind of a bee have you got in your bonnet? Do you imagine you're Mr. Sexton Blake?"

"I am a detective, miss, honest," declared the lad. "I'm employed by a big swell of a millionaire to protect his lovely daughter from being kidnapped by a Society villain who loves her for her father's money."

"You go chase yourself!" snapped the girl, tossing her head. "I've had enough of your nonsense!"

She flounced away, and Tinker grinned. He couldn't wonder that his presence was regarded as a blot on the immaculate cleanliness of the dairy-shop; for he was more ragged and dirty, and more thoroughly disguised, than he had ever been before when working for Secton Blake.

From head to foot he loked like a waif of the gutters. His shabby, shapelesscap was too big for him, and drooped over his ears.

He wore no collar. His boots were in holes, and a bit of string was tied round one of them to keep if from falling off.

And grease-paint, and other artifices, had so altered his features that no one could have traced in them the remotest resemblance to Blake's young assistant.

"I'm about fed up with this sort of thing," he said to himself, as he sipped his milk and munched his bun. "I've been at it for nearly a week, and there's nothing doing yet. When Mr Desboro leaves the house he goes alone to a restaurant, or a cafe, or a theatre, and he doesn't talk to anybody. And when he's at home he doesn't have any callers. He's either playing the game on his own, or he's afraid to meet the real blackmailer anywhere. I'll have to stick to it, though. As for that Sherbroke chap, I guess he's too much afraid of the police to go near the house in Ponter Street."

Having finished his frugal luncheon, Tinker rose, ostentatiously wiped the chair he had been sitting on with a grimy handkerchief, left a copper on the table, and slouched out.

"Good riddance!" the waitress called after him.

"It's a pity you wasn't taught manners when you was young, my girl,' the lad retorted. "You're too old to learn now."

CHAPTER 8.

AT eight o'clock one evening, while on the way to his post of duty, Tinker went into a newsagent's shop in a quiet little thoroughfare near Ponter Street, and came out with a packet of cigarettes.

It was several days since he had chaffed the dairy waitress, but he looked the same waif of the gutters. His appearance was unaltered, except that he wore a greasy muffler around his throat.

He walked for a few yards, and stopped to light a fag at the entrace to Rayburn's garage; and then, being in no hurry, he lingered to watch a man in his shirtsleeves who was cleaning a car and chatting with another man.

The former was Jim Harris, an employee of the garage. He had just come on nightduty, and the man he was talking to was a friend who had dropped in.

"I saw you at the Red Lion last evening," the latter remarked. "Who was the bloke you were with?"

"Is name's Leary, and 'e's a chauffeur," said Jim Harris. "That's about all I know of 'im. 'E' 'as 'is own cab, and there it is yonder, that blue one. Three days ago 'e put it up 'ere, and 'e 'asn't 'ad it out since. As a matter of fact, 'e's been sleepin' in it."

"Sleeping in his cab—eh? What's the idea?"

"E told me what, Creech. I appears 'e's been 'ired steady by a wealthy company promoter, round in Lennox Gardens, who's expecting any night to be called by telegram to Paris to do a big deal there in the morning, and 'e wants to be driven sharp to the Croydon Aerodrome as soon as 'e gets the message. That's why Leary 'as been sleeping in is cab—so 'e can pop off quick if 'e should be rung up on the telephone. What 'e does with 'imself in daytime I dunno."

"A queer sort of a tale, it strikes me."

"It does sound a bit thick. I guess its all right, though."

"Is the fellow asleep over there now, Jim?"

"No, 'e's been and gone. 'E said 'e was going to 'ave a 'alf-pint at the Red Lion, and 'urry back."

Tinker had heard the conversation, but he was not interested in the tale of the man Leary. He went on, and when he had turned a corner into Ponter Street he walked slowly, his hands thrust into his pockets, wishing he was at home by the fire instead of on duty on this bleak and chilly autumn night.

As he drew near to Mr. Charles Desboro's residence, he noticed that it was all in darkness, and as he reached the gate he saw beyond him, by the glow from a lamp, the approaching figure of a burly policeman.

He had not been seen himself, he was sure, and he was anxious not to be seen. He would probably be arrested on suspicion for loitering in this aristocratic street.

He paused by the gate, which was partly open, and, on the impulse of the moment, he slipped through into the patch of garden and crouched in the shelter of a clump of shrubbery to one side of the tiled path.

"I hope to goodness nobody will see me from the house!" he thought.

The policeman's measured tread came nearer and nearer. He loomed in sight, stopped to flash his lantern, and passed by.

Tinker waited a little while before he rose to his feet, and he was gliding to the gate when, startled by stealthy footsteps behind him, he glanced over his shoulder.

Two constables were darting towards him, and the next instant he was in their grasp.

"We've got you, my lad!" said one. "Don't give us any trouble!"

Tinker was too surprised and bewildered to offer any resistance, and it would have been useless if he had. Tightly held by the arms, he was led hastily along the path to the house.

The door had already been thrown open by a servant, and when Tinker and his captors had entered the hall, where now the electric light had been switched on, the door was pushed softly shut.

The constables let go of the lad, and one of them thrust him down on a bench; and as he sat there, his face in shadow, his mind worked quickly and shrewdly.

He was not deceived. It was all clear to him. A cunning trap—doubtles a trap with murder for its object—had been set for Denis Sherbroke; and he, Tinker, had fallen into it.

These men in uniform were not real policemen. They were accomplices of Charles Desboro, and they were thus disguised, as officers of the law, to divert suspicious should anubody see them leaving the house with the youth for whom they had been watching night after night.

All this passed swiftly through Tinkers mind, and it occured to him also that very likely the chauffeur, Leary, who had been sleeping in his cab at nights at Rayburn's garage, was another member of the gang, and had been held in readiness to aid their plans.

"I'll bet I'm right," the lad reflected. "Mr. Desboro would have been afraid to have Denis Sherbroke arrested. He wanted to get rid of him for good and all. What will they do with me? That's the question. I dare say they will find out their mistake, and if they don't I'll have to tell them."

Only a brief interval had elapsed since Tinker had been brought in, and he row heard footsteps overhead.

A tall, handsome man in evening dress, with a blonde moustache, came down the stairs to the hall, Charles Desboro had arrived on the scene.

"So you have caught the fellow?" he said.

"Yes sir, we tripped him up neatly," replied one of the constables. "He was hiding in the shrubbery at the front."

"I thought he would venture back one of these nights. I will telephone to the neighbouring garage and have a cab sent round."

"Very good, sir. It will be best to have a cab. We will take our prisoner to Scotland Yard, and——"

The man broke off abruptly, and drew a sharp breath as he got a good view of Tinker's face in the light.

"Good heavens, sir, we—we have made a mistake!" he faltered. "We've got the wrong party!"

"The wrong party?" Charles Desboro exclaimed in consternation. "What do you mean?"

"It's a mistake! This-this isn't Mr. Julian Sherbroke's son!'

"The devil is isn't! Are you sure, Hewitt?"

"I an dead certain, sir. I've seen young Sherbroke, you'll remember. He is a bit taller than this fellow, and a trifle heavier built. And he don't look the least like him."

"So you've brought a stranger in here! A ragamuffin of the gutters!"

"You shouldn't blame us, Mr. Desboro, begging your pardon. We only obeyed our orders. The fellow was hiding in the shrubbery, and——"

"Curse you for an imbecile, Hewitt! You're a pair of blithering, blundering idiots! You in particular!

You, who've seen young Sherbroke, talked to him, spent hours in his company!"

"But it was dark in the garden, sir, for one thing. And it never occurred to us that it might be somebody else who was——"

"It should have occurred to you! Why the blazes didn't you flash your lantern on him? I've a good mind to——"

Fury stifled Charles Desboro's voice, and on the instant he was transformed into a human tiger. A golden glint, like tiny points of fire, played in his steel-blue eyes. One corner of his lips curved inward, showing his teeth. His fist clenched, he drew his left arm up and back, level with his shoulder, and held it so as if he was about to strike.

"You blundering idiots!" he repeated in a snarling tone. "You imbeciles! It was for a less mistake than you've made I smashed Starkey, in Vienna, three years ago!"

The bogus constables shrank in terror form their infuriated chief, and the servant who was standing by the door—he appeared to be the butler—turned white.

But no blow was struck. Charles Desboro let his arm drop, and in a trice his passion was gone, leaving a grey pallor on his cheeks.

"You've had a warning!" he said. "Don't forget it! You won't get another!" There was a brief silence. Fortunately no one glanced at Tinker, who was striving to hide his agitation. His brain was reeling. He felt as if everything was swimming round him.

"Gosh. I know him now!" he said to himself. "My word, what a discovery!"

He had suddenly learned who Mr. Desboro was. He knew him well, and, knowing he was equally well known to the man, he was in mortal terror lest his identity should be suspected, and his facial disquise rubbed off. If so his life would not be worth a moments purchase.

"What shall we do with the fellow, sir?" asked the constable who had been addressed as Hewitt.

Charles Desboro smiled grimly.

"I think I shall telephone for the cab," he replied in a low, tense tone.

"I wouldn't sir, if I were you."

"Why not?"

"Because I don't believe any harm has been done, sir."

"I am not so sure of that, Hewitt. However, we will see."

By now Tinker had pulled himself together, and was prepared for the ordeal he expected.

His life was at stake, hanging by a thread; but he sat calmly on the bench with his chin raised, with a sullen, dogged expression on his grimy face, while Charles Desboro scrutinised him closely, intently, studying every detail of his features.

Had not the light been artificial the lad would have been lost. As it was the grease-paint and pencil marks were not detected by Charles Desboro, and what vague suspicion he had entertained was lulled. He was led to think it was a genuine ragamuffin he was gazing at.

"Who are you?" he demanded. "What's your name?"

"Billie Smith, sir," Tinker answered. "I'm an orphan. I 'aven't got no father and mother, and I've got no 'ome."

"How do you live?"

"Any old way I can, sir. I 'ang out in Whitechapel mostly."

"You're a young crook, I dare say. You came to the West End to-night to break into some house, and you chose mine, eh?"

"No, sir, I din't," whined Tinker. "I wasn't going anywhere in particular. I seen a policeman coming, and that's why I slipped into your garden and 'id in the bushes."

"That's a poor excuse," said Charles Desboro. "I haven't any doubt you meant to——"

"The boy's story is true, sir," the man Hewitt interrupted. "Croxted and I were watching him from round the corner of the wall, and he hadn't much more than crept into the shrubbery when a constable passed by."

"Was the fellow still in hiding when you seized him?" Charles Desboro inquired.

"No, sir, he had got to his feet, and was moving towards the gate."

"You think he was about to leave the garden, then?"

"I am sure he was, sir. He couldn't have seen or heard us until we grabbed him."

Tinker's spirits roe. The peril he feared most had been averted, he felt. But he was still apprehensive. What if he should be handed over to a genuine constable?

"Don't 'ave me arrested, sir!" he begged, screwing a dirty knucke into his eyes. "I wasn't goin to break into your 'ouse—'onest I wasn't! Let me go, please!"

Charles Desboro hesitated. His suspicious had been further lulled by Hewitt's statements, yet he wasn't altogether satisfied.

"Don't you live in Baker Street, my boy?" he rapped out sharply.

Not a muscle of Tinker's face twitched.

"I dunno where Baker Street is, sir," he muttered, in a puzzled tone. "There ain't one in Whitechapel."

"Do you know Sexton Blake?"

"Do I know 'im? Ravver! Lummy, sir, 'e's the detective bloke what pinched me once for stealing some jewels! 'E let me off because I promised 'im I'd keep straight, and if 'e was to find out——"

Tinker's voice faltered, and he sprang to his feet. There was terror in his eyes.

"Don't send for Mr. Blake, sir!" he cried boarsely. "Not 'im! 'E'd get me a year, 'e would! I'd ravver be took to the police-station! But give me a chance, sir, won't you? It ain't as if I'd broken in 'ere. I was only 'iding in your garden!"

Charles Desboro shrugged his shoulders. He was quite satisfied now. He stepped to the door and opened it.'

"Clear out!" he bade. "You can go." "You're a toff, you are, sir!"

"Clear out my boy! Be quick about it!"

"Yes, sir, thank you.

The door was softly shut behind Tinker as he left the house, but he did not hear the latch click.

Judging that he was under observation, he stopped in the gateway, and stood there for a few seconds, peering around him, as if he was afraid of being seen by a constable.

Then he slepped out of the garden, and at a leisurely pace he walked along Ponter Street to Sloane Street, where he climbed to the top of a 'bus.

He changed to another one at Hyde Park Corner, and a quarter of an hour later he let himself into the house in Baker Street with his latchkey, and mounted the stairs to the consulting-room.

The bloodhound, stretched on a rug, languidly flopped his tail, and Blake, who was sitting by the fire, loked up from the book he was reading. He glanced at his watch.

"It's only a little past nine o'clock," he said, "What's amiss that you are back so early?"

"I have some news for you," replied Tinker, who was fairly bursting with excitement.

"You have shadowed Mr. Desboro to some West End residence, eh?"

"No, guv'nor, it isn't that."

Tinker related the whole story of his adventure, beginning with the conversation he had overheard at Rayburn's garage. He omitted the most important part of the narrative, though.

When he had finished, Blake frowned at him.

"You reckless, careless youngster!" he said severely. "You have had a narrow escape. I wonder Mr. Desboro didn't discover you were disguised."

"I wonder myself he didn't," said Tinker. "I fooled him, though."

"Luckily for you, my boy."

"And the game was well worth the risk, guv'nor, for I discovered who Charles Desboro really is."

"Indeed? Who is he?"

"He is Basil Wicketshaw!"

It took a great deal to stir Secton Blake's phlegmatic nature, but he sprang to his feet now, a startled exclamation on his lips, and stared incredulously, in black bewilderment, at the smiling lad.

Basil Wicketshaw! One of the most daring, dangerous, clever, and resourceful crooks in the world! Blake's old enemy! The man who had baffled him on numerous occasions, slipped from his clutches again and again when he was sure he had him!

Tinker was enjoying his triumph.

"Yoy needn't gaze at me as if I was daft," he said. "It's a dead certainty."

Blake shook his head.

"I can hardly believe it," he declared. "I had a good look at Mr. Desboro in the Northern Capital Bank that morning."

He was disguised," said Tinker. "You know how clever he is at making-up."

"I am not convinced. The last we heard of Wicketshaw he was running a gammingden at Manilia, in the Philippine Islands. He would have been afraid to venture back to England."

"He's back right enough, guv'nor, and he is living in Ponter Street, in the name of Desboro. You can take that from me straight."

"Why are you so sure?" asked Blake. "You haven't told me yet."

"I'll tell you now," Tinker replied. "I'll give you the clearest proof. Basil Wicketsaw is left-handed, you will remember. Well, when he flew into a rage with the bogus constables he clenced his left hand, and drew his arm back, as if he was going to hit out. That's an old trick of his."

"Anything else, my boy?"

"Yes. His dark-blue eyes flashed as if they were shot with gold. You've seen that often. And he sucked in his lips at one side, showing his teeth. Two more old tricks of Wickeshaw's, guv'nor. Three in all. What do you think now? Am I right?"

Blake nodded. He was convinced. He could not dispute the assertion in the face of the lad's statements, And he should not have been so incredulous at first, knowing the prince of rogues as well as he did.

"I suppose there can't be any doubt about it,' he said, dropping into his chair again. "The use of the left arm, the golding glint in the eyes, and the sucking in of the corner of the lips—that's Basil Wicketshaw to the life, and Charles Desboro is Wicketshaw. Many a man has been betrayed by ineradicable mannerisms. In Wicketshaw's case they are involuntarily displayed—the first tow of them—only in moments of the most violent rage."

"And that's what gave him away to me," Tinker replied. "But is Basil Wicketshaw the real and original blackmailer? How about that?"

"I am pretty certain he is not," said Blake, after brief reflection. "No, there is somebody behind him, somebody who has been prominent in Society for years. With all his cunning and cleverness, and the acquaintance with prominent people he has enjoyed from time to time in assumed names, Wicketshaw could not have discovered the dark secrets, the family skeletons, which drove Sir Bruce Maitland into exile abroad, and led to the suicide of the Marquis of Barleven, the Honourable Gertrude Haysboro, and my friend, Eric Milvern. Nor is it likely he could have found out anything about Mr. Julian Sherbroke's first marriage in Uruguay many years ago. No, my boy, he has been playing second fiddle to someone, possibly a woman, who is as ruthless and mercilessas himself."

"Then we can't have him arrested yet, guv'nor."

"Oh, no; it is not to be thought of, badly though the police want him. We should gain nothing by disclosing his identity to Scotland Yard, for he hasn't the documents in the Sherbroke case in his posession.I an certain. We'll have to wait, and be patient. It is of vital importance to run the real blackmailer, the Society vampire to earth; and that can be done only by keeping Basil Wicketshaw under surveillance, as far as possible. Or Desboro, as we will continue to call him.

"As for the events of to-night, it is obvious Desboro and his accomplices have been watching for Denis Sherbroke to put in an appearance—it was a shrewd idea, the bogus constables—and the man Leary, who has been in readiness night after night with his cab at a neighbouring garage, is one of the gang. It looks as if they meant to murder the young fellow, and perhaps throw him into the river, should they catch him. But I doubt if he will be so foolish as to make a second attempt at the house in Ponter Street. I wish I could find him. He could tell an interesting story of things that happened in Uruguay, and it might help us to——"

Blake paused and filled his pipe.

"I fell rather uneasy, " he went on. "There is no telling what Denis Sherbroke will do. Suppose you go back to Ponter Street, and keep watch until a late hour."

"Just what I was thinking of," Tinker replied, "I had better change my disguise first, though."

"By all means," Blake assented. "You mustn't go as you are. It would be asking for trouble."

It did not take Tinker long to prepare. He set off a few minutes later, wearing a faded bowler, and a shabby suit of blue serge. A bird's-eye handkerchief was knotted about his throat, and he had an automatic pistol in his pocket.

He took a cab to Knightbridge, and walked the rest of the way; and he had not gone far along Ponter Street when he saw a blue taxi coming from the direction of Rayburn's garage—saw it swing round, and saw it stop in front of Charles Desboro's residence.

The chaueffer's back was turned towards Tinker, who was within about twenty yards of the house. At once, risking discovery, he darted forward to the adjoining dwelling, which was flush with the street, and with quick and noiseless tread he slipped into the wide portico, and crouched behind one of the massive pillars.

He was none too soon. Mr. Desboro's butler appeared, stepped to the gate, and looked to right and left.

Then he raised his hand as a signal, and out of the house came the two bogus constables, leading between them a tall youth with a small moustache. They crossed the pavement and got into the taxi, and the servant, who had followed them, spoke to the chauffer in a low tone, yet so distinctly that he was heard by the concealed lad.

"The shortest route. Carey,' he said. "Victoria Street and the Embankment to Blackfriars."

"Right you are," the chauffeur replied. "I have my instructions.'

The cab glided away, and the butler returned to the house and shut the door. Tinker waited for a moment, and then crept out from the portico.

"They've got him!" he said to himself. "They've got Denis Sherbroke! And there isn't another taxi in sight! What the deuce am I to do?"

Suddenly he thought of something, and was off like a shot. He walked rapidly past Charles Desboro's residence, and then, quickening his pace, he hastened on to a side street and turned into it.

A few more yards, and he was at Rayburn's garage. Jim Harris, the man on night duty, was standing inside the open doorway, and a light was burning in the office at the rear of the premises.

"I want your help." Tinker said breathlessly. "I'm Sexton Blake's assistant. I've been working on a case for him, and——"

"What are you trying tc put over me?" Jim Harris interrupted, staring at the lad in derision.

"I'm not lying!" Tinker earnestly declared. "That man Leary, who has been sleeping here at nights in his cab, has pitched you a yarn. He's a crook, and he's just been round to a house in Ponter Street to pick up two other crooks, and a young fellow they've kidnapped."

"You're not kidding me, are you?" asked Jim Harris.

"Dead straight, I'm not! It's the truth. We've got to go after the men in a cab or a car. They haven't much of a start. They're going by Victoria Street, and the Embankment. I'm afraid they mean to murder the young fellow. I'm sure of it!"

"So Leary is a crook, eh? I thought there was something queer about 'is tale. There was a telephone-call for 'im a bit ago, and when 'e left with 'is cam 'e said——"

"Never mind what he said! Don't waste time in talking. If we hurry we may catch up with the blue cab on the Embankment. I've told you the truth. You'll be sorry if you refuse. There will be murder done!"

"I believe you," said Jim Harris, nodding. "I guess you're not pulling my leg. You're sure that's the way the party are going—along the Embankment?"

"Yes, I heard the instructions given to Leary," Tinker replied.

"Well, I'll come with you. We'll take the two-seater Wolseley over there. It will overhaul any cab that was ever——"

"For Heaven's sake, stop talking and——"

"'Old your 'orses, my lad! The boss is 'ere, and I'll 'ave to tel 'im where I'm going. I'll say there's somebody want's to 'ire, a car and chauffeur for an hour or so."

Jim Harris hurried to the office, spoke briefly to Mr. Rayburn, and hurried back.

He snatched his coat from a peg and put it on, and a few seconds later the Wolseley car, with Tinker and the man on the driving-seat, slid out of the garage, ran round into Ponter Street, and went racing towards Grosvenor Place in pursuit of the blue cab.

"It I could think of any objick other than what you've said," observed Jim Harris, "I might think you 'ad a box of tricks up your sleeve."

"You wait and see," replied Tinker. "We have a big job on, and afterwards you can drive me to Baker Street, if you like, and I'll introduce you to my guv'nor.

CHAPTER 9.

TINKER had made no mistake, of course. It was Denis Sherbroke he had seen from his hiding-place in the portico.

A little while before the reckless youth had got access to the garden at the rear of Charles Desboro's residence, intending to lie concealed in the shrubbery until a later hour, and then make a second attempt to get the documents which he believed to be in the desk in Mr. Desboro's study.

But vigilant eyes had watched his movements, and he had promptly fallen into the hands of the two constables, who had marched him into the house and confronted him with Charles Desboro.

The conversation between the two had been limited to a dozen words or so. Mr. Desboro had not even mentioned the youth's name, though he knew who he was, and knew why he had broken into the house on a previous occasion.

And Denis, well aware that Charles Desboro knew, had prudently kept his mouth shut. A cab had been telephoned for, and when it arrived he had gone sullenly and quietly with the constables, not doubting that they were genuine officers of the law.

His arrest was a hard blow to him, but he had a ray of hope to cling to.

"If I can get an interview with some big police official," he reflected, as he was driven away from the dwelling, "perhaps he will believe my story, and let me go. And there's Mr. Sexton Blake, who helped to save me from prison three years ago. I shouldn't care to tell him, though. He would take up the case himself, and that wouldn't suit me. I want to cheat that scoundrel Desboro by my own efforts, so my father will be more readily forgive me. And I'll do it yet, somehow or other, if I have the chance."

Yes, if the were to have the chance. But he would be a fool to count on that. His hope faded. There were two serious charges hanging over him, and whether or not the police should credit his amazing story, he would certainly not be set free. It was improbable that even Sexton Blake could accomplish that.

The cab was gliding down Grosvenor Place now, and presently it crossed the Buckingham Palace Road, and swerved into Victoria Street.

"You are taking me to Scotland Yard, I suppose?" said Denis, who was seated between the two constables.

"Yes, your old friend Inspector Widgeon is very anxious to see you," one of the men answered. "He's credit to the Yard, he is, He suspected you would make another attempt at Mr. Desboro's residence, and he set a trap for you."

"Why didn't he send you in plain clothes? It's the usual thing, isn't it?"

"No, my lad, it isn't. Not always."

The cab crossed Parliament Square, and bore to the right, turned from Bridge Street on to the Embankment, and went rapidly on.

And now Denis, who had been absorbed in gloomy thoughts, looked from a window and had a glimpse of the private gardens at the back of Whitehall.

"I say, we've passed Scotland Yard!" he exclaimed.

"Yes, I know we have," replied the man Hewitt.

"How's that? Why did you lie to me? Where are we going?"

"Don't get excited, y lad, It's all for the best. Out of sympathy for your father, Inspector Widgeon and Sexton Blake decided that instead of putting you on trial, should you be arrested, they would send you abroad again. They have fixed things with the skipper of a vessel which is lying in the Thames below the Tower Bridge, and that's where we are taking you. It's nothing to grumble about, is it? You can consider yourself lucky."

"That be darned for a tale!" said Denis.

He said it to himself, though. That Sexton Blake and the inspector should have arranged beforehand to ship him abroad in the event of his being caught, and without seeing him, was utterly absurd.

Of a sudden the truth flashed to his mind with almost stunning force. He was not deceived. These men were not real constables.

They were disguised accomplices of Charles Desboro, and he was afraid—with good reason—that they meant to murder him, and throw him into the river.

While he was in Mr. Desboro's house, Denis had merely glanced at his captors, both of whom were clean-shaven.

He gazed furtively and closely at them now, and traced in the features of one of them a likeness which took his thoughts back to Uruguay.

"I know you, Mack Hewitt!" he cried.

With that he sprang to his feet and gave a lusty shout for help. He was at once dragged down, and before he could shout again one of the men dealt him a blow on the jaw, and the other seized him by the throat. He struggled as hard as he could, unable to utter a sound, until he was nearly suffocated.

His senses swam, and when he recovered clear consciousness his wrists were tied and a handkerchief was bound tightly over his mouth.

"You—you scoundrels!" he wheezed.

"We ought to have gagged and bound the fellow at the first, as I told you," one of the men said to the other. "He might have jumped out of the window, Mack."

Mack Hewitt laughed.

"I wanted to see how he would take it," he replied. "I was ready to tackle him.'

Denis tugged and strained at his wrists, but he could not loosen the cords. The cab shot by Charing Cross, and it was about to glide under Waterloo Bridge when the chauffeur pulled up abruptly to avoid a tramcar which was crawling slowly from the mouth of the Kingsway tunnel.

And at the same moment, to Denis Sherbroke's intense relief, a police-inspector, who was standing near, stepped to the open window and peered through it.

"What's this?" he demanded. "Where do you men belong?"

"B Division, sir, Chelsea," Mack Hewitt glibly answered.

"Where are you taking your prisoner?" asked the inspector.

"To Cannon Street Station, sir, and down to Rochester, where he is wanted for burglarly. He was caught at a house in Pimlico this morning."

"Why have you gagged him?"

"He isn't gagged, sir. His mouth was badly cut while he was resisting arrest."

"It sounds a bit fishy to me. Take off the fellow's bandage. I want to talk to him."

"Certainly, sir! We are in a bit of a hurry, but——"

With that Mack Hewitt thrust his arm from the window, grasping a life-preserver, and as quickly he struck at the inspector, who staggered and fell as the weapon crashed on his head. And the next instant the chauffeur started the cab, and drove on at dizzy speed. A hue and cry rose, and soon faded in the distance.

Mack Hewitt looked back.

"It's all right!" he declared; "there's no other cab coming after us."

"There will be, Mack," said his companion. "Hadn't you better tell Carey to go a different way?"

"No fear! Several persons heard what I told the inspector, and they know now I was lying, so the safest way for us will be past Cannon Street Station."

"Yes, that's true. I see the idea."

Denis was bitterly disappointed. He had rather have been in the hands of the police than in the clutches of these scoundrels. He had identified one of them as Mack Hewitt, and he had learned since that the chauffeur was Gavin Carey.

He was completely helpless. If he was to be murdered, and he so believed, there would be no chance of escape for him.

Hewitt looked back again.

"We've done the trick, Croxted," he said, "There's something in sight a long stretch behind, a cab or a car, but I'll bet it don't come any closer to us. Carey will see to that. He has his eyes open."

The blue cab had darted across New Bridge Street at Blackfriars, and was in Queen Victoria Street.

It turned into Cannon Street, and raced steadily and switfly on—by Eastcheap and Mark Lane and Trinity Square, past the Tower and the Royal Mint, by Upper East Smithfield, down Nightingale Lane, and round by the docks to the district of Wapping, where it stopped in a quiet and gloomy street.

It was the end of the journey. A throbbing noise swelled faintly in the rear for a moment, and was drowned by the hotting of a tug.

The two men got out of the cab with their prisoner, and spoke a few low words to the chauffeur, who at once drove away in the direction of Shadwell.

And Denis, dreading the worst, was led by his captors along a narrow alley, to a flight of stone stairs, at the bottom of which a small boat was tied to a ring.

Fifty or sixty yards off shore, out in the Lower Pool, a vessel could be seen swinging at her moorings—a large, rakish-looking vessel, with lights burning fore and aft.

Mack Hewitt pointed to it.

"There's your ocean liner waiting for you, my lad!" he said, with a chuckle. 'The tramp-steamer Calabar, commanded by Captain Dan Bludsow. You're going a good many thousand miles with him before you put foot on dry land. You won't have to pay your fare. Carey has fixed that, He's a pal of the skipper, who's been expecting you at any time."

So the scoundrels did not mean murder! It was such a great relief to Denis that he felt almost cheerful.

But when he was seated in the stern of the boat with Mack Hewitt, while the other man bent to the oars, his heart sank to the depths of depression.

He was to be shanghaied. Yes, that was the word for it. He was going on the tramp steamer to some far-distant country, on a voyage that would probably last for weeks and months. And then, he supposed, he would be put ashore to shift for himself.

It was a crushing blow to his hopes and plans. He would lose all he had been looking forward to, he was afraid—paternal forgiveness, the withdrawal of the old charge against him, and the girl he loved.

He had been beaten by Charles Desboro, who had shrewedly hit on this means of getting him out of the way.

"I dare say by the time I get back to England, if I ever do," he reflected, "that villain Desboro will have squeezed a hundred thousand pounds out of my father, and he and his accomplices will have disappeared. I wish to goodness I hadn't gone to Ponter Street to-night!"

The boat slid alongside of the vessel, and was made fast to the bottom of a ladder.

It was no easy task for the two men to climb with their prisoner, who was still bound and gagged, but, without mishap, they reached the top of the ladder and stepped on to the deck.

They had not been heard, for a stiff breeze was blowing. Their arrival was expected, however, and three men immediately came towards them from a shadowy part of the deck, into the glow of a swinging lantern.

Two were ordinary seamen, and the third, who wore a peaked cap and a shabby suit of blue serge, was obviously the skipper. He was a big, burly man, red-faced, clean-shaven, except for a scanty fringe of black beard.

"So you've caught your bird at last, eh?" he said gruffly.

"Yes, he fell into the trap to-night," Mack Hewitt replied.

"Well, if he hadn't, you'd have missed me," said Dan Bludsoe.

"Missed you?" Hewitt repeated. "How's that? You told Carey you weren't sailing for several days yet."

"So I did. But I'm sailing with the tide at daybreak to-morrow, as it happens. I got all the cargo into the hold sooner than I expected. The rest of the crew will soon be coming on board. I gave them a couple of hours leave."

"And about the voyage, Dan? I think Carey said your first port of all was Mombasa."

"Not a bit of it. I'm calling at Freetown and Loanda and Durban and Zanzibir, but you can take it from me this young fellow won't be put ashore until we're in the port of Mombasa. And then, if he tries to kick up a row, I'll charge him with being a stowaway."

"That's the place—Mombasa. When are you likely to arrive there?"

"It will be three or four months, I reckon. I'll keep my part of the bargain. And what of the money? Have you got it with you?"

"Of course I have, Dan."

Mack Hewitt drew the skipper aside. They held a short and whispered conversation, and a packet of banknotes changed hands.

Then they turned their attention to Denis, who had been making furtive and futile efforts to get his wrists free.

"Come along, my lad!" bade Dan Bludsoe. "And let me give you a word of advice. If you behave yourself, you'll have nothing to complain of. If you don't—well, you'll get a taste of a rope's end and be slapped in irons. That's the sort of a man I am!"

The skipper descended the companion-way, carrying a lantern, and Hewitt and Croxted followed with Denis, who was thrust into a small, cramped cabin which had a tiny porthole.

The door was locked on him, and he sat down on the edge of a bunk and listened to the retreating footsteps.

Presently he heard the faint creaking of oars, and knew that his captors were pulling ashore in the boat.

He had no chance of escape. A few more hours, and the tramp steamer would sail with him, bound on a voyage of months around the coast of Africa, and he would be a helpless prisoner on board until the vessel reached Mombasa, where he would be turned adrift.

CHAPTER 10.

A FEW moments after Hewitt and Croxted landed at the water-stairs and disappeared in the alley, a youth, who had been lying flat on an adjacent wharf, lowered himself to the stairs, got into the boat, cast off, and fitted the cars to the rowlocks.

The youth was Tinker. The Wolseley car had held steadily and warily to the chase from Blackfriars, where Jim Harris and the lad had glimpsed the blue taxi ahead of them, to the bottom of Nightingale Lane, and it had been only a couple of hundred yards in the rear, moving very quietly, with its lamps out, when the occupants of the cab got out of it and the chauffeur drove on towards Shadwell.

Tinker had hastened forward alone, and from the mouth of the alley he had seen the two men and their prisoner embark in the boat, and pull in the direction of the moored vessel.

His fears thus allayed, believing as he did that Mr. Desboro had previously arranged to be rid of Denis Sherbroke by having him shanghaied, Tinker had quickly retraced his steps to the car paid Jim Harris, told him he would not need any assistance from him, and sent him back to the garage.

He had then hurriedly returned to the alley, and climbed to the wharf which jutted to one side of the water-stairs; and while lying there, within a short distance of the vessel, he had seen by the light of a lantern the two men talking to the skipper on the deck—had seen Denis Sherbroke taken below, and had seen Hewitt and Croxted come ashore.

It was a dangerous enterprise. He would almost certainly be discovered, and if so there would be trouble; but as he was armed with an automatic he was fairly confident of success.

"It isn't as if I had to deal with Desboro's men," he reflected, as he bent to the oars. "The skipper isn't that kind. He has been paid for the job, and I dare say I can strike fear into him, and force him to set Denis free."

The tide was on the flow, and Tinker let it carry him some yards above the stern of the vessel before he pulled close alongside of it, opposite to the Middlesex shore.

Where he had tied the boat at the bottom of the ladder, he listened for a few moments, and then, satisfied that he had not been seen or heard, he very cautiously mounted the ladder until he could get a view of the whole vessel.

He could hear confused voices, but there was nobody in sight. He had his chance.

He stepped on to the deck, glided stealthily to the companionway, and descended to a narrow passage, where he stood peering about him in the gloom. He dared not call out, lest some of the crew should be sleeping below.

Taking an electric-torch from his pocket, he moved to one side, and stopped at a door that was locked.

The key was in the lock, and without hesitation he turned it, pushed the door open, and played the flashlight beyong him.

He was on the threshold of a small cabin, and Denis Sherbroke was sitting on a bunk, staring in surprise.

Tinker slipped over to him, tore the handkerchief from his mouth, and untied his wrists.

"Hush!" he bade in a whisper. "Don't talk loud! It's all right! I've come to set you free!"

"Thank heaven!" said the youth in a low tone. "But how did you know I was here? Who are you? You don't look like one of the crew."

"I'm not. You used to know me. I'm Tinker, Sexton Blake's assistant, and I followed you in a car from Ponter Street to Wapping."

"You can't fool me! You're not Tinker!"

"I am, honest. Only I'm disguised. Come along, while we have the chance. There's a boat waiting for us. Mind you don't make any noise."

Tinker put the flashlight back in his pocket, and with Denis at his heels he crept quietly from the cabin, and up the companionway.

And he had no more than stepped on to the deck when his heart gave a quick throb, and he whipped out his automatic.

"Darn the luck!" he muttered. "Keep cool, Denis! Leave the palaver to me!"

They were discovered. A couple of yards in front of them stood the skipper, and close behind him were the two members of the crew. On Dan Bludsoe's face was an expression of blank stupefaction.

"What the blazes!" he ejaculated, with an oath, as the pistol was pointed straight at him. "What do you mean, you help, by sneaking on board my ship, and letting this young fellow out of his cabin? Put that gun down! Be quick about it!"

"I'll bore a hole through you if you're not careful!" Tinker replied, in a truculent tone. "I'm not afraid of you! Stand where you are! If any one of the three of you lifts a finger I'll shoot him! I cam on board to rescue my pal, and I mean to do it!"

"The devil you will!" snarled the infuriated skipper, showing his teeth. 'The lad's going on a voyage to Africa for his health, and I reckon you'll have to go with him!"

Tinker laughed. "I don't think!" he said. "We're not sailing with you, either of us! We're going ashore, old son, or whatever your name is!"

"It's a name you won't forget—Dan Bludsoe!"

"Well, Mr. Dan Bludsoe, you had better keep your temper and listen to what I've got to say to you. I'm going to talk to you straight! You don't want a row, I'm jollysure, and we don't want one either. This isn't police affair. You needn't be frightened. You let me and my pal go quietly, and you won't hear any more of it, I'll promise you."

"I'm hanged if I will, you impudent brat!" spluttered Dan Bludsow.

"You cant help it," said Tinker. "I've got the whiphand. Suppose I was to fire a shot in the air and blow a police-whistle? What would happen? It wouldn't be long until you were in Wapping police-station."

"If you were to try to bring the police, my lad, you would soon be at the bottom of the river with a cracked skull."

"Don't get the wind up, captain. What's the use? You've been paid to shanghai my pal, and you won't lose the money. So what have you got to grumble about? Come, stand back, and let us pass!"

Dan Bludsoe did not move, though the pistol was still pointed at him. He turned to the two sailors.

"This young crowing cock is only bluffing, men,' he told them. "he won't dare shoot."

"Daren't I?" said Tinker. "You'll see!"

He spoke defiantly, but he knew his bluff had failed. The situation was desperate now. In all likelihood, it seemed, the Calabar would sail in the morning with two prisoners on board.

What was to be done? Tinker had no intention of shooting, of course, either to kill or cripple.

"We're in pretty tight corner," he whispered to Denis Sherbroke.

Denis nodded. he had been listening to the conversation with his fists clenched, and was spoiling for a fight.

"We'll have to rush the three of them." he murmured. "There's nothing else for it."

"I'm afraid not!" Tinker replied. "I'll have another try first, though."

And with that, clinging to a slender hope, he stepped a little closer to Dan Bludsoe, and jammed the pistol almost into his face.

"I'll show you if I dare shoot or not!" he said fiercely. "Will you let us go, or must I——"

"You're trapped, you fool!" the skipper interrupted in a jeering tone. "Look behind you!"

Tinker did not look. On the instant he tumbled to the trick. But the words startled him, none the less.

He involuntarily lowered his arm, and before he could raise it he was covered by two revolves which the two sailors had quickly jerked from their pockets.

Dan Bludsoe roared with laughter.

"The boot's on the other leg now!" he declared. "Get below, both of you, and as quick as you can! Your pal will have company on his voyage to Africa!"

For a moment Tinker hesitated, boiling with rage; and then, as he was about to throw himself recklessly on the skipper, his attention was attracted by the sound of creaking, splashing oars from the direction of the Surrey shore.

He saw a long, lean boat with several men in it gliding down-stream within a hundred yards of the vessels, and he knew at a glance what it was. His heart gave a throb of joy.

"That's done it, Mr. Dan Bludsoe!" he exclaimed. "there goes one of the Thames Police galleys! Do you see? You'll let us go now, I'll bet! If you try to stop us we'll shout for help, and I'll fire every darned chamber of my pistol! The police will come on board, and the lot of you will be arrested! Stand back, you scum! Stand back!"

Thy did stand back—three baffled, frightened men, in terror of the Thames Police. They dared not run any risk. They knew an alarm would be raised should they attempt to make a move.

There was a murderous glitter is Dan Bludsoe's eyes, and he and the sailors swore bloodcurdling oaths. But not one lifted a finger to stop Tinker and Denis, who darted swiftly by them and ran across the deck to the left side of the vessel.

They rapidly swarmed down the ladder, and they were adrift in the boat, with Tinker at the oars, before the police-galley had passed by the steamer on the Surrey side.

"If it hadn't been for that galley,' said Denis Sherbroke, "you and I would have been carried off to Mambasa. We've had a narrow escape."

"A miss is a good as a mile," Tinker replied. "It was a mighty close shave, though. So you were to have been taken to Mombasa—eh?"

"Yes, that's what you saved me from, and I'll never forget it. How did you do it, Tinker? I can't imagine, unless you happened to be near when I was put into the cab at Ponter Street."

"I did happen to be there. It wasn't by chance, old chap. I know at lot more than you think I do, and we have a lot to talk about. But not now. We'll wait a bit."

They were some yards from the Calabar now. Glancing over their shoulders, they saw dusky figures watching them from the deck.

"They're taking it very quietly," Tinker remarked.

"They can't come after us," said Denis, "for the rest of the crew have gone ashore with the ship's boat."

As the men Hewitt and Croxted had landed at Wapping, Tinker judged it best to avoid that locality, and rowed down for a short distance against the tide to Ratcliff, where he ran the boat on to a strip of mud and gravel between two wharves.

A narrow passage, and a dark little thoroughfare, brought Tinker and Denis to Broad Street, and here they bore to the left, and went along the Shawell High Street to George Street.

Tinker was perfectly familiar with the neighbourhood, as he was with all of the East End—and practically all of London.

"There's no chance of a taxi hereabouts, Denis," he said. "It's just struck me I'm as hungry as a bear. How about you?"

"I'm hungry myself," Denis assented.

"Suppose we have some grub, then, as we're not in a hurry?"

Where can we, Tinker?"

"I know of a fairly decent place close by. Black Dave's, in Upper East Smithfield. No frills—no swallow-tailed waiter—food sort of checked at you—eat with your knife if you want to. But everthing's clean. We'll feed there, and afterwards we'll pick up a cab at the Mint, or at Aldgate."

They had no distance to go. Five minutes later they were sitting at a small wooden table at the rear of a long, low-ceilinged room, drinking tea from large cups of coarse, chipped china, and devouring thick slabs of bread-and-butter.

The other customers of the cheap eatinghouse were mostly rough seafaring men. The waiter was a Chink, and Black Dave the proprietor, who sat at a high stool by the door, was a swarthy Jamaican.

"Feeling cheerful now, old chap?" asked Tinker, with his mouth full.

"A good bit more cheerful than when I was on board that tramp-steamer," Denis Sherbroke replied, in rather a dull tone.

A feeling of constraint fell between them, and for a little while they went on with their meal in silence.

Denis was wondering how much Tinker knew; and Tinker, on his part, was wondering if he could win his companion's full confidence, and get him to Baker Street.

At length he guardedly approached the subject.

"I was watching Charles Desboro's house in Ponter Street to-night," he said. "That's how I happened to see you carried off in a cab by those two bogus constables."

"Why were you watching?" Denis inquired. "Did Mr. Sexton Blake send you there? Does he suspect that Charles Desboro is a crook?"

"Yes, he has his suspicions of the gentleman," said Tinker. "It was you I was keeping my eyes open for, though."

Denis gave a quick start.

"You were keeping your eyes open for me?" he repeated. "Oh I understand now! It was because of the affair of a week and more ago, whe I broke into Mr. Desboro's house for a good reason. I left finger-prints behind, and they were identified as mine at Scotland Yard. There was no mention of that in the papers, but, if course, Mr. Blake learned from the police, and that is how he came to put you on my track."

"That's right, He heard from Inspector Widgeon."

"And he is very angry with me, I suppose, because I returned from South America."

"No, he isn't a bit angry, Denis. The fact of the matter is, he knows just why you came back to England, and why you broke into Mr. Desboro's house. So there you are!"

Denis Sherbroke stared in consternation and amazement.

"How the deuce did Mr. Blake find out?" he asked.

"He tumbled to it," Tinker replied. "The guv'nor was led to believe, in the first place, that your father was bein blackmailed. So he called at his offices in the City, and Mr. Sherbroke admitted he was in the power of a Mr. Charles Desboro, of Ponter Street, who had in his possession certain documents which must have been stolen by somebody at a village up-country in Uruguay. Your father told the guv'nor he had paid fifty thousand pounds to Desboro, and had promised to pay another fifty thousand at the end of a month, when the documents would be given to him."

"So Mr. Desboro has already had fifty thousand pounds from my father, Tinker?"

"Yes, a week or so ago. That is what the guv'nor discovered, and afterwards, when he learned about the finger-prints from Inspector Widgeon, and remembered you have been in Uruguay, he suspected you had tumbled to the game out there, and come back to try to get the documents from the blackmailer, for your father's sake."

"So I did. Its all true. That's why I broke into Charles Desboro's house, and I would have broken in again to-night if I hadn't been caught."

"You've been a darned fool, to put it bluntly," said Tinker. "You ought to have come straight to the guv'nor with your story, and got him to help you. You know what those documents related to, I suppose?"

"I don't," Denis declared. "I haven't the least idea. It is a mystery to me. You know, don't you?"

"Your father told Mr. Blake," Tinker answered evasively. "But it is a private and confidential matter, and the guv'nor keeps such things pretty much to himself. I can tell you one thing, though. It is nothing to your father's discredit—nothing he need be ashamed of."

"I have been sure of that from the first, Tinker, By the way, does my father know I am back in London, and what I have been doing?"

"No, he believes you are still out in Uruguay. Mr. Blake thought he had better not to let him know. He has been working on the case. He couldn't arrest Charles Desboro, as he had no proof against him, so he has had me set a watch on the house. And I got into a nasty scrape myself to-night, not long before you were——"

Tinker paused abrumptly.

"Good heavens, look!" he gasped.

The door had just been opened, and Mack Hewitt and Croxted had entered the restaurant, with Gavin Carey at their heels.

They saw the two lads at once, and for a moment they stared at them in dumb stupefaction.

"I'm blowed if there isn't young Sherbroke!" cried Hewitt. "How the blazes did he escape from the vessel?"

Tinker and Denis were on their feet in a trice, and turning to the rear of the room, they knocked down the Chinese waiter in their haste—flung open a door—ran through a kitchen where a woman was cooking—and ran out to a yard.

With a shrill clamour ringing in their ears, they scrambled over a low wall, and dropped into an alley; raced along that, and emerged from it in a quiet street.

They were hotly pursued. They could hear Hewitt and the other crooks shouting with rage. But by rapid sprinting, and dodging round corner after corner, they gained steadily on their pursuers.

The blind course they held to brought them at length to Dock Street, and then, the hue and cry having faded behind them, they whipped across Royal Mint Street, and walked calmly up Aldgate East Station.

"We left without paying our bill," said Denis, with a grim smile.

"No fear!" Tinker reufully replied. "I hadn't any loose silver, so I put a ten-shilling note on the table, and I forgot to pick it up when we bolted. I've half a mind to go back for the change."

Seeing no cab in the vicinity, they went on towards the City, and found a taxi in Leadenhall Street. They got into it after Tinker had given instructions to the chauffeur, who drove along Cornhill, and down Queen Victoria Street.

Denis was uneasy.

"Where are we going?' he inquired.

Tinker hesitated.

"To my place," he answered.

"This isn't the way to Baker Street."

"Not the nearest, I know. I told the man to drive rather a long way round, so we would have plenty of time to talk."

"Well, you can drop me before we get to Baker Street, and I will take another cab to my lodgings."

"Where are they, Denis? Where have you been living?"

"I had rather not tell you, if you don't mind."

Tinker did not press the point. He wasn't going to let the youth give him the slip—not if he could help it.

He spoke of his unpleasant experience in Charles Desboro's house, and of the pursuit of the blue taxi in the Wolseley car.

And then, after a little urging, Denis told the whole story of his amazing adventures out in Uruguay; speaking first of his life on the estancia of San Pablo, and then of his discovery of the men Hewitt and Carey in the mission-chapel at the village of San Jacinto, of what they had done there and in the padre's house, of his subsequent narrow escapes from death, of the means by which he had got a passage to England on the steamer Trinidad, and of his arrival at Euston Station with the men, where he had overheard the address in Ponter Street they gave to the cab-driver.

"I took a big risk, Tinker," he continued. "I had promised I would never come back, and I knew what it would mean if I was arrested—a couple of years in prison. If I were to be arrested before I could do anything, I mean. But there was another way of looking at it. Fate had played me a strange trick up in that Uruguayan village, and given me a chance such as I couldn't have hoped to get in a thousand years.

"A chance of redeeming what I had lost in the past by mad follies. It was that that lured me back to England. I believed that if I could steal the packet of letters, and the page cut out of the church register, from the blackmailer, and thus save by father from being forced to pay a huge sum of money, he would readily forgive me, and would use his influence to have that old charge against me withdrawn. And I had another motive—a girl I love. She had faith in me before and after my disgrace, and the thought of her kept me straight while I was out in Uruguay. And now that I've returned——"

Denis paused for a moment, showing emotion.

"Do you blame me for shadowing Hewitt and Carey to England?" he went on. "If you had been in my place, Tinker, wouldn't you have done the same thing? Wouldn't you?"

Tinker nodded.

"I jolly well would," he declared. "I'd have jumped at the chance, as you did. No, I don't blame you, old chap. You've been a silly ass, though. You should have come to the governer, and told him all you have told me, and got his advice and his help. He wouldn't have had you arrested. You needn't have been afraid of that."

"I wasn't," said Denis. "It was for another reason I din't got to Mr. Blake I was sure he would have taken the matter in hand, and I wanted to recover the documents on my own, without any help from anybody, so all the credit would be mine, and my father would be the more willing to forgive me. And his forgiveness will put me right with the police and with the girl I've spoken of."

"Well, I don't suppose you mean to work on your own now, after what has happened to-night?" Tinker replied.

"Of course I do," Denis said stubbornly. "I'll stick to it, and when I have got the documents I'll bring them to Mr. Blake, and let him to the rest."

"It won't be a bit of use, old chap. Apart from the risk of trying to break into Charles Desboro's house a third time, the documents aren't there."

"They aren't? How do you know?"

"It's my govenor's opinion. Denis. He is sure Mr. Desboro isn't the real blackmailer. He believes there is somebody higher up, and that person has the letters, and the page of the register."

"Who is the person, Tinker?"

"That's what the gov'nor has been trying to find out. He hasn't even a suspicion as yet."

"Then he had better leave it to me. I'll find out who the person is, and I'll get the documents."

Tinker was irritated.

"Can't you see you are tallking nonsense?" he said, in a sharp tone.

"I'm going to get the documents myself," Denis vowed. I'll show you what I can do. I'm not goint to let you or Mr. Blake spoil my chance."

There was a short interval of silence. Tinker lit a cigarette, and Denis sat gazing from a window.

The taxi had travelled by way of the Strand and Piccadily and Berkeley Street, and it had now passed the grounds of Devonshire House, and was skirting the east side of Berkeley Square.

"It's a pity you're so darned obstinate," Tinker remarked. "At all events, you must come home with me and have a talk with the guv'nor."

"I had rather not," Denis quietly answer, "I don't want to talk to Mr. Blake."

"He won't eat you, old chap. He'll only give you some good advice."

"I'll think about it, Tinker. Perhaps I had better come."

Denis had hardly more than uttered the words when he sprang quickly to his feet, and as quickly he threw open the door on the right, stepped to the footboard, and leapt from it backwards.

The cab was moving rapidly, and it had gone, some yards and as about to swerve towards the bottom of Davies Street before Tinker could stop it.

He jumped out to the right, and, bidding the chauffeur wait for him, he hurried to the rear of the cab.

He saw Denis Sherbroke running beyond him to the right, saw him whip round the upper corner of Bruton Street, and raced after him as fast as he could.

But when he reached the corner, in the brief space of a few seconds, there was no sign of the youth in all the length of the street, much to his surprise.

"That's very queer!" he muttered. "What the deuce has become of the fellow? I was close behind him. He couldn't have got more than a third of the way to Bond Street, at the most!"

Tinker walked slowly along the north side of Bruton Street, perring down every area, and into every portico, until he was within a short stretch of Bond Street.

Then he crossed over and looked into all the areas and doorways on the south side of Bruton Street as he retraced his steps to Berkeley Square.

"Confound the fellow!' he said to himself, as he stopped on the corner to glance behind him. "He tricked me neatly. He must have got into one of those empty dwellings by a basement windown. Well, I be sorry one of these days he gave me the slip. He's a darned plucky chap, though. I must give him credit for that."

Tinker returned to the waiting cab, and without gratifying the chauffeur's curiosity, he drove home to Baker Street.

It was less than an hour past midnight—events had moved in rapid sequence—and Sexton Blake had not gone to bed yet. He was lounging in a big chair by the fire, smoking a pipe, when the lad entered the room.

"What have you been doing?" he draled, as he rose. "You look as if you had been walloing in a dustheap."

"I've been wallowing in adventure," Tinker declared. "My word, there's a lot happened since I went back to Ponter Street, guv'nor!"

He related the whole story, from begining to end, and when he had finished Blake shook his head gravely and narrowed his eyes.

"It was keen, shrewd work," he said. "You did uncommonly well. But what a pity those men discovered you and Denis Sherbroke in Black Dave's restaurant."

"I know it is," Tinker assented.

"Yes, it is unfortunate," Blake continued. "The men will go to Charles Desboro to-night with their tale, and Desboro will suspect—believe, in fact—that it was you who rescued Denis from the skipper of the vessel, and that I have had you watching his house."

"It will give him a fright, won't it, guv'nor?"

"Exactly. And I didn't want him to be frightened, my boy. Desboro will make some prompt move, I dare say, to bring matters to a head. Very likely he will go to Julian Sherbroke, accuse him of opening his lips to me, and demand the other fifty thousand pounds. As for young Denis, his courage and zeal, his dogged determination to get the documents without help have blinded his discretion. So you believe he crept into some empty house in Bruton Street, eh? I have just been thinking that——"

Blake did not finish the sentence, He broke off, and a vague look of conjecture crept into his eyes.

"No, there is no telling what Charles Desboro will do," he said, "now that he will be led to suspect me. You must keep a stricter watch on him than before, Tinker, no matter what the risk. I may take a hand in the game myself," he added, "but it won't be to-morrow night. I have an appointment at my club, and afterwards I am going on to Lord Maltraver's reception."

CHAPTER 11.

ON the following evening Sexton Blake dined at his club in Pall Mall with his old friend, Sir Roger Murchison, the famous traveller and explorer, and when he left there at nine o'clock, immaculately attired in evening dress, he strolled round to St. James's Square, where innumerable private cars were parked.

Accompanied by other persons, he trod on a red carpet, beneath an awning, and was ushered by a servant into Maltraver House, a large and imposing dwelling which was the town residence of Lord Maltraver and his wife.

They were staunch Tories, and they were giving a reception to-night in honour of the new

Conservative Government, of which Lord Maltraver was a member.

Several hundreds of guests were present, all from pre-eminent walks of life, not one but had some claim to distinction.

Having received a hearty welcome from his host and hostess, Blake strolled here and there, stopping to talk to little groups of friends of his, now cracking a joke with one of his Majesty's judges, and now discussing the merits of vintage portwith a bibulousbishop.

A length he ascended the stairs, and as he was going along the hall, on his way to the ball-room, he paused by the open door of a small smoking-lounge which was empty except for one person.

Standing by the fireplace, with a cigar in his mouth, and his hands in his pockets, was Mr. Julian Sherbroke.

He beckoned to the detective, and Blake, after throwing a glance to right and left, entered the room.

"How are you, Sherbroke?' he said. "You have fled from the crush—eh?"

"Yes, I've been talking till I'm hoarse," the millionaire replied. "I was glad to find a quiet spot."

"You don't look very well."

"I know I don't And I'm not feeling well, either. What have you been doing? Any news?"

"No, not yet. I thought I might have heard from you, Sherbroke."

"I had nothing to write about, for nothing has happened. Matters are at a standstill."

There was a brief silence. The faint frou-frou of silken skirts came from the hall—drew nearer to the door—and ceased. Blake and his companion had not heard the rustling noise.

"I've been worried since the day you called at my office." continued Julian Sherbroke, in a peevish tone. "I wish I hadn't told you the story, and let you help me. I was a fool to break my promise to that scoundrel Desboro."

"Oh, no, you were not!" Blake declared. "No harm has been done. On the contrary, it was fortunate you did tell me."

"What was the use? The fellow is too clever to let himself be caught in your clutches. You can't trip him up. At all events, I want you to drop the affair, and leave it entirely to me."

"I have no intention of dropping it, be assured."

"I insist on it. Blake. I won't let you take any steps whatever. I am afraid. I would do anythign to avoid exposure. Money is no object to me. I hate the idea of being blackmailed, naturally; but when the time-limit has expired I shall pay Charles Desboro another fifty thousand pounds, after he has given me the documents, and that will be the end of the matter."

"The matter is not going to end in that way," Blake replied. "It is my duty to prevent you from being blackmailed, and I an going to see you are not. You will hear from Charles Desboro in a day or so, I imagine. He will probably call on you, or write to you, and if he does either you must at once communicate with me."

"No, I will not," Julian Sherbroke said doggedly. "I refuse. It would be a different matter if you could get the documents from the scoundrel, but as there isn't a chance of that——"

Blake raised a warning finger as he heard footsteps coming up the stairs. A moment later several gentlement entered the smoking-lounge, and, leaving Mr. Sherbroke with them, Blake went out.

He passed on to the ball-room and stood in the doorway, listening to the strains of the orchestra, and absnet-mindedly watching the dancers swinging to and for to the measure of a fox-trot.

Julian Sherbroke's injunction to him had gone in one ear and out of the other.

"I must baffle that fellow Desboro," he said to himself. "He has bled Sherbroke of fifty thousand pounds, and he shan't get another penny from him. I'll spoil his game somehow or other. But I don't see my way clear as yet. It is difficult problem."

Betwen ten and eleven o'clock that night a handsome Packard car, driven by a chauffeur in a private livery, turned from Knightsbridge into Sloane Street, glided down that thoroughfare for some distance, and pulled up at the edge of the pavement.

A lady stepped out of it—a tall and beautiful woman of less than forty, with dark hair, lustrous black eyes, and a complexion that was like ivory faintly tinged with olive.

She wore an evening-frock made by the most expensive costumeier in the Rue de la Paix, and a string of superb diamonds glittered on her neck.

But the splendour of her gown, and the flaming fire of her jewels, were hidden by a grey cloak which swathed her graceful figure from head to foot.

The fur collar of it was muffled about her throat and chin, leaving only her eyes and the tip of her nose visible.

"You will wait here, James," she said to the chauffeur. "I don't want you to drive any farther because the friend I am going to visit is seriously ill, and must be kept very quiet."

With that the lady hurried away. She disappeared around the corner of Ponter Street, and when she had walked for a short distance she stopped in front of a dwelling, entered the portico, and rang the bell.

The door was opened shortly by the butler, and before he could prevent her the lady had brushed by him into the hall.

Her features were still hidden by the fur collar, and she raised it a little higher as she spoke.

"Is Mr. Desboro at home?" she asked.

"Yes, madam, my master is at home," the butler replied, in a stiff tone, "but I doubt if he will——"

"I wish to see him, and at once," the lady interrupted, an imperious ring in her voice. "Don't keep me waiting."

"If you will give me your card, madam, or your name, I will——"

"I won't give you either, my good man. You need not announce me. I know where to find your master. Let me pass, please!"

The butler, who had been barring the way, hesitated for a moment; and then, as a pair of dark eyes flashed angrily at him, he reluctantly stood to one side.

And the lady, crossing the hall to the left, opened a door, stepped into the library, and closed the door behind her.

Charles Desboro rose from a chair by the fire, turned round, and stared in amazement.

The lady moved towards him, and lowered the collar of her cloak.

"It is I, Charles, she said quietly.

Charles Desboro gazed at her in anger and surprise.

"Good heavens!" he exclaimed. "You Are you mad, Highness? What possessed you to come here, to my house?"

"I had to come," the lady answered. "It was necessary. I have news for you. Most alarming news."

"What is it? Tell me quickly!"

"Be patient, Charles I have come straight from the reception at Maltraver House in my car. I left it in Sloane Street. Sexton Blake was at the reception, and so was Julian Sherbroke. I saw Mr. Sherbroke go into an empty smoking-room, and shortly afterwards I saw the detective go in. I crept close to the door and listened, and heard them talking of you."

"Of—of me, Highness?"

"Yes, of you, I did not hear all of the conversation. I was disturbed by some gentlemen coming upstairs, and had to steal away. But I heard quite enought."

"Go on!" Charles Desboro said hoarsley. "What did you hear, Highness? What did you learn?"

"I learned this, Charles," the lady replied, a vicious glitter in her eyes. "Julian Sherbroke has broken his promise! he has told everything to Sexton Blake, and Sexton Blake is on your track!"

CHAPTER 12.

SEXTON BLAKE left Maltraver House towards twelve o'clock. As soon as he got home he changed his clothes, and he was pottering about the consulting-room, in his old, shabby smoking-jacket and shabby slippers, trying to decide which of his collection of rare tobaccos would be best for breaking in a new and ornate pipe of German meershaum, when Tinker came striding in with flushed cheeks and sparkling eyes.

Jerkin off his faded bowler, he flung it into a corner, and dabbed with a handkerchief at the grease-paint on his face.

Blake read the signs. He knew something had excited his young assistant.

"Be careful!" he bade. "You barely missed that Chinese porcelain jar, which is worth a couple of hundred pounds. What's the matter with you? Are you rehearsing your part of an East End hooligan?"

"Ask me another!" Tinker replied. "I'm going to be a reputable member of Society again. No more rags and tags for me!"

Blake was slightly puzzled.

"Am I to understand that Charles Desboro has disappeared?" he inquired.

"No fear, guv'nor! He is still hanging out in Ponter Street. I don't think he will need any more watching, though."

"What on earth are you talking about, my boy?"

"The gentleman has had a visitor to-night. That's what. The proud and haughty Lady Clara Vere de Vere. In other words——"

Tinker paused for an instant.

"In other words guv'nor," he continued, in a serious tone, "the beautiful Duchess of Windermere has called on Mr. Charles Desboro!"

Blake gave a quick start, and nearly dropped the meershaum pipe he had taken from the rack.

"Impossible!" he ejaculated. "Incredible!"

"The Duchessof Windermere!" Tinker repeated. "It wasnt anybody else! You can take it from me I'm right!"

"Then she must be the real blackmailer, my lad!"

"Sure thing, guv'nor! She must be!"

Blake nodded. He was not so sceptical now, for his mind had swiftly recalled what he knew and had heard concerning the lady.

Hermione Duchess of Windermere! The beautiful aristocrat, queen of Mayfair, who was at the top of the social ladder!

There was a strain of Spanish blood in her veins. Her mother, belonging to a Madrid family of ancient lineage, had married an English baronet.

They had settled in England, and ten years ago their lovely daughter Hermione had married the Duke of Windermere.

He was seventy at the time, more than double his wife's age, and three years ago he had died.

He had left only a moderate fortune to his widow, for his estate had been sadly reduced by high taxation, and the death duties demanded by the Crown had made a further hole in it.

"It staggers you, guv'nor' doesn't it?" said Tinker, after a pause.

"It did at first," Blake assented. "It doesn't seem so incredible now. The Duke of Windermere was a comparatively poor man. It has been common talk for several years that theDuchesshas been living far beyond her means. People wondered how she contrived to keep up such extravagant state at Windermere House, in Grosvenor Square.

"And there is another point to be considered, my boy, in view of the amazing discovery you say you have made. The old duke was the biggest gossip and scandal-monger of the Victorian and Edwardian reigns. He sought for scandal. He did not wait for it to come to him. But he was too discreet to talk of all he leanred. He kept most of his secrets for posterity, and put them down in writing. To my certain knowledge he left a volume of memoirs in manuscript, which was not to be published until thirty years after his death. And in all likelihood that manuscript fell into the hands of——"

Blake broke off.

"I haven't heard your story yet," he said. "Are you positive there is no mistake?"

"I'm dead sure, guv'nor," Tinker replied. "But I'll leave it to you to judge. I was hiding in an area, over the day, when a tall, slim lady, who was wrapped from her head to her feet in a grey cloak, came along Ponter Street. She stopped in front of Mr. Desboro's house and rang the bell. As soon as the door was opened she walked in, and when she came out, half an hour later, I shadowed her to Sloane Street, where a car driven by a chauffeur in livery was waiting for her.

"I picked up a taxi and followed the car, which went straight to Windermere House. The lady got out, and I saw a gorgeous footman open the door of the house as she was crossing the pavement, and saw him bow to her as she passed in. So there you are!"

Blake nodded again.

"You have stated a clear case," he said. "It was the Duchess of Windermere who called in Poter Street, and the duchess is the society vampire whose existence I suspected from the first. She got possession of the volume of manuscript left by her husband, the memoirs filled with scandalous advantage. She had been dipping into the pages of them, raking up family skeletons, victims with the help of Basil Wicketshaw, alias Charles Desboro, who probably had an acquaintance with her previously.

"What a terrible, atrocious woman! She hounded Eric Milvern to death—and the others I have mentioned. By heavens, what a satisfaction it will be to me to expose her, and bring her to justice with Basil Wicketshaw!"

In Blake's eyes, under the knit brows, was a stern and ruthless glitter. He regarded a blackmailer as the most detestable human being on earth.

"There's no mistake about her being the Duchest of Windermere," said Tinker. "Not a bit of it.

But Charles Desboro has often figured in society in different names, so isn't it possible the lady called on him for some reason other than we suspect?''

Blake shook his head.

''No, it is not,'' he declared. ''Why did she leave her car in Sloane Street? Why didn't she drive all the way to the house in Ponter Street? Because she feared the car night be seen standing there by sombody who knew it by sight. I can readily account for her visit. I was at Maltraver House to-night, Julian Sherbroke was there, and the Duchess of Windermere also was amongst the guests. Mr. Sherbroke was alone in a small smoking-room, and I went in to speak to him. The duchess must have seen the two of us there as she was passing the open door, and she stopped, hiding in the hall by the doorway, to listen to our conversation.

''We talked in ordinary tones, as there was no one else in the room; and Julian Sherbroke mentioned the fact, I remember, that he had told me all about Charles Desboro and the blackmailing game. The listening lady heard that, and probably everything else. And that is why she drove from Maltraver House to see Charles Desboro. She was alarmed. She had no doubt I was on the track of her accomplice. And she must have given Desboro a bad fright and a shock, though his suspicious must have been roused by the circumstances of young Denis Sherbroke's escape from the vessel, of which he must have informed las night or to-day but those men.''

''Well, that settles it, what you've told me,'' said Tinker. ''The duchess certainly listened to you and Mr. Sherbroke talking, and if she is the chief blackmailer—and we can be user she is—she has the documents of the case.

''Of course she has,'' Blake replied. ''She would not have left them in the possession of Charles Desboro, since he had the risky task of conducting the negotiations.''

''What the deuce are we to do, then? What we discovered to-night doesn't help us much. How are we to trip up Mr. Desboro and the lady?''

''That is the problem, my boy. We cant obtain a search-warrant against the Duchess of Windermere. We have nothing to justify such an application. And we can't break into her residence.''

''Well, guv'nor, it looks to me as if Charles Desboro and the lady would get the other fifty thousand pounds from Mr. Julian Sherbroke, and we couldn't arrest them. There is nothing else for it, unless we could get the documents. And if we did get them, by some means or other, what would be the use? Mr. Sherbroke would not bring a charge against Desboro.''

''No, he would not. He is stubborn about that, and there is some excuse for him. He would give his while fortune to save his daughter, Lady Morpeth, from shame and disgrace. I have to do that myself, and I also want to punish this wretched woman and her accomplice. As for the documents, I have been wondering if there is any means of getting at them. It might possibly be done, but it would be at grave risk to you and me, and to——''

Blake paused, a troubled look on his face. While talking he had filled his pipe from one of the tobacco-jars on the cabinet, and he now lit it, and sat down.

''I am going to recall something to your mind, Tinker,' he said. ''Three years ago and more, on the evening before Denis Sherbroke sailed for South America, he asked my permission to call on a girl he was fond of.''

''I remember,'' Tinker replied.

''The girl was a Miss Muriel Treverton,'' Blake went on, ''the dauthter of Harry Treverton, the banker.''

''I remember,'' that, too, guv'nor.''

''And her father lived in Bruton Street.''

''I didn't know that. Or I had forgotten it. Bruton Street? That is where Denis Sherbroke disappeared last night. My word, guv'nor, I sholdn't wonder if he has been living in Mr. Treverton's house! If it is close to the corner of Berkeley Square, and Denis had a latchkey, it would account for——''

''That's enough,'' Blake interrupted. ''We'll drop the subject for the present. I have some instructions for you now. Get up early to-morrow, and go to Ponter Street, and watch Charles Desboro's house I have an idea he may go to Mr. Julian Sherbroke's residence, or to his offices in the City. Should he do either you will promptly telephone to me, and if I am not at home you will leave a message with Mrs. Bardell. In any event, come back early in the evening.

''Thats all, Tinker, And now be off to bed. I want to think.''

Tinker was not a bit inclined to go to bed. He was anxious to know what his master proposed to do. At a second biding he left the room, however; and for a couple of hours Blake sat smoking by the fire, seriously and gravely considering what was in his mind, now rejecting it as too dangerous, and now giving it fresh considration.

"I'll take the risk, if it can be arranged," he said to himself, as he tapped his pipe on his heels and rose. "It is the one and only way."

Tinker was up and gone by nine o'clock the next morning, and Blake was out of bed a few minutes later, and splashing in his cold tub.

He had his breakfast, and read the paper, and wrote a couple of letters. And shortly before eleven o'clock, after giving a message to Mrs. Bardell, bidding her say he would not be absent long should Tinker telephone, he left the house.

He hailed a taxi, and drove to the corner of Bruton Street, where he got out; and then he walked along the north side of Bruton Street, and rang the bell of a stately residence that was very close to Berkely Square.

A servant opened the door to him. He inquired for Mis Terverton, and at the same moment a pretty girl appeared. She had heard the inquiry, and she looked in surprise at the detective.

She did not know who he was, but observing that he was a well-dressed and gentlemanly person, she took him into the library. She was inclined to think she had misunderstood his remark to the servant.

"You asked for Mr. Treverton, didn't you?" she said. "My father is in the South of France."

Blake shook his head.

"I called to have a few words with you," he replied.

"With me? I don't know you."

"Blake is my name, Miss Treverton—Sexton Blake, And I wish to see Denis Sherbroke."

The girl grew very white.

"How—how should I know anything about him?" she stammered.

"You know a great deal about him," said Blake. "He has been living here. Don't deny it, please. It will be useless. But don't be frightened. I only want to talk to the young gentleman."

"Is that all? You are't goint to arrest him?"

"No, I assure you I am not, Miss Treverton. You can believe me. I was a good friend to Denis three years ago, and I am here as his friend now. He has nothing to fear from me."

"I am so glad. You did frighten me at first, when you told me who you where. I was sure——"

The girl paused. She had recovered from her agitation, and the colour had flowed back to her cheeks.

"You are right, Mr. Blake,' she said quietly. "Denis Sherbroke is in the house. He was in trouble, in danger of arrest; and I persuaded him to live here for a time as my cousin, in the absence of my parents. I didn't think there was any harm in it. I knew Denis had returned from South America for a good reason, a creditable reason, and——"

"You know why he came back?" Blake interrupted.

Yes, of course I do. He told me all."

"Well, Miss Treverton, fetch him to me now. Tell him not to be uneasy. I am anxious to help him in his task, and I think he may be able to help me. He learned the night before last that I was——"

Blake broke off abruptly. The door had just been opened, and Denis Sherbroke walked into the room. He gave a slight start as he saw the detective, but he did not show any alarm. He did not even change colour.

"So you have found me, Mr. Blake he said. "I thought it likely you would, after learning from Tinker of my quick disappearance in Bruton Street the other night."

Blake nodded.

"That's right," he answered. "I remembered the young lady living in this street you called on, with my permission, three years ago."

"Well, you might have let me alone," Denis continued. "I have a certain thing to do, and I won't be interfered with.

"Yes, the whole story—all you told him. I don't blame you for coming back to England. You ought to have come straight to me, though."

"You know why I didn't, Mr. Blake. I mean to get the documents from that villain Desboro, and I am going to do it somehow or other. I want to give them to my father with my own hands, and tell him I recovered them for his sake by my own efforts, without any help from the police. It wasn't cricket of you to run me down, even as a friend. You learned of the matter from my father, and cut in between me and Desboro. Won't you drop the game, and let me have my chance?"

"Your chance?" Blake repeated. "Would you be foolhardy enough to try a third time to break into Charles Desboro's house?"

"Yes, I would!" the youth declared.

"If you succeeded—which is imposible—you would not find the documents in Mr. Desboro's desk, or anywhere in the house. They are not in his possession."

"They—they are not? Are you sure, Mr. Blake?"

"He has not got them, my boy. You can believe that."

"Tinker told me the same, sir; but I thought he might be trying to deceive me, so I wouldn't make another attempt."

"No, he told you the truth. Charles Desboro is merely an agent, so the speak, of the real blackmailer. And the documents are in the possession of that person."

There was a look of consternation on Denis Sherbroke's face. He had doubted Tinker, but he could not disbelieve Sexton Blake.

"Do you know who the real blackmailer is?" he asked.

"I have my suspicious," Blake replied.

"Tell me the name of the person, and where he lives, and give me a week to get the documents. Will you?"

"No, I won't do that. You have been playing a fool's game, against hopeless odds, and there must be no more of it. Come, my boy, be sensible. Let us work together. You need my assistance—you can accomplish nothing without it—and I think you can help me. Nothing is more difficult than to get the better of a blackmailer, but——"

"That is just what I told Denis, Mr. Blake!" the girl broke in. "I have been trying to persuade him to stop risking his life, and go to you. But he wouldn't listen to me. He is very obstinate. Perhaps you can persuade him."

"I dare say I can," Blake answered. "I will have a confidential little talk with him, if you don't mind."

Muriel Treverton took the hint. She left the room, and Denis sat down in a chair by the fire.

There's a girl in a million for you. Mr. Blake," he said, a note of emotion in his voice. "She had faith in me before I went wrong, and she has been loyal and faithful to me ever since. The truest kind of love—that's what it is. I knew I could depend on Muriel to give me a helping hand, and she did. She lent me money, and sheltered me in her father's house, and encouraged me to hope that everything would come right some day."

Blake nodded absently.

"Yes, she is a noble girl, is Miss Treverton," he said, "and for her sake you must be reasonable. I have a certain plan in mind, and my object in coming here this morning was to talk to you about it. I should not care to take it on myself, so you must——"

"If there is anything to be done I will do it on my own," Denis sullenly interrupted.

"Have patience," bade Blake. "If the plan succeeds the credit will be yours, not mine. I won't tell you now what it is. I will only ask you a couple of questions. If you had a chance of getting those documents—a chance of a most dangerous nature—would you take it?"

"Indeed I would!" Denis exclaimed. "I shouldn't hesitate for a moment, no matter what the risk. You try me, sir!"

"I am going to," Blake assented, "If I see the way clear. And now tell me if you are acquantied with the Duchess of Windermere? I have an idea you are."

"I often met the duchess in Society, in the first year after I came down from Oxford."

"Do you think she would know who you were if she were to see you now, without your false moustache?"

"Yes, I dare say she would recognise me, I haven't changed much. But what has the Duchess of Windermere got to do with——"

"You will know later," said Blake. "I want you to come home with me now. I will explain everything to you at luncheon. Tell Miss Treverton you are going to my place, and will spend the night there."

The youth went off at once, and Blake stood by the fire smoking a cigarette, a grave expression on his face.

It was indeed a dangerous and daring plan he had conceived, solely on the strength of Shrewd deductions. If it were to succeed, well and good. If it should fail the consequences would be disastrous, and in more ways than one.

CHAPTER 13

SHORTLY after eleven o'clock that night, when the Duchess of Windermere came home in her car from a theatre, a little group of men were standing in shadow over by the railings of the Grosvenor Square Gardens—three plain-clothes detectives from Scotland Yard, and Sexton Blake and Inspector Widgeon, the latter with a search-warrant in his pocket.

And at the back of Windermere House, where was a large garden, Denis Sherbroke way lying flat on a balcony that projected from the first floor of the residence.

To one side of him was a French window, which was not locked, and the window opened from one of the suite of prive apartments occupied by the duchess.

"I'm a darned fool to be here," Inspector Widgeon said to Blake, as he saw the lady enter the house, "and you are a bigger one. I never heard of such a mad-cap enterprise."

"It is worth the risk, isn't it?" Blake replied.

"Yes, if it comes off. But if things go wrong you know what will happen."

"I do, my dear fellow. In all likelihood young Sherbroke and I will appear in the dock at Bow Street to-morrow."

"You will, Blake, mark my words. And for young Sherbroke it will be a short step from Bow Street to Brixton. As for you, I will not oppose your application for bail."

"Thanks, Widgeon. Very kind of you. But don't count your chicken before they are hatched."

The inspector remarked that his chickens were as good as hatched, or something to that effect and Blake bent his gaze on the dwelling opposite.

He was in keen suspense. Very soon he would know the result of his plan.

The Duches of Windermere was in the hall, hesitating by the open door of the dining-room. Cold supper was laid there for her, but she was not hungry. She had dined at the Corona before going to the theatre.

She had the butler open a half-bottle of champagne, and, having drunk a small glass of the wine, she went upstairs to her luxuriously furnished sitting-room, where soft-shaded lamps were burning, and a fire was crackling in the grate.

Her maid was waiting for her, and when she had helped her off with her wraps, and carried them in the adjoining boudoir and returned her mistress sent her away, saying she would not need her again to-night.

Denis Sherbroke, out on the balcony, was trembling with excitement, his eyes fixed on Hermione, the beautiful Duches of Windermere, who was standing pensively in the rosy glow of the lamps.

She took a gold-tipped cigarette from a case, lit it, and chose a French novel from a bookshelf; and then, as she was about to sit down by the fire, she heard a rustling, scraping noise.

She saw a shadow outside the French window, and the next instant it was pushed open and there darted into the room a youth in dusty, shabby clothes, and a ragged cap. There was a wild in his eyes, and he was pale with fright.

"I—I'm trouble!" he panted. "You're got to help me!"

The duchess gazed at the shabby figure in anger and scorn.

"Stand perfectly still!" she bade. "And don't tell me lies! You are a thief! I am going to call my servants, and have them——"

She stopped abruptly, catching her breath, and stared open-mouthed.

"You-you are Denis Sherbroke!" she gasped. The youth nodded.

"I thought you knew me at first," he said, speaking in an agitated voice.

"You here!" exclaimed the duchess, "Julian Sherbroke's son! You have dare to break into my house!"

Denis moved a little nearer to her, and held out his arms appealingly.

"Please help me!" he begged, shaking like a leaf. "Dont's let me be caught! I'll tell you the truth! I came here to-night to search for those papers—you know what I mean—and Sexton Blake and the police were outside, over by the garden ralings. They saw me, and knew who I was! They chased me round the corner, and I climbed the wall, and dropped into your garden, and got up to the balcony by a tree. They're after me! They want me for that old charge. Do hide me somewhere! Don't let me be arrested!"

The duchess was alarmed.

"What papers are you talking about?" she asked. "I don't understand!"

"Oh, yes, you do! I've been spying on Mr. Charles Desboro, as you know. You called on him last night, and——"

"So that is why you came to my house to-night! You silly fool! I'm not afraid of you! I shall hand you over to the police!"

"No, duches, you daren't! I haven't told you yet why they were outside with Mr. Blake! They are after you, too! I heard them talking! They have a search-warrant!"

"A search-warrant! I don't believe it!"

"It's the truth, duchess! They have found out you have the papers!"

"What can have led them to suspect that?"

"I don't know, unless they learned from Mr. Desboro! I have an idea the has been arrested! And now show me where to hide, duches! Tell the police you haven't seen me! I think they are ringing the bell!"

The Duches of Windermere did not answer. She was terrified. Her brain was fairly reeling. Charles Desboro must have betrayed her, she thought.

Ignoring the presence of Denis Sherbroke, she did exactly what he had hoped she would do.

Snatching a steel paper-knife from a table, she hasted to a Chesterfield couch, ripped the convering of it open with deep and rapid slashes, thrust her had in, and drww out a bulky envelope that was sealed.

Meaning to burn it, she hurried towards the fireplace; but before she could reach it Denis siezed her by the arm, swung her round, and tore the envelope from her.

"That's mine!" he declared. "That's what I came for!"

The infuriated woman, realising she had been tricked, at once flung herself at the youth, raving in a passion.

For a fee seconds they struggled, swaying to and fro; and at length, giving Denis' wrist a twist, the duchess jerked the envelope from him, and tossed it on to the blazing fire.

She had no more than done so when Denis broke her hold of him and gave her a push that sent her reeling to the couch.

Then he sprang to the fireplace, plucked the scorched envelope from the flames, darted to the door, and was gone.

He sped along the passage, and went tearing down the stairs to the hall, aimed a blow at a servant who tried to stop him, reached the frot door, and threw it open.

"I've got the documents, Mr. Blake!" he shouted, flourishing the envelope. "I've got them!"

Sexton Blake and Inspector Widgeon ran across from the gardens, followed by the three plain-clothes men; and the whole party, accommpanied by Denis, entered the house, brushed by a little group of bewildered and agitated servants, dashed up the stair, and hurried into the sitting-room.

They were just too late. The Duchess of Windermere was lying on the rent couch, in a limp attitude, a greenish froth oozing from her lips.

There was a glassy stare in her sightless eyes, and in one hand was clenched a tiny empty phial of blue glass.

Blake felt her pulse.

"She is dead!" he exclaimed. "She has taken poison!"

"Clear proof of her guilt,' said the inspector, as he sniffed at the phial.

"Her possession of the documents would have been sufficient to prove that, Widgeon."

"Well, she has cheated the law. And now for Charles Desboro, eh?"

"Yes, at once. We shall learn from Tinker whether or not he is at home."

Leaving one of the plain-clothes men behind, the rest of the party, with Denis Sherbroke, hastened from the house.

They picked up a taxi in Grosvenor Square, drove to Ponter Street, and stopped within fifty yards of Charles Desboro's residence; and a moment later, as they were about to get out, Tinker appeared.

"You have missed the gentleman, guv'nor," he said. "Mr. Desboro has been gone for at least twenty minutes. He went off in a cab, and I heard him tell the chauffeur to take him to Lord Morpeth's house in Curson Street."

Lord Morpeth's house!" Blake repeated in consternation. "I know why he has gone there, I believe! We must go after him as quickly as we can! Get in, Tinker," he added. "You can come with us."

CHAPTER 14.

THAT night, as it happened, Mr Julian Sherbroke had dined at his son-in-law's residence in Curzon Street. After dinner the little party of three—Mr. Sherbroke, and Lord Morpeth and his wife—had retired to the library; and they were sitting there, at a game of cards, when there was a rap at the door.

It was opened at once, and a tall, handsome gentleman in evening-dress, with a blond moustache, walked into the room, and closed the door behind him.

"I must apologise for this intrusion, my lord," he said calmly, "and for persuading your servant that it was not necessary to announce me. Desboro is my name—Charles Desboro. I called to see your lordship, but as Mr. Sherbroke is here, and my business relates more to him than to you, I will address myself to him, and I trust you will not interfere."

Lord Morpeth and Julian Sherbroke were on their feet, the latter obviously agitated.

"You can guess what I want with you, Mr. Sherbroke," said Charles Desboro, in an icy tone. "You have broken your promise. You told Sexton Blake everything, and put him on my track. You have played me false, and you must pay for it. It is your habit to always carry a cheque-book, I believe. Have you one with you now?"

"Yes, I have," Julian Sherbroke huskily assented.

"Very well," Charles Desboro continued. "You will come with me to my house now, and then give you the documents you are so anxious to have, and you will give me a cheque for one hundred thousand pounds drawn to bearer."

"I—I am willing to do that, if you will wait until to-morrow."

"No, it must be to-night at once. If you refuse I will reveal something very unpleasant to Lord Morpeth and his wife."

Julian Sherbroke hesitated.

"I will go with this gentleman, Morpeth, if you will excuse me," he said. "It is a matter of private business, and——"

"Private business, be hanged!" Lord Morpeth angrily interrupted. "Do you suppose I am blind? A hundred thousand pounds for certain documents! You are being blackmailed, I am sure! Let this impudent fellow say here what he has to say! You are not going with him!"

"I must, Morpeth. Really I must!"

"You will not! I shan't let you! Don't be coward! Don't be frightened by this scoundrel's threat! Let him reveal his secret, whatever it is! I'll wring it from him if you won't!"

"No, no, Morpeth! Leave the affair to me, I beg of you! It is not anything disgraceful, but I would much rather pay than——"

"You shan't pay a penny, Sherbroke! I will see that you don't!"

Charles Desboro shrugged his shoulders. "It will be much better if you do not interfere, my lord," he said suavely. "Mr. Sherbroke wishes to pay, and you can't dissuade him."

"Hold your tongue, sir!" bade Lord Morpeth, "Mr. Sherbroke will listen to me, not to you!"

There was a brief, tense silence, while Lady Morpeth gazed in apprehension at her father. Julian Sherbroke's face was a study of conflicting emotions. What should he do? He felt that he exposure of the secret was inevitable, whether or not he should yield to the extortionate demand, and of a sudden his courage rose.

"I have already paid you fifty thousand pounds, you cur, and I will pay you nothing more!" he declared. "Now do your worst!"

The challenge was flung in Charles Desboro's teeth. He was beaten. He knew it. Only one thing was left to him, and that was revenge.

But he kept his fury under control, and turned to Lord Morpeth.

"Your lordship will kindly bear in mind that I have been foreed to he disclosure I an going to make to you," he said quietly. "It will be a shock to you. Many years ago, when Mr. Sherbroke was out in Uruguay, he married the nice of a Spanish padre, who lived at the village of San Jacinto. The girl's name was Mercedes, and her mother had married Pedro Valdez, a notorious bandit, and a half-breed of low caste, who has hanged for robbery and murder.

"Mr. Sherbroke's wife died, leaving him with a child. He returned to England, kept his Uruguayan marriage a secret, and sent for his child. He had her brought up and educated at a convent school in France, as his ward; and subsequently he brought her to his home in London, in the name of Evelyn Kerr.

"And you, my lord, ignorant of the girl's parentage, and of the sordid history of her grandparents, married her in the belief that she was——"

An oath burst from Lord Morpeth's lips, and clenching his fists, he dealt the blackmailer a smashing blow that Knocked him down. The man scrambled to his feet, and was promptly knocked down again by Julian Sherbroke.

Once more he got up, cursing with rage; and now, as both men rushed at him, he whipped a pistol from his pocket and held them at bay. Slowly he backed to a French window, flung it open, darted out to the garden at one side of the house—and as quickly disappeared in the darkness.

"Let the follow go," said Julian Sherbroke, "We couldn't catch him if we tried."

Lord Morpeth nodded, and turned to his distressed and weeping wife. His face was very tender.

"Don't cry, Evelyn!" he bade. "It's quite all right! You have nothing to worry about, my dear! Love is stronger than pride. Have you no faith in mine?"

He had hardly spoken when the door was opened, and Sexton Blake and Inspetor Widgeon entered the room, followed by Tinker and the two plain-clothes men. Blake glanced around him.

"Where is Charles Desboro?" he asked. "He has been here, hasn't he?"

"Here and gone," replied Lord Morpeth.

Widgeon and his men at once hastened in pursuit, through the window to the garden.

Lord Morpeth related to the detective all that had occured, and when he had finished he slipped his arm around his wife's waist, and kissed her.

"The disclosure doesn't make a bit of difference to me, Blake," he said. "I have a reputation for stiff-necked pride, I know. But I married my wife for love, and I don't care a hang for her family history. I wish her father had come to me at the first. It would have saved him fifty thousand pounds, and a lot of worry.

"I wouldn't like to go deep into my own family history," he added, with a smile. "I believe one of my ancestors was killed in a common brawl hundreds of years ago, and one fled abroad after stabbing a friend in a quarrel, and another was hanged for persistently killing the king's deer on Exmoor in the reign of Henry the Eighth."

Lord Morpeth paused. "Have you been on the track of that rascal Desboro?" he inquired.

"Yes, for some time," Blake answered. "But there was somebody higher up. You will be astounded to hear that the real blackmailer was the Duches of Windermere. So I learned last night. I went to her house to-night with the police, to arrest her, and we found her lying dead on a couch in her sitting-room. She had taken poison."

The beautiful Duches of Windermere! Lord Morpeth and his wife gazed at each other incredulously.

It was a staggering surprise to Julian Sherbroke also, and now he had another surprise; for Denis Sherbroke, who had been waiting in the hall, made a dramatic entrance into the room.

"This will explain why I broke my promise, and came back to England," he said, as he gave his father a bulky envelope, which was scorched at the edges. "It contains the stolen packet of letters which you wrote to your first wife when you were in Uruguay, and the page which was cut from the register in the mission chapel at San Jacinto."

It was Sexton Blake who told the story to the bewildered man—the whole story from beginning to end, including an account of the adroit and dangerous means by which the youth had induced the Duchess of Windermere to reveal the hiding-place of the documents.

"You have reason to be proud of Denis," he continued. "For your sake, Sherbroke, he risked his freedom and his life. It is greatly to his credit that he succeeded, and I shall make it my business to see that the old charge which has been hanging over him is withdrawn."

Julian Sherbroke clasped his son's hand.

"I am more than proud of you, my boy,' he said. "We will try to forget the past. You will come home with me to-night, Denis, and start life afresh. That you have recovered these documents means everthing to me. The secret which I did wrong to conceal will no longer haunt me."

Footstep were heard in the garden, and Inspector widgeon and The Scotland Yard men came into the room. They had failed. They had not discovered any trace of Charles Desboro.

Blake shrugged his shoulders. "It is just as I expected," he said. "We will hurry along to Ponter Street now, but I am quite sure we shall not find the scoundrel there. And I very much fear we won't find him at all."

There is not much more to be told. The tragic death of the Duches of Windermere, and the fact that she had been a society blackmailer, caused a great sensation.

Basil Wicketshaw, alias Charles Desboro, eluded errest. It was learned that he had succeeded in escaping abroad, and the men who had been his accomplices had probably gone with him, for the search made for them in London was of no avail.

As for Denis Sherbroke, he had the reward his courage and daring deserved; and when he was married to Muriel Treverton, shortly after Christmas, Sexton Blake and Tinker were honoured guests at the wedding.

THE END.

First Published in the Sexton Blake Library in 1927

THE CRIME IN THE WOOD

A Tale of a Curious Murder and of a Sinister and Complex Mystery that was Solved by SEXTON BLAKE and His Young Assistant, TINKER

THE PROLOGUE.

HughClontarf'sVisitor—The Teviot Memoirs—Sir Ralph Athelstan's Demand—A Firm Refusal–An Attempt at Blackmail—Baffled—The Last Word.

HUGH MALLISE CLONTARF, not to mention several other names he was entitled to use, was in somewhat of a dilemma.

The look of perplexity and irritation on his face deepened to a frown, and, pushing his chair back a little from the big, flat-topped writing-table at which he was seated, he bit the end of his pencil while he gazed absently at the litter of manuscript and notes in front of him, at the heap of reference books, and at his secretary sitting opposite to him.

"It's no use," he remarked, in a petulant tone. "I can't grasp the meaning of that paragraph. It is too abtruse and complicated. I'll have to think it over carefully, and I am not in the mood now. Confound the book! It will turn my hair grey before I have finished."

"Suppose you let me have a try, sir?" said the secretary.

Hugh Clontarf shook his head.

"No, I won't do any more this afternoon," he replied. "You can go, Creed. We will get on with the work again this evening."

Parrish Creed put the cover on his typewriter, and, remarking as he rose that he would be in the library should he be wanted, he left the luxuriously furnished room.

Hugh Clontarf sat still for a few moments, his thoughts remote from the literary work he was engaged on. He was a handsome young man of thirty, tall and well-built and fair, with dark blue eyes and a blond-moustache; a young man to be envied for his good looks and ancient blood, his comfortable income, and his old country house in one of the loveliest parts of Surrey.

Presently he got up from his chair, and, when he had lit a cigar, he strolled over to one of the large windows, and stood there with his hands in his pockets.

It was an attractive view that met his gaze. Beyond him a gravelled drive swept across the well-kept grounds of Ranmore Lodge to the wrought-iron gates, to one side of which was a small rustic lodge.

Beyond the gates the drive led in to a private road, and the road, after running for a number of yards through the woods, swerved in the direction of Dorking.

The April day was drawing to a close. The sky was aflame with colour. Birds were twittering sweetly, and rooks were cawing and circling above the tree-tops. A cock-pheasant strutted boldly out from the shrubbery, and crossed the lawn with mincing steps.

A faint, throbbing noise was heard in the distance. It swelled louder and nearer, and at length there appeared, at the bend of the road, a taxi-cab which looked as if it had seen its best days, and was driven by a bearded old man in a glazed hat.

"Who the deuce can that be?" Hugh Clontarf muttered, in an irritable tone. "I can't imagine. It is somebody old Davy is bringing from Dorking. I wish people wouldn't disturb me!"

The taxi glided up to the gateway, ran up the drive, and swung round in front of the house.

Hugh Clontarf could not see it now. He turned away from the window, and shortly afterwards there was a rap at the door, and it was opened by a servant; a lean, swarthy man of middle-age, clean-shaven, whose attire was very different to that of English servants. He spoke the English language perfectly, however.

"A gentleman has called, sir," he said, handing his master a card. "He has private business with you, he told me."

On the card was engraved the following: "Sir Ralph Athelstan, 198, Hamilton Place, Piccadilly, London, West."

It was not an unfamiliar name to Hugh Clontarf, though he had never met the owner of it, and never seen him. He changed colour, and for a few seconds he did not speak. A curious expression crept into his eyes, and faded from them. He hesitated. He could not at once decide what to do.

"You can show the gentleman in, Kashar," he said slowly. "I will see him. I think I know what he wants."

The servant withdrew, and Hugh Clontarf had a little time for further reflection—time to come to a definite conclusion—before the visitor was ushered into the room.

He was a man of about fity, immaculately dressed, and of striking, handsome appearance, with aristocratic features, dark hair and eyes, a fresh complexion, and a close-cropped iron-grey moustache.

"I must apologise for intruding on you, Mr. Clontarf," he began. "You know who I am, I believe."

Hugh Clontarf nodded.

"I remember my uncle speaking of you on several occasions," he said, in a peculiar tone; and, ignoring the hand that was offered to him, he pointed to a chair, and bade his visitor be seated. "I was rather surprised to hear from my servant," he added, "that you had business with me."

Sir Ralph Athelstan's friendly attitude stiffened.

"Why should you be surprised?" he asked, as he sat down. "You can guess what my business is, I dare say."

"Yes, I can guess."

"And you have been expecting a visit from me, perhaps."

"On the contrary, I have not."

"Well, Mr. Clontarf, if you will kindly let me explain——"

Sir Ralph Athelstan paused for a moment and his glance swept the room, resting on the big writing-table, with its litter of papers and volumes.

"I have been abroad for a considerable time, shooting big game in East Africa," he continued. "It was not until I returned to England last week that I learned of the recent death of your uncle and my friend, Lord Roderick Teviot; and learned also that he had left a large sum of money to you, on the condition that you revised and rewrote, and had published as his memoirs and biography, the letters, notes and diaries in his possession."

"That is quite right," Hugh Clontarf assented. "You have the facts correct."

There was another brief pause.

"As you are doubtless aware," Sir Ralph Athelstan went on, "your uncle and I were on very friendly terms, though I was some few years younger than he was. We were together in India, where I held a high position under the Government, and Lord Roderick was a diplomat at the Court of Delhi. We were both somewhat wild and reckless in those days, and the two of us were concerned, in a very unpleasant way, in what was known as the Serampur Turf Scandal. It was over a race in which two horses of mine ran. Someuglycharges were made—no names were mentioned publicly—but Lord Roderick's influence saved him, and I was equally fortunate."

"I have full knowledge of the affair," Hugh Clontarf drily replied. "I had it from my uncle's lips. His version of it differs entirely from yours, however. I was given to understand that you had a grudge against him, that you deliberately tried to blacken his character, and that he helped you out of the scrape to protect himself."

"It is untrue!" Sir Ralph Athelstan declared. "Absolutely untrue!"

"I prefer to believe what my uncle told me, if you will pardon me. His memory could not have been at fault."

"You have been misled, I can assure you. But we won't argue the question. I will only say that Lord Roderick must have had a faulty memory in regard to something that happened eighteen years ago. To come to the point, Mr. Clontarf, did your uncle instruct you to write up the story of the Serampur Turf Scandal from the material he left you?"

"He did. He had a chapter mapped out to guide me."

"You have written the chapter?"

"Yes, Sir Ralph, it is completed."

"And my name appears in it?"

"Frequently. There are a number of references to you—and to the horses you ran in the race."

"Is the chapter in print yet?" Sir Ralph Athelstan inquired.

"Not yet," Hugh Clontarf replied. "I have sent only the first chapters of the book to the publishers."

"And they are——"

"Henson and Halbury, of Bedford Street."

"It is not too late, then, for you to suppress the turf story."

"Suppress it? I shall do nothing of the sort! I supposed that was what you came for!"

The words burst sharply from Hugh Clontarf's lips. He was flushed with indignation. Sir Ralph Athelstan twisted the ends of his scrubby moustache, but did not speak until he had his temper under control.

"I can persuade you to change your mind, I think," he said quietly.

"You cannot," Hugh Clontarf declared. "Don't deceive yourself."

"I have a very particular reason for making the request."

"I don't doubt it, sir. You probably have several."

"Will you let me make my position clear, Mr. Clontarf. I am going to be very candid. I have a titled relative, a man of high rank in the peerage, who is seventy-five years of age. He allows me an income of ten thousand pounds a year, and I am down in his will as the sole heir to his estate, which is worth half a million and more. He has a good opinion of me. He believes that I am the soul of honour, that I have never done anything in the slightest degree discreditable. He is a voracious reader, especially of biography and memoirs; and if he were to read the chapter about the Serampur Turf Scandal—as he certainly will, should it appear in the book—he would stop my allowance, and cut me out of his will. And even if the book escaped his attention, the story would be poured into his ears by malicious people, distant relatives of his, who would like to see me disinherited."

Hugh Clontarf shrugged his shoulders.

"It is very unfortunate," he admitted. "I appreciate your position."

"I was sure you would," Sir Ralph Athelstan replied. "And now that you know what I stand to lose, I hope you will consent to do what I wish."

"I cannot. It is impossible."

"It can make no difference to you Am I to believe that you are determined to ruin me? It would be comtemptible of you."

"Listen to me, Sir Ralph. I have reasons of my own for refusing. There are two sides to the question. I am rather sorry for you, though you really don't deserve any sympathy. But my position is this. I am bound by a sacred obligation. I have given a pledge which I cannot break, nor have I any desire to break it, under the circumstances.

"The blame is wholly yours. You have brought the threatened exposure on yourself. From the time of the turf scandal until the day of his death my uncle was under a cloud, so to speak. His intimate friends and his acquaintances never forgot the affair. He knew that they suspected him, and he felt it most keenly. He was too proud to take them into his confidence and justify himself. He was a kindly, considerate man. He bore you no malice. During his lifetime he spared you at the sacrifice of his own honour.

"On his deathbed, however, he took a different view of things. He sent for me, and told me the whole story of the Serampur scandal; gave me instructions, and exacted from me a solemn promise that I would clear his name and vindicate his character. And it is my duty to do so, no matter what the cost may be to you. That is how I stand."

"A promise to the dead is one thing," said Sir Ralph Athelstan. "An obligation to the living is another."

"An obligation?" Hugh Clontarf repeated. "What do you mean?"

"I mean this. Your first duty is to shield me from the disastrous consequences of a fabrication which I cannot refute."

"Be careful, sir! You imply that my uncle's version of the affair was deliberately untrue."

"No, I assert that either Lord Roderick's memory was at fault, or he was misled by false information at the time of the Serampur scandal."

"I know better than that. He had more than information. As for his memory, it was not impaired to the last hour of his life. Your statements are weak and illogical. If you have a clear conscience you could not have had any reason for fearing you might be injured by the publication of my uncle's memoirs. Why, then, did you come to me to-day?"

"Simply because I have always thought Lord Roderick might be under a misapprehension in regard to me," Sir Ralph Athelstan answered.

"He was not," said Hugh Clontarf. "You can take my word for it."

"I am afraid I can't. I did not expect to meet with so much opposition. I have everything at stake, everything to lose, and I beg that you will——"

"It is useless, sir, to discuss the matter any further. It will be only a waste of breath."

"That is your last word!"

"It is all I have to say to you. You have had your trouble for nothing. I refuse your request, finally and absolutely."

"It is not all I have to say, Mr. Clontarf. You are in comfortable circumstances, but one can never have too much money. Will you accept twelve thousand pounds to suppress the chapter about the turf affair? I can raise that amount."

Hugh Clontarf sprang to his feet, hot with anger.

"You insult me, you scoundrel!" he cried.

"I do not," replied Sir Ralph Athelstan. "I am making you a friendly offer."

"It is an insult to me, and to my dead uncle! You would have me take a bribe to let his reputation remain tarnished by your villainy, by the swindle you perpetrated at Serampur eighteen years ago!"

"You lie, Mr. Clontarf!"

"That is enough! Go now, please! Gŏ at once!"

Sir Ralph Athelstan bit his lip and flushed. He was breathing hard, striving to keep his passion within bounds. Aristocratic gentleman though he was, son of a noble family, there was the strain of the primitive caveman in his blood.

"I will go when I have finished!" he exclaimed. "Not before! You have refused to oblige me as a favour, and you have refused to take my money! Very well! I warn you now that if the chapter I object to appears in the book I will bring an action against you for criminal libel! You will have to pay heavy damages, and very likely you will go to prison!"

Hugh Clontarf laughed.

"I am not in the least afraid," he said. "You can do what you please."

"I mean it!" declared Sir Ralph Athelstan. "You will see! I will have you in court!"

"I advise you to consult a solicitor first. He will tell you that the truth is never a libel."

"But the story of the turf scandal is not true! It is a tissue of lies, concocted by Lord Roderick from sheer spite!"

"Oh, no, it is not! I have the clearest proofs in my possession. Written proofs. They were given to me by my uncle."

"Indeed! What are they?"

"They consist of various documents. One is a deposition sworn to by a jockey who rode your horses at the Serampur races."

Sir Ralph Athelstan turned almost white.

"Where are these extraordinary documents?" he savagely demanded, throwing a glance at the desk. "Here?"

Hugh Clontarf smiled and shook his head.

"No, I sent them to a bank in London after I had written the chapter," he replied.

"Ah! You were afraid that——"

"I thought I had better put them in a safe place. And now clear out of this, sir, before I lose my temper. You have strained it to breaking pitch."

Sir Ralph Athelstan had failed. Beaten at every point, with disgrace and black ruin staring him in the face, he hesitated for a moment, loth to depart, his features twitching. His fists were clenched, and there was an ugly, menacing glitter in his eyes.

"You have not heard the last of this business, Mr. Clontarf!" he said, his voice husky with rage. "If you publish the memoirs with that chapter in it, you will do so at your peril!" Mark my words!"

With an oath he turned on his heel, opened the door, and was gone. And Hugh Clontarf, standing at the window, heard the crazy old taxicab start, and saw it go rattling down the drive.

"The scoundrel!" he muttered. "Thinking I would take a bribe! I don't care a snap of my fingers for his threat! He won't do anything to me!"

He was right. He had nothing to fear from the man who had just left him in anger. But none the less, Sir Ralph Athelstan's visit to Ranmore Lodge, and the rejection of his request, were to have sensational and far-reaching consequences.

End of Prologue.

CHAPTER 1.

A Cry in the Night—Ben Partrick Investigates—The Struggle in Ranmore Woods—The Two Gamekeepers—The Dead Man—An Early Summons for Sexton Blake.

THERE were gamekeepers on the watch, prowling about with the stealth of panthers seeking their prey. Ben Partrick, professional poacher and vagabond, had caught a glimpse of one of the men, and had heard the rustling treadof another; which accounted for the fact that his movements were more than usually vigilant to-night.

He had been in gaol a number of times for indulging in his favourite pursuit, and he did not want to go there again if he could help it.

With a gun under his arm, and some wire snares in his pocket, the incorrigible rogue stole warily and quietly through Ranmore Woods; now pausing to listen, and to peer into the darkness with eyes trained to keen vision; now skulking from thicket to thicket, and now making a detour to avoid a spot which was bathed in the dim glow of the moon, that was riding behind a rack of scudding clouds.

That there should be keepers in the vicinity was a personal grievance to him. He resented it. He had to earn an honest living—he could never be brought to believe it was dishonest—as well as they, and they didn't have to work as hard for it as he did.

On many nights they had not troubled him. They had avoided his regular beats, so to speak, and let him have his fling.

To-night they suspected his presence, he was sure; and he was afraid to visit the snares he had set, afraid to set any new ones, and afraid to discharge his gun at any pheasant he might discover nestled in the foliage above his head.

"Darn the luck!" he grumbled. "It isn't fair! I've got to live the same as anybody else. I dare say I'll have to go home with empty pockets. I'll try the Abinger Woods first, though, if I can get that far. Perhaps there aren't any keepers there."

Of a sudden, a sound broke the hushed silence, floating to the poacher's ears from somewhere beyond him, and at no great distance.

It was a short, sharp cry that trailed into a husky shout, and ceased. The cry was heard once more, and on the instant it was stifled.

And now, forgetting the risk of falling into the clutches of the gamekeepers—he supposed one of them had tackled another poacher—Ben Partrick took to his heels, and ran as fast as he could in the direction from which the cries had come.

When he had gone for thirty or forty yards, he stopped for a few seconds to listen, and heard faint, strange sounds which were unlike anything he had ever heard before. He hastened on more cautiously, making as little noise as possible, and stopped again by a wide-girthed tree that was close to a footpath.

Here he dropped flat on the ground, beneath a spreading clump of bushes, in such a position that the tree did not obstruct his view.

"It looks as if there was going to be murder done!" he muttered. "I had better keep out of it! I wonder who they are!"

In a shallow glade which the path crossed, indistinctly visible in what feeble moon-light penetrated the foliage, two men were locked together, and were struggling desperately and almost noiselessly. One of them was tall, and the other appeared to be a head shorter.

The sight held Ben Partrick spellbound. He watched the men, gruesomely thrilled and fasincated. He was certain neither of them was a keeper, though they were only blurred, shadowy forms to his vision.

They were fighting to the death, it seemed, for one had a grip on the other's throat. For several minutes they swayed and bent reeled this way and that, scuffled to and fro on the grass; the while the smaller man's efforts gradually relaxed, and the taller one pressed his advantage.

At length there was a dull thud. The struggle was at an end. The small man was lying motionless on the ground, in a twisted heap, and the other was stooping over him, fumbling at his neck with both hands.

The poacher did not stir. He was still spellbound. A few more moments elapsed, and then, his sinister work completed, the tall man stood erect, and peered into the gloom; glided swiftly off to the right, and vanished in the cover.

Rapid crashing steps were heard now. Somebody was approaching from the left. A stalwart gamekeeper burst out from the thickets, and, having glanced at the prostrate figure in the glade, he gave a lusty shout.

There was an immediate response, followed by more rapid steps in the bushes; and shortly afterwards a second gamekeeper came on the scene.

"Hallo! What's wrong?" he exclaimed.

"Case of murder, I should say!" the other replied as he struck a match.

"Murder? You don't mean it!"

"It appears to be! What do you think of this, Sandy?"

"Ah, you're right, Bill! Is he dead?"

"Yes, there's no breath of life in him. He hasn't been dead long, though ."

"Who did it?"

"I've no idea, Sandy. I didn't see anybody running. I heard a sound like a fall a bit ago. That's what brought me in this direction."

Ben Partrick hugged the ground, scarcely daring to breathe. Were he to be discovered here he would be accused of the crime. The two gamekeepers were examining the body, striking match after match.

"A man murdered in Ranmore Woods!" said the one who had arrived first. "It is a queer business, Sandy!"

"It certainly is!" the other answered. "It beats me! Look at the cord around the poor fellow's neck! He was strangled with it! And from the funny clothes he is wearing, and his brown skin, he must be a foreigner of some sort."

"That's what he is. I've seen lascar sailors like him at the docks in London."

"I have, too, Bill. The queerest part of it is that I've never laid eyes on the man before."

"Neither have I. He can't belong anywhere in this neighbourhood, or we should know him by sight. I wonder if it was Ben Partrick who killed him? I have no doubt the rascal is prowling about in the woods to-night."

The keeper who had been addressed as Sandy shook his head.

"No, he couldn't have had anything to do with the murder," he declared.

"Why not?" asked his companion.

"It stands to reason, as Sexton Blake would say if he was here. Look at the footprints on that patch of damp earth. The prints made by two men while they were struggling."

"Well, what of them?"

"You can see, Bill, that both of them had rather small feet. And Ben Partrick wears boots like clodhoppers."

"So he does. We can't suspect Ben. You ought to be a detective yourself, Sandy. You seem to have a mind for that sort of thing."

"It's easy enough. What you call deduction. Which means that you take one thing to start with, and work it out, and build up other things around it, until you find a clue to——"

"You've been reading of Sexton Blake's cases in the newspapers, Sandy, and so have I. It's not going to help us to solve this mystery, though. We had better inform the police, instead of wasting time talking."

"That's right. I'll get my bicycle and ride to the police station at Dorking. And you stay here with the body. One of us must do that."

"I will. But I'll slip home first and fetch a lantern."

"Come along, then, Bill. And when you get back, mind you don't disturb the footprints. They will be helpful to the police, and I shouldn't be surprised if they were to send for Sexton Blake, as this is a very mysterious kind of a murder."

"I wish they would, Sandy. It would be a treat for us to see Mr. Blake working on a case—eh?"

The two gamekeepers strode off, and they were hardly more than out of sight when Ben Partrick crept from behind the tree, and picked up something that was lying on the footpath—something he had seen one of the men drop while they were fighting. He glanced at it and slipped it into his pocket; and as he went his way, in the direction of the Abinger Woods, thunder pealed, and a flash of lightning blazed from horizon to horizon.

A storm was theatening, and soon it burst. A gale sprang up and rain fell in drenching torrents, beating down on the scene of the death struggle and pelting on the face of the murdered man.

★ ★ ★

Roused from heavy slumber by a hand tugging at his arm, Tinker awoke with a start, and, lifting his head from the pillow, he gazed around him in bewilderment while he rubbed his drowsy eyes.

The light of day was shining in at the window, and Sexton Blake was standing by the bedside in a dressing-gown and slippers.

"What is it?" the lad exclaimed. "What's wrong?"

"Nothing!" Blake replied. "Get up and dress."

"What for? Is it breakfast-time already? Have I overslept myself?"

"No, it is only seven o'clock. We are going to the country."

"To the country? How is that, guv'nor?"

"I have been talking to my friend, Inspector Stracey, of Dorking, on the telephone. He got through to me a few minutes ago. He wishes me to come down there, and I told him I would."

"Is it murder or burglary?" Tinker asked.

"Murder," said Blake. "A man has been found strangled in a plantation on Lord Ranmore's estate. The inspector has been to the scene of the crime, where the body was discovered by a couple of gamekeepers. And as the victim is a foreigner, and is apparently a stranger to the neighbourhood, Stracey thought the case would interest me. And I dare say it will.

"Dress yourself quickly, my lad," he added, as he turned to go. "I want to leave as soon as possible. I have rung up the garage, and they are sending our car round."

CHAPTER 2.

At the Scene of the Murder—No Clues—Blake's Deductions—A Baffling Mystery—A Visit to Colonel Roylance—The Identity of the Dead Man—Some Information about Hugh Clontarf.

BEFORE half-past seven o'clock that morning, Sexton Blake and his young assistant, Tinker, accompanied by Pedro, the bloodhound, were on their way down to Surrey.

At a few minutes to nine they stopped in front of the police-station at Dorking, and when they had picked up Inspector Stracey, who was waiting here for them, they drove on for a couple of miles, left the car by the roadside, and went on foot through Ranmore Woods to the spot where the murder had been committed.

The two gamekeepers, Sandy Kelke and Bill Lambert were on the scene; and by the inspector's orders they had not touched the body.

Blake had his own methods of investigation, and he followed them in this instance. He bent over the dead man, scrutinising him closely; next he questioned the keepers, and learned from them what little they could tell him.

"I don't see the footprints you mentioned," he said, as he looked at the damp and sodden earth. "Did it rain here last night?"

"Yes, sir, there was a very heavy shower," Sandy Kelke replied. "Quite a tempest."

"When?" Blake asked. "Before or after the murder?"

"Shortly afterwards, sir. Lambert and I were caught in it as we were going across the plantation."

"It is a great pity. The prints have been entirely obliterated. Otherwise my bloodhound might have been able to track the murderer."

"Possibly he was a poacher, Mr. Blake," Inspector Stracey suggested.

Blake shook his head.

"I don't think so," he answered. "I can't entertain that theory, under the circumstances."

As he spoke he turned to the corpse. He bent over it, and, grasping it carefully, he moved it aside. To his disappointment there was not a single footprint on the space he had laid bare.

His next step was to search the flimsy blue garments—a tunic and a pair of tight-fitting trousers—that were on the body.

He found nothing whatever in the pockets, and now, his preliminary investigations finished, he removed the cord that was twisted and tied around the neck of the dead man.

Then he knelt by him, and for fully a minute he examined his throat, pressing it here and there with his finger.

"It is curious!" he remarked as he stood erect. "Very curious! Have you ever heard of the Thugs of India, Stracey?"

"I have read something about them," the inspector replied. "They are a band of robbers, I believe."

"Robbers and assassins," said Blake. "A religious sect who worship the goddess Kali, and put their victims and enemies to death by strangulation. Look at this cord. It is made of woven silk, and it is similar to those used by the practisers of Thuggee. It is one of them, in fact. The genuine article."

"The real thing? Are you sure?"

"I am quite sure, Stracey. I have a Thuggee cord at home in my collection of souvenirs of crimes. I took it from the neck of a Hindu merchant in a bazaar at Allahabad—and caught the assassin afterwards."

"And this dead man? Is he a——"

"He is a Hindu, of course. That is obvious to me. Furthermore, he had been in England for a considerable time, for his shoes are well-worn, and they bear the stamp of a Northampton firm of boot-makers."

"He belonged to the sect of Thugs, perhaps."

Blake shrugged his shoulders.

"Possibly," he said. "I doubt it, though. The circumstances of his death are peculiar. You can see on his throat purple bruises made by fingers, and they were caused by much stronger pressure than were the marks left by the cord. I can tell to a certainty that he was strangled by the hands of the murderer, not by the silk-cord. That was twisted round his neck after he was dead."

"Afterwards?" said Inspector Stracey. "Why? On the chance that he might revive?"

"Or for another reason. To divert the police on to a false scent."

"I see. You suggest that the man was murdered by some person who, though not a Thug, himself wished the police to believe he was."

"I was thinking of that, Stracey. But it is rather a far-fetched theory. I may be wrong."

Blake had made no progress as yet. All he could judge was that he had a very sensational affair to deal with.

He filled his pipe, and lit it, looked at the corpse again, and put further questions to the men Kelke and Lambert, and to the inspector as well.

They could not give him any information. Each and all of them asserted that they had never seen the dead man before, and that to the best of their knowledge no Hindu had been living in employment, or otherwise, anywhere in the neighbourhood.

"I ought to know," continued Inspector Stracey, "and so should the gamekeepers. They have been on Lord Ranmore's estate for years."

Blake's brows were knit.

"That storm in the night probably washed out clues which would have been valuable to me. As it is, I am at a loose end. I can recall few cases more extraordinary than this one. Stracey," he said, in an irritable tone. "Here we have a crime which, on the face of it, appears to have been committed by a native of India. Who is the victim? Why did he come to this lonely plantation, and where did he come from? Who murdered him? And why? What was the motive? Furthermore, why kill the man by the clumsy and lengthy process of strangulation, when a knife thrust, or a sharp blow on the head, would have finished him quietly and expeditiously?

"Was the dead man going through the woods alone? Was the murderer with him, or was he stalking him? Was there a quarrel between the two men? No, if there had been the keeper Lambert, who arrived first on the scene, would have heard angry voices, whereas he heard only the sound of a fall. And that fall marked the end of the struggle, when the victim was dead or dying."

"I don't wonder you are puzzled," the inspector remarked. "The case admits of various theories. I can think of several."

"What are they, Stracey?"

"The most likely one, it seems to me, is that the man was decoyed here, lured to his death, by some person familiar with this part of the country. Don't you agree with me?"

"In part, yes. But if the trap was set for the victim—a deliberate murder—trap—why was he not killed by a blow, or even with a knife? And why was the silk cord put around his neck after he had been strangled?"

"You answered that question yourself a bit ago."

"I answered it? How?"

"Don't you remember, Mr. Blake? You intimated that the murderer wanted the police to believe that the man had been strangled by a Thug."

Blake nodded vaguely. He glanced at the rain-drenched earth, as if he was trying to read signs which were not there, and turned to the gamekeepers.

"Have any people moved into the neighbourhood recently, Lambert?" he inquired.

"No, sir," Bill Lambert replied. "Not for a year or so."

"What is the nearest house?"

"Ranmore Lodge, half a mile to the north. It belongs to Mr. Hugh Clontarf, a wealthy young gentleman."

"Is he married?"

"No, sir. He is a bachelor."

"Did you come from that direction when you found the body?"

"I came the other way, sir. From the direction of Lord Ranmore's residence."

"Does the footpath lead to Mr. Clontarf's place?"

"It leads close to it, sir."

"Is Lord Ranmore at home at present, Lambert?"

"No, sir, he isn't. His lordship is at his town house with his family and the servants. His country house is closed."

Blake was none the wiser for the questions he had put. He chafed under a sense of utter helplessness. How was he to discover the identity of the murdered man? He pondered briefly and decided what to do.

An old friend of his, he had remembered lived at the Elms, a rather pretentious place which lay a mile to the south, towards Abinger Hatch.

Colonel Roylance, now retired, had a private income, and was a widower with a pretty daughter. He had a wide acquaintance in the surrounding country, and Blake felt, therefore, that he might get some useful information from him.

"I am going to the Elms, my boy," he said to Tinker. "I shan't be long."

"The Elms?" Tinker repeated. "Colonel Roylance lives there, doesn't he.?"

"That's right," Blake assented. "I want to have a talk with him. I will leave you here with the inspector. And by the way, Stracey," he added, "you can let the keepers go home now. They have been up all night, and they can't be of further assistance to us."

The men were loth to depart. They would have preferred to remain, and see what the day brought forth. They trudged off towards their cottages, however; and Blake, taking Pedro with him, turned in another direction, and retraced his steps across the plantation to the road; got into his car, and drove rapidly to the Elms.

Colonel Roylance was at home, he was informed by a servant. He sent in his card, and was shortly taken to the library, where the colonel, an elderly gentleman with a florid complexion and a grey moustache, was seated in an armchair, with one foot swathed in bandages and resting on a footstool.

"Hallo, Blake!" he exclaimed, as he shook hands with him. "Glad to see you! I can't get up! I've been having the deuce of a time with the gout! The old complaint! So you have brought your bloodhound along with you! Are you down here on professional business?"

"I am, as it happens," Blake answered. "There was a murder in the neighbourhood last night."

"Good heavens! You don't mean it!"

"Yes, a very mysterious one, Roylance. A Hindu was found strangled in Ranmore Woods."

Colonel Roylance gave a quick start.

"A Hindu?" he repeated. "What was he like?"

"A man of middle age, clean-shaven," Blake replied.

"By Jove, I thought so! I know who the fellow is! He must be Kashar Das! I am sure of it! There isn't another Hindu in a radius of miles around!"

"And who is Kashar Das, Roylance?"

"A servant in the employ of a friend of mine, Hugh Clontarf, who lives at Ranmore Lodge, not far from here."

"I dare say you are right. No doubt you are. It is strange, though, that neither of Lord Ranmore's gamekeepers, nor Inspector Stracey of Dorking, had ever seen or heard of the Hindu or even knew there was one living in the neighbourhood."

"That is easily accounted for, Blake. I don't suppose Kashar Das has been outside the grounds of Ranmore Lodge since he came here. And the other servants, a woman and a maid—there are only the three of them—also live on the premises."

Blake was elated. He had identified the victim of the murder, and he now related all the details of the crime to Colonel Roylance, who listened to him with close attention.

"A most amazing affair!" he declared. "If I am baffled by it, you can imagine what my feelings are. The Hindu strangled to death in Ranmore Woods and some time after midnight! Almost incredible! I wonder if he has been missed!"

"In all probability," Blake replied. "But it is too early in the morning as yet for Mr. Clontarf to have taken alarm."

"I don't think the disappearance of Kashar Das would disturb him much," said the colonel. "He is too absorbed in his work. He is writing a book."

"So he is a literary man. You are well-acquanted with him, I presume."

"Very well indeed. I have known him a long while. He is a charming fellow, one of the best. For some months he has been——"

Colonel Roylance broke off.

"He will be shocked by the murder," he continued. "Kashar Das strangled by a silk cord! A cord such as those used by the Thugs of India! How sensational! What are your theories?"

"I haven't got any," Blake answered, a trifle sharply. "You have thrown a partial light on the mystery, and I want you to give me what further assistance may be in your power. Tell me all you can about Hugh Clontarf. How is it that——"

"I will tell you to start with," the colonel interrupted, "that nothing could be more absurd than to fasten your suspicious on him."

"I don't suspect anybody. I am a detective as you are aware. I am working on this case, and I should be neglecting my duty if I did not begin my investigations with the employer of the murdered Hindu. You should realise that."

"I do realise it, Blake. I understand."

"Please go on, then. Who is Hugh Clontarf?"

"He come of a good family. He is a relative on the distaff side of the late Lord Roderick Tevoit. He is a 'Varsity man, educated at Oxford and Heidelberg. He inherited Ranmore Lodge from his parents, and they bought the place from the father of the present Lord Ranmore. He is popular with county-society in Surrey, and he entertains a great deal. Or rather he did until recently, when he engaged in literary work. But that is another story. Did you happen to be acquainted with Lord Roderick Teviot, of Troon Court, Ayrshire?"

"I knew him fairly well," Blake replied.

"So did I," said Colonel Roylance. "I met him in India, in Egypt, at Malta, in other countries where I was on military service. A wonderful and fascinating man! He was not only a diplomat of the greatest ability, with a splendid record at all the British embassies in Europe, but he was a famous traveller, explorer, and savant. And he was a personal friend of so many crowned heads, was so deeply in their confidence, that in his later years he was generally known as the 'Intimate of Kings.' During his lifetime he preserved numerous letters and documents, and kept voluminous diaries and notes, with the intention of embodying them in an autobiography. He did not carry out his intentions, however. It was not until——"

The colonel paused for a moment.

"When Lord Roderick Teviot died, about six months ago," he resumed, "his will was found to contain three clauses relating to his nephew, Hugh Clontarf. For one thing, all his letters, and papers, and diaries, and a rough draft of the book he had in comtemplation, were to be handed over to his nephew, who was to receive ten-thousand pounds on the condition that he revised and re-wrote the book from the material in his possession, and to have it published under the title of 'Memoirs of Lord Roderick Teviot.'

"By the terms of the second clause he, the nephew, was to be assisted in his task by a certain Parrish Creed, a clever young man who had been Lord Roderick's private secretary. And the third clause stipulated that Hugh Clontarf was to take into his service, and treat with kindness and consideration the Hindu Kashar Das, who had been Lord Roderick's devoted body servant for a number of years.

"These provisions were readily accepted by Hugh Clontarf. He brought Parrish Creed and Kashar Das to Ranmore Lodge, and settled down to his painstaking task. And since then he has been practically a recluse living mostly in retirement. He let it be understood that he did not want to be disturbed by his friends until his work was finished, and his wishes have been respected."

The story interested Blake. He was inclined to think in a vague sort of a way, that there might be a link between the murder of the Hindu servant and the terms of Lord Roderick Teviot's will. He had seen the will mentioned in the papers, he remembered now; and he had also read an announcement of the forthcoming volume of memoirs.

"When did Kashar Das enter Lord Roderick's service?" he inquired. "And under what circumstances?"

"Sixteen or seventeen years ago, while Lord Roderick was at the Court of Delhi," Colonel Roylance answered. "He took a liking to Kashar Das, and kept him with him during his subsequent wanderings. And when he came home to Troon Court, shortly before his death, the Hindu accompanied him."

"What knowledge have you of Parrish Creed, the private secretary?" Blake went on.

"Little or none. I have never even seen him. But he isn't at Ranmore Lodge now."

"He is not, Roylance. How is that?"

"He resigned, Clontarf told me, two or three weeks ago. He had more lucrative employment offered to him."

"What became of him? Do you know?"

"N0, Blake, I don't. I believe he went abroad somewhere."

"And a new secretary has taken his place?"

"Yes, Hugh Clontarf has engaged another one. I haven't seen him, either, and I can't tell you what his name is. But what is the use of asking me all these trivial questions?"

"It is all in the day's work, so to speak," Blake said lightly. "I am getting on bit by bit."

"I should banish Ranmore Lodge from my mind, if I were you," the colonel replied. "You won't find the key to the mystery there. There is no lady in the affair. No jealous lover. The cook is an elderly woman, and a widow. And the housemaid is a slatternly wench who has no followers."

Blake nodded.

"I had no such suspicion," he said. "Hindus hold themselves strictly aloof from all woman except those of their own race and caste. I am going to put another question to you now, and you must not let it irritate you. Tell me first if you have been a frequent visitor to Ranmore Lodge."

"Yes, I have dined there a number of times."

"Very well. Do you know if Hugh Clontarf had in his possession one of the silk-cords used by Thugs?"

"I don't believe for a moment that he had. I never saw one. He wasn't interested in such things."

"Lord Roderick Teviot might have had one, Roylance, as he was in India for a long period."

"I don't know if he had or not. And I don't care. Lord Roderick had a collection of queer weapons, and other curios, which he picked up in wild countries. But he left them in his will to the public museum in the town of Troon. And it is a far cry from Troon to Surrey. I can't imagine what you mean by——"

Colonel Roylance paused. He scowled, and twisted his moustache; imprudently shifted his gouty foot a little, and swore at it.

"Hang it all, Blake, I tell you again you are on the wrong tack!" he exclaimed. "Hugh Clontarf is the last person in the world you can suspect of the murder! I don't like your insinuations! They hurt me! And what's more. Clontarf and my daughter are engaged to be married!"

Blake raised his eyebrows.

"He is going to marry Gwenda?" he murmured. "It is news to me."

"They became engaged some months ago, before Lord Roderick Teviot died," said the colonel. "It is not generally known yet."

"Is your daughter at home?"

"No, she is travelling in Italy with friends. When she returns—I am expecting her almost any day—she will break into Hugh Clontarf's seclusion, I'll warrant. She is impatient to see him again."

"Hasn't he been seeing anybody since he began to write the memoirs of his uncle?"

"Very few people, Blake. I am the favoured one. I had luncheon at Ranmore Lodge a couple of weeks ago."

Blake looked at his watch, and rose. He had drawn blank, with one exception. He knew the murdered man must be Kashar Das, and that was all. He was still in the dark as to the motive for the crime, and the identity of the murderer.

"I'll have to go back now," he said. "Tinker and the inspector are waiting for me. Thanks for the information, Roylance. If I learn anything I will let you know."

"I would go with you," the colonel replied, as he shook Blake's hand, "if it wasn't for this confounded foot. I have finished with port! I'll never drink another glass of the cursed stuff!"

CHAPTER 3.

The Face in the Bushes—A Cunning Trick—Waiting for Pedro—A Disastrous Shower—Hugh Clontarf Comes on the Scene—Blake Goes to Ranmore Lodge—A Futile Search.

IT was a dreary and gruesome vigil for Tinker and Inspector Stracey waiting there in the glade by the murdered Hindu whose swollen features, distorted with agony, had stiffened like plaster in rigors of death.

Not a sound broke the hushed silence. No bird chirped. No rabbit ventured from cover. No pheasant or partridge strutted in the tall grass.

It seemed as if the little creatures of the woods, winged and furried, were instinctively shunning the spot where lay the victim of a dastardly crime.

The inspector, seated on a flat stone, moodily smoked a pipe, and racked his brains for a clue that would win him praise from Sexton Blake.

And Tinker, too restless to sit still, wandered about with lagging steps, went slowly here and there, ranging in a narrow circle beyond the corpse, the while he scanned the ground in the slender hope of finding a footprint which had not been obliterated.

The day had begun well, calm and sultry, with a clear sky. But as the morning wore on, dark clouds gathered, and when Blake had been gone for an hour the clouds had spread from horizon to horizon, and the distant muttering of thunder presaged a storm.

"We're going to have another shower, and it will be a heavy one," remarked Inspector Stracey, as he tapped his pipe on his heel. "You and I will get a soaking, I am afraid. I wonder what is keeping Mr. Blake so long? I wish he would return."

"He istalkingto Colonel Roylance," said Tinker. "Perhaps he will learn something from him."

"And perhaps he won't. If Lambert and Kelke didn't know anything about the Hindu, it isn't likely the colonel will."

"I'm not so sure. He visits all the country people for miles around, and he may——"

The lad broke off abruptly.

"Look!" he whispered. "Look there!"

"My word, I see!" gasped the inspector.

"Another Hindu! The—the murderer!"

"That's who it is, my boy! Good heavens!"

They stood spellbound, petrified by what they saw. A dozen yards or so beyond them, in the direction of Ranmore Lodge, the bushes at the edge of the glade had been drawn apart, and a face was peering from the rift in the green foliage—a swarthy face, light brown in colour, surmounted by a white turban and fringed with a black beard.

It was visible for a second or two. Then it suddenly vanished, and at the same instant Tinker and Inspector Stracey shook off the numbing lethargy that had gripped them, and dashed forward.

They plunged into the thickets at the spot where they had seen the face, and stopped to listen. All was quiet, but as they pressed on they heard, from straight in front of them, a crackling, crashing noise.

"There he is!" cried the inspector. "Hurry, my boy! This way! We'll get the fellow!"

They scrambled through the trees and bushes as fast as they could, straining their eyes ahead of them, and stopped again in a marshy hollow where the grass was emerald green. They could not hear a sound now, nor could they see a single footprint on the soft, wet earth.

"The fellow didn't come this way after all," said Inspector Stracey. "I could have sworn he did."

Tinker had been sure of it, too. He was puzzled. He glanced around him, and, stooping he picked up a stone, bigger than his fists, which had lodged in the cleft of a bush close to the ground.

"Ah! Look at this!" he exclaimed. "It has just been dug out of the earth, for it is dry on one side, and damp on the other!"

The inspector nodded.

"That's right," he assented. "I see what you mean. It was the stone crashing through the foliage we heard. The man threw it in this direction to fool us, and bunked off in another. A darned clever trick, wasn't it?"

"We were too easily fooled," the lad said ruefully. "We might have suspected it was a trick."

"No use talking of that now. We must try to find the man. I wish Mr. Blake was here with his bloodhound."

"We had better wait until he comes, inspector, and let Pedro do the searching. I dare say he will be able to get the man's scent, and follow it."

Inspector Stracey was of the same mind. They retraced their steps, and as they reached the glade they heard a rustling noise beyond it. Sexton Blake was coming, and a moment later he appeared, with the dog trotting by his side.

"The murderer has been here, guv'nor!" Tinker eagerly blurted out. "We've seen him! Another Hindu, wearing a white turban!"

Blake stared. "Another Hindu?" he repeated, in an incredulous tone. "Nonsense! It must have been an illusion!"

"Not a bit of it!" declared the inspector. "We saw the man's face as plainly as we can see yours! He was just over yonder, peeping at us from that thicket."

In a few words Tinker related all that had happened, and Blake, bewildered by what he had been told, was about to lead the bloodhound into the bushes, when there was vivid flash of lightning, followed by a deafening thunderclap.

Big drops of rain were already falling, and almost at once a heavy, drenching downpour set in.

"Of all the confounded luck!" grumbled the lad.

It was too late to do anything now. The rain was beating, savagely, forcibly on the earth, lashing it in torrents, and spurting up from it like clouds of watery spray.

The little party hastily sought for shelter, and took refuge beneath the spreading boughs of a wide-girthed tree that was dense with foliage.

"We have lost a fine chance, sir," said Inspector Stracey.

"Absolutely lost it," Blake bitterly replied. "But for this unfortunate storm, we should probably have caught the murderer. As it is, there will be nothing to help Pedro. Every vestige of scent will be destroyed. It is a great pity."

For half an hour, while the bloodhound whined and whimpered—he had an aversion to thunder and lightning—the tempest raged with the utmost fury, accompanied at intervals by a shrieking gale; and when at length the wind dropped and the sombre clouds brightened, and the rain trailed into a drizzle as fine as a Scotch mist, the ground looked as if a flood had swept over it.

In places it was hard-beaten, in others churned to a mire; here strewn with clipped leaves and twigs, there lashed to furrows, in which water glistened. To discover the faintest trace of a footprint anywhere in the plantation would have been an impossibility.

During the storm Blake had told Tinker and the inspector all he had learned from Colonel Roylance, and the three now discussed the extraordinary thing which had happened while he was absent.

Why, after an interval of a number of hours, had the murderer ventured back to the scene of his crime, and so boldly shown himself? Inspector Stracey had a theory, and so had Tinker.

"The explanation is quite simple, guv'nor," said thelad. "It occurred to the Hindu this morning to hide or bury the body of his victim, if it hadn't been discovered yet. That is why he returned. As for his showing his face so openly, I don't suppose he knew how much of it was exposed. He was as startled at the sight of us as we were at the sight of him."

Blake shook his head.

"Not bad, my boy," he replied. "And not correct. Next, Stracey!"

"I should suggest," said the inspector, "that the fellow lost something last night, and he came back this morning to search for it."

Blake shook his head again.

"It is a plausible theory," he answered, "and so is Tinker's. You are both wrong, though unless I am greatly mistaken. My theory is this, and it is based in part, not entirely, on the fact that the man split the bushes with his hands, whereas he could have seen as distinctly if he had peeped through the foliage. He came back to the scene of the murder with the deliberate purpose of showing himself. He knew you and the lad were here—he had been prowling about previously—and he wanted you to see him."

"He wanted us to see him?" Inspector Stracey repeated. "Why on earth should he?"

"Simply to make you believe that the murder had been done by a Hindu, to deceive you in that respect."

"To deceive us, sir? But—but the fellow was a Hindu!"

"No, Stracey, he was not. He was disguised as one. It was to mislead the police that he used the silk-cord to strangle his victim, and he returned to strengthen the suspicions he judged the Thuggee cord had given rise to. It was a daring thing to do, but he thought it worth the risk."

"You are right, guv'nor!" said Tinker. "I'll bet you are!"

The inspector's face was a study.

"It beats me!" he declared. "You are a cleverer man than I am, Mr. Blake, and I think myself you must be right. I don't dispute it. But you could knock me down with a feather. If I had to deal with this case on my own it would tie my brain into a knot. I am glad you are going to help me to——"

"Look at Pedro!" interrupted the lad.

The bloodhound's big ears were slightly cocked, and the fur on his back was bristling. He growled in a low key.

Footsteps were heard now. Somebody was approaching. Blake glanced at his companions, and put a finger to his lips; thrust a hand into his pocket, and grasped a pistol.

The steps drew nearer, moving slowly; and out from the thickets into the glade, by the footpath, came a good-looking young man of about thirty, tall and fair, with dark blue eyes and a blond moustache. He carried a stick, and wore a cap and a mackintosh.

He stopped abruptly—gazed at the little group—gazed from them to the body of the Hindu, and uttered an exalamation of horror.

"Good heavens, Stracey, what does this mean?" he cried. "My poor servant! Is he dead?"

"Yes, sir," the inspector replied. "He was murdered in the night, Mr. Clontarf—strangled with a silk cord. Two of Lord Ranmore's gamekeepers found the body. They sent for me, and I telephoned to my friend Mr. Sexton Blake, and had him come down here to help me with the case."

"Sexton Blake! Hugh Clontarf exclaimed, offering his hand to the detective. "I am very glad to meet you, sir. I have often wished I could make your acquaintance. Inspector Stracey is fortunate in having you to assist him.

"This is a shocking business," he went on, his voice husky with emotion. "My Hindu servant murdered! Could he have had a fight with a poacher?"

"I think not," said Blake. "It is a most mysterious affair. You can throw some light on it, perhaps."

"None whatever. All I can tell you is that Kashar Das disappeared in the night. So I was informed an hour ago, and I at once set out to search for him, coming by the footpath."

"Why by the path, Mr. Clontarf?"

"Because it is a short cut to the village of Ranmore. I thought the Hindu might have gone there for some reason."

"I see. Whether he was going to the village or not, he didn't get any farther than this spot, where he was attacked in the dark."

"And cruelly murdered! I can't account for it! Have you made any discoveries, Mr. Blake?"

"Only that the dead man was in your employ. I had the information from Colonel Roylance, of the Elms."

Continuing, Blake spoke of the peculiar manner in which the Hindu had met with his death, and mentioned briefly what he had learned from Colonel Roylance regarding the inmates of Ranmore Lodge.

Hugh Clontarf nodded.

"Yes, only five of us," he said. "The cook and the maid, Kashar Das, my private secretary, and myself. And we were all on the best of terms with the Hindu. He had no enemy in the house. No acquaintances outside of it. He hasn't been anywhere since he came from Troon Court in Ayrshire, where he was formerly in my uncle's service, as you have been told."

"It would appear," replied Blake, "that he was murdered by one of his own race."

"From the fact that he was strangled with a silk cord of the kind used by the Thugs of India?" said Hugh Clontarf.

"There is stronger evidence, sir. Another Hindu, a man with a white turban and a beard, was prowling about here before the storm. He was seen by Inspector Stracey and my boy. They chased him, but he got away."

"Another Hindu? Most amazing, Mr. Blake! That tends to deepen the mystery, instead of to clear it up! Who was the fellow? What motive could he have had for the murder? Where did he come from?"

"From London, probably, to keep an appointment here in the plantation with your native servant."

"I can't believe it, sir. It is incredible. I could swear Kashar Das never saw a man of his own race all the time he was at Troon Court with my uncle, Lord Roderick Teviot. And since he has been at Ranmore Lodge, as I have told you——"

"Facts are stubborn things," broke in Blake, who did not care to speak of his belief that the murderer was not a real Hindu. "The evidence is contrary to your statements, Mr. Clontarf. I will go over to your place with you now. I would like to have a look at your dead servant's room, and talk to you of certain matters."

He turned to the inspector.

"You had better go to the village at once, Stracey," he said, "and arrange to have the body removed to the local inn, the White Lion. I will join you there later. Tinker will stay here, and I will leave the dog with him."

Inspector Stracey set off on his errand and Blake held in the opposite direction along the footpath with Hugh Clontarf, who was greatly distressed by the tragedy.

The path led them through the woods to a small side-gate which gave access to the garden of Ranmore Lodge, and when they had entered the house unobserved by the servants, Hugh Clontarf took the detective upstairs to the bed-room that had been occupied by Kashar Das.

They made a thorough search, and, having found nothing that could possibly have any bearing on the crime, they went down to the library. Blake accepted a cigar, and let the young man mix him a whisky-and-soda.

"It must be very annoying to you," he remarked, "to have this terrible thing happen when you are in the midst of your literary work."

Hugh Clontarf shook his head sadly.

"It is much more than annoying," he answered. "I feel it keenly. I have lost a friend as well as a servant. Kashar Das was as devoted to me as a faithful hound is devoted to his master. I wish I could help you to bring the guilty party to justice. Aren't you going to have the other Hindu sought for?"

"The police will attend to that," said Blake. "I am chiefly interested in discovering the motive of the crime. Once that is accomplished, the rest should be easy. Has Kashar Das received any letters since he has been in your service?"

"None, I am certain. He could not have had any correspondents in this country or anywhere else."

"Had he any relatives in India?"

"There may be some, Mr. Blake. I can't say."

"He spoke English, of course. Could he write it?"

"No, he could neither read nor write our language. He was a simple, kindly, industrious fellow, with not a thought above his work. That was of a varied nature. He acted as my valet, and often helped the cook and the maid."

"Could a written or verbal message have been delivered to him yesterday?" Blake asked.

"There was none," Hugh Clontarf replied. "I inquired of the other servants."

"Did they hear Kashar Das go out in the night?"

"Neither of them. I questioned them closely when I learned that he was missing."

"How did he leave the house, Mr. Clontarf?"

"By the kitchen door. It was found unlocked this morning. He must have gone, and met his death, before the heavy shower we had about midnight; for there was no trace of his footprints in the garden or in the woods."

Blake shrugged his shoulders.

"The other shower, the one this morning, was more unfortunate," he declared, "for it obliterated the footprints of the Hindu who was prowling around the scene of the murder. If it hadn't been for the rain, my bloodhound Pedro would have got the fellow's scent and tracked him down."

"By Jove, I wish he had!" exclaimed Hugh Clontarf, looking the detective straight in the yes. "What a chance you lost!"

"The miscreant will be caught, and probably very soon. I suspect who he is, I may tell you."

"Ah, I am glad of that!"

"I doubt if he was really a Hindu, though. He may have been merely disguised as one. I believe he was, indeed."

"What an extraordinary thing, Mr. Blake! I think it is the most amazing murder I have ever heard of!"

Hugh Clontarf's face expressed only interest and surprise. The remarks about the bloodhound and the Hindu had not led him to betray any sign of uneasiness. He had not even changed colour.

So Blake had observed with satisfaction. He would have been loth to suspect the young man of having any guilty knowledge of the murder.

He kept an open mind, however. It was at Ranmore Lodge, he was sure, he must seek for the key to the bundle of mysteries.

And to find that hidden key he must leave no stone unturned in his preliminary inquiries.

"Has Kashar Das been in good spirits of late?" he continued.

"He has been the same that he always was," said Hugh Clontarf. "Quiet and stoical, like all Orientals. I never noticed any difference in him."

"Was he on good terms with your former private secretary?" Blake asked.

"With Parrish Creed? Yes, he served him as faithfully as he served me. There was at no time any friction between them."

"Mr. Creed resigned his berth not long ago, Colonel Roylance informed me."

"That is right. A couple of weeks ago, Mr. Blake. He found life in the country rather too dull for him. He had a better offer, and he accepted it."

"What became of him? Where is he now?"

"He has gone to Constantinople, as tutor to the sons of a wealthy Turkish pasha living in the Grand Rue at Pera."

"You have since engaged another secretary," said Blake.

"Yes, a clever fellow of the name of Leighton—Charles Leighton," Hugh Clontarf replied. "He furnished the best of references, and he has been with me for about ten days. He also was on good terms with Kashar Das. He is an amiable chap who wouldn't harm a fly."

"I would like to meet him. He is at home, I suppose?"

"No, he isn't. He is in town, as it happens."

"In town? When did he go?"

"Yesterday morning, Mr. Blake. I sent him up to consult some books of reference, and make notes from them, at the London Library in St. James' Square."

"When will he return?" Blake inquired.

"I am expecting him to-morrow," said Hugh Clontarf. "But I could wire to him to come back at once, if you wish."

"No, no, that won't be necessary! Don't trouble. By the way, has Charles Leighton ever been in India? Can you tell me?"

"I believe not. He hasn't spoken of that country."

"Have you ever been there, Mr. Clontarf?"

"No, never in my life."

There was a short pause. Blakesippedhis whisky, and gazed around the library. Hugh Clontarf, his face still grave and sad, puffed at his cigar and thoughtfully contemplated the detective.

"I wish I could help you," he murmured. "I can't throw any light on the crime, though. I can't conceive any motive for it. All I can say is that the murderer must be somebody I don't know. You would like to question the servants, perhaps!"

"Yes, I may as well," said Blake. "I had better see them before I go."

Hugh Clontarf left the room, and came back presently with the cook and the house-maid, who were of the ordinary type of country servants.

They had been told of the murder of Kashar Das, and were much agitated, as well as flustered, in the presence of the famous detective. But they gave coherent answers, without hesitation, to all the searching questions he put to them; and, having learned precisely nothing, he sent them away.

"They don't know anything, Mr. Clontarf," he remarked. "It is pretty obvious that I shall have to look elsewhere for a clue to this sensational case."

Hugh Clontarf placed his hand on the detective's shoulder.

"Will you help me?" he said earnestly. "You are working for the police. Will you also work on my behalf? Will you do all in your power to avenge the cruel death of my devoted servant?"

"I intend to," Blake replied. "You can be assured, my dear fellow, that I will do my very best. And in the end I will put a rope around the neck of the man who murdered Kashar Das."

"I hope you will. It will be a great satisfaction to me, sir. Don't spare any expense. I can afford to pay whatever fee you may ask."

"We won't discuss that now. Sometimes I do not charge for my services. It depends."

Blake rose to go. Hugh Clontarf went to the hall with him, and, opening the front-door wide to let the light in, he pointed to a full-length portrait of himself that hung on the wall.

"My uncle had that done, a year ago, while I was visiting him at Troon Court," he said. "It was painted by Macrae, the Scotch artist."

"A clever man," Blake answered. "I know him."

"It is a striking likeness, isn't it?"

"Very striking, indeed, Mr. Clontarf. It could not be better."

They shook hands, and Blake, remarking that he would probably call again, left the house and walked slowly down the drive with a look of vague conjecture in his eyes.

"I wonder?" he said to himself. "I wonder why Clontarf showed me that portrait?"

He returned through the woods to the scene of the murder to find that the body of Kashar Das had already been removed to the inn at Ranmore.

Tinker was waiting for him with the bloodhound, and when he had told the lad of his interview with Hugh Clontarf they hastened to their car and drove to the village, which was excited over the tragedy.

They had luncheon with Inspector Stracey, and early in the afternoon, leaving the inspector to pursue his investigations, they set off for London.

"It is a baffling case, my boy," said Blake, as they went spinning along the village street. "I don't in the least know what to make of it as yet. I am at a deadlock. But of one thing I am sure. The key to the mystery lies within the four walls of Ranmore Lodge."

CHAPTER 4.

The Furnished Lodge—Hugh Clontarf at Work—The Marks on the Drive—Footsteps in the Dark—The Fight in the Planatation—Blake Meets Colonel Roylance—At the Elms—The Girl's Strange Story.

IN the purple dusk of the evening, as the moon was throwing a pale glow above the horizon, a man in rough tweeds and a cap was lying flat on the grass at the edge of the garden of Hugh Clontarf's residence.

Beyond him was the house, showing lights at several windows; and to his left, by the gates was the small rustic lodge. All was quiet. There was no sight or sound of life.

The man was Sexton Blake. Three days has elapsed since the murder of Kashar Das, and meanwhile the detective had left the conduct of the case to Inspector Stracey, in order to give him a chance to show his skill.

But the inspector had made no progress whatever, as Blake had learned; and to-day, leaving Tinker at home, he had come down to Dorking by train, and walked over to Ranmore Lodge, through the wooded country; had found the main gates and the side gate locked, and had squeezed through a prickly hedge into the garden.

Why he was here he could scarcely have explained. He had no definite purpose in view. He had only suspicions, and they were of the flimsiest fabric. He could not have analysed them.

Yet he still had faith, more than faith, in the theory he had mentioned to Tinker on the day of the crime—that the key to the mystery lay within the walls of the dwelling from which the Hindu servant had gone forth in the night to meet with a tragic death.

Though it was not likely he had anything to fear, prudence bade Blake be very careful. There was no telling what might happen. It was possible, he felt, that somebody was watching for him; and he was the more inclined to think so because the gates were locked—secured with padlocks—at this early hour of the evening.

At length he rose to his feet, and, bearing to the left, he glided to the rustic lodge, which was in darkness.

He opened the door, and took a flashlight from his pocket, switched it on, and saw a small room that was cosily furnished with a carpet, a couch, a table, and a big armchair.

On the couch were a steamer-rug and a couple of cushions. On the table were a book and a newspaper, a bottle of whisky and a glass, and a packet of cigarettes.

"This is very interesting," Blake said to himself. "Somebody, it would appear, is in the habit of spending the day here. Who? Not one of the servants. Not Mr. Clontarf. And not Charles Leighton, the private secretary. Yet there are only those four people, unless I have been deceived. It looks as if I had been."

His suspicions strengthened by what he had observed in the lodge, he shut the door, and hesitated for a moment; then made his way across the grounds, in the shadow of the trees and shrubbery, and crept round to one side of the house, where he stopped at the edge of the thickets.

There was a lighted window opposite to him, and now he could hear a faint, clicking noise, a sound that was familiar to him.

At the risk of discovery he stole over a strip of open lawn, and, crouching beneath the window, he cautiously raised his head an inch or so.

Through the narrow slit at the bottom of the drawn blind he could see clearly into a room where Hugh Clontarf was seated at a writing-table, his fingers busily tapping the keys of a typewriter. No one else was there.

The young man was alone in the room, and there could be no doubt he was engaged in the task of re-writing the memoirs of his uncle, Lord Roderick Teviot.

He paused, pressed his hand to his brow, and went on with his work, puffing at a pipe. Again he paused and glanced at something on the table, which was littered with letters and manuscripts, notebooks and reference volumes, and printers' proofs.

Where was Charles Leighton, the secretary? Why was he not performing his duties, assisting his employer? Had he not returned yet from London? He was to have come back on the day after the murder, Hugh Clontarf had said.

"The mystery deepens!" Blake murmured. "I doubt if the secretary is still in town. He may be, though. Or perhaps it was he who killed Kashar Das, without Hugh Clontarf's knowledge, and he has disappeared from fear of being suspected."

He withdrew from the window, darting back to the shrubbery, and when he had retraced his steps for some distance he turned aside for a couple of yards and stopped at the margin of the drive.

He played his flashlight on the gravelled surface, moving it here and there, and slipped it into his pocket. He had made another interesting discovery.

"Ah, the marks of tyres!" he said to himself. "A car has been here and gone. And to-day, I imagine. Visitors, or a visitor, for Mr. Clontarf. I wonder who?"

Hugh Clontarf did not own a car. He had no garage. Who, then, had come in one to Ranmore Lodge? None of the country people, it was to be presumed. It was doubtful if any of them would have disturbed the young man, knowing that he was averse to callers while he was writing his book.

Blake was disposed to attach some significance to this discovery. He would have liked to take a more comprehensive survey of the house from all sides, but he was afraid to risk it.

He was deterred by the reflection that the private secretary might have come back from London, and be prowling about somewhere in the large garden.

Concluding to go to the Elms and have dinner with Colonel Roylance on his own invitation, he squeezed through the hedge by the gap at which he had entered, sought for and found the footpath he had trodden before, and held to it. He could dimly make it out in spite of the overhanging foliage, as the moon was above the horizon now.

He went slowly along, deep in thought and conjecture; and he had passed the scene of the murder and was within three or four hundred yards of the road when he came to a bed of velvety moss.

It completely muffled his tread, and in the silence he heard the sharp snapping of a twig behind him. Suspicion flashed to his mind at once.

Was there somebody on his track? Had he been shadowed from Ranmore Lodge? He glided on for half a dozen yards, and stopped. He could plainly hear stealthy footsteps now.

He hastened on a little farther, and stopped again. And again he heard the pursuing steps.

It was as he suspected. Some person was coming warily after him. He had been followed.

"Is it a gamekeeper?" he thought. "Or a poacher? No, I don't believe it is either."

It was very dark here in the woods, for the trees were dense and close together, and the glow of the moon did not penetrate them.

Blake felt decidedly uneasy. A foe in the open he did not fear. He could meet him on equal terms. But an enemy in ambush he dreaded as one dreads a poisonous reptile that strikes without warning.

What should he do? Match craft with craft? That would be best. He would stand his ground.

He turned in the direction from which he had come, and with his flashlight in one hand and an automatic pistol in the other, he peered into the murky gloom and listened with strained ears.

For a few seconds—they seemed as many minutes to him—there was hushed silence. At length he heard a faint rustling noise, and as he flashed on the light, stabbing the darkness with a luminous streak, he had a vague glimpse of a crouching figure that was within a yard of him, and was in the act of leaping.

He had no time to shoot. Before he could pull the trigger a heavy body launched itself at him, and the next instant he was down, battling for life with the invisible tracker.

He knew instinctively that his antagonist was a powerful man—a big, burly man—and was perhaps the stronger.

Blake knew also that his object was murder, and he would not have hesitated to shoot him had it been possible. But he had lost both his pistol and his flashlight as he fell.

It was almost a noiseless struggle. Neither of them uttered a word. They sought strenuously, with crackling muscles, with laboured breathing, floundering from tree to tree, from copse to copse, beating the grass flat, crushing fern and bracken, rolling over and over, now one uppermost, and now the other, each striving for an advantage.

It was Blake who scored first, and just when his strength was beginning to fail him. He got a grip of his assailant's throat, and in spite of the other's efforts to break it he clung desperately like grim death, squeezing harder and harder.

He felt the man's hold of him gradually relax, heard him wheeze and gasp in the agonies of suffocation; and finally, by a sudden wrench, he tore himself free.

In a trice he was on his feet, and the other was up as quickly, spluttering oaths in a husky voice.

"Curse you!" he raved. "Where the devil are you?"

As he spoke he sprang, a black form etched on the blacker darkness. But Blake eluded his clutch, struck at him and missed, and then very wisely took to his heels.

Shots were fired at him as he ran. He heard the rapid reports of an automatic, heard the vicious hum of bullets, heard them rake the foliage above his head, and heard his enemy still coming in pursuit of him.

He was not hit. The firing ceased, but he was not rid of the man yet. Bloodcurdling oaths and crashing footsteps rang to his ears, and from not far behind him.

"The scoundrel!" he muttered. "Who the deuce can he be? I am certain he isn't Hugh Clontarf. He must have followed me from the garden of Ranmore Lodge, though, meaning to kill me at a distance from the house. And Clontarf probably knows nothing of it."

The pursuing steps sounded nearer. Another shot was fired. Blake raced blindly on and on, scrambling amongst the trees and thickets, not knowing in which direction he was going.

He paused for breath and resumed his flight. He could see a silvery glow beyond him now. It grew brighter, and in a few more yards he came out from the woods on to a road that was bathed in the light of the moon. He saw a small car standing close to him, and saw the occupant of it staring in amazement.

"Hallo, Roylance!" he cried. "You here!"

"By Jove, it's Blake!" exclaimed the colonel. "What's wrong? Who has been shooting?"

"I'll tell you presently! We had better not stop here!"

"Good heavens, you have been in a fight! I wish you could see yourself!"

"Yes, I have been in a bit of a scrap. I was attacked in the woods."

Blake got into the car and sat down by the side of Colonel Roylance, who drove swiftly on along the lonely road in the direction of his residence, while he listened to the story of the detective's visit to Ranmore Lodge and his thrilling adventure in the plantation.

"Extraordinary!" he declared. "By gad, you had a narrow escape! Who attacked you? The Hindoo who murdered Kashar Das?"

"Very likely," Blake replied. "But he swore at me in good English, not in Hindustani."

"Well, he certainly wasn't Hugh Clontarf."

"No, Roylance, he was not. He was a much bigger man. Moreover, when I left Clontarf was at work on his book, pounding the typewriter, as I have told you."

"Your assailant was a poacher, perhaps—or a gamekeeper who mistook you for a poacher."

"Neither one nor the other. The scoundrel followed me with murderous intent, and he nearly succeeded."

The colonel was so bewildered that he lost control of the car for an instant, and nearly ran it into a hedge.

"The fellow must have been the murderer," he said. "It is the only explanation. He is anxious to get rid of you because he knows you are working on the case. And it would seem that he is living somewhere in the neighbourhood."

Blake nodded, and changed the subject.

"I was on my way to your place when I met you," he remarked, "to invite myself to dinner."

"I will be glad to have you," Colonel Roylance replied. "You had better let me put you up for the night."

"Thanks for the offer, but I must go back to town by the 11.30 train for Dorking."

"Very well. I will drive you over. I have been in Guildford most of the day discussing business matters with my solicitor. By the way, I forgot to tell you that Gwenda has returned from Italy. She arrived this morning, and she meant to go over to Ranmore Lodge this afternoon to see Hugh Clontarf. She would be back in time for dinner, she told me."

Blake did not answer. He was thinking of the furnished room in the rustic lodge and of the tyre-marks on the drive. He had not mentioned them to the colonel.

The lights of the Elms were visible now, shining out of the darkness. The car rolled through the gates and up to the house. A servant opened the door and informed his master that Miss Gwenda was at home.

Colonel Roylance took the detective to a bed-room and waited while he had a wash and brushed his dishevelled clothes. Then they went downstairs to the library, and they were sitting there, having a drink before dinner, when Gwenda Roylance came in.

She was a very pretty girl of twenty, with brown hair and eyes. She shook hands with Blake, who she had known since childhood, and as he was talking to her, speaking of her trip to Italy, the colonel interruped.

"You have been crying, Gwenda," he said. "What is wrong? Have you been to Ranmore Lodge?"

The girl's lip quivered.

"Yes, I walked over after luncheon," she replied.

"And you saw Hugh?"

"No, father, I didn't."

"Indeed! How is that?"

"He refused. It was cruel of him. I can't understand it. He would be glad to see me, I thought, as I have been so long in Italy. But—but he wouldn't——"

Gwenda paused for a moment.

"I was very badly treated," she continued, in an indignant tone. "Brutally treated. I found the gates locked, though they have never locked before. I went round to the side gate, and that was locked, too. So I slipped through the hedge, and I was crossing the lawn, when a man called to me from the rustic lodge by the gateway. I didn't pay any attention to him. I walked on to the house and rang the bell. Loake, the maid, opened the door; and before I could say a word to her the man came up to me. He was a big man, heavily built, and I didn't like his looks.

"He asked me what I wanted. I told him who I was, and that I had come to see Mr. Clontarf; and he said Hugh was very busy with his work, and couldn't be disturbed on any account. I lost my temper, and insisted on seeing him. That made the man angry, and he took me roughly by the arm, and marched me down to the gates, and unlocked them, and put me out in the road."

"The impudent rascal!" cried Colonel Roylance. "He ought to be soundly thrashed. I shall go over there myself, and complain to Hugh! He will see me, you can be sure!"

There was a grave expression on Blake's face.

"Didn't you have even a glimpse of Mr. Clontarf, Gwenda?" he inquired.

"Yes, I saw him looking from a window as I was led away," the girl answered. "He disappeared at once!"

"The man who handled you so roughly must have been Charles Leighton, the private secretary. What was he like?"

"He was a big man, as I have told you. And he was dark and clean-shaven."

"Was he in the rustic lodge when you entered the garden?"

"Yes, I saw him come out of it just before he called to me."

"Has there been a lodgekeeper since you have known Mr. Clontarf. Gwenda?"

"No, never. The lodge wasn't occupied. There was no furniture in it."

"It is furnishednowand apparently the private secretary has been installed there. Did Mr. Clontarf write to you while you were in Italy?"

"Regularly, Mr. Blake. I had a letter from his every week."

The colonel was flushed with anger.

"A nice state of affairs, I must say!" he exclaimed. "Absurd! Aggravating! Padlocked gates! No visitors admitted! Clontarf refuses to see Gwenda, though he has been engaged to her for months! Outrageous! And that fellow Leighton playing watch-dog in the rustic lodge, when he is supposed to be helping to compile the memoirs of Lord Roderick Teviot! Has the impudence to throw my daughter off the premises! The scoundrel! I shall certainly have a talk with Hugh!"

"You had better not," Blake demurred. "Leave it to me. I will go there to-morrow, taking Gwenda with me, and I'll guarantee Mr. Clontarf receives both of us."

"Perhaps, if you get into the grounds."

"There won't be any difficulty about that Roylance. The gates will be unlocked for me."

"Well you can try it. But why do you want to call on Hugh Clontarf? About the murder, Blake?"

"That willbe my pretext. It is the man Leighton I wish to see. I am rather curious in regard to him."

A servant rapped on the door, opened it, and announced that dinner was ready. And, with knit brows, puzzled by what he had learned, Blake followed Gwenda and her father to the dining-room.

"There will be some interesting developments in the case very shortly, I imagine," he said to himself. "I shall have Tinker set a watch on Ranmore Lodge, and without delay."

CHAPTER 5.

Tinker on Duty—The Claret-coloured Car—A Glimpse of the Lodgekeeper—The Man with the Bottle—At the White Lion at Ranmore—A Bibulous Customer—Sexton Blake Arrives—Instructions for the Lad.

THAT night Tinker was given explicit instructions by Sexton Blake, and at eight o'clock the next morning, after an early breakfast, he left the house in disguise, and took a taxi from Baker Street to Charing Cross Station.

He travelled down to Dorking by train, and set off on foot from the little Surrey town, striking across country. And before eleven o'clock he was at his post of observation, which commanded a view of Ranmore Lodge and the garden.

He was concealed in abelt of woods, stretched flat on the grass beneath a copse of bushes, and within a yard of the private road that ran south from the entrance to Hugh Clontarf's residence.

From where he lay he could see, almost directly in front of him, the wrought-iron gates, the rustic lodge, and the sweeping drive beyond it.

No one was visible in the lodge. The gates were not only unlocked, but were wide open; and the reason was obvious, for a small claret-coloured car, with a chauffeur in livery on the seat, was standing in front of the house.

It was the first thing the lad noticed, and he gazed at it thoughtfully.

"I believe I know that car," he murmured. "Yes, I'm sure I do. I wonder who brought it here?"

Half an hour elapsed, and nothing happened. Then a gentleman appeared alone from the dwelling—he could not be seen distinctly—and got into the car, which had its hood up.

The chauffeur swung it round, and it slid down the drive and out at the gateway, giving Tinker a fleeting glimpse of the profile of the occupant as it shot by.

The door of the rustic lodge was opened now, and from it came the man Gwenda Roylance had described—a big man of heavy build, dark and clean-shaven, with surly features.

He might have been a professional boxer. Anybody less like a private secretary could no easily be imagined, yet he was supposed to be filling the post vacated by Parrish Creed.

He shut the gates, and padlocked them; and, instead of returning to the lodge, he walked up the drive to the house, and entered it.

"It's not likely anything else will happen," Tinker reflected, "I wish it was time for me to get something to eat, and meet the guv'nor."

Another half-hour dragged by monotonously, and at length the peaceful silence was disturbed by shuffling footsteps that were approaching from behind the lad. He crouched flatter in the copse, and drew a spray of foliage over his head.

A middle-aged man came along the road on unsteady legs and stopped close to the gates; a disreputable, unwashed, bibulous-looking man, with bleary eyes, a red nose and a red face, and unshaven cheeks and chin. He wore a shabby velveteen jacket and trousers of whipcord; ragged boots, and a ragged cap.

With a grimy hand he drew a flat bottle from his pocket, and raised it to his lips; drank half of the contents, and replaced it. He took hold of the gates now, rattled them, and swore at them.

He waited for a few seconds, and then, muttering incoherently, he shook his fist at the dwelling, turned on his heel, and went slowly back in the direction from which he had come.

"A poacher or a tramp!" Tinker said to himself. "I wonder what brought him here? I shouldn't care to meet the fellow on a dark night."

He glanced at his watch. It was twelve o'clock. He concluded to go now, and, rising to his feet, he threw a last look at the house, slipped furtively across the road, and struck into a footpath which was a short cut through the woods to Ranmore Village.

A brisk walk of twenty minutes brought him there, and he entered the White Lion, where he sat down at a table in a corner of the tap-room, and ordered a couple of sandwiches.

Several rustics were drinking at the bar. They presently went out, and shortly afterwards, when Tinker had finished his luncheon, the door was noisily pushed open, and in came the bibulous-looking individual who had been to Ranmore Lodge.

He lurched to the bar, and leaned heavily against it. George Harnett, the landlord, regarded him with a scowl.

"You're drunk!" he said severely.

"You're another!" the man retorted. "I'm ash shober as you are!"

"What do you want, Ben?"

"I want you to fill my bottle. And you can give me a pint of beer, and a couple of packets of Woodbines, and two ounces of baccy—the best baccy you have."

"You can pay for them, Ben, I suppose?"

"Me pay? Of course I can!"

The man dived into his pockets, taking from one the flat bottle, and from another three crumpled Treasury notes of a pound each. He detached one of them, and slapped it on the bar.

"There y'are, George!" he mumbled. "There's your Bradbury!"

The landlord stared.

"It's a lot of money for you to have, Ben Partrick!" he said, in a suspicious tone. "Where did you get it?"

"None of your business!"

"It wasn't come by honestly, I'll bet."

"By honest labour, George, and sweat o' the brow. I've been doing odd jobs o' work lately."

"Tell that yarn to the marines—not to me! You don't know what it is to work! And there's nobody in this neighbourhood would employ you."

"Wouldn't they?" sneered the bibulous party. "All right! B'lieve me or not, it's the truth! Want the money, or don't you?"

"I'll take it," George Harnett replied. "But, if you ask me, it's not honest money."

"Thash a lie! Didn't I tell you it's carned by sweat o' the brow! I'll have you know I'm a reformed character!"

"You'll never reform, Ben. You've been poaching in Ranmore Woods again, and smuggling the game up to London to be sold."

"I've stopped poaching, I say! No need to poach! And what if I haven't stopped, George? Does the game belong to Lord Ranmore? No, it b'longs to everybody! Wasn't there a cock pheasant and a hen pheasant on the Ark with old Father Noah? Wasn't there? Answer me that!"

The landlord did not continue the discussion. He filled the flat bottle with whisky, and produced the beer, the cigarettes, and the tobacco.

Ben Partrick emptied his tankard, insisting the while that he was a reformed character and had no need to poach; pocketed his purchases, lurched to the door, and reeled out of the room.

"A funny chap, that," remarked Tinker, who had been listening with more than casual interest.

"He's a wicked old rascal," George Harnett declared. "Been in gaol a dozen times."

"You don't believe he earned the money?"

"No fear, my lad! And I doubt if he got it by selling game. He's been up to something else."

"Where does he live? In the village?"

"A little way out. He has a ramshackle cottage on the Guildford road, at the edge of the fir plantation by the abandoned quarry. He's the biggest poacher in Surrey. As for the money he has on him, I was told this morning he's been seen with more than that."

A throbbing noise in the distance brought Tinker to his feet. He paid what he owed, and hastened from the inn just as a car came along the road and stopped. Sexton Blake was driving it.

"I didn't expect to find you here so soon," he said. "Nothing doing at Ranmore Lodge, I suppose?"

Tinker shrugged his shoulders, a mannerism he had learned from his master. "I am not so sure," he replied. "A couple of things happened."

He told of the claret-coloured car, and of the curious behaviour of the poacher at the gates of Mr. Clontarf's residence; and repeated what he could remember of the conversation between Ben Partrick and the landlord of the White Lion.

Blake's eyes narrowed.

"Did you notice the number of the car?" he inquired.

"No, it went by too quickly," Tinker answered. "The number doesn't matter, though, for I know the car. There are a lot of them in London all alike. It belongs to the Knightsbridge Motor Car Service Company. The chauffeur wore their livery."

"That's all right. And the man Partrick? He went to Ranmore Lodge, and tried to get into the garden! Swore at the locked gates! And he is flush with money! He told the landlord he had no need to poach! Rather significant, eh?"

"That's how it struck me, guv'nor. I have an idea he may know something about the murder of Kashar Das."

Blake nodded vaguely.

"You needn't go back to Ranmore Lodge," he said. "Take the first train to town, go to the Knightsbridge Motor Car Service Company, and find out who hired one of their cars for a trip to Surrey. I think you will easily get the information."

"And what shall I do afterwards?" Tinker asked. "Come back here?"

"No, you can stay in town until I return. And now I must go off. I am due at Colonel Roylance's place at one o'clock. I am having luncheon at the Elms, before Gwenda and I call on Mr. Clontarf."

"You had better be careful. Ranmore Lodge isn't a safe place for you."

"I dare say it will be safe enough in daylight, my boy. But if I am not home by ten o'clock to-night, and you have not received any message from me, you can inform the police."

With that ominous remark Blake drove on towards the Elms, and Tinker, turning in the opposite direction, went briskly on his way to Dorking.

CHAPTER 6.

At Ranmore Lodge—Admittance Refused—Mr. Leighton Changes his Mind—The Meeting of the Lovers—Hugh Clontarf Breaks off the Engagement.

WHEN Blake drove off in his car from the Elms after luncheon, accompanied by Gwenda Roylance, he was not sure it was a wise thing he was going to do. He had no fears for himself, but he was reluctant to expose the girl to any risk. He had strong reasons, however, for wanting to take her with him.

As for Gwenda, her heart was torn between pride and affection; she resented her ill-treatment of the previous day, yet she was inclined to forgive her lover.

She was not much concerned about the mysterious murder of the Hindu servant. She supposed the police would soon solve the mystery, and she took it for grant, of course, that Hugh Clontarf had no knowledge of the crime.

It was three o'clock when the car pulled up in front of the gates of Ranmore Lodge. They were still locked, and though Blake called repeatedly, no one came from the rustic lodge, nor did he see any person there.

He thrust the crook of his stick into the bars of the gates, and raffled them loudly. There was no response.

"They aren't going to let us in, I am sure," said Gwenda.

"They will if they have seen me," Blake replied, "and I dare say they have."

He was right. He waited for a moment, and was about to shout when a servant, an elderly woman, appeared from the house. She hastened down to the road, a key in her hand.

"Is Mr. Clontarf at home?" Blake inquired.

"I—I don't know," the woman answered. "I can't tell you."

"We wish to see him. Let us in, please."

"Yes, sir. Mr. Leighton said I should."

The woman unlocked the gates, pulled them open, and stood aside. Blake sent the car spinning up the drive to the dwelling, and, getting out quickly with the girl, he rang the bell.

Loake, the maid, opened the door, and without a word she showed the visitors into a room to the left of the hall. It was the same room into which the detective had peeped through a window.

A dark, clean-shaved man was seated at the writing-table, which, as before, was strewn with books and papers, and proofs from the publishers. He rose to this feet, and bowed curtly.

Blake observed bruises on his cheeks, and had little or no doubt that he was face to face with the person who had attempted his life in the woods.

"You are Mr. Leighton, I presume?" he said.

The man nodded.

"Yes, I am Charles Leighton, Mr. Clontarf's private secretary," he assented.

"We have come to see Mr. Clontarf."

"I am afraid you can't see him to-day, sir."

"We must. I dare say you know who we are?"

"I know the lady is Miss Roylance. I was to tell her, if she called again, that Mr. Clontarf intended to write to her."

"You also know who I am, I think?"

"I can guess. I suppose you are Mr. Sexton Blake, the detective who is helping Inspector Stracey with the murder case."

"I am," Blake replied. "and it is in connection with the murder I have called. That is my business with Mr. Clontarf, and I insist on seeing him."

Charles Leighton shrugged his shoulders. "I am sorry," he said, "but you can't see him to-day. He is not at home."

"Where is he?" Blake asked.

"He has gone up to London to keep an appointment."

"When will he be back?"

"He expects to return this evening, sir."

Gwenda was bitterly disappointed. Blake glanced closely at the secretary, who returned his gaze without a sign of discompose.

"I am sorry, sir," he repeated. "Perhaps you will call to-morrow. I may tell you, though, that it is difficult to see Mr. Clontarf at any time."

Blake felt his temper rising. He was irritated by the man's bland, suave attitude, and, moreover, he was certain he had lied.

"It is partly on Miss Roylance's account I have called to-day," he said. "Some curious things have happened. I can't understand them, and I should like to have an explanation."

"Some curious things?" murmured Charles Leighton. "I have no idea what you mean."

"Oh, yes, you have!" Blake sharply declared. "You know quite well. This young lady is engaged to Mr. Clontarf, yet when she called yesterday he not only refused to see her, but you dragged her roughly to the gates, and threw her into the road."

"I simply did what my employer told me to do."

"He gave you such orders?"

"Not exactly. He could not be disturbed, and as Miss Roylance was determined to see him I had to force her to go."

"Why are the gates always locked?" Blake continued. "Why have you been occupying the rustic lodge? Why has Mr. Clontarf hedged himself about with such precautions? One might think he had an enemy he was afraid of."

Charles Leighton smiled insolently.

"It is his nerves," he replied. "You must make allowances for that. He is almost a mental wreck. You cannot realise how tremendous, how exacting, is the labour involved in compiling the memoirs of his late uncle. It leaves him no time to visit or entertain his friends. He is compelled to live like a recluse. The task has been preying on his mind, and exhausting his energies. He has been under a heavy strain, and will be until the work is finished."

"You are helping him, are you not?"

"To some extent, Mr. Blake. He works at night, while I work by day."

"Is there any necessity for haste? Are the publishers waiting for the book?"

"Yes; it must be completed by a certain date. That is why we are rushing it through."

Gwenda had been listening with flushed cheeks, with a gleam of indignation in her eyes. She was not satisfied.

"I have been treated shamefully," she exclaimed, "and I won't have it! Mr. Clontarf's behaviour is insulting!"

"You must remember how busy he is," Charles Leighton answered, "and what a strain there is on his mind."

The girl tapped the floor with her foot. "That isn't any excuse," she protested. "Surely he can spare a little time. You can tell him from me that he must remove his silly padlocks, and let me come here as often as I wish."

"His work absorbs all of his time, Miss Roylance."

"I don't believe it! I shall see him to-morrow if I have to break into the house!"

There was an ugly expression on Charles Leighton's face now.

"As you are so insistent," he said, in a sneering tone. "I will give you a message which has been entrusted to me. That I did not give it to you before was because I wanted to spare your feelings. The truth of the matter is this. Mr. Clontarf has come to the conclusion that you and he are not suited to each other."

Gwenda stared in consternation.

"He wishes our engagement to be broken off?" she faltered. "Is that his meaning?"

"Yes, in plain words that is exactly what he means. He realises he has made a mistake, and thinks he ought to set you free."

"He told you so?"

"I have repeated the message as I had it from him, Miss Royance."

The girl's lip quivered, and a look of bitter pain crept into her eyes. But as quickly her pride was in arms, and she gazed at the secretary scornfully.

"Very well!" she cried. "I am glad I have found out my mistake before it was too late! The engagement is at an end! Mr. Clontarf has broken it—not I! He need not be afraid I will try to force myself on him! I will never speak to him again! Never see him again! He is not the man I thought he was! When he knew he was tired of me, knew he didn't care for me any longer, why didn't he tell me so? It would have been more honourable! He could have written to me while I was in Italy, instead of waiting until I came back, and—and humiliating me by——"

Gwenda's voice faltered, and she paused overcome by her feelings. It was a cruel blow to her, for she had been very much in love. She turned to the detective, her eyes moist.

"I want to go now!" she half-sobbed. "Take me home, please, Mr. Blake!"

Blake did not stir. His anger had been roused.

"Have you spoken the truth?" he demanded of the secretary. "Did Mr. Clontarf give you the message you delivered to Miss Roylance, or did you invent it?"

"I did not!" Charles Leighton hotly exclaimed. "I had it from my employer! What do you mean by insinuating that I am a liar? What have you got to do with Mr. Clontarf's affairs?"

"I have more to do with them than you think, perhaps!"

"That's enough! I won't stand any further impertinence from you! You may bully other people, but you can't bully me! Be off with you now!"

"Be careful how you talk to me, you impudent rascal!"

"I'll do more than talk if you don't clear out!"

As Charles Leighton spoke he moved forward in a threatening attitude, and Blake, his temper beyond control, clenched his fists and let fly, dealing the man a blow on the jaw that sent him crashing to the floor.

"That will teach you to keep a civil tongue in your head!" he cried.

By the time Charles Leighton had staggered to his feet, Blake and the girl had left the house. They hurried down the garden to the car, got into it, and drove away.

Gwenda was grief-stricken. For a little while she wept silently, stifling her sobs, trying to hide the tears that trickled down her cheeks.

Blake let her alone. He did not speak to her—his mind was absorbed in the mystery of Ranmore Lodge—and she did not speak to him until they had nearly reached the Elms. And then she said, half to herself:

"I suppose there are excuses to be made for Hugh. He has been working too hard on the book."

Blake did not answer. He was deep in thought, pondering over a glimmer of a theory, a mere shadow of one, which, though it slipped from him now, was to develop later into something very tangible.

CHAPTER 7.

The Man who Hired the Claret-coloured Car—What Blake Remembered of Sir Ralph Athelstan—A Visit to the Publishers—An Interesting Conversation with Mr. Hendon—The Secret Chapter.

BLAKE stayed to tea at the Elms, tried with poor success to soothe Colonel Roylance's indignation at his daughter's treatment, and drove back to London, arriving home at nine o'clock in the evening.

He told Tinker of everything that had occurred at Ranmore Lodge, and the lad then reported on the instructions his master had given to him. He had been to the garage of the Knightsbridge Motor Car Service Company, and had got the desired information.

"The man who hired the claret-coloured car this morning for a run to Surrey," he said, "was Sir Ralph Athelstan, of Number 198, Hamilton Place. I have heard of him, guv'nor, and no doubt you have, too."

Blake nodded.

"I know him," he replied. "I have met him once or twice. Sir Ralph Athelstan belongs to a very good old family. He is the seventh baronet, and he has several wealthy and titled relatives. He is heir to one of them, I believe. He is a bachelor, popular in society, and a member of two or three of the best clubs in London. He was a famous cricketer in his day. He has been in the Civil Service abroad, has shot big game in Africa and India, and has the reputation of losing a couple of fortunes on the Turf. As for the rest, he used to sail a yacht at Cowes, and I think he at one time owned some race-horses."

"Why do you suppose Sir Ralph Athelstan called on Mr. Hugh Clontarf?"

"I don't know. It isn't the first time he has been to Ranmore Lodge, I imagine."

"Social visits, perhaps."

"And perhaps not, my boy. If my memory is not at fault, Sir Ralph Athelstan was mixed up in some scandalous affair—I can't recall what it was—a number of years ago. And I am also under the impression that he was a friend of the late Lord Roderick Teviot, the uncle of Hugh Clontarf. And as that young man is engaged in writing the memoirs of Lord Roderick, the fact may have some connection with——"

Blake paused for a moment.

"The thread is probably not worth following," he added. "It is not likely to help me to throw any light on the murder of Kashar Das. Yet I should like to learn something about the forthcoming book. I will call on Henson and Halbury, the prospective publishers, to-morrow, and see what they can tell me."

"If you ask me, guv'nor," said the lad, "it isn't worth while."

Blake thought differently, and he was in the same mind the next morning, when, after breakfast, he took a taxi to Bedford Street, and was shown into the private office of Mr. Edward Henson, the head of the publishing firm. Mr. Henson was acquainted with the detective, and had a cordial greeting for him.

"Good-morning, Mr. Blake," he said, rising from his desk. "Sit down. Take that armchair. I am very glad to see you. And I would be even more glad if I could believe you had come with a proposition to write your memoirs for me. Memoirs of eminent people go splendidly with the public."

Blake smiled.

"I am afraid I haven't any time to spare for literary work," he replied.

"I hope you will consider the matter seriously," urged Mr. Henson. "I am very much in earnest. The book could be published in a couple of volumes, at two guineas for the set. It would run into many thousands of copies. It would be translated into a number of foreign languages. In addition to the English rights, you would have royalties on the American rights, the Colonial rights, and the Continental rights."

"It sounds very alluring," Blake admitted. "You can't tempt me, though. I am more interested in somebody else's memoirs than in my own. That is why I have called."

"Indeed? To what do you refer?"

"To the memoirs of the late Lord Roderick Teviot, which you have announced for early publication. I am aware, I may say, of the terms of Lord Roderick's will, and of the fact that his nephew, Mr. Hugh Clontarf, is engaged in writing the book from his uncle's notes and diaries, and other material."

"Just so," Edward Henson assented. "And Mr. Clontarf, unfortunately, is very prominent in the eyes of the public at present. An amazing affair that, the murder of the Hindu servant in a plantation in Surrey! I understand you are helping the police with the case. Have you discovered any clue?"

"Not yet," said Blake. "It is still a baffling mystery."

"Well, I dare say you will soon clear it up. But I am wandering from the subject. We were talking of Lord Roderick Teviot's memoirs. In what way are you interested in them?"

"Not in any way, personally speaking. I presume you have most of the manuscript in hand?"

"The greater part of it, Mr. Blake."

"And you have read it?"

"I have read every line, and also rough drafts of the chapters not yet completed.

"You can tell me, then, if Sir Ralph Athelstan is mentioned in the memoirs to his detriment. In other words, will the publication of the book blacken his character, injure his social standing?"

Mr. Henson looked somewhat startled.

"You put me in a dilemma," he said gravely. "I fear I can't give you any information."

"It is important that I should know," Blake answered. "I have a reason which I cannot divulge to you now."

"And I am bound to a pledge of secrecy."

"To Mr. Clontarf?"

"Yes, to Mr. Clontarf. That is my position. Would I be justfied, do you think, in breaking the pledge?"

Blake hesitated for a moment.

"I think you would be," he said. "provided I regard what you might tell me as confidential, as, of course, I should."

"Very well," replied Mr. Henson. "If you feel that I ought to confide in you, I will do so. I should certainly not tell anybody else. Did you ever hear of the Selampur Turf Scandal?"

"I did, now that you have refreshed my memory," said Blake. "I had forgotten it."

"It occurred out in India, about eighteen years ago, and Lord Roderick Teviot and Sir Ralph Athelstan were implicated in it. Sir Ralph was subsequently vindicated, and so was Lord Roderick, to a great extent. To the end of his life a shadow of suspicion rested on him, however, and most unjustly. He was the innocent scapegoat, and Sir Ralph was a designing villain. He had a grudge against Lord Roderick Teviot, and he deliberately tried to ruin and disgrace him."

"There is a chapter in the book relating to Sir Ralph Athelstan, I suppose."

"There is, Mr. Blake. It is locked in that big safe yonder with the bulk of the manuscript. It gives the true version of the Selampur Turf Scandal, and, furthermore, it is supported by written proofs. Though Lord Roderick Teviot could at any time have vindicated his honour, he held his tongue, preferring to suffer in silence while he lived. But it was his express wish, his command, that after his death the truth should be disclosed and his reputation cleared."

"Did Sir Ralph Athelstan make any attempt to have the chapter suppressed?" Blake inquired.

"I can't say," Mr. Henson answered. "I don't know. To the best of my knowledge, Mr. Clontarf has never seen or heard from Sir Ralph Athelstan. All I can tell you is that he brought the chapter dealing with the Turf affair to me in person, that he bade me keep it locked in the safe, that he had me promise I would not speak of it to anybody, and that the printers and proof-readers were to be bound by a similar promise of secrecy."

"That is rather curious. It suggests that Mr. Clontarf had an interview with Sir Ralph Athelstan, and that he was afraid he might try to get to the manuscript."

"It does suggest that. It is the only explanation. But if Mr. Clontarf has had a talk with Sir Ralph about the chapter, why didn't he tell me?"

"Ah, why not? I don't understand it. When did he bring the chapter to you?"

"One day last week."

"When is the book to be published?" asked Blake.

"Very shortly," Mr. Henson replied. "It will be on sale in a little more than a month, I hope."

"Has anything been paid on it?"

"Not yet. Mr. Clontarf is to have a cheque for a thousand pounds, on account of royalties, on the day of publication. I shan't be risking anything. The memoirs of Lord Roderick Teviot are bound to have a tremendous sale."

Blake had got all the information that was to be had. He knew now, he believed, why Sir Ralph Athelstan had gone to Ranmore Lodge. He thanked Mr. Henson, and, somewhat perplexed by what he had learned, he went home to luncheon, and told Tinker of his conversation with the publisher.

"It doesn't amount to much, does it?" he resumed.

"You know what I told you," said the lad, "that it wouldn't be worth while for you to call on Mr. Henson. What you learned from his is very interesting and sensational, and all that sort of thing. But the Selampur Turf Scandal and the murder of Kashar Das are as far apart as the poles."

"It would seem so," Blake assented. "I dare say they are. Apparently, from what I should judge, Sir Ralph Athelstan, being aware that his villainy would be exposed after the death of Sir Roderick Teviot, came to Hugh Clontarf, and tried to bribe him to suppress or destroy the chapter relating to the Turf affair. Mr. Clontarf refused, and that would account for the instructions he gave the publisher."

"There is another way of looking at it, guv'nor. Mr. Clontarf may be playing the part of a scoundrel."

"How so, my boy?"

"Perhaps he took a bribe from Sir Ralph, promised to suppress the chapter, and doesn't intend to keep his word."

"Possibly. Your theory is not as plausible as mine, though. Hugh Clontarf bears the highest character in Surrey, and he is in no need of money. I doubt if he would have accepted a bribe from Sir Ralph Athelstan, especially with the intention of deceiving him. It is hard for me to believe he would have played so mean and wicked a trick on a man who, after enjoying immunity for eighteen years, and meanwhile leading a clean life—I think the Selampur affair is the only thing to Sir Ralph Athelstan's discredit—is threatened with social disgrace through the publication of Lord Roderick's memoirs, and probably with the loss of a fortune as well. No, I can't entertain such a theory. And yet—and yet——"

Blake broke off and shrugged his shoulders irritably. A shadow of a suspicion had flashed upon him, and had slipped out of his mind as quickly, before he could grasp it.

"I wonder if the inquest will throw any fresh light on the murder?" he continued. "It is to be held to-morrow, by the way. You and I will be there, Tinker, and afterwards I may have a talk with that poacher, Partrick. I am rather curious to know where he got his money."

CHAPTER 8.

The Inquest—The Verdict of the Jury—Blake has a Talk with Ben Partrick—The Poacher's Strange Story—Danger.

THE inquest on the body of Kashar Das was held the next day, at the White Lion in the little village of Ranmore.

Sexton Blake and Tinker motored down to give evidence, and other witnesses were Inspector Stracey and the two gamekeepers, Lambert and Kelke; the servants from Ranmore Lodge, and Hugh Clontarf and Charles Leighton, whose bearing under the coroner's fire of questions was perfectly cool and composed.

No fresh statements were made. No light was thrown on the mystery. A verdict was rendered to the effect that the Hindu had been wilfully murdered by some person unknown.

The coroner remarked that he was glad to hear Mr. Sexton Blake had the case in hand, and the proceedings were finished. The witnesses dispersed, as did the crowd of people who had flocked to the inn more to see the famous detective than for any other reason.

Blake had a consultation with Inspector Stracey, and then he and Tinker drove over to the Elms, where they had luncheon with Colonel Roylance and his daughter, and stayed for tea.

They returned to the village late in the afternoon, and Blake, having made inquiries of the landlord of the White Lion, left the lad there to wait for him, and set off on foot in the direction of Guildford.

His destination was the place where Ben Partrick, the poacher, lived; and he reached it in a brisk walk of a quarter of an hour. It was a suitable spot for the abode of a lawless man.

The cottage, a ramshackle little structure with a patch of cultivated garden in front of it, stood a number of yards back from the road and on much higher ground, nestled on a grassy shelf that projected midway up a hill.

Immediately behind it the continuation of the hill rose at a steep angle, clothed with fir-trees, and close to the left was a sheer drop into an abandoned quarry, at the bottom of which was a deep pool of water.

In all directions the country roundabout was thickly wooded, and there was no other habitation in sight or anywhere near.

Having ascended the hill by a twisting path, Blake rapped twice on the cottage door and got no answer. He pushed the door open and saw that the poacher was not at home.

A sweeping glance at the wretched room, which had a floor of red tiles, showed him a narrow bed that was dirty and in disorder, a deal table with dishes and bottles on it, and a couple of rickety chairs.

Should he go in and wait? He hesitated and was about to withdraw when he heard footsteps approaching along the road. On a sudden impulse he shut the door and slipped hastily round to the back of the cottage, where he crouched by a small and grimy window, and peeped through it.

He could hear the steps drawing nearer. They were mounting the path now, and presently Ben Partrick appeared in the doorway. He was obviously quite sober. His movements were steady.

His first act was to pull from one of the capacious pockets of his velveteen jacket a young hare and toss it under the bed. He drank from one of the bottles on the table, and then, dropping to his knees, he prised up a lose tile from the floor and revealed beneath it a shabby wallet, took from the wallet a packet of Treasury notes, and thrust one of them into a pocket of his waistcoat.

Having replaced the wallet and the tile, he produced a tobacco-pouch and clay pipe, drank from the bottle again, and sat down in one of the chairs.

Blake had been watching him, and now with noiseless tread he went round to the front of the cottage and walked quietly into the room.

"Hallo, Partrick!" he remarked in a cheery tone. "I have attended the inquest on the Hindu to-day, and I thought I would drop in to see you."

The poacher sprang to his feet, struck dumb. There was a look of perplexity, more than of fear, on his unshaven features. It was evident he did not know who the visitor was.

"I am a London detective," Blake continued. "I am helping the police with the murder case. Sexton Blake is my name."

Ben Partrick's expression did not change. He betrayed no uneasiness. He studied the detective's face for a moment, though, before he spoke.

"I've heard a lot about you, sir," he muttered. "Everybody has."

Blake nodded.

"There was a crowd at the inquest," he went on, "but I didn't notice you."

"I wasn't there," said the poacher. "I don't often go to the village."

Blake sprang a question.

"By the way, did you happen to be in the Ranmore Woods the night Kashar Das was killed?" he asked.

As he spoke he gazed straight at Ben Partrick, who did not flinch under the searching scrutiny. Not a muscle of his face twitched.

"No, sir, I wasn't out anywhere that night," he answered. "I was at home in bed."

"Are you sure it was the same night?" Blake inquired.

"I could swear to it, sir."

"When did you first learn of the murder, Partrick?"

"Not until the afternoon of the next day. I had the news from the postman who came by my cottage."

Blake seated himself in a chair and lit a cigarette. Though he had failed to shake Ben Partrick's composure, he was inclined to disbelieve the statements which had been made to him.

"It is a mysterious affair, this murder," he resumed. "I am very anxious to clear it up, and I had an idea you might be able to help me."

"Me help you, sir?" the poacher replied in a puzzled tone. "I don't know why you should think that."

"It is because of something I heard the other day," said Blake. "You were in the White Lion at Ranmore. You made some purchases and displayed three Treasury notes of a pound each. Harnett, the landlord, accused you of having come by the money dishonestly, and you told him you had stopped poaching and had been doing odd jobs of work."

"So I have been, sir. That's right. The money was earned."

"How much had you in all?"

'Only the three pounds, sir."

"For what people in the neighbourhood have you been working, Partrick."

"I—I forget who they were."

"Nonsense! You couldn't have forgotten. You are trying to deceive me."

There was a short pause. Having observed the hidden hoard beneath the tiled floor, Blake knew to a certainty now that the poacher was lying to him.

"Tell me this," he bade sharply. "Why did you to to Ranmore Lodge the day before yesterday and rattle at the locked gates?"

Ben Partrick was caught off his guard. He stared at the detective in dismay, a look of apprehension in his eyes.

"Why did you go there?" Blake repeated. "Why?"

"I—I wanted to see Mr. Clontarf," stammered the poacher.

"What about? What business had you with him?"

"It was Mr. Clontarf I got the money from. That's why I went to his place."

"He paid you for work done?"

"No, sir, it was a gift?"

"A gift of three pounds? Do you expect me to believe that tale, Partrick? It is absurd!"

"It's the truth, sir! Mr. Clontarf did give me the money, and I thought I might get a bit more out of him. I had been drinking too much that morning, else I wouldn't have had the nerve to——"

Ben Partrick stopped for a moment, overcome with confusion, and pulled himself together.

"I've not lied to you, sir," he continued. "I'll tell you the whole story, and you can believe me or not. It hapened one night last month over in Abinger Woods, and close to the River Wharle. The moon was shining bright, and I was setting a snare by a tree when I heard footsteps and voices—or rather a voice. I slipped behind the tree and watched. And who should come along but Mr. Hugh Clontarf. He hasn't any hat on his head, and he was talking to himself in a queer sort of a way, mumbling the words as if he was a bit daft. I'd have let him go by if it hadn't been that he was walking straight for the river, and didn't seem to know it was there, though he was within three or four yards of it.

"So I stepped out in front of him and spoke to him. And before I could warn him of his danger he clenched his fist and let fly at me. He was frightened, I dare say, because he thought I was going to attack him. He was in an ugly mood, and I had to defend myself. I hit back at him, and from blows we came to grips. We fought hard for a couple of minutes, and I was getting the worst of it when we tripped and fell, and Mr. Clontarf struck his head on a stone. He lay there like a dead man, and I was afraid I had killed him.

"I didn't wait to see. I went off in a hurry, and after a while I bucked up courage and crept back. As I come close to the river I heard voices and stopped. I crept a little nearer, and saw Mr. Clontarf on his feet and two men holding him. I couldn't see the men plainly, for the moon was under a cloud at the time; but I think one of them was a gentleman of the name of Creed, who lived with Mr. Clontarf at Ranmore Lodge. They all moved away, and I went home afterwards, feeling a bit worried for fear I would get into trouble. I didn't hear anything of the affair, though, and I had almost forgotten about it when——"

Ben Partrick paused and struck a match to light his pipe, which had gone out. He appeared to be wondering how he should finish his tale.

"Go on!" bade Blake. "What else?"

"The next time I saw Mr. Clontarf," the poacher resumed, "was on the road one morning near Ranmore Lodge. And as he gave me a nasty look, I apologised to him for what I had done. He stared at me in surprise, saying he didn't know what I meant. I told him about the fight, and he hadn't any recollection of it. He said he lost his memory that night and wandered away from home, and Mr. Creed and another friend of his had searched for him and found him, and taken him back. And then he gave me the three pounds, sir. It was a gift because he was sorry he had attacked me."

"That's all you have to tell me, Partrick, is it?"

"That's all, sir. There isn't anything more."

"Mr. Clontarf didn't give you money because you told him you had some knowledge of the murder?"

"Of course not. I don't know anything about the murder."

Blake did not care to press the subject any further, now that his vague suspicions had been strengthened. He had better play a wary game, he felt. As for the poacher's story, he was in two minds as to how much credence to give to it.

On the whole, he was disposed to believe that part of it which related to the fight in Abinger Woods, and to believe also that the subsequent conversation between Mr. Clontarf and Ben Partrick in the road had taken place. But he was quite sure, and with good reason, that the poacher had lied in regard to the money.

"When did you meet Mr. Clontarf in the woods?" he asked. "How long ago was it?"

"Between three and four weeks ago, as far as I can remember," Ben Partrick replied.

"Describe the spot as best you can," said Blake. "Don't hesitate."

"I can tell you exactly where it was, sir. In an open space by the River Wharle, and about thirty yards from a footbridge that crosses the stream. It was under a big oak-tree, with spreading boles, that Mr. Clontarf and I had the fight."

"In which direction did he go with the two men after they found him? Towards Ranmore Lodge?"

"I suppose he did, sir. I didn't notice."

"When did you meet Mr. Clontarf in the road hear his house, Partrick?"

"Only a few days ago, sir."

"Before or after the murder of the Hindu?"

"It was afterwards, Mr. Blake," the poacher answered. "All I have told you is true, and perhaps you can prove it if you wish." He pointed to the front of his jacket. "You can see there's a brown button missing, can't you? I lost it the night of the fight in Abinger Woods. It was torn off my coat, and I dare say it is still lying somewhere on the ground near the big oak-tree."

Blake shrugged his shoulders.

"Never mind about the button," he said. "It wouldn't prove much. I am satisfied with your explanation of the money," he added, with intent to deceive. "If you came by it honestly, that is the end of the matter. But don't tell any person that I have had a talk with you. Hold your tongue, and——"

"Look, sir, look!" Ben Partrick interrupted. "The window! Somebody is peeping in at us!"

Raising his eyes to the window at the rear of the room, Blake had a glimpse of a shadowy face that vanished on the instant. He whipped out of the cottage, and dashed round to the back of it.

He was too late. He could not see the man, but he could hear him climbing the wooded slope, and at once he gave chase, followed by the poacher.

The dusk of evening was falling now, and it was to Blake's disadvantage. Guided by the crashing sounds above him, he ascended through the fir-woods as fast as he could, bearing to the left in the direction of the old quarry.

Twice he had a dim, fleeting view of the fugitive beyond him, and he had gone a short distance in pursuit when two pistol-shots were fired at him in quick succession.

Both narrowly missed him. A third shot grazed his arm, and as he dodged to one side he slipped on a bed of moss, lost his balance, and fell backward.

In vain he tried to check himself. He slid rapidly past Ben Partrick, rolled over and over amongst the thickets, toppled out from them at the brink of the quarry, and plunged headlong into space.

With a heavy splash he dropped into the pool at the bottom, going deep under; and, rising to the surface, he swam for a few yards to a ledge, and scrambled on to it.

Close to him was a winding cart-trick, and by that he mounted to the road, where he stopped to wring the water from his dripping clothes.

He was thus engaged when the poacher appeared on the scene, and now Tinker came running from the direction of the village.

"Are you all right, guv'nor?" cried the lad, as he reached the spot.

"Quite all right," Blake calmly replied, "except for a drenching. What are you doing here? I told you to wait at the inn for me."

I wondered what was keeping you so long," said Tinker, "and I thought I would come to meet you. I heard the shots, and saw you fall into the quarry. And I saw the man who fired at you. What did he do?"

"He was looking through a window of the cottage while I was talking to Partrick. You saw him, you say? How was that?"

"I had a glimpse of him in the open from the road as he darted over the top of the hill into the woods.

"Did you get a good view of him, my boy?"

"I didn't see him distinctly. But I noticed that he was wearing a white turban."

"A white turban? Then it was the same man who——"

"He must have been the murderer, guv'nor. There isn't any doublt about it. My word, you had a narrow escape!"

Ben Partrick's face was a study. He gazed speechlessly at the detective for a moment, a look of terror in his eyes.

"A man with a white turban!" he exclaimed. "You think it was the Hindu who is supposed to have murdered the other Hindu?"

"It would seem so," Blake drily assented.

"I wonder what brought him to my cottage?" said the poacher, in a tremulous voice.

"He followed me, I dare say."

"And he heard all I told you, sir!"

"Very likely he did. It depends on how long he was listening at the window. You needn't be alarmed, though. I don't suppose the fellow has any designs on you."

"No, he—he couldn't have."

"Not if everything you told me was true, Partrick."

"It was, Mr. Blake. Every word of it."

"Don't worry, then. You probably won't see any more of the man."

Ben Partrick's apprehensions had obviously not been allayed. The look of fear was still in his eyes.

Without another word he returned to his cottage, slowly and thoughtfully; and Blake, remarking that he would dry his clothes at the White Lion, set off at a brisk pace with Tinker towards the village, and repeated to him as they went along what he had learned from the poacher.

"It is an amazing story, guv'nor," said the lad. "I can hardly believe it. Do you?"

Blake nodded vaguely.

"I am inclined to believe the greater part of it," he replied. "It may be all true, with the exception of Partrick's tale of the money, and if so—well, it should point to a very startling theory."

"What theory?" asked Tinker.

"Never mind," said Blake. "I won't talk of it now. I have an idea in my head, and I want to think about it."

CHAPTER 9.

The Next Day– Blake Goes to Abinger Woods—The Lost Button—The Path by the River—The House on the Road—A Significant Discovery—What Tinker Learned.

AFTER breakfast the next morning, Blake and Tinker drove down to Ranmore in their car, and left it at the White Lion, where they separated.

The lad went in the direction of Ranmore Lodge, to obey instructions which had been given to him; and Blake, who was familiar with the neighbourhood for miles around, struck across-country to the Abinger Woods.

It was with no very definite purpose that he was going there, for the slender suspicion he had conceived on the previous day had almost entirely evaporated since. He was still in the mind to believe Ben Partrick's story however; and he felt that he would like to obtain proof of it, if possible.

Arrived at the woods, he had no difficulty in locating the spot the poacher had described to him. It existed.

Here was the open space, with the big oak-tree to one side of it. The little River Wharle was close by, and a short distance to the left of it could be seen the footbridge that spanned the stream.

Blake searched thoroughly and patiently, tramping over the whole surface of the glade, and in the end his patience was rewarded.

Much to his satisfaction he found in the tangled grass, between the boles of the oak-tree, a brown button similar to those he had seen on Ben Partrick's velveteen jacket.

"Ah, here it is!" he murmured, as he picked it up. "This confirms the fellow's story, as far as it goes. He fought with somebody, and I dare say the person was Hugh Clontarf. But I am no nearer to solving the mystery. I am not so sure though. The suspicion still sticks in my mind—a suspicion that would account for everything if it was right. I wonder if it is?"

Had two murders been committed, not one? Thus reflecting, with no purpose except to return to the village by the nearest route, Blake followed the course of the river to the left, and crossed it by the bridge.

A little farther on he stumbled on a footpath, and it lead him to a road, where he turned in the direction of Ranmore. To one side of him was a plantation—and on the other side—the side on which he was walking—was the high brick wall of a garden.

Presently he came to double gates of wood, set between stone pillars on which the name of the place, Laurel Grange, was painted in white letters.

He noticed the name as he was passing by, and the next instant he stopped abruptly, uttering a low exclamation. He had just heard footsteps and voices in the garden, and had also distinctly, unmistakably heard hisown name spoken.

"By Jove, that's queer!" he said to him self. "Very queer! What the deuce can it mean?"

The footsteps were drawing near. He heard the voices again, but could not catch what the speakers were saying. At once he hastened across the road, and into the woods; slipped behind a tree, and peered cautiously from it.

He had taken to shelter none too soon. One of the double gates was opened now, and two men appeared. One of them was a gentleman of middle age, wearing spectacles, with a brown moustache and a beard that was round in shape.

And the other Blake recognised with bewilderment as Charles Leighton, Hugh Clontarf's private secretary.

The two exchanged a few words, and shook hands. The man with the beard stepped back into the garden, and shut the gate; and Charles Leighton, having lit a cigar, came to the opposite side of the road, and entered the plantation close to where the detective was concealed.

He was going towards Ranmore Lodge, and when his footsteps had faded to silence Blake left his hiding-place, and went on his way.

His curiosity had been roused by what he had seen. He could not account for it. Was it to be reconciled with his dim suspicions? No, apparently not!

"I must make some inquiries about that house," he reflected. "It was to let, furnished, I remember, the last time I was by here. And that was last year."

Blake reached the White Lion at one o'clock. He sat down at a table in a corner of the tap-room, and ordered something to eat; and when he had finished his luncheon, and filled and lit his pipe, he spoke to the landlord.

"I passed Laurel Grange this morning," he said. "When I was last in the neighbourhood the place was to let, furnished. You can tell me who lives there now, perhaps."

George Harnett nodded.

"The house was taken about a year ago, sir," he replied, "by a Dr. Gavin Todd. He is a Scotsman, I believe."

"I didn't see his name on the gates," remarked Blake. "Is he a practising physician?"

"No, sir, he isn't. He keeps a rest-home. That is what he calls his place. He takes in private patients, people of means, who have nervous disorders, and need rest and careful treatment."

"His name has a familiar ring to me, Harnett. I imagine I have heard it somewhere or other before."

"Very likely, sir. Some motoring gentlemen who stopped here for dinner one evening last month were talking of Dr. Gavin Todd, and it appears, from what they said about him in my hearing, that he was in serious trouble several years ago, when he had a rest-home in Yorkshire. There was a scandal over the affair. He detained a wealthy patient he hadn't any right to detain; because the relatives wanted him to be kept in confinement. An action was brought against the doctor, and he had to pay heavy damages."

"Ah, yes, I recall the case," said Blake. "It was in the papers. I didn't pay much attention to it. Has Dr. Gavin Todd any patients at Laurel Grange?"

"He has a few, I have heard," George Harnett answered.

"Has he made friends in the neighbourhood? Is he acquainted with Mr. Hugh Clontarf?"

"Not to my knowledge, sir. I doubt if he is. The doctor doesn't go anywhere. I have never laid eyes on him."

"Does he bear a good character?"

"So far as I can say, he does, Mr. Blake. I don't suppose the people hereabouts know anything of——"

The landlord broke off to serve a couple of customers who had entered, and shortly afterwards, as Blake was thinking of Dr. Davin Todd, the door was opened and Tinker appeared. He came over to his master, and sat down at the table. Blake had been expecting him.

"Anything doing at Ranmore Lodge this morning?" he asked. "You look as if you had some news for me."

"So I have," the lad replied. "It will keep, though."

"Out with it. What is the news?"

"You first, guv'nor. How did you get on? Did you learn anything?"

"Yes, I learned a great deal."

Blake briefly told Tinker of his discovery of the lost button, of what he had seen at Laurel Grange, and of what he had heard of Dr. Gavin Todd from the landlord of the White Lion. The lad whistled under his breath.

"My word, you've got me guessing!" he declared. "So Ben Partrick didn't lie! You found the button he lost in Abinger Woods! You saw Mr. Clontarf's secretary at Laurel Grange, talking to the doctor! And you heard him mention your name!"

"Yes, most distinctly," Blake answered. "In what connection I don't know, though."

"It's queer, isn't it? Why do you suppose Charles Leighton went to see Dr. Gavin Todd?"

"To pay a friendly call, perhaps."

"I don't think! And neither do you, guv'nor! What do you make of it? What is your theory?"

"I haven't any theory to suggest—not yet."

"Well, there is something in the wind. Something as mysterious as the murder of Kashar Das. I shouldn't wonder if Mr. Clontarf and his secretary were having some person kept a prisoner at Laurel Grange."

Blake smiled and shook his head.

"Let me have your news now, my boy," he bade. "Is it as interesting as mine?"

"More so," Tinker replied. "I kept watch on Ranmore Lodge from the same place as before, in the woods opposite to the gates. There wasn't anything doing for a while—Charles Leighton must have left to go to the Grange before I arrived—and I was feeling bored, when I heard footsteps approaching. Somebody passed very near to my right, and stopped. I was afraid I would be discovered. I scarcely dared breathe. I lay as flat as I could, hugging the ground, and got a glimpse of a man within two or three yards of me. All I could see of him were his legs up to the ankles. The rest of his body was hidden by the dense bushes. He was standing perfectly still by a big tree, not making a sound.

"He remained there for about a minute, and after he had gone, and I couldn't hear anything more of him. I crawled to the spot where he had been. I wondered why he had stopped by the tree. I looked at it and noticed a hole in the trunk as high up as my shoulder. I put my hand inside, and——"

The lad paused.

"I put my hand inside," he continued, in a low tone, a thrill of excitement in his voice, "and took out a cardboard box. I opened the box, and found a white turban, a false black beard and moustache, a bottle of brown stain, and a sponge and a cloth."

"Ah!" murmured Blake; and for an instant his eyes sparkled.

The deduction he had drawn at the first, that the Hindu who had been seen in the Ranmore Woods on the morning after the murder of Kashar Das was not a real Hindu, had been proved to the hilt.

"I told you so!" he remarked.

"I know you did," said Tinker. "It was a shrewd shot."

"You put the box and its contents back in the hollow tree, I suppose?"

"Of course I did, guv'nor!"

"That was right. It would have been a mistake—a grave mistake—had you brought them with you. It might have ruined what chances we have of arresting the murderer."

"He was almost as near to me as I am to you. My heart was in my mouth while he was standing so close. If I had been discovered he would have killed me as he killed Kashar Das."

"Don't jump to conclusions," said Blake. "We can't be certain he is the actual murderer. He is the man who twice played the part of the bogus Hindu, though. Either he has been carrying the turban and the other things about with him, and he stopped at the tree to replace them in their hiding-place; or he wanted to make sure they were still in the hole."

"At all events," Tinker replied, "the man was certainly Charles Leighton. He was on his way home from Laurel Grange when he stopped."

"Did you see him go into the garden of Ranmore Lodge?"

"No; I didn't have a glimpse of him after he left the tree."

"Did you hear him unlock and open the gates?"

"I didn't hear a sound guv'nor."

"It is possible, then, that the man was not Mr. Clontarf's private secretary."

"But there can be hardly a doubt that he was. You must admit that. And it stands to reason also that the person who played the part of the bogus Hindu murdered Kashar Das."

"I won't admit anything, my boy. The case is too complicated, it has too many threads, for me to express any definite opinion about it as yet. I am getting a grip of it, however. I dare say it won't be long until——"

Blake broke off abruptly.

"You haven't had your luncheon," he added. "Order it now, and when you have finished we will go back to town. The sooner we are away from this neighbourhood the better."

"You think we are in danger down here?" asked Tinker.

Blake shook his head.

"There are others who are in danger," he answered, "and I want them to think they are not."

CHAPTER 10.

A Summary of the Case—Tinker Breaks into Laurel Grange—What the Lad Heard—An Unlucky Fall—A Daring Ruse—Caught.

AFTER breakfast the next morning, when Blake had glanced over the newspaper, he told Tinker not to disturb him, and sat in silence for a long while in his big "thinking-chair," as he was in the habit of calling it, smoking pipe after pipe.

At length he rose, and sat down to his desk; wrote on a sheet of paper for a few minutes, and handed it to the lad.

"Look at this," he bade. "It is a summary of the case. Read, ponder, and digest it."

What he had written ran as follows:

"Hugh Clontarf, by the instructions of his deceased uncle, Lord Roderick Teviot, undertakes to write the latter's memoirs from material supplied to him. He is assisted in his task by Parrish Creed, and he has in his employ a Hindu servant. Both of them were formerly in the service of Lord Roderick. Parrish Creed resigns, and Clontarf engages another man, Charles Leighton, to fill the post of secretary.

"At about that time Clontarf wanders off at night to the Abinger Woods, suffering from a lapse of memory. He meets the poacher, Partrick, and has a fight with him, and is afterwards discovered in the woods by two men, one of whom was presumably Charles Leighton. He subsequently meets Partrick again, and tells him he has no recollection of the fight.

"Kashar Das leaves the house mysteriously at midnight, and the next morning he is found strangled in Ranmore Woods. The same morning the bogus Hindu purposely shows himself near the scene of the murder.

"Gwenda Roylance goes to see Hugh Clontarf, and he refuses to receive her. He has padlocked the gates, and the secretary is keeping a watch for visitors in the rustic lodge. Clontarf has instructed his publisher to preserve the strictest secrecy in regard to a certain chapter of the memoirs.

"Sir Ralph Athelstan, whose reputation will be damaged by the publication of that chapter, calls on Clontarf. It was probably not his first visit. The poacher displays Treasury notes at the White Lion, and tells the landlord a false tale. Gwenda Roylance goes again to Ranmore Lodge, accompanied by myself, and learns Clontarf deliberately wishes to break his engagement to her.

"The bogus Hindu prowls about Ben Partrick's cottage, listens to my conversation with him, and attempts to shoot me. On the following day the poacher's statements as to what happened in Abinger Woods are verified by the discovery of the button he lost from his coat, and Charles Leighton is seen coming out of Laurel Grange, where Dr. Gavin Todd, at one time concerned in a scandal, receives patients who require a rest.

"Queries: Why did Parrish Creed resign his position? Why was Kashar Das murdered? Who killed him? Is it Charles Leighton who has been playing the part of the bogus Hindu? Why did Hugh Clontarf take such precautions against visitors? Why was he anxious to break his engagement to Gwenda Roylance? Was the money Ben Partrick has hidden in his cottage given to him by Hugh Clontarf? If so, for what reason? Why did Charles Leighton go to Laurel Grange? And what understanding, if any, exists between Clontarf and Sir Ralph Athelstan?"

Tinker read the summary very carefully.

"You don't expect me to answer all these questions, do you?" he said.

Blake shrugged his shoulders.

"Not likely, as I can't answer them myself," he replied. "I wanted you to have a clear comprehension of the various aspects of the case. Yet there is one thing you might be able to deduce, or to suspect, if you used your wits."

"I can use my wits all right. I can't see what you are driving at, though. I can't imagine."

"Can't you? Well, never mind."

"You needn't be sarcastic, guv'nor. I haven't got any brains."

"I am not sarcastic. It is not in the least to your discredit that you fail to grasp a slender theory which occurred to me only after long and puzzling reflection. It may be altogether wrong. I don't know. There is another theory, a less startling one, which is nearly as plausible."

"What are the two, guv'nor? Tell me."

Blake ignored the request. Dropping into his chair again, he filled a pipe, and said quietly:

"You are going to break into Laurel Grange to-night!"

Tinker stared.

"The deuce I am!" he exclaimed. "What for?"

"To learn what you can," Blake answered. "To try to get some information for me."

"You want me to find out what patients Dr. Gavin Todd has?"

"No; that would be too risky. And probably impossible. But you may have an opportunity of hearing a conversation between the doctor and somebody else—a conversation which will throw some light on Charles Leighton's visit to the house."

"Oh, that's the idea! Right you are! But the chances are I'll be caught."

"If you get into a scrape I will contrive to get you out of it. I shall be near at hand. And both of us will be disguised. You must be extremely careful, though. It is most important that Dr. Todd should be left under the impression that a burglar broke in. Otherwise, should be suspect your identity, a great deal of harm might be done."

"What time to-night?" asked Tinker.

"Not too late," Blake replied. "Before the doctor has gone to bed."

"Any particular instructions for me, guv'nor?"

"Not until we get there. We will start early in the evening, and hide the car somewhere in the vicinity of Laurel Grange."

Blake rose as he spoke.

"Luncheon won't be ready for a couple of hours yet, my boy," he added. "We will go for a stroll, and take Pedro with us."

★ ★ ★

Between nine and ten o'clock that night, Blake and Tinker left their car in the shadow of a clump of trees on a strip of common which was in a lonely part of Surrey, and setting off on foot, they traversed a plantation, and came in half a mile to a road at a point where it skirted Laurel Grange.

They separated here after a short conversation. Blake remained in the woods, opposite to the entrance to the doctor's place; while Tinker glided across the road, and with skill born of long practice clambered nimbly to the top of the high wall, swung into the boughts of a tree, and climbed down to the garden.

His next step was to unfasten the gates, which were merely barred on the inside; and, that done, he advanced amongst the trees and shrubbery, keeping to the left of the sweeping drive.

He stopped for a few moments, and listened, peering in all directions. Was there a dog about? Or a watchman? Apparently not. There was no sign of either.

Nor was it likely Dr. Gavin Tood observed any such precaution. Even if he had some mysterious patient—somebody in whom Sexton Blake was interested—he could not have any reason to fear a visit from the detective, or from the police.

Reassured, Tinker moved on until he could command a view of the dwelling, which had a large porch with a balustrade on top.

He noticed that the walls to right and left of it were thickly clothed with ivy, and then, with the stealth of a cat, he worked round to the rear by one side, and returned to the front by the other.

He had seen lights at several curtained windows. He knew that some of the inmates, if not all, had not yet retired for the night.

But that did not deter him. On the contrary, it was better for his purpose. If he were to wait until everybody had gone to bed he would have no opportunity of learning anything.

Where should be make the attempt? He hesitated, and decided to try to get in at the front, as no lights were visible here.

"I am glad the guv'nor isn't far off," he said to himself, as he stole forward. "It is going to be a pretty risky undertaking, no matter how careful I may be."

Grasping with both hands the tough tendrils of ivy that grew on the wall to one side of the doorway, Tinker climbed up inch by inch, as noiselessly as he could. He was afraid the tendrils would yield and let him fall; but they supported his weight until his head and shoulders were above the top of the balustraded porch.

Then he felt the ivy giving way, and just in time, as it crackled and sagged, he clutched at the caught the balustrade, and swung over it. He listened. No alarm had been raised.

He had a French-window to deal with now, and it was an easy problem. He forced it with a small jemmy such as burglars use, and pushed it open; listened again, and stepped through into a hall that was dimly lit.

The house was very quiet. Faint sounds floated from somewhere below, but there was hushed silence on the upper floor. the rooms occupied by the patients must be here, and they were probably all in bed and asleep.

Tinker was in a quandary. He had precious little chance, he reflected, of getting any information.

He crept along the hall, wondering if he hadn't better go down to the lower floor; and he was drawing near to the top of the staircase when he heard, from behind a door on his left, a sound that was like the creaking of a chair.

He stopped, and, glueing his eye to the keyhole, he got a glimpse of a blurred figure, and of a table with a bottle and glasses on it.

"There are a couple of persons in there, I believe," he murmured.

He straightened up to listen, and now a man's voice, speaking with a north country accent, came to his ears:

"Will you have another whisky, Dodson?"

"I will, doctor, if you don't mind," another voice replied. "Thank you."

"Help yourself. And don't be stingy with it."

"I don't like it too strong. It is uncommonly good stuff."

"It is that. Fifteen years old if it's a day. I get it direct from a firm in Edinburgh."

There was a brief pause. One of the persons in the room was Dr Gavin Todd, of course; and his companion, from the respectful way in which he spoke, was very likely one of the domestic staff of the rest-home.

"What were we talking about?" Dr. Todd continued. "Ah, yes, I remember! We were having a little discussion. Your argument was that I am playing a dangerous game."

"So you are, to my way of thinking," said the other.

"I don't agree with you, Dodson. You haven't grumbled before. What has struck you all of a sudden?"

"I don't know. My nerves are a bit shaky to-day. I have a sort of a premonition that you and I are going to get into serious trouble."

"Nonsense, man! There's no fear of that. I am justified, you will bear in mind, in keeping the fellow under my roof. And he is a very lucrative patient. It will mean two thousand pounds in my pocket. And there will be a couple of hundred for you."

"I can do with the money, doctor. I am afraid of the risk, though."

"Risk? Where does the risk come in? Nobody suspects the fellow is here, and no one will. He will be released as soon as the book of memoirs is ready for publication, and that will be the end of the matter."

"There's no telling. What about that mysterious murder in Ranmore Woods? Who strangled the Hindu?"

"That's for the police to find out. It doesn't concern us, Dodson."

"I'm not so sure. Sexton Blake is working on the case, and he is a clever man—far more clever than any one at Scotland Yard. I have an idea there is some connection between the murder and other things that have happened, and if so Mr. Blake will get to the bottom of it all, and his suspicious will be drawn to you. That's why——"

"Don't talk like a fool! Dr. Todd angrily interrupted. "You irritate me! Finish your drink, Dodson, and be off to bed! I hope you will be in a more sensible frame of mind in the morning!"

The discussion was not resumed. Tinker was satisfied with what he had learned, however; and now, supposing the doctor's companion was about to depart, he prudently beat a retreat, considering a daring idea that had occurred to him while he was listening to the conversation.

"I won't leave the house yet," he said to himself, as he crept in the opposite direction to the French-window by which he had entered. "I will hide somewhere below until they are all in bed, and then I will try to find the mysterious patient. Or prisoner, rather. I can guess who he is."

A couple of yards brought the lad to the top of the staircase, and he had hardly more than begun to descend when the door by which he had been listening was suddenly opened, and a ray of light streamed on him.

In his haste to elude observation he made a false step, and his foot slipped. He reeled to the banister, clutched at it and missed, and toppled heavily forward. Unable to stop, he slid and rolled to the bottom of the stairs, and landed with a crash in the lower hall.

"A burglar!" shouted a voice above him. "A burglar, doctor!"

An alarm had been raised, and a clamour was ringing in Tinker's ears as he scrambled unhurt to his feet. What should he do? Try to escape by the front door? No, he wouldn't have time.

On a quick impulse he darted to a door on his right, and threw it open; slipped through, and softly shut the door behind him.

He meant to get away by a window, but as he was groping rapidly and blindly across the floor—he was in darkness—he collided violently with a table, and overturned it. He fell with it, and a shower of objects, large and small, rained upon him, bruising his head and body.

While he lay there for a few seconds, half-dazed, he heard rapid steps and shrill voices, and before he could rise the lights were switched on.

He saw now that he was in the library, and saw also, scattered around him, the things which had fallen from the table—a lamp, books, a silver pen-tray, little statuettes of bronze and ivory.

Tinker remembered now, in a flash, how important it was that he should be taken for a genuine burglar. He was concealed from view by the table, which was between him and the door; and at once he snatched the silver pen-tray and two of the bronze figures, and thrust them into the pockets of his coat.

Then he got quickly up, on shaky limbs; and the next instant he was in the grasp of Dr. Gavin Todd, and a lean, clean-shaven man with a sallow complexion.

"You scoundrel!" creid the doctor. "You audacious villain!"

"You needn't be so rough!" Tinker whined. "It's a fair cop! I'll give in, sir!"

None of the inmates of the house, it seemed, had gone to bed yet. The servants had already appeared, and were gathered in the doorway; a cook, two maids, an elderly butler, and a diminutive boy in a mulberry-coloured livery with brass buttons.

They looked on, talking excitedly, while Dr. Todd searched the prisoner, and took from his pockets the pen-tray, the jemmy and the bronze statuettes.

Tinker offered no resistance. He was so bruised and sore from the two falls that he could not have escaped had an opportunity offered.

Would his identity be suspected, he wondered uneasily? It was not likely, he concluded, as he was made up for the part of a burglar. Not only were his features deftly disguised, but his boots had rubber soles, his clothes were of course material and were provided with capacious pockets, and a dirty bird's-eye handkerchief was tied around his neck in place of a collar.

One thing did worry him, though. What would be the outcome of his capture? Would Sexton Blake contrive to rescue him? Could he rely on that?

"An ugly-looking rascal, isn't he?" Dr. Todd remarked.

"Atrocious, sir," assented the man Dodson. "An absolute type of a criminal face."

"It couldn't be worse! Vicious and degraded! The fellow can't belong anywhere in this part of the country. I daresay he is a London crook."

"No doubt he is, doctor. Came to Dorking or Guildford by train, I should think and tramped over here."

"It is fortunate he tumbled down the stairs, Dodson. He must have been prowling about above."

Dr. Todd bound the lad's wrists together with a handkerchief, and grasping him by the shoulder, he shook him savagely.

"Who are you?" he demanded. "What is your name?"

"I 'aven't got any," Tinker answered, in an aggressive tone.

"You sullen brute!" snapped the doctor. "It will be the worse for you if you refuse to speak. Did you come alone? Or did you have an accomplice with you?"

"I came on my own. I didn't 'ave anybody with me."

"How did you get in, you rascal!"

"It was easy enough. I climbed up by the ivy to the top of the porch, and broke a French-window open."

"I see. What put it into your head to choose my place for a burglary?"

"Because I've seen it before. I thought rich people lived here, and it would be a safe crib to crack."

There were no more questions. Tinker had passed the ordeal well. They believed what he wanted them to believe—that he was a professional crook from London. But the worst was to come, and he was very apprehensive.

By what means Blake would try to set him free he did not know. There had not been any definite understanding between them.

The doctor had a car, he presumed. What if he were to be promptly carried off in it, on the way to the nearest police-station in Surrey? In that event it would be next to impossible for his master to rescue him. He clutched at a glimmer of hope.

"Don't be 'ard on me, sir!" he pleaded. "You've got back what I stole! Give a bloke a chance!"

Dr. Todd laughed in scorn.

"Let you go?" he repeated. "Is it likely? No, you scoundrel, it will be the police for you! And a few years in prison. It won't be the first time you've been there, I'll warrant."

"What's are we to do with the fellow?" asked the man Dodson. "He ought to be taken to Dorking, or to Guildford."

"One or the other," the doctor replied. "But we will have to keep him here until to-morrow, I suppose. We can't use the car. I am afraid there is not enough petrol for——"

He paused abruptly. Somebody had just begun to pound on the front door, and Tinker's heart throbbed with relief. He hadn't a doubt that Sexton Blake, who was also disguised, had come to play some daring game.

"Who can that be?" Dr. Todd exclaimed.

Dodson hastened from the room. He was heard to unlock and open the door. There were voices in the hall, and a moment later, to the lad's dismay, Dodson came in with a strapping big constable of powerful build.

CHAPTER 11.

On the Way to the Village—Shots from the Woods—Sexton Blake to the Rescue—Safe Away—Tinker's Theories

CONSTABLE MACK PUGSLEY, of Ranmore Village! Amateur boxer, zealous guardian of the peace, and the terror of mischievous, law-breaking youths for miles around!

He had attended the inquest on the body of Kashar Das. He had seen Sexton Blake and Tinker there, had talked to them, had drunk beer at their expense at the White Lion. Would be recognise the lad now? Or at least trace something familiar in his features?

Tinker was afraid he would. His heart was in his boots. But the constable merely stared at him, and looked away.

"So you've caught a burglar, sir!" were his first words, addressed to Dr. Todd.

"Yes, we caught him red-handed, with stolen property in his possession," the doctor replied. "That silver tray, and the bronze figures, were in his pockets. He got into the house by climbing the wall to the top of the front porch, and forcing open a window. But how do you happen to be here? You were on your round of duty, perhaps."

"That's right, sir. I was coming along the road when I heard the shouting. I hurried as fast as I could, and entered the garden by the gates, which weren't fastened. You are lucky to have caught this fellow. He has a mug like a Guy Fawkes. One need only look at him to see he is a crook."

"Exactly. A professional crook. He has admitted that he came down from London. He refused to give his name."

Tinker scowled, though he felt like grinning.

"I don't mind telling you who I am," he said, in a surly tone. "My name is Slick. Sam Slick."

"Don't try to be funny!" growled the constable. "Any accomplices?"

"Not me! No fear! It's my 'abit to work alone."

"Your next job of work, my lad, will be hammering stones at Dartmoor. And it will last a while."

With that Constable Pugsley turned to the doctor again.

"You have bound the prisoner's wrists tightly, sir?" he inquired.

"As tightly as I could," said Dr. Todd. "He won't be able to get his hands free."

"Well, I'll take him along now."

"I would take you both in my car, officer, but, unfortunately, there is not sufficient petrol for——"

"It doesn't matter, sir. I will march the fellow to Ranmore, and have the landlord of the White Lion drive us to Dorking. You will have to appear at the police-station to-morrow."

"Certainly. I will be there by ten or eleven o'clock in the morning."

"Very good, sir. I will tell the superintendent."

The constable hesitated, observing that it was a warm and dry night. The hint was taken.

The boy in buttons, despatched to the larder, returned with a bottle of beer and a glass; and when Constable Pugsley had slaked his thirst he left the house with Tinker, who was almost in cheerful spirits now.

Dr. Todd and Dodson accompanied them as far as the gates, and stood gazing after then as they set off in the direction of Ranmore.

"No trick, mind you!" bade the constable, taking a tight grip of his prisoner's arm. "If you try to give me the slip I'll bash you one on the head, you know!"

"Don't worry," said Tinker. "I'd 'ave a fat chance of getting away from a big, hulking fellow like you, wouldn't I? You look as if you could knock me out with three fingers."

"So I could. I've won a dozen boxing matches."

"'Ave you? I 'ope you're in practice, for you may 'ave to put your dibs up pretty soon."

"Ho! Indeed? What do you mean by that?"

"Nothing much. I was only wondering if my pal, Battling Bill, might be 'anging about anywhere. 'E's an ugly customer to tackle."

"Battling Bill, the Bermondsey Chicken? I—I thought you hadn't any accomplice? You told me so!"

Tinker did not answer. He merely laughed, and the laugh dispelled the sinister suspicions his remarks had given rise to. Constable Pugsley believed he was joking.

"I wouldn't mind tackling half a dozen of your pals, my lad," he boastfully declared. "I could knock them all out."

No harm had been done, though Tinker had spoken very foolishly. He felt like joking. He appreciated the humour of the situation. That Sexton Blake would rescue him he hadn't a doubt. He was absolutely certain of it.

But as he went briskly on, as the distance from the gates of Laurel Grange increased, he grew vaguely uneasy. He had gone three or four hundred yards, and nothing had happened yet.

What was wrong? Where was Blake? Why had he not taken action? He was to have waited in the plantation opposite to the gateway. Could he have entered the garden after the alarm, slipped round to the rear of the house, and been there at the time when he, Tinker, left by the front door? It seemed to be the only plausible explanation.

"Where's your Battling Bill?" chuckled Constable Pugsley. "Where is he, eh?"

"You go to blazes!" the lad irritably retorted.

They went on and on, following the lonely road with a plantation on each side of them, until they were more than a quarter of a mile from Dr. Todd's place.

Tinker's anxiety had turned to a sickening fear, and he had lost hope of rescue, he was sure he would ultimately be landed at the Dorking police-station, when the unexpected happened.

Of a sudden a loud shout, and a couple of pistol-shots, rang from the wooded cover on the left. Immediately there was another shout, another shot.

The constable uttered a startled exclamation, and jumped nearly off his feet. He let go of Tinker, who at once darted away from him; and at the same instant a man who wore a black mask, and had an automatic in his hand, appeared at the edge of the plantation.

"Don't shoot!" yelled Constable Pugsley, throwing up his arms. "Don't shoot!"

With that he took to his heels, running towards the village as fast as he could. The lad whipped over to the woods, and Blake, who was laughing heartily, untied the handkerchief that bound his wrists together.

"Funny, wasn't it?" he said.

"It wasn't funny for me," Tinker indignantly replied. "Why didn't you do it before?"

"Because it was more prudent to wait until you were a good distance from the house. I have been following you."

"I see, guv'nor. I didn't think of that."

"You were stupid. You might have known."

The frightened constable was still running, his figure dim in the murky gloom of the night. And now a faint clamour was ringing in the direction of Laurel Grange. The pistol-shots had been heard there.

"Come along," bade Blake. "We will have to be quick."

"There is nothing to worry about," said Tinker. "Dr. Todd has a car, but he is short of petrol. We shan't be pursued."

"You didn't make a mess of things, I hope. They didn't suspect who you were?"

"No fear, guv'nor. They took me for a professional crook. I tricked them neatly. I was caught with the plunder in my pockets—a silver pen-tray and a couple of bronze statuettes."

"Good lad! And what did you learn? Anything? But you needn't tell me now. Wait until we are homeward bound."

They struck across the plantation, walking rapidly and silently, and in less than a quarter of an hour they reached their car, and without delay set off for London.

They talked as they went spinning along the quiet country roads. Blake did not know just what had happened, it appeared. He had heard the clamour in the doctor's house, and had seen the lad marched away by Constable Pugsley. That was all.

He listened to Tinker, who repeated the conversation he had overheard between Dr. Gavin Todd and the man Dodson, and gave an account of what had befallen him afterwards.

"All's well that ends well," he continued. "No harm has been done. They haven't the remotest suspicion that you sent me there."

"Fortunately not," Blake replied. "As for the information you got, it is of the greatest value. I know what it means."

"So do I," declared Tinker.

"Do you? What, my lad?"

"It is as plain as daylight, isn't it, that Sir Ralph Athelstan is a prisoner at Laurel Grange?"

There was a twinkle in Blake's eyes."

"Indeed?" he murmured. "Perhaps you will tell me how you arrived at that concusion."

"I couldn't have arrived at any other," said Tinker. "Nothing could be more obvious considering what I learned about the claret-coloured car, and what Mr. Henson told you. Sir Ralph Athelstan has been kicking up a row over the chapter in Lord Roderick Teviot's memoirs relating to the Selampur Turf Scandal. He has threatened to do this or that. He went again to Ranmore Lodge a couple of days ago, and Mr. Clontarf and Charles Leighton attacked him and drugged him and carried him off to Laurel Grange and made an arrangement with Dr. Todd to keep him there for a time."

"With what motive?"

"Because they were afraid he might break into the office of the publishers and steal the manuscript of the book."

Blake shrugged his shoulders.

"Your wits are rusty," he answered. "You will have to find a much stronger motive than that."

"It is rather weak, come to think of it," Tinker admitted.

"I should say so, especially in view of the fact that Dr. Gavin Todd is to receive two thousand pounds."

"Well, guv'nor, I can suggest a better explanation. A far more plausible one. Mr. Clontarf has taken a bribe from Sir Ralph Athelstan—a large sume of money—to suppress the chapter. He has promised to do so, and he isn't going to keep his word. He fears Sir Ralph will find out, and that is why he wants to keep him at Laurel Grange until the memoirs have been published. How does that strike you?"

"Not bad. It is not the right solution, though. You are wide of the mark. What about the murder of Kashar Das?"

"That is a side issue, guv'nor. I don't suppose it has any connection with Lord Roderick Teviot's memoirs.

"On the contrary, my lad, there is a link between the two."

"I would like to know what it is. I can't see it."

Blake smiled.

"I will tell you this much," he said quietly. "Dr. Todd's mysterious patient is not Sir Ralph Athelstan."

"Who the deuce is he, then?" exclaimed Tinker. "Tell me that, if you are so sure I am wrong!"

There was no answer from Blake. His mind had wandered. For mile after mile he drove swiftly on, deeply absorbed in speculation, scarcely conscious of his firm hand on the steering-wheel, not uttering a word. And it was not until the lights of suburban London were sparkling close ahead that he opened his lips to speak.

"If you had been sent to prison for six months for burglary, my boy," he said in an absent tone, "it would have been well worth the information you got for me."

"Really?" snapped Tinker. "I don't think! You wouldn't have cared if I had, I suppose!"

"It would have been worth it," Blake repeated. "I have a comprehensive grip of the case now. I am ready to make fresh moves. There will shortly be dramatic developments, and a very sensational finish."

"What is the first move? What do we do next?"

"I am going to Laurel Grange to-morrow, Tinker, to see Dr. Gavin Todd."

"With the police, guv'nor?"

"Alone, and as a visitor. I will not be a welcome one. That goes without saying. But I shall have nothing whatever to fear."

There was nothing more to be had out of Blake. Deep in thought again, paying no heed to Tinker's occasional remarks, he drove the car on to the garage in the Marylebone Road.

CHAPTER 12.

Ben Partrick Goes to Ranmore Lodge—Prepared for Dinner—At the Side Gate—A Talk with Mr. Clontarf and Mr. Leighton—The Arrangement for the Morrow.

CAUTIOUS footsteps, stopping now and again for a moment, broke the hushed silence of the night. A dusky figure loomed out of the darkness, and along the stretch of private road leading to Hugh Clontarf's residence, moving with slow and stealthy tread, came Ben Partrick.

He was uneasy, suspicious. He was not at all sure it was safe for him to come here to-night. But he wasn't a coward. He had been playing a very daring game, and he meant to play it to the finish, no matter what risks he might incur. Should danger threaten him he would be prepared for it. In a pocket of his jacket, ready to be drawn at an instant's warning, was an old service revolver, loaded in every chamber, which he had got hold of somewhere or other.

Having reached the gateway to Ranmore Lodge, and peered at the drive beyond it, he bore to the left and went warily round by the stiff, high hedge to the small gate.

He stood listening for a few seconds, then rapped softly. Almost at once the gate was unlocked and opened, and as the poacher stepped through into the garden and was confronted by Hugh Clontarf's private-secretary, his hand slipped to his pocket and fastened on his revolver.

"You are late, confound you!" said Charles Leighton, as he shut the gate. "Why have you kept me waiting?"

"I'm not very late," Ben Partrick sulkily replied. "It's not more than ten o'clock is it?"

"Nearly half-past. Where were you when I was at your cottage and put the note under the door?"

"I was at the White Lion at Ranmore, I dare say."

"The more fool you! You were warned not to drink too much!"

"I didn't. All I had was a pint of beer. I found your note when I got home, and I knew what it meant, though there was no name to it, and nothing about any place. It only said I was to come at ten o'clock to-night."

"I thought you would understand, Partrick. Did you suppose I would be such a fool as to sign my name and tell you where to come?"

"What do you want with me?" asked the poacher. "That's what I'd like to know."

"There is a very important matter to be discussed," said Charles Leighton. "Mr. Clontarf will explain."

"All right, sir. But if you try any tricks——"

"Don't be absurd, Partrick. We don't mean you any harm. Come along!"

They crossed the garden to the house, and Charles Leighton, opening the door, bade his companion be quiet, and took him from the hall into a small smoking-room that was furnished with leather-padded chairs and a couch and an oak table.

Hugh Clontarf was standing by the fire-place in evening-dress, his hands in his pockets. He nodded to the poacher, and pointed to the table on which were decanters and glasses and a box of cigars.

"Help yourself, my man," he said.

Ben Partrick did not need to be told twice. He poured a stiff measure of whisky into a glass, lit a cigar, and sat down.

Hugh Clontarf glanced at his secretary, and neither spoke for a moment. There was veiled malevolence, ill-concealed, in their eyes.

"What's that bulging from your pocket, Partrick?" Hugh Clontarf asked.

"It—it's a revolver," stammered the poacher, who was more in dread of the master of the house than he was of Charles Leighton.

"Why did you bring it with you?"

"Not for any particular reason, sir. I'm in the habit of carrying it about with me."

"You were afraid of treachery, I imagine. You haven't anything to fear from us, Partrick. You have from somebody else, though."

"I have? What do you mean, sir?"

"You shall hear presently, after I have talked of other matters," said Hugh Clontarf. "I happen to know you had a visit from Mr. Sexton Blake, the detective, one evening recently."

Ben Partrick changed colour.

"Yes, he came to my place," he assented. "But I was careful what I told him, sir. Only how I had a fight with you in the woods that night, and I met you afterwards, and you gave me some money because——"

"Never mind about that. I had it all from Mr. Blake himself. He told me he had seen you. He wanted me to verify your story, and I did."

"That's all right, then."

"No, Partrick, it isn't all right. Not as far as you are concerned. Sexton Blake has got it into his head that it was you who killed the Hindu in Ranmore Woods."

"He—he couldn't have, sir! He must believe the murder was done by the other Hindu—the one who has been prowling about the neighbourhood, and was hidden behind my cottage the evening Mr. Blake came to see me."

"Don't deceive yourself," Hugh Clontarf replied. "Sexton Blake has been making inquiries, and he has found a farm labourer who saw you hurrying away from the Ranmore Woods on the night of the murder, within a few hundred yards of the spot where the Hindu was killed. You are likely to be arrested, and, if you are, you will probably swing."

Ben Partrick's face flushed. His eyes blazed. He was a slow-witted fellow, else he would have realised that he was being imposed on.

"Me swing?" he cried. "Not me! If I'm accused I'll tell the truth, sir! I'll say that——"

"It wouldn't matter what you said," Hugh Clontarf interrupted. "Your tale would sound too ridiculous for belief."

"Would it? What about the watch? You're forgetting that!"

"Oh, no, I am not! Your possession of the watch would make things worse for you. I should swear you stole it from me."

"That I—I stole it, sir?"

"Yes, I could easily fasten the crime on you in a way that would satisfy the police."

"It would be a cursed lie! We'll see! That's all. I'm not afraid of you! I'll bet Mr. Sexton Blake will believe me!"

Hugh Clontarf and Charles Leighton exchanged glances—sinister glances. At that moment the poacher was in deadly peril, though he was not aware of it. He was thinking of what he had been told, and was too stupid to see that it was all a bluff.

His passion had cooled now, and he was ghastly white. There was terror in his eyes. And that gleam of terror, and his pallid, twitching features, averted the crisis. Hugh Clontarf's savage expression relaxed.

"You have been talking like a fool, Partrick, and you know it," he continued. "If you have come to your senses I will get on with what I was going to tell you. I will explain why I wished to see you to-night. You are a contemptible rascal. You have played a dirty, sneaking game. You took advantage of me, exorted money from me because you thought I was in year power—because you had the watch hidden where you knew I could not get at it. You demanded an extortionate sum for it, and I refused to pay. In spite of it all, however, I want to do you a good turn."

"I like that!" Ben Partrick sneered. "You are a lot worse than I am!"

"We won't argue," said Hugh Clontarf. "I don't care for the threats you have made. Why should I? Who would believe the word of a disreputable scamp of a poacher? But to come to the point. You can stay at home, if you prefer, and run the risk of being arrested and hanged. On the other hand, if you are wise, you will clear out of the country. I am willing to help you to do so."

"Me clear out of the country?" Ben Partrick repeated. "I'm darned if I will!"

"Think carefully before you decide. Wouldn't it be for the best?"

"I'm not so sure, sir. Where would I go?"

"I would suggest that you go to Canada, in a false name. You would like it there. You could make a good living by hunting and fishing. And you would have nothing to fear in that distant land."

"I don't believe I'd have anything to fear if I stayed in England, either. You're too anxious to be rid of me."

"For your own good, Partrick. Remember that Sexton Blake suspects you, and is on your track."

"I could clear myself," the poacher said sullenly.

"You could not," declared Hugh Clontarf. "I have a good reputation, and you have a very bad one."

"Well, what if I was to take your offer? How about money, sir?"

"You shall have a thousand pounds, Partrick."

"A—a thousand pounds?"

"Yes, in cash. And your expenses will be paid."

It was a tempting offer to Ben Partrick. His eyes sparkled. He hesitated, considering the proposal. There was not a shadow of suspicion in his mind.

"I'll do it," he said, with sudden resolve. "When shall I go?"

"The sooner the better," Hugh Clontarf replied. "I would advise you to be gone within the next twenty-four hours."

"Will it be safe for me to wait as long as that, sir? What of Sexton Blake?"

"He isn't ready to arrest you yet, Partrick. He is trying to get further evidence against you."

"Then I'll be off in the morning, sir."

"No, not so soon as that," said Hugh Clontarf. "I must have time to make the necessary arrangements. Do you know the old red barn that stands in a field, off the Guildford road, and is about a quarter of a mile from a road that leads to Abinger Hatch?"

"Yes, I know it. I've been there often," said the poacher.

"Very well, Partrick. I will meet you inside the red barn—I don't want anybody to see you standing outside—at nine o'clock to-morrow night. I will give you one thousand pounds in cash, a passport, a railway ticket, and a ticket for your passage across the Atlantic. You will then walk over to Guildford, take a train to London, spend the night there, travel down to Southampton the next morning, and sail for Canada the same evening."

"I will be there, sir. Nine o'clock, to-morrow night at the red barn."

"Or a little before nine. If I should not have arrived, you will wait for me. I have told you now what I am going to do for you. And you, on your part, will being the watch with you, and hand it over to me when you have received the money."

"Of course I will," Ben Partrick readily agreed. "It's only fair I should, as you are sending me abroad and giving me a thousand pounds."

"That is understood," Hugh Clontarf answered. "I am to have the watch. And, meanwhile, not a word of your plans to any person, remember."

"Not a word, sir. You can trust me. But, if you don't mind my speaking of it, I'll be needing some decent clothes. I can't travel in these old things, looking like a tramp."

"Quite true, Partrick. You shall have ten pounds now. You can walk into Guildford in the morning, and buy what you need there."

Hugh Clontarf took some Treasury notes from his pocket.

"Here you are," he said. "You have your instructions. Don't forget a word of them. You can go now. Mr. Leighton will let you out at the gate. Good-night."

Ben Partrick put on his greasy cap, glanced wistfully at the decanters on the table, and departed with the private secretary.

Charles Leighton returned in five minutes, and laughed as he mixed himself a whisky-and-soda.

"The credulous fool!" he said.

Hugh Clontarf shrugged his shoulders and smiled.

"Not a glimmer of suspicion!" he replied. "Swallowed it all! You had better go to bed now, Charlies," he added, "and get a good night's sleep. You will have a great deal to do in London to-morrow."

CHAPTER 13.

Blake Goes to See Dr. Gavin Todd—Satisfactory Results—A Summons to Scotland Yard—A Message from Tinker—Back to Surrey—At the Poacher's Cottage—Tinker's Story—Pedro on the Trail.

IT was on a Wednesday night, the day after Tinker fell into the clutches of Dr. Gavin Todd, that Ben Partrick went to Ranmore Lodge. And on that Wednesday, to go back a little with the thread of the story, Blake drove down to Surrey alone in his car to call on Dr. Todd, starting on his journey after luncheon.

On presentation of his card he was promptly admitted to Laurel Grange. He entered the house with a cool and confident bearing, satisfied that he had nothing to fear; talked to the doctor for an hour, and stayed to tea with him; parted from him on amicable terms, and drove back to town.

And the tale he told to Tinker that evening, while they sat at supper, had literally a stunning effect on the lad.

He knew everything now, as far as related to the mystery of Laurel Grange. He discussed that and other matters with his master until a late hour of the night, and before he went to bed Blake gave him some instructions.

"My next step will be to put the screws on the rascal of a poacher," he said, "and get a confession out of him. I want you to go down to Dorking by train to-morrow, taking your bicycle with you, and keep a furtive watch on Ben Partrick's movements. He knows I suspect him, and I am rather afraid he will disappear, or that somebody else may smuggle him away by fare means or foul. I shall probably join you later in the day, my boy. I have been neglecting my correspondence, and it is absolutely necessary I should write some letters."

Tinker set off after breakfast the next morning, and Blake was busy with his correspondence until one o'clock, when he had his luncheon.

He would then have left for Surrey—he was uneasy about the poacher—but he was detained by a client who wished him to undertake a private case, a request which he had to refuse.

And when finally be dismissed his caller and was on the point of ordering his car, Inspector Widgeon rang him up on the telephone and told him he would like to see him at once.

Blake could guess the reason. He left the house in an irritable mood and took a cab to Scotland Yard. The inspector was in his room overlooking the Embankment, at a desk littered with papers.

"Ah, here you are!" he said. "Sit down. It's the Surrey police. I have heard from Inspector Stracey, of Dorking, in reference to the mysterious murder of that Hindu near Ranmore Lodge. He isn't satisifed with the way you have been conducting the case. He complains that you are keeping him in the dark. He don't know if you have made any progress or not."

"I know he doesn't," Blake sharply replied. "What of it?"

"It is hardly fair to Stracey, is it?"

"You can call it unfair. I have reasons for keeping him in the dark. The best of reasons."

"That's just like you, Blake. Secretive or nothing. Perhaps you won't mind telling me how you are getting on."

"I have not been idle, I can assure you."

"I suppose that is a roundabout way of saying you are at a deadlock," InspectorWidgeon answered. "Why don't you tell Stracey so instead of being so darned mysterious?"

Blake smiled."

"Really, my dear fellow," he answered, "you are very amusing at times. But why did you send for me? To criticise my methods?"

"Dear me, no! You are beyond criticism, aren't you? The fact of the matter is the Surrey police wish the Yard to help them, and I wanted to know if you needed any help. We can't spare a man at present. They are all busy."

"It doesn't matter. I have a firm grasp of the case. I can see throught it. You can tell Inspector Stracey from me that it won't be long until I apply to him for a warrant for the arrest of the murderer or murderers of Kashar Das. That's all. Good-bye, Widgeon. I should have been on the way to Surrey by now if you hadn't rung me up."

"If you ask me, Blake, I think you are getting a bit too big for your boots."

Blake did not reply to the inspector's parting shot. He went hurriedly downstairs and out of the building, hailed a taxi, and drove home. On his desk was a telegram that had been delivered during his absence. It ran as follows:

"News for you. Come as soon as you can, and bring Pedro. Dog may be useful. Will meet you at the White Lion or on the road to the cottage. If not, come there.

"TINKER."

What was the news? What move on the part of the poacher could have prompted the message? Blake was uneasy. He imagined all sorts of things. Stepping to the telephone, he rang up his garage and ordered his car to be sent round at once.

"I wish I had gone down this morning," he said to himself. "It may be a serious matter if Ben Partrick has disappeared."

In a quarter of an hour he was on the way. He travelled as fast as he dared, but he had to go slowly across London, and what with that and a delay caused by engine trouble, he did not get to the White Lion at Ranmore until after seven o'clock in the evening, when the sun was low on the horizon.

Tinker was not at the inn. He had not been there. Blake drove on towards Guildford, seeing nothing of his young assistant on the road. And as he stopped by the footpath that led to the poacher's humble home he lad appeared in the doorway and waved his hand.

"Come along, guv'nor!" he called.

Blake got out of the car, and with the bloodhound trotting at his heels, he hastily ascended the winding path.

"What has happened?" he exclaimed. "Isn't Partrick here?"

"No; he's gone," Tinker replied.

"Gone? How long ago, my lad?"

"I don't know. Not a great while, guv'nor. He isn't coming back, I'll bet. I'll tell you all about it. I have something to show you first. Come in and look."

They entered the cottage, and Blake gazed around him in consernation. There were obvious deductions to be drawn from what he saw.

On the floor lay a piece of thick string tied in knots, and a crumpled sheet of wrapping paper that bore the label of a Guildford firm of haberdashers.

And strewn on the bed were all—with the exception of the man himself—that had made the poacher a familiar and disreputable figure in the neighbourhood for years—his treadbare velveteen jacket, fustian trousers, khaki shirt, greasy cap, leather gaiters, and thick, coarse boots caked with mud.

"He shed his clothes, guv'nor," remarked the lad, "as snakes shed their skins for new ones. He was a sight."

Blake nodded.

"It is the very thing I was afraid of," he said. "The fellow has been tampered with. Those scoundrels have——"

Pausing abruptly, he knelt on the floor and prised up the tile he had seen the poacher lift when he was watching him from the window. There was nothing beneath it. The wallet containing the Treasury notes was gone.

"I thought so," declared Blake. "The man hasn't any intention of coming back."

"No fear!" Tinker answered. "He took his money with him."

"What do you know? Let me have your tale. Was Ben Partrick here when you arrived this morning?"

"No, guv'nor, he wasn't. I hid my bicycle in the woods on the other side of the quarry, and crept behind the cottage and peeped through the window. The poacher wasn't in, and I hung about killing time as best I could until he returned late in the afternoon carrying a big parcel. Then I peeped in at the window again and saw everything he did. He had a whole outfit in the parcel—a cheap suit of pepper-and-salt mixture, a bowler-hat, a flannel shirt, collar and tie, socks and boots. He put them all on and shaved himself. And when he had finished he raised that lose tile and took a wallet from under it. I don't know what was inside."

"Treasury notes. Did he have any more money?"

"He had a little. Two or three Bradburys and some loose silver."

"Go on my boy."

"Partrick wasn't in any hurry to leave. He sat down and lit his pipe and drank whisky out of a pocket-flask. I knew he meant to bunk off, and I was not sure if you would want me to follow him or not. I was expecting you every minute. You didn't turn up, so I got my bicycle and rode to the village and sent the wire on the chance of your being still at home."

"It was very sensible of you," said Blake. "I am glad you did. And then you returned, eh?"

"Yes, I rode back," Tinker replied, "and crept behind the cottage again. The poacher was still here, and as I was afraid of being discovered I crept a little way up the hill and lay down on a bed of moss. I waited a long while for you to come, and finally I——"

He paused for a moment.

"I'm sorry," he continued, "but I grew drowsy and fell asleep. And when I got awake Ben Partrick was gone."

"You shouldn't have been so careles. No harm has been done, though, as we have the dog. How long is it since you got awake?"

"About an hour, guv'nor."

"And how long were you asleep?"

"Perhaps half an hour. Not more than that."

"At the most, then, the fellow has been gone for an hour and a half."

"That's right. But I don't suppose he has gone that long. What are we to do—go after him?"

Blake nodded a vague assent. His brows were knit, and there was a look of speculation in his eyes.

"As I told you, my boy, it is what I feared," he said. "Partrick has been paid to clear out. Those scoundrels have persuaded him to leave the country because he knows too much about the murder of Kashas Das. There isn't a doubt of it. He intends to walk to Guildford or Dorking or some interlying station and travel to London by rail. I wonder in which direction he went? Towards Guildford, most likely. We may be able to overtake him. It is possible. We will have to try, at all events."

"And if he gives us the slip, guv'nor?" said Tinker.

"If he should," Blake replied, "I will wire a description of him to Charing Cross and to Scotland Yard."

They went down to the road at once and ran the car into a plantation that was close by, returned to the cottage and let Pedro sniff at one of the poacher's old boots.

It was enough for the sagacious bloodhound. He readily picked up the scent outside the door, and, wagging his tail, he set off at a slow trot, leading Blake and Tinker up the wooded hill on a diagonal course.

The sun was below the horizon now. Dusk was falling, and it would soon be dark.

CHAPTER 14.

The Poacher's Precautions—At the Red Barn—Trapped—A Fight in the Dark—Blake and Tinker Arrive—A Running Duel—The Dead Gunman—Ben Partrick's Dying Confession.

DULL-WITTED as Ben Partrick was, though he had credulously swallowed what he had been told at Ranmore Lodge, he was not altogether a fool.

Knowing as he did what good reason Hugh Clontarf and Charles Leighton had to be afraid of him, a vague suspicion had crept into his mind during the day, and had not been dispelled by the whisky he had drunk at Guildford and afterwards.

It was still in his thoughts, haunting him in a dim shape, when he started off from his cottage in the evening in his new raiment and with his Army service revolver in his pocket.

He need not have left so soon, but he was more afraid of Sexton Blake than of the two men—he supposed they would both be there—whom he was going to meet at the rendezvous.

He was in fear of arrest. He was quite convinced that Blake suspected him of the murder of the Hindu, and he was stupid enough to believe that a strong case might be built up against him in spite of the statements he could make.

And there was another worry in his mind as well. A misfortune had happened to him in the morning. It was not in his power now to keep his share of the bargain with Hugh Clontarf, and he doubted if his explanation would be credited, true though it would be.

"If they don't want to take my word for it they can come back with me," he reflected, "and see for themselves, I can show them I didn't lie."

Ben Partrick was in no particular hurry. He had ample time. Nor did he go by the most direct route, for he was anxious to elude observation.

He knew that the sight of him in his new clothes and new hat would rouse suspicions, so he went by a roundabout way on a detour, keeping to cover as much as he could.

He traversed plantations and skirted meadows, skulked by the side of hedgerows, and now and again crawled along dry ditches. And at intervals alluring visions swam in his brain, temporarily banishing his morbid thoughts—visions of a thousand pounds in cash, of a great ocean-linerbreastingthe Atlantic waves, of life in a far, wild land where game was not preserved and there was no fishing rights.

For three miles he held to his circuitous course, trudging leisurely and warily across country, while the twilight faded into the darkness of night. And the moon was floating above the horizon, a globe of pale orange, when at length he came out from a wood to the edge of a road and saw the red barn.

It was a landmark in the neighbourhood. For several years it had not been used, and it was falling to decay now.

It stood on the other side of the road, fifty or sixty yards back in a field. To right and left of it were dense plantations, and behind it was rising ground clothed with scrubby thickets.

There was not a farmhouse or dwelling, not a cottage within half a mile in any direction. From far off the rattle of wheels and hoofs throbbed on the still air. No other sound broke the silence.

Ben Partrick was a little ahead of time, as he had meant to be. It was no more than a quarter to nine o'clock, he was sure.

He stopped at the verge of the woods in the black shadow of the trees, and for five minutes he waited there motionless, with tensely strained ears, scanning the red barn as a soldier might scan the enemy's position.

He was nervous. The sinister suspicions were in his mind again. Did treachery lurk yonder? he wondered. Had a trap been set for him?"

He had in his pocket a flash of whisky, bought at Guildford, which he had not touched yet. He took it out and drank half of the contents, and very soon he felt inclined to laugh at his fears.

"I'm a fool!" he muttered. "There's nothing to be afraid of. If my fine gentlemen had wanted to do me in they wouldn't have brought me here, miles from anywhere. Why should they? They could have come to my cottage and knocked me on the head and heaved me into the quarry pool, and no one would have been the wiser."

The poacher emptied the flask and threw it into the woods. He was still somewhat apprehensive, but the whisky had given him false courage, and he went forward boldly enough, striding across the road and passing through a gateway into the field.

He did not pause until he came to the big double doors of the red barn. They were not locked. He pulled one of them open, and it swung shut behind him, creaking on rusty hinges as he stepped inside.

He moved on for two or three yards, and stopped. He was in almost pitch darkness. For a moment he stood perfectly still, peering around him with eyes that were trained to keen vision.

And of a sudden he perceived to one side a couple of vague figures that were gliding noiselessly towards him in crouching attitudes.

He was so frightened that he forgot the revolver that was in his pocket. He gave a startled gasp, and at once, in a frenzy of terror, he leapt at the dusky forms and hurled himself on top of them.

There was a bloodcurdling oath, a dull crash. Ben Partrick was on the floor in the grip of the two men. And as he struggled with them blindly in the dark a shrill cry burst from his lips:

"Help! Help!"

That cry of distress, ringing faintly to the ears of Sexton Blake and Tinker, told them something tragic was happening. They were within a couple hundred yards at the time, following the bloodhound as he traced the poacher's scent through the woods.

"My word! Partrick must be in trouble!" exclaimed the lad.

"He has fallen into a trap," Blake declared. "I am not surprised. I am afraid we will be too late to save him."

They hurried forward as fast as they could with Pedro baying loudly at their heels, broke from the woods to the road, and sped across it to the gateway.

And they had barely entered the field when three men dashed out of the red barn, one by one, separated by spaces of three or four yards.

It was obvious at a glance, from their size, that neither of the first two—they were men of less than average height—could be Hugh Clontarf or Charles Leighton. As for the third and rear man, the moonlight clearly revealed him as Ben Partrick.

Blake seized the bloodhound by the collar, and as he and Tinker hastened on, both armed with automatics, they witnessed a lurid little drama.

The leading man, whether or not he was armed, was bent only on escape. Gaining on the others with every stride, he swerved to the left of the barn in the direction of the scrubby hill behind it.

But the other two carried on a duel as they ran, the foremost man stopping and turning frequently to discharge a pistol at the poacher, who returned the fire with his revolver, the while he yelled like a fiend.

"Somebody is going to be killed, I'll bet!" panted the lad.

The running duel continued for a few seconds, the weapons spitting flame in quick succession. Then of a sudden Ben Partrick flung up his arms, reeled and dropped. And at the same instant the man who had shot him stumbled, pitched to the ground, and did not move.

The man in the lead had got a good start by now, and he reached the base of the hill and disappeared amongst the thickets just as Blake and Tinker came to the scene of the double tragedy.

"Will you let Pedro go after him, guv'nor?" asked the lad.

"No, I won't risk it," Blake replied. "The fellow probably has a pistol."

The poacher and his assailant were lying limp and motionless on the grass a short distance apart. Blood was trickling from a bullet-hole in Ben Partrick's chest, and, thinking at first he was dead, Blake went to the other man, who had been shot in the throat, and must have been killed instantly.

He was a lean, clean-shaven little man of about thirty. Blake gazed at him closely and recognised him.

"Look, my boy!" he bade. "We know this fellow. We saw him last year in New York, at police headquarters at the City Hall."

"So we did!" Tinker exclaimed in amazement. "I believe he is the Bowery Kid, a notorious gunman!"

"That's quite right," Blake assented. "He and another gunman fled to England several months ago to elude arrest, and Scotland Yard has been trying to find them."

"Of all the queer things, guv'nor! The Bowery Kid! The fellow who escaped must have been the other gunman! What the deuce do you suppose they came down here to Surrey for?"

"They were hired to murder the poacher, of course. Hugh Clontarf and his secretary were afraid to do the deed themselves. They had a trap set for Partrick, and he fell into it."

There could be no doubt that such was the case. The two American gunmen, bribed by greater villains, had been concealed in the red barn, waiting for the poacher.

They had not had it all their own way, however. They had been put to flight, and one of them had been killed at the moment when he shot Partrick.

All was quiet. The shooting had not attracted any attention in this lonely neighbourhood. But suddenly the silence was broken.

A throbbing noise was heard from somewhere beyond the scrubby hill, and it faded swiftly in the distance as Blake and the lad were listening.

"The scoundrels must have come down in a car," said Tinker.

Blake nodded.

"And the other gunman has gone off in it," he answered. "I don't know who he is. They know at Scotland Yard, though."

"Well, it's a pity the poacher is dead."

"It is more than a pity, my boy. It is disastrous, in a sense. I expected to get an important statement from his concerning the murder of Kashar Das. As it is, I may not be able to——"

"What's that, guv'nor?" the lad interrupted. "It sounded like a moan!"

They hurried over to Ben Partrick, and found to their surprise that he was not dead. He was conscious. His eyes were open, and he was making feeble attempts to rise. Blake knelt by him, and lifted his head, and shoulders.

"I wish we had some brandy, Tinker," he said. "The fellow is dying. You can see that. If we could only rally his strength for a while!

"Try to talk, Partrick!" he added. "What do you know of the murder in Ranmore Woods? Tell me before you die! There isn't any hope for you! Tell me!"

Ben Partrick looked up, his face distorted with pain. There was recognition in his glazing eyes. He knew the detective, and wanted to confess; but he was too far gone to speak coherently.

"The dirty villain!" he muttered. "Mr. Clontarf, sir! I was to meet him at the red barn to-night, and—and he was to give me a thousand pounds—for going out to Canada! He lied! He—he set a trap for me. There were two men hiding! I don't know—who they were! We had a fight, and I got the better of them, and—and——"

"Never mind about that," Blake interrupted. "What of the murder? You saw it done, didn't you?"

" I saw it all," the poacher went on. "I was there."

"And it was Hugh Clontarf who——"

"That's right! Mr. Clontarf, sir! He strangled the Hindu! He lost something while he was fighting with him, and I—I picked it up afterwards, and——"

"You picked up something he lost, Partrick? What was it?"

"It—it was a watch!"

"What did you do with it? Where is it? Tell me!"

"I lost it, sir! It was hidden near my cottage—in a hole—under the bank—and when I went to get it—this morning—it slipped from my fingers, and—and——"

"How did you lose it? Tell me where to search for it! Be quick!"

"It fell, sir! You—you will have to——"

They were Ben Partrick's last words. His voice choked. He gasped for breath, and, after a brief, convulsive struggle, he died, passing away in Blake's arms.

"Poor fellow!" said Tinker. "I can't help feeling a bit sorry for him, rascal though he was."

"It is unfortunate he didn't live long enough to sign a written statement," Blake replied, as he rose to his feet. "However, I dare say we shall be able to find the watch Hugh Clontarf dropped at the scene of the murder."

"I dare say we will, guv'nor. When the poacher spoke of the watch being hidden in a hole under the bank, he must have meant the base of the hill behind his cottage."

"I should think so, my boy. I don't know what else he could have meant. We will have to try to-night. The sooner the better."

"What about the bodies? We are miles from anywhere. The nearest house is at Abinger Farm. Shall I go there, and——"

The lad paused, listening to footsteps. A rural policeman was approaching along the road, almost at a run. He reached the gate, came through into the field, and hastened to where Blake and Tinker were standing.

They recognised him as a man of the name of Christie, who had been at the inquest on Kashar Das, and he knew who they were.

"Ah, it's Mr. Blake!" he said, as he stopped. "What is wrong, sir? I heard pistol-shots in this direction a bit ago, and——"

The constable broke off as he observed the two bodies on the grass. He looked at the gunman first, then at the poacher.

"Good heavens, sir, it's Ben Partrick!" he cried in bewilderment. "Is he dead?"

"They are both dead," Blake answered. "They shot each other."

"And the other man, sir? He's a stranger to me! To the best of my knowledge I have never seen him before!"

"I don't suppose you have, Christie. He is a crook from London."

"And he shot and killed old Ben? How did it come about, sir? What was there between them?"

Blake was cautious. The longer the true circumstances of the double tragedy were suppressed, the more it would be to his advantage; for he was not ready as yet to make any move against Hugh Clontarf and Charles Leighton.

So he told the policeman only as much as he cared to tell him, which did not amount to much. He did not mention the gunman who had escaped. He merely suggested, in his brief statements, that the poacher had encountered a crook who was prowling about in the neighbourhood for no good, and that there had been a pistol-duel between the two.

Constable Christie was no satisfied.

"I don't understand it," he said. "Partrick is wearing a new suit of clothes, and new boots, and a new hat. I wonder where he got the money to buy them?"

"By selling poached game, perhaps," Blake replied.

"He always spent his money on drink, sir. He didn't care if he looked like a scarecrow. It's very funny his buying new clothes. And what's more, it's queer he should have come to the red barn, so far from his home, at this early hour of the night."

"So it is. There is a lot of mystery about the affair, I will admit."

"What brought you and your boy here, Mr. Blake, if you don't mind my asking?"

"To look for the London crook of course."

"Ah, I see! I dare say you have been on the fellow's track, and——"

"I am sorry," Blake broke in, "but I can't stop to talk now. I must get to my car, which I left two or three miles away. I will then drive to Dorking, and send Inspector Stracey here. Meanwhile, Christie, you will have to stay with the bodies.''

The constable assented rather reluctantly, and Blake and Tinker set off at once with the bloodhound.

They did not return by the circuitous route Pedro and followed. They held to a straight course across country—they had their bearings—and came in a couple of miles to the poacher's cottage.

Behind it, stretching for half a dozen yards along the base of the fir-clad hill, and running up to a height of six feet to the edge of the woods, was a slope of bare soil and gravel.

Blake and the lad examined it by the light of an electric torch. They discovered several shallow cavities, but Hugh Clontarf's watch was not in any of them, and they did not find it anywhere in the vicinity, though they scoured the grass and thickets above the slope and at the bottom of it.

They finally abandoned the quest, and, going down the path of the road, they got into their car, and drove towards Dorking, wondering what to make of Ben Partrick's statement.

Had he told a deliberate lie? No, not with his dying breath; nor would he have had any motive for doing so. The watch was not on his person. His pockets had been searched.

Whre, then, was it? Under what circumstances had he lost it? If it had simply slipped his fingers as he was taking it from the hole under the bank—those were his words—how could it have vanished so completely?

''Perhaps the fellow's mind was wandering when he spoke of the watch,'' said Tinker. ''It may be hidden in the cottage.''

Blake shrugged his shoulders.

''I don't know,'' he murmured. ''I will have another try to-morrow.

CHAPTER 15.

The Next Day—Another Futile Search—At the White Lion—Tinker has an Inspiration—The Quarry Pool—The Lad's Diving Operations—Success—Under Fire—Saved by Blake—Tinker's Find.

BLAKE and Tinker returned to London that night, breaking their journey at Dorking to inform Inspector Stracey of what had happened; and without delay the inspector and a couple of constables went in a car to the scene of the two murders, and removed the bodies of Ben Partrick and the gunman to the White Lion at Ranmore.

The news of the double tragedy soon leaked out, as sensational news will; and the village street was thronged with curious people, assembled from the surrounding neighbourhood, when Sexton Blake and his young assistant drove through the next morning, on their way to the poacher's cottage.

They did not stop. They went straight on, and spent two hours and more in searching diligently and patiently for the missing watch. They probed deep into the surface of bare earth as the base of the wooded hill, from end to end and top to bottom, and raked as with a fine-toothed comb and grass and bushes in a wide radius.

They scoured the ground on both sides of the cottage, and in front of it, and made a thorough search inside as well, tapping every inch of the walls, pulling the bed apart, and lifting every tile from the floor.

Again they failed. They did not find the watch, and, keenly disappointed they drove back to Ranmore between twelve and one o'clock, and ran the car into the garage; sat down at a table in the tap-room, and ordered luncheon.

They noticed at a corner table near by, but did not pay any attention to, a man who was a stranger to them. He was a man of about forty, shabbily dressed, with a thick, black moustache, and a puffy, florid complexion; and he was leaning lazily against the wall, apparently half-asleep, with a soft hat drawn low over his eyes.

Blake merely glanced at him. He was more interested in the yokels, some in smocks, who were slouching in and out, and drinking beer at the bar while they talked noisily of the mysterious murders.

''It seems to me, guv'nor,'' Tinker remarked at length, when he had nearly finished his luncheon, ''that we are at a deadlock.''

''So we are,'' Blake moodily assented. ''Or very much like it.''

''You don't know what our next move is going to be, then?''

''No, I don't. I haven't decided yet.''

''What's the matter with Laurel Grange, eh?''

''I don't want to take any steps in that direction at present. I would rather wait. The murder of Kashar Das comes first.''

''But you haven't evidence enough to arrest anybody, have you?'' said the lad.

Blake shook his head.

"Unfortunately not," he replied; "in spite of what the poacher told us before he died. It is not sufficient. If only he had told us more! I wish we could find the missing watch! That would alter the situation to my advantage."

"I don't believe it will ever be found, guv'nor."

"I am afraid not, my boy. I haven't the remotest idea what can have become of it, unless——"

"Unless what?"

"Unless somebody else sought for it and found it while we were at the red barn last night, or early this morning."

"Perhaps somebody did, guv'nor. I never thought of that."

Blake nodded absently. He took his pipe from his pocket, and as he was filling it the door was opened, and Inspector Stracey entered the room. He caught sight of the detective, and came over to him.

"I thought I might find you here," he said. "Any fresh news?"

"Nothing fresh," Blake answered.

"The other gunman—you haven't learned who he is, sir?"

"No, I haven't made inquiries yet, Stracey. I have had too much else to occupy my mind."

The inspector, who had no knowledge of Ben Partrick's dying statements, sat down to the table.

He leaned across, and engaged Blake in conversation; and Tinker, who had been wanting to get away, now seized the opportunity that offered.

He rose, remarking that he was going for a stroll; and when he had left the inn he walked slowly and thoughtfully along the Guildford Road.

It was his intention to make another search for the missing watch. What a feather in his cap it would be, he reflected, if he were to find it! How pleased Blake would be with him!

He was not sanguine. Far from it. He knew there was hardly a chance in a thousand that he would succeed. He was pretty sure, however, that the watch was somewhere in or near the poacher's cottage.

Assuming that the gunman who escaped had been to Ranmore Lodge last night to report the disastrous failure of the trap at the red barn, Hugh Clontarf or Charles Leighton might have gone to the cottage at an early hour this morning to look for the watch, and had found it.

The lad's ardour was chilled. He stopped, half-inclined to turn back; and as he stood hesitating he recalled again Ben Partrick's dying statements:

"I lost it, sir!" I was hidden near my cottage—in a hole—under the bank—and when I went to get it—this morning—it slipped from my fingers, and—and——"

They were the man's dying words, and he had added with his last breath, just as he died:

"It fell, sir! You—you will have to——"

He had let the watch fall as he was taking it from a hole in a bank. Where had it fallen! How could it have disappeared? Why had not the poacher been able to find it?

Tinker racked his brains, and of a sudden an inspiration flashed upon him. It was so simple, so plausible, that he was surprised he had not thought of it before.

"I believe I am right!" he said to himself. "There can't be much doubt about it!"

He was sanguine enough now. In cheerful spirits, almost certain that he had solved the mystery, he hurried on his way to the home of the murdered man.

He climbed the footpath, and, bearing to the left of the cottage, he went along the base of the wooded hillto the top of the abandoned quarry, and stretched himself flat on the ground at the edge of it.

Thrusting his hand beneath him, he fumbled at the surface of the cliff, and discovered a small cavity which felt to the touch as if it had been hollowed out with a knife.

Then he peered warily over the brink, and his heart gave a quick throb as he perceived, a few inches below the cavity, a narrow shelf, on which lay a little heap of loose, powdery soil mixed with tiny flakes of stone.

How it had got there was obious. It had dropped on to the shelf while the poacher was digging into the cliff with a knife.

"My word, I was right!" Tinker murmured. "The watch was hidden in the hole, and as Ben Partrick was taking it out yesterday morning it fell into the pool! That is how he lost it!"

Greatly elated by his discoveries, the lad retraced his steps to the road, and descended into the quarry by the winding cart-track, to the margin of the deep and tranquil pool; and then, by a succession of projecting ledges, he crept along one side of the pool until he was directly beneath the spot where he had been lying on the ground.

He was going to try to recover the watch, and he did not suppose it would be a very difficult task. He had a clear idea as to where he must search for it.

Having stripped to the skin, he plunged headforemost into the water, and dived to the bottom, groped here and there, and rose to the surface for breath.

Again and again he plunged in, staying under as long as he could. Four times he dived, and after the fourth attempt he was shivering with cold, and his eyes were blurred. But he was not discouraged yet. He would have another try.

Once more he dived, and this time, as he was groping over the bottom in a wider radius, he had a glimpse of something that glittered like a bright pebble.

He reached for it, clutched it, and gripped it tightly in his hand. He had found the watch.

Up he came with it, almost exhausted; and now, as he was about to clamber out on the ledge, he heard a sharp report, and a bullet hummed close to his ear.

Glancing above him, he saw the figure of a man at the top of the cliff, at a point opposite to the road.

Instantly he dived again, just as a second shot was fired at him; and going deep down, he swam under water in the direction from which the shots had come, that he might get out of harm's way, and rose inside of a shallow cleft, which he had observed at the base of the rocky wall.

"The scoundrel!" he muttered. "It was either Clontarf or Charles Leighton! He must have been watching me!"

Submerged to the chest, he clung to a jutting stone, and looked at the small gold watch he had dredged from the bottom. Would it cost him his life!

He was in a place of shelter, a little cavern in the cliff, but how long would he be safe here? His enemy could easily get in range by working round to the opposite side of the quarry, and he was probably doing so now.

All was quiet. There was not a sound. Several minutes elapsed, while Tinker waited in keen suspense, chilled to the bone.

At length, to his horror, he caught sight of the man creeping amongst the bushes on the rim of the cliff, and near the road.

The moving figure was only dimly visible. It stopped and crouched, peering below; and at this critical moment, when Tinker was in deadly peril, the throbbing of a car came to his ears from the direction of Ranmore.

The man in the bushes did not fire. He hesitated, and as the throbbing noise rang louder he suddenly vanished. He could be heard in flight, running towards the poacher's cottage.

The danger had been averted, and with a thankful heart, his teeth chattering with cold, Tinker swam to the ledge, and clambered on to it.

And a moment later, as he was pulling on his clothes, the car stopped in the road, and Sexton Blake appeared at the top of the quarry. He saw the lad, and waved to him.

"Hallo!" he called. "What on earth have you been doing?"

"Swimming, of course!" Tinker cheerily called back. "What did you think, guv'nor?"

He hastily finished dressing, and went round by the ledges of rock to the foot of the cart-track. Blake was standing there, a puzzled expression on his face.

"I got tired of waiting at the White Lion for you," he said irritably, "so I set off for the Elms to see Colonel Roylance. I pulled up the car a bit ago, to light my pipe, and I thought I heard a couple of pistol-shots in this direction."

"So you did," Tinker replied.

"And as I drew near the quarry," Blake continued, "I saw a man rise from the bushes at the top of the cliff, and dash off towards Ben Partrick's cottage."

"That's right. The man was Mr. Clontarf, or his private secretary. It was he who fired the shots, and they were fired at me."

"At you? And what brought you here, my boy?"

"This, guv'nor."

As the lad spoke, he took the watch from his pocket and handed it to his master. Blake stared at it in bewilderment, and Tinker gave him a full account of all that had happened.

"That was clever of you, my boy!" Blake declared, patting him on the shoulder. "Very clever indeed! Really brilliant! I was stupid not to have thought of it myself. But you should have returned to the inn, and told me what you were going to do. I would have come with you, and mounted guard while you dived."

"It doesn't matter," Tinker answered, "since you turned up in time to save my life. The fellow was about to shoot at me when the sound of the car frightened him away."

"You had a narrow escape," said Blake. "As for the man who tried to kill you, whether he was Hugh

Clontarf or not, he was sitting close to us when we were having our luncheon."

"Close to us? The man with the black moustache and the soft hat, who was asleep in the corner? I remember him."

"He wasn't asleep. He was very much awake. He was listening to our conversation. He went out shortly after you did, and he must have followed you here, keeping in the cover of the woods."

"Ah, that's how it was, guv'nor!"

"Exactly! The man was Charles Leighton in disguise, I believe, and he was sent to the White Lion by Hugh Clontarf. He thought we might be there during the day, and his object was to find out, if he could, if we had found the watch on the poacher's body last night.

"Well, he learned that we hadn't, and that is why he shadowed me. He suspected I was going to the cottage to make another search."

"Yes, I dare say."

Blake was examining the watch now. He snapped the lid open, and his sparkled with satisfaction.

"What's this?" he exclaimed. "An inscription inside—'To Hugh Clontarf from his uncle, Lord Roderick Teroit.' A very damaging piece of evidence—eh?"

"It is pretty bad," Tinker assented. "Will it be enough, though?"

"I should think so," Blake replied. "There is other evidence, remember, of a circumstantial nature. By the way, does the man know you dredged the watch from the pool?"

"No, guv'nor, he don't."

"Are you sure?"

"I am quite certain. He couldn't have seen the watch, for I had it clasped tightly in my hand all the time."

"So much the better," said Blake. "If you are right no harm has been done. Mr. Clontarf and his precious secretary will remain at Ranmore Lodge, believing they have nothing to fear for the present.

"We will be off now, my boy," he added, as he began to ascend the cart-track. "This isn't a healthy neighbourhood for us. I have changed my mind about going to the Elms. We will drive back to London, and discuss our plans for the morrow. The birds will not have flown by then."

"You are going to arrest them?" asked Tinker.

Blake nodded.

"Before it is too late," he said. "It would be imprudent to wait any longer."

CHAPTER 16.

The Following Day—A Startling Development—The Rifled Safe—Blake's Suspicions—A Visit to Scotland Yard.

THE next day was to be an eventful one, even more so than Sexton Blake anticipated. He rose at the usual hour, and he had finished his breakfast, and was reading the morning paper, when he was called to the telephone.

It was Mr. Henson who was speaking, and what Blake learned from his was of such a startling nature that, after a few words to Tinker, he hastened from the house, hailed a taxi, and was driven to the premises of Henson and Halbury, the publishers, in Bedford Street.

He went straight through to the private office, and Mr. Henson, who was waiting there, pointed to the large safe that stood by the wall.

"Look!" he bade. "What do you think of that?"

It was an obvious burglary. The safe had been blown open—there was a hole burnt through the massive door—and the contents were in confusion. Letters and papers were scattered about on the shelves.

"I made the discovery when I arrived this morning," Mr. Henson contined, "and I telephoned to you immediately. There were two men concerned in the affair, I imagine. One kept watch at the mouth of Clare Court, to give warning of danger; and the other got in by that small window yonder, which opens on to the court. You can see where the iron shutter was violently wrenched from its fastenings. As for the safe, it was opened by means of oxygen gas and a blow-pipe."

"And the chapter was stolen?" said Blake. "The chapter of Lord Roderick Teviot's memoirs relating to the Selampur Turf Scandal?"

"Yes, it is gone," replied Mr. Henson.

"Only that one chapter!"

"Only that one, Mr. Blake. The rest of the manuscript isstill there—or what portion of it is not in the hands of the printers."

"Was there any money in the safe?"

"No, not a penny. The chapter is all that is missing."

Blake nodded.

"The motive is clear, then," he said. "There is only one person we can suspect, and that is——"

"Sir Ralph Athelstan," the publisher interrupted. "No one else could have had any motive for the theft."

"Just so. I doubt if Sir Ralph Athelstan was the actual thief, though. He probably hired a couple of crooks."

"Yes, I dare say you are right."

"You haven't disturbed anything, Henson?"

"I have touched nothing except the manuscript of the book. Everything else is as I found it. There aren't any finger-prints. There is no clue of any description."

Blake had a look for himself. He scrutinised the door of the safe, and the inside of it; went to the window, and thoroughly examined that.

"Not a single finger-print," he remarked. "The burglar was too clever to leave any. He was an expert cracksman, I am satisfied. This is a very unfortunate business. The chapter has been destroyed by now, of course."

Mr. Henson smiled.

"It doesn't matter if it has been," he said.

"It doesn't matter?" Blake repeated. "I should say it does. What do you mean?"

"I haven't told you yet that the missing chapter had already been set up in type."

Ah, I see! Only proofs of the chapter were stolen? If it is in type it can be reproduced!"

"Exactly. The burglar had his pains for nothing, Mr. Blake. Publication will not be prevented. Two sets of proofs of the chapter were struck off. The one was stolen, and the other I took home to read last night, intending to post it to Mr. Clontarf. But I forgot to bring it with me this morning."

"And the chapter in its original form? The manuscript? Where is that?"

"I took that home also, to compare with the proofs. It is in a safe at my house."

"So no harm has been done!" said Blake. "I am glad to hear that."

"It will be a blow to Sir Ralph Athelstan," Mr. Henson replied, "to find that his object has been foiled."

"I am not so sure. He had certain suspicions, I believe. He wanted to verify them, and he has succeeded in doing so. And now tell me, Henson, when will the memoirs will be completed."

"They are completed now. I had the last chapter of the manuscript from Mr. Clontarf yesterday, by post. He has been working very hard of late."

Blake shrugged his shoulders.

"Naturally he would," he said. "I can understand that. By the way, have you sent word to him of the theft?"

"Not yet," Mr. Henson answered. "I was going to."

"Have you informed the police?"

"No; I thought I had better consult you first."

"That was right. Let the matter rest as it is. Don't call the police in, and don't inform Mr. Clontarf of what has happened."

"He ought to know, considering the instructions he gave me regarding the chapter."

"He must not know to-day. To-morrow you can do as you please. It won't make any difference then."

"And what about Sir Ralph Athelstan? I am afraid you will not be able to get any proof against him, Mr. Blake."

"Probably not; nor do I wish to. That is all, Henson. I will be off now. Remember my instructions. Good-morning!"

Blake was gone as he spoke. He walked down Bedford Street to the Strand, a look of perplexity in his eyes, and picked up a taxi, drove home, and told Tinker all that had happened.

"I am rather worried," he continued. "There is no telling what the outcome of the affair wil be. Sir Ralph Athelstan has been badly treated, I am sure. He suspected as much, and I dare say he has already learned that his suspicions were correct."

"And you are afraid he will try to get even with Hugh Clontarf?" asked Tinker.

"That is why I am uneasy," Blake assented. "There is no reason to be, perhaps. Sir Ralph may lie low for a day or so."

"And he may not, guv'nor. Hadn't I better keep him under observation?"

" I think not. No, I'll chance it. Even if Sir Ralph Athelstan should be in a revengeful mood, it is not likely he will——"

Blake paused.

"There are more important things to be thought of," he said, glancing at his watch. "The sands are running out. I am going to Scotland Yard now, my boy, to make arrangements with Inspector Widgeon. And I want to see him about another matter as well. He may have news for me. You know he told me last evening, when I walked to him on the telephone, that he would have a couple of his detectives search for Buck Corrigan, the other American gunman who came to England with the Bowery Kid, and that he would probably be found and arrested to-day."

"And if he isn't?" said Tinker. "It won't alter your plans?"

Blake shook his head.

"Certainly not," he replied. "I am ready to strike at the murderers of Kashar Das."

CHAPTER 17.

Sir Ralph Athelstan Goes to Ranmore Lodge Again—Treachery Laid Bare—Sir Ralph's Demands—Hot Words—A Desperate Fight—The Police Arrive—The Arrest of the Murderers—A Sensational Disclosure.

TIRED and dusty, and in a very bad temper—it was aggravated by the fact that the car in which he had come from London had broken down three miles from his destination—Sir Ralph Athelstan arrived on foot at Ranmore Lodge that night between eight and nine o'clock, as darkness was falling

He refused to give his name to the maid who opened the door to him, and reluctantly, at his insistence, she admitted him, took him to the cosy little smoking-room on the ground-floor, and hastily withdrew.

Hugh Clontarf was here alone, sitting in a lounge-chair by the table with a cigar in his mouth. It was obvious to him at a glance that the baronet was in a temper, but he welcomed his cordially enough.

"Hallo, Athelstan!" he said. "I'm glad to see you. Sit down."

Sir Ralph Athelstan frowned.

"I prefer to stand, thank you," he replied, in an icy tone.

"Will you have a drink? And a cigar? Help yourself!"

"I won't have either, Clontarf. I will accept no hospitality from you."

"Why not? What's wrong? Have you come to insult me? You have no reason to."

"Haven't I? Don't deceive yourself. I have come to tell you that I have found out what a despicable cur you are."

"Be careful!" bade Hugh Clontarf, springing to his feet. "Don't call me names! What do you mean? You must be mad!"

Sir Ralph Athelstan stepped nearer to him.

"I am going to have a reckoning with you," he said in a low boice that was tremulous with suppressed passion. "Some time ago I came to see you, you will remember, and tried to persuade you to cut out from your uncle's memoirs the chapter relating to the Selampur Turf Scandal. You refused, and I dropped the matter. Subsequently, however, I receive a letter from you. I called again, and on that occasion we struck a bargain. You agreed to suppress the chapter, if I would give you twenty thousand pounds, and half of that sum you have already had from me."

"That is quite true," Hugh Clontarf assented. "What of it? I have not broken my word."

"You lie! You have broken it! You have been playing the dirtiest kind of a game!"

"You are talking nonsense, Athelstan! You are wrong, I can assure you! If you will wait until the book is published you willseethat——"

"I have no need to wait. I have discovered your perfidy. You can guess how. I will tell you this much. The chapter is not only to be included in Lord Roderick Teviot's memoirs, but it is now in type, and proofs of it have been struck off."

"How—how do you know? There must be some mistake! I instructed the publishers to——"

"Don't keep on lying, Clontarf! It is useless! There is no mistake at all! I am not afraid to admit that, suspecting treachery, I had a professional burglar break into the offices of Henson & Halbury in Bedford Street, and open the safe. That is how I came into possession of the proofs of the chapter you swore you would suppress. Now what have you got to say for yourself?"

Hugh Clontarf was silent for a moment. White to the lips, his features twitching, he stared in consternation at the man he had so basely betrayed.

"I—I tell you again," he faltered, "there must be some mistake. I can't understand how it happened."

"You told the publishers to cut the chapter out?" asked Sir Ralph Athelstan.

"Most certainly I did!"

"That is another lie, you infamous scoundrel! You meant to trick me from the first! You ought to be shot! I am tempted to thrash you within an inch of your life! I will spare you, though, on conditions. In the first place, you will see to it that the chapter is suppressed; and you will prove to me, by a letter from the publishers, that it is not going to be included in the memoirs. Is that clearly understood?"

"Yes, of course," Hugh Clontarf readily assented. "I will see to it. You needn't worry."

"You will have cause to worry," said Sir Ralph Athelstan, "If you fail to keep you promise. You are liable to a heavy penalty, to several years in prison, for extorting money under false pretences."

"The chapter will not appear in the book. What else do you want?"

"What else? The ten thousand pounds you have had from me! You will refund it, Clontarf!"

"But I am entitled to it. If I am going to save you from exposure by cutting out the chapter about the——"

"Never mind about that," Sir Ralph Athelstan interrupted. "You deserve to lose the money, for the way you rooked me. You shan't profit by your villainy to the amount of a single shilling. Youwill have to be satisfiedwith what you may get from the sale of the book. I must have the ten thousand pounds at once. To-night! I will take your cheque."

"I can't do it," said Hugh Clontarf, in a sullen tone. 'Notto-night. You will have to wait for a day or so."

"Why must I wait? Why can't you give me a cheque?"

"For the simple reason that the money is not available at present. It has been converted into securities, Athelstan, and they are in a bank in London."

"I don't believe it! It is another lie!"

"It is not! I am telling you the truth! If you will be sensible, and give me a little time——"

"Not an hour! Not five minutes, Clontarf! I will wring the money out of you! You are trying to play me false again, you cursed trickster! You won't succeed, though! I am not to be fooled!"

They glared at each other, Hugh Clontarf's demeanour had suddenly, swiftly changed. There was a menacing glitter in his eyes. He was at bay now, and he showed his teeth.

"I've stood enough of your insults!" he declared, with an oath. "More than enough! Don't try to bully me, you impudent dog! I won't have it! I am not afraid of your threats. Clear out of this! Be quick about it! I have a temper myself, and if you provoke me any farther——"

"You yellow cur!" cried Sir Ralph Athelstan, flushed with rage. "I am going to teach you a lesson you won't forget in a hurry!"

He clenched his fist, and let fly, striking like lightning. A blow landed on Hugh Clontarf's chin, and toppled him against the table. He overturned it, and fell with it, crashing to the floor amidst a litter of broken glass and spilt whisky.

He jumped up, spluttering curses; and as he was reaching for his pocket he was knocked down again. And now Charles Leighton, who had been listening from the hall, hastened into the room.

"What's all this about, Athelstan!" he demanded. "Stop it! What the devil do you mean?"

Sir Ralph Athelstan laughed.

"Another swindling rogue—eh?" he exclaimed. "Birds of a feather. I'll serve you as I served your accomplice, you rascally crook!"

Once more he launched out with his fist, and hit hard. Charles Leighton had no chance to dodge the blow. Taken off his guard, he staggered backward—reeled to the wall—dropped like a log—and lay there half-stunned.

Meanwhile Hugh Clontarf has scrambled to his feet in a mad fury. He whipped a pistol from his pocket, fired, and missed. Before he could fire a second shot the weapon was struck from his grasp, and Sir Ralph Athelstan had him by the throat.

They were at grips, locked together; and of a sudden, as they were swaying to and fro, the door was thrown open, and at once the room seemed to fill with men.

There were only six in the party, however—Sexton Blake and Tinker, Inspector Widgeon, Inspector Stracey, and two Scotland Yard detectives.

In a trice Hugh Clontarf and the enraged baronet were torn apart, and Sir Ralph Athelstan, himself unmolested, stood aside, and looked on in blank amazement.

There was a mad whirl of confusion, a clamour of strident shouts, and bloodcurdling oaths, and clatter of falling chairs; a dizzy kaleidoscope of bodies that writhed and strained and twisted while they lurched and plunged from wall to wall, and recoiled to plunge again.

It was a short struggle. In a couple of minutes it was all over. Battered and dishevelled, with collars awry, Hugh Clontarf and his private-secretary were flung on to the couch, where they sat tugging at their handcuffed wrists, and whispering apprehensively to each other in low, breathless sentences.

In the hall, outside the open doorway, the terrified servants were standing. Inspector Stracey spoke to them, and shut the door.

Blake glanced at Sir Ralph Athelstan.

"I can guess what you are doing here," he said curtly. "You can be thankful you aren't under arrest as well."

"You can arrest me if you life," the baronet replied, in an aggressive tone. "I came to denounce a pair of infernal swindlers."

"I thought so. And you learnt you had been swindled, Athelstan through the crook you hired to break into the office of Henson & Hilbury, the publishers, of Bedford Street."

"You can't prove that, Mr. Blake."

"Probably not. And I am not sure I want to. There are mitigating circumstances. Your punishment will be severe enough as it is. I imagine. I have some knowledge of the position you are in, and I know all about the chapter of Lord Roderick Teviot's memoirs, which relates to the Selampur Turf Scandal. These men extorted money from you under false pretences, I suppose. They led you to believe the chapter would be cut out of the book."

"Yes, exactly," said Sir Ralph Athelstan. "That was the understanding I had with Hugh Clontarf, and he deceived me, as I have discovered. It was a rascally trick."

"It was," Blake assented. "How much money have you parted with?"

"Ten thousand pounds. And I was to have paid ten thousand more."

"Well, sir, you have been doubly deceived. You have had no dealings whatever with Hugh Clontarf. You did not pay him a penny."

"I most certainly did, Mr. Blake!"

"You certainly did not, Sir Ralph! You have dealt with a daring and cunning impostor! This man is not Hugh Clontarf!"

Sir Ralph Athelstan stared in stupefaction, struck dumb. The dramatic secret had been revealed. It had been known to Blake and Tinker since the former's visit to Laurel Grange, and the police had been told this evening.

There was a moment of tense silence, and then Blake turned to the two prisoners, who had been taken by surprise by his statement.

"It is a great satisfaction to me," he said, "to bring to justice two such scoundrels as you are. Parrish Creed, alias Hugh Clontarf, you and your accomplice, Charles Leighton will be charged with the wilful murder of the Hindu servant, Kashar Das. And you will be further charged with inciting two American gunmen, one of whom is dead, and the other in custody, to murder the poacher, Ben Partrick."

Parrish Creed was ghastly pale.

"You will find you have made a mistake!" he exclaimed. "Where is your evidence?"

"You haven't got any, Blake!" declared Charles Leighton. "You can't prove anything against us!"

Blake shrugged his shoulders.

"Don't delude yourselves," he replied. "I have enough evidence to hang you both."

With that he took the gold watch from his pocket.

"This was dredged from the quarry pool near the poacher's cottage," he went on. "Partrick lost it there. He picked it up near the scene of the murder in Ranmore Woods. He saw the Hindu strangled, and he told me with his dying breath, Creed, that you were the murderer. To be more precise, he said Hugh Clontarf was—which amounts to the same thing. The watch belonged to Mr. Clontarf. It was a gift to him from his uncle, Lord Roderick Teviot, and there is an inscription inside of it to that effect. I know where Hugh Clontarf is, as it happens, and I know also that the watch has not been in his possession since the night he wandered away from Ranmore Lodge. He left it at home, and you very foolishly carried it about with you."

Blake paused, and bent his gaze on Charles Leighton.

"It was you who played the part of a Hindu to mislead the police," he continued, "and I have discovered in a hollow tree, outside the grounds of his house, the turban and false beard you wore, and the brown stain you used for your face and hands. As for the murder of Ben Partrick at the red barn, I may tell you that the American gunman, Buck Corrigan, was arrested in the East End to-day, and has made a full confession."

Charles Leighton glared savagely at the detective, and an oath burst from Parrish Creed's lips. They looked at each other in consternation, with fear in their eyes, realising that nothing could save them from the gallows.

Sir Ralph Athelstan was astounded.

"So these fellows are guilty of the mysterious murders in the neighbourhood!" he cried. "And the one I believed to be Hugh Clontarf is an impostor! Who are they really, Mr. Blake? Do you know?"

Blake nodded.

"I found out this afternoon," he answered. "I had the information from the American gunman I have mentioned. Parrish's real name is Burke, and Leighton's name is Preller. They are both crooks. They went to New York some few years ago, and operated there. It was then they met Buck Corrigan, and after they came back to England they kept in touch with him, and thus learned recently that he had come over to this country with another gunman, and was staying at an address in the East End of London.

"Meanwhile, after their return, Parrish got the position of private-secretary to Lord Roderick Teviot in Scotland, doubtless through false references; and he subsequently filled the same post with Hugh Clontarf."

"And then what?" asked Sir Ralph Athelstan. "What does it all mean? Why was the Hindu servant murdered? And where is Mr. Clontarf?"

"I can't tell you now," said Blake. "The whole story will be in the papers to-morrow evening."

"And I will be shown up? Can't you keep my name out?"

"I intend to. I will see to it, because I have some slight sympathy for you."

"Can I persuade you to do more than that for me, Mr. Blake? Won't you—won't you try to have the chapter about the Turf scandal suppressed? I stand to lose a fortune—and inheritance from a wealthy relative who believes me to be a man of unblemished honour?

Blake's face hardened, and he shook his head.

"It is impossible," he coldly replied, "I can do nothing for you in that respect, Sir Ralph, nor would I if I could. The chapter will be included in the memoirs, and you know why. You did Lord Roderick Teviot's a grievous wrong. His reputation was tarnished while he lived, and now that he is dead justice must be done to his memory. He must be vindicated before the world."

Sir Ralph Athelstan did indeed stand to lose much. The publication of that sinister chapter, the revelation of his sin of many years ago, would rob him of a vast inheritance, and involve him in social ruin and disgrace.

But he accepted the detective's decision calmly, without another word. He knew any further appeal would be useless.

The two prisoners were waiting in sullen silence. Down in the road, outside of the gates, were standing the two taxis which had brought the raiding-party to Ranmore Lodge. It was getting late. Blake turned to Inspector Widgeon.

"Let us be off with these rogues now, Widgeon," he said. "The servants are trustworthy. We can leave them in charge here in the morning, and thoroughly search the premises. We will give you a lift, Athelstan, if you like," hę added, "should you be going our way.

CHAPTER 18.

The News Reaches and Elms—Gwenda's Distress—A Visit to Laurel Grange—Dr. Todd's Patient—Recognition—Hugh Clontarf's Recovers his Memory.

THERE was sorrow, and the shadow of tragedy, at the Elms the next day. For part of the morning Gwenda Roylance had been in her bed-room, now pacing the floor in agitation and suspense, now lying listlessly in a chair for a few moments, while her pretty face twitched with grief, and occasionally her eyes filled with tears.

It was nearly twelve o'clock when she heard a throbbing noise, and gazing from a window, she saw a car approaching, and recognised the driver of it.

She darted from the room, and flew down the stairs to the hall, threw open the door, and hastened out to the porch just as the car stopped in front of the house.

"Oh, Mr. Blake!" she breathlessly exclaimed. "I am so glad you have come! I—I have——"

Her voice faltered and choked, and tears crept into her eyes again. Blake remaining in the car, looked at the girl closely.

"My dear child, you have been crying!" he said. "What is the matter?"

"I heard the news, not an hour ago!" Gwenda replied. "The butcher's boy told the cook!"

"I am sorry. I wanted to spare you the shock. I should have been here in time had I not been delayed on the road. What have you heard?"

"Everything, Mr. Blake! What happened at Ranmore Lodge last night! That Hugh Clontarf and his secretary were arrested, and will be charged with the murder of Kashar Das and the poacher! Only it wasn't really Hugh! They say he was an impostor! I can hardly believe that. It can't be true, surely!"

"Yes, it is quite true," Blake assented. "An impostor."

"Where is Hugh, then?" asked the girl, her lip quivering. "What has become of him? Is he dead? Has—has he been murdered by those wicked men?"

"Murdered? No, no, nothing of the sort! Don't be alarmed. Mr. Clontarf is alive and well. At least he is in good health, and in safe hands. He is in the neighbourhood, staying with a gentleman who lives no great distance from here. I have known for some days where he was."

"You knew, Mr. Blake? And you didn't tell me! Why not?"

"I had my reasons. It was best that the secret should be kept for a time. I meant to tell you this morning, but unfortunately you had the news before I could——"

Blake broke off.

"Where is your father?" he continued.

"He has driven over to Ranmore Lodge, to make inquiries," Gwenda answered. "I begged him to go. I have been terribly worried. There is so much I don't understand. Does Hugh still love me? He hasn't changed?"

"Of course not. He has always loved you."

"And I thought he had tired of me! I have been heart-broken about it! I am longing to see him! When can I?"

Blake smiled.

"To-day," he said. "You will see him in a few minutes. I am going to take you to him. I have sent a telegram to the gentleman he is staying with, and he is expecting both of us. Get your hat, Gwenda, and we will start at once. I will tell you all about Hugh Clontarf while we are on the way.

The girl's eyes sparkled.

"I won't keep you waiting, Mr. Blake!" she cried, as she hurried into the house. "I will be back in a minute! Oh, how glad I shall be to see Hugh again!"

★ ★ ★

It was not far to Laurel Grange. The gates were wide open for the expected visitors, and the car rolled through into the garden, and along the winding drive to the house.

The man Dodson opened the door, and nodding respectfully, he took Blake and Gwenda to a reception-room. Dodson withdrew, and shortly afterwards Dr. Gavin Todd appeared.

He came in bland and smiling, with words of friendly greeting; shook hands with the detective, and bowed to the girl, whom he knew by sight.

He had not heard of the arrests at Ranmore Lodge, and Blake did not enlighten him.

"How is the patient to-day?" he asked.

"About the same, sir," Dr. Todd replied. "No better, and no worse."

"There will be no harm in our seeing him?"

"Oh, no, Mr. Blake! On the contrary."

"You think the experiment I mentioned to you several days ago may be a success, doctor?"

"There is a chance of it. A very strong chance, sir. I have had much experience with cases of mental trouble. Let us put it to the test."

The three went upstairs, and into a large room, comfortably furnished, where a man was standing by a window. A handsome young man of thirty, tall and fair, with a blonde moustache.

"Some people to see you, Mr. Clontarf," said the doctor.

Hugh Clontarf turned in a slow, listless manner. He gazed dully, vacantly at Blake and from him to the girl, regarding her as if she was a stranger of whom he had no knowledge.

For a moment he showed no interest, and then, of a sudden, his expression changed. His cheeks flushed. He started forward.

"Gwenda!" he cried, opening his arms. "Gwenda, my darling!"

The next instant the girl was nestled on his breast, her hands clasped around his neck, her lips pressed to his lips.

"Hugh!" she half-sobbed. "Hugh, dear Hugh! So you know who I am! Oh, I am so thankful!"

Blake and Dr. Todd nodded to each other greatly pleased. The experiment had succeeded. The threads of a severed memory had been joined together by the recognition, and now, as Hugh Clontarf released the girl from his embrace, and glanced around him, a look of utter bewilderment crept into his eyes.

"Where am I, Gwenda?" he exclaimed. "I have no idea!"

"You are at Laurel Grange, a home for private patients," the girl answered. "Dr. Todd has been taking care of you."

"I know the doctor. He has been very kind to me. How long have I been here, darling?"

"Quite a long time. For several weeks, Hugh."

"For weeks? What does it mean? Who is the gentleman you have brought with you? He is a stranger to me, Gwenda!"

Blake spoke for himself.

"It does not matter who I am," he said. "I am a friend of Miss Roylance, and I came with her because I was interested in your case. You lost your memory some time ago, Mr. Clontarf, and it has been suddenly restored to you. Have you no recollection of the events which led to your being in the care of Dr. Todd?"

Hugh Clontarf shook his head.

"Up to a certain point, not afterwards," he replied. "It was the book I was writing—my uncle's memoirs. It was hard, strenuous work. It was too difficult for me, as I had never done anything of the sort before. It preyed on my mind and nerves, until finally, one night, I felt as if my brain would burst. I was afraid of going mad. I remember leaving the house, and wandering aimlessly through the woods in the darkness, and—and——"

The young man paused, and pressed his hand to his brow.

"I can't remember anything else," he declared. "No, nothing more. It's no use trying. No, I can't do it."

He dropped into a chair, and sat gazing into vacancy, trying to recall what was lost from the cells of his brain. He was absorbed in his thoughts, oblivious of all else. Gwenda bent over him, and kissed him. He paid no heed to her.

"We had better leave him now, sir," Dr. Todd whispered. "He will be quite all right in an hour or so. There will not be another lapse of memory."

They quietly left the room, and went downstairs. Blake had a short conversation with the doctor, giving him to understand that he would take Hugh Clontarf home on the following day; and then, declining an invitation to stay for luncheon, he departed with the girl, whose sorrow had been turned to rejoicing.

"You will have luncheon at our place, won't you?" she said, as they were spinning along the road.

"No, I won't stop to-day," Blake replied. "I must get back to town. I will drop you at the Elms, and you can tell your father I will see him some time to-morrow, probably in the evening."

CHAPTER 19.

Hugh Clontarf Returns to Ranmore Lodge—At the Elms—Sexton Blake Tells the Story.

AT nine o'clock in the evening of the next day Sexton Blake was sitting in the library of the Elms with Colonel Roylance and his daughter, smoking an excellent cigar, and feeling very cheerful over the results of his clever work.

He had been busy in London during the greater part of the day. In the afternoon he had come down to Surrey, and taken Hugh Clontarf from Laurel Grange to Ranmore Lodge.

He had dined with him there, and had a long talk with him; and he had just driven over to the colonel's place for the purpose of giving him and Gwenda a full account of the sensational and mysterious case.

"As I have already mentioned," he said, "Charles Leighton made a confession to-day, in the slender hope of being able to save his neck. And from his statements, from what I have learned from Mr. Clontarf, and from what Sir Ralph Athelstan has told me, I have got a complete understanding of the whole affair from beginning to end. It shows how the veriest trifle may lead to momentous events. Curiously enough, nothing would have happened, there would have been no murders had no imposture, had not Sir Ralph Athelstan called on Hugh Clontarf—the real one—and offered him a heavy bribe to suppress the chapter of the memoirs relating to the Selampur Turf Scandal, which Mr. Clontarf indignantly refused to do. The matter would have rested at that no doubt, but for the fact that Parrish Creed overheard the conversation between the two, and foresaw how he might profit by it. He laid his plans very craftily. His first step was to resign his post of private-secretary, and, having taken Charles Leighton into his confidence, he got him into the position he, Creed, had vacated.

"Omitting details of no particular importance, Parrish Creed stayed in the neighbourhood in disguise, and saw Charles Leighton from time to time. And he also saw Dr. Gavin Todd—he had known him in the past—and induced him for a monetary consideration to admit Hugh Clontarf into his house, and keep him there for a certain period. The young man was to have been abducted. That was the intention of Creed and Leighton, and they were helped to carry it out by what occurred just when their plans were ripe.

"In a state of mental distress, suffering from the strain of his literary work, Hugh Clontarf wandered away from home on night. He met the poacher, Ben Partrick, and had a fight with him; and he was subsequently discovered in the woods, with his memory quite gone, by Creed and Leighton. And with the assistance of another man who was with them—a friend of Creed—they smuggled Mr. Clontarf off to Laurel Grange.

"The next move in the game was for Parrish Creed to make himself up as the very double of Hugh Clontarf, and step into his shoes. That accomplished,theywrote in the name of Clontarf to Sir Ralph Athelstan, who came again to Ranmore Lodge, and agreed to pay twenty-thousand pounds to have the chapter omitted from the book; and was basely deceived, as you are aware.

"Some little time passed, while Parrish Creed, a man of superior education, worked on the memoirs with the aid of Sir Roderick Teviot's notes and diaries. Then danger threatened the conspirators. Kashar Das found out that his supposed master was an impostor, denounced him to his face, and fled from the house to inform the police; and was followed by Creed, who overtook him in Ranmore Woods, and cruelly murdered him. There was a struggle first, and it was witnessed from hiding by the poacher, who afterwards picked up a watch belonging to the real Hugh Clontarf which Creed had dropped. Seizing his advantage, Partrick extorted money from Parrish Creed, and paid for his folly with his life. In the meantime I had been led to suspect that Creed was an impostor, and that Hugh Clontarf was at Laurel Grange, with his memory gone. And I was right. I saw Dr. Gavin Todd, and he was so badly frightened that he owned up, told me of the arrangement he had made with Creed and Leighton, and readily agreed to obey my instructions."

Continuing Blake spoke briefly of other things—of his reasons for suspecting that Hugh Clontarf was at Laurel Grange.

"I cannot recall a more amazing plot," he resumed. "The motive, of course, was to keep Hugh Clontarf out of the way until the memoirs were finished and turned in, when Creed and Leighton would have disappeared with Sir Ralph Athelstan's money, and with an advance payment of a thousand pounds from the publishers of the book. Fortunately, however, the scoundrels have been completely baffled. I dare say Parrish Creed and Charles Leighton will be hanged. I don't see how they can possibly escape the last penalty of the law. As for Lord Roderick Teviot's memoirs, they will include the chapter dealing with the turf scandal of eighteen years ago, and Sir Ralph Athelstan, for whom I have some slight sympathy, will suffer a heavy punishment. He will lose a fortune, and will be socially ostracised as well."

Blake paused for a moment.

"I am glad for your sake, Gwenda," he said, "that no harm has been done. Hugh Clontarf is none the worse for what he has gone through. Now that the book is off his hands, he is looking forward to his marriage. And it will not be long, I dare say, until you are the mistress of Ranmore Lodge."

THE END.

First Published in the Sexton Blake Library in 1929

DOWN AND OUT!

CHAPTER 1.
The Night Alarm!

ALL through the evening and far into the night, a great gale had been sweeping through Yorkshire. The wind had howled over mountain and moor and dale, while the rain had lashed and splashed and drenched every inch of the county of broad acres.

Dentwhistle Moor in the West Riding had caught the full fury of the tempest. The village of Dentwhistle itself had partly escaped by reason of the sheltering shoulder of the mountainous Caukle Fell, but half a mile away, one little stone cottage had rocked and rocked in the rushing mighty wind, almost like a boat in a raging sea.

This cottage stood on the high moor, exposed to every wind that blew, at the head of the great mountain-limestone quarries, which formed the district's staple industry, and kept most of the able-bodied villagers employed.

In this lonely cottage—there was no other human habitation nearer than the village, save one—lived old Luke Samways and his wife. Samways had been a quarryman himself for most of his working life, but some years before our story opens, a fall of limestone rock had made a hash of his right leg, and left him permanently lame. From that time, therefore, he had filled the responsible, but somewhat less strenuous, office of timekeeper and night-watchman, a position which carried with it the tenancy of the little stone cottage referred to.

Although called night watchman, his duties rarely necessitated his being up later than ten o'clock, and at that hour, after a final "look round," he had retired as usual on this night of storm.

Accustomed to the moors in all their varying moods from the time he was a child, old Luke scarcely heeded the raging gale, but like the healthy man with an easy conscience that he was, fell to sleep almost as soon as his grey and grizzled head touched the pillow.

With his wife it was otherwise. A town dweller in earlier life, she had never become quite inured to wild moorland weather, spite of her thirty-odd years of happily married life with her husband. Ordinary storms she could stand—and sufficiently forget—but the terrific tempest of to-night had been something that she could not ignore. It had kept her awake till past midnight with its fierce howling. Then, as at last there came a lull, she too fell asleep.

But for barely five minutes! Then something made her start awake instantly, and sit bolt upright in bed!

The violence and suddenness of her movement awoke her husband, too.

"Why, lass, what is't?" he asked. "Why 'ow thou'rt tremblin'? Shakin' like a leaf? What ails tha, Bessie, dear?"

She did not answer a second. Only gasped and trembled.

Luke hopped out of bed and switched on the electric lantern standing on the floor near by—the lantern he used on his quarry rounds. Its bright rays fell on his wife's face.

"Why lass, thou'rt as white as paaper! Thou'st been skeered. Whaat's skeered thee?"

"A gunshot, Luke! I heard a gunshot!"

"Nay, nay, tha couldn't a done! Thou must a dreamt it, or belike 'twere the wind! Hark to it now. It's clappin' and yappin' like muskets now. 'Twas the wind tha 'eard!"

"No, Luke, no!" She was out of bed now with a wrap around her. "'Twas a gunshot I heard for sure! And hark to that—merciful Heaven! Hark to that! 'Tis another gunshot!"

There had come a sudden lull in the wind again, and in the lull had come the unmistakable report of a firearm.

"By gum, lass, thou'rt right!" cried the man. "That was a gun—or a revolver more like!"

"As 'twas before!" gasped the woman all trembling and pale. "And hark to that! 'Tis somebody shoutin'! Somebody screamin' for help! Heaven save us! 'Tis as if murder were bein' done!"

"Nay, nay, 'tis nowt as bad as that, Bess," answered Luke as he hurried his clothes on. "'Tis nobbut more than poachers! Bide tha 'ere while I go and have a look round. I'll be back soon, so don't tha tak on, my lass!"

He spoke as comfortingly as he could for his wife's sake. Since the time of the great war, her nervous system had been peculiarly affected by the sound of firearms, owing to the shock of an air raid during a temporary stay in London. But although he spoke thus consolingly, he inwardly had little belief in the words he had used. Poachers? What was there to poach in that district? Or was it the least bit likely poachers would be out on so wild a night as this?

Mercifully the rain had stopped some time before, but the wind, though intermittent, was still blowing great guns at times. It made his electric lantern swing violently as he hobbled towards the great quarry near by, and to cast big, weird, distorted shadows upon what once had been green turf, but was now a wide, white stretch all covered with the dust of limestone, and heaped up with chips and quarried boulders.

It took him but a few seconds to reach the hut at the top of the quarry which served as timekeeper's office. The door was looked as he had left it, and a flash of his lantern through the window showed it to be empty.

Nothing wrong there, nor anywhere about the quarry entrances so far as he could see. No sign of recent footprints in the whitened wet spaces, no sounds from anywhere.

From whence had those shots come, then? Certainly not from the village. That was too far off, and was to leeward of him, so that even if the shots had been fired there, they would never have been heard.

"Help! Help! Help!"

The cries came suddenly to interrupt his speculations. Frantic cries, borne on the wind, which had lulled as to sound bit was still blowing with some power.

They pulled him up suddenly, making him swing round and face the other way. At the same moment, footsteps came hurrying from the direction of the cottage he had just left. It was his wife, more scared-looking than ever, but brave all the same.

"Luke—Luke—the green bungalow!" she gasped. "'Tis from there the shoutin's come!"

"T' green bungalow—Mr. Dolby's plac(? But thou'rt right, lass, thou'rt right. Theer be the shouts agen! But get tha back to the cottage, Bess. 'Tis no fit night for thee to be out. I'll see what's amiss!"

Lame though he was, he hobbled past his wife at a great pace, leaving her to return indoors while he himself went on towards the place mentioned, namely, the "Green Bungalow."

This was barely two hundred yards away, but was hidden from view by a shoulder of the big hill. It was a building of concrete and wood, and was the only other human habitation nearer than the village.

It had been built a few months before by the gentleman who lived there—Mr. Nicholas Dolby. Lived there, that is, at night time and week-ends only. For Mr. Nicholas Dolby was junior partner in the firm of Messrs. Sharron and Dolby, Solicitors, and spent his working days in their offices at Lummingstall, the manufacturing town ten miles away where he practised.

Hating town life and loving the quiet of the country, he had built a comfortable bungalow among the hills, motoring to and from Lummingstall every day. Being a bachelor and unable to get servants to stay in such a lonely spot, he lived quite alone, being cooked for and attended to by old Mrs. Samways who lived close by. Luke also lent an occasional hand in cleaning the car and doing a turn at the little garden, so that he knew the place and Mr. Dolby quite well.

Rounding the shoulder of the hill, and approaching quite close to the green bungalow, an astonishing, not to say alarming, sight met his eyes.

Outside the wooden garage, which was a short distance from the bungalow, stood a tall, spare man. He was attired in a dressing-gown and slippers. His head was bare, his hair unkempt, his face deadly pale, his eyes distraught!

He was standing quite close to the garage door, facing it, while in his right hand was a heavy walking stick. This he was clutching by the wrong end, with the heavy knob raised in air, ready as it seemed to bring it down on the head of somebody evidently shut up in the shed, and who apparently, he feared, might try to break out at any moment.

The moon had come out from behind dense clouds a moment before, revealing the strange scene in all its details. A single glance, therefore, enabled Luke Samways to recognise the figure at once.

"Mr. Dolby!" he panted. "What be all the din? I heerd shots and shoutin's. What's bin happenin'?"

At sound of his voice the solicitor turned a white scared face quickly round.

"You, Samways? Thank Heaven you've come! There's a burglar inside!"

"A burglar, sir?"

"A most desperate ruffian! I caught him breaking into the bungalow! He shot at me but missed, and I managed to stun him with my stick!"

"Heaven save us, sir! T' missus was right, then. 'Twas murder that might a bin done. And t'ruffian's in theer now?''

''Yes. But may come to the break out at any moment. Hurry to the village for the police. My telephone's out of order. Hurry to the village for help at once!''

CHAPTER 2.
Murder is Discovered!

LUKE SAMWAYS hobbled off at a pace astonishing in a cripple. His brain was all in a jumble. Nothing like this had ever come his way before. Burglary—attempted murder. These terrible things were quite alien to the placid though busy life he had led for years in that remote Yorkshire village.

Truly remote was Dentwhistle, a little world of its own, so to say, tucked away amid the rocky hills, far from the busy haunts of men.

Yet not so far away as to distance after all. On a clear night or day great manufacturing towns could be discerned all around it, or rather, the distant haze and smoke of them. Less than twenty miles eastward lay Bradford, with Leeds beyond, while over the Lancashire border lay Burnley to the north-east, and Rochdale to the south-west at almost equal distances. But while those towns teemed with life and noise and bustle, much of the great triangular tract in which Dentwhistle lay remote and quiet as if they had been a hundred miles from any such hive of industry.

Even to-night, with the atmosphere cleared by the dying tempest, the lights of some of these far-distant places could be made out. But Luke Samways had no eyes for them. No thoughts either for aught save the important errand he was on—to get help.

Burglary—attempted murder! These were things right outside his ordinary ken. Now that they had come, it was little wonder that the terror of them should engross all his mind.

Fancy such things coming to such a quiet, retiring, peace-loving man as Mr. Dolby. Such a placid, mild, almost meek gentleman as he was. And none too robust, either. Not the sort you'd willingly pit against a desperate ruffian. Yet he'd tackled this midnight thief, and in spite of being shot at, had boldly faced him, and had managed to stun him with his stick.

''A good plucked 'un, spite o' lookin' so skeered arter it all!'' was the watchman's inward comment as he hastened along. ''Nobbut a good plucked 'un 'ud atackled a chap wi' a revolver like that. Ha, yon's the village, and yon's the pleece-station. Oim 'opin' Constable Stack'll be at 'ome!''

Constable Stack was at home, just preparing to start out on his night beat. He was startled and excited enough at Samway's news, for serious crime had rarely come his way. But he faced the job eagerly enough, and just waiting to enlist a couple of quarrymen as helpers, at once set off with Luke Samways on the return journey.

★ ★ ★

Mr. Dolby was relieved enough to see them come. He was still on guard with his knobby stick outside the garage. Still very pale, too, but resolute and full of pluck all the same.

He wheeled round at their footsteps and advanced a pace or two as he caught sight of the policeman's helmet in the moonlight. Constable Stack saluted him respectfully. He not only knew him as a resident of Dentwhistle, but as one of the leading solicitors of the neighbouring town of Lummingstall.

''Startlin' news Samways has told me, sir. Hope you ain't come to any harm?''

''Nothing to speak of, thank you, constable,'' replied Mr. Dolby, with a somewhat sickly attempt at a smile. ''But it wasn't the scoundrel's fault that he didn't kill me stone dead. He fired at me point-blank, but by a stroke of luck I managed to knock his revolver-hand up and the bullet went harmlessly in the air!''

''Where is the weapon, sir? He hasn't got it still, I hope?''

''Oh, no! I managed to stun him with my stick before he could fire a second time, and the revolver fell from his hand. I haven't had a chance to look for it yet, but no doubt we shall find it somewhere about. In those bushes perhaps.''

''We must search later, sir. What about the villain himself? Come to yet?''

''I think not. I've heard nothing of him. After knocking him out with my stick I carried him inside and locked him in. I fancy I've heard him groan once or twice, but can't be sure.''

Long time for him to remain insensible, sir. We'd better have a look at him.''

''Here's the key, constable,'' the solicitor said, taking it from his pocket.

''Sticky, sir. There's blood on it!''

Mr. Dolby shuddered.

''Is there? I didn't notice. I was too excited. Must have come from that scoundrel when I cracked him on the head."

Constable Stack turned to Samways and the others as he fitted the big key into the door.

"Be ready in case he's waiting his chance to make a dash. Spread yourself across the doorway!"

But there was no need for anything of that sort. As the constable threw the door open and flashed his bull's-eye inside the figure of a man was to be seen all huddled up on the ground.

Stack was kneeling beside him in a moment, his hand to the man's heart.

"He's not dead! I haven't killed him, surely?" asked the solicitorpaintingfor breath and with face twitching distressfully.

"Oh, no, sir! His heart's beating, but he's unconscious still. My word, sir, but you fetched him some knock, not but what I'd have done the same thing myself under the circumstances. Look at this bump. Makes his head about twice the size it ought to be. We'd best get a doctor to him. Will one of you chaps go back to the village and fetch Doctor Alford?"

"Ay, I'll go!" replied one of the quarrymen, and hurried away.

"Strong petrol smell about this place," said the constable with a sniff. "Best carry this chap into the bungalow if you don't mind, sir. He'll come to quicker there!"

Two helpers lifted the unconscious man and carried him across to the bungalow, placing him on an old couch in the kitchen.

"Can't do much till the doctor comes, so if you don't mind, sir, perhaps you'll please give me an account of what happened!" and Constable Stack took out his notebook.

"Certainly, constable, not that there's a great deal to tell," answered Mr. Dolby, and in the manner of a trained lawyer told his story briefly and to the point.

He had retired to bed somewhere between ten and eleven, and had been asleep for an hour or more, when he found himself suddenly sitting up wide awake. What had happened to him he didn't know. For a moment he had thought it must have been the noise of the gale, but a second after he had heard other sounds that made him leap out of bed and rush to his window, which, like the rest, was, of course, on the ground floor.

Looking out, he was amazed, not to say startled, at seeing a man gliding away from another window towards the garage, whose lock he started to pick, evidently with the intention of stealing the car inside.

Hastily donning his dressing-gown and seizing a heavy stick, Dolby had rushed out and challened the fellow. At once the burglar had turned on him menacingly with a revolver. There had been a brief struggle, during which the weapon had gone off in the air. Then having managed to stun the ruffian with his stick, the young solicitor had locked him inside the garage and shouted for help, which had come a few minutes later in the shape of Luke Samways.

"You saw him coming away from one of the bungalow windows, sir? Which window was it?" asked the constable, looking up from his notes.

"The window belonging to the best bedroom," answered the lawyer; and then his face suddenly contorted and he gasped out: "Good heavens! I'd forgotten!"

"Forgotten what, sir?"

Mr. Dolby didn't answer for a second. He stood where he was with a sudden great agitation upon him. With a catch of his breath he blurted out:

"I'd forgotten amid all the excitement that somebody was sleeping in that room. I'm usually alone, but to-night my partner, Mr. Sharron, is staying with me. He's sleeping in that room!"

"The very room the thief was coming away from. And you haven't been to see if old Mr. Sharron's all right. We'd best see now!" cried Stack.

"Yes, at once. Come this way."

They were out of the kitchen and along the passage in a moment. Mr. Dolby led the way right to the other end, hurrying and visibly anxious.

"Here's the room!" he said, controlling himself. "Mr. Sharron's old, as you know, and he's been ill for a long time, so we mustn't excite him too much. I'll just see if he's all right, so wait here a moment."

He opened the door softly and tiptoed into the room so as not to alarm the sleeper. But two seconds later, as he advanced towards the bed, there broke from him such an agonised cry as immediately brought the constable and the others hurrying into the room.

"What is it, sir?"

"Look—look!" almost screamed Nicholas Dolby. "Poor old Mr. Sharron! Look at him! He's—dead!"

CHAPTER 3.
The Grief of Nicholas Dolby.

ALL stared at the figure on the tumbled bed, aghast. All saw in a flash that Mr. Dolby's word were true, and the sight appalled them!

First to recover himself, the constable stepped right up to the bed to take a closer view of the already set features of the old man who lay there.

"Dead—dead for sure!" he murmured with a slow shake of his head. "How did he die! Can't see any—— Merciful heaven! Look here!"

His charged speech came as he turned the bedclothes farther back. They were all wet with blood as was the old gentleman's blue-striped sleeping suit.

"He's been shot!" exclaimed the constable. "Here's the bullet wound, see!"

"Shot!" echoed Dolby emotionally. "Then that scoundrel of a burglar shot him, just as he afterwards tried to shoot me! Must have been the shot that woke me. Constable, it's murder—wilful murder"

"Looks like it, sir. But the bullet seems to be in the groin. Queer for a wound like that to have killed him so soon, don't you think, sir?"

"Ordinarily, perhaps, yes. But not in his case. His heart was so weak! He's been ill for a long time. The shock would be enough to cause death! Oh, my poor, dear old friend and benefactor!"

And kneeling down beside the death-bed, Nicholas Dolby covered his face with his hands and broke down in uncontrolable grief.

The constable and the others looked pityingly on at the younger solicitor's sorrow, for all knew something of the true relationship which had existed between them—a relationship to be explained presently, and indicated in the younger man's use of the words "friend and benefactor."

But there came a quick interruption to this poignant scene. Steps were heard in the passage, and a moment later Dr. Alford entered the room.

★ ★ ★

His trained eye told him at a glance the truth about the body on the bed. It shocked him greatly. First, because he had been fetched to attend merely to an unconscious man, not to a dead man at all. Second, because Mr. Sharron was a man he had known in years past.

Shock, however, did not prevent him from doing his duty. In a moment he was beside the dead man, examining the bullet wound in his thigh, and searching for other possible injuries.

He, like the constable, was a little surprised that the old lawyer should have died so soon from a leg wound, but on hearing Mr. Dolby's account of the heart disease of long standing, agreed that he might have died from shock.

"Or he may have been choked to death!" he added. "There are marks on the throat, but the bruise hasn't properly come out yet. But about his heart—he was medically attended for that, of course?"

"Oh, yes, first by Dr. Pettry, of Lummingstall, but that was two years ago. It was on Dr. Pettry's advice that he practically retired from business, and went to live at Southport."

"Ah, yes. I must see Dr. Pettry. There'll have to be a post mortem, of course. But I expect he's been medically attended at Southport too?"

"Oh, yes. I forget the name of his doctor there, but that can be easily ascertained from his nurse. Mr. Sharron has, as perhaps you know, been a widower for many years, and had no near relatives."

"Quite—quite! There'll be quite a lot of things to do later, but just now I must see this other man—this burglar. It was on his account you sent for me, I believe. Where is he?"

"In the kitchen, sir!" It was Constable Stack who answered. Mr. Dolby seemed incapable of doing so. He was looking at his old friend and benefactor again, and the sight of him lying there dead, seemed altogether too much for him.

"What's happened? Where am I?"

It was the burglar who gasped out those words. He had been brought to after a few minutes, under the ministrations of Dr. Alford.

During thse few minutes as he lay unconscious on the couch, they had been able to take careful stock of him. He was quite a young man, not more than thirty-two. He was moderately tall and quite well built, but thin and ill-nourished, while his face just now was, of course, very pale as a result of the blow on his head which had rendered him unconscious. His clothes were shabby and threadbare, and soaked through with the rain, as if he had been long out in the wild storm. His boots were very down at heel, with holes in the soles. They had let in the water.

Already Constable Stack had removed those boots, had examined them closely with certain significant nods of the head and had then carefully placed them on one side. In addition, he had made many notes in his pocket-book, as to the man's condition and other things.

Now as the man at last spoke, he turned to him, still with his notebook in his hand.

"Why as to that," he said drily in reply to the fellow's gasped questions, "seems to me you ought to be able to tell us about that. What's your name?"

"Wilson—John Wilson!"

Constable Stack wrote the name quickly in his book, then whispered to the doctor: "What about charging him sir? It's a case of murder—I shall have to charge him with that!"

"Not at once!" the medical man said hastily. "He's very weak at present. Give him a few minutes anyway to recover. Perhaps he'll tell us something about himself first. You can charge him when he's a bit stronger."

The policeman nodded, and turned again to the man who was now half sitting up on the couch rubbing his injured head.

"Now, John Wilson, how come you to be trespassing on private property at this hour of night?"

"I'm sorry, but I came to get shelter," answered the man nervously. "I've been on tramp. I've come from London. Been on tramp for three weeks. I was making for Burnley. But I got caught by the storm out on the moors yonder. I was wet and tired and hungry. Pretty well fit to drop, I was. That's why, when I spotted this house, I made for it, hoping to find some sort of shelter where I might get a bit of sleep."

"You've tramped from London and were making for Burnley," echoed the constable, who had rapidly pencilled the words down. "Why were you going there in particular?"

"Because I'd hopes of getting a job!"

"Why there more than anywhere else?"

"Because I know a gentleman there. Or did know him a few years ago. In the war, that was. I served under him in Flanders—at Ypres, and other places."

"Who was he?"

"Lieutenant Straker! Leastways, he was then. Now I suppose he's plain Mr. Straker. Mr. Adrian Straker. Manager of some big ironworks at Burnley, he is. I see that by chance in a paper. That's what put it in my mind to go and see him in the hopes of a job. Heaven knows I want one bad enough, with a wife and poor little kiddy nigh on starvin'."

"So you're married then? Where do your wife and child live?"

"London. Islington. They lives in a garret at No. 34, Tubb Street."

More rapid note taking by the constable, then further whisperings with the doctor, till he turned again to the suspect with—

"Well, John Wilson, I've heard your explanation, and—well it don't quite fit in with what's happened!"

"How do you mean?"

"You must consider yourself in custody!"

"In custody——" the man panted. "What, just for innocent trespassin'!"

"No—I charge you, John Wilson, with murder!"

"Murder! Great and merciful——"

"Stop! Let me finish! The charge is the wilful murder of Mr. Richard Sharron, by shooting him with a revolver!"

"Great heaven! It's false—it's——"

Again the constable pulled him up.

"Let me finish! My duty is to warn you that you needn't say anything, and that anything you may say will be used in evidence against you!"

"I don't care!" Wilson's face was contorted, and his voice rose to a shriek. "I must speak! This charge—it's horrible—it's monstrous—it's——"

He said no more. Overtaxed by emotion and strain, his strength gave way, and he fell back on the couch and his senses fled from his a second time!

"Gone off again—fainted!" pronounced the doctor, bending over him.

"Ah, couldn't stand the pressure, sir, eh? He didn't expect to be charged so soon with what he's done. Almost like being caught red-handed!"

"I suppose there can be no doubt he did it, constable!"

"How can there be, sir? That yarn of his about coming to the place for shelter is about the lamest I've ever heard."

"Certainly sounded very thin!"

"He'll swing, sir; he'll swing, you can bet. I've absolute proof already that he went into the dead man's bed-room!"

"Proof!"

"Ay, sir, here!" The constable took up The accoused man's boots and turned them over to display the sodden, broken soles. "He left plain prints of these behind him!"

"Heavens! Did he though?"

"Yes, one on the window-sill and another actually on the stained boards close to the bedside! 'Twas one of the first things I noticed, and there's absolutely no mistakin' this broken left sole!"

The doctor took another look at the unconscious man.

"He'll be coming to in a minute," he said. "You'll be taking him off then, I suppose?"

"Not till the inspector comes, sir. I've already sent a chap to telephone to Lummingstall for him. Till he arrives I must wait here to look after the dead body as well as the prisoner!"

"Quite! That reminds me. Mr. Dolby's in the other room still. He's terrily cut up at this tragedy, poor fellow."

"Not surprising, sir. They do say as old Mr. Sharron had always been more than a kind friend to him. Reg'lar made him, accordin' to all accounts."

"So I've heard. Well, I must see him and try to get him away from these morbid surroundings."

"You mean he'd better not stay on here at the bungalow, sir."

"Quite! I must persuade him to come and stay with me till after the inquest, at any rate."

★ ★ ★

"Mr. Dolby, my dear fellow, I know how very distressing this must be to you, but you mustn't let it get you down. I get you not to brood on it, or you'll get ill yourself. You mustn't brood on it, you really mustn't?"

It was Dr. Alford speaking to the young solicitor. The scene was the doctor's house in Dentwhistle village, whether he had persuaded Nicholas Dolby to return with him overnight. The time was the next morning, and the two men were seated at breakfast together. They had risen quite early in spite of the fact that they had retired late.

The solicitor certainly seemed in need of the advice given him. His distress was most obvious. His face seemed positively torn with anguish, while his eyes were the eyes of a man who had hardly slept at all, but whose mind had been kept on the rack by fierce grief.

"Thanks, doctor," he answered, in a none too firm voice, "I'll do my best to smother my feelings, but it's a job. This is a blow—the most terrible blow of my life. I can't tell you what Mr. Sharron has been to me. The kindest friend man ever had. Whatever little success I have achieved in life has been solely due to him."

"Oh,come, your own efforts and ability and——"

"Yes, I know all that. Butit wasMr. Sharron who gave me the chance to show them. Without him I might have been in the workhouse. He befriended me when I was a poor orphan. He had me educated, he articled me at his office without a ha'penny of fee. He pushed me on and on, and two years ago, when he could no longer attend to business himself, he made me his partner so that I might have a free hand with everything. Yes, he was the kindest friend a man ever had, and now—now to think he should have come to such an end! And last night of all nights! If anything could make it more bitter it was that!"

He was on the verge of breaking down—at a point, in fact, when the doctor thought it better to humour his mood, sad though it was.

"What exactly do you mean, Mr. Dolby? Such an occurrence would be terrible at any time. Why should last night be worse than——"

"Because he was my guest—the only time he has ever been my guest!"

"Really!"

"Yes. As you know, I'm a bachelor, a lonely man. Till Mr. Sharron retired from business more than two years ago, and made me his partner, I never had a home to which I could invite him. I was always in lodgings up to then. But when, through his kindness, my means allowed, I built the green bungalow out on the moors yonder, and bought a car to carry me to and fro. I grew to love my lonely little home, and I always looked forward to the time when I could invite Mr. Sharron to it. For a long time I feared his health would never allow of such a thing. But yesterday, when he came to the office, I found he was well enough. So I asked him, out, and—and——"

"How did it come about?" the doctor inquired gently, to keep the young lawyer from breaking down.

"Mr. Sharron came to the office quite unexpectedly yesterday afternoon. A friend had motored him over from Southport, sixty miles away. I was delighted to see him, especially as he was so much better. He was indeed greatly better after his long rest, and actually announced his intention of getting into touch with the business again. To that end we went through a lot of old deeds and documents together. But the work tired him after a few hours. I saw that a long motor journey back to Southport would be too much for him, so I invited him to pass the night at my bungalow out here."

"Which he accepted?"

"Eagerly—almost joyfully, I might say. And when we got out—Idrove him in my little car—he was as enthusiastic about my little home as I was myself."

At that moment there came a knock at the door, and a maidservant entered.

"It's a police officer, sir; wants to see you. Inspector Yarrow from Lummingstall!"

Dr. Alford bent forward and touched his guest on the arm.

"The police, my dear friend! They've probably news." He turned to the maid: "Show the inspector in, please!"

Inspector Yarrow entered. He was a big man with a heavy moustache and clear, shrewd eyes.

"'Morning, inspector! Any fresh developments?"

"Oh, so, so, sir!" Yarrow's eyes twinkled trimphantly. "Not very much perhaps, but enough. Enough to tell us we've got the right man. John Wilson killed Mr. Sharron without a shadow of a doubt!"

"You seem very certain. What's happened?"

"Why, in addition to footprints in the dead man's bed-room, which we've proved were made by Wilson's broken boots, we found Mr. Sharron's wallet in his pocket!"

"In Wilson's pocket, do you mean?"

"Yes. It contained fifteen pounds in Treasury notes, besides one or two documents. John Wilson's the man without any doubt at all. He'll swing for it!"

CHAPTER 4.
A True Friend's Plea!

NEWS travels fast nowadays, faster than it ever did. Within an hour or two of the events related in the previous chapter, all London was echoing with the "Green Bungalow Tragedy."

Evening paper posters made those three ominous words familiar everywhere, while special editions told London's millions all there was to know about it.

Practically all, that is. There was no mystery out it. The murderer had been caught, not quite red-handed it is true, but nearly so, thanks to the prompt action and courage of the dead lawyer's partner, Mr. Nicholas Dolby. All the newspapers were full of that—the courage of the junior partner, and his deep grief at the loss of his old friend and benefactor.

The one consolatory feature of the whole grim and ghastly business was that the murderer had been arrested. For that John Wilson, out-of-work ex-service man and tramp-burglar, had done Richard Sharron to death, nobody had any sort of doubtIt was a plain case. A tragic drama, but with no mystery about it. Old Richard Sharron, a highly respected Yorkshire solicitor, had been murdered. John Wilson had been arrested for that murder. Later he would be tried, condemned to death, and hanged! That was all there was to it. Having read the grim story, most people were ready to dismiss it from their minds, so complete did it seem.

So thought even Sexton Blake, the famous detective; so certainly thought Tinker, his assistant, as he, like his master, went through the afternoon papers at their Baker Street chambers.

It was part of his job to cut from the newspapers the stories of current crimes as they came to be reported, and to index them up for possible future reference. In this way Sexton Blake's shelves had accumulated thousands of cases, of which only a small percentage were ever afterwards referred to. It was to this "limbo" that Tinker, in his mind, already relegated the "Green Bungalow Tragedy," even as he read it.

"Hardly worth indexing up, is it, guv.?" he remarked, after some exchange of views on the detailed accounts both had just read. "Never likely to want it, are we?"

"Perhaps not," agreed Blake, who was so full of Tinker's mind that he had already turned his attention to other matters in the newspaper he was reading. "We're not in the least likely ever to want it. Still, just keep it as a record. Now about that passport forgery business. Look up all the papers connected with it, and——"

But Tinker wasn't to do anything of the sort. Before Sexton Blake could even finish his sentence there came the sound of a taxicab suddenly pulling up at their door in Baker Street, followed by a long and peremptory ringing of their bell.

"Somebody in a hurry, guv."

"Yes, an impatient and excited client, I should say."

"Some duchess lost her favourite Pekinese, and wants you to find it, or——"

Tinker was interrupted this time by steps on the stairs. Following a "Come in!" to her tap, Mrs. Bardell, the housekeeper entered.

"Gentleman to see you, sir. Seems very hagitated, and begs you to see him at once!"

Blake took a proffered card from the tray, and gave a jump!

"How queer!"

"What is? Who it is, guv.?"

"Mr. Adrian Straker, Manager, Paragon Iron Foundry, Burnley," read out Blake.

Tinker snatched at the evening paper.

"Why, that's the man referred to in the Green Bungalow case, surely?"

"Quite! That's the odd thing about it. He's the gentleman mentioned by John Wilson, the accused man." Blake thought hard for the fraction of a second, then said quietly to Mrs. Bardell: "Show the gentleman up at once!"

Half a minute later and Adrian Straker was in the room. A young man—about thirty-five. Tall, well-built, good-looking, brainy and energetic and terribly excited. So excited that, as was plain, he had all his work cut out to hold himself in.

"How do you do, Mr. Straker?" Blake, who liked the look of him, gave him his hand. "What can I do for you?"

"Let me thank you, sir, for seeing me. I've come about—about that!" His quick eyes had fallen on the afternoon papers spread out on the table with the big headings uppermost: "Green Bungalow Tragedy!" "Have you read it, sir?"

"Why yes, only a few minutes ago. You are the Mr. Straker mentioned there? Why have you called on me?"

"To ask you to take up the case—to beg you to take up thecaseon Jack—that is, on John Wilson's behalf. To get you to clear him of this horrible charge!"

"Eh, what—a big order, isn't it?"

"It may seem so, sir, but I'm sure you could——"

"But the case is black against him. Everything points to—— Why are you interesting yourself on his behalf?"

"Because I believe he's innocent!"

Blake stared at his visitor, wondering if in his intense excitement he had taken leave of his senses.

"On what grounds do you base your belief, Mr. Straker?"

"Because he says he's innocent!"

"Bit flimsy that, isn't it? I've read the details, and though it's early days, the police case seems complete—absolutely complete already. Everything points to Wilson's guilt!"

"I don't care! I'd believe Jack Wilson's word against everything!"

Again came Blake's doubt as to his visitor's sanity, and again he decided in his favour.

"What do you know of him?"

"Nothing but good. I knew him all through the War. I was a lieutenant, he was a private. Part of the time he was my batman, and once"—Straker voice quavered with emotion as memory stirred within him—"once at Ypres he saved my life at the greatest risk to his own. Jack's the bravest chap who ever lived. As to doing this—this terrible murder, why, he couldn't—he couldn't!"

Such passion had come into Adrian Straker's voice as touched Blake. In a world which, generally speaking, is so forgetful and ungrateful, the detective revered gratitude as one of the greatest virtues. And he saw that the foundry manager's whole being was steeped in gratitude. Nevertheless, he felt he must not let this sway him too much. He must keep a level head.

"Aren't you letting your war memories run away with you, Mr. Straker," he said in gentlest reproof. "You mustn't, you know. I can quite understand your feelings towards a man who saved your life, but when that man has committed a ghastly crime——"

"He hasn't—he hasn't!" protested Straker hotly. "I tell you he couldn't do such a thing. Without his word, I should have known that, but I've seen him—this morning. I was allowed to have a few minutes' interview with him, and he told me—he swore to me that he was innocent!"

"But in face of all the circumstances? Why, the fact that the papers deal with the matter so fully—they tell us practically the whole of the police case—shows how little doubt there is about his guilt!"

"Oh, I know it looks black-terribly black! But Jack denies it all! He denies that he entered the bungalow at all, let alone the bed-room where the dead man was found!"

But his footprints were found actually in the room. More significant still, the dead man's wallet was found in his pocket. How does he explain these things?"

"He—he can't explain them!" cried Straker, pacing the room all pale and agitated. "They baffle him completely. There is some mystery about it all. That's what I want you to elucidate, sir. That's why I've come to you. I promised poor Jack long ago that I'd stand his friend if ever he needed one. And now he does need one. I want to keep my word. Take up the case in his interest, I beg you to!"

"I can't—I'm deeply sorry, but I can't. I've other things to do, and to do this would be—a waste of time!"

"Oh, no, no; don't say that, sir! I'm not a rich man, but I'm comfortably off. I've got a first-class job. I can find a few hundreds for Jack's sake. A thousand or two for that matter. If money will help to clear him——"

"It's won't, I fear! It's good of you to offer to stand by him like this, Mr. Straker. I admire you for it. But it would be wasting your money. The case is hopeless. It's so strong against him that nothing I nor anybody else could do could break it down. Once again, I am sorry, but I cannot take up the case!"

"You will not save an innocent man's life?" cried Straker despairingly.

"You mustn't put it that way—you really mustn't. If I could believe he was innocent——"

"He is—he is!"

"In face of the evidence already published, I cannot believe it. To my mind it is black—dead black against him! How then could I hope to save him?"

Something like despair was in Adrian Straker's eyes as he suddenly jerked up his head, and said in hollow tones:

"Then save me!"

"Save you—what do you mean?"

"Just that! Save me, Mr. Blake! Save me from a life of misery and self-reproachings! Oh, don't you understand how I feel? I believe Jack innocent, against all the world. Yet because the police and all the world believe him guilty, he may go to a shameful death! Don't you see if I do nothing and such a terrible thing as that should come about, that I could never forgive myself? I, who owe my life to him, who swore to be his friend! How could I ever forgive myself if I should fail in that? How could I ever sleep? How could I ever have one moment's peace day or night. That-that is what I meansir, by saving me! Take up the case! Do your best, even though you should fail. I do not think you would fail. But even if you did, I should at least have the consolation of——"

Sexton Blake gripped his hand and pressed it fervently.

"I admire your firm friendship for Wilson," he said. "If just to satisfy you I will make inquiries. I'll make a start at once!"

CHAPTER 5.
Sexton Blake Goes North.

SEXTON BLAKE caught the four o'clock express from King's Cross. It was due at Bradford at 8.26 that night. At Bradford he intended to hire a car and drive out to Lummingstall, lying among the mountains some twenty miles or so away. It was a nuisance having to change, but it seemed the best way, and he had chosen it from several alternative routes.

In the reserved first-class compartment with him were Tinker and Pedro, his famous bloodhound. Adrian Straker was not with them. He intended to return to Burnley by a later train, and had arranged to meet Blake the next day. Full of profound gratitude to Blake for consenting to take up the case, and eager to help all he could himself, he would willingly have accompanied him, but for a task—a duty, rather, as he regarded it—which would detain him in London a few hours longer.

That duty was to go up to Islington, seek out the wife and child of his old friend and soldier-servant, Jack Wilson, and render the monetary help of which they stood in such dire need.

So it came to pass that Blake travelled without him. He wasn't a bit eager or happy. In fact, he was very reluctant and miserable. He had consented to take up the case purely out of pity for Adrian Straker.

As to the case itself, Blake had no hope of doing any good with it; not a shadow of hope of saving John Wilson. Even from the evidence published—and the police might well have something else up their sleeve—his doom was as good as sealed. Beyond all reasonable doubt Wilson had committed the murder. He would be tried. He would be found guilty and condemned to death. That seemed sure. Nothing could save him.

No wonder Sexton Blake was glum on the journey. He felt he was engaged on a fool's errand, and nobody likes to feel that. So, apart from some desultory conversation as they sat at dinner in the restaurant car, he spoke but little on the more than four-hours' journey. Tinker, who fully shared the hopelessness regarding their mission, quite understood the reason for his silence, and therefore made but few attempts to rouse him out of it.

Arrived at last at Bradford, Blake sought outside the station for a taxi to take him out to Lummingstall, but found a difficulty. Several drivers were engaged for jobs later in the evening which would prevent their going so far; others hadn't enough petrol for so long a journey; still others were disinclined for a night jaunt among the mountains with so much rough weather about.

"I know where you can get a good car, sir!"

It was a station "cab-runner," who had been following them about, waiting to pick up a tip.

"Where?"

"Garridge just round t'corner, sir."

"Right-ho! Lead on!"

Rinker's Garage, to which the man led them, wasn't a very classy place, but it served. They got an old, big, closed saloon car which promised to suit their purpose, and a driver who knew the way. In a very few minutes they were off.

Through Buttershaw and as far as Halifax the road was quite "towny," but from there a secondary road quickly led them to Bodgery Moor. Here all was wildness and loneliness. Hills—almost mountains—led to great high stretches of bleak moor, interspersed here and there with woods, over which the wind tore, if not with the fury of last night's gale, at any rate, with sufficient power to imbue the journey with the spirit of adventure.

An adventurous journey it was to be! Rocking in the wind, the somewhat ancient car was making quite good speed along a section of road heavily shadowed by woods on either side, when it came suddenly to a stop by the abrupt jamming on of the brakes!

"Hallo! What's up?" cried Blake, leaning over the saloon partition towards the driver's seat."

Round came the driver's face with a scared look on it. But the direct answer to Blake's question came from somewhere else, and somebody else.

"Hands up!"

The startling words came from a masked man standing in the road just ahead of the car and beside the bonnet. In his hand was a revolver, which was covering the driver.

Near him were three other men, also masked, and also with raised revolvers covering Blake and Tinker in the rear part of the car.

"Duck, and hold Pedro down!" whispered Blake hoarsely, and then did an astounding thing.

Vaulting instantly over the low partition, he bundled the unnerved driver ouf of the seat, jumped into it himself, seized the steering-wheel, and in a second had the car in motion again.

Plop—plop—plop! came three bullets aimed wildly, as the astonished highwaymen scattered to save themselves from the plunging car. There came a jangling of glass.

Plop—plop—plop—plop—plop! came again as the car cleared them and shot forward. For a quarter of a mile the old bus in Blake's hands did marvels in the way of speed. Then he, too, pulled up, and swung his head round.

"All right, laddie?"

"Yes, thanks, guv'nor. Some of the bullets plugged into the car, but we weren't hit."

"You're all right, driver?" asked Blake.

"Yes, sir," answered the shivering man beside him, and lifted a scared white face. "But what a close shave, sir! Whatever would have happened if you hadn't hopped into my seat. I couldn't have driven on to save my life."

"Driving on was the only way to save it,' said Blake dryly. "Those ruffians meant mischief."

He alighted and stared back along the road.

"No sign of them!" said Tinker, joining him and looking back.

"No, they've scooted before now. Hiding in the woods, no doubt. We must give information to the police at the next village."

He turned to the still trembling driver as once again he took the driving-wheel.

"Any hold-up like this taken place about here before?"

"Not here, sir, so far as I know. But there have bin one or two cases the last few weeks. One out by Beedleham, and another by Snaggar Snout, in the north Ridin'. Supposed to be done by the same gang, them two jobs was. They robbed the motorin' party and trussed 'em, all up. This may have bin the same crew."

"Shouldn't be surprised. Anyway, we're well out of it"; and, without further talk, Blake got going again.

The only other halt was at the next village, where Blake pulled up at the wayside police-station to lay information. Then he drove on to Lummingstall.

Driving straight to the police-station there, he dismissed the car, the driver of which, however, announced his intention of delaying his return till the following morning. He seemed thoroughly shaken and in no mood to risk a recurrence of another hold-up.

CHAPTER 6.
"No hope! John Wilson's for it!"

SEXTON BLAKE struck lucky. Inspector Yarrow was in. He was immensely pleased and flattered to meet the famous criminologist. But even his joy at that was eclipsed by his amazement on hearing why he had come.

He was almost incredulous that a man of Blake's outstanding perspicacity should have started on such a "wildgoose chase."

"Clear John Wilson!" he exclaimed, raising his bushy eyebrows as he repeated Blake's own words. "Why, you can't have realised the strength of the evidence against him!"

"I do realise that it's pretty strong," said Blake rather lamely. "But I was hoping there might be a chance."

"There isn't an earthly, Mr. Blake! Neither your nor anybody else can save John Wilson. That chap's for it, if ever a criminal was!"

Blake smothered a sigh. The local officer's opinion was practically his own. His loathness to admit it and chuck up the sponge at the outset was only born of pity for Adrian Straker, and the fact that he had given his solemn word that he would tackle the case without prejudice, and do his very best on the prisoner's behalf. For this reason he found himself forced into a false position, and compelled to endure Inspector Yarrow's banter and very real—though good-natured—scorn.

"Astonishing to find you believing in his innocence, Mr. Blake!" he exclaimed.

"In accordance with our country's laws, I am entitled to assume it tillhis guilt is proved, inspector."

"Oh, quite so, quite so! Yarrow's shrewd eyes were twinkling with triumph. "I don't know how much you know of the case, but if you knew what the magistrates will be told to-morrow morning, you'd agree that his guilt was proved already!"

"That so? Well, I won't ask you what the magistrates will be told in the morning, inspector, because I shall be in court to hear it. But you won't mind giving me the leading points, eh?"

"Not at all, not at all! I'll give you two facts, anyway. You may or may not have seen them already. Mentioned in the papers, I mean. Fact one: The prisoner's bootprints were found in the bed-room of the murdered man. Fact two: The wallet containing money, which belonged to the murdered man, was found in the prisoner's pocket when we searched him!"

"Yes, I did read as much in the newspapers," assented Blake dismally, feeling more and more the falsity and stupidity of his position.

"Yet you've undertaken to try and clear him! To my mind, those two facts alone are enough to hang the fellow."

Blake was inwardly inclined to agree. More and more he regretted his promise to Adrian Straker, and right willingly would he have taken it back if his sense of honour had allowed.

As it wouldn't, he must put as bold a face as possible on it and go through with the business.

"Quite sure they are his bootprints, I suppose?" he asked, in the manner of a drowning man clutching at a straw.

"Oh, lor, yes!" Yarrow proceeded. "No good challenging that, my dear sir. I'll save you time on that score right away. The bootprints were left on a strip of Indian matting that lay beside the bed. I've had them photographed. Here are the prints, developed exact size. And here are the boots which made them. Test them for yourself."

He had stepped to a corner, where there was a big bag containing the "exhibits" for the police court next monring. From it he took the objects named, the big photographic prints, and the pair of dilapidated boots, and placed them before Blake.

The latter took up the prints first. Was that a startled look which immediately sprang in his eyes as he looked at them? If it was, he said not a single word as to what it was that startled him. But he looked long at the prints before setting them down.

Then he took up the boots, and turned them soles upwards. They had originally been stout, but had now worn to a pitiful thinness. The heels were right down, while the soles were actually in holes. Strips of brown paper had been placed inside them by the wearer, in a hopeless attempt to make them wearable. Quite a hopeless attempt. The heavy rain of the previous night had soaked the paper to a pulp.

Blake examined them with the utmost minuteness, then placed them down and looked across at Yarrow.

"Any doubt?" the inspector queried, with quizzing eyes.

"About what?"

"About the prints being made by those boots?"

"None at all. So much is certain."

Again Blake was looking at the photographic prints.

"No doubt about these being John Wilson's boots, I suppose?"

"Guess not!" said Yarrow drily. "They were taken straight off his feet by Constable Stack. Those prints seem to interest you a lot, Mr. Blake!"

"Interest—they positively fascinate me!"

"Good prints, eh? As good as I've ever seen. Remarkable prints, to my mind."

"Quite! Made by remarkable feet!"

Sexton Blake spokes solemnly, yet in his manner as well as the words there was such a suspicion of quaint banter as made the inspector look up.

"Don't get you quite, Mr. Blake. In what way are the feet remarkable?"

"Don't know that I can quite tell you. Only they seem so to me."

It was an enigmatic answer. It conveyed no clear meaning to Inspector Yarrow. Only irritated him. He asked again, pressingly.

"How do you mean the feet are remarkable?"

"Oh, well, they seem very flat."

The mollified inspector burst out laughing.

"Do they? I didn't notice that. Very likely they are. Lots o' men are flat-footed."

"Quite!" Blake paused half-absentmindedly. They he asked suddenly: "Where is Wilson?"

"Here, at the station. In the cells at the back."

"Can I see him?"

"Not till the morning, I'm afraid. He's asleep now. Rare job the doctor had to get him off."

"Gave him a draught, you mean?"

"Had to. Doctor Filsome was afraid if he didn't sleep he'd go crazy."

"Bad as that?"

"Storming nearly all day. Raving that he was innocent, and asking us to tell his wife he was innocent. That's why the doctor gave him a draught, but even that didn't look like acting at first."

"How was that?"

Inspector Yarrow rasped his chin.

"Well, the doctor can't be sure about it, but he's got a strong suspicion that Wilson's a drug-taker!"

"Gee, that's the first I've heard of that! A penniless tramp! How could he get drugs?"

"What's the matter with burgling a chemist's shop?" said Yarrow, with a shrug of his heavy shoulders. "Anyway, Dr. Filsome said he showed symptoms of a man who doped. Don't know how he knew, but that's what he said. Seemingly that's what stopped the sleeping-draught from acting at first."

"But it has acted since. Well, that means I can't see him till to-morrow. That being so, I'll quit."

"Where are you staying, Mr. Blake?"

"At the Unicorn. I'll cut along now. My assistant, Tinker, went on ahead to see about the luggage, and he'll be waiting for me."

CHAPTER 7.
A Planned Affair!

TINKER was waiting for him, most impatiently. Not at the Unicorn Inn (which was only a stone's throw away) but in the street.

Blake met him half-way and instantly saw by his face that he was excited.

"What's up, laddie?"

"Don't quite know, guv, but suspicious things have been happening. That fellow who drove us in the car——"

"What about him?"

"He's a wrong 'un."

"What makes you think so?"

"The pals I saw him meet. Three of 'em. The very three, if I'm not mistaken, who held us up!"

"Heavens, boy, what do you mean? Tell me exactly what's happened."

Tinker did. When Blake had settled with the driver, it was on the understanding that he should drive Tinker and Pedro along to the Unicorn Inn and help with the luggage. But the moment the detective had departed, the fellow's manner had changed. Instead of being respectful to the point of servility, he had become suddenly brusque and defiant. He had certainly driven across to the Unicorn Inn, but that was all. Instead of helping to get the baggage inside, he had dumped it down on the pavement and then driven off, with no more than a morose explanation that he was in a hurry.

"Hurry for what?" interposed Blake. "He wasn't going back to Bradford to-night. He said he was going to stay at Lummingstall till the morning."

"Just so, but I don't thing he meant it. Got something up his sleeve all the time, I fancy. Anyway, his sudden change of manner made me suspicious. So, leaving the porter to look after Pedro and the luggage, I rushed after him."

"Were you able to follow him?"

"Yes. By a bit o' luck he didn't drive far. Pulled up in a back street not far away. Outside a pub called the Blue Boar. He didn't get down, but just yonked away with his horn. It was a signal, as I saw. In a minute a fellow came out, waved to him, then went back into the pub. A minute after he came out again. Two others were with him, and all three got into the car, which at once drove off."

"And you think they were the three who held us up?"

"Well, I couldn't be sure, of course! Couldn't get a look at their faces on the road on account of the masks."

"But you did here in the street?"

"Just a glimpse. Villainous faces they were. Hard-bitten, with steely eyes. Reg'lar racecourse-tough type. I couldn't follow the car, or I would have. Wasn't another car about, for one thing, and for another I couldn't leave Pedro for long."

"Quite! Don't know where the car was going, I suppose?"

"Don't know at all. Nothing was said above a whisper, and they were off in a second or two. But it all struck me as a very funny business."

"No doubt of that. All the queerer if those three men were the actual three who held us up. That would point to a deliberate plot, of course."

Blake thought hard for ten seconds, then said:

"Laddie, we must get back to Bradford to-night!"

"Think they'll have gone back?"

"Don't know, but they may have. Anyway, we've got to see. If it was a plot to hold us up, it looks as if—— It's just an off-chance, but it's too important to miss. We'll get back to Bradford to-night. Don't suppose we can overtake them, but if they go back to that garage—— Come along, laddie, I must get Inspector Yarrow to help in this."

Inspector Yarrow jumped to the job at once. Blake had previously mentioned the "hold-up," so that he already knew the bare facts. Without knowing in the least what was really in Sexton Blake's mind, he could at any rate see that the driver might have been in league with a highwaymen gang, and have conspired with them to work the hold-up for purposes of robbery. It never occurred to him (as it most certainly did to Blake) that this affair might have any bearing on the murder of Richard Sharron. Nor did it occur to him that it was a personal attack on Sexton Blake. To him, it seemed hardly likely the attackers would know the identity of the detective at all. They would simply regard him as a man who was worth robbing, and make their plans accordingly.

Even so, the affair was sufficiently serious on its own account, and therefore he was quite ready and eager to render the aid now asked.

He gave orders for a big car to be obtained and half a dozen officers to get ready to accompany him and Blake.

While this was being done, he rang up the Bradford police and asked them to set a watch on Rinker's Garage, pending their arrival from Lummingstall.

That being arranged, and the car and police officers ready, the whole party, every man armed with a revolver, set off in a few minutes on their adventurous night ride.

Although they did the twenty miles to Bradford in very fast time, they failed to overtake the fugitives.

Nor could they get any news on arriving at Bradford. The two plain-clothes men set by the Bradford police to watch Rinker's Garage reported "nothing doing." The car for which they had been instructed to look out, had not returned.

It then had to be considered whether inquiries should be made inside the garage as to the character of the missing driver. This was decided against by Blake on his hearing from the local police that the place was already under suspicion.

Rinker—as the proprietor called himself—had only been established in the place a few months. In that brief time he had earned for himself a somewhat shady reputation. There had as yet been no definite charge against him, but he was strongly suspected of having had dealings in stolen cars. The police, therefore, had had him under observation for some time, on and off.

In view of this, Sexton Blake now decided to wait a bit—till next day, at all events. Meantime, the local police would keep a close all-night watch on the place. If the absent driver returned by the next morning, they would detain him for inquiries as to his overnight doings. If he didn't return, they would similarly inform Blake, who would then be guided by events in his future action.

Blake himself, together with the rest of the party from Lummingstall, waited at Bradford an hour or more on the chance of Reuben Gunn (that being the absent driver's name) turning up. But he didn't turn up, and Blake and the others returned to Lummingstall, leaving the Bradford police to the task of watching.

★ ★ ★

"Think Reuben Gunn will go back in the morning?"

It was Tinker asking the question of Blake that night, when at last they found themselves alone at the Unicorn Inn.

"It's a toss-up, laddie. The fact that he does or does not return, ought to throw light on things, though."

"How?"

"Well, if he doesn't go back, it'll look as if the three men he met were actually the three who held us up."

"That's so. I think they were the same, but of course I can't be sure. But I say, guv! Supposing, for the sake of argument, they were the same, what do you think it all means?"

"It would prove that the hold-up was a planned affair!"

"Yes, of course; but what was the extent of the plan? What was their object in holding us up? Was it just robbery, do you think?"

"Can't make up my mind yet. It might have been just that. That chap loafing about the station yard may have been in co. with an ordinary hold-up gang on the look-out for anybody who seemed worth robbing."

"That would make it very chancy work, wouldn't it? What I mean is most ordinary travellers would have got a taxi in the station yard."

"Quite! That's an argument in favour of its not being an ordinary hold-up for robbery, but something more!"

"You mean——"

"Well, ordinary passengers would only want to go short distances. We failed to get an ordinary taxi because we wanted to go a much longer distance."

"And you think that loafer knew that?"

"He could easily get on to it. Didn't you notice how he followed us round. Directly he saw his chance, he came forward with his offer and took us round to Rinker's. That suggests he'd been specially told off to look out for us."

"Guv'nor, you are making a plot of it! How'd a gang here get to know you were coming to Bradford at all?"

"By their other pals shadowing us in London! They could have seen me booking at King's Cross!"

"But how——"

"The thing's simple. At this end, a gang could easily have known about Adrian Straker's departure for London, while their pals there could easily have shadowed him to Baker Street. The rest would be easy to fix up."

"But Adrian Straker came from Burnley?"

"Yes, but he'd been over to Lummingstall to see John Wilson.

"A special visit to a man under arrest, would be quite enough to attract attention from men on the look out for things of that sort."

"Gee whiz! But you're racing ahead, guv'nor! You're linking up to-night's affair with the very murder itself! You're talking of a gang and plots, as if they might have killed Richard Sharron!"

"Why no?"

"Do you think a gang did?"

"It's too early to make up one's mind. One can't decide till one get's more evidence!"

"But you're beginning to think John Wilson may be innocent?"

"I am!"

"Yet you were dead against any such idea when you started?"

"I was."

"What's made you alter your opinion—this hold-up?"

"That's only secondary. It may or may not corroborate my primary idea."

"What is your primary idea?"

"One I got when Inspector Yarrow showed me those photographs of the bootprints!"

"But they're his trump cars! The very things he most relies on to prove Wilson guilt!"

"And yet the very things which, after all, may prove his innocence!"

CHAPTER 8.
Committed for Trial!

AFTER breakfast the next morning, Sexton Blake and Tinker were on their way to the police station to see the prisoner.

All was in readiness for them. Inspector Yarrow was not there, but he had left the necessary instructions. The visitors were conducted to the prisoner's cell at once. The policeman who conducted them at once went away, leaving them alone with the suspected man.

John Wilson was amazed to see Sexton Blake, whose great name and fame was known to him, as it was to all the world. For a moment he was inclined to resent the visit, believing, as was not unnatural, that the great detective was acting in conjunction with the police.

But on Blake's informing him that he had come at the request of Adrian Straker, his eyes lit up and the heavy expression of his grief-stricken face lightened for a moment.

"God bless him!" he murmured brokenly. "Mr. Straker promised to stand my friend years ago, out in Flanders, and he's doin' it now. I knew he would—I knew he would! He's nigh the only friend I've got in this world; the only one who believes me innocent o' this terrible crime!"

Sexton Blake watched him narrowly. Wilson didn't strike him as being of the criminal type at all—certainly not the type that would commit a brutal murder for the sake of a few pounds. Moreover, he was terribly thin and emaciated. Looked as if he were half-starved, and that he and a good square meal were not regular acquaintances these days. Evidence this—negative evidence, of course, but still of some value—that he was not an habitual criminal, for your habitual criminal doesn't allow himself to go hungry.

For so young a man—he was only thirty-two—he looked strangely old. But this was due to his hollow cheeks, his slightly greying hair, and his wild, lustreless eyes. In their turn all of these things might have been caused by anxiety and suffering arising out of his poverty, and especially out of the terrible position in which he now found himself.

Or they might, of course, have been caused by something else!

Drug-taking, for example! Was he a doper? According to Inspector Yarrow, the police-surgeon had suggested it, but was it probable?

Blake thought it highly improbable, and his experience in such matters was certainly equal to the average provincial police-surgeon's.

Still, something had suggested to Dr. Filsome that the man had been under the influence of drugs. He must have had some good reason for thinking that, and, therefore, it was a matter to bear in mind.

Other things, however, must be gone into first.

"Well, well, Wilson," said Blake soothingly, in response to the prisoner's speech. "It's something to have one good friend who believes in you. Let that help you to keep up your heart. Who knows but what others may come to believe in your innocence, too. I have promised Mr. Straker to do all I can to arrive at the truth, so if arriving at the truth will help you——"

"It will, sir, it will!" cried the young man passionately. "It's all I ask for. If only the truth can be discovered! Heaven grant it may, if only for the sake o' my dear missis and little kiddie!"

"As to that, Wilson, you may be able to help as much as anybody!"

"How can I help, sir?" Wilson cried hopelessly. "I've already told the police all I know about it, but they don't believe me. Nobody believes me except Mr. Straker. Everybody else thinks I killed this old gentleman. And I didn't. I swear I didn't! I swear I didn't even know he was in the house—or who was in the house."

Blake listened and watched him intently. If this man was lying, he was one of the most accomplished actors in the world, was his thought.

He encouraged him gently with:

"Please tell me what you've already told the police. I want to get at the truth first hand. Tell me everything you know. Every little detail, just as it happened!"

Wilson began. Up to a point, his story—told with many a suppressed sob and break in his voice—was a repetition of what Sexton Blake already knew from the newspaper accounts, and from the added details told him by Adrian Straker and Inspector Yarrow.

In brief, that part of his recital amounted to what has already been set forth in this story.

Ever since the war he had, like too many others, been unable to secure a permanent job. He had had several that promised for a time to be permanent, but for various reasons—bad trade and other things—they had failed him after a time. He had been various things at various times. A warehouse clerk, a porter, an insurance agent, a canvasser on commission, a clerk again and a porter again.

But all the jobs—most of which had been most precarious even while he held them—had failed him in the end. At times he had drawn the dole, but there came a time when even this failed, owing to some technical default beyond his own control.

Several weeks of semi-starvation had followed. During that time he had tramped all over London in a vain search for work. Only the most strenuous efforts by his young and delicate wife had kept the wolf from the door. Quick and clever at needlework, she had managed to earn just enough per week to pay their rent and buy them dry bread.

In that way they had lived—say, rather existed—until John Wilson could stand it no longer. The work denied him in London—Heaven knew he was eager and willing to take anything—he would seek in the provinces. Anyway, if he could no longer support his wife and child, he would no longer be a burden on her meagre earnings.

Like many another down-and-out, he had gone on tramp in search of work. Striking northward, he had reached the busy Midlands, hoping to find a job there. Failing, he had been in doubt as to his next move, when the chance sight of an old newspaper gave him an idea.

The newspaper contained the prospectus of a new iron-foundry company, and contained the name of Adrian Straker as manager. This filled him with a new hope. Because in this Mr. Adrian Straker, he recognised one whom he had known in the Army. Moreover, on account of some signal service he had rendered him, Adrian Straker had promised always to be his friend, and had told him to be sure to apply to him if ever he were in need of a friend.

Of a naturally independent spirit, Jack Wilson had never so far troubled him. Now, in his great need, he decided to apply to him for work.

During his tramping he had communicated with his wife as often as he could afford the stamp to do so, and at this juncture he wrote to tell her of his intention to make for Burnley, in which Lancashire town the iron foundry was situated.

After days of weary tramping, during which he had sufferd many privations, he had reached that part of Yorkshire, beyond Lummingstall, in which our story opened.

Near to the village of Dentwhistle he had been overtaken by the great storm. Drenched through and hungry, and well-nigh exhausted by the violent gale, he had looked about for some sort of place where he might get shelter from the storm and rest for his weary limbs.

It was then that he found himself a little beyond the great quarry and within a little distance of the green bungalow. The sight of the shed—the garage—a little way off, suggested that here was the very place, where he might sleep for a few hours. With that idea he made straight for the place.

Then happened—according to Wilson's statement—a most dramatic thing! He had scarcely reached the garage and started to try to open the locked door, when a sudden rush of footsteps behind him made him jerk round his head!

But before he could properly turn, a ımanı had thrown himself right at him! The man was carrying a stout bludgeon. This he swung aloft, and, before Wilson could do anything to defend himself, he brought it across the side of his head with such terrific force as to knock him clean out!

"And that," concluded John Wilson chokingly, "is all I know about it. That's all I remember until I found myself brought to in the kitchen of the bungalow, with the policeman and the doctor and other people bending over me!"

"Then you know nothing of the murder of Richard Sharron?" asked Sexton Blake.

"Nothing—nothing, I swear it, sir!"

"You never went into his bed-room?"

"I never went into any room! I never entered the bungalow at all!"

"Yet, as you know, your boot-prints were found on the window-ledge, and actually beside the dead man's bed?"

"The police told me so yesterday, but it's all a lie—a cruel, horrible lie! I never entered the room at all!"

"How then do you account for the bootprints being there!"

"I don't account for 'em, sir—I can't! How can I? I swear I never entered the room—never even went near the window. I swear it—I swear it! Merciful Heaven, sir! Don't you believe me?"

Sexton Blake didn't answer for a moment. He remained silent—in deepest thought. The passionate vehemence of the man's denial impressed him. So, indeed, had the whole of his story, so different in its later part from that recounted by the police.

"Don't you believe me, sir?" demanded the distracted prisoner again.

And then Blake suddenly came out of his silence and spoke.

"Wilson, I want to look at your feet! Your bare feet. Will you let me?"

"I don't see what—— But, of course, sir, of course!"

John Wilson removed the old socks and slippers which had been provided him by the police.

"Raise you feet!"

The man obeyed, and Blake examined them closely, noting their exact shape.

"Tinker, that bag!"

Tinker passed a small handbag they had brought with them. From it Blake took two pieces of cardboard, carefully prepared with some chemical substance, which he placed on the floor of the cell.

"Stand up, Wilson! Right! Now place your feet on these cards—one on each. Press hard as you can—with all your weight!"

The prisoner obeyed, his eyes full of wonder as to the meaning of these things.

"Step off!"

The man stepped off. Blake took up the cards and examined them with a face like a mask. He placed them carefully in the bag, and took something else out—a pair of worn boots. Not so old or broken as Wilson's own had been, but sufficiently worn for his purpose.

"Put these boots on!"

While Wilson dumbly obeyed, Blake took out two more pieces of cardboard, prepared similarly to the others.

"Now stand on these! Press hard again, with all your weight. That's right! Yes, that's enough! You can take the boots off again!"

While Wilson was doing this, Blake was intently examining the second pair of cards. These he also placed in his bag. His face wa still like a mask.

But suddenly it relaxed a little as Wilson handed him the boots back.

"Wilson, you told me just now that you had never entered that room?"

"And I tell you so again, sir. I'd say the same thing with my dying breath! I never did. Don't you believe me?"

Sexton Blake's hand shot out. His already relaxed face wreathed into a smile—a smile of real kindness.

"My lad, I do believe you! There's my hand on it!"

"You do, sir—and do——" sobbed the poor fellow. "How can I thank you for saying——"

"Don't thank me, but keep up your heart, lad! Don't despair. I believe what you say—that you never entered that room!"

"But the police believe that I did!"

"The police are mistaken. They'll have proof—from me—that you didn't go into that room!"

"How can you prove it, sir—how can you?"

"It may take time to prove it, but I'll do it. Till I do, you must have patience. You must remain under suspicion and a prisoner. You must place yourself in my hands. Be guided by me entirely! Will you agree to that?"

"Gladly and gratefully, sir!"

"Very well, then. Not a word to anybody as to what I've said or done now. Keep absolutely mum about that. In fact, say nothing till I give you the word!"

"I'll be guided by you in everything, sir. I don't see the meaning of what you've done, sir. Those footprints, I mean. May I ask what they——"

"Don't ask anything yet, my friend. I'll tell you in good time. Till then trust me. You're to be brought before the magistrates this morning?"

"Yes, sir."

"The proceedings will be merely formal. Not much more than evidence of arrest, I expect. The police will then apply for an adjournment and will get it. Seven or more days adjournament. That will be all to the good. It will give time to intruct a solicitor, and to get you properly defended at the next hearing. Now before I go, just one or two more questions."

"As many as you like, sir."

"The prosecution says you killed Richard Sharron by shooting him. It says too that you fired a revolver at Mr. Dolby just as he knocked you down with a stick. That, of course, isn't true?"

"Of course not, sir. How could it be?"

"You hadn't a revolver in your hand?"

"I had not, sir. I've never possessed such a thing. If I had, it would have gone long enough ago."

"What do you mean by that?"

"Why I mean I should have sold it—as I have had to sell many others things—to buy food for my wife and child," Wilson answered bitterly.

"Ah, I see what you mean. Now about the shots. You didn't fire them, yet it's certain they were fired! Two of them. We have that on the evidence of Samways, the night-watchman, and his wife. The question is, who fired them?"

"That's beyond me, sir."

"Oh, quite so, but did you hear them—either of them?"

"No, sir. I heard no shot at all."

"Yet you couldn't have been far off the bungalow when they were fired—the second one at all events."

"I heard nothing of the sort, sir. Perhaps that's not so astonishing after all, considering how the wind was roaring."

"Perhaps not," said Blake thoughtfully. "From which direction did you approach the garage? From the quarry side?"

"No, sir. I came the other way."

"Then the wind was at your back?"

"Yes."

"And would blow the sound away from you. That would account for your not hearing the shots, even if they fired while you were near. That's all now," Blake said, looking at his watch. "I shall see you at the court later on. I may or may not speak to you then. Meantime, I repeat, not a word to anybody about all this. So long for the present."

With another handshake, Sexton Blake quitted the cell, leaving the prisoner far more hopeful than he had been before, but not a little mystified as to the meaning of what he had done and what he meant to do!

CHAPTER 9.
Blake's Deductions.

SOMEBODY else was mystified too—Tinker! He refrained from questions until they were alone in their own room at the Unicorn Inn, but then he opened out.

"What's all this, guv? You started on this job thinking Wilson hadn't an earthly. Now suddenly you tell him you'll clear him! What's done it?"

"His footprints!"

"What about them? That's the most puzzling part. All that trouble you went to getting those cards ready with the chemical stuff. What does it all mean?"

Blake was opening the bag. He took out the cards and laid them on the table.

"Look at 'em!" he said laconically.

"Well, what about 'em guv? Don't see anything every extraordinary about 'em!"

"Quite so. Now look at these! These are a duplicate set of photographs of the bootprints found in the murdered man's bed-room. I got them from Inspector Yarrow. Compare them with the impressions made in our presence!"

"How can I compare 'em? One set are made with boots on; the other barefoot."

"Oh, well, compare them with these others. The ones made with the old pair of boots Wilson put on."

He spread those cards out too, and Tinker spent a minute in comparing one set with the other.

"Don't see how you can compare these very well either," he said. "How can you? The pairs of boots were quite different. Different soles and heels and——"

"Never mind about that, laddie. It doesn't affect the matter really. My point is independent of actual detail."

"Then I don't see your point."

"Do you see something else? Waiving the difference in the boots, do you see anything similar about the rival prints."

"Why, yes, the length is exactly the same, and the curious outer curve of the foot is the same. But that only tells against Wilson."

"Standing alone it would tell against him—strongly," agreed Blake. "But it doesn't stand alone. There's the inner side of the foot to consider. Do the one set resemble the other in respect to that?"

"It's impossible to say, I was just going to mention that. In the inspector's set the inner side shows as clearly as the other. In your set, in spite of all the trouble you took, it hardly shows at all!"

Blake's eyes suddenly sparkled.

"Now you've hit it, laddie. Hit it at last! Surely you see that the inspector's prints—these impressions which are as perfect on the inner side as on the outer, could only have been made by a man with abnormally flat feet!"

"The puzzling phrase you used last night!"

"Nobody unless they had very flat feet could have a print as perfect as that simply by standing on a mat. You couldn't, laddie. I couldn't! John Wilson certainly couldn't either! He has a high instep, and consequently a very pronounced arch to his foot. With such a foot, the impression left might be quite distinct on the outside, but the inner side would hardly show at all. Wilson couldn't do it, though at my bidding, he tried with all his weight!"

"Why?"

"Because the natural poise of the body allows of very little pressure coming to the inner side. To make such a perfect impression as these, would require a man not merely to be flat-footed, but knock-kneed as well. John Wilson is neither. He is quite straight-limbed and has a perfectly arched instep."

Tinker's eyebrows were lifted high in amazement.

"This is too much, guv'nor! You yourself admitted last night that undoubtedly those prints on the bed-room rug were made by Wilson's boots!"

"By his boots—yes. But not when he was wearing them!" was Blake's amazing answer. "Those bootprints were, so to speak, faked!"

"How?"

"By somebody who held the boots in his hands—not on his feet at all!"

"Guv'nor!"

"I mean it. The prints are far too distinct and perfect to have been made by a man just standing up—far too equal as to the inner and outer sides!"

"But why should anybody do a thing like that?"

"To throw suspicion on the owner of the boots, of course!"

"Yes, I know, but who would want to do it?"

"Who else but the real murderer?"

"Some other than Wilson!" gasped the astounded Tinker. "Who could it be?"

"Too early to say yet," said Blake. Then, after a brief pause: "There was another curious thing about those bootprints, too!"

"What was that?"

"The clear impression on the rug was partly due to there being some oily stuff on the broken soles. Petrol, I fancy."

"Quite likely, isn't it? There may have been petrol on the floor of the garage?"

"Perhaps. But John Wilson hadn't been in the garage before the murder! We know that on the evidence of the chief witness against him."

"Mr. Dolby?"

"Exactly! He has stated that the door was locked and that Wilson was trying to open it. That's the only point on which Mr. Dolby and Wilson seem to agree in their conflicting statements. How came the petrol on Wilson's boots before the murder, then?"

"He must have picked it up on the road somewhere."

"That's possible, though not probable. But even if he did, it wouldn't have remained on them in a clear patch. Remember, he had walked through the storm. The heavy rain would have washed his boots, while his walk through the wet grass would have wiped away nearly all vestiges of the petrol. These footprints on the bed-room rug are far too distinct and clear to have been made in the ordinary way. The petrol must have been on them like a thin coat of paint. The whole thing points to most careful preparation."

"Then how do you account for it?"

"I'm not trying to—yet. There isn't time now, for one thing." Blake was looking at his watch. "Getting towards half-past ten. Time we got round to the police-court!"

CHAPTER 10.
John Wilson Astounds Blake!

THE little police-court at Lummingstall was crammed full. Everybody in the place had known old Mr. Sharron, and had held him in highest respect. Their curiosity to hear details of the cruel crime, and see the man accused of it, was therefore natural.

Among those who had managed to obtain a place in the court was Adrian Straker. He had returned to Burnley by a late train overnight, and had motored over to Lummingstall just in time for the proceedings.

Sexton Blake had only time to shake him by the hand and to whisper a cheering word or two, before the usher called "Silence!" made him pass to his own seat, just as the magistrates entered the court.

Directly they were seated, John Wilson appeared through a side door. He was attended by two policemen, and was at once placed in the dock, quite close to which Sexton Blake had placed himself.

Just before the proceedings began, Blake leant close to him to whisper:

"Don't forget what I told you! Not a word about what happened at our interview. Mum's the word! Keep your mouth shut and eyes open! For the rest, trust to me. I'll watch your interests!"

John Wilson murmured his thanks, then faced the bench as he heard his name called out. In a moment the clerk of the court was reading the charge, and the hearing began.

As Blake had foretold, the proceedings were to be purely formal. As yet no lawyers were in it, and it was Inspector Yarrow who made the opening statement.

All the same, he went a little farther than Sexton Blake had expected he would. For after briefly outlining the charge, he announced his intention to calling two witnesses. First, Constable Stack, who would give evidence of arrest; secondly, Mr. Nicholas Dolby, the murdered man's partner, who would give some account of certain things which had preceded the arrest.

This was duly done. Constable Stack related the facts as we already know them. Then Nicholas Dolby was called.

As he stepped into the box and was sworn, John Wilson, who had been provided with a chair on account of his wounded head, suddenly sprang to his feet and gave vent to an exclamation.

"Silence!" roared the usher.

But it was Sexton Blake who soothed the prisoner in his sudden strange excitement.

"Keep quiet!" he whispered. "Say nothing now! No good will come of it—only harm. Whatever you want to say, tell me later!"

Wilson subsided into his seat. But his lips were still quivering as he stared with all his eyes at the mane in the witness-box. As to that man, Nicholas Dolby, he looked a picture of absolute distress. His face was pale and drawn, his figure bent, while his eyes had in them the look of a man who had suffered much and slept but little.

And when, in quavering accents, he gave something of his life story and told of all the kindnesses he had received at the hands of old Mr. Sharron, there was hardly anyone in court but who realised how much he was suffering, and how deeply he was feeling the loss of his dear old friend, who had been put to death by the hand of a foul assassin.

Following this personal history, which partook of a tribute to the dead man's memory, he told, in low but clear tones, all he could tell of the murder. These things amounted to a repetition of what has already been related in an earlier chapter of our story.

As he left the witness-box and was making his way back to his seat, he came face to face with the prisoner in the dock. It was the signal for the latter once more to spring to his feet and give vent to some exclamation.

This action, which was accompanied by a movement towards the front of the dock and a violent throwing out of his arms, was interpreted as an attempt on his part to wreck vengeance on the man who had just testified against him.

Instantly, therefore, two or three policemen threw themselves upon him, while one snapped a pair of handcuffs promptly on his wrists.

Then, as Wilson sank back again exhausted by the struggle and wrapped in a sullen silence, Inspector Yarrow once more rose to his feet and addressed the Bench.

"That, your worships, is as far as I wish to carry the case to-day. On the evidence given, I respectfully ask for an adjournment of seven days."

"Very well," returned the chairman; "your application is granted. We adjourn the case for seven days. The prisoner will be remanded in custody. Remove the prisoner!"

And Wilson was hurried from the court.

All the way back to the cells he showed signs of the most intense excitement. More than once he half-turned round to Blake, who was following, as if he were bursting to tell him something.

Not till they had reached the cells, however, and were quite alone, did Blake address himself to him. When at last he did, it was to say:

"You seem terribly excited, my friend!"

"I am, sir. So would you be! There's been some terrible mistake, or else I've gone mad!"

"What do you mean?"

"That man Nicholas Dolby!"

"What about him?"

"He swore he was the man who knocked me senseless!"

"Well, so he did, surely?"

"No, no! He wasn't the man who did it at all! It was somebody quite different."

"Eh—what?" Blake had given a start of surprise. "This is something new! So two men attacked you? You never said so before!"

"No, no! There weren't two men—only one! But he was quite different from Nicholas Dolby."

Blake stared at him incredulously.

"Are you sure?"

"Positive! When Nicholas Dolby went into the box and swore it was he who had outed me, I was amazed! That's why I shouted out. That's what I tried to explain in court."

"I'm glad you didn't anyway! This is a most astounding thing you're saying!" Blake looked at him as if he half-thought he might be mad. "Are you quite certain about it?"

"I was never more certain about anything in my life."

"But it was dark, and the storm was raging at the time."

"No, sir, the rain had stopped then, and the moon had come out. I got a glimpse of the fellow's face just before he up with his bludgeon, and—well, it wasn't Nicholas Dolby!"

"Who was it, then?"

"I don't know. But it was an older man than Dolby—much older! A man of sixty, I should think!"

"So old? Surely you could have mastered——"

"I had no chance, sir. He was on me before I could properly turn round. And although he was that age, he was strong. Very broad, powerful-looking fellow! That's another difference between them. Dolby's taller and slimmer."

"You mention a bludgeon! Mr. Dolby says a walking-stick—the one the police produced. Which was it?"

"What I call a bludgeon, sir! A short, thick thing with a heavy knob. Certainly it wasn't the walking-stick I saw in court."

"This man—this elderly assailant. How was he dressed?"

"Long-grey ulster—or perhaps it was an old dressing-gown. Came right down to his heels, and he held it up as he ran. The collar was pulled up close round his throat, and cap was drawn low over his eyes!"

"This is strange, most strange. It needs the most careful thinking over. But I'm glad you didn't blurt this out in court—very glad. . . . Now what?"

"Hist!" whispered Wilson suddenly. "There's somebody at the spyhole—listening!"

Blake whipped round swiftly and darted silently towards the cell door. As he did so, something seemed to flit away from the spyhole fixed in it. In an instant Blake had the door open. The next, and he had fixed a powerful grip on the collar of a man who was just rising erect. The man was not a police official, but a rather rough-looking workman with a hang-dog expression and cunning eyes.

"Here, I say, what's the meaning of this?" demanded Blake, and shook him like a rat.

"Leggo, leggo! What yer a-doin' of? I'll have the law on yer for this! Leggo afore yer chokes me, will yer?"

"Who are you? What are you?" demanded Blake sternly, and transferring his hold from collar to arm.

"I'm Bill Perkins. I'm an honest workin' man, I am. I'm a plumber. I've bin seein' to the pipes in the bath-room."

"Then take my tip, Perkins, stick to your job. When you come here to plumb, plumb, don't pry! Stick to clearing out pipes; don't try stopping up spyholes!"

"Who was a-doin' of it?" asked the man sullenly.

"Didn't I catch you with your eye to that spyhole? Weren't you spying and listening to what was going on in that cell?"

"Me!" cried Perkins, bristling with indignation. "Me do a thing like that! Wot do yer take me for—a Prooshun?"

"But I caught you bending down!"

"To tie up me bootlace. 'Ow else could I tie up me bootlace wi'out bendin' down, I'd like to know?"

Blake didn't answer that question. He didn't believe the man, but felt convinced that he had been looking through the spyhole. Still, as that might just have been idle curiosity, he didn't attach much importance to the incident, and in any case he had scared the main quite enough.

"Well, I'll give you the benefit of the doubt, Perkins. So get back to your pipes!" he said.

"Finished 'em," answered the man, shouldering his tool-bag, which he had placed on the floor. "I'll pop off. An' mark me, mister, this is the larst time I'll ever come to a bloomin' pleece-station."

"An admirable resolution, Perkins," laughed Blake, as he watched him depart. "Hope you'll keep it."

★ ★ ★

"I think it's all right," remarked Blake to John Wilson as he went back to the cell. "I don't think the fellow was really listening."

"But I'm almost sure he had his eye to the spyhole, sir."

"Perhaps he had, but I think it was idle curiosity—nothing beyond that."

"But he may have heard what you'd been saying, sir?"

"I hope not—I think not," Blake said thoughtfully; "but I'll make sure that he had a right to be here, when I see Inspector Yarrow presently."

And this he did when, after a little more talk, he bade good-bye to John Wilson. He didn't see Yarrow, however, because the inspector was not at the station. But he saw the sergeant-in-charge, and was informed that although Perkins was personally unknown to him, a plumber had been at work most of the morning, on some defect in the pipes attached to the prisoners' bath-room at the rear of the police-station. Satisfied so far then, Blake dismissed the incident from his mind.

Before many hours were over, however, it was to recur to his mind with an unexpected significance!

CHAPTER 11.
Conflicting Clues.

MEANTIME he had other things to think about. The morning's happenings had given him much food for thought. The police-court proceedings, and what Jack Wilson had told him afterwards.

Especially the latter. That, indeed, was most startling. He didn't know quite what to make of it. Although hazy about many things, he had made up his mind about certain others. One was that Nicholas Dolby had been the man who had knocked Wilson out. The solicitor had, of course, openly said that, while Luke Samways' statement made a quite clear that it was Dolby who had stood guard over Wilson after locking him up in the garage.

Ha! According to Samways, Dolby had been wearing a long dressing-gown also. Such a loose, flowing garment altered a man's figure considerably. It might easily make a slim man look more bulky than he really was.

Had Wilson been mistaken? Seeing Dolby in ordinary attire in the police-court might well make him believe that he was some other and different man from the one who had attacked him. True that the arrested man spoke of other differences, but on such a wild night, and half-dazed by exhaustion as he was, he might easily be mistaken.

Blake felt, therefore, that he need not attach too much importance to this latest revelation. All the same, he must keep it in mind, for did not the idea of there being a third man about fit in with his new-born theory of Wilson's innocence?

Back at the Unicorn, he had just recounted the latest events to Tinker, when Inspector Yarrow looked in. His face looked excited and not a little worried.

"Glad to have caught you, Mr. Blake. I want your opinion about something. There's a hitch—a complication!"

"So—what's that?"

"I've come to the conclusion there was a second man in it! Wilson had an accomplice!"

"What makes you—what's happened?"

"This!" Yarrow took a fat wallet from his pocket, opened the canvas flap, and selected a photographic print.

"Hallo, fingerprints?" exclaimed Blake. "Whose?"

"The murderer's!"

"You speak dead sure!"

"They were on the dead man's throat! You knew there'd been some throttling going on?"

"Dr. Alford told me there were some throat bruises, and I saw them for myself when I examined the body."

"Well, I had 'em photographed. This is the result!"

"Know whose they are?"

"No, but I know whose they're *not*. That's where the complication comes in. They're not John Wilson's! I've compared 'em."

"That's one up for Wilson, then?"

"I don't say that. I'm dead sure he was in it. This only shows he had a partner."

"Yet you didn't find his bootprints in the room—only Wilson's!"

Yarrow shuffled irritably.

"Give me time, Mr. Blake. I told you it was a tangle. It'll need a bit of time to straighten it out."

"Quite! But why couldn't the chap have worked independently of Wilson? Why couldn't Wilson have been out of the murder altogether?"

Yarrow shook his head resolutely.

"No, I don't give you that. Wilson's bootprints were found there, and another's fingerprints. That spells a pair. Two of 'em were in it. I've got Wilson already. And I'll get the other."

"Wish you all the luck. You've struck it right, though, with that print. Got a second copy?"

"Like one?"

"Yes. I may be able to lend you a hand in bagging the chap who left his trademark on the dead man's throat. Many thanks!" And Blake pouched the photographic print the other handed him.

He was silent a minute, then he asked:

"What about that revolver? Found it yet?"

"No. Mr. Dolby thought it must have been thrown among the shrubs or grass, but my chaps couldn't find it. That puzzled me at first, but it doesn't now."

"Why?"

Yarrow tapped the photographic print.

"This second chap! He must have picked it up before he scooted off. Which reminds me that I must be scooting off, too. I've a lot to do."

"He's getting a hustle on, guv'nor," remarked Tinker when Yarrow had hurried away. "What do you really think about these fingerprints?"

"They confirm my belief that somebody else murdered Richard Sharron, laddie."

"Somebody working in co. with John Wilson, do you mean?"

"No, I don't believe that part of Yarrow's theory. I believe Wilson to be quite innocent. But these fingerprints are tremendously interesting and important."

"Guv'nor," said Tinker, with a sudden thought, "do you think it likely that the chap who choked poor old Mr. Sharron might also be the man who knocked Wilson out?''

"I should think it's very probable. Nothing more likely.''

"You would?'' Tinker stared incredulously. "Then you think Wilson wasn't mistaken, after all? But I say, guv'! If it was another chap who bashed him on the head, why on earth should Nicholas Dolby say that he did it?''

Blake gave him a curious glance.

"I didn't say I thought it was another man.''

"But it must have been if——'' Tinker broke off. He had caught a most strange expression in the detective's eyes. "Oh, I say, guv'nor, you don't think it was Dolby who——''

"Knocked Wilson out? I do. Hasn't he said so himself?''

"I don't mean that. I mean—I hardly know how to say it. But—but—I say, do you think it was Nicholas Dolby who murdered——''

Blake held up a warning finger.

"I'm going to get hold of Nicholas Dolby's finger-prints! I think I know a way. Pass me that small bag.''

Tinker obeyed. Blake took out a big sheet of blue paper—brief size, and handed Tinker a pen.

"Now, laddie. I want you to take something down at my dictation. The more like a lawyer's clerk that you can write, the better I shall like it!''

CHAPTER 12.
The Missing Wallet.

MR. NICHOLAS DOLBY sat in his private office at the corner of Market Square, Lummingstall.

His face was pale and drawn, and he looked terribly woebegone. Grief at the death of his old friend and benefactor seemed to have affected him deeply, while the ordeal at the police court that morning had clearly added to his distress.

He looked anything but fit for business, yet business must be attended to, and there was none among his several clerks to whom he could entrust it.

There were a lot of things to attend to, for the late years the business had greatly grown. The growth, be it said, was mainly due to Mr. Dolby himself. If old Richard Sharron had done a fine thing for Dolby by making him his junior partner, he had, at the same time, done a fine thing for himself, in that the skill and ability and hard work of Dolby had resulted in a great extension of their clientele. In all Yorkshire there wasn't a shrewder lawyer than Nicholas Dolby, and many were the ironmasters and mill-owners of Bradford and other great neighbouring towns who had discovered this, and, as a consequence, placed their legal business in the hands of this very capable attorney.

Spite of the great distress of mind which his pale face all too plainly reflected, he was forcing himself to concentrate on business. Many deeds and other legal documents were on his desk, and his brow was deeply knit as he scanned their contents.

A tap came suddenly at his door, and a clerk entered.

"Gentleman to see, you, sir. Wants to swear an affidavit.''

"Who is he, Docker?''

"Gives the name of Rowlands, sir. Farmer-looking man.''

"One minute then!''

Mr. Dolby started to clear his desk of all the deeds and documents, then changed his mind as he moved across the room to what had in former years been Mr. Sharron's seat.

"I'll see him at this desk. Show him in.''

The caller came in. He was an oldish man, with close-clipped side whishers on his hard-bitten face. He was dressed in an old-fashioned tailed coat, Bedford cord breeches, and leggings. In his hand he carried a soft tweed hat.

"Afternoon, sir,'' he greeted, in a somewhat raucous voice. "Sorry to trouble ye, but I got a paper form my lawyers in London this marnin', and a letter sayin' I was to swear a happydavid. So seein' by your plate as you was a commissioner for oaths——''

"Quite so—quite so,'' interposed Mr. Dolby affably. "Sit down, Mr.——''

"Rowlands, sir, be my name. Joe Rowlands, and hoss-dealin' be my business in life. Goes all over the country, I do.''

He dived a hand into a capacious breast-pocket, and pulled out a legal-looking paper.

"That be the dockyment, sir. Ye'll see that it consarns the sale of a couple o' hosses, and that the party I sold 'em to says as 'ow——''

"All right, Mr. Rowlands," interposed Mr. Dolby, with a faint smile on his pale face. "There's no need for me to know what the document is about. I merely witness your signature. You have read it, and you are ready to swear that the contents are true."

"That I be, sir."

"Very well, then, if you'll take this Testament in your right hand and kiss it. That's right. Now if you'll sign your name here—your full name. That's right. Now I'll witness your signature in this other space!"

He took the document from his horse-dealing client, and signed it in the allotted space. As he handed it back, he fiddled a moment with his fingers, remarking as he wiped them with his handkerchief:

"The document's a bit sticky, Mr. Rowlands."

"Be it, sir? I was readin' it over at breakfast this marnin'. I allus takes traycle wi' me porridge. Mebbe a dab o' that must 'ave got on the paper. I apolergise and thenk ye, sir. 'Ow much do I owe ye?"

And having paid the statutory fee which the solicitor named, the horse-dealer took his leave.

It was market day at Lummingstall, and he made his way to the enclosure where the "lots" of cattle were still being auctioned. Quite a natural thing for a horse-dealer to do.

But he didn't stay long. After looking at the sheep and several horses with a critical eye, opening one or two of their mouths to look at their teeth, he seemed suddenly to decide that there was nothing there he wanted to buy.

With a lithe ash stick swinging in his hand, and chewing a wisp of hay taken from a wagon, he strolled down one street and up another, until by a somewhat circuitous route he reached the Unicorn Inn.

Quite a number of farmers and cattle dealers were gathered about the inn both inside and out. He lingered among them in a perfectly natural manner for a few minutes.

Then he suddenly slipped from the crowd, and disappeared up the stairs into a private sitting-room on the first floor.

Inside that room sat Tinker. He looked up as his master entered.

Sexton Blake, alias Rowlands, gave a satisfied grin.

"Got what I wanted all right. Quite a good impression of Dolby's finger-prints, I fancy. Nearly spoilt it, though. The stuff couldn't have been quite dry. Dolby remarked how sticky the paper was. Now let's see the results!"

He dived his hand into his pocket, and then his grin faded.

"It's gone!" he gasped.

"The paper?"

"The paper—my wallet—the whole shoot? Somebody has run the rule over me?"

"Gee! Must have been a smart man to pick your pockets!"

"Must have been one of the b-hoys! One of the regulars, and a star man at that. Tinker, lad, we're up against a gang!"

"What do you mean?"

"The deeper we go into this case the more of a tangle it becomes."

"Dolby's in it, you mean, and has got smart accomplies?"

"There are some smart fellows in it whether Dolby is or not."

"But he must be. You as good as said so before. That's why you went to the trouble of dictating that affidavit and pretending your London solicitor had sent it, so that you could get Dolby's finger-prints. And now somebody's pinched your wallet containing the prints. Of course, Dolby's in it. He must have got suspicous of that stickiness and had you followed."

"Even so, he would needed to have had an expert piclpocket on hand. No ordinary man could have done the job so neatly."

"That's true enough, guv. Even a don at the game must have had a nerve to put it across you."

Blake remained quiet a minute, thinking hard.

"I'm not sure we ought to jump to conclusions," he said. "The wallet may not have been pinched at all. Come to think of it I may have dropped it."

"How could you?"

"I did a good deal of stooping in the market. When I was feeling the sheep and bending to stroke the horses' pasterns, and so on. The pocket's big and the wallet was heavy and lopsided."

"How d'ye mean?"

"Well, it had several things in it, including two bullets."

"What bullets?"

"The two I pouched last week when we were investigating that shooting affray at Newport. By the way, it'll be rather serious if I don't get them back. I must advertise the loss, laddie, and offer a reward for the return of the wallet. I must get out some handbills at once. There's a printer round the corner. I must see about it now."

He hurried out at once. The recollection of those two spent bullets had given him fresh concern, furnishing as they did vital evidence in another grave case he had in hand.

"The handbills will be distributed presently," he explained when he returned a few minutes later.

"Haven't given your own name, have you, guv'nor?"

"No. The wallet contains no mention of it. I've offered a reward of two pounds and asked the finder to return the wallet to the police-station. Which reminds me, I must let Yarrow know about it or he'll be puzzled."

They found the inspector in when they arrived. He still had the grave look that had marked him previously. He was still worrying over the suspicion he had mentioned earlier—viz., that there was a second man in the murder with John Wilson.

That belief was founded, as we know, on the discovery that the fingerprints found on the dead man's throat had not been made by Wilson.

When, therefore, Sexton Blake told him of the latest development in connection with those fingerprints, he was simply amazed.

"Mean you suspected Mr. Dolby of the murder?" he exclaimed.

"No, I don't!" Blake's tone was almost snappy with emphasis. "I was anxious to see his fingerprints, that was all. I got them as I've explained. And now I've lost 'em, together with other things. I'll be real glad to get that wallet back."

"I'll let you know at once if anything turns up," answered Yarrow, and fell into deep thought when Blake had gone.

Nicholas Dolby! Was it possible he could have done the murder? Such a thing as that had never so much as occurred to Yarrow. Dwellers in little towns often become little-minded, the effect of environment, and to none does this more strongly apply than to officials. Yarrow was an official in a small provincial place, of which Nicholas Dolby was one of the most prominent citizens, and it had never occurred to him that so highly-respected and properous a citizen could possibly be guilty of a foul and dastardly crime.

CHAPTER 13.
In Peril on the Moor.

ON the way back to the Unicorn, Blake was thoughtful, too. His thoughts led him to a decision, for he suddenly said:

"Laddie, we've a job for after dark this evening. I'm going over to Dentwhistle to have another look at the Green Bungalow. If we are up against a gang, I don't want them to see us. Not that we've long to wait. It's beginning to get dark already."

Within an hour, and wearing only slight disguises, they had started for Dentwhistle in a hired car. Blake was in the driving-seat, while Tinker and Pedro sat behind. The detective preferred to drive himself for two reasons. First, because it ensured greater secrecy; second, because he had had enough of hired drivers for the time being. He remember the traitorous Reuben Gunn, who had not returned to Rinker's Garage, and about whom he had so far had no news from the Bradford police.

Their ten-mile run over the moors to Dentwhistle was accomplished fast and safely. There was next to no traffic on those lonely, hilly roads, and the little car was a demon at hills.

But fast as they went, something went faster. On one of the very loneliest stretches, a two-seater went past them like a flash.

"Mad fool!" was Blake's comment. "That's the sort of speed-merchant who deserves to break his neck!"

"See who it was?" Tinker asked, leaning forward.

"No, I was looking after my own job."

"It was Nicholas Dolby!"

"What, a broken-nerved chap like that driving at such a pace."

"He wasn't driving. Another chap was doing that. His chauffeur, I expect."

"Doesn't employ one, as a rule. Always drove himself, I'm told."

"Must have hired a driver since the shock of Richard Sharron's murder upset him. He's not going on to the green bungalow, is he?"

"Oh, no! Yarrow tells me he can't bear the sight of the place now. He's staying with Dr. Alford for the present. He lives at the end of the village. We have to pass the house on our way to the quarry moor. I'll show you. It'll be just as well to make sure Dolby's there—if we can."

There was no difficulty about this, as it proved. Passing through Dentwhistle at a slower pace, Blake slackened still more as they approached Dr. Alford's at the end of the village.

It was a detached place, standing pleasantly back from the road behind a shrubbery and two clipped yews. Beside the house was a little outbuilding that served as garage.

Blake's intention had been to pull up a little beyond the place, and then, by walking back, try to discover whether Nicholas Dolby was there. As it chanced, there was no need to do this. For the doors of the garage stood wide open, and was lighted up. In the light, both Blake and Tinker caught a clear sight of a man standing beside a two-seater car, which had evidently only just been taken inside.

The man was Nicholas Dolby, and he was alone. The man who had driven him from Lummingstall was nowhere in sight.

"He's there all right, so that's that," whispered Tinker.

Sexton Blake nodded, and, quickening up, drove towards the quarry moor in silent thought.

★ ★ ★

"Ever see anything as plain as this, laddie?"

It was Blake asking Tinker the question. They were inside the bungalow.

The subject of the detective's query was a footprint on the outside sill of the window belonging to the room in which Richard Sharron had been found murdered. The window was opened wide, and Blake was leaning out.

"Don't know about that," Tinker answered. "The bootprint's fairly distinct still, considering the time it's been there. That's no account of the petrol, and the fact that there's been no rain since, I suppose. But how you can sort of say it's the plainest thing you've ever seen, I don't quite——"

"I don't mean the bootprint itself, laddie. I mean, what it indicates."

"What does it indicate?"

"Fake!"

"You said that about the other print."

"This confirms it. The absurdity of there being a bootprint here at all! Why should there be? A man escaping from this room not only need not stand on this sill, but it would be a positive inconvenience to do so!"

"You mean——"

"He'd kneel! He'd just scramble on to it from this side and then slither over to the ground. His feet would hardly touch the sill at all. Try it."

Tinker tried. As Blake had said, there was no need to touch the sill with his feet—a slight scratch of the heel was all that showed in his case. It required, indeed, a special effort to stand upright on it, and took time.

"Gee whiz! You're right, guv'nor," he said. "It would have delayed a man's escape if he'd stood up."

"And a man who's just done a murder doesn't usually delay unnecessarily in getting away. This bootprint, like the other, was made deliberately by somebody holding the boot in his hand. It was done to throw us off the right scent by fixing suspicion on John Wilson!"

"That means, somebody must have taken Wilson's boots off. He mentioned nothing about that."

"He didn't know. It was done while be lay senseless in the garage. The presence of the petrol on the soles proves that."

"Then, it must have been Nicholas Dolby! Yet, you told Yarrow you didn't suspect Dolby of the murder!"

"I don't suspect him!" Blake answered, with the same emphasis as before.

"Can't make you out, guv!" exclaimed the puzzled Tinker. "If you didn't suspect him, why did you go to all that trouble to get his fingerprints?"

"Fingerprint records are useful in any case, and—well, I wanted to make quite sure he hadn't choked Richard Sharron. I hadn't much doubt about it, but I wanted proof."

"And you haven't got it, after all! You've lost the fingerprints and your wallet into the bargain. Will you try to get Dolby's fingerprints again?"

"Don't think it'll be worth the trouble. We shall see! But we'll get on with our search, and then get back to Lummingstall."

For the next three-quarters of an hour they continued their search of the bungalow. More than once during that time, Blake brought his lens into operation, and more than once made notes in his pocket-book. But whether any of these things indicated any clue of importance, he didn't say.

Completing their search, they left by the back door of the bungalow. This brought them quite close to the low hedge behind which they had left their car.

As they approached this, Pedro suddenly made a dart forward, and started to circle round and round the car, growling angrily the whole time. This was all the more strange, since he had behaved himself so well during the time they had been inside. Although he had done a good deal of sniffing around, he had shown very little excitement, except when he had come near to the bed in which the murdered man had lain.

"Hallo! What's up with Pedro?" Tinker asked, as they saw his antics now.

Blake looked grave.

"Seems as if somebody's been about."

"No signs of any fresh footprints, or anything."

"That's so. Well, it may be just fancy on Pedro's part. It's clear there's nobody about now, so we'll push on."

Pedro was the very soul of discipline—he had been brought up that way from a puppy. Therefore, when Sexton Blake ordered him into the car he obeyed. But he did so with such apparent reluctance that Blake wondered whether he was doing right in not trying to account for the dog's excitement.

It led to a change of mind even as he started to crank up.

"We must see what's up, if we can, laddie," he exclaimed suddenly. Then to Pedro: "Come along, old chap—find—find!"

No second bidding was necessary. The bloodhound leapt out of the car eagerly. Once more he began his eager circling movements, his nose ever to the ground, his tail straight out and quivering.

Every second his excitement grew, until all in a moment he moved away from the narrow road and across the patch of scrub which had been fenced in as part of the bungalow property.

Blake, with torch flashing, scanned the ground again for footprints. He found them in plenty here, but immediately discarded them as worthless, because this was a spot on which the police and others had gathered since the murder, and where, if there was any fresh trail, it had been crossed and re-crossed by a score of others, and so made untraceable by sight.

But not by scent! Pedro proved that by immediately following what must, as it seemed, be a new trail.

It led through a small wicket gate in the fence, and away over a corner of the moor proper. Following this trail for some distance they saw some dark object looming up out of the darkness.

"A cottage!" whispered Tinker.

"Yes, the night-watchman's!"

"Pedro's making for it!"

"So he is. Wonder if old Luke Samways has been up to the bungalow lately. If he has that would account for it. We'll find that out."

Blake had met the night-watchman twice before. First when Inspector Yarrow had introduced him; second, when he had attended at the police-court at Lummingstall.

When, therefore, he knocked at the cottage door a minute later, he was immediately recognised, his disguise being but a slight one.

Explaining why he had called, Blake asked him if he had been up to the bungalow.

"Ooay, this afternoon, sir, aw was oop theer just t'ave a look round. 'Twas just afore dusk."

"You've seen or heard nobody else about?"

"Not a soul, sir, not since t' lads went away whoam from t' quarry. And that was 'fore darkness coom."

"Thank you, Samways, that about settles it then. Good-night!"

"Must have been Samways Pedro scented," remarked Tinker as they made their way back to the car.

"Yes, I suppose so," Blake answered reflectively. "Well, anyway, we've done all we can. We'll shove off now."

They were off in earnest now. For a mile or so all went well. The car, oldish though it was, travelled fast and as smoothly as any other could have done considering the roughness of some of those moorland roads.

But presently there came a change. This was after they had got clear of the great quarries and the village and were running over a particularly desolate stretch of moorland. A perilous stretch, too, the road winding like a twisted knifeboard round the slope of a hill.

To their right the hill ran upward, but to their left it shelved down in a manner to steep as to suggest a precipice.

It was in very truth a precipice, as daylight would have shown, for the split in the hills along that stretch was part of "Vyebury Fault," one of the great mountain breaks for which Yorkshire is famous. Could they but have seen, they would have realised that they were driving along the edge of a deep ravine, with only some dozen feet or so between them and its treacherous edge!

And as ill-luck would have it, it was just at this point when something seemed to go wrong. For no apparent reason the car began to sway and rock, and a moment later gave a violent lurch. The next instant, and it pitched forward and sideways. At the same moment came a snapping sound, and something went bowling away sideways from them. In the glare of the lamps both saw what it was.

A wheel—their front near-side wheel!

As Blake jammed on his brakes, they saw it go spinning down the few feet of sloping road and then disappear from sight over the edge of the chasm!

Bad, but worse was to follow! If the brakes were acting, it was only inadequate. For that matter, what brakes could hold up a car on such a slope? The vehicle was slithering down, propelled by its own weight as well as by the only partly-checked engine.

Frantically doing his best, Blake was forced to recognise the situation.

"Jump, laddie!" he roared. "Jump for your life!"

Tinker stooped to Pedro's collar. Hoisted thus to his feet out of a sleep, the bloodhound at a word leapt from the skidding car, followed by Tinker.

As he jumped, the latter saw Sexton Blake rise in his seat and make a move as if to jump too, but his own leaping brought the body of the car between him and his master, and pitching forward into the road, he could see no more of the detective.

What he could see by the light of the still-glaring lamps was the car itself, slithering to the edge of the ravine, and then over—to fall into the unknown depths beyond!

CHAPTER 14.
Is it Foul Play?

TINKER lay still for a couple of minutes. He had pitched on to the road with some violence. Fortunately he had kept his head up, but the impact of his shoulders had knocked the breath out of him and dazed him.

Never quite knocked out, he was well enough in a little while to sit up. Under the spell of nature's first law, he ran his hands over his bruised ribs and shoulders, and was thankful enough to find that no bones were broken.

The next thing he realised was that Pedro was bending over him, trying to lick his hand.

"Old chap, old chap," he muttered gratefully as he patted the dog's head. "You all right? But the guv'nor—where's the guv'nor?"

He stood erect, full of sudden uneasiness. He looked about him in the darkness, but could see nothing of Blake. He took his electric torch from his pocket and flashed it about. Still he could see nothing of Blake.

"Guv'nor—guv'nor!" he called aloud, but no answer came.

Suddenly his dazed senses cleared. What had happened came back to him in a flash. He remembered seeing the car skidding over the chasm's edge. Sexton Blake had been standing up in it as if about to jump clear. But had he jumped? Had there been time, or had——

There had been no time to jump. The car had certainly gone over into the abyss—Tinker had seen that—and Blake must have gone with it!

In that event, from the framing of the rest of his thought, Tinker had to shrink. Again he braced himself. He must face whatever was in store for him. Sexton Blake had disappeared, was neither to be seen nor heard. He must be searched for and found. Heaven grant that when he was found it might not be too late!

"Pedro—Pedro!" Tinker cried out now, and turned to where he had last seen the bloodhound.

He got a second though milder shock. The dog was nowhere to be seen either, nor heard. Usually at the word of command he would come bounding forward. Now there was no sign nor sound of him.

This puzzled Tinker for a moment, but only for moment. The next he realised what had happened. Guided by some subtle instinct, the dog had gone to search for his master. Which way had he gone?

Tinker had not long to wait to learn that. Even while he strained his eyes this way and that in search of the dog—calling out his name every few seconds—he got light on the subject.

An answering bark reached him. It came from somewhere in the ravine! Not from that point of it that lay immediately beneath him, and which was where the car had hurtled over, but from some distance away to the right.

"Pedro—Pedro!" he yelled again, and this time the answering bark came from far down in the ravine, almost directly beneath him.

Not only that, but the barking was continuous, and had in it a note of alarm whose meaning Tinker at once guessed.

Pedro had found his master—had found him helpless, and was now giving voice to let Tinker know!

"All right, old boy, I'm coming!" he cried, for all the world as if Pedro was a human being.

He started along the sloping road to the right. From somewhere along there the bloodhound had found a way down. Perhaps the same way would serve his ends. He must see, anyway.

He had not to go far. Barely sixty yards along he found a slight break in the edge of the road. It marked a path which wound down the face of the precipice—not so steep here—and right down into the bed of the ravine.

Tinker's heart was in his mouth. Not on account of the dangerous path—for it was mightily dangerous on so dark a night—but on account of what was in his mind.

Sexton Blake—his beloved master—what had happened to him? Pedro had found him, he felt certain, and in a few minutes he would find him, too.

Heart and brain were too full of deadly fears. All he could do was to descend the perilous path with all speed, and then, turning to the left, hasten along the bed of the ravine towards the fateful spot from which by this time Pedro was sending forth a continual baying that sounded to Tinker's imaginative mind like a death knell!

An agony of suspense lasting three or four minutes, and then he reached the spot towards which he had toiled.

It was Pedro who gave him the first intimation of this. With alternative barks and pitcous whines, he came forward to meet him, then turned to lead him to the spot.

In the gloom, Tinker could see only a tangled mass. Switching on his torch, he saw a sight that stabbed him like a knife. Amid a juble of boulders—some loose, some fixed in the ravine's bed—lay the car. It was a sheer wreck, parts of it smashed to fragments, others twisted and contorted. The bonnet was a flattened, shapeless thing, the engine a silent ruin of pulverised fragments!

But Sexton Blake—where was he? That was the one all-absorbing question to which he sought an answer. It was the bloodhound who provided the answer.

Even while Tinker gazed aghast at the smashed car, Pedro was trying to force his way in among the wreckage. His tearing and scratching drew Tinker's attention that way. Scrambling over a big boulder he came to where the dog was, and flashed his torch again.

At once he saw—saw a sight which froze his blood! Right amid the debris, sprawled out between the splintered hood and the twisted chassis, was a human form—Sexton Blake!

He was lying on his breast, with his face slightly turned away, and his head a little raised, amid a heap of the car's cushions and tumbled leather upholstery.

Even at that early stage Tinker felt thankful that these things had in some measure broken Blake's fall and prevented him coming into direct contact with the rocks. Also, that a section of the car's upper part had been held clear of the detective's head by the peculiar position of the brass rods belonging to the hood.

The realisation of these circumstances lightened Tinker's heart a little. Previously he had been horribly oppressed by the fear that Blake would be dead! How could he escape death after such a plunge into space? Hitherto he had thought that nothing short of a miracle could save him.

Now the miracle seemed to have happened, or something like it. His falling among the cushions and massed upholstery, and the warding off of falling debris by the curious position of the brass rods, were surely a dispensation of Providence almost amounting to a miracle!

With hope rising in his grateful heart, Tinker set to at once to rescue his master from amid the wreckage.

Ten minutes of hauling and lifting, and he had cleared away sufficient of the debris to enable him to crawl through to where Blake was.

Gently lifting him, he turned him over on his back, and with his torch fixed in a niche he gazed on his face.

It was very white—deathly white almost—and he lay very still. But he was not dead. Although unconscious, he was still breathing. Tinker was able to detect that almost at once, and he got to work in an endeavour to bring him back to his senses.

Usually he carried an emergency flask with him, but the fact that he hadn't it with him now filled him with chagrin. This was short-lived, however, for an thrusting his fingers into the detective's pockets he found a phial containing some small glass globes. He recognised them at once as containing a certain chemical which was among the most powerful restoratives known to medical science. Blake had of late carried them about with him, and Tinker knew their use perfectly, having seen the detective administer them to other people.

Taking once of the tiny globes from the phial, therefore, he wrapped it in his handkerchief and crushed it. Averting his own face to avoid getting the potent fumes, he clapped it over the unconscious Blake's mouth and nose, and held it there for the space of a few seconds.

These globules were a recent discovery. Blake had obtained them in Vienna, while attending to great International medical conference there. They represented the latest and greatest discovery in the way of respiratory and cardiac restoratives, and were deemed to be a great advance on anything hitherto used.

In this intance their effect was truly wonderful. Some half-dozen instinctive inhalations—for Blake was not breathing consciously—and there came an astonishing stimulation of heart and lungs.

Within thirty seconds of Tinker's withdrawing the handkerchiefr, a tinge of colour stole back into Blake's cheeks, while a few seconds later he opened his eyes.

"Hallo, Tinker, old lad!" came in a faint murmur.

Tinker took his hand in a comforting grip.

"Dear old guv'nor!"

"What has happened? I—I can't quite recall."

Tinker told him. Blake nodded his head slowly.

"Ah, yes, I remember now. The car."

"Something went wrong with it, guv."

"Something was made to go wrong with it, laddie—while we were in the bungalow. Somebody must have done something. Weakened the wheel—filed the hub—or something."

"But——"

"That wheel would never have spun off like that unless. It struck me directly I saw it."

"Who could have——"

"Remember how Pedro behaved. Went mad with excitement. I felt sure that meant somebody had been about."

"But we decided that must have been Luke Samways in the afternoon."

"We were wrong. Must have been somebody later. While we were inside the bungalow. Trail must have led beyond Samways' cottage. We ought to have tried further——"

Blake broke off suddenly. He had spoken jerkily all through. Now he began to pant for breath and to go pale again.

"You're feeling bad, guv?"

"My side. Hurts a bit. Ribs bruised. Lucky to get off with that. Wonder I wasn't killed outright after such a fall. Wonder I came to so quickly."

"That was this stuff, I expect, sir," Tinker said, showing the phial.

"Ah, you found that in my pocket! Amyl compound. You gave me one?"

"Yes, and it brought you round in no time."

"They're wonderful for that. Only the effect wears off so soon. They let you down again, and—I feel queerish again, laddie!"

Blake broke off. His hand had gone to his side, his face had gone deadly pale again.

He had swooned!

CHAPTER 15.
A Sinister Silhouette!

TINKER gazed at the white face and still form in agonised dismay. The fainting had come suddenly, and he had nothing else handy in the way of a restorative. Nor dare he leave Blake's side to get help.

Yet help must be obtained. He must be carried to a house of shelter, and a doctor must be got to him. How could he bring such help?

In his extremity his thoughts worked like lightning. He remembered that Blake had a police whistle in his pocket. In an instant he had fished it out and risen to his feet.

A moment after, and the whole ravine was echoing to the sound of the shrill blasts he was blowing on it. Blast after blast he blew till the whole air was full of the startling sound!

Hardly had these echoes died away than there came another sound that filled Tinker with alarm!

It manifested itself at first by a mysterious rumble from somewhere high up the precipice. Tinker's glance flew upward in a second, but in the darkness he could see nothing.

But in three seconds he knew what it meant. The rumbling came closer, growing in volume as it came, and taking on the sound of some heavy mass, alternately bumping against limestone projections, and tearing through the stiff and scrubby bushes that grew against the cliff's face. Then:

Crash!

It was the fall of a ponderous boulder as it thundred on to the rocky bed of the ravine, and smashed itself into fifty flying fragments like an exploding shrapnel shell!

The fall came within eight yards of where they were, while a chunk of stone narrowly missed Tinker's head as it hurtled through the air.

Following the first shock of alarm, Tinker's first thought was one of profound thankfulness that he had placed Blake beneath an overhanging ridge of rock which completely sheltered him from any such accident.

It must be an accident, of course? The boulder must have been loosened by the motor-car as it slithered over the edge.

That was Tinker's thought for a moment. The next he knew that he was wrong—that it was no accident!

For, in that next moment, came another hurtling rock, to be followed by a perfect fusillade like an avalanche!

Smash—crash—smash—crash!

To right and left of him the descending boulders fell, splintering into a hundred heavy missiles, and filling all the air with chalky dust and dangerous chips! One great lump fell plump upon the overhanging rock beneath which Blake was lying, but the protecting roof easily withstood the onslaught and saved him from harm!

But the nearness of the peril filled Tinker with the greatest alarm! Blake was safe where he was from such a bombardment, and he himself had so far escaped hurt, but how long would he do so?

For this was no accident surely! It was being deliberately done! Enemies were at work high overhead! Enemies who, knowing Blake was there, were using these diabolical means to put paid to his account!

Who were they? Was it possible to see? He must try!

Whispering to Pedro to follow him, he made a sudden dash across the ravine. Reaching the other side, he found a narrow crevasse that penetrated steeply into the opposing hillside.

Scrambling some twenty feet up this, he reached a point from where he could see the top edge of the precipice from which the avalanche of rocks had been hurled, and over which the car had plunged. Something at that moment favoured his intention. The bank of backing cloud broke, and the moon peeped out to light up the top edge of the precipice!

Against that clear edge and plainly silhouetted against the skyline, he saw a figure! The figure of a man stooping down, and pressing with all his might against a huge boulder!

Over the edge it came! Down—down the cliff it hurtled, bumping against projections and tearing through scrubby bushes! Then smash—crash—smash—crash, as before, and another shower of flying fragments as before!

Another cloud of chalky dust, too, which shut out Tinker's sight of that sinister figure high up on the cliff-top. When it had cleared away, the figure was no more to be seen!

With all his blood on fire now, Tinker once more took out his police whistle and blew blast after blast upon it. Once more it awoke the echoes, but this time they were not the only sounds that came in answer!

For along the bed of the ravine came hurrying footsteps, and in the midst of them a sonorous shout:

"All right, all right—we're coming!"

A minute later they had come—Constable Stack and half a dozen quarrymen from Dentwhistle. In that quiet district the blasts of the police whistle had penetrated right to the village.

Locating the sounds as coming from Vyebury "Fault," (and divining some sort of accident over the edge), the constable had hastily got together a band of volunteers, and had set out to render aid by the nearest way, namely along the rough bed of the ravine itself.

CHAPTER 16.
Tinker on the Trail.

TINKER sat alone deeply depressed. The time was rather more than an hour later; the scene, a room at the Quarrymen's Rest—the little old wayside inn at Dentwhistle.

In an adjacent room Sexton Blake lay in bed. Thither he had been carried, on a hurdle for stretcher, by the constable and his helpers; while Dr. Alford, who lived at the other end of the village, had been immediately sent for.

On examining the detective, he was in nowise surprised to hear that Blake had complained of pain in his side, when he discovered that two of his ribs were broken! This injury, added to the severe shock to his nerve centres from that terrible plunge in the car over the precipice, was also responsible for his second swoon.

"Lucky to get off with that!" he had declared. "The marvel is that he wasn't killed outright!"

Tinker himself had of course already thought that, but it was cold comfort at the best. When, in response to his further questions, the doctor told him that it might be several hours before the detective came back to consciousness, and that it would certainly be several days before he would be able to get about again, it was not a bit surprising that Tinker should be weighed down with depression.

He tried to shake that off. He knew he must. There was pressing work to do. With Blake out of action, he must work double tides. He could do nothing by waiting at Blake's bedside. The doctor was kindness itself, and he was going to send in a nurse. He, Tinker, was therefore free to start on the work waiting to be done.

His most pressing job lay at the top of the cliffs. At the point where that unknown murderous ruffian had rolled those rocks over. He had scooted off suddenly at the second sound of the police whistle. He must try and track him.

"Come on, Pedro!" he said suddenly, and leapt up.

"We've got to try and track that scum who tried to kill the guv'nor!" he explained to the bloodhound as they set out in the darkness.

Clouds had obscured the moon again and the night was dark. That didn't matter much. He wasn't going to depend on sight. Pedro was to do the tracking by scent, if possible. Still, sight was to play an important part in it, as will presently be seen.

Leaving the village, Tinker followed the road they had gone in the car. As he tramped along with the bloodhound on the leash, his brain got busy with the events of the past few hours. Particularly with the few words Sexton Blake had spoken in that brief interval when he had come back to consciousness.

Foul play! He had suggested foul play!

Had there been? It looked like it. Such a sudden collapse of the car could hardly have come by any other means. That wheel had spun off in a way that truly suggested a partly-filed hub, just as the detective had said. Tinker wished now that he had searched for the wheel in the ravine to make sure. Amid all the anxiety about Blake, and the general excitement, he had forgotten that. Well, the wheel must be searched for later. The chief thing now was to track the man.

The spot where he had been was easy to find—ridiculously easy. Reaching a certain point along the road, close to where the car had gone over, Tinker found his tracks in abundance!

In such abundance that Tinker, trying his master's methods, deduced that the villain wasn't a practised crook, but an amateur at the game.

His boot tracks were everywhere, in the soft grass patch, and on the bare chalky places nearer the edge of the chasm. Bootprints with odd characteristics! For while the left foot showed as a whole with great distinctness, the right foot was never imprinted in that way. Only the tracks of the toe of it, here and there! The actual toe print in the grassy places, and the scratch of the toe-piece in the chalk!

And what were these other strange marks that accompanied the boot-prints everywhere almost? Round, deep-dented marks that might have been made by a stick upon which the man had pressed with all his weight. Not an ordinary walking stick—too thick. More like a broomstick. Why had the man carried such a thing as a broomstick with him?

As a lever perhaps? He may have used it to work the boulders free, and to lever them over as he pursued his murderous job?

That was the ready explanation Tinker found for the curious marks. But he didn't bother much about that side of the question. His chief concern was to follow the man wherever he had gone, and these curious marks might help in the tracking.

He had found a spot where the man had lain full stretch, evidently to peer over the edge, and here he began his task. He called Pedro to the spot, and bade him take his fill of whatever scent might be there.

That the bloodhound knew what was meant, and that he got what he wanted from his sniffing, became plain. In ten seconds he was bristling with excitement. Then, with tail on the quiver and standing straight out, he backed from the cliff edge and began circling about. After a few seconds of this he turned to the left, and began to amble along the road back towards the village.

"Stuck it!" was Tinker's inward exclamation, and turned to follow the bloodhound.

For nearly half a mile he followed the trail without a hitch. Then came the first check. It was at a junction of roads. One branch led on to the village, the other turned off towards the great limestone quarries.

Here the man seemed to have hesitated. His tracks were all about. That definite left boot and that indefinite right boot, with only the toe showing. And here also, with only the toe showing. And here also, as on the clifftop, the marks of that everlasting broomstick! Oh, yes, the man must be the veriest amateur at the game! No real professional crook would have left his trade mark all about in this fashion!

The check lasted but a few seconds. Then Pedro was off again. He had forsaken the main road, and was taking the side way—the trolley road leading towards the quarries. And here again in the chalky surface were the tell-tale marks in plenty of boots and "broomstick," to confirm as correct the choice the bloodhound had made.

Tinker was able to see this by the light of the moon, which now and then was breaking through the clouds again. If the man had used the broomstick as a lever for the rocks, why then should he have carried the betraying thing so far? Why also should the marks of it be so plentiful? As plentiful as an ordinary walking-stick would have been, yet surely far less convenient to carry. And, come to think of it, judging from the end, what an extra thick broomstick it seemed to be!

The trolley-track led to one of the slopes leading right down into the quarry bed; but, arrived at that point, the bloodhound did not pursue it any further.

Instead, he took a narrow footpath which ran like a strip of white tape along the top of the quarry and only a few feet from the edge. Here again the marks of boots were occasionally apparent where the chalk was soft, and always near to them those other marks of the stout broomstick.

After traversing the full length of the rim of the quarries, the path suddenly turned away into a slight dip, and led straight towards a small solitary house.

Luke Samway's cottage! Tinker had, of course, been there before with Blake earlier that night, and recognised it in a moment.

Pedro was making straight for the door! No, he wasn't. Within fifteen paces of the door, and just inside a fence built of slabs of chalk and wooden piles, which enclosed a space half yard, half garden, the dog turned aside from the house and ambled towards a shed standing on the farther side.

Straight for this he made—straight for the door of the shed without a second's hesitation. The door was closed, and in a moment the bloodhound's paws were scratching on its panels with the fierce energy of impatience to pass through!

Tinker stopped him at that in an instant. The sound of the scratching might betray their presence, and that was the last thing he wanted.

In silence he paused a moment. He looked towards the cottage. There was a light inside the room he guessed to be the sitting-room. No appreciable sound came from it. No sound came from the garden, either. Plainly the night watchman and his wife were safe indoors, and nobody else seemed to be about.

Out went his hand to the latch. The shed door was unlocked, and opened inwards to his push. He passed inside—Pedro going with him—and closed the door softly behind him.

Pedro had rushed past him to the further side of the shed.

His heavy snuffling came across the darkness to Tinker's ears. An eager snuffling telling of the end of his quest—of a "find"!

What had he found? Tinker switched on his torch. In a second he saw.

A stout crutch was hanging from two close-set nails in the wall. Its base was shod with a rubber ferrule and was covered with moist chalk and other soil, and it was at this that Pedro was snuffling so excitedly!

But only for a moment now that it had been shown to Tinker. Then the dog turned aside, and sniffed across the floor of the shed to the other side.

An old box stood there—a box without a lid, and half full of odds and ends. But it wasn't among these that the bloodhound started to rout. It was behind a space between the box and the wall.

Excitement marked him again at once, and Tinker went across. A flash of his torch, and he saw the cause of this fresh agitation.

A pair of boots! Not a real pair, but two boots striking in their oddity! One was of ordinary type, but the other was a surgical boot, with a sole some four or five inches thick!

The toe of this was similarly covered with white moist chalk, as was the whole sole of the other boot!

In a moment Tinker knew the meaning. Luke Samways was a cripple. One leg was shorter than the other. These were his boots.

CHAPTER 17.
Tinker's Deductions.

TINKER caught his breath. That last thought carried with it so many implications. His brain, all afire now, beat back on them step by step.

Those boots belonged to Luke Samways for certain. So did the crutch. The crutch was the "broomstick." That was certain, too. The moist chalk on the ferrule proved it. Besides, come to think of it, a broomstick would never have been carried so consistently like a staff as to make marks beside the boot-prints with such unfailing regularity. But a crutch would—must inevitably—make such marks wherever the crippled carrier of it went.

It followed, then, that it must be Samways whom he had been tracking! Granting that premiss, it must be Samways who had hurled those rocks over the ridge! That meant that he had tried to kill Sexton Blake and him—Tinker—too, for that matter!

Beating still further back, Tinker's reason told him that Samways must have known that Blake and he were down in the ravine—the exact spot—since it would have been utterly impossible for anybody to identify faces or figures from above.

That meant, then, that Samways must have engineered the "accident" to the car! It must have been he who had tampered with the wheel! He could not, of course, have guaranteed where the "accident" would take place, but he would know that the car must collapse soon, and probably by going ahead along the road before the car started, he had actually been a witness of the collapse and the plunge over the cliff!

Anyway, he had engineered it! Come to thing of it, who more likely! He lived close to the green bungalow. While Blake and he were inside he could easily come up to where they had parked the car, and do his foul work unheard and unseen.

Then again, hadn't their first trail led straight to his cottage? It was true that on their visit then Luke Samways had been at home. But what of there? He might have started out directly they had gone, and by some short cut through the quarries still have been a witness of the "accident" which he had foully planned from a distance off.

Having got so far in his deductions, Tinker found his heart pumping hard with excitement. For what did these things portend? Other things of an equally, or even more terrible character!

Whence rose Samways' desire to kill Sexton Blake? Fear, surely! Fear of what? Detection in regard to some serious crime already committed?

Great heaven! Tinker felt his heart almost stop at this sudden thought! Was it possible that Samways had been concerned in the first mystery—the murder of Richard Sharron?

Tinker suddenly shook himself. He felt he was getting out of his depth. The swift current of events and the deductions arising out of them had swept him into deep waters. Much more of it and he would be engulfed. He decided to see Blake first.

He must go before Samways should chance to come out of his cottage and find him there.

Without waiting any longer, Tinker pulled the door of the shed softly after him, and hurried away back to the village.

Reaching the Quarrymen's Rest, he led Pedro through a back door which he had used before, and made for the staircase leading to the bed-room in which Sexton Blake was.

The passage from the door to the foot of the staircase led past the inn snuggery, the door of which now stood partly open.

As he passed this he saw that the room was full of people, the usual collection of quarrymen and other villagers, and one or two strangers in addition. The sound of a familiar voice pulled him up suddenly, and from a point in the dark passage from where he could see without being seen, he stared in at the man whose voice had arrested him.

It was Luke Samways!

He was drinking spirits from a steaming glass, and it was plain from his face and husky, incoherent voice that he had already imbibed far more than was good for him.

This was a double surprise. First, to see Samways there at all; second, to find him in such a condition of advanced inebriety. To have got to that state must have taken time, and he couldn't surely have been there long?

Going slowly and silently up the stairs, Tinker thought out the possible explanation. The night-watchman must have been drinking before setting out for the ridge road. (That would account for his carelessness as to his tracks.) Then, having returned to his own cottage, he must have immediately made for the village inn after changing his boots and depositing the crutch in the outhouse. It seemed a little odd that he hadn't used his crutch for his second outing , but the journey being shorter, he probably didn't feel the need of it, but had contented himself with an ordinary stout walking-stick.

The fact that the suspected man was on those very premises, only made Tinker the more eager to tell Blake what had happened, and the more anxious to consult him as to what was to be done. How he hoped that the detective might have sufficiently recovered for this purpose!

But in this he was disappointed. Sexton Blake was still unconscious, no better and no worse than when he had left him two hours before. The nurse whom Dr. Alford had sent for from Lummingstall, told him that.

"He's not likely to come to for some hours," she informed him. "In addition to the broken ribs, the doctor thinks he must have met with some internal injury that's affected his brain."

The ominous words made Tinker jump.

"No, I don't mean anything serious to the brain,' the nurse explained hastily, "but enough to keep him unconscious for a time. Sleep is the best thing for him. As the doctor says, when he does wake up he'll probably be all right. Except for his broken ribs, of course. They'll take some little time to get right."

With that Tinker had necessarily to remain content. However much he wanted to consult Blake, it couldn't be done. He must needs wait till the detective was well enough before confiding to anybody the details of what had happened that night.

"I'll wait till the morning, anyway," Tinker decided. "The delay won't matter much. The guv'nor may be better tomorrow. If he is, I can tell him. If he isn't, I can decide whether to tell the inspector."

Thinking thus, he went to bed and tried to compose himself to sleep. He was about to drop off when he was rudely awakened by voices outside.

It was closing time, and the revellers had been turned out. Loudest among the boisterous voices was Luke Samways. He was loudly protesting that he was "all ri'" and could walk alone, but with such vehemence and thickness of utterance as belied his words.

Jumping out of bed and looking out of his dark window, Tinker beheld him. In the glow of the inn lamp he could see his contorted face and bleared eyes, and could tell that he was helplessly drunk.

He was being persuaded to go home quietly, and the last Tinker saw of him was his being led by two labouring men along the dark lane leading to his lonely cottage on the moor.

CHAPTER 18.
Inspector Yarrow on the Warpath!

INSPECTOR YARROW was a very efficient officer. Of the plodding, methodical sort, he never allowed the grass to grow under his feet, but kept on in the way he had mapped out for himself in his own stolid way.

While at this stage he never wavered in his belief in John Wilson's guilt, circumstances had forced him to the belief that there was a "second man in it."

The chief of those circumstances were the finger-prints found on the dead man's throat. Discovering that they were not Wilson's finger-prints, he had modified his theory about the murder to this extent.

While still holding to the idea that Wilson had played a leading part—perhaps had actually fired the bullet which had entered Richard Sharron's thigh—he was forced to believe that a second man had done the choking.

Who was that second man? Some other tramp, an associate of Wilson's? A second vagabond, who, with Wilson, had planned to burgle the green bungalow, and had been spurred on to greater crime by the turn of events?

That seemed the most likely theory, but it did not exclude from the inspector's mind other possibilities. It was quite likely that some local man, some ne'er-do-well with whom Wilson had struck up an acquaintance, might have taken a hand in the terrible crime.

With his mind thus inclined, it will be easily understood how eager he was to lend a ready ear to anybody able to give him any information on this point.

Thus, when Tinker motored over to see him at Lummingstall the next morning—he had hired another car for this purpose—he welcomed him with open arms.

This visit followed on a decision by Tinker, on finding still no change in Sexton Blake, to confide to the police-inspector his adventures of last night.

Yarrow listened in amazement.

"I'm not a bit surprised to hear this about Luke Samways. I've always had it at the back of my head that he might be in it."

"You mean in the murder of Mr. Sharron?" exclaimed Tinker, not trying to hide his surprise.

"Sure! I told Mr. Blake almost from the start that there was a second man in it."

Tinker let this exaggeration pass without comment.

"Seems to me there must be more than a second man in it. A whole gang, I should reckon, considering all the things that have happened."

"Well, it may be so," said Yarrow loftily. "I haven't had much chance of probing into John Wilson's past yet. When I do, I shan't be surprised to find he's an old hand—a habitual crook. That being so, it wouldn't be surprising to hear that he'd got some of his pals to lend him a hand."

"In the murder, do you mean?"

"No. I don't think there were more than two in that, and Samways may well have been the other." It was almost amusing to watch Yarrow behaving as if he had suspected the night-watchman from the very start. "The gang wouldn't come in till they found that Wilson was in trouble. Then they'd try and get him out of it. That's the most natural thing in the world."

Tinker didn't comment on this either. He might well have done. More confused thinking than the local police-officer was indulging in would have been difficult to find. For he seemed to forget—which Tinker didn't—that Sexton Blake had been working on John Wilson's behalf, and that therefore it was wildly improbable that any "crook pals" of his would set themselves to attack the man who was trying to prove him innocent. But Tinker couldn't hope to rescue Yarrow from this morass of muddled thought, so much leave him to wallow in it for the time being.

Cutting further cackle he got to the "hosses" by saying:

"As to Luke Samways, what are you going to do about it? Arrest him?"

"Not yet. I must watch him first to get more evidence. I shall put a plain-clothes man on to shadow him for a bit. Then if I get any information, I shall act according."

Tinker left it at that. It was all he wanted. Pending Sexton Blake's recovery to direct operations, he preferred this shadowing to an actual arrest which might prove premature. He knew how Blake was always against precipitate action, and always believed in giving a criminal sufficient rope to make sure of hanging him. In this case, that phrase would have a literal as well as a figurative mean, Tinker thought grimly.

★ ★ ★

With Tinker gone, Inspector Yarrow got to work. Having, so to speak, got his teeth into the possibility of Samways being involved in the murder—as certainly he seemed to be in the attack on Blake—he proceeded to chew and digest it.

The result was that he quickly persuaded himself that Samways was in it—in the whole plot! More, he almost persuaded himself that this belief was not merely the outcome of what Tinker had told him, but that he had suspected the night-watchman's complicity from the start!

In this frame of mind he set to work, and it was not many minutes after Tinker's departure before a plain-clothes police-officer was on his way to Dentwhistle, with instructions to keep an eye on the neighbourhood generally, and on Luke Samways in particular.

That fixed up, Yarrow went out to conduct certain inquiries on his own, not only in and about Lummingstall, but by means of telephone and other messages, in more distant parts of the neighbourhood.

Thus he passed the greater part of the day. If he did not glean much helpful information, he certainly remained full of hope that eventually he would do so.

And he indulged in a lot of dreaming! Always ambitious, he began now to swell with a desire to win promotion by solving this complex mystery of the murder and the after events.

It was the first time in his official career that such a big thing had come his way. Certainly it was the first time he had ever found himself associated in a case with such a big man as Sexton Blake.

And now he was! Not so much associated with him, as pitted against him! Yes, actually that, since Blake had been retained to clear from the murder charges the man who he—Yarrow— had arrested.

Returning to headquarters at Lummingstall after dark that evening, he found a small package on his desk in the office. It was addressed to him, tied up with string, and rather elaborately sealed with dabs of red wax. It was addressed to him personally, and was "registered."

"Came by the six o'clock post, sir!" explained the constable who had taken it in.

Yarrow tweaked through the string with his penknife, and opened the parcel. Instantly his eyes stretched wide with astonishment, while from his throat gurgled the words to himself:

"Sexton Blake's wallet!"

CHAPTER 19.
A Bombshell for Blake!

NO mistake about that. The first glance proved it. Inside the flap of the brown leather thing were the initials "S.B." Moreover, a half-sheet of writing-paper contained these words:

"Enclosed is the wallet advertised on handbills. It was picked up by the sender among some straw in Lummingstall market-place. Contents returned as found."

That was all. No name, no address! No sort of claim of the reward offered! The anonymous message was in printed characters, as was the address on the postal wrapper.

Returned anonymously! That was queer. What did it mean?

Although Yarrow asked himself that question, he didn't waste time speculating on it. He was too eager to know if the contents were indeed intact, as the message said. Not knowing exactly what the wallet contained at the time Blake lost it, he would not be able to check this.

But he knew of two things it had contained. Bullets?

Sexton Blake had mentioned bullets. Yes, and here they were—two exploded, flattened things!

And the paper—the affidavit! The document by means of which Sexton Blake had tricked Mr. Dolby into giving his finger-prints. Yes, that was there, too, finger-prints and all!

This was an important thing—this recovery of the wallet. Not on account of the fingerprints, for, of course, Mr. Dolby could have had nothing to do with the murder—even to suggest such a things was absurd!—but on account of the other things which the wallet contained. The bullets, for example. They were connected with some other case which Blake had in hand, and formed an important link in his chain of evidence. There were other private documents, too, the loss of which had made him anxious to get the wallet back. Oh, yes, it was an important recovery, and Sexton Blake would be intensely glad to hear the wallet had been regained.

Inspector Yarrow therefore went to the telephone and rang up the exchange. In a minute he had got through to the Quarryman's Rest at Dentwhistle. Another minute, and he was talking to Tinker at the other end.

"How's Mr. Blake—well enough to speak to me?" he asked.

"Sorry, he isn't, inspector. He's still unchanged. Still unconcious!" replied Tinker.

"H'm, I'm sorry to hear it. I hoped he'd be well enough to hear what I'd got to tell him!"

"You've had news? Anything important?"

"Not as bearing on the murder mystery. But important to Mr. Blake! His wallet has turned up!"

"By Jove, has it, though? How did you get it?"

Yarrow explained over the wire, adding:

"He'll be glad to hear about it, I'm sure."

"He certainly will. I'll tell him directly he's able to understand. About those fingerprints on the bogus affidavit. Done anything about 'em yet?"

"No; I've hardly looked at them. What is there to do about them?"

"Well, I didn't know whether you'd compared 'em with those others."

Inspector Yarrow's reply came back in withering tones.

"Not much use doing that! I don't know what was in Mr. Blake's mind when he went to all that trouble to get them. Struck me as an absolute waste of time. Will you come over for the wallet?"

"I can't to-night. The doctor says the guv'nor may come back to his senses any time now. I want to be about when he does. I'll tell him about the wallet at the first opportunity. That'll ease his mind. Meantime, if you'll please keep it till I can come to Lummingstall, I'll be glad."

"Very well, I'll lock it up in my safe!"

★ ★ ★

That is what Yarrow started to do directly he had hung up the receiver. But he didn't do it!

Halfway across the room to the safe he suddenly halted with the affidavit in his hand.

Why shouldn't he examine those fingerprints? Nothing in it, of course, seeing they belonged to Mr. Nicholas Dolby. He was a highly-reputable professional gentleman—one of Lummingstall's leading townsmen. It was an insult to suspect him, it was an insult even to have taken his finger-prints.

Still, thought Yarrow, he might as well just take a look at them out of curiosity.

Yes, he would examine them, so that when Blake did ask him such a question, he would be able definitely to answer him; able to tell him straight out that the finger-prints bore no resemblance to those found on the murdered man's throat; that it was utterly and absolutely ridiculous ever to have supposed that they would resemble them!

He returned to his seat. He opened a drawer of his desk and took out the photograph of the finger-prints found on the murdered man's throat, and also a big, round magnifying-glass.

A second or two later, and he started on the task of comparing one set of finger-prints with the other.

He studied them for two or three minutes in a casual, almost careless way. Then something suddenly riveted his attention. It made him apply himself to his task with closer interest. Much closer interest! His eyes stretched wide—then wider.

Then he positively leapt from his seat with such a look in his eyes as told of the greatest inward excitement!

★ ★ ★

As Tinker had said over the telephone, the invalid was expected to return to consciousness at any time now. Dr. Alford, who had been in and out at every opportunity during the day, had noted the favourable signs, and had foretold a happy issue out of them.

One of the most important signs was that Blake's sleep had become more natural and, as a consequence, pulse and heartbeat had become more normal.

The knitting up of the broken ribs, which had been surgically set, would naturally take time, and would necessitate Blake's being bandaged for a week or two. But the feared injury to his head had proved to be but slight, and, with sleep putting this right, there was no reason why the patient should not soon come back to his senses and be reasonably well when he did at last wake up.

It was chiefly because Tinker wished to be close at hand when this desired state of things should come about that made him disinclined to go over to Lummingstall that night. Otherwise he would certainly have motored over to get possession of the wallet.

As it happened, he might safely have done so, for it was many hours before Blake did at last come to—the early hours of the morning, in fact.

But when he did it was well worth waiting for. Because Blake woke up wonderfully well! Leaving out his broken ribs—and the pain from these was greatly diminished by now—he was practically himself again. His brain was quite clear, and his voice was fairly strong as he greeted the delighted Tinker.

Not that he, or Tinker either, said much during the first few minutes. Emotion gripped them too tightly for talk—emotion born of gratitude for mercies vouchsafed. The thoughts filled both of them of how much worse things might have been.

But with these first few emotional minutes over, Blake expressed his willingness to talk, and to hear from Tinker all that had occurred since the frightful moment when the car had collapsed and hurtled over into that dreadful chasm.

"It's wasn't an accident, guv'nor," Tinker told him. "It was part of a diabolical plot to get rid of you!"

Blake nodded his head.

"As I thought!"

"And as you said when you came to for a moment. I soon found out that it was so!"

"How, laddie, how?"

"A few minutes after, when a vile scoundrel started shoving rocks over the cliff! You might have been killed, only luckily you were well protected by a great boulder!"

"Gee! Who could the murderous cur have been?"

"I found that out. With Pedro's help I tracked him. Who dod you think it was?"

"I won't try to guess. Tell me!"

"It was Luke Samways!"

"Luke Samways!" Blake's voice drew out the repeated name in a long, incredulous echo. "Surely not! It's impossible!"

"It isn't, guv! It's true. I tracked him. I've proof!"

"I—I can't believe it. Old Luke Samways! It sounds incredible. But tell me about your proofs! Tell me all—every detail!"

Tinker did so. He told him of the crutch tracks, of the odd boot tracks; of the discovery in the outhouse of the chalky boots and the chalky crutch. He finished by telling of Samways' drunken carousal at the Quarrymen's Rest.

Sexton Blake listened intently. Time after time he shook his head as if in doubt, yet how could he ignore all this evidence which Tinker had piled up.

"You have done well, laddie," was his first comment when Tinker had finished. "Luke Samways! Of all people to be mixed up in a vile plot like this, I should have said he was about the last. It seems almost impossible to believe it!"

"How can you do anything else, guv, after what I've told you?"

"Oh, I know, laddie, I know. Don't misunderstand me. You've done well—extremely well. You've discovered things that make it look as if he must be guilty. Yet—yet—you must forgive me— but I'm bound to say I can hardly believe he is guilty!"

"But how can he be other than guilty?"

Whatever Blake might have said was left unsaid. An interruption came. The bed-room door opened, and Dr. Alford entered. Usually calmness itself, he was now plainly agitated.

"Why, doctor, what's——"

"Haven't you heard the news—the terrible news—about Mr. Nicholas Dolby?"

"No. What about him?"

"He's been arrested?"

"Good heavens!"

"Yes, Inspector Yarrow arrested him at my house an hour ago, on the charge of murdering Richard Sharron!"

CHAPTER 20.
Still Another Arrest!

A BOMBSHELL bursting in the room could hardly have surprised Sexton Blake more.

"Why's Yarrow done it?" he asked in amazement. "What evidence has he got?"

"Plenty, apparently," answered the agitated doctor. "Enough to hang him, he told me!"

"But what is it? What's the nature of it?"

"That I don't know, Mr. Blake. I only saw Yarrow for a minute, and naturally he wouldn't say much. But he may call and see presently, especially as I told him you'd come back to consciousness."

"And he's still in the village, then?"

"He said he was going to be for a bit. From something he said, I fancy he's going to arrest a second man as well!"

"A second man! Who on earth can that be? What game's he playing at?" Blake was frowning, and spoke angrily. "I do hope he's not going to spoil things by making premature arrests!"

"You think the arrest of Nicholas Dolby is premature?" asked the doctor with some eagerness, for the apprehension of the man who had been his guest for the last few days had shocked him considerably, and he would willingly have believed him innocent.

"I don't know what evidence Yarrow has, but I should have said so!"

"You don't think Dolby killed Mr. Sharron?"

"I should have said not—but again, I don't know what Yarrow may have discovered since I was placed hors de combat. Where is Dolby now?"

"In the village lock-up for the time being. I gathered that when the second arrest had been made, the two prisoners would be taken over to Lummingstall."

"Who can the second man be?" queried Blake again.

The answer came from Tinker. A noise outside in the village street had drawn him to the window, and he was looking out.

"Gee-whiz, it's Luke Samways!" he exclaimed.

"What do you mean, laddie?"

"Samways is the second man! They've got him down there—in the street! He's handcuffed! They're taking him along to the village lock-up!"

Blake tried to rise up in his excitement, but the doctor restrained him.

"I do hope Yarrow isn't going to mess up things. Is Yarrow in charge of him, laddie?"

"Yes, with a couple of constables. Samways is hobbling along between them."

"Then run after Yarrow, and ask him if he'll please look me up after he's caged his bird! Jingo! How I hope he's not caging the wrong birds! Hurry, Tinker."

Tinker was off like a shot. He was back in two or three minutes, with the news that Inspector Yarrow would call on him directly he'd arranged about the prisoners being conveyed to Lummingstall.

"He said he was coming in any case, sir. He'll be along in a few minutes."

Those few minutes were a time of suspense for Blake. The news seemed to have excited him greatly, and the waiting for details seemed to make him chafe so much that Dr. Alford felt compelled to interpose.

"I'm not sure, Mr. Blake, that I ought to allow you to go into this matter. Your temperature is quite high enough already, and if——"

"Don't put obstacles in my way, I beg you, doctor. I simply must see Yarrow and hear what has led up to these amazing arrests. I do hope he's not making a fool of himself over them, but I'm half afraid——"

He didn't finish his sentence. Steps on the stairs interrupted him. A tap came at the door, and to the doctor's "Come in!" Yarrow himself entered.

He came straight across to Blake's bedside with a jaunty air.

"Heard you were better, Mr. Blake. Glad of it—very glad of it!"—and he took the patient's hand.

"Thanks, inspector. But what's all this I hear? You've been moving since I saw you last—during the last few hours."

"Ha, you've heard about it? The doctor's told you? Oh, yes, I should have told you about it if you'd been well enough. But as you were laid up, I couldn't. The time had come to strike, so I struck."

"Nicholas Dolby and Luke Samways, eh? You've taken them both?" said Blake with some dryness in his tone.

"You've got it. Surprised?"

"Very. Samways hadn't been thought of when I last saw you. If Dolby had, you'd ruled him right out!"

"So had you, Mr. Blake, so had you!" chortled Yarrow.

"I still do! I don't believe for a moment that Dolby killed Richard Sharron!"

Yarrow's eyes flashed a momentary resentment of the other's tone. Then his look changed to a triumphant grin.

"That's because you don't know what I know! Yet you ought to have known it first."

"What do you mean by that?"

"You were on the right track. That affidavit you faked up—the fingerprints on it!"

"Dolby's fingerprints? What about them?"

"They're the same as were found on the murdered man's throat!"

"Eh, what? What are you saying?" Blake sat up in his excitement.

"Identically the same." said Yarrow. "I've compared them with the photograph and—well, they're it! And I found something else on it, too!"

"Good heavens! Blake's excitement was growing intensely. "Are you sure?"

"Absolutely positive! No doubt about it at all. Like to see for yourself? Here's your wallet, and here's the photo!"

Blake opened the wallet and took out the faked affidavit. His hands trembled violently as he unfolded it, proof position of the way the excitement had shaken his nerve centres.

With the document opened, he stared at it for one moment. Then, without any warning at all save one stifled moan, he slipped down on his pillow, the papers fluttering from his hand!

"Fainted!" The doctor had darted forward. Anger mingled with the concern on his face. "It's been too much for him in his weak state. I was afraid it would be. I warned him!"

CHAPTER 21.
Nicholas Dolby's Silence!

THE earlier charge against John Wilson of murdering Mr. Sharron, had caused a great sensation in Lummingstall, as has already been made clear.

But that was as nothing compared to the sensation made the next morning when a second prisoner was placed in the dock and charged with the same offence. The stir that made among the inhabitants was nothing less than stupendous.

It was not be be wondered at considering the position. The prisoner who was now charged was no other than Nicholas Dolby, the dead man's partner. No ordinary partner either, but the man who had been made a partner by Sharron—itself an act which marked, so to say, the culminating kindness of one who had been Dolby's life-long friend.

Remembering that—the whole story was common knowledge—and remembering how Nicholas Dolby himself had always been the first to acknowledge Mr. Sharron's kindness to himself, and how he had never expressed himself in terms otherwise than of the deepest gratitude—remembering these things we say, it seemed altogether incredible that the grateful beneficiary should have killed his benefactor. The thing seemed so far to exceed belief as to stamp the charge on the part of the police as absurd—ludicrous—impossible!

This lack of belief increased the public curiosity, and they crowded the court to suffocation point in their desire to hear what possible justification the police could have for bringing such a ridiculous charge against one of their town's most highly-respected professional men.

They got more than one surprise. The first was Inspector Yarrow's confident air. Nothing suggestive of bluff about him. Only the manner of an efficient officer quite sure of his case—quite certain that he had got the right man!

Surprise the second was the demeanour of Nicholas Dolby. Instead of the clear-brained, alert man of law whom all had been accustomed to—for he himself had practised in that court quite a lot—he was utterly broken and dejected. Absolutely hang-dog!

Called upon to plead, he amazed not only magistrates and onlookers, but even Mr Gregg—one of his fellow-solicitors in Lummingstall who had been retained to defend him—by remaining utterly silent.

"Come, come, prisoner at the bar," urged the Clerk of the Court. "Answer the question. Do you plead guilty or not guilty?"

But still the prisoner kept silent—mute as an oyster. It was only after several whispered urgings by Mr. Gregg that Dolby nodded his head sullenly.

The defending solicitor turned to the bench.

"My client pleads 'Not Guilty!'" he said.

Naturally the plea was accepted, but it seemed strange that the prisoner had not made it himself, eagerly and emphatically. It created a bad impression, sowed the first seeds of prejudice against the accused man. As he sat in the dock with downcast eyes and woe-begone expression, even people who had refused to believe in the possibility of his guilt, began to wonder if——

But Mr. Gregg was speaking:

"In justice to my client," he was saying: "I think it should be explained that this terrible charge has come upon him with such surprise as to overwhelm him. Following on the recent death of the very old and dear friend whose loss he is mourning, the terribly ironical charge of compassing that death has come as an unspeakable shock. This has handicapped him greatly in instructing me. This places me at a great disadvantage in cross-examining witnesses, and therefore——"

Mr. Letbury, solicitor for the prosecution, rose with:

"Nothing will be done to handicap the prisoner's defence. No witnesses will be called to-day, except to give evidence of arrest. When that has been given, I shall ask for an adjournment."

"Very well," assented Mr. Gregg.

In the briefest possible way the prosecution solicitor then outlined the charge and called Inspector Yarrow. Standing in the witness-box, Inspector Yarrow said that, acting on information received, he had, early on the morning of the previous day, proceeded to the house of Dr. Alford at Dentwhistle where Nicholas Dolby was staying, and had then and there arrested him and charged him with the murder of Richard Sharron.

Up rose the defending lawyer.

"Did my client make any show of resistance?"

"Oh, no, sir."

"He consented to go quietly?"

"Quite, sir."

Mr. Gregg paused and bent over his papers. He was seemingly at a loss what else to ask, as he well might be. It was the prisoner himself who prompted him. He suddenly stood up and beckoned. It struck everybody, because it was the first and only time he seemed to rouse himself to take any interest in the proceedings.

Mr. Gregg bent towards him, and their heads remained together for a minute or two in whispered consultation. As a result, Mr. Gregg turned to the witness-box again and asked:

"Inspector Yarrow. You mentioned just now that in making this arrest you had acted on information received. May I ask what was the exact nature of that information?"

"I don't think I ought to answer that at this stage, sir."

"I think I am entitled to the information. I press for an answer!"

Here the prosecuting solicitor interposed:

"The information asked for will be given in evidence at a later hearing. My friend will then get it in the ordinary course. I respectfully submit, gentlemen"—this to the magistrates—"that it's against public policy to forestall what is to be sworn evidence, by anything in the nature of a casual statement."

"We uphold your objection," said the chairman, and Mr. Gregg had reluctantly to submit.

With the evidence of arrest completed by a constable being put into the box, Mr. Gregg said a little dismally:

"I reserve my further cross-examination."

Up got Mr. Letbury again.

"That is as far as I wish to carry the case to-day, your worship. I ask for a remand of the prisoner in custody for seven days."

"Yes," nodded the chairman.

And that completed the hearing for that day. But not the excitement. As will now be seen, a small but most important thing was to happen.

CHAPTER 22.
The Man with the Flat Ear!

THE court was empty save for two people. Those two were Mr. Letbury and Inspector Yarrow.

"The man's guilty sir. Apart from evidence, his face shows it!"

"Possibly," said Mr. Letbury. "I must admit the prisoner's loook and demeanour were all against him. Still, we don't hang people on their faces. The public executioner would be kept pretty busy if we did. We must have evidence."

"And we've got it, sir," answered Yarrow. "Notice how eager Dolby was to know what it was?"

"I did. Nothing struck me more than his suddenly rousing up to ask about that. It struck me as strange—considering how deadly that evidence is—that he should ask about it, and demand to see it."

"So it did me, sir. Because those fingerprints are deadly. Once they are produced, it will prove beyond all doubt that he was the man who choked Richard Sharron to death!"

"Quite so—quite so. That is, of course—what I mean to say is—I suppose there's no doubt at all about the fingerprints being the same?"

"Good lor, no, sir! I've gone over them two or three times most carefully. There's not the smallest doubt. But would you like to see for yourself?"

"Yes. I shall have to see and compare them for myself before the adjourned hearing, so we may as well go through them together now. Where are the photographs and the bogus affidavits?"

"Among your papers, sir. You'll find them in the dossier I handed to you."

"Ah, yes! Let's have a look!" The solicitor drew out a sheaf of papers from a huge envelope, big enough to take foolscap without folding. "Here we are—the photograph, at any rate. The other will be—where is the other?"

He spoke that last words with some petulance. He had gone quickly through all the papers without finding the one he wanted. He went through them again—slower this time—and his brows knitted.

"It isn't here!" he said. "You couldn't have given it to me!"

"But I did—I know I did, sir. With the others!" exclaimed the inspector. "It must be there. Let me look, I shall spot it at a glance, sir!"

Yarrow didn't spot it at a glance. He didn't spot it at all.

"It's gone, sir!" he gasped.

"Gone! But how could it go? I haven't budged from this seat! How can it have gone?"

"Can't say, sir." Yarrow looked almost distracted. "I only know I gave it you with the other papers, and now it's gone. Our strongest big of evidence—the clinching thing! It must have been stolen!"

"Stolen? Impossible! Why, and by whom?"

"What price the man with the flat ear?"

The last words came from the back of the court, and made them both swing round. It was no other than Tinker who had uttered them!

He was standing in the doorway of the court and apparently had just returned. For he had been present all through the brief hearing, but had gone out at the finish of it.

"Who are you?" demanded the solicitor sternly.

"Inspector Yarrow will tell you, sir," and the inspector did.

"Why, I'm pleased to meet you, Mr. Tinker. Pleased to meet anybody so closely associated with the famous Mr. Sexton Blake. But what on earth did you mean by those words just now, about the man with the flat ear? Who's he?"

"The man who came and spoke to you just before the hearing began, Mr. Letbury."

The solicitor rubbed his chin in perplexity.

"I don't remember anybody—oh, yes, I do! A man came up to ask me something. A tall, thin, farmer-looking chap, with a hatchet face."

"And ferret eyes and a flat ear!" Tinker added.

"I didn't notice those things. But what about him? He's a farmer or something like that. He's got a dispute on about the sale of some farm implements, and wants to consult me about it. I told him to call at my office later on to-day. You don't think he had anything to do with taking that document?"

"It's gone, anyhow, and he was the only person who came near you. And I don't think he is a farmer!"

"Why not?"

"Well, I've seen him before for one thing."

"When—where?"

"Night before last. Over at Dentwhistle. He was standing drinks to Luke Samways with some other strangers."

"H'm. That may be queer. At the same time there may be nothing in it. He's to call on me at four o'clock this afternoon, so I shall be better able to judge then."

"If he calls. I rather doubt it."

"Why?"

"Because I think he's a fraud. He pitched that yarn about consulting you, so as to pinch that paper. I think he's one of the gang Mr. Blake's been after for some days."

Yarrow made a fidgety movement. This mention of a gang again rather irritated him, but he said nothing.

"I don't see why he shouldn't call on me," the solicitor said. "He seemed genuine enough."

"Don't think he will, sir, for another reason," asserted Tinker. "He's gone off in a car to Burnley."

"How do you know that?"

"Saw him start. I watched him from the moment I recognised him in court. That was when he moved up to speak to you. I watched him all the time, and followed him when he left the court. He joined some pals waiting with a big car near by, and I heard them tell the driver 'Burnley.'"

"Wonder you didn't follow if you were so suspicious," put in Yarrow.

"No need. Somebody else is following, Barry, one of the guv'nor's confidential men. He arrived here this morning. I wired for him directly I knew the guv'nor would be out of action for a time. Barry's gone after the car on a motor-bike, so we may hear more about 'em later."

Mr. Letbury looked thoughtful. He was impressed by what Tinker had told them, and he turned to Yarrow.

"Rather serious that, inspector?"

"Nothing like so serious as it might have been, sir," replied Yarrow.

"Why not?"

"Because I'd already established the fact that the fingerprints on it were identical with those found on the dead man's throat!"

"Ah, yes, I see what you mean. We can easily take Nicholas Dolby's fingerprints again, eh?"

"Just so, sir. And it's suggested a nice little dramatic coup which we can bring off at the next hearing. I'll tell you what I mean later on."

"Right, inspector. I must cut off now. If that farmer chap does turn up, I'll let you know."

"And I'll let you know if I get any news from Burnley," said Tinker. "I'm going over to the guv'nor at Dentwhistle now, I'll 'phone you from there."

Without further parley, Tinker hurried off. After a little more talk, Yarrow and Mr. Letbury also separated.

While the inspector was certainly disturbed by the incident, since it suggested enemies working actively against him, the loss of the actual document did not greatly worry him.

He had had plenty of opportunity to examine it and compare the fingerprints thereon with those found on the throat of the murdered man. He had so compared them, and he had established beyond all doubt, that the fingerprints were the same. Therefore, since the document had served its purpose, its loss did not greatly matter. The theft of it had come too late to save Nicholas Dolby from the incriminating evidence—the absolutely deadly evidence—it contained.

To anybody calmly reviewing the course of recent events, it would have seemed rather more than strange, that since the document had been successfully filched from Sexton Blake's pocket, it should have been returned to Inspector Yarrow, and so allowed him to establish that deadly evidence. The second robbery of the document indicated a desire of the enemy to keep it out of the possession of the police. That was not to be wondered at. But why should it have been returned after the first robbery?

That was a problem that baffled Yarrow altogether. It took him so completely out of his depth that he jibbed at wading in to consider it at all.

He resolved to waive all the puzzling side issues and tangled details, and to keep to the main question. Sexton Blake had cleverly obtained Dolby's fingerprints on that bogus affidavit, while he, Yarrow, had discovered that the fingerprints on the document tallied in every detail with the fingerprints found on the dead man's throat.

That meant that it was Dolby who had killed Richard Sharron. It was proof of his guilt which nothing could shake.

CHAPTER 23.
Inspector Yarrow's Coup Goes Wrong!

A FULL week had passed and the day for the adjourned hearing had come.

For Tinker that week had been a time of disappointment, gloom, and suspense. Barry's visit to Burnley had yielded next to nothing. He had certainly followed the car to a public-house in that town, and by entering the bar had heard one of the four men who had travelled in the car, address the suspect as "Larry Dwyer." He had also seen them with their heads together over certain documents. But whether one of these was the stolen affidavit he could not get near enough to see, but since it was on blue paper, considered it might well be.

Gathering from their talk that they intended to stay the night at Burnley, he, too, booked a room, with the intention of further watching their movements.

To his dismay, on rising in the morning he found that Dwyer and the others had gone. Barry had been early, but they had been earlier, and they had taken their leave in the car by which they had come, before daybreak.

Where they had set out for, Barry could not discover. Primed with the number of the car and a full description of the men, he made many inquiries in and about the town. He drew blanks everywhere. Nobody of whom he inquired could give him any sort of definite information. Depressed at his failure, he had returned to Dentwhistle to report, and to lend Tinker a hand in any other direction that might become necessary.

As a matter of fact, however, neither he nor Tinker had been able to do very much during the rest of the week. This was mainly because they did not quite know in what direction to exercise their activities. Never before had they so utterly felt the lack of Sexton Blake's guidance and advice.

And that, during this time, was absolutely impossible to get. Because, during all those weary nights and days, Blake still lay in a condition in which he could not be questioned or worried in any way with current events.

It was true that once or twice he regained partial consciousness, but for the most part he lay in a comatose state. This was all the more curious because during that time his body was rapidly on the mend. The broken ribs were knitting up splendidly. As far as his physical condition was concerned, he showed every sign of being fit as a fiddle in extraordinarily quick time.

Consequently, his state of coma puzzled the doctor not a little, and he was glad to act on Tinker's suggestion to get a specialist—an old friend of Blake's—down from London to see the baffling patient.

The specialist diagnosed the case as one of a curious kind. It was due, in the first place, to a severe shock to the nerve centres from the plunge over the chasm, and, in the second, to some emotional crisis arising out of the sight of the document which Inspector Yarrow had handed him, and which must have given Blake a secondary shock of a somewhat severe sort.

This latter pronouncement, which the specialist made with all confidence, only served to puzzle Tinker the more. He could conceive of no other than a pleasurable emotion coming to Blake, on finding that the missing document had once more been found. How, then, could that have caused such an "adverse shock," as the physician suggested? Yet the latter was quite certain it must have been an "adverse shock" of some kind.

As to recovery, that might be a slow process, or it might come about with the suddenness of the sock itself. One thing was sure, that when the recovery did come, it would be a lasting one. The great improvement in his physical condition ensured that.

During Blake's periods of semi-consciousness—if his state could be so called—some rather odd things had occurred. While incapable of coherent speech, or of answering questions, he had, in a sort of partial delirium, given vent to some strange impressions.

These all had a bearing on the tangled problem he had been investigating, and in nearly every instance brought Inspector Yarrow's name into it.

"Hope Yarrow doesn't make a fool of himself!" "Don't spoil things by premature action, Yarrow!" "Don't arrest Dolby on any account—yet!" "Wait till we know more!" "These other people may have been in it but we haven't spotted the principal yet!"

Such were some of the definite phrases that emerged from a mass of incoherencies during his semi-delirious mutterings. To Tinker they seemed highly pregnant with meaning. Yet what precisely did they mean? What was really lying in Blake's brain to be thus half-hidden, and yet half-revealed by these subconscious ravings?

Tinker would have given much to know, but, alas, it was impossible!

This, then, was the position a week later, when the day for the adjourned hearing had arrived.

The court was even more crowded than before. The stage was set for as thrilling a scene as that or any other police-court had ever witnessed!

Once again a prelinary survey revealed some little surprises. First among these was the entirely different demeanour of the prisoner. Nicholas Dolby had become a changed man from the previous week.

No longer did he appear as a weak, broken, depressed creature. He was now once again the energetic, alert, clear-brained and clear-sighted man that had won him his position as one of the smartest lawyers in the district.

Anxious he still was, of course. Innocent or guilty, to be placed in the dock charged with murder, is a position to breed anxiety. But mingled with that perfectly natural state was a suggestion of intense and righteous indignation at having such a monstrous charge hurled at him. And in his general bearing, and in his many whispered consultations with his advocate, Mr. Gregg, was an air of confidence, an indication of sureness that he would be able to clear himself, and would emerge from his terrible ordeal with his name cleared and his character and reputation trimphantly vindicated.

But Inspector Yarrow was confident, too. More so even that last week. If ever man was sure of his case, Yarrow was that day!

A duel then between two men who were equally certain of victory! Which was to win?

With the stage set, so to say, the curtain went up on the second act—the vital act—of this real life drama.

Certain preliminaries passed without challenge from the prisoner or his solicitor, Mr. Gregg. These preliminaries included a reading over the evidence of arrest given the previous week.

Then came the first witness. This was Constable Stack, who recounted the circumstances under which Richard Sharron had been found dead—killed, as was at first thought, by the bullet wound in the thigh.

This witness was not questioned by Mr. Gregg. The latter had previously announced his intention to postpone his cross-examination till a later occasion. This was a little surprising to the general public, who did not know its inner meaning. The secret of that remained for the time being in the clever brains of the prisoner himself and his defending solicitor.

Perhaps it had to do with the dramatic coup which Inspector Yarrow had planned. They may have got some hint that it was intended to spring some devastating surprise on them, and maybe they were reserving all their energies to fight that!

Dr. Alford went into the box. He gave his evidence in a subdued and somewhat sad voice—as if he gave it reluctantly. Well he might, for he knew it must be against the man whom he had treated as a friend and a guest, and who had actually been arrested in his house!

Not that it was he who was to point the direct accusing finger at the man in the dock. Only the indirect. His evidence was to lead up to other evidence, to be given presently by Inspector Yarrow himself, and it was that which was to fix the guilt upon Nicholas Dolby.

What Dr. Alford testified to was the simple fact that Richard Sharron had not died from a bullet wound, but from suffocation. He had been choked to death by a man's hands. Further he bore witness that in the subsequent bruise induced by the terrible pressure, certain fingerprints had been photographed by the police in his presence, and prints from the negative were to be put in evidence by the police.

Presently these prints were put in—by Inspector Yarrow. When he went into the box, a few minutes later, it was felt by most of those present that the crucial moment was approaching.

There was something about the inspector's bearing that suggested finality! Something about the way in which he carried his sheaf of documents that conveyed the idea that among them he carried the trump card that would win the final trick!

And, in very truth, the great moment was approaching when the dramatic coup which the police officer had planned in conjunction with the prosecuting solicitor, Mr. Letbury, was to be brought off.

★ ★ ★

Nearly half an hour had passed. Inspector Yarrow had told his story in detail, and had replied to questions put to him by Mr. Letbury.

Then had come the most critical part—his cross-examination at the hands of Mr. Gregg. He had entered into this with the same easy confidence which had marked his manner throughout, and had answered the questions of the defending solicitor without any sort of hesitation or doubt.

For a time. Then had come a gradual change. With the tenacity of a bull-terrier, Mr. Gregg had stuck to his task, and had begun to badger him till Yarrow showed signs of getting rattled.

All the same, conscious of triumph presently, the police officer kept his head. With shrewd brain measured against shrewd brain, it became a duel of wits.

"Now, sir"—it was Mr. Gregg speaking—"you have asserted many things in your evidence-in-chief, among them some very startling ones. One very startling thing in particular to which I will now come."

At these words—addressed rather to the Bench than to the witness—Mr. Gregg squared his shoulders ere he faced full at Inspector Yarrow again.

"The most startling assertion—a most terrible accusation from my client's point of view—was to this effect: That the fingerprints found on the dead man's throat were made by Mr. Nicholas Dolby! Do you still maintain that?"

"Yes, sir. Most certainly."

"on what evidence? You have produced none."

Pardon me, sir. I stated in my evidence-in-chief that I had compared the finger-prints most carefully."

"With what?"

"With an impression of the prisoner's finger-prints!"

"Where is that impression?"

Inspector Yarrow hesitated, and looked across at Mr. Letbury, who had already risen to his feet and now interposed with:

"I thought I had already made that clear in my opening. The impression of the prisoner's finger-prints was obtained to a certain document by Mr. Sexton Blake, who has been engaged in this mystery in an unofficial capacity."

"Then why has Mr. Sexton Blake not been called to testify to this?" snapped Mr. Gregg.

"Because, unfortunately, he is too ill," answered Mr. Letbury. "Had he remained well, he undoubtedly would have compared the prints. As it was, Inspector Yarrow made the comparison."

"With what? Where is this precious document? This alleged impression of my client's finger-prints? I demand its production!"

Mr. Letbury answered:

"We are unfortunately unable to produce it because it has been stolen!"

"Stolen!" Mr. Gegg echoed the ward in a voice of thunder. "I protest against that. The assertion is only made to prejudice my client!"

"No, no, nothing is farther from our intention," replied Mr. Letbury. "Perhaps I should not have used the word stolen. I beg to withdraw it and substitute lost. The document has been lost!"

Mr. Gregg threw down his brief with a fine gesture of absolute disgust.

"Lost! Stolen—why not 'or strayed'?" he cried, and got his reward in a burst of laughter.

"Yes, yes," he commented when this had died down, "it would really be a laughing matter were it not so serious to my client. Really, really, I ask was ever such a piffling case presented in a court of law before? First, a most important witness fails to appear; secondly, a most damaging statement is put forward as evidence without a shred of proof."

He turned once more to Inspector Yarrow.

"You still assert that the finger-prints found on the dead man's throat were made by Mr. Dolby?"

"I don."

"Your sole evidence in support of that is your comparison with a second set of finger-prints alleged to have been taken by Mr. Sexton Blake? That is your sole evidence?"

"It is sufficient! It is conclusive!"

"But Mr. Sexton Blake—the all-important witness—is not here to give evidence?"

"Because he is too ill to attend."

"While the alleged document is not produced?"

"Because it has been stolen—that is, it is missing!"

Once again came that magnificent gesture of scorn from the defending solicitor.

"Missing witness—missing document! Do you seriously expect their worships to accept such flimsy evidence as this?"

"I do. I propose to give them proof that it is true!"

"How?"

Now was the turn of Inspector Yarrow for a triumphant gesture.

"I ask that the finger-prints of the prisoner at the bar be taken now—at this moment! They can then becompared with the photograph, and their worships can be guided by the result."

This was Yarrow's coup, and a buzz through the packed court marked the sensation it made.

If Mr. Gregg was taken aback he did not show it. He merely smiled as he faced the magistrates.

"I think that is quite a good suggestion. I welcome it as the readiest means of clearing my client of every vestige of suspicion. If your worships approve, please let it be done."

The chairman and the other magistrates nodded.

"Just one thing, though," said Mr. Gregg. "Who is to make the comparison of these two sets of finger-prints? It is rather technical work, and needs an expert."

"The expert is here," interposed the prosecuting solicitor. "Anticipating the need, we communicated with Scotland Yard. They answered us this morning by sending Inspector Travis, one of their chief finger-print experts. I trust my friend is ready to accept him as adjudicator in this matter?"

"Quite!" agreed Mr. Gregg. "Let us get on with it!"

But now a momentary objection came from quite an unexpected quarter—from the prisoner himself.

As a police officer approached him with the necessary materials for taking his finger-prints—these had been brought specially into court for that purpose—Nicholas Dolby suddenly asserted himself.

"Why am I to submit to this indignity?" he demanded angrily. "I am innocent! Why should I be submitted to this monstrous indignity?"

The faintest of faint smiles hovered on Yarrow's face for a second, while another sensational buzz passed through the court.

The prisoner's outburst, natural and righteous in some circumstances, was suspicious under these. Surely if he were innocent he sought to welcome the suggestion eagerly, since it would establish his innocence! Yet he was protesting—objecting! Did that mean that he was afraid?

Mr. Gregg, his solicitor, was whispering to him—advising him—pleading with him, it seemed. His pleading won. The lawyer turned to the bench.

"My client is naturally indignant at this odious affront, but is willing to be advised by me. He consents to having his finger-prints taken!"

It was done amid tense silence. It took but a few moments, everything being ready and the apparatus of the most effective kind.

Something else had to be done to fix the impression, but that only took a minute or two. Then all was ready, and the clerk of the court handed the two sets of finger-prints to Inspector Travis of Scotland Yard.

In workmanlike way the famous expert got to work with a powerful pocket lens. The silence could be felt as all watched him. No wonder. On this expert's decision depended the life of that other man in the dock!

Yet, as he scanned alternately one set of finger-prints and then the other, the expert gave no sign of what was in his mind. No emotion played upon his face at all, it remained a grave, impassive mask.

Five minutes passed—ten minutes—a time of almost unbearable suspense. Then the expert rose to his feet and addressed the bench.

"I have finished, your worships."

"You are ready to give your decision—under oath?"

"Yes, sir."

Inspector Travis was placed in the witness-box. The oath had been administered. Every eye was on him. The clerk of the court asked the vital questions:

"You have compared the prints taken of the fingers of Nicholas Dolby, the prisoner at the bar, with those found on the dead man's throat?"

"I have."

"Are the two sets identical?"

"They are not!"

"Not? Then your evidence is to the effect that Nicholas Dolby did not strange Richard Sharron?"

"He could not have done so! The two sets of finger-prints are only similar in superficials. In essentials they are absolutely different!"

Mighty the buzz that swept through the court now. It was hushed by Mr. Gregg rising to his feet with triumph in his eyes.

"That is conclusive," he cried. "On the prosecution's own evidence the innocence of my client is established beyond all doubt. I ask for his immediate discharge without a stain upon his high character!"

CHAPTER 24.
Sexton Blake Straighens the Tangle!

NICHOLAS DOLBY was a free man! Inspector Yarrow was a depressed man! One of the most depressed men in the world. He felt utterly crushed!

And utterly bewildered too! How it had all come about he couldn't begin to understand. Twenty-four hours passed to find him just as puzzled and nonplussed as he had been at that final dramatic moment in court, when Inspector Travis, of Scotland Yard, had exploded his myth, and, so to speak, hoisted him on his own petard!

Then, as he sat miserably in his office, came the first bright bit of news. A telephone message from Dentwhistle. It was to say that Sexton Blake had recovered consciousness at last, and would be glad to see him at the earliest possible moment.

Yarrow was pleased, of course. Greatly pleased at Blake's recovery. But it didn't raise his spirits in regard to the other matter. How could it? He had made an utter fool of himself over those finger-prints. He didn't know how he had done it, but he had.

Asked if he had anything to say about the prisoner being discharged at once, Yarrow had openly challenged Inspector Travis' verdict, and had asked to compare the fingerprints for himself.

The challenge had been accepted. He had seen the fingerprints.

Inspector Travis had stood beside him, had pointed out difference after difference, discrepancy after discrepancy; had proved utterly and absolutely that the two sets of fingerprints were not the same!

And Yarrow had had to admit that. In answer to the further questioning of the defending solicitor, he had not only to admit that he had made a terrible mistake, but abjectly to apologise to the magistrates for having done it, and for having brought such a grave charge against Mr. Dolby on quite inadequate evidence.

It had been the bitterest time of his life. What with Mr. Gregg's revilings, and the chairman of magistrates' stern reproof about official carelessness and inefficiency, he had never felt so wretched in all his police career.

And now, even if that career was not finished, even if presently his terrible blundering might not entail reduction in rank, or possible suspension from duty, it was all up with his chances of promotion.

Deservedly so, for his blunderings had been grievous indeed; how on earth had he come to make them? How had it happened that his previous comparison of the fingerprints had led to his bold accusation of Nicholas Dolby, while his second comparison, under Travis' guidance, had shown them to be entirely different, and made it impossible that Dolby could have been the murderer?

For the life of him he could not account for his amazing mistake. He was not conscious of any aberration of mind at the time of making the first comparison, yet that alone would account for his hideous error.

Such was his state of mind when, after twenty-four haunted hours, he received the message over the telephone, saying that Sexton Blake had recovered his senses, and wished to see him.

Wished to see him! Was Sexton Blake also going to revile him—to crow over him for his miserable blunder? He hoped not—he thought not. Sexton Blake wasn't the sort of crow over a fallen colleague. He was far too big a man. Well, he would go over to Dentwhistle and see him.

He started out at once, miserable as ever. Little did he dream of the tremendous surprise Sexton Blake had in store for him!

★ ★ ★

"I tell your, inspector, you mustn't reprove yourself too much. You haven't blundered as much as you think you have! You have made mistakes, and you made a tactical error in arresting Dolby prematurely. But though you made a bloomer, it isn't as grievous as you think, nor is it of the kind you think!"

It was Sexton Blake speaking, as he sat up in bed at the Quarrymen's Rest, at Dentwhistle, and he was speaking to the humiliated and contrite Yarrow.

Tinker and Dr. Alford were also present. From them had Sexton Blake already heard the story of the amazing court scene of yesterday, the story being repeated and the blanks filled in by Yarrow himself on arrival.

The inspector heard the famous detective's words in a kind of dream. He could hardly believe his ears.

"Not so grievous as I think," he groaned. Why no man could have made a bigger ass of himself than I have!"

"Oh, yes, they could. I tell you that although you've made a bloomer, it isn't so bad as you think, and it isn't of the kind you think. You've been tricked!"

"Tricked?"

"Yes. The enemy are a cunning lot. More ingenious and daring that you gave them credit for!"

"Cunning—ingenious—daring! I don't get you, Mr. Blake!"

"I'm not altogether surprised. You see, inspector, you and I were working on this business along different lines. While you were following up your own suspicions, I was following up mine which were different. Unluckily I was put out of action at a critical time. Had I not been, I should have taken action doubtless before now, and the upshot would have been different."

"Tell me what you mean," gasped Yarrow. "Tell me this first. How could I have made that mistake about Dolby's fingerprints? When your wallet was returned to me and I made the first comparison, I made out the fingerprints to be absolutely indentical with those found on the dead man's throat!"

"Yes."

"Yet when Dolby's fingerprints were taken in court, they turned out to be absolutely different from the other set."

"Quite so!"

"Why do you say 'quite so'? Weren't they the same?"

"Of course not!"

"But you distinctly told me that the fingerprints on the affidavit were Dolby's?"

"So they were. I still say that."

"But——"

"That paper returned in my wallet wasn't the original affidavit at all. It was a forgery!"

"Eh, what?"

"An impudent but clever forgery! I saw that directly you showed it to me! Do you remember?"

"Of course I remember. It was just then that you seemed to get a shock and went off into a faint!"

"That was what gave me the shock. The discovery that my affidavit—the document Tinker had most carefully written out—had been closely imitated! It was one of the most impudent forgeries I've ever known!"

"Heavens! but I still don't see why it was done."

"The motive was a subtle one. It was done to gain time—to give some of the principal villains time to get away!"

"How?"

"Consider this: Supposing the wallet had contained the actual affidavit I had drafted? That would have shown the real fingerprints of Nicholas Dolby. Supposing you had compared those with the others on the photograph—what would have happened?"

"I should have discovered they bore no resemblance and should never dreamt of arresting Dolby!"

"Exactly! There would have been no red herring drawn across the trail. You would have devoted your energies to getting on the track of the real murderer, instead of wasting a precious week in charging Dolby!"

"You mean to say that Dolby lent himself to this trick? Allowed himself to be charged with murder so as to give the real murderer a chance to get away?"

"Yes. He knew perfectly well he could clear himself when it came to comparing his fingerprints with the others. And it gained time for the other—has, in fact, given him a clear week to get away."

"But if you're right, it clearly shows that Dolby was in it, even if he didn't do the actual killing!"

"Of course he was in it, and of course I'm right. It's a case of the most elementary deduction."

"But the real murderer put his fingerprints on the forged document. Why did he do that? Bit of a tactical error, wasn't it?"

"Might seem so from one point of view, but there were sound reasons for it. Two, anyway. Reason No. 1, is that it wouldn't be easy to get anybody else to give his fingerprints to a document connected with a murder case!"

"They might have got another member of the gang, surely, instead of the actual murderer giving away his trade mark like that."

"Mightn't be easy to induce him. Besides that, there was another important reason. Other fingerprints wouldn't have done. They had to be the murderer's in order to ensure an arrest being made and time being gained."

"I see what you mean. They knew that on getting the document back I should assumre that they were Dolby's?"

"Exactly! They also guessed you would at once compare them with those on the dead man's throat, and, finding them similar, that you would arrest Dolby. In that way they'd gain time."

"Yes, quite, only——"

"Only what?"

"Well, you see, Mr. Blake, supposing you'd been all right, you would have defeated their purpose by twigging that the document was a forgery."

"Yes, I know. But they knew I was out of action. They'd taken care I should be. That's another sign of their diabolical cunning. They guessed you'd have to deal with the document, and that you wouldn't detect the forgery. It wasn't easy, for it was cleverly done. That, by the way, affords further evidence of their working in with a highly accomplished gang. The cleverness of the double theft affords further evidence still."

"Look like it, certainly. That makes it all the more remarkable that they should have employed a poor yokel like Luke Samways to help them."

Blake shook his head.

"They didn't!" he said emphatically. "That was just a blind, I'm certain. Part of the red-herring trail they've been giving us. Some of the gang got Samways out of the way that night. Lushed him up in the bar downstairs. Plain why they did that."

"Why?"

"To get hold of his boots and crutch, and so mislead Tinker in the way they did."

"Then Samways wasn't in it at all?"

"No more to do with it than you or I. You haven't charged him yet?"

"No, I was waiting for further evidence against him."

"You'll never get it. You'll have to drop the charge and release him. Poor Jack Wilson will have to be released, too. That'll require a certain formalities, of course, but when he is released, we shall have to try and get him some compensation."

Yarrow nodded. By this time he had quite come to realise that Wilson was quite innocent, and had been the victim of unfortunate circumstances.

"How far do you think Dolby was in it?" he asked suddenly.

"Up to the neck!" answered Blake. "I believe he connived at the murder. I firmly believe him to have been an accessory after the fact. I shan't be surprised if we dicover he was an accessory before the fact as well!"

"Gee! I wonder who could have done the actual murder?"

Blake didn't answer that question immediately. He suddenly closed his eyes and pursed his lips, the while he thought hard. Then he said slowly:

"I'm not sure—yet!"

"But you suspect some particular person!" exclaimed Yarrow.

Very strongly!"

"Good heavens! Who?"

"I can't say—yet. I'll name no names—yet. But it's somebody with a strong hold over Nicholas Dolby!"

"That's a sure thing, or Dolby would never have shielded him by allowing himself to be arrested. But, of course, that's explainable. If Dolby was an accessory, he had to agree to the others wishes to save his own neck!"

Blake moved his head slowly.

"That's all true, but there's another reason. The hold the murderer has over Dolby is of a different and a stronger kind."

"Don't get you—don't begin to get you! Won't you tell me what's in your mind, Mr. Blake!"

Before Blake could answer that there came an interruption. Barry hurried in.

"A cablegram from New York, sir," he said, and handed it to Blake.

The latter read it. It was in code, but he quickly deciphered its meaning. As he did so his set jaw relaxed, and he turned to Yarrow with a grim smile.

"You asked me a question a minute ago, inspector. I couldn't have answered it then. I can now! You asked who the murderer of Richard Sharron was!"

"Yes—yes, you've got it?"

"I have. His name is Jacob Ludford."

"Jacob Ludford! Never heard it before. Who is he? A friend of Nicholas Dolby?"

"More than that—closer than that! He's Dolby's father!"

CHAPTER 25.
An Astounding Confession!

SHEER amazement held Inspector Yarrow spellbound for a minute. When he could find his tongue it was to gasp out:

"Nicholas Dolby's father! What in the name of heaven do you mean?"

"Simply what I say."

"But I thought his father had been dead years, ever since he was a child! Even Mr. Gregg in court yesterday, in speaking of the cordial relations between the two partners, referred to Dolby's gratitude to the man who had shown him lifelong kindness ever since he was a tiny orphan boy. That was his exact phrase—'a tiny orphan boy.'"

"A very good phrase, too, to touch the hearts of the magistrate. I've no doubt Mr. Gregg believed it. Everybody did. But it isn't true, nevertheless. Dolby's father is still alive."

"Why has Dolby concealed the fact?"

"For the same reason that he changed his name from Ludford to Dolby. Jacob Ludfordis one of the biggest scoundrels unhung. It's about time now that he did hang. He should do before long, for this cablegram is the last link in may chain of evidence, and proves him to have murdered Richard Sharron."

"How does it do that?"

"It's from the New York police. They identify the fingerprints found on Richard Sharron's throat as Jacob Ludford's!"

"How on earth could they have seen the fingerprints?"

"I had them telegraphed from London before I was taken ill. My friend, David Manistry, of the 'Daily Searchlight,' helped me in that with their wonderful new television installation. I'll tell you all about this and other things concerning Ludford later on. Isn't time at the moment. We've got to get busy."

"What to do?"

"First this is to wireless all ships that have sailed from Liverpool during the past week."

"What's the idea?"

"It's likely Jacob Ludford may be aboard one of them. It's almost a sure thing he was one of the men who gave Barry the slip at Burnley. If he hasn't sailed already, he'll try to soon. Therefore all the ports must be warned and watched. Barry must get across to Liverpool and put that in hand right away."

"Can't I lend a hand?" asked Yarrow.

"There's a job in Lummingstall for you, inspector. You've got to arrest Nicholas Dolby again!"

"Eh—what? I think I've had about enough of arresting Dolby!" exclaimed Yarrow, with a shudder.

"The charge will be different this time. 'Being an accessory to the murder,' instead of being the actual murderer. You'll be on quite safe ground this time, I assure you."

"When am I to do it?" the inspector asked dismally, not seeming to relish the job a bit.

"I'll give you the tip. But before the arrest is made, before even he gets a hint of this new charge, I'm going to see him."

"You—are you well enough?"

"Quite! My body's been well enough for days past, and now that I've come back to my senses—oh, yes, I'm well enough. Know where Dolbye is?"

"In Lummingstall. Staying at the Lion Hotel. I'm told he went back to this office directly the magistrates discharged him as if nothing had happened. He's there to-day too. Marvellous nerve, considering how utterly broke he seemed at the first hearing!"

"We should find him then if we went over now?" said Blake looking at his watch.

"I daresay he'll be there till six o'clock."

"Good! Then we'll go together. I just want a few minutes with Barry to give him instructions, then I'll be ready."

★ ★ ★

For a man who had been in the dock and stood the charge of murder, Nicholas Dolby looked remarkably fit and well.

So thought Sexton Blake, when, a couple of hours later, he sat facing him in his office at Lummingstall. Blake had been admitted only after some little difficulty. Dolby had sent out word refusing to see him at first, and only the detective's persistence had made him change him mind.

Now that they were together, the solicitor had mounted the high horse; had adopted the scornful and indignant manner of a man who had been shamefully ill-treated.

"Now then, Mr. Sexton Blake, what do you want?" he asked with blustering arrogance.

Sexton Blake was used to handling all sorts of men. He could handle the blustering and arrogant type as easily as any.

"If we're going to have a talk, Mr. Nicholas Dolby, mightn't it as well be a civil talk?"

"Civil!" fumed and lawyer. "Civility to you! To a man who has had the insolence and audacity to bring an outrageous charge against me!"

"Hadn't you better keep to the facts?" Blake's quiet, almost soft tones, were in striking contrast to the other's thunder. "I didn't bring the charge against you. I have never brought any charge against you!"

"It was through you, anyway. It was you who disguised yourself and played cursed trick on me with a pretended affidavit! It was that that led to my being charged in so monstrous a way! It is mean spies like you who——"

"Think it's wise to start calling names?" put in Blake. "It's not at all a nice or polite game, and sometimes it leads to recriminations, doesn't it?"

"Recriminations! Confound you, what do you mean?"

"Well, calling names is an easy game, isn't it, at which two can play!"

"Look here, you infernal imitation policeman! Don't sit there making your vile insinuations, or I'll call in witnesses and make you pay dearly for it!"

"That's for you!" Blake said with an airy wave of his hand. "If you like to have witnesses to hear me call you by a certain name, do so!"

Dolby sprang out of his chair.

"I've had enough of this!" he cried, edging round so that he stood with his back to his desk facing Blake. "What do you mean by those last words? What do you mean by a certain name? Out with it!"

"No, I won't out with it!" responded Blake. "I'll get on with the business. I came to ask a certain question. You're a lawyer, and my question is in the cause of law and justice. Will you answer it?"

"How can I say till you've asked it? What is it?"

Blake paused just one second, fixed the blustering solicitor with his eyes, then asked:

"Where is Jacob Ludford?"

What a change came over the lawyer! In an instant all the arrogance seemed to ooze out of him, while the flush of indignation faded from his face and left it grey and bloodless, every little nerve of it quivering! It was sheer will-power that enabled him partly to master himself and to gasp out in hoarse tones:

"Jacob Ludford! What do you mean—who do you mean? The name is strange to me. I know nobody——"

"Oh, yes you do! Come, come, think again! By answering my question, you will save the police some trouble, and may possibly do yourself some good. Now then where is—— Oh, no you don't!"

The last four words were a sudden exclamation. As Blake uttered them he leapt forward—heedless of his barely-healed ribs—and in a moment had pinned the lawyer's arms to his sides.

Simultaneously a shot rang out, and a bullet buried itself harmlessly in the floor at Blake's feet! The next instant and the detective had wrenched from the lawyer's grasp the revolver he had suddenly drawn from a drawer of the desk against which he had been leaning!

The game was up. By that impulsive action Nicholas Dolby had thrown in his hand.

At the sound of that shot, two clerks came running in from the outer office, looking very nervous. A moment after, and three men came dashing in from the street.

They were three police officers, with Inspector Yarrow at their head. And they were not nervous!

"Take him!" cried Blake. "I charge him with firing a revolver with intent to do me grievous bodily harm! Other charges will follow, but that will do for the time being."

"No, it won't do!" shrieked Nicholas Dolby as the handcuffs snapped upon his wrists. "Make another charge now! The most serious charge! Charge me with murder. Listen! Take note of my words—my confession! It was I—Nicholas Dolby—who killed my later partner and benefactor, Richard Sharron!"

CHAPTER 26.
The Full Truth at Last.

IT was twenty minutes or so later. Nicholas Dolby was for a second time under arrest, lodged in Lummingstall police-station. Beyond making his astounding confession, he had refused to say another word, but surely he had said enough!

In the inspector's private office at the same police-station, Yarrow and Sexton Blake sat together. The former's face was a study in amazement and bewilderment. That "astounding confession" had in his own words "fairly got him down."

"Is it true?" he asked Blake, not for the first time, though Blake had not answered till now.

"No!"

"Then why's he made it?"

"To try and save his father—Jacob Ludford!"

"Mean to say he'd do such a thing—a vile scroundrel like him?"

"Oh, it's not quite the noble act of self-sacrifice it might seem. There's a little bit of filial affection in it, no doubt, but there's something else as well. He's made this pretended confession in order to gain more time. If he can persuade us to stop looking for Jacob Ludford, it'll give him a still better chance of getting away!"

"But if we fail to find Ludford, he'll risk his own neck, won't he?"

"He knows perfectly well he won't. Remember, he's a lawyer, and a cunning one at that. He knows perfectly well that no judge ever acts on uncorroborated confession. It's unlikely that the court would even accept his plea of guilty in a murder charge. Anyway, the judge would never act on his confession alone. He'd require corroborative evidence. The murder would have to be proved. And we can't prove that Nicholas Dolby killed Richard Sharron, because he didn't. Dolby knows we can't prove it. Therefore, he doesn't mind putting up this bogus confession!"

"I still don't quite see his game!"

"Surely you do. Dolby himself sees it very plain. If he's charged with the murder—he alone—it means we waste weeks. Supposing we got him committed for trial, as we should do. Weeks and weeks—perhaps a month or two before the Assizes. What then? At the last minute, just as we think we're pinning him down, out he comes with that rebutting evidence. Those fingerprints on the throat! They're not his! He'll prove they're not his! Down breaks our charge of murder. We could then charge him with other things; but he'd escape hanging, and meantime Jacob Ludford would have got clean away!"

"Ha! I see what you mean now!"

"But we're not going to fall into the little trap he's laid for us. We're not going to charge him with committing the murder. We're going to fix him with being an accessory to it! And we're going to play for time. Just as much time as it takes us to lay Jacob Ludford by the heels. Once we've got 'em side by side in the dock, we can proceed with the capital charge!"

★ ★ ★

"What about Jacob Ludford, Mr. Blake?" It was Yarrow asking again, after a few minutes' pause. "How did you find out about him? How did you find that Dolby was his son? There are fifty things I want to know. I'm all in a fog."

"Let me dissipate the fog. Let me tell you the full story as I've gradually come to know it."

It took some time to tell the tale in all its details, but this was the gist of the first part of it.

Nicholas Dolby wasn't an orphan—as for years it had been supposed he was—at the time kindly old Mr. Sharron had taken him under his wing. He was the only child of Jacob Ludford, an arch-crook!

Some twenty years before, while practising as a criminal solicitor in London, Mr. Sharron had come into contact with him. As the outcome of a charge of manslaughter, Ludford had been sentenced to imprisonment for life, being lucky to escape the charge of murder—and hanging!

Out of pity for the criminal's young son, Nicholas—then a small boy—kind hearted Mr. Sharron had had him educated, and had afterwards taken him into his office. There he had proved so industrious and competent, that the elder solicitor had given him his "articles," pushed him on, and ultimately given him a share in the business as junior partner.

But born of such a father, Nicholas Dolby—he had changed his name from Ludford at Mr. Sharron's own suggestion, so as not to handicap his future—had a criminal streak in him. This he indulged when Mr. Sharron was suddenly struck down by illness and was compelled to leave the management of the business to him. Left to himself, Dolby began to realise certain securities entrusted to the firm's charge, and to misappropriate the money!"

He had thought he was comparatively safe in doing this, inasmuch as he thought Mr. Sharron would never be well enough to take any hand in affairs again.

The sudden and unexpected return of the senior partner to business scared him. His scare rose to panic when he found that it was Mr. Sharron's intention to go through all the manipulated bonds and securities the next day!

Now all this had happened at a strangely dramatic moment. It coincided with the sudden visit of Jacob Ludford to his son. Some two years before Ludford had been released from prison, and had smuggled himself to the United States.

His long years of imprisonment, which might have been expected to wean him from criminal paths, did no such thing. After a few months in America, he had got into trouble there. Robbery was the crime he committed, and for this he served a term of fifteen months, at the end of which he had been deported.

Shipped back to England, he had first of all got into touch with some members of the crook gang to which he had formerly belonged. These men had broken away from the main gang in London, and of late had made Liverpool their centre.

It happened just then that certain members of the gang were in low water, and were urgently in need of funds to carry out some big robbery they had for some months been planning. Needing five hundred pounds for this purpose, and finding himself so near to the neighbourhood where his lawyer son lived, Jacob Ludford resolved to try and get the money advanced by him.

Thus it had come about that on the very night Mr. Sharron had decided to stay at the green bungalow, Jacob Ludford was also being sheltered there by his son!

"So much,' said Blake, when he had come to this point in his story, "I found out from certain correspondence I found at the bungalow, and from certain innocent but significant information I obtained from Mrs Samways, who, as you know, did the cleaning there. And practically that's as far as I can speak with certainty."

"And it's quite a lot," said Yarrow. "You astound me at having found out so much. It carries us to the night of the murder, but breaks off before it gets to the murder."

"That's so," agreed Blake. "As to what took place on the fatal night. I have no absolutely definite knowledge. There's a hiatus which still needs filling in. But, knowing what happened before, and also what happened after, it isn't a very difficult matter to fill it in."

"You mean you can guess what happened?"

"I think so. Especially as the guessing is helped by the results of various inquiries I've made as to the character of Jacob Ludford, as well as of his son."

"And what is your guess about it all?"

"Well, I've reconstructed the events of that night this way," went on Blake. "I think that on Ludford's asking for that five hundred pounds, Nicholas Dolby had to refuse him. This because he hadn't got the ready money. Though he had misappropriated a lot of cash, he had kept none of it. Dolby is a born and reckless gambler. What he gained by crime he lost by mad plunging Bookmakers and bucket-shop keepers have scooped the pool.

"Ludford, I fancy, must have doubted his son's imprecuniosity. To convince him of its reality, Dolby confided in him the story of his defalcations. More, he told his father of Sharron's intention to go through certain documents on the morrow, and the great danger in which this placed him. He made it transparently clear that he was on the verge of exposure, ruin, and probably imprisonment.

"This roused the crook-father. I've reason to believe that he's always been a heavy drinker. I believe he drank heavily that night, and I believe that in his bemused brain grew a scheme to kill Richard Sharron, as the only means of saving his son from utter disgrace and ruin."

Blake paused a moment. A far-away look was in his eyes as he reconstructed the terrible thing that had happened that night. Then he went on:

"I believe that that night he did kill Richard Sharron! While the old man lay asleep, he stole in on him and choked him to death!"

Yarrow gasped.

"And the bullet wound in the thigh!"

"Was fired for one of two purposes. Either because in his death agony poor old Richard Sharron put up some resistance, or to put us off the scent."

"How do you mean?"

"Take our attention off the throat bruise, and make it look like the act of a burglar. I'm rather inclined to think it was the latter—a deliberate attempt to fasten suspicion on a burglar—to be exact, on Jack Wilson!"

"Ha, where exactly does Wilson come in?"

"As a perfectly innocent man! Of that I'm dead sure. We can believe Jack's tale just as he told it. He was a tramp. Beat to the wide. Hungry, exhausted, and drenched to the skin, he was just seeking shelter that night—that and nothing more."

"Just at the time when the murder was being done?"

"At that precise moment."

"But how did it come about?"

"Something like this. Whether Nicholas Dolby took a hand in the actual murder or not, I can't say. But he was there—knew it was done, probably knew about it while it was being done. And just as it was being done he probably heard a sound outside. Looking out, he caught sight of Jack wilson trying to open the garage door."

"Ha, and he rushed out and held him up with the revolver?"

"No, not Dolby. It was Jacob Ludford who did that! That explains what Wilson meant—I told you the story—of its not being Dolby who knocked him out with the bludgeon. It was Ludford."

"But it was Dolby whom Luke Samways saw and——"

"Just so. It was Dolby who planned that. He knew it would be all up if Ludford were seen about. On the other hand, he saw a means of cleverly manipulating circumstances so as to clear himself and his crook-father by fastening the crime on somebody else!

"That somebody—Jack Wilson—was ready to his hand! Things had happened that called for prompt action. A shot had been fired. Somebody might hear it—Luke Samways, for example—and come to see what was amiss!

"Dolby acted on that hypothesis. He doubtless discovered from the light in the cottage hard by that Samways was moving about. What did he do? He first helped his father to lift Jack Wilson into the garage and place him on the floor. Then, carrying out the evil scheme he had thought of, he removed Wilson's boots. With these in his hands he returned to the room where the dead body was. There he made clear imprints of the boots, not only on the floor, but on the window-ledge. Then he returned and put the boots on Wilson's feet again!"

"And after that?" panted Yarrow, aghast at the way the case had been reconstructed.

"After that he did what we know. He knew by this time that Samways was about. Instantly, therefore, after hiding Ludford away, he fired the revolver again and then set up his shouts for help!"

"Which quickly brought Samways along?"

"Exactly, and the rest we know."

"And the revolver—what became of that?"

"It was found by my dog Pedro, among some scrub in the quarry. I found that the weapon belonged to Ludford."

"Ah, Ludford! By the way, Mr. Blake, how on earth did you first get on to the idea of his being Dolby's father?"

"An old birth certificate which I found among some other papers at the bungalow. It happened to coincide with Dolby's birthday, and that set me thinking and raking about. It didn't take me long then to discover that Nicholas Dolby was really and truly Nicholas Ludford. Full of wonder as to why he had changed his name, I went on, and found out all about Jocob Ludford's career as a crook years ago. An old diary found among Mr. Sharron's papers at Southport helped me greatly in that and other matters!"

"Well, you've done the trick this time, Mr. Blake! Done it splendidly! Beaten poor me all ends up! Only one thing remains to be done now, and that is to capture Jacob Ludford himself. Think you'll do that?"

"I've every hope. Barry's busy in Liverpool wirelessing and doing other things. I've every hope we shall get news of Jacob Ludford before long!"

CHAPTER 27.
Conclusion.

SEXTON BLAKE proved to be right in his confidence, but it took some five weeks to happen. Then came the calbed information that Jacob Ludford and two companions had been arrested as they stepped ashore from a steamer from Liverpool at Rio de Janeiro, in Brazil.

This was in accord with the instructions of Sexton Blake—who had circularised all possible ports by wireless and cable—and the message further said that the men would be detained pending further instructions from the English police, to whom, of course, Sexton Blake had by now handed the case over.

Those instructions did not take long in the giving. Following certain extradition formalities, Inspector Yarrow—accompanied by other officers, including one from Scotland Yard—made his first journey across the Atlantic.

A few weeks later, and the police party arrived back at Lummingstall with the redoubtable Jacob Ludford and the other two prisoners in charge.

Pending their return, Sexton Blake had more than once visited Nicholas Dolby, who was in prison on remand. More than once he had given the solicitor a chance to mitigate his own share in the infamous crime of murder by revealing the full truth of the share Jacob Ludford had played in it.

But now, in very truth, Dolby did show a redeeming side to his character. Embezzler, plotter, unscrupulous villain though he was, he yet showed that he retained some spark of humanity and a considerable share of filial affection. Though it was pointed out to him that he might save his own neck by telling the whole truth about the murder, he refused resolutely to do it. He would not split on the man who was his father, vile scroundrel though that man was!

Indeed, it touched Sexton Blake not a little to see how Dolby tried to screen his father by taking all the guilt to himself. For he stuck to his confession all through, and when he heard that Ludford had at last been captured, it only had the effect of making him more vehement than ever in his protestations that he was guilty and that his father was innocent.

All in vain these protestations—utterly vain! When in due course the full case was unfolded at the police court, Sexton Blake was able to prove beyond all doubt that the murder had been committed in the way he had already outlined to Inspector Yarrow.

Such evidence was put forward as proved that it was Jacob Ludford who had strangled Richard Sharron, and not Nicholas Dolby at all. At the same time, the younger man had been an accessory both before and after the fact of murder. Therefore, whatever a judge and jury might later on decide about the measure of his infamy, his guilt was abundantly sufficient for the magistrates to commit him for trial with his father.

★ ★ ★

But Nicholas Dolby was destined never to come before an earthly judge. Only a few days before the date fixed for the trial at York Assizes he was found dead in his cell. Dead by his own hand, so the verdict of the coroner's inquest said. Poisoning was revealed by the post-mortem. It had to be assumed that the poison had somehow or other been smuggled into the prison, though how was never exactly discovered.

★ ★ ★

Jacob Ludford, his infamous father, was duly arraigned for the crime of murder, found guilty, sentenced, and in the fulness of time launched into eternity, to give an account of his stewardship.

The two men who had been arrested with him, together with four other men taken in Liverpool, were also duly put on trial on lesser but still grave charges. They were proved to belong to a gang which had devoted its energies to burglary, forgery, and other crimes, and who had for long given the police much trouble, not only in the North of England, but in London also.

It was these men who had assisted Dolby and Ludford in the concealment of the capital crime, and who had taken part in the various assaults on Sexton Blake which have been detailed in our story. They were quite properly sentenced to lengthy terms of penal servitude.

Luke Samways was, even as Blake had said, quite innocent. He had taken no sort of part in the attack on Blake that night in the ravine, but had been merely a pliant tool in the hands of the conspirators. Long before the trial came off, he had been discharged from prison without a stain on his character, unless the stern magisterial admonition to "leave the drink alone" may be classed as such.

So, too, had Jack Wilson been discharged long before the great trial came off. Discharged, of course, without any sort of stain on his character. In regard to him, it was generally felt that he had been a most unfortunate victim of circumstances, and that he had been most unjustly dealt with. Therefore Sexton Blake's efforts to get him compensation were strongly seconded by the magistrates and other influential people, and met with success.

This, however, was not the only compensation Jack got. Bestirring himself on the young fellow's behalf, his old friend and comrade-in-arms, Adrian Straker, obtained for him a most comfortable and quite well-paid job in a seaside town.

Here Jack is now living happily with his wife and child—now quite restored to health. Jack's job is a semi-official one, so that if during the next seaside holiday you chance to go to——

But no, we had better not reveal the name of the town. If we did, Jack might find himself the subject of too much curiosity, and, in his own words, he has had "quite enough publicity to last him his lifetime."

THE END

THE MISSING MILLIONAIRE

THE VERY FIRST SEXTON BLAKE STORY

First published in the Halfpenny Marvel, 1893

THE MISSING MILLIONAIRE

CHAPTER I

The Detective and His Visitor—A Strange Story of Treachery—The Missing Millionaire

"MR. FRANK ELLABY wishes to see you, sir."

"Good!" answered Mr. Sexton Blake. "Let him come up, and at once."

The clerk withdrew, and his master gazed thoughtfully at the grimy window of his office in New Inn Chambers.

"So," he muttered, "my wealthly client has come at last, thanks to the influence of my friend Gervaise, of Paris. I wonder what kind of mission it is he has in hand that is to bring me in such high rewards? Gervaise says it may keep me busy for a year or two."

Sexton Blake belonged to the new order of detectives. He possessed a highly-cultivated mind which helped to support his active courage. His refined, clean-shaven face readily lent itself to any disguise, and his mobile features assisted to clinch any facial illusion he desired to produce.

The door again opened, and a tall, handsome man, whose cheeks were bronzed by travel, and whose grey eyes were large and prominent, entered.

"Mr. Blake, I believe?" he said, as he paused on the threshold.

"Very much at your service, Mr. Frank Ellaby. Pray take a seat, and let me hear what I can do for you. Mr. Gervaise prepared me for a visit from you. But I am quite in the dark as to the nature of the business you desire me to undertake."

"It will prove more troublesome than dangerous," said the visitor, with a slight smile. "I will tell you my story, and then you will understand exactly what I want.

"My sister and myself were left orphans before we had finished our schooling. Some friends sent her out to Australia, where I believe she obtained a comfortable situation. It is unnecessary for me to bore you with a description of my struggles for existence. When I was about twenty I, like thousands of other men, old and young, took a sever attack of gold fever. I was determined to get to the Antipodes by hook or by crook, and try my luck at the diggings. If I came across my sister, well and good, although I did not start with any design of finding her. I had one object in view, and one only—that was wealth!

"I have obtained my desire," he added, with a heavy sigh, "But my heart is empty, and my life desolate!

"Out in Australia I met a man and his wife, with whom I became so friendly that he and I became partners in a claim, at which we toiled for months without finding one grain of gold. He was some years older than myself, and he went by the name of Calder Dulk. I don't supose it was his real title, for I know now that there was nothing true about him.

"In those days I would have trusted him with my life. He, again, was younger than his wife, who was a tall, majestic woman, of French extraction wonderfully accomplished, fiercely ambitious, and altogether unscrupulous.

"I always mistrusted her, and, unfortunately, I had not the art to conceal my dislike.

"Just when we were despairing of ever having any luck, and were thinking of seeking our fortune in some other part, we struck a rich vein of the precious ore, and found ourselves wealthy.

"Like many before us, this sudden success turned our heads. Nothing would do but we must hasten to Melbourne and enjoy ourselves.

"A few days after we arrived there I accidentally found the house where my sister lived. I got ther just in time to bid her good-bye for ever. She was dying. A beautiful, golden-haired girl of perhaps four years of age was playing in the room.

"'Frank,' gasped my sister, "I swore to the mother of little Rose there, when she lay on her deathbed, that I would protect her child until she came of age. Take the same oath to me, Frank, so that I may die in peace.'

"There was, of course, no refusing this request at that awful moment, so I most solemnly took the vow she wished.

"'In that cabinet, standing in the corner over there, you will find some papers which will explain who her parents were,' my sister continued, speaking with great difficulty, for life's lamp was at its last flicker. 'When you have perused them you will understand how precious she is, and how important it is that she is well guarded till she becomes a woman and can cliam her own!'

"As she ceased speaking she pressed my hand in hers. Smiling on me, she passed into the eternal sleep.

"This sad event so distressed me that I could do nothing in connection with the child or anything just then, Calder Dulk led me away from the place to the hotel where we were staying. He advised me to remain alone and keep quiet until the morning, which I did.

"When the morrow came both he and his wife had disappeared, and they had taken every ounce of gold I possessed with them! Nor was this all. They had run off with the child, too, not forgetting to secure the papers relating to her birth, to which my sister attached so much importance.

"I need not tell you what my emotions were under this stinging reversal of my fortune, at this horrible breach of faith, and at my inability to keep the oath I had so recently made to my dying sister.

"I was powerless to follow them, for I had not sufficient money even to pay the hotel bill. There was nothing I could do but return to the diggings, and by hard labour again woo the favour of the goddess of chance.

"I swore then in my heart that, if I ever did attain wealth, I would spend every farthing of it, if necessary, in hunting down the traitor who had betrayed me, and in finding the child who was so infamously stolen from my protection! So, Mr. Sexton Blake, I am here to obtain your co-operation in this search, which must never cease till my end is attained!

"How long is it since this double robbery was committed?" asked the detective.

"Fourteen years."

"Whew! That's a long time. Dulk and his wife may be dead; the girl has become a woman——"

"And a beautiful one, too, I am sure. You see," Mr Ellaby explained, "for a long, long time my luck was so bad that I scarcely succeeded in keeping body and soul together. It is only recently that the wheel of fortune has taken a turn. Then, as always happens, gold poured in on me till I as tired of gathering it."

"Have you heard anything of these people since?'"

"Absolutely nothing. But your friend, Gervaise, of Paris, believes that Madame Dulk has visited the French capital quite recently. While there she plundered the aristocracy in a most grand and daring manner. No one answering the description of her husband was seen to visit her. As she has undoubtedly left France, it is surmised that she is either in England or America."

"A very wide address," said Blake, with a smile. "If she is a high-toned adventuress, and is in London, she will be easily found. But you are giving me a tall order. When Stanley was sent to Africa to find Livingstone, his search was at least limited to one continent. The whole world is before me. But I will do my best——"

"Do that, and whether you fail or succeed, you shall have your own reward. Day and night I shall be at your service to aid you, and you may direct me as you choose."

"We will work together, and I can promise you heartiness on my part. But, I fear if we find Calder Dulk that I shall have helped to bring about a murder."

It was the detective who spoke.

"What do you mean?" demanded Ellaby.

"Simply this: you wish to meet him, *so that you kill him!"*

"When I get him will be time enough for me to decide what I shall do with him," replied the other. "I know you cannot give me any useful advide off-hand. It must let you have a little time to digest my story. Meanwhile, will you lunch with me? I have been away from England so long that it will be safer for both of us if I trust to you to select the restaurant."

"With pleasure," said Blake. "Let us stroll as far as Charing Cross. I think best when I am walking. Come round this way," he added, when they stood in Wych Street, and he pointed to St. Clement's Danes. "I must give a minute's call in Arundel Street."

Two other men were watching them from a neighbouring doorway. They took great care not to be seen.

"That's our man," said one to the other, indicating Frank Ellaby. "Once we secure him we shall be as well off as anyone need ever want to be. He's worth millions! You shadow him, Scooter, and make no mistake about it. If you let him give you the slip it will be as much as your skin is worth."

"No, thanks," laughed the first speaker. "That job is not in my way at all."

In the narrowest part of the Strand, between the two churches, the detective and Frank Ellaby became separated in the roadway, and by some evil chance to latter was knocked down and run over by a carelessly-driven hansom cab.

He was carried to the opposite pavement in an insensible condition.

Mr. Sexton Blake feared that he was killed outright.

A tall, handsome woman pressed her way through the crowd, which at once surrounded the injured man.

Her hair was as white as snow, and her eyes were coalblack in colour. It was a face time had treated tenderly. It was determined and commanding, too.

"Let your friend be brought to my house," she said to Blake. "It is close here—only round the corner in Norfolk Street. He may die before he can be taken to the hospital. A doctor lives opposite to where I reside."

Gratefully indeed did the detective accept this opportuned proposal. Apart altogether from the common sympathies of humanity, which were strongly developed in Blake, he had selfish reasons for desiring to keep this exceedingly wealthy client alive.

It happed, fortunately, that the front apartment leading off the hall, in the Norfolk Street house, was a bedroom, and here they laid the unconscious man.

In a few minutes Dr. Tuppy, from opposite, was by his side making a careful examination of his injuries.

"One rib fractured," he said. "Severe scalp wounds. No danger. Quiet, good nursing, and my advice will soon put him on his feet again. He must not, on any account be removed for some days. I don't know, madame——"

He paused to be supplied with the name of the lady who had called him in.

"Vulpino," she said, in a musical voice.

"Well, I don't know, Madame Vulpino, whether you can possibly allow the gentleman to stay in your rooms, but I can assure you that he can only be conveyed out of them, at present, at the risk of his life."

"I would not turn an injured dog from my roof," said madame, with a touch of emotion. "He shall stay here till he can be taken away with safety. I have an elderly woman with me who will nurse him——"

"Excellent," said the doctor.

"Believe me, he shall want for nothing."

"You are indeed a good Samaritan, madame," declared Blake. "My friend is a man of means, and any expenses you may be put to——"

She closed his speech with a proud wave of her hand, which clearly indicated that she would not accept any money recompense for the inconvenience she was putting herself to.

"Now, my dear sir," said Dr. Tuppy, "*you* can do nothing more for your friend. He is in excellent hands. I will see the nurse, and give her my instructions. He will soon recover consciousness, and then he must have absolute quietness. Of course, you may come round in the morning and see how he is."

Blake, quite easy in his mind, left his new client in the house in Norfolk Street, and set about a careful consideration of the problem which had been put before him, and attending to such other matters as he had in hand.

The next day, at ten o'clock, he called to see how Ellaby was progressing.

The door was opened by a typical specimen of the London lodging-house "slavey."

"Well," he said, good humouredly, "how is my friend this morning?"

'Wot friend? Oh, the gent as was ill yesterday. He's gone."

"Gone? Impossible! How did he go?"

"That's just what missis says when a lodger gets out without paying what he owes. Why sir, how can I tell you how they goes?"

"Madame Vulpino is in, I suppose?" said the detective, as he tried to persuade himself that the girl was talking foolishly, and at random.

"She has gone, too," was the answer. "That was her room he was taken into. Her time was up last night, and she went, and paid up, too. She gave me half-a-crown, and told me not to bother her when she was getting her luggage into the cab. So I didn't. I just went to sleep in the kitchen. My misses was out at the time."

"Will you let me look into Madame Vulpino's room?" said Blake, more perplexed than ever detective was yet.

"Why, of course I will, sir," laughed the girl. "You can come and live in it if you like to pay the rent regular, and gas, and coals, and boots is extra, and I does the boots.''

There was no doubt about it. Frank Ellaby was not in that house, nor could any information be obtained as to how he had left it. To make matters worse, no one knew anything about Madame Vulpino.

As for Dr. Tuppy, he simply shrugged his shoulders.

''You are all strangers to me,'' he said, ''and I only know three things about you. First, you call me from my lunch in a dreadful hurry. Second, the removal of the patient last night was quite against my instructions, and will probably kill him. Third, I have received no fee!''

''Frank Ellaby has fallen into bad hands,'' thought Sexton Blake, as he made his way to his office, feeling very vexed with himself. ''Not only into bad hands, but, I fear, powerful ones. I must try and rescue him, whatever it costs me. There can be little doubt that he has been followed from Australia by some desperate gang, who know how wealthy he is. They have succeeded in capturing him in the simplest way possible. They have him in their power, while he is quite helpless It means a race now between my brains and another London mystery, and I'll back myself to win!''

CHAPTER 2
Frank Ellaby Finds Himself Bound and Helpless in a Cab—At the Old Water Mill.

To keep the events in this remarkable history abreast of one another as much as possible, we will leave the detective to take his own way of discovering the whereabouts of his rich client, and concern ourselves with Mr Frank Ellaby's own movements.

When he regained his senses he found that he was gagged, and bound hand and foot.

He was in some kind of vehicle which carried no lights. As it jolted along a rough, dark road, it rattled like a ramshackle old four-wheeler. He was stretched along it from the back to the front seat. A piece of plank covered the space between, and gave him additional support.

His injuries occasioned him great pain. At present his senses were numbed, as though the effects of some powerful drug were still clinging to him. He dimly recalled the accident which had befallen him. From then to now was a blank.

He consoled himself at first with the thought that he was being conveyed to some infirmary where he would find ease, and receive kind treatment. But if this was the intention of those who had placed him in the cab, why was he gagged and bound?

The air grew keener, and the part through which they passed more and more silent, till Frank judged that they must now be in the open country. Suddenly the vehicle pulled up with a jerk, which nearly sent the injured man to its other side.

''Wake up, my beauty,'' said a rough voice.

The door of the cab opened, and Frank's body was prodded playfully with a heavy bludgeon.

''We have reached our destination. You must try and walk into our picturesque country retreat, for vou are a bit too heavv for me to carry.''

By the aid of the bright moon, Ellaby saw that the gaunt, spectral building which stood before him and back from the road in murky ugliness had been a water-mill.

The big wheel was there yet, dripping with slimy weeds. The moon's rays made the still water look green and murderous. The house itself was as forbidding a structure as it is easy to imagine.

The door of the evil place opened. A man carrying a lantern emerged and came towards them. He wore a mask. His voice appeared familiar to Frank, though, at that moment, he could not identify it.

''Is it all right, Bill Bender?'' he asked, addressing the rough driver.

''Quite right. Now, my young swell, I'll just undo the strap which holds your legs, and with a little support from me, you will be able to walk inside. Why, bless me, If you haven't got a lovely gold lever, as big as a turnip, and a chain strong enough to hold a horse. I'll take care of these trifles for you, and if you want any civility from me, you had better make no fuss about this little incident.

''You see,'' continued the ruffian, ''if I have any of your nonsense I can given you a touch with *this*''—he tapped the prisoner's head with a life-preserve—''or you can have a dose of *this*.''

He produced a pistol, and the barrel gleamed in the moonlight.

''But there,'' he added, with a coarse laugh, ''it won't be any good for you to try on anything. We are a thousand miles from everywhere, as the saying is, and if you try to escape, all you will find will be a water grave."

They had removed Frank's gag now. Although he was in great pain he addressed them with the utmost coolness and assurance.

"I am to ill and weak to make any attempt to escape, especially from any place which promises warmth, rest, and shelter. Pray help me in, and let me lie down."

"We have ventured to take a few liberties with you to-night," said the man who wore the mark, "but we do not contemplate treating you with violence. To-morrow, however, will show us whether you are a reasonable, or an unreasonable, man—whether we must resort to force or not."

"To-morrow will be time enough for that or any other discussion. To-night my pain is so great I can hardly stand. I beg of you to take me indoors. The man who guards me to-night will have an easy task."

"I am glad to see you take matters so coolly. You shall have all the attention this place affords. Let me warn you. You are as far from human aid here as though you were in your tomb."

CHAPTER 3
A Threat of Torture—Left to Starve to Death.

"How is your patient getting on now?" The man who had worn the mask asked this question of the ruffian he had called ' BillBender."

The former was sitting before a well-spread table, enjoying a hearty meal, and the latter had just returned from the room which was to prove Frank Ellaby's prison.

"Beautiful!" was the answer. "I never saw a man in his position take things so cool and comfortable. He could not be more contented in his own hotel."

"I'd rather he made a fuss. He'll prove all the more troublesome to us in the end. These calm, determined men are more difficult to deal with than excitable people."

"We can soon knock the nonsense out of him. What made you cover up your face with that mask to-night, Mr. Calder Dulk?"

"Why, you see," came the slow answer, "after he has paid his ransom, I don't want it to be in his power to take proceedings against me when he is once more free."

"When he is once more free?" repeated Bender, with a low chuckle. "You don't mean that he ever shall get free? One you have got his money, he will only be a danger to you alive. *He'll have to go where the rest have gone."*

"I neither contemplate, nor do I recommend, violence," said Dulk, with a queer look in his eyes; "when we obtain possession of the cash, I shall leave him here, and you can do what you like with him."

"Thanks; and I shan't forget to keep my eyes on you, either," muttered the rascal.

Frank was put into a comfortable bed, in a warm room, and he was well supplied with everything in the way of nourishment he could desire.

He felt that whoever had bandaged his injuries had done the work with some skill.

There was no window to the apartment, and all escape from it was prevented by a iron-bound oaken door, which was secured by bolts and an iron bar on the outside.

Except for the fact that he was a prisoner in that sinister building, and probably in imminent peril of his life, he might have felt as contented there as in any other place he could have been taken to.

After a long and grave consideration of his present position, he came to the unjust conclusion that Mr. Sexton Blake had proved a scoundrel, and for his own ends had made him a prisoner.

"Yes," thought Frank, "it must be Blake. Not another soul in London knows who I am, or what I am worth! I wonder how much he will want to set me free? I wonder whether I shall ever yield to his infamous demands? I think not. He has played a dangerous game, and he shall suffer for it, Unless they kill me outright. He could not have planned the accident which befel me, but my helplessness may have suggested this cunning plot. Opportunity is the great tempter. I suppose to-morrow my gaolers will tell me their intentions."

When he awoke on the following day, he felt refreshed, and so hungry, that he looked forward eagerly for the appearance of breakfast.

Frank had a remarkably strong constitution, which travel, hardship, and exposure had hardened, and not shattered.

In spite of Doctor Tuppy's prognostication, his sudden and queer removal had not retarded his

recovery. He felt in himself that a few days would see him on his feet again, and in fair health.
His only visitor the next day was "Bill Bender."
He brought a jug of coffee and a couple of slices of bread and butter.
"We are not goint to feed you up with high-class food," said the man, "because it might fire your blood, and we mean to keep you nice and cool."
This fare, rough as it proved, was very welcome to Frank.
"Now," continued the ruffian, drawing a packet of papers from his pocket, "I'm going to leave these things with you for your careful and best consideration. One is a cheque on the London Joint Stock Bank for twenty thousand pounds. Oh, my fine millionaire! we've got friends in Paris, who told us which was your London bank."
"Gervaise, of course," Frank thought; "he has planned this with Sexton Blake. I have plunged my head right into the hornets' nest."
"All you have to do,' continued "Bill Bender," with a grin, "is to sign this cheque, and then, in case you should not have so much cash as that at the bank, here's a little power of attorney for you to put your name to. It authorised Mr. Cornelius Brown to reliase on any stocks or shares, bonds or certificates, personal or real estate, you may possess. Once you have signed these different documents, and we have secured what we have justly earned, you will be free to leave this place and enjoy yourself as you may think best. So it just rests with you, Mr. Frank Ellaby, how long you remain here. We can wait for years, if necessary. *You have not one living person on earth likely to trouble themselves whether you are alive or dead!"*
How true this was Frank knew only too well, and to his sorrow.
"I can't prevent you from leaving the papers here," he said quietly; "but I will never sign one of them as long as I live!"
"That's what you think now, but we will make you change your mind soon."
"I should be a fool to sing."
Frank spoke carelessly. "So long as you want my authorisation to those papers, you will keep me alive for the gratification of your own greed; but once that is satisfied, it will not matter to you whether I am alive or dead. While I am alive I have hope."
"Well, I never thought of that! How clever you are! But, look here; this matter has been put into my hands, and I am going to work it off quick. I don't suppose you are a bit more frightened of death than I am; but there's something worse than that, and it's *torture.* If you won't come to any reasonable terms, *I'll starve you into submission!* Do you hear?"
"You cur!" said Frank, contemptuously. "Why, you would run a mile from me, if I had my strength, and we were on equal terms. As it is, I'll bring you to the earth!"
On the little table by the bedside the man had placed a metal inkpot and a pen, with the papers to which he wished Frank to put his signature.
The prisoner seized this pewter inkstand, and hurled it, with all the force he could command, full in the face of his brutal custodian.
The blow was unexpected, and Bill dropped to the ground like a log of wood.
Frank thought that the moment for his escape had come, and he tried to struggle into his clothes.
Alas! he was so weak that he had to sink on to the bed, and cling to it, trembling from the effects of his recent exertions.
This gave "Bill Bender" time to regain his feet, and he soon had his prisoner back again between the sheets.
"So that's a sample of temper, is it?" snarled Bill. "I shall look our for you in future. You take my advice. Sign those papers while you have a chance. I'm a bit rough to deal with when I'm put out, and you have marked my figure-head for life. Until those papers are signed you don't get bit nor sup from me."
With a curse Bill left Frank Ellaby to recover from his prostration as best he could.
For two days Frank had neither food nor drink given him.
In one way he suffered terribly, but this heroic treatment helped his injuries to heal up in a miraculously short space of time.
He then began to consider whether, after all, he had not better attach his signature to the documents which were still at of his bed.
If he did not do the bidding of these wretches, it was certain they would starve him to death!
Circumstanced as he was he could lose nothing by agreeing to their terms. If he ever did get free he promised himself that he would punich Mr. Gervaise, of Paris, and Mr. Sexton Blake, of London,

most severely for their villainy. He hoped, too, that he would be able to make them disgorge the money they had wrenched from him.

Little did he imagine that both these wrongly suspected gentlement were at that very moment doing all they could to find and rescue him!

The next time "Bill Bender" put his head into the room, with the question whether his prisoner had come to his senses yet, Frank Ellaby said—

"I have signed all you wished me to. Bring me something to eat and to drink. When you have got your money I suppose you will see that I am released from here?"

"Not much," said Bill, with a coarse laugh, as he thrust the papers into the breast pocket of his heavy overcoat "Now, listen to me. If you had not been so obstinate, I would have done fair and honest by you. But you've bee pig-headed, and you've kept me from my pleasures and enjoyments. More than that, you have marked my face. The consequence of which is that *I'm going to leave you here to starve. You can't escape. No one can come to you. Here you shall remain and slowly starve to death."*

With this speech the ruffian left the room, bolting and barring the door behind him.

"He tells the truth for once," groaned Frank, "there is no help of hope for me. I see nothing before me but a dragging out of an existence which will be torture till the end of its last thread!"

CHAPTER 4

Gervaise, of Paris, Appears on the Scene—The "Red Lights' of London—The Newspaper Boy's Story—Finding the Old Mill—Dragging the pool—Discovery of a Body.

"So far all my searchings have been in vain. I have failed to find any trace of Mr. Frank Ellaby."

So said Sexton Blake to his fellow-worker, Detective Gervaise. of Paris, to whom he had telegraphed directly it became know that the millionaire had disappeard.

"I blame myself very much for this catastrophe,' said Gervaise, gloomily. "I should have described that woman to you, and have put you on your guard against her. She was as anxious to secure Ellaby as he was to find and punish her. She wanted me to shadow him before he called on me to get information concerning her. I intended coming to England, to put on her track, and I calculated that your speedy discovery of her would bring a substantial reward from our wealthy friend. You have already guessed that this Madame Vulpino and Mrs. Calder Dulk is one person. This unfortunate accident has played havoc with my plans. Fate seems to have worked altogether in favour of Ellaby's enemies."

"On the night of his disappearance," said Blake, "the woman, accompanied by a shabbily-dressed man, drove from Norfolk Street to Charing Cross Station, where she took two ticket for Paris. She and her companion both entered the Continental train, but it is quite certain they never went by it. They must have left it when it was on the point of starting."

"The booking to France was a mere blind—to lead you on to a false scent. There can be no doubt that the woman is still in London, and probably not far off. Very likely the man who accompanied her was Dulk himself. Within a day or so someone will turn up at the London Joint Stock Bank with a cheque signed by the missing man. As we have warned the authorities at the bank to detain any such messenger, I hope to reach the conspirators through that means. There can be no doubt that their object is to extort money from their prisoner——"

"And when they have succeeded what will become of him?" suggested Blake.

"Ah, that is just where all the danger comes in," said Gervaise gravely.

"I wonder if the 'Red Lights, have any hand in this kidnapping?"

"Who and what are the 'Red Lights,' my friend?"

"It is a new and formidable society of professional lawbreakers of every class. Its conception was due to the fertile brain of a young, well-educated fellow named Leon Polti. It was his idea to join together into one powerful association the most expert operators in all branches of cime. The cleverest burglar throws in his lot with the most accomplished forger, and so on through the whole list of police offences. The notion is a brotherhood of crime, with meeting places, and correspondents all over the country, working for the comon good of their own combination, and to the hurt of honest people.

If Polti could realise his highest ideal and conduct such a gigantic organisation, on strictly business principles, and with keen method, I fear the police would be beaten at every turn, and crime would be triumphant in the land! Luckily, rogues never do agree together for long.

"They will observe no laws—not even their own. So Polti's vast scheme will remain a dream, and nothing else, to the end of time. This case we have in hand looks something like the work of his gang. Watching and waiting for the rich man coming from Australia, and sending the woman over to Paris to shadow him, suggests his methods. I daresay I can find him. He knows me. We will see if we can discover anything of his doings."

At this point their conversation was interrupted by the appearance of a shaggy, flaming head of red hair, which thrust itself into the office through the half-opened doorway.

"Well," interrogated Blake, "what do you want?"

"Please, governor, I'm the boy wot stands about the top of Essex Street, selling papers, and you've given me many a 'brown,' you has."

A body followed the head, and there stood disclosed to the two detectives, a short, bright-faced boy, who looked like nothing so much as an animatedbundle of rags. His tattered trousers barely touched his knees, and strips of time-eaten cloth fluttered round his thin, discoloured arm.

"I've got no 'browns' for you to-day," said Blake, waving his hand impatiently.

"Oh yes, you has, sir," the street boy answered, with a knowing shake of his glowing locks. "Wait till you 'ear wot 'ive got to tell yer, and then I think you'll be good for a 'bob.' It's like this 'ere. Tommy Roundhead says as 'ow you want to find out about a 'toff' as was taken out of a house in Arundel Street, late Thursday night. Well, I can tell you all about that 'ere. 'Cos, why? I helped in the job myself."

"If you can help me to find that gentleman," said Blake, with sudden energy, "I'll make a man of you! We won't trouble about shillings. Pounds and pounds shall be spend on you."

"We can decide what to do when we have hear his tale," said Gervaise, with more caution.

"It's like this, governor. I was walking down Arundel Street, wondering where I should pitch myself for the night, when a four-wheeler drives up, and stops at that house. The driver jumps off the box, and I see, at once, that he weren't a reg'la cabby. 'Ere young Vesuvius!' 'ee cries, "old the' osses 'ed.' The door of the 'ouse opens without him knocking or ringing. I sees that there's a sort of bed made up in the cab. In a minute or two the driver comes out with another man. Between them they carries a third man, who, if he ain't 'as lost 'is senses. They puts this helples chap inside, and the coachman, springs on to his box again. 'I shall be there before you,' says the man who is standing on the pavement. He pusts his 'and in 'is pocket, and, after fumbling about a bit, he pulls out 'arf a sovereign. 'Take that," he says to me, 'I ain't got noffink smaller.' He walks away quick.

"'Well,' thinks. I, 'if I gets 'arf a quid for 'olding the 'oss while they puts the swell *into* the cab, perhaps I shall get a bit more if I'm there to 'old it when they take 'im *hout'*. So I gets up on the back of the cab, and clings on. But, bless you! I was taken right away to Barking. I didn't get of because I made sure the cab would be coming back again. At last we stops before a tumble-down old water-mill. Then the driver brings out a blunderbuss, or sumfink deadly, and a reg'lar hold-fashioned life-preserver. I take to me 'eels in case they should want to give me one on the 'ed. I waits about hoping to see the cab go back. But they puts in the stable there, and I'as to walk. I falls in with a tramp, and he sneaks my half sovereign. Then the police collars me for being a vagabond, and that's how it is I ain't been at my hold pitch the last day or two."

"This is new indeed!" exclaimed Gervaise. "Can you lead us to this old mill?"

"It's a hawful lonely place," said the boy, "but I think I can find it again."

"Le us go at once," suggested Gervaise.

"We must lose no time," agreed Blake, meditatively, "but we need to go to work with extreme caution. I don't lie that remote water-mill. It looks murderous in my eyes. I our man is still there, and alive, his gaolers may offer a desperate resitance. The quickest way will be to take the train to Barking."

"Can't do it, governor," declared the lad; "I shall never find the place if I don't go the same way as that four-wheeler did."

So they hired a hansom, and it took half a day to light on the spot where "Bill Bender" hadthreatened Frank Ellaby with bludgeon and pistol.

"The place is deserted," said Blake. "I fear the worst."

"We shall have no difficulty in getting in," said Gervaise, as he threw the weight of his body against a rotten and illsecured back-door, which at once flew open.

The rats infesting the place scampered before them as they walked through the musty passages and gloomy rooms.

Upstairs they came on a heavy door, barred and bolted on the outside.

Their hearts beat high as they undid these fastenings.

They felt sure they were on the point of entering the room where Mr. Ellaby had been kept prisoner.

Would they find him there now, was the question which trembled on the lips of both, but neither spoke.

They were not hopeful of discoveirng him alive, for he had not answered the shouts they had raised on entering the building. Was his murdered body to meet their horrified gaze?

"Empty, as I expected," said Gervaise. "What a strong room it is? It might have been built for a prison cell. He has been here, that is quite clear. There is his bed, his writing materials——"

"And" said Blake, "an absence of water and of other food!

"They left him to starve to death!" Gervaise added excitedly, "but he has escaped by tearing the fire-grate from its settings. See how loose the bricks behind are. He could not have had great difficulty in making the hole through which he must have crawled. There is a room beyond—long, narrow. We must follow his example, and see where it leads to."

"His footprints on the dusty floor can still be traced," said Blake. "The open window at the end shows he escaped that way. Why has he not communicated with me?"

"Because," answered Gervaise impressively, "his body lies at the bottom of that still, black-loking pool. You observe, this window is exactly over the old wheel of the water-mill. He must have stepped on to it. His weight would make it revolve; he would be hurled into the water. Probably one of the flanges would strike his head, and render him insensible. Then the weeds would catch him in their deadly embrace.

"See! There is his hat floating on the green scum! We must have this water dragged!"

As soon as they could procure drags and other aids, the pond was most effectually dragged.

After some hours' work, and with much difficulty, they brought a corpse to the bank, about which lank weeds still clung.

"Unhappily, we are too late to preserve the life of Frank Ellaby, for here his body undoubtedly lies. The one thing left for us is to make our very best effort to bring his murderers to justice."

It was Gervaise who spoke.

"And that we will do as certainly as we stand here," answered Sexton Blake.

CHAPTER 5.
The Vicar's Secret—A True Lover—The Cheque for £20,000—Arrested.

IN this chapter we must take the reader to the old-fashioned Sussex village of Downslow, and to the ivy-clad rectory there, in the library of which sat the Rev. Frederick Briarton, in grave conversation with Ernest Truelove, a farmer's son, who was on the eve of leaving his old home for London, with the intention of entering one of its medical schools and winning a surgeon's diploma.

"I will not conceal from you my satisfaction at knowing that you have won the love of my dear Rose," said the clergyman, "for I have confidence in your high regard for truth and honour. I am old, and it is idle for me to hope that I can be much longer in this world. I shall die the happier for knowing that Rose has linked her life with one who will do his utmost to shield her from its storms. But, my dear boy, I have a secret to confide to your keeping, which may make you desire to withdraw from the engagement you have entered into."

"Nothing can possibly happen to make me do that," said Ernest fervently.

"Prepare yourself for a shock, my friend. *Rose is not daughter of mine!* I do not even know who her parents are."

"You have succeeded in surprising me," said young Truelove. "I love Rose for herself alone, and I care not whose child she is!"

"She is the essence of goodness and purity. Many years ago I was chaplain to one of Her Majesty's prisons. A few days before I resigned that appointment to commence duties at a small living in Yorkshire, which had been presented to me, one of the female convicts, a handsome and accomplished woman, sent for me, and, upon her knees, implored me to protect a little girl her arrest and sentence had comp elled her to leave in the care of some rough, illiterate people living at Hammersmith. She said that the child was not her own, that it had a great futura before it, and that when she was released she would repay me for my trouble, and restore the child to its proper sphere. As I had not been blessed with any children of my own, I was ready enough to adopt Rose. My poor dead wife grew devotedly attached to her, and she was brought up as our own daughter. The time soon came when I began to feel terror lest her convict guardian should appear at our home, and blight its happiness by claiming our darling Rose.

"By the will of an uncle I was practically compelled to change my old name of Sparrow to the one I now bear—Briarton. I have moved about a good deal, too, and perhaps that is why the woman has not found me. I am glad to have eluded her. I would go very much against my moral grain to have to deliver up so pure and gentle a girl to a woman who has once worn a convict's dress. I have never had the courage to tell Rose the truth. She firmly believes herself to be my child."

"Let her die in that faith," said Truelove, promptly.

"It would be cruel to her to tell her the truth now, and no useful purpose would be served. She herself is too good for me to believe that her parents were bad. I will work hard, and in a little over three years I shall secure my diploma; then I can give her a name which shall be her very own, and she can defy anyone who may wish to claim her."

After this, Ernest spent a long time with Rose herself, till the hour came when he had to drive to the station and catch his train. They had repeated their mutual vows over and over again.

When evening prayers were said in the vicarage, the rector introduced a fervent one for the safety and prosperity of Ernest Truelove, amid the pitfalls and temptations of the huge metropolis.

Meanwnile this young gentleman, having spent an hour or so in Brighton, was dashing on to London at express speed, his regrets at leaving his old friends and the scenes of his youth lightened by this sense of the vivid change which wa no to colour the daily routine of his life.

His only fellow-passanger was a young fellow who looked about his own age, but he might have been older. Slight in build, with a creamy skin, and large dark,fascinating eyes, a round smooth chin, and a delicate mouth, he was decidedly effeminate in appearance, and yet there Inrked in his every graceful movement a suspicion of sinewy and uncommon strength.

The two had easily fallen into conversation, and this had led to an exchange of cards.

The stranger's bore the name of—

"Leon Polti."

"So," said the latter, to whom the innocent Ernest had confided much of his past history and many of his plans for the future, "you want comfortable lodgings in the centre of London? Ah! Now I don't think you can do better than take up your quarters at the house where my sister and I are temporarily located—99, Bernard Street, Russell Square, It's no distance from Charing Cross Hospital. The landlady is the most obliging creature I ever met with, and the cooking is capital. I know she has a bed and sitting-room to let. Probably you don't mind if they are a bit high up. You can drive home with me to-night. There will be no harm in seeing the place, even if you should elect not to take the apartments."

"I am very much obliged to you," said Ernest. "I have no doubt the place will suit me very well indeed. I suppose, though, I shall have to go to an hotel to-night?"

"Not a bit of it! If you like the accommodations, Madame Dulk, the landlady, will make you perfectly comfortable at once."

Ernest was charmed with the house and with his new friends.

The same evening he dined with Mr Polti, and he saw that this gentleman lived in quite high style. The table was spread with delicacies, in and out of season, and there were famous wines.

"My sister is out of town to-night,' said his host. "I hope to introduce you to her to-morrow."

On the following morning he encountered a dark young lady on the stairs. The likeness to Leon Polti was so striking that he could not doubt her near relationship to that gentleman, so he ventured to address her.

"Oh, yes," said, with a laugh, which disclosed a set of brilliant teeth, "I am Nizza Polti. My brother has told me so much about you. I hope we shall be great friends. Some business has called him away; he will not be back for a few days. But," she added, "Madame Dulk generally sit with me in the evening, and any time you like we shall be glad if you will join us."

The days passed very pleasantly with Ernest. Some evenings he saw Nizza, and on others Leon. Their own affairs so fell out that they were never able to be together when young Truelove was in the house.

One evening as Leon was sitting with the medical student in the latter's room, Madame Dulk tapped at the door, and brought word that a gentleman waited below to see Mr. Polti on most urgent business.

"Bother him!" said Leon. "Can't he come in the morning?"

"No. He says it is imperative that you see him now."

"He shall wait till I have finished this cigar, at any rate. Tell him so, whoever he may be. I hate these inquisitive people," he added, with a yawn, to Ernest.

When he did at last deign to descend the stairs he found Calder Dulk waiting for him. He took him into another room.

"You have an odd way of disturbing one at most inconvenient moments," said Leon. "Well, what is it you want me for?"

"The rat in his cage has eaten his cheese," replied Dulk, harshly, annoyed at the other's assumption of cool indifference. "In other words, Mr. Frank Ellaby has signed all the papers you made out for him to put his signature to. I've got them with me. It's for you to turn them into good current gold. Our part of the business is finished, and that has been the roughest and the worst section of it. Now you can put in some of your 'fine' work, as you call it."

"I'm afraid you have come in a sneering mood, Dulk." Polti drawled his words out lazily. "And really is dces not become so jovial a fellow as yourself. *What has been done with Ellaby?*"

"I left him to 'Bill Bender.' *You* know what he generaly does with them."

"It's always force, and never persuasion, with you people," said Leon contemptuously.

"These papers seem to be all right," he continued. "They shall have my attention as soon as possible, and you will all know the result."

"That won't do for me," said Dulk fiercely. "I mean having the lion's share of this plunder. Why, if it hadn't been for me you would not have known of the existence of this Frank Ellaby. But for my wife's promptitude it might have taken you months to capture him. Those papers represent an actual little gold mine. It is through our work, and through the work of no one else, that they have been obtained, and we mean being *paid in full!* You talk about us all being equal. You are like the man in the play. He wanted *his* followers to be equal so long as he was chief. No doubt you would like to be crowned 'Monarch of Criminals,' and 'King of Crime,' and al that kind of thing; but we are not quite such fools as to give way to you."

"You amuse me, Dulk," said Leon, throwing himself back in his chair, and smiling dangerously. "Perhaps you will condescend to remember that, but for me, there would have been no house in Arundel Street to take your victim to—the man you have twice plundered. But for me there would have been no old mill in which to torture him into subjection. But for me you would not now have good broadcloth on your back. But for me the only possible roof for you would be the strong one of the gaol. You want the lion's share of this money? You shall have it all, my friend. Take back your papers; do what you will with them. I wash myhands ɔf the affair, of you, of your wife. You cannot play either the rôle of knave or honest man. Well, I am better without you. Good-night."

"Leon, Leon," plead Dulk, with a white, anxious face, "don't talk like that! You know I dare not work those papers! Come, come; forgive me! I spoke hastily; I did not mean what I said. Take the papers again. Work as you choose with them; I make no conditions."

"Make conditions!" repeated Leon. "Theworld must turn inside out before *you* will ever be able to dictate to *me.* Leave those documents. Go away. I will see what can be done. It is a risky business, and I know the hazard better than any of you. If a hitch occurs, there must be instant flight from here."

"Yes," said Polti himself, when he was alone; "I see that I am in most danger from my own followers. They would kill me to gain possesion of Frank Ellaby's money. Dulk is the most likely man to strike the first blow. Knowing where my peril lies I can evade it. Extreme caution and swift flight will save me, and nothing else. I thank thee, Fate, for throwing that innocent youth Ernest Truelove in my way!"

On the following morning the studen again met Nizza Polti on the stairs.

"My brother has been unexpectedly called away this morning before you were awake," she said in her pretty way, shedding the full light of her eyes on his face. "He wants you to do a small favour for him, and I am sure you will. It is only to get a cheque cashed at the Lond Joint Stock Bank, and meet him to-night at Charing Cross Railway Station with the money. He is going to Paris with it."

"I shall be delighted to be of any service to him, *and to you,*" said Ernest. "Whey! this cheque is for £20,00! Quite a fabulous amount!"

"My brother's transaction often run into five figures." she answered, with a smile. "If the cheque were for a small sum, I could do the business myself. He prefers to trust it to you, because you are stronger and cleverer than I am."

"Directly I have had my breakfast I will go to the bank," declared Ernest, in his impulsive way.

"There is not such a great hurry. So long as you are at the bank by eleven o'clock, that will do."

Just as Ernest was leaving the house a cab drew up at the door. To his great surprise, it contained Rose and the Rev. Frederick Briarton.

It chanced that just as these two reached the house, Madame Dulk was standing at the dining-room window, and she had a clear view of them.

She drew back hastily. Gleams of satisfaction shot from her eyes.

"At last I have found him!" she said to herself. "The clergyman to whom I confided the child. Doubtless that is Rose herself, grown into a beautiful woman. I will lose no time in regaining my prize. My husband and Polti and the rest may have *their* big hauls, but I shall now be better off than any of them!"

"Dad had to come up to London by the very first train on some business in the City,' Rose explained.

She was flushed with excitement, and with the delight she felt at seeing her lover again. "So I coaxed him to let me come, too."

"We thought we would give you a surprise," laughed the vicar, "and join you in a little lunch, if you have such a handy thing in the house."

"Only too delighted to see you," said Ernest; "but I must go to the City myself. We can all go together in the cab you have come by, and talk as we go.

"My business is with the Joint Stock Bank," he added, "and it won't occupy many minutes. After that I shall be entirely at your service. What do you think, Mr. Briarton? I'm going to change a cheque for twenty thousand pounds!"

The figures were sufficienlty large to impress the rural clergyman, and to awe Rose.

Ernest briefly explained how he chanced to be in possession of so valuable a piece of paper.

They watched him, as he, with a great air if importance (which he could not resist), entered the bank. They saw him emerge from its portals, and then a dreadful thing happened.

A tall, broad man tapped him on the shoulder.

Before he could say a word a pair of handcuffs were thrust on his wrists. Two other men came from across the road with a seeming air of authority. They were seized, too, and treated in the same way.

The police had taken Ernest Truelove into custody. They had also arrested Mr. Gervaise, of Paris, and Mr. Sexton Blake, very much to the complete dismay of both these notable detectives.

Calder Dulk and Leon Polti watched these proceedings from a safe corner, and then made off with all the speed possible.

Poor Rose uttered a cry of distress, and the Reverend Mr. Briarton sprang on to the pavement and was at once in the midst of the excited group, standing shoulder to shoulder with Mr. Frank Ellaby!

CHAPTER 6.
The Release of the Prisoners—Flying from Justice—"I will Kill You Both."

"So I have made a good haul, and caught you all at once," said Ellaby, with a grim smile. "I am sorry you have turned out a rogue, Gervaise, for I had formed another opinion of you. I did hope that you, Sexton Blake, were honest, yet you have joined in as vile a conspiracy against my life and fortune as man could devise. As for you," he added, addressing Ernest Truelove, "you have a noble, manly face, which makes me sorry to see you associated with these rascals."

"I do not know what all this means," declared the Rev. Frederick Briarton, "but I do aver that this young gentleman never did a dishonourable action in his life, and, if you dare to detain him, it will be at our own peril. He was simpl y asked to get this cheque cashed by people who lodge in the house where he has apartments."

"It was Leon Polti's sister," Ernest commenced.

"Ah!" Blake interrupted, "this, as I guessed, is the work of the 'Red Light,' and I hope we shall be able to capture and convict the whole gang. I forgive you, Mr. Ellaby, for thinking I had something to do with your kidnapping; but had you gone to Scotland Yard, instead of to the City Police, you would have heard that Gervaise and myself have toiled day and night to rescue you. Only yesterday we discovered and old mill. We had the pond dragged, and we found one body which, at first, we thought was yours——"

"No, I am still alive," said Frank, "though I did get a ducking there. I hope, Blake, your tale is true."

"If we all drive to Scotland Yard, you will soon be satisfied on that point. It's my opinion, Mr. Ellaby, that this young man has simply been the dupe of the daring Polti crowd."

"I am a clergyman of the Church of England," said Mr. Briarton; "and I have known Ernest Truelove for many years. I am convinced he is incapable of committing a criminal action. I must insist on his immediate release from custody."

"Oh, Rose, Rose!" said Ernest, as his *fiancée* joined the throng. "I do wish you had been spared the pain of seeing me so disgraced."

"So your name is Rose?" questioned Frank Ellaby, regarding her fair, fresh young face with interest. "Many years ago I had a little girl stolen from me bearing that name. She must be about your age now. I would give much to find her."

"That is a matter we can discuss some other time," declared the rector, and with such significance that a sudden hope sprung up in Frank's heart. "Ernest Truelove must be released!"

It took very little time to prove how far from the truth was the charge against Messrs. Sexton Blake and Gervaise, to whom Mr. Ellaby made a most handsome apology.

Nor was it long before this gentleman was persuaded to withdraw every imputation against Ernest Truelove; and later, when he knew more of him, he decided to make him reparation for the wrong to which he had been subjected.

They all journeyed to Bernard Street, hoping to effect the capture of Madame Dulk and Nizza Polti, if not of Polti himself.

No one answered their repeated knocks or continuous rining of the bell.

"The birds have flown," said Blake. "No doubt Mr. Truelove was shadowed to the bank. When he was seen to be taken into custody the warning note was sounded, and the ducks have taken unto themselves wings and vanished. Gervaise and I will see that the railway stations and the wharves are watched. Every effort shall be made to prevent the escape of the culprits. Now we know them there should not be any difficulty about this. You gentlemen had best make yourselves comfortable at some good family hotel where I can visit you later on, and report progres. Say the Silver Bell, at Charing Cross. I really don't think you can help us now in any way. Too many cooks, you know, spoil even good broth."

"All my personal belongings are in that house," said Ernest, ruefully looking up at its windows.

"I daresay you will get our luggage all right," returned Gervaise, with a smile, "but that is a department of our business which can well afford to wait. We have got a moment to lose, so farewell, my friends!"

Gervaise was right. Every second was previous. Already much valuable time had been squandered.

Even as he spoke, Calder Dulk and Nizza Polti stood on the platform of King's Cross Station ready to step into a fast train soon to start for one of the Northern centres.

The appearance of Mr. Frank Ellaby outside the bank had filled Dulk with the direst consternation. He judged there could be no safety for him in England now, especially as Ernest was in custody, and could put them on the track of Madame Dulk, who had gone he knew not where.

"Ah!" he said, when he and Nizza had settled themselves in the carriage, and the train was almost on the move, "we shall get out of London all right, and then entire escape won't be so very difficult."

The whistle sounded, and the great engine gave on mighty gasp of relief.

They were on the move, when the door was torn open, and a man threw himself into the carriage.

"Keep still," he yelled, placing himself opposite them. "If you move an inch I'll shoot you both like the dogs you are."

He pointed a pistol at each head.

"So," he continued, "you've got possession of the plunder, and you mean to cheat me out of my share—me, who has done all the work, too! It isn't the first time you have tried on that game; but it shall be the last. You look very pretty in that woman's disguise, Leon Polti; but it won't work with me, because I know it. I always swore if a pal played me false that I would kill him. *I mean to kill you both!*"

They knew that their first stoppage was Peterborough, and that they were completely at the mercy of this desperate man, who was none other than Bill Bender, and who laughed to scorn the terrors of the law.

CHAPTER 7 .

A Struggle for Life—Thrown from the Train.

IT was some time before the two men recovered from their surprise.

"Don't be a fool, Bill Bender. We have not got a farthing of Frank Ellaby's money. The game is up;

the detectives are after a lot of us. We are flying out of London, and mean to lie quiet in the country for a time; that's why we are in this train."

It was Calder Dulk who spoke, half pleadingly, and with somewhat of a reassuring tone to Bill Bender, who still covered him and Nizza Polti with his pistols.

Dulk looked very helpless with the muzzle of the deadly weapon pointed straight at his heart.

"You always were an idiot, Bender," said Nizza, talking in his natural voice—for Nizza and Leon were one.

The disguise was so perfect that only very few of his own followers knew that he did not possess a sister.

By the aid of this change of costume he had more than once deceived his confederates, and passed freely out from among them, when very little would have made them tear him to pieces.

"Put those silly things down. They are more likely to hurt you than me."

"I am glad you have turned up," Leon added in his cool, business way. "I wanted to see you. I fancy we may yet get hold of that money, and want *your* help, my friend Bender."

They had emerged from King's Cross tunnel now, and were beginning to whiz along at a rate which soon promised exciting speed.

"None of that for me," said Bill. "I've had lots of it from you, and I know you. Now then, young gentleman in the skirts, tumble up the gold. You had the cheque right enough, and you've got the money."

"Certainly I had the cheque," acknowledged Leon quietly, "but you don't suppose I was going to be so foolish as to present it myself?"

"No," growled Bill, "you've all been clever enough to leave me to be the only one who can be identified as being connected with this job. One wears a mask and the other hides himself. Then you try to do me out of the money and leave me to swing, while you enjoy yourselves with wine and other luxuries."

"I sent a young country friend of mine to the bank to get Frank Ellaby's cheque cashed," Leon spoke impressively, "and I suppose he got the money. Dulk and I watched from a safe distance to see if things were all right. All we know is, that when our young friend left the bank he was taken in charge by the police. Just pay particular attention to this, Bill—*Frank Ellaby was there, too, waiting for him!*"

"What!" exclaimed BIll, so astonished at the news that he relaxed a trifle of his vigilance.

"How could he have escaped from the mill? I made sure he was a corpse by this time. He won't rest till he finds me. Yah!" he exclaimed, with a sudden change of demeanour, "you think I am a kid, and you are trying to put me off with those fairy tales till we stop somewhere, where you think you can get help. Come on, pay up, or I'll fire."

"Don't be so thick-headed, Bill; I tell you we have not got the money. Besides, I should never think of swindling *you;* you are too useful to us. Why don't you search us? Perhaps that will satisfy you. You can commence with me."

"So I will," said the thoughtless ruffian, laying his pistols by his side.

Leon was full of tricks. This proposal was only a ruse to put Bill Bender off his guard, and to enable them to deprive him of his weapons.

It would have succeeded admirably had not Leon been *too* quick.

He stretched his white hand over to secure the deadly weapons before Bill had half risen from his seat.

The burly bully saw what was intended, and Leon was felled to the floor of the carriage, rendered insensible, and his body kicked under a seat in less time than it takes to write these lines.

Thinking *his* opportunity had come, Calder Dulk now sprung on Bill Bender, to be received by him in his powerful grip.

Dulk was a man of weight and muscle.

Knowing the one he had to deal with, he was sure this must prove a struggle for very life.

Nothing would ever now persuade Bill that there had been no intention to deprive him of his share in the cheque obtained by such desperate means. His teeth were set. His eyes stood out of his head. His whole system throbbed with one idea, and it was a fierce one—to crush Dulk.

This so absorbed his every faculty that he did not hear the rush through the air of the train, the rattle of the carriages, or the frequent wild shrieks of the engine.

No pleadings for mercy from human tongue could touch him!

Dulk's veins rose up his forehead, knotted and black. His face was horror-stricken. He knew that a relentless demon was grappling with him, and it could only be by a superhuman effort that he could escape the death sentence written on that implacable face.

Strive his utmost he did, straining every muscle and nerve.

At one moment the two stood silent, and looking as firm as a pair of Roman wrestlers cut in marble. When the train gave a lurch they were thrown heavily with it. Then came a fierce, panting struggle on the floor. Some seconds one had the advantage, to be quickly wrenched from him by the other.

As they managed at last to struggle to their feet, they never for an instant released their hold on each other.

A thick hot breath fanned their cheeks as a blast from a furnace all the time. The solid seating on each side of them in the narrow passage of that compartment made it difficult for either to throw the other.

So each strove with slow, persistent effort to reach the pulsating throat of the other.

Bill Bender was the first to win in his deadly effort.

As his thumb and finger closed on Calder Dulk's throat, a groan of triumph escaped him. Now he could throw his whole weight against his victim, for with the latter's lack of breath the muscles of his arms and legs relaxed.

The two fell against the carriage door. A third of Dulk's body was already out of the open window, which had no protecting rail in the middle of it.

Just then they were entering a tunnel.

"You are best out altogether!" growled Bill, lifting up the legs of the man, and letting him drop out into the darkness.

A crimson flash of light from the fire of the engine illuminated his ghastly white face as he was swallowed up by the relentless black of that stifling excavation.

"It's Leon Polti who has the money; that's certain, or he would not be got up like a girl," muttered Bill, and he at once commenced to roughly search that gentleman.

"The other has got it after all!" he cried, in disgust. "There all that money lies on the line for any navvy or porter, or anyone to have for the finding. I *must* have a try for it."

The signal towards the exit of the tunnel was against the train, and it slowed.

Bill took advantage of this opportunity, and he dropped gently off the footboard into the gloom.

Leon, now he was lone, sprang to his feet, and, taking down a small bag from the luggage-rail, he quickly made a complete transformation in his dress.

When the train stopped at Peterborough, and he stepped gingerly from his carriage, he appeared in such attire as would have befitted the most exacting up-to-date Bond Street swell.

"I am glad Bill and Dulk have both gone *that* way," he reflected, with an amiable smile. "It is an experience they are not likely to recover from, and they were beginning to get troublesome."

CHAPTER 8 .
The Drugged Coffee—Coronet or Grave?

WHILE the detectives were pursuing their investigations, Frank Ellaby's party engaged quarters at that cosy and eminently respectable hostelry, the Silver Bell.

Here it naturally followed that Ernest should seek the companionship of Rose, and that Mr. Briarton and Frank Ellaby should exchange confidences one with another.

"From what you have told me," said the latter, "I have little doubt, in my own mind, that your Rose and the little girl my dying sister entrusted to my care are one and the same.

"The woman from whom you received her said no idle words when she declared that the child had a great future before her, for I can give her much wealth.

"Though I never like Calder Dulk's wife, I did not regard her as a criminal, though, seeing that she robbed me, the news need not surprise me. Odd, indeed, it is that I should once more be thrown into her clutches.

"Someone has truly said that we all live our lives twice over. Certainly, our experiences have a way of repeating themselves in the strangest manner.

"I quite agree with you, that it would be unwise to say anything to the young lady at present touching her real identity, which I fear we shall never discover, unless we can force that woman Dulk to give up the papers she stole from my sister's escritoire.

"If we once catch her, a promise to withdraw my prosecution against her may work wonders."

"I trust that she and her evil companions may soon be brought to justice," said the clergyman. "They might have ruined my friend, Ernest Truelove, who is so honest himself that he suspects no one. I will remain in London a few days, and see how the search progresses."

"Dad," cried Rose, entering the apartment at that moment, "there is to be a splendid concert at St. James's Hall tonight. Do, please, let us go."

"Certainly. We will all go," laughed Frank. "I will send round to the box-office and secure seats at once. Should Blake want us, we can leave word where we are to be found."

The concert-room was crowded, and on leaving it they became involved in the whirl of a fashionable crush.

Frank Ellaby had called for a cab. While they waited for it a rush from behind separated Rose from her friends.

"This way, miss," said a man to her; "the cab is waiting for you."

She followed the fellow in all simplicity, and soon she was sitting inside a soft, delicately-perfumed vehicle, which drove off at a furious rate before she realised what she had done.

A lady, beautifully dressed, sat facing her.

She smiled kindly on the young and agitated girl.

"There is some mistake. I have lost my friends. Oh, pray forgive me for getting into your carriage instead of into our cab. Please tell your coachman to stop," cried Rose in alarm.

"I saw your mistake, and it amused me," said the lady, "I dearly love a little joke. Tell me where you wish to go to my man shall drive us there."

"But my friends——" Rose commenced.

"You will be home before them, and will have the laugh against them. That is all. They deserve a taste of anxiety for losing you. The Silver Bell Hotel? I know it quite well. My house lies the same way, but it comes first.

"We will pause there for a moment, if you don't mind, and then I will take you to your own people."

The splendour of the equipage in which she found herself, and the aristocratic bearing of the white-haired lady, who patronised her with such an easy grace, were sufficient to lull all suspicion of foul play in Rose's mind.

"Indeed, she felt that she was an intruder there, and she considered her hostess very gracious in treating her with such good humour.

They pulled up outside a large but dismal-looking house.

"Here we are at my home" said the lady. "Come in with me, if only for a minute. Nay, I insist. You are too nervous to be left alone. Come! we shall yet reach the Silver Bell before your folks get there."

The door of the building opened, and without hands it seemed. Silently is closed behind them, leaving them in a dark passage.

"Take my hand," said her conductress in a more commanding voice.

"I will lead you to the light?"

Rose began to feel frightened now, but she had no choice but to follow her guide along the black corridor, down a number of steps, then to the still open air, again into another building, and up a high flight of stairs.

"Open for us Belus—open!" said the woman.

Rose was now conscious that some creature was walking in front of them.

She could hear its breath coming and going quickly, but its footfall made no sound, and she wondered whether it was a monkey or a human being.

Suddenly her eyes were blinded by a great flood of light.

She stood in one of the most lavishly-furnished rooms her imagination could conceive.

She saw that "Belus" was a dreadfully attenuated man. His skin was dry and yellow, and his flesh all withered up like that of a mummy, to which he bore a strong resemblance.

The horribleness of his appearance was increased by the fact that he had lost one eye, and one arm was gone.

These injuries were all on his left side, and they suggested that he had at some period of his existence been involved in a terrible accident.

"Belus has been with me many years," said the strange lady, "and he is very faithful."

"Unto death," declared the ghastly-looking Belus.

"It is well said," laughed his mistress. "Unto death! Get us coffee," she added.

"Indeed, indeed," protested Rose, "I must not stay. Do, please, let me go to my friends. They will be quite upset at my disappearance."

"We will leave here within ten minutes," said the lady, smilingly. "The coffee will revive you. I shall feel hurt if you do not take it."

It proved a delicious decoction of the glorious Arabian berry, and it was served in tiny gold cups chased in a most elegant way; but it had not the effect of stimulating Rose. On the contrary, it made her so drowsy that in a couple of minutes she was sound asleep on the luxuious sofa on which she had been induced to sit!"

Her hostess stood over her, and regarded her prostrate figure with an expression of evil triumph.

"What is this?" asked Belus, creeping to her side, "revenge or merely simply villainy?"

"Greed," answered the woman shortly. "This girl is worth much money to me.

"Hark! That is the duke's knock. Take care he does not enter here. Nor must he know of this girl's presence in this house. The time is not yet ripe for the disclosure I have to make. Go to him. You may tell him that I am here, and would see him on a matter of grave importance.

"Do my bidding well, my faithful Belus, and I will reward thee."

"Yes," muttered the man, as he seemed to melt from the room, "as you did before, with the loss of an arm and an eye. Your rewards are perfect, and so shall be my revenge!"

"Ah! my beautiful Rose," reflected the woman, unable to take her eyes off her prisoner.

"What is to be your fate? Are you destined for an early grave, or will you soon wear one of England's noblest coronets?"

CHAPTER 9
One Thousand Pounds Reward—The Duke of Fenton—A Sudden Death.

"WHERE is Rose?" demanded Ernest, as the three men clustered round the cab.

"She was by my side a second ago," said Frank Ellaby.

"It is but this moment that I spoke to her," declared Mr. Briarton. "It is ridiculous to suppose she has lost us."

They looked around in every direction. They waited till the crush had spent itself, and the pavement was pretty clear, and to their confusion they could see nothing of her.

They returned to the hall; she was not there.

The neighbourhood was searched, police and cabmen questioned, and they could gain no tidings of the missing lady.

The extraordinary mystery of her disappearance appalled them. It was as though she had been suddenly swept off the face of the earth.

They made haste back to the hotel, hoping against hope, that, by some possibility, she might have reached it first. Only disappointment awaited them.

The clergyman and Ernest Truelove were both plunged into the deepest distress and consternation.

Frank Ellaby, too, was gravely concerned. It seemed absurd that he should no sooner find the girl he had been searching for all these years than he should allow her to be snatched from him again.

"It is past all comprehension," he said, "that with three of us to guard her, she should be taken from us in this miraculous way. It makes one believe in the supernatural. If money will bring her back she will soon be with us again. I will offer a thousand pounds reward for her recovery. The advertisements shall be sent to-night to all the daily papers."

"I thank you heartily for that generous decision," said Ernest, "but we must strain every nerve to find her ourselves."

"And pray fervently to the One above to bless and protect her," said Mr. Briarton.

Before the missives to the newspapers could be dispatched, Sexton Blake called on them to report such progress as he had made in the hunting down of the "Red Lights."

The discovery of the body of a murdered man in the pool by the old mill had made this a police business.

Mr. Blake's efforts were confined solely to the interests of Frank Ellaby, who had now greater reason than ever for desiring to secure Calder Dulk and his desperate wife.

The detective listened to the story of Rose's disappearance with some surprise.

"I can only suppose," he said, "that this is the work of the daring woman who stole the young lady before. How she managed to accomplish her purpose so easily, and in the full blaze of Piccadilly, I do not know.

"Doubtless her object is extortion. She is determined not to let you escape her, Mr. Ellaby. If the young lady is in her power, I can promise you that I will soon bring about her release. Now that I know this woman Dulk, it will not be long before I find her.

"They are an exceedingly slippery gang to deal with. For instance, I have absolute proof that Calder Dulk and Nizza Polti left King's Cross this morning by the North express, which makes its first stoppage at Peterborough.

"I wired to that old cathedral city to have these two people detained until I arrived there, and formally charged them. No one answered their descriptions was to be found in the whole train!

"Indeed, it chanced that there was only one lady 'on board,' and she is the daughter of a well-known clergyman.

"The train goes at a break-neck speed all the way, the guard is certain that no one left it *en route,* and that Nizza Polti and her male companion were in their carriage when is started from King's Cross.

"They have managed to do the vanishing trick to perfection."

"If that gang have succeeded in capturing poor Rose, they hold a trump card. I shall not dare to proceed against them for fear of imperilling her life. They are quite capable of using her as a shield to protect them from my vengeance."

It was Ellaby who spoke.

"That is true," Blake allowed ruefully. "But if they escape your active hostility, they have still to reckon with the police.

"The offer of a thousand pounds reward will bring a communication from some of them, I'm sure."

While this conversation was taking place in the Silver Bell Hotel, another, and even more important one, was being carried on in the strange house whither Rose had been so cleverly conveyed.

Madame Dulk had left her beautiful and unconscious prisoner still reclining on the luxurious couch.

Entering another apartment, more superbly furnished than the first, Madame found a tall, stoutly-built, aristocratic gentleman waiting for her.

He had keen, grey eyes, which glittered under his grey, heavy eyebrows. His white hair was clipped short to his military-looking head, and his moustache was well trimmed and intensely black.

"I received your message," he said in a cold haughty tone, "and I have come. What have you to tell me now?"

"Will your Grace not deign to take a seat?" said Madame, humbly. "The missing child is again found. Of course she has grown to be a woman now. She is beautiful, and would ornament the highest station in the land."

"Tut!" he spoke impatiently; "what an old story this is! Woman, if you are in difficulties and want money, why not tell me so, and take you chance whether I give it you or not? Why do you always try to touch my purse by some untruthful story?"

"Never, your Grace, never in my life!" protested Madame. "I have been mistaken before—that is all. I have never wilfully deceived you. This time I have made no error. I have seen the minister who took possession of her when I was in prison. She is with him now.

"But the danger which threatens you is to be found in the fact that the brother of the woman who had her as a baby in Australia is here, and with her. He came over expressly to find her, and to vindicate her rights.

"He is enormously rich, and he will spend all he is worth in striving to establish her true identity. With my assistance he might learn this in half-an-hour.

"Now it is for your Grace's consideration whether you will submit to be compelled by law to accept this young lady as the daughter of your late elder brother, and allow her to take over the estates you now posses.

"You can arrange matters with me so that the proof of Lady Rose Fenton's existence can be for ever destroyed, and she herself be removed to some safe place abroad.

"As she has never known the joys of the position she is legally entitled to, she can never miss them."

The Duke of Fenton, resting his head on his hand, sat for some minutes without speaking.

"It is a hard problem to solve," he muttered. "If I had only myself to consider, this girl might take her place in our family without hindrance from me. I doubt whether it would be good for her. One has to be bred up to a coronet to wear it with ease.

"But my son, my dear and only son! The sudden appearance of this cousin of his would play sad havoc with his financial position!

"What do you propose, Madame?" he added in a louder tone, and looking up sharply at her.

"I propose that you should have a few days to prosecute your own inquiries about the Rev. Briarton and his so-called daughter," was the woman's prompt reply.

"While you are thus engaged, I undertake to get possession of the young lady, and have her snugly housed at the big place in Bedfordshire.

"Then I will hand her over to you with all the proofs as to her birth, parentage, and so on.

"Then it will be for *you* to decide what to do with her. You are already satisfied that such a lady does exist."

"Your terms?"

"The difficulties are great; the dangers not to be despised——"

"Your terms?" he repeated, waving his hand impatiently.

"Two thousand pounds!"

"Set about your business," he said. As he rose he allowed a deep sigh to escape him.

"Remember, not a hair of her head must be injured; not a cruel word must be said to her.

"Do not forget that the blood of the Fentons flows in her veins. Woe betide you if you do not pay it proper respect!"

He strode from the room, and out of the house, with a grand, haughty air.

At his carriage door his valet waited for him. The man had made such haste to get there that he was out of breath.

The few words he did utter were sufficient to send the proud nobleman reeling into his equipage as though he had been stabbed to the heart.

"What can have happened?" asked Madame, nervously.

She had followed "his Grace" to the door.

"His son is dead," said Belus, who was by her side. "His only son has been struck down suddenly in the billiard-room of his club; heart disease, they say.

"So much for pride of birth and the joy of riches! These aristocrats despise us and trample on us, but they all have to die—oh, yes, they all have to die!"

CHAPTER 10.

Rose Awakes—A Long Ride—The Country House—Leon Polti's New Plot.

WHEN Rose did at last recover her senses her brain was dizzy and numbed, and her muscles felt sore, as though she had been bruised. Heavy curtains were drawn across the windows, the lights were still burning, so she did not know whether it was night or morning.

She felt as though she had been unconscious for a long, long time. Her recollection returned slowly, and in a blurred, indistinct form.

"Thank goodness, you are once more in possession of your faculties," said Madame, who was sitting by her side. She spoke with great fervour.

"Your papa has only just gone away. Do you know you have lain there like one in a trance for two days?

"The doctor says it is one of the most singular cases he has met with in the whole of his professional experience. He fancies that a small clot of blood must have gone into one of the minute blood-vessels of the brain, and pressing on that important organ, rendered you insensible.

"He advised us that directly consciousness returned to you all danger was passed, and that you would be your old self again, as by a miracle. So you must rise now, and take some sustenance.

"Then I will convey you to a pretty place in the country, which your friends have taken for you, and where they are waiting you."

The poor girl, still suffering from the effects of the powerful drug which had been administered to her, listened to these words in hopeless bewilderment.

Judging from her own feelings, had she been told that she had lain there a week, she would have believed the tale. At any rate, she could do nothing now but obey her hostess. What little strength she had was swallowed up in wonder.

An appetising meal was put before her. She partook sparingly of it, yet it revived her. She was soon ready, and anxious to leave that place, hoping most devoutly that she was really to be taken to her father—or rather to the good old man she had all these years regarded as being her parent.

But for the fact that as she passed out of the front door she saw a patch of blue sky above her, walking into the vehicle which was waiting was like stepping from one room into another.

The fact was, a large "pantechnicon" had been backed close up to the entrance to the house, and its folding doors at its end being opened, made a closed-in passage from the hall of the dwelling to the interior of the van.

So no strange, curious eyes could see Rose leave that residence, and all view of the street she was in was shut out from her.

A swing lamp hanging from the roof diffused a pleasant light through the interior. The floor was heavily carpeted.

There was a comfortable sofa, some easy chairs; a good solid table stood towards the far end, and handy to it were lockers containing crystal, cutlery, wines, and food.

An old-stove made cooking possible, and a speaking tube rendered instructions to the driver easy.

It was certainly the warmest way of travelling by road that could well be devised.

There were many conspicuous evidences to prove that Rose was not its first passenger.

When Madame and her prisoner had once entered the van, the man, who was to drive them, closed the doors sharply, and barred them.

The horses started off at a sharp trot.

"Now, my dear," said Madame, decisively, "make yourself comfortable, and don't attempt any fuss, or bother me with stupid questions. You are with friends, and that is quite enough for you to know. Later on you shall be told all the fine things that are in store for you!"

"But," faltered poor Rose, "am I not to be taken to my father?"

"Why, of course you are! Have I not told you so? There now, amuse yourself with some of the these books while I read the paper."

It was, perhaps, as well for Rose that she was too dazed just then to feel any particular alarm. It all felt like a dream, and not an entirely unpleasant one.

She attempted to read, but drowsiness assailed her, and she continued to drop into short, fitful sleeps, which seemed to tire her more than refresh her.

They had a comfortable lunch, for which she had but small desire, and then came a cup of tea, which failed to refresh her.

On, still on they went, keeping up a round pace all the time. They had four good horses, and Rose fancied that these were changed at least once during one of their many short stoppages.

It must have been towards evening when Madame herself dropped into a doze. The atmosphere of that van was close, and conducive to sleep.

Rose languidly picked the newspaper off this lady's lap.

For some reason, which she herself could not have explained, she was rejoined to see that its date was the one following the night she visited the St. James's Hall.

So she had *not* been unconscious for two days, as she had been told.

Then her eyes caught sight of the advertisement, offering one thousand pounds reward for her safe recovery.

Her friends were on the alert, and she felt sure that she would soon be free.

She did not think it possible that in law-abiding England anyone could be long detained against his will, except in a prison or a lunatic asylum.

For her own safety's sake, she determined to take things quite calmly, to show no excitement, and to obey any reasonable command she might receive.

It would require an effort to hide her anxiety, and some courage to affect cheerfulness, when she was all terror in her uncertainty as to what designs her captors had on her.

She felt strong and brave enough to play the difficult part she had set before herself, and by enacting it well she hoped to soon effect her own escape, even if Mr. Briarton failed to find her.

The moon showered its light on them, and the stars twinkled with a frosty brightness when they at last drew up before a large, old-fashioned, substantial country house, which stood in the midst of thickly-timbered grounds.

The hall door was open, and in the yellow glow of the gas was seen the from of Leon Polti.

"You here?" cried Madame, in a tone of distinct anger. "Why have you come to this place?"

"I expect for the same reason as yourself!" he answered, lightly. "For safety. Everything has failed—all has gone wrong. We are all scattered like chaff before the four winds!"

"Enough!" said the woman, curtly. "You and I will discuss business matters later. This way, my dear Rose. You will find your room has been made very comfortable for you."

"I wonder who her pretty friend is?" muttered Leon, as he threw himself on a sofa before a bright fire in one of the sitting-rooms.

"The conditions of our confederation compel me to make you welcome, Leon Polti, anywhere and at any time. But I am sorry you are here to-night. I wish you had not come.

"Besides, I have done with the 'Red Lights' for ever! Some of you are clever enough men, and you do great things when you work alone. When together, all you seem to do is to get in each other's way.

"I, at any rate, can afford to do without you."

The was what Madame said when she rejoined him.

"Ah," said Leon, with a cynical smile. "You have thought so before to-night. I have some news for you—your husband is dead!"

"Dead?" she echoed, starting to her feet. Then she fell back in her chair, and again repeated the dread words, "Calder Dulk dead?"

"Well, I saw Bill Bender throw him out of a quick-going train on to the rails and in a tunnel. He seemed half dead before he left us. I don't think he can possibly be alive."

"You saw this, and raised no hand to protect him?"

"I was almost insensible myself. It's a miracle I escaped the same fate. Bender believes that we played him false. He'll do his best to kill me if he ever catches me. As for being here, I won't trouble you for long. All I want is to hide for a few days. By the way, who is your young friend?"

"That, Leon Polti, is my own particular business. She is worth more to me that all your abortive schemes put together would have been, even had you brought them to a successful issue. And I share with no one!"

"Don't you," Leon muttered, after Madame had left him to his own reflections.

"Let me look at that advertisement again. 'One thousand pounds reward.' Ah! A nice little sum.

"Yes, as far as I can judge, the description of the missing lady tallies with that of the one who has just arrived. What an odd thing they don't give her name? Some reason for it, I suppose. 'Clothes marked, R. B.—Apply Proprietor, Silver Hall Hotel."

"It would be rather amusing were I to snatch this pleasant little prize from your grasp, Madame Dulk? I want a thousand pounds quite as much as you do.

"Nothing can be done till the morning, when I will contrive to get a look at the stolen beauty."

CHAPTER 11

Sexton Blake has News—The Last of Calder Dulk—A Duke's Repentance—Baffled by Suicide—A Message from Rose.

A FEW days had passed, and to the surprise of Sexton Blake no one had yet made any serious application for the thousand pounds reward so widely advertised.

Suggestions, descriptions, and offers of help they had from all parts of the country, but nothing that promised the quick return to Rose.

As Mr. Briarton and Frank Ellaby were discussing one of their gloomy breakfasts, Mr. Sexton Blake entered the coffer-room, and took a chair at their table.

"I have some news," he said disconsolately. "I have found Calder Dulk."

"Good!" cried Frank, "through him we may get Rose, if his wife has had anything to do with the dear girl's disappearance."

"I fear he is past giving help to us, or to anyone. Someone has been before you with his vengeance. Dulk is dead!"

"How did it come about?" asked Ellaby, in a low tone.

"His body was was found in a tunnel, on the Great Northern Railway. It must have dropped from the North express I told you he and Nizza Polti took tickets by.

"He might have fallen out by accident, or he might have committed suicide; but both these theories are negatived by the fact that his throat, even yet, bears the impress of a powerful thumb and finger, which must have exercised sufficient pressure there to throttle him."

"Surely Nizza Polti had not enough strength——"

"Dear me, no. Indeed, it seems pretty clear that there never was any sister, and that is how I and Scotland Yard have been so often tricked on to wrong scents. Leon and Nizza are one.

"I managed at Peterborough to get permission to examine all the luggage that had come by that particular train, and which had been left in the cloak-room.

"This chanced to consist of one petite portmanteau. It contained a regularly built-up woman's costume, such as are used by female impersonators on the stage, only more delicately manufactured, to suit a drawing-room. The wig was a work of art. *Now* I understood why no Nizza could be found in that train. Leon had entered it at King's Cross as a girl, and had left it at Peterborough in his proper male attire.

"It turns out, too, that a man answering the description of the fellow who left you to starve at the water-mill, jumped into the carriage in which Polti and Dulk were, just as the train was on the move.

"Bill Bender, they call him. There is not a worse ruffian unchanged. I suppose he and Dulk quarrelled—quarrelling is the one great characteristic of the criminal character—and Bill Bender strangled him, and then threw him on the line.

"So far the murderer has made good his escape. But the police are keen after him all over the country, and after the whole gang.

"I think we shall see a quick extinction of the 'Red Lights of London.'"

Ernest Truelove just then returned from an early lecture at his college. Truth to tell, his mind was too much stirred with anxiety for the safety of Rose to benefit from the learning which had been poured into it.

"I suppose you have no news of Miss Briarton!"

His tone was one of reproach and hopelessness.

The grief which he could never escape from had made its impress on his face.

"You are wrong, Mr. Truelove, this time," said the detective, with a faint smile, "I bring you great news. No less a personage than the Duke of Fenton himself shall restore Miss Rose Briarton to you. Perhaps, my dear sir, you will read that letter, and aloud."

He handed an envelope to the astonished clergyman, who opened it and repeated its contents, which ran as follows:—

"Rev. and Dear Sir,—

"We, as solicitors to the Duke of Fenton, are instructed by his Grace to ease your anxiety as to the welfare of the young lady to whom you have so kindly acted as guardian for some years past.

"He believes that it is within his power to bring about her return to you with little or no delay.

"With this view he desires that you meet him at our offices to-day at 12 o'clock, when he trusts to be in a position to discuss with you this young lady's real position in society, and her prospects, with more freedom than is consistent with such a purely professional communication as this.

"We are, Rev. and Dear Sir
"Your obedient Servants,
"Martindale & Co."

"What does this mean?" asked Mr. Briarton, wonderingly, "and what *can* the Duke of Fenton have to do with my Rose?"

"Simply and briefly," and Sexton Blake, "the facts seem to be these. Martindale and I were schoolboys together at Winchester, and knowing I had this matter in hand, he confided the true state of affairs to me last night.

"It is clear that the late Duke of Fenton (the present Duke's elder brother), was a somewhat adventuresome young man, and that during his travels in Australia he fell in love with, and married, a lady who had everything to recommend her except birth and fortune.

"He persuaded her to keep the union a secret until he had at least seen his parents, and had endeavoured to win their countenance to this wedding of wealth with poverty. The ship he sailed in from Melbourne unhappily sand, and he, with many others, was drowned.

"His wife lodged with your sister, Mr. Ellaby, and in her house she died suddenly, before she could know her husband's sad fate.

"I need not tell you how Miss Ellaby left the child to your care, or how the papers establishing her right to the title of Lady Fenton excited the cupidity of the Dulks. I have ascertained that during their voyage home husband and wife quarrelled.

"It was the present duke who got Madame Dulk sentenced to imprisonment for endeavouring to obtain money under false pretences.

"She produced the child, but at the critical moment her husband went off with the documents necessary to establish its identity. In fact, it was the usual criminal bungle.

"But though the duke, for his own protection, sent this woman to gaol, he quite believed her tale, and when she was released, he had some other transactions with her, for she was then able to produce the documents she had so much wanted before.

"She and her husband had now come to some sort of agreement again.

"When the duke heard that Rose had really been found again, he did not forbid this woman to secure her. He wavered between his good impulses and his bad ones.

"He had not made up his mind what to do about his niece, when his only son was struck down with awful suddenness. The duke has taken this catastrophe as a warning from above, and he has now resolved to freely recognise Lady Rose Fenton, and to accord her the revenues and privileges which are her due.

"So, if you please, we will hasten on to Hanover Square, and keep this appointment with Messrs. Martindale and Co. Whey, gentlemen, you don't look just as delighted as you should with my great news."

"It seems," said Mr. Briarton, "that if we recover Rose it will be but to lose her at once in the turmoil of fashionable life."

"A medical student can scarcely aspire to the hand of a duke's daughter," said Ernest, in a crestfallen way.

"I could have given her as much money as she could ever reasonably spend," muttered Frank Ellaby.

"Nonsense!" cried Sexton Blake. "If the young lady is worth troubling about at all she will be just as good, and as lovable, bearing a title as if she remained a simple miss.

"I can't understand how it is," the detective grumbled, "but I get more dismayed when I give people good news than when I have to take them bad. It is the detective's lot to always be received in the opposite way from that which he has a right to expect."

Shortly afterwards they left the house but did not go far in a westwardly direction. They were soon stopped by the hoarse cries of newspaper vendors, who were already abroad with the ghastly tidings of—

"SUICIDE OF THE DUKE OF FENTON!"

It was too true. The untimely cutting off of his much-loved son had driven the nobleman to this rash act.

"We are as far from finding Rose as ever," groaned Mr. Briarton.

"I fear so," said Mr. Blake, "his lawyers know nothing at all concerning her whereabouts."

On their return to the hotel, Mr. Briarton was informed that a rough-looking man was waiting in the minister's sitting-room to see him, and that he had some very important information for them

They all went up, but it chanced that Frank Ellaby was the first the enter the apartment.

"What!" he cried, recognising the burly figure standing defiantly with his back to the window. "I'm glad I have you at last, Bill Bender!"

He would have made a spring on to his old gaoler, but Bill Bender seized a heavy cut-glass water-bottle which was near at hand, and raising it high above his head, cried—

"Move a step, and I'll brain you!

Sexton Blake, who had followed Frank in, caught the situation with half a glance.

He made a dart round through another room on to the balcony outside. Springing through the window of Mr. Briarton's room, he caught Bill from behind, and had him on the floor before that powerful gentleman was aware of his presence.

At the same moment Ernest Truelove sprang to the detective's help.

"Don't kill me!" gasped Bill, "you'll never forgive yourselves if you do. I've got a message—a message from the young lady—from Miss Rose Briarton!"

CHAPTER 12

The Discovery of Rose—An Awful Tragedy—The End.

LEON POLTI'S amiable intention of delivering Rose up to the people of the Silver Bell Hotel, receiving the reward for her restoration, and so baulking Madame Dulk's well-laid plans, would have taken very quick effect but for the fact that during his morning ramble through the grounds he detected the form of Bill Bender skulking among the trees.

A feeling of cold terror struck him, for he knew that this desperate character had only one purpose in being there—it was to kill Leon. The latter was sure that so far Bill had not seen him—had, indeed, only guessed that he might be at this rendezvous. So he crept quickly back to the house, revolved to remain in hiding until his enemy should grow tired of watching.

He had one consolation, and it was that while Bill lay waiting for them outside, Madame Dulk would not date to venture out to set her schemes in motion either.

"It's a bitter reflection that I should be caged up here and powerless to denounce the murderer of my husband, when he might be so easily taken," declared that lady angrily.

"All might have gone well had we left this Frank Ellaby alone. The unlucky plot emanated from you and your husband. Now the hue and cry is out after us hot and active," said Leon.

"Bah! I have no fear of that. What can they prove against me?"

"Sufficient to send you into penal servitude for life. The sooner we are both out of the country the better."

"True. But your way shall not be my way. I have some little business to settle, and that accomplished I shall be able to take care of myself in future."

"That is exactly my case," muttered Leon to himself, "and both our interests revolve round that young girl."

Aloud he added. "So long as Bill remains on guard outside we are powerless to do anything."

"If you were a man, you would go out and kill him," and Madame contemptuously.

"And attract the attention of the police to this only remaining refuge? No, thanks, all we can do is to wait."

Polti was not the only one who had seen Bill Bender lurking in those woods. Rose, at first much to her alarm, had encountered him in one of her brief walks, and promising his rich rewards, had persuaded him to take her message to Mr. Briarton, at the Silver Bell Hotel. Bill had means of scaling the high walls which surrounded the grounds, but it was impossible for her to do so.

Bill's surprise at finding himself face to face with Frank Ellaby can well be imagined. It is not surprising that he blamed himself for having walked into a trap so simply laid for him.

"Now, look here," said the desperado, when they allowed him to regain his feet, though they had securely bound his hands. "If you want to rescue that young lady, I know where she is, and I will take you to her. But you'll have to let me got scot free afterwards. If you can't agree to those terms, my lips remain closed for ever—you may all perish before I'll give you any help."

"Remember, Bill," said Blake, "we are not the police, and we can't control them. Take us to where Miss Rose Briarton is confined, and we will give you your freedom right enough; but you will have to take your chance as to whether the police get you or not."

"That's a chance I take very day," growled the ruffian. "Come on, I'm your man. Not one of you must leave my sight. I'm not going to have you giving information. The places lies between Bedford and St. Neots. It don't take very long to get there!"

They reached their destination in due course.

As they stood in front of the park-like gates of the principal drive they opened, and Polti, closely muffled up, emerged into the high road. He was alone, and in a smart gig, to which was harnessed a strong, spirited horse.

At sight of Bill he uttered a cry of dismay, and slashed the beast in front of him unmercifully.

But there was no escape for him!

With a roar like that of a tiger Bill sprang on to the back of the vehicle. By sheer muscular strength he dragged his heavy body up on to the seat by the side of the driver.

Here commenced a fierce and awful struggle for life!

The tugging and jerking of the reins, the swaying of the gig, the dreadful mutterings of the combatants, maddened the high-spirited horse.

Getting the bit between its teeth, it tore madly forward, blind to all before it!

"See!" cried Ernest, in a tone of horror, "where the road takes a sudden bend in skirts a cutting, which makes a sheer drop of forty feet into that turbulent stream. Will that excited animal hold to the highway, or go over?"

Not until the horse reached the edge of the cutting did it realise its danger. With a sudden jerk it turned, as if to get back to the highway and safety once more.

As if by a miracle, the sudden jerk caused the shafts to snap off short, and the traces, which held the horse, were torn in two. The animal retained its footing, but the gig, with the two men, went over the awful height.

And still they struggled, though they were descending to their doom!

They disappeared down the deadly chasm into the deep, fast-running water!

When they were found it was seen that, in its descent, the gig had turned completely over, and had buried Leon and Bill under it at the bottom of the stream, so they had no chance of swimming for their lives, even if they were conscious when they reached the water.

This dreadful tragedy had been witnessed from one of the upper windows of the mansion by Madame Dulk. Except that the horror of it fascinated her for a moment, it occasioned her no regret. She turned away with a shrug of her shoulders.

The telegram she held in her hand concerned her more deeply. It told her of the suicide of the Duke of Fenton. It urged her to meet the sender of it at St. Neots that night.

It was signed "Belus."

"So the duke has gone," she murmured, "and with him my last hope of immediate wealth and safety. The documents proving the legitimacy of Rose are still in my possession, and should be valuable. But I dare not offer them to Frank Ellaby and to Mr. Briarton. It would be one more crime to the list they have against me.

"They had best be destroyed. They shall never benefit any person but myself, for I have gone through much to secure and retain them."

From her travelling bag she withdrew a packet of papers. In the act of casting them into the fire, she paused.

"Even yet they may be of service," she reflected.

At that moment she heard the voice of Frank Ellaby and the others, as they ascended the principal stairs.

"The end has come! They are here to take me!" she ejaculated in terror.

"But they shall never have these precious proofs."

The documents she had sinned so deeply to obtain she cast on to the burning coals, and the flames greedily devoured them.

The voices came nearer and nearer. They passed her room, and next she heard a joyous cry from Rose, as she was once again in the clergyman's embrace, and in the sunshine of her lover's glad welcome.

Quickly and silently Madame ran into her bedroom. Seizing her cloak and hat, and securing her valuables, she crept down the back staircase, out of the house on to the free, wide road.

She met Belus at St. Neots that evening. To her dismay he was accompanied by a couple of the London police inspectors, who very adriotly decorated her wrists with a pair of handcuffs, and conveyed her straight to the London train, which was already in the station, impatient to commence its rush to the Metropolis.

The two officers from Scotland Yard informed her that they had secured sufficient evidence against her to warrant any judge in sending her to prison for fifteen years.

"When you in your fury threw that lamp at me, and burned half my body away, I swore to be revenged on you," cried Belus, thrusting his malicious, evil face into the carriage window.

"And my time has come now. Take her away, gentlemen—take her away to her righteous doom!"

With a scream of satisfaction the engine dashed forward, and was soon lost in the darkness of the night.

★ ★ ★

Frank Ellaby, being in doubt as to what he should do with his wealth, has showered most of it on Rose and Ernest, those fortunate young people who in a few months' time are to be made man and wife.

Sexton Blake has been well rewarded, and he and Mr. Gervaise, of Paris, are partners.

"I did the best I could for you in the matter," he once said to Ellaby; "but it was not so much as I wished."

"Thank goodness!" said the Rev. Fred Briarton, "we have been the means of suppressing those terrible people, the 'Red Lights of London.'"

"Yes," agreed Frank; "we have managed to clear away four desperate criminals at least."

THE END.